T0286100

THE
MET
GALA
&
TALES
of
SAINTS
and
SEEKERS

Also by Bruce Wagner

Force Majeure
Wild Palms (graphic novel)
I'm Losing You
I'll Let You Go
Still Holding
The Chrysanthemum Palace
Memorial
Dead Stars
The Empty Chair: Two Novellas
I Met Someone
A Guide For Murdered Children (writing as Sarah Sparrow)
The Marvel Universe: Origin Stories
ROAR: American Master, The Oral Biography of Roger Orr

THE
MET
GALA
&
TALES
of
SAINTS
and
SEEKERS

TWO NOVELLAS

BRUCE WAGNER
ILLUSTRATED BY MATT MAHURIN

Arcade Publishing • New York

Copyright © 2024 by Bruce Wagner

All rights reserved. No part of this book may be reproduced in any manner without the express written consent of the publisher, except in the case of brief excerpts in critical reviews or articles. All inquiries should be addressed to Arcade Publishing, 307 West 36th Street, 11th Floor, New York, NY 10018.

Arcade Publishing books may be purchased in bulk at special discounts for sales promotion, corporate gifts, fund-raising, or educational purposes. Special editions can also be created to specifications. For details, contact the Special Sales Department, Arcade Publishing, 307 West 36th Street, 11th Floor, New York, NY 10018 or arcade@skyhorsepublishing.com.

Arcade Publishing® is a registered trademark of Skyhorse Publishing, Inc.®, a Delaware corporation.

Visit our website at www.arcadepub.com.
Please follow our publisher Tony Lyons on Instagram @tonylyonsisuncertain.

10 9 8 7 6 5 4 3 2 1

Library of Congress Cataloging-in-Publication Data is available on file.

Jacket design by Brian Peterson
Cover painting: *Saturn Devouring His Son* by Francisco Goya (c. 1820–1823)
Illustrations by Matt Mahurin

Print ISBN: 978-1-64821-041-9
Ebook ISBN: 978-1-64821-042-6

Printed in the United States of America

THE MET GALA

1

ON A LATE SEPTEMBER EVENING, a young actress window-shopped the grail of barren Rodeo Drive boutiques whose pharaonic facades, in curious tradition, are demolished and rebuilt each eighteen months for no rhyme or reason. Rick Owens was already doing the family's clothes for the Met Gala but being on the lookout for ideas never hurt.

Waiting for the crosswalk light to ghost-blink green, she swiped IG to a coven of randy ninetysomethings. So random: Closeup Danskin crotch-selfies, splayed, linty, and dyson'd—hoovered?—into camel toes (sans humps), no doubt choreographed by the fun-loving memory care staff for a scandalous rec room bacchanal. With broken brains and one osteoporotic hip in the grave, the hellish vaudevillians mimicked influencer smiles pretty well. The Zoomy, zoological impulse was universal: to *present*, like the rutting walking dead.

The only job she'd booked was a commercial for Chantix; never got a callback for her audition as a deranged TikToker on *The Morning Show*. Her best friends were Kaia Gerber, Malala, and Willow Smith, *so why am I such a loser?* But then the miracle happened. Early that morning, at the stroke of the first midnight of her twenty-first year, bluesy, still sleepwalking, just three months out of hospital after what she campily called The Attempt, Candida Coldstream (christened with her mother's favorite '70s song—Tony Orlando and Dawn—believe it), got deliriously soaked in a deepfake whiff of serenity and suddenly knew holiness. She ugly cried at the California Queen-size epiphany of this voluptuously ragged world . . .

The Santa Anas buttonholed her in front of Saint Laurent like an old flame with issues. (Saints and Santa's abounded.) The wind used to paw at her but she was too small to understand; now that she was *of age*, as her mother Corinne kept saying, they were back on bended knee, lick-gusting six-gun proposals of marriage. How could a cis or nonbinary or non*anything* resist? Her downy arms erupted in tenderly satanic gooseflesh ecstasies. She felt twitchy, witchy, regnant, pregnant—

—and said aloud at the shock revelation:

I'm wet.

A dented dirty Tesla broke the mood by nearly jumping the curb. Stumbling back, she thudded into a plate of stained YSL glass.

A madman sprung forth with a camera.

"Sadie! Sadie! Sadie?"

Since she'd gone red, people on the street mistook her for Sadie Sink. A snappy friend told her, "You're Sadie but you've got mad Sarah Snookitude." She only really wanted to be Emma Corrin.

The pap stared down her counterfeit face, grunted, and sped away.

Apparently, he didn't even know she was Candida Coldstream . . .

Loser!

2

When she got home, Charlie was in the enormous cinema rewatching *Pretty Baby: Brooke Shields.* Candida thought her little sister looked exactly like Emma Corrin, mostly because Emma was *Candida's* obsession. But Charlie only wanted to look like Ellen Page before he was Elliot.

Staring at the screen, Charlie said, "Doesn't she remind you of Mom?"

"Maybe the energy? The smile . . ."

"It's so crazy that Brooke was in *Playboy* when she was ten."

"*Not* true."

"Fact check it online, bitch. She just *talked* about it."

"*What.* Like, a centerfold?"

"Left-of-centerfold. Showed her lil puss though."

"Oh my god."

"The eyebrow hair had yet to migrate. Ya gotta love Teri for making that happen."

"Who's Teri."

"Her mom, dumdum. Her pretty baby mama."

"How was that even legal, Charles?" She always called them Charles.

"I'm gonna do it," they said. (Charlie eschewed *hir, it, per,* or *ver,* the pronouns of so many friends.) "I want everyone to see my lil gaper in *Vogue.* Mom told Anna Wintour to fucking make it happen, and Anna's *mulling.* Ariel Nicholson's *lobbying.*" They tittered. "Bill Nighy thinks me voguing the gaper 'is naughty and brilliant.'" (The latter, in shitty British.) "I love Bill. Gonna show him my cuntie in *Loon*din town. Or wherever."

Candida's sixteen-year-old sibling, assigned male at birth, was named for the Revlon perfume—another of Mom's kitschy '70s hit parade-isms—and kept it when they transitioned. Charlie had a darkly funny, vindictive streak. When their Harvard lit professor accused them of using AI to write an essay on Bataille's *Story of the Eye,* they dredged the Facebook swamp and discovered that a decade ago, Mercutio Schecter—Department of Comparative Literature Emerita, Stéphane Bancel Professor of Romance Language and Literatures—"liked" a *Crazy Amazing Songs* Facebook post, singling out "Only Women Bleed." For such heresy, he was fired by Dr. Petra O'Tom, director of the Diversity and Inclusion Task Force, who quickly deleted a laughing/cry-face/triple-heart link to a news story of the de-tenured professor being doxed, sod-omized, then beaten as he crawled from his home when it was set afire. Corinne wasn't thrilled with the prank because she was a dear friend of Vince (aka Alice Cooper, though no one called him by his birthname apart from her and Keith Richards) but wagged a finger at Charlie and laughed at her baby's rotten bravado.

Bored with Brooke, Candida said, "Talula told me about the Houseless Hook-Up Challenge. Have you heard?"

"You are so fucking old, Dida. TikTok hates your oldness."

"Like, it started in London as a Skeetl sketch with, like, actors—they call the houseless 'rough sleepers' in the UK, don't you love that?—but then it became a thing. You take antibiotics for like a week or ten days and then you fuck, like, a random unhoused person. People get their confidence up with Klonopin, Adderall, mushrooms, whatever. It's like Burning Man."

"The Burning Man sick burn. But is it *woke*?"

"Um, I guess? Kinda. It's kinda superpowery."

Charlie mock-sighed. "Just strive to be based, Dida. And don't tell Malala about the challenge."

"I *am* based, my Edgelord. I'm so based, I'm woke."

"Then do it! Live your best pathetic, inauthentic life."

3

Charlie was ecstatic about the upcoming Met Gala.

Anna Wintour was a family friend and this year's honoree (TRACTOR BEAM: THE ART OF RICK OWENS) had been Corinne's idea—she discovered RO thirty years ago in LA when she met his wife at Les Deux Café, the restaurant Michèle owned. The three scavenged the Supply Sergeant on Hollywood Boulevard for army blankets and duffel bags; Rick was obsessed with cutting them up to make clothes. Only a triad of living designers had been so honored at the legendary ball: Saint Laurent, Rei Kawakubo, and now Rick.

Charlie had just returned from Paris after spending a week with RO, who was dressing the Coldstream clan for the ball. Rick was warm, brilliant, and mad relatable, yet hermitlike, fearless, and severe—they wanted to live like Rick did, an untouchable art guerrilla god dropped down in a cemetery of power, the seventh arrondissement, amidst the rose and wisteria of parliament (the Palais Bourbon and Ministry of Defense) and the handsome stormtroopers on guard . . . a dream-survivalist who lived in fascist bunkers of concrete and travertine, filled with morphine drips of *objets d'arts*: sarcophaguses, twenty-foot-long Onagadori rooster feathers, sadistically impractical Balla chairs, and sorrowful George Minne kneeling boy sculptures, Toto toilets of crystal and onyx, floors covered in Swiss army blankets, tattered cashmere, and shaved mink, and super real sculptures of himself on each floor. (Their favorite was the one of RO, a big black *objet* shoved up his ass, pissing into another Rick's mouth.) They would live as *he* did, taking arcane, impromptu side trips to places like Lago di Garda, where the designer once luxuriated in the final tub Mussolini soaked in during his wartime confinement or pilgriming to Sankt Martin to commune with the sculptures of Walter Pichler, each housed in customized buildings—Rick's favorite was in a space called House for the Torso and the Skullcaps—or excursions to Egypt's Valley of Kings. They wanted to be like Rick and make their home in the heart of a necropolis though yearned as well to be a fallen idol, dethroned, fugitive, but still the daemon of Time, abundance, and poetry—an exiled supervillain with an immense, misunderstood heart.

Rick told them *everything*—thirty years of what his eyes saw at sex clubs, the sorrows of boyhood, and his homophobic father—and Charlie did the same, even about the chronic bacterial smells and infections of their neovagina . . . how they'd worn Corrine's over-unders since they could walk, a pastime that electrified them just as the Santa Anas did Candida . . . and at ten, alone in the temple of their mother's three-story walk-in (more museum than wardrobe), the act of slipping into the mauve, bona fide Cassini shift that Jackie Kennedy wore one Easter Sunday in '63 made them ejaculate. The ensuing shame—not about the stimulus, which they considered nondeviant—was directed at the repulsively banal, despotic outgrowth between their legs that clockwork-hardened, flared and burst, even when Magic Taped to banishment. To have a *hole* instead, a bunker, would be the holiness, its imagined odors and ardors a mystic privilege.

One winter at the Amangiri Resort in Utah, Charlie went on a private tour. The guide saw something high on a tree and motioned for them to be quiet before handing over binoculars. They focused, looked, and thought: *A small songbird, nbd.*

"See what's next to it?" whispered the guide. The bird was tearing long strings out of something. "That's a deer mouse—the shrike impaled it on a branch. Shrikes use anything sharp, even barbed wire when it's handy. They're also known as 'the Lords of Pain.'"

The butcher bird haunted their dreams for months.

They saw themself skewered—the writhing, loathed boy body that ruled their fate with impunity. The visions of impalement became prophetically surgical: mouse, frog, and meaty insect replaced by Charlie's cock, pinned like the thorax of a butterfly on a spreading board, pecked, torn, and devoured, like the myth they studied at Waldorf school, Saturn swallowing his sons as they were born. The anguished child begged Corinne to *do something* but she said the intervention "must wait till you're legal." Hence, Charlie embarked on self-amputation and almost succeeded. When they overdosed on Candida's antidepressants, a mother's instinct forced her hand and she used every resource available to keep her baby alive, of which there were many—the family were angel investors of the trillion-dollar generative AI chipmaker Nvidia, and the largest shareholder of the Goliathan asset managers BlackRock, Blackstone, BlackAdder, and BlackBlack.

When they were eleven, the clandestine vaginoplasty was finally done at a hospital with some echoey iteration of the Coldstream Family Tree etched in Statuario marble on every building from Obstetrics to Oncology. Perforce ("legal"), the news was withheld.

It was Anna Wintour, one of the few entrusted to know the truth, who suggested, with boyfriend Bill's urging, that it would be brilliant to go public just before they all showed up at the Gala—with an alibi that the surgery was fresh, to avoid problematic speculation.

4

RO came to LA and Corrine's chauffeur drove the stone-grey Rolls Ghost to their old Hollywood stomping grounds. Rick was sad to see Supply Sergeant had closed.

"I'm a ghost riding around in a Ghost," he said. "Are you my Virgil?"

She laughed. "Well, I'm certainly not your virgin. But I'll always be . . . your *Virgo*." Rick was a cuspy Scorpio and liked to tell her the stars had organized their mutual loyalty.

He wanted to see skateparks, so they went to El Sereno and Manhattan Beach before ending up in Venice—then headed up the coast to an Ando house in Carpinteria that Corrine was leasing for a million a month and thinking of buying. (When Rick asked how many houses she owned, she didn't know the answer. "But I must have *more*," she said. "Such is my maison d'etre.") Tadao Ando was the decade's god of trophy houses; the Kardashians had one, Beyoncé had one, and Tom Ford used to, on twenty thousand acres in Santa Fe.

Rick talked her out of it.

"Ando—and John Pawson—are too clean," he said. "I like Aman hotels but don't want to live in one. I love a broken-into monastery or sketchy end-time pillbox. You've *got* to get a book called *Bunker Archeology*—these amazing photographs of abandoned German bunkers on the French coast. Michèle and I are obsessed." He peered through the vaulting space toward the movie screen-size window facing the ocean before looking around the room again. "You could dirty it up but then it'd be a Coldstream, not an Ando. Why give Ando all the credit?"

On the way to the Little Beach House in Malibu, Rick was laughing over something he read on the internet about the need to develop a vaccine for "Malibu Cove-id," the syndrome of people obsessed with buying as many adjacent properties as possible—like the Chrome Hearts couple that trolls were calling "Zillow Zombies."

~

Candida and Talula were there with Kaia and her boyfriend, Austin Butler, whom RO loved in *Elvis*. When Candida introduced him to the designer, Austin was speechless, finally saying aloud, trancelike, "I just shook hands with Rick Owens." Rick asked Austin to walk in his next show and the actor blurted "Yes! Thank you! Yes!" and jerked his head for nearly a minute, as if having a myoclonic seizure.

As the group departed, Lizzo jammed up and held Corinne's bejeweled hand. "This my lady *right here*," she huskily intoned, looking only at Rick. "*Lady Corinne Coldstream* is my fuckin *soul sister*." Everyone giggled and gossiped then Lizzo said she would see him in New York for her fitting and was so sorry she couldn't go to Paris because she was touring. She kissed each of them three times, a Swiss tic picked up while visiting Tina Turner's deathbed. She gave RO her love to his wife ("My *other* witchy soul sister") then swept out with the servile entourage that respectfully had stayed in the shadows during the encounter.

"She seems to have bounced back from the scandal," said Rick.

"Oh, she *bounces*, and you just better be on high ground when she lands. Do you have enough fabric for her?" said Corinne. For a moment he thought she was serious. "She's shooting up too much Lizzempic—that's for diabetics who identify as fucking walruses. *Well*," she mused, "you *could* cut up a parachute. No! *I* know what you should do: get a shipment of army blankets from Zelenskyy, stains and all! You *know* how you love to 'dirty it up' . . . Sean Penn'll have some. Keepsakes he masturbates into while dreaming of getting the Peace Prize."

Someone she didn't recognize made a beeline for them. Corinne whispered contemptuously, "Can't anyone leave us alone?"

"I'm so sorry to interrupt but wanted to introduce myself. I'm Dr. Petra O'Tom." The nervously officious woman put her hand out and Corinne, nonplussed, shook it. "Director of the Harvard Diversity and Inclusion Task Force. *Former* Director—I'm with the ACLU now."

"Ah!" said Corinne. While a bell didn't ring, it tinkled. "This is Rick Owens."

They shook hands though it was clear the crasher didn't know who he was (Rick loved when that happened). "I just wanted to tell you how *wonderful* your Charlie was throughout the *whole ordeal*—how very brave and strong your daughter is. And wanted to thank you for your enormous contributions, not just to the university, but to *things trans*. And to the ACLU."

"It's my pleasure," said Corinne, wishing she had a stun gun.

"Did you hear about the crash?" The trespasser shook with the adrenaline aftershocks of having stumbled into such a fortuitously status-raising tête-à-tête. "Jane Bookman, one of *the* most important people in the movement, was on her way to Tonga, which has an *abysmal* trans rights record. In fact, there are *zero* rights for trans people at *all*. They want to throw them into prisons, torture and kill them! Jennifer Pritzker graciously loaned her jet to Jane for the conference, and the plane went *down*. They *said* 'mechanical problems' but there is . . . *suspicion*."

"Oh?"

"The government was *not* happy about the conference. But there's a problem that I'd like to get your quick input on. It would be of such value . . . Jane Bookman, *I'm sure you know*, is the one who convinced the NEA to change 'mother' to 'birthing parent.' Jane's done *so* many marvelous, groundbreaking things with language. It's because of *Jane* that AOC tweeted about 'menstruating people'—"

"What is the problem?" said Corinne impatiently.

"They found the black box—the recorder that's on planes—washed up on one of the Vava'u Islands. I've read the transcripts—terrible, *terrible* to listen to—I cried!—which have not yet been publicly released. *For good reason*. The *problem* is that right before the crash, Jane is *screaming*—" She paused, looking over her shoulder as if someone might be listening. "What she was *screaming* was . . ."—she looked around again—"'Mother!' *She used the M-word*. Now, she wasn't in the cockpit so it's muffled but there is *no question* it was her, and *no question* that she said 'Mother.' *Several times*. 'Mother! Mother!' The last one sounds like 'Mama' but that doesn't help us."

"I'm not understanding."

"How are we to *explain*, Mrs. Coldstream?" She wrung her hands. "While I certainly understand—off the record—*why* she said it—I can *assure* you there are those who do *not*. Understand. There are those who say, 'You simply do not use that word, full stop! You die on that *hill*. You die on that *cloud*.' Oh, there are rumbles, rumbles that it—Jane—*reeks* of controlled opposition—that she was some kind of TERF spy . . . Who's behind it? Is it Walsh? Is it Rowling? I just can't believe personally that Jane . . . and *certainly* don't know what *I* would have done—knowing that my life was ending—how could any of us? I won't sit in judgment of a person who had precious seconds left—but *do* hope I would have screamed the right thing. That I'd have—somehow—been on 'the right side of history' . . . but *how* are we to justify that *word* when she was such an extraordinary warrior *against* it? *How* can the ACLU escape the optics of . . . of *complicity*? I'd be *so grateful*, Corinne, if you became part of the conversation."

5

Talula and Candida left the Little Beach House and headed to Venice.

The odd couple met on the psych ward, in Acute Inpatient lockdown. Talula's dad was a musician in Jeff Goldblum's band, The Mildred Snitzer Orchestra, and she tried to kill herself too. Candida was a little nervous about introducing "Lula" to Kaia because the new friend was five years younger. (Talula was funny though. She took one glance at Rick Owens, whom she'd never heard of, and said he looked "like a Navi.") Kaia was always asking Candida to help get Malala to guest on her IG book club, but Talula didn't even know who Malala was, let alone that she'd won a Nobel Prize at Lula's age. When Austin informed that Bob Dylan won it too, Talula did a deadpan Aubrey Plaza. Austin thought Dylan won it for Peace and Kaia laughingly said he won it for Literature. Anyway, Kaia thought it was sweet that Candida took the broken girl under her own broken wing and spontaneously offered Lula a job hostessing at the family restaurant, Café Habana, in the Malibu Lumber Yard. Talula responded with an affable Aubrey Plaza.

Candida generally got a pass for everything because she was so "real"—her unlikely, relatable defeatedness—and her family did so much. The Coldstreams had given billions to charter schools and literacy foundations, BIPOC educator collaboratives, abortion rights groups, transgender prisoner justice, climate change, and of course the Malala Fund. Part of Candida got off on rubbing the nose of the world in her own loserdom, but when Charlie devilishly forwarded internet hater comments that called her "Rob" (as in the dead loss, zero-sum Kardashian), it still stung. Anyhow, the deepfake Santa Anas birthday miracle revelation embraced the notion that if people thought she was Rob, well then, she'd Rob the rich and give to the broken-winged poor.

"It would be *amazing* to have Malala on Book Club," said Kaia, who could be persistent once she got a big idea.

"She's amazing," said Austin. "Like, an actual saint."

Kaia and Malala had only met once, at Wallis Annenberg's house, the day before the Oscars. Rihanna and Taika Waititi and Ke Huy Quan and Adam Sandler were there, and Ralph Lauren, who designed Malala's silver gown and hood. But Kaia had made her point and thought it best to pivot. "I've reached out to Salman Rushdie through Bill Maher, who's a friend of Mom and Dad's. It's so *interesting* that Sir Rushdie was hurt in kind of the same way Malala was. So awful!"

"Crazy unforgiveable," said Austin. "Really Shakespearean."

"He's already written a book about what happened! I hope he's coming to LA soon . . . they're both so *unimaginably brave*. It's funny because so many writers want to do my show now! I may have to turn one down but don't feel good about it because she's Black. That sounds awful but people in the community—I kind of sought their counsel?—told me to, like, tread carefully."

"Which community?" asked Candida.

"The writing community? Mostly?" When she was insecure, Kaia ended sentences with a question mark. "I mean, I've reached out to *different* communities, but people are totally paranoid to talk about it—her."

"What has she written?"

"It's tricky," she said, sneaking a look at Austin, who knew all about it. "She *says* she wrote five bestsellers—she *does* have a huge following on IG and TikTok—and people seem to love her work. But there aren't any physical books."

"They're online?" asked Candida.

"It's Melanchta Coleridge, have you heard of her?" Candida shook her head. "The *New York Times* was going to do a story about how she hadn't really *written* any—none that anyone's seen, anyway—but her lawyers stopped it. And I guess when it came out that they were going to do this kind of 'hit piece,' *so* many people said they'd cancel their subscriptions . . . So, the *Times* wound up doing a really nice story about her—I'll send it to you—but it's really more about the plight of POCs who've been *disallowed* to enter the mainstream of writers and readers and critics—something I *totally agree with*." She allowed herself a small laugh. "I *would* have her on but I'm not sure what we'd talk about!"

"So, there *aren't* any books?" said Candida. "Or there *are*, but she won't let people see them?"

"I guess it's complicated. But writers are complicated!"

"Maybe you could talk about *that*," suggested Austin. "I think what she's doing is actually brilliant. 'The writer who hasn't written.' Ha! Why *shouldn't* that be celebrated?"

"I think you're right, babe," said Kaia, a lightbulb going off. "Austin's so smart."

"Kerouac wrote a dozen books before they allowed him to publish," said Austin. "And no one saw *them* either. The only people who'd read *On the Road* were Ginsberg and Burroughs. Or maybe just Ginsberg . . . it took ten fucking years for someone to say 'Hey, this is genius! Why don't we publish it?' There's so much crap out there anyway."

Proud Kaia tenderly touched his cheek. *"You're* a genius."

"Well, then," he said, playfully debonair. "You should just interview *me.*"

Kaia started talking about the idea of being a writer and how interesting it was to never share your work; what a lovely challenge to use one's imagination ("Isn't that a reader's superpower?") to construct an oeuvre that checked all of one's personal boxes. "A writer can be pret-a-porter or they can be haute couture," she said, slipping into the lingo of her day job. "Depending on who's doing the imagining." Austin called it "knitwear AI," which Kaia again thought was genius, though it went over (or under) Candida's head.

When Talula changed the subject to the Houseless Hookup Challenge and its premise, Kaia and Austin laughed, thinking it an outrageous joke. An under-table kick from Candida stopped her friend from saying more.

6

They slowly drove down the alley that paralleled the boardwalk.

Talula was stoned and vaping nonstop. Over and over, she said, "I'm geeked up on the geek bar—it's giving geek—it's giving geek—I'm *giving.*" When she asked Candida if she'd done the course of Amoxicillin, Dida said yeah but only for a few days. Lula read her to filth. *"Fucking not enough!* It has to be at least a *week.*"

"Sorry!" said Candida. "Did you?"

"Fuck yeah. *Ten days.* It's an antibiotic with benefits: I had zero breakouts."

"Of the syph?" she joked.

"Oh my god, my *friend,* who's named after a fucking *yeast infection,* didn't take the full course!"

"Should we do a Get Ready With Me?"

"'Watch Dida and Lula prep for their houseless hookup!' That's *genius*. For Finsta."

"It's giving burner. Did you bring pepper spray?"

To show she was carrying, Talula quick-patted her Jacquemus bag—Candida's gift on her Sweet Sixteenth. Then Talula looked past her to the svelte, shorthaired, nearly fashionable woman rummaging in a dumpster. Her mouth dropped and she said, "Oh my god."

"What," said Candida.

"It's *Loni Willison*."

"Who?"

"The model who was married to Jeremy Jackson."

"Who's Jeremy Jackson."

"From *Baywatch*. She was, like, a *fitness covergirl*. You have *no idea* how awesome this is . . . I've been so bingeing *Baywatch*!"

"That's her? The whatever?"

"She's like on the internet *every day* being interviewed by like these *Brit reporters*, they're *obsessed*. She and Jeremy were strung out and he tried to kill her but Loni wouldn't press charges. She started working for a plastic surgeon in Beverly Hills, lost her job, lost her mind, and went houseless." She took out her phone and showed Candida a video of the actress on *The Daily Mail*. "*No*," said Talula, scrutinizing it in disbelief. "No!"

"*What?*" said Candida.

"Look! They're fucking talking to her in front of the *exact same dumpster*."

She rushed from the car and Candida followed. When the woman turned to face them, Talula said, "Oh my god, I am such a fan! I literally have all your *Glam Fit* covers!"

"That's very kind," said Loni cordially, before going back to rummaging. She wore a dozen silver rings on her dirty, broken fingers.

"You look *amazing*. I mean, I know shit happened, but you still have *such* fucking style."

"So do you," said Loni, with a toothless smile. Candida sniffed a chemical odor and couldn't wait to tell Charlie that it strongly reminded her of the perfume they were named after. Just then, an old man approached with a crack pipe. He was street-ancient, with a shock of white hair erupting from his scabby, bald head. He wore a tattered suit and a Celine Dion t-shirt.

Ignoring the guests, he said "Madame L, I am pleased to present your delivery"—then made a little bow and held out a baggie-wrapped glass pipe, as if presenting a bauble to the queen. "The crack is how the light gets in."

Loni took it from his hand and said, "How very kind, Professor."

"Courtesy of LA County. These sweet *cherubs* gave me wonderful little boxes of Narcan too. Narcan is the opiate antagonist of the people—in case someone asks."

"You're funny," said Talula, winking at Candida as if to say, "He's our man."

Loni turned to the girls. "Someone asked the Professor if he was homeless. You know what he told them? He said, 'No, I just don't happen to be home at the *moment*.'"

"Which I wasn't," said the old man mischievously.

Talula told him they had food in the car (a Happy Meal for their quarry, from the McDonald's opposite the Little Beach House) and the Professor talked a blue streak as he and Talula sat in back while Candida kept watch from the driver's seat. Doing it in the vehicle was a favorite of Houseless Hookup challenges, a technique borrowed from porn "dogging" videos where cuckold husbands drove their wives to sex parks. A married couple would wait until loiterers gathered round like the horny walking dead; after jittery pas de deux, arms reached through open windows to explore the body of the squirrely adulteress . . .

Candida was supposed to be making an iPhone movie but was too nervous to get it together and Talula was too stoned to take note. As he daintily munched a quarter-pounder, all she could think of was to ask why he was called the Professor.

"Well, I *am* one—or was. But I suppose those two are the same."

"My dad used to be a teacher!" said Talula.

"'To be' and 'to have been' coexist. The world is a *duality*; you're too young to know this. Listen and ye shall learn!" Fumbling at his pants, Talula asked his name. "Mercutio," he said, a glimmer in his eye, for he could always count upon the name's power to delight.

"Baz's movie!" said Candida, breaking the fourth wall. "Romeo's best friend . . . "

He smiled at her, sighed, and said, "Among scholars at last."

"I love Claire Danes *so much*," said Talula, grabbing his dick.

He giggled, squirmed, and feinted with surprise as she went down on him, then began a scary string of coughs. Candida thought he was crying, and he might have been. He giggled again. "O Romeo," said the Professor, knowing/not knowing what was going on. "That she were—oh! Ah! Yeeeee!" He hack-barked a bolus of chewed food, dancing in his seat with the renewed bronchial seizures, but Talula's percussive, rollercoasting head was all business. When he recovered, he said, "That she were an open-*arse*, and thou a poperin pear!" He didn't get hard but Talula, hepped up over her Happy Meal, unclamped long enough to chastise her friend.

"You're supposed to be filming, Dida!"

7

Corrine, Charlie, and Rick went to the Disney Concert Hall to see Ryan Murphy's *Salome*, staged by the French-Senegalese filmmaker Mati Diop. Charlie's friend, the TikToker Vinnie Hacker (twenty-five million followers) and Anna Wintour's daughter Bee went along. Bee was in town without her husband Francesco, who was in Capri. Charlie loved that Francesco used to date Lana Del Rey.

RO was obsessed with *Salome*. On the way, Charlie asked Rick what the opera was about. Rick smiled and said, "Each man kills the thing he loves. Some do it with a bitter look, some with a flattering word. *The coward does it with a kiss.*" They sat in the same row as Malia Obama, Spike Lee and Deva Cassel, a few seats ahead of Donald Glover, Lily Gladstone, and Eric Andre. Hunter Schafer was there with the Antiguan, trans, differently abled model Aaron Rose Philip, who was riding around in an amazing wheelchair designed by Jeremy Scott and Tadao Ando. Rick said it was almost the best *Salome* he'd ever seen, and nothing had really been changed "from the Strauss" except that the cast was Black, save for Herod, the dissolute Tetrarch, who was still white.

Charlie couldn't believe how great it was. Herod kills his brother and marries the widowed sister-in-law. Then he gets a hard-on for the sister-in-law's kid, Salome (his former niece, now stepdaughter), but Salome only wants to fuck a prophet—John the Baptist—a gaunt, amazingly beautiful nonbinary imprisoned in a dungeon of the palace. The tempted saint ultimately rebuffs her, making Salome crazy. When Herod says that he'll give her half of his kingdom if she strips for him, Salome says she will, but she wants something *else*. The king or tetrarch or whatever agrees and jacks off while she does the Dance of the Seven Veils. When Salome finishes, she drops the bomb: "I want you to kill the prophet." Herod freaks and tells her it's not within his power—so Salome does it herself. She cuts off J the B's head, puts it on a silver plate . . . and tongue-kisses the bloody skull!

As they left the theater, Corinne said to Charlie, "I dream of doing that to your father every night. Without the kiss."

∼

They were at Giorgio Baldi for a late dinner.

Candida's friends Suzanna Son and Halle Bailey were there. Corinne said hi to Carrie Mae Weems and Barry Manilow, then Lady Gaga rushed over, threw her arms around RO, and kissed Corinne three times. She kissed Charlie too, looked deep into their eyes and earnestly said, "You are the most beautiful girl in the world." Turning to the rest, she said, "Aren't they? Aren't they the most beautiful girl in the world?" Before she left, Gaga whispered in Charlie's ear, *You need to write about your amazing fucking journey*, loud enough for the whole table to hear. Bruce Willis' wife came over to thank Corinne because the Foundation was a major donor to aphasia research.

When the merry band of Salomettes were at last alone, Charlie said, "A friend of mine who's an amazing animator just did a short film about Bruce Willis. It takes place after he dies. I guess only boomers know who Willis is but in the short, he becomes super-popular with Gen Beta."

"Like Robert Evans," said Vinnie.

"Whoever that is," said Charlie. "So, Willis's weepy, creepy wife—the estate, whatever—makes a honey hole deal for Deepfake Bruce to make movies, ad infinitum. What happens though is, towards the end of every new film, the Willis avatar—and no one knows why—keeps getting corrupted, keeps getting *aphasia*, and the coders can't figure out why."

"That's so dark!" laughed Bee. "But it's *so* going to happen—not the aphasia part! Like in a hundred years, Tom Cruise'll be in *Top Gun 53*."

"Still doing his own stunts. Still a Scientologist."

"Still stunting as cishet."

"Don't forget Bill Nighy!" said Corinne. "Your mother's boyfriend will be in the fortieth sequel to *Living*."

Rick said he loved *Living*, then started talking about the amazingly beautiful silent film of *Salome* that Alla Nazimova starred in and paid for—he ordered everyone to watch it on YouTube ASAP—and how Alla built cottages on Sunset Boulevard that eventually became the Garden of Allah Hotel. After she went bankrupt because *Salome* was a giant fail, Alla sold the Garden but was still living there when she died. Vinnie said that if Alla Nazimova were alive now, she'd for sure have to get rid of the *Nazi* part and just be Alla Mova. Corinne nonsensically sang *Blame it on the Bossa Nova* then suggested Alla B. Praised. Rick offered Alla B.

Toklas, ending the riff, but no one got the reference, not even Corinne. Everyone was high and nothing mattered.

Vinnie announced that Bruce Willis was trending on the lists of celebrities not expected to make it through the year, which didn't make sense to RO, "because it's just aphasia." Vinnie said Paul Giamatti was on a bunch of lists too, "probably because he looks like he's eighty but he's only fifty-six," and Bob Odenkirk was still 8-to-1 because of the heart attack he had when they were shooting the last season of *Better Call Saul*. Rick grew pensive and brought up something curious he'd noticed about obituaries. It seemed like the cause of death wasn't mentioned anymore, even when the person was young and the death came out of nowhere. Clumps of healthy young athletes were dropping dead each day—cricketers, footballers, swimmers, and whatnot—and people not known to be drug addicts were dying in their sleep with no explanation or follow-up. "They call it SADS," said Rick. "Sudden Adult Death Syndrome."

"That's so sci-fi," said Bee. "Like *Blade Runner*. Maybe we're just all replicants, being quietly 'retired.'"

Rick said, "One day, like a time capsule thing, parents will say, 'A long time ago—in a galaxy far away!—when someone died, people used to want to know what happened. *Especially* if they died young. It was the main thing: How? *How* did they die? And their kids'll be stunned. Like, *What?* What the fuck. You know, '*Why?* Why would anyone want to know that, why would anyone want to know how someone died? That's so crazy!'"

Charlie said, "Soon it'll just be, 'He left.' 'She left.' 'They left.'"

"It's *total* science fiction," said Bee.

"I like it," said Corinne. "Who cares? It's too intimate—it's none of anyone's business. It's not even the business of the person who *dies*. Besides, I *like* 'She left.' I like it *aesthetically*. It's like leaving a party. 'Where's Corinne?' 'She left.'"

"It totally reminds me of that movie Francesco and I watched online," said Bee. "*The Time Machine*. A guy travels 100,000 years in the future, where people die and no one cares. Everyone's gorgeous, everyone's androgynous, they wear these lame white togas and have mass picnics in the woods. Everyone's laughing all the time. Suddenly, someone starts drowning and they take a quick look. They smile, laugh, and go on eating as the person screams for help, then goes under."

After dinner, Charlie and Vinnie went off together and Rick had to go downtown so Corinne drove home alone. She thought about the gown he was making for her and had an outrageous idea. Rick adored the secret Courbet displayed in her Bel Air home—the notorious closeup of a woman's bushy labia that the artist called *L'Origine du monde/The Origin of the World*—the painting had been in the family for twenty years and was currently mired in a legal drama following Corinne's divorce from Dax, her children's father. (The whole *monde* had been artfully tricked into believing that the masterwork hung in the permanent collection of the Musée d'Orsay, when in fact the museum possessed a flawless copy, courtesy of the preeminent forger, David Henty.) Rick Owens was lionhearted; as an homage to the gloryholes he'd seen in gay clubs, his models once infamously walked the runways in pants with crotch cavities exposing their cocks. Corinne thought, why not do the same, but with the *anus*—was that not the true origin of this godforsaken hell-bound world?

She wanted to burn down the world's origin and hysterectomize its future too.

Asses to ashes, dust to dust . . .

8

Driving to Rick's PH at the Chateau the next morning, foul visions of devil's garments still spun Corinne's head, joyriding her pulse. She knew he would love the idea but there was an architectural problem that needed solving: how would anyone be able to *see* what she called "my gory hole"?

Grotesquely contrived, Madonna-style contortions were definitely out. Then, the *aha* moment arrived: *she wouldn't show it at all.* She would take just *one* in-studio photograph—by Pigozzi, Slimane, or Juergen Teller—on her knees, legs spread, with a fingerless glove-assist to showcase the waxed, rose-grey death dimple in the framed center of a lambskin portal. Laughing out loud, she thought, *Rick's womenswear line 'Cyclops' is gonna take on a whole new meaning.* No Gala goer would be able to unsee the iconic image of the decade—a crater hidden in plain-ish sight by the zillionaire mother of all moons during Wintour celebrations.

It was all too genius.

While funny-texting with Rick—his replies made her howl—she blew through a stop sign, struck a pole, and slammed into a squalid, parked RV.

Corinne heard ear-piercing shrieks but was immobile, pinned by the airbag.

A voice cried, "Ellas estan muertas! Mis bebés! Mis bebés estan muertos!"—she hadn't run into a pole at all. She craned her neck and saw little bodies in the road.

The deranged hollers resumed.

9

She had a concussion and was released after an MRI. Because of the investigation, the Ghost (she had a fleet of them; this one's color was Belladonna Purple) was impounded. At first, Corinne told police that she hadn't seen the nanny *or* her charges; then managed to recall the blur of the trio as they dashed in front of the roller "like kamikazes." Blood was drawn for drug and alcohol levels and Corinne demanded they do the same with "whoever was responsible for those children." The man who lived in the RV that she plowed into had been urinating on the sidewalk when the accident happened and escaped harm.

The nanny's leg was broken, and the twins were dead.

Dodging the burgeoning news vans that were already on a stakeout swarm, the security team wheeled Corinne from the ER and into the bowels of the medical complex before finally resurfacing at a distant loading zone, where she was sealed into a Black Badge for the ride to Holmby Hills.

From her bed at home, high on opiates, Adderall, and Klonopin, she fielded ten thousand calls and emails. The bogeyman was social media and the family machine responded with alacrity; an immersive crowd-botting campaign was launched by Coldstream PR that didn't so much break the internet as drown it in sorrow, compassion, and prayers for the tragedy of the dead children and their parents—while simultaneously, sotto voce, promoting the antiquarian, much-maligned tradition of waiting for all the facts to come in. But the campaign for restraint couldn't stop photos of the twins from being posted alongside those of decap'd babies (real and AI-generated), nor did it stop edgelords from calling for Corinne's arrest and execution while certifying the socialite as the FUCKING BLACKROCK CZARINA and further attesting THE CUNTSTREAMS OWN GATES, SOROS, AND K. SCHWAB!!! The machine patiently mounted its defense, counterpoising such assertions with an avalanche of firsthand testimonials from thousands of regular folks whom the Foundation had helped in large and small ways before and after the turn of the century, from micro-loans to life-saving surgeries. Thanks to longtime family fixer Murray Cadence, a remunerative arrangement was hastily made between the twins' parents and Coldstream legal that forestalled them from speaking to the media. The only real problem "at this time," said Cadence, were phone records. If those were subpoenaed, they would prove that she was texting RO when the collision occurred, "which would not be helpful."

He was working on that.

Hilaria Baldwin, Sofia Vergara, Bruce Willis's wife—and many others—selflessly reached out to the wounded matriarch. More than twenty years ago, Corinne slept in a cot beside Sofia when she had radiation for thyroid cancer, something the actress never forgot. "It is of course *terrible*," she commiserated. "Such an accident—is awful and life-changing. *It totally change your life*, but it *happen*. The universe force you to become, how to say, *spiritual*. This happen to Howard Hughes! Did you know this, *mi Corinne?*— Howard Hughes he hit some body on Sunset Boulevard too—and the judge, he *clear* him! This happen to *Laura* fucking *Bush*! She kill a boy with her car, at seventeen. She no kill pedestrian, though . . . Gavin Newsom the fucking *governor* run over his eight-year-old sister with golf cart! He kill her! This is *fact*. And the nanny! The nanny of Katherine McPhee and David Foster! She hit by old lady and dragged through car dealership! I wish it was *your* nanny she got killed, not those babies! It happen to *so many people*, Carina! You *will* be through with flying colors! *Mi Corinne-Corazón* . . . I will sleep in cot by your bed like you do for me! *Ángel precioso* . . . Lord help us, they were *twins*—so terrible! But you are *strong*, Corinne-Corazón. *Always* you are strong—not weak like that old man whose foot on the brake kill ten at Santa Monica Farmer's market! He senile like El Presidente! Ha! Haha! We must laugh, Carina, no? To see you smile is so nice! When we cannot cry no more, we must laugh. . . . We are talking *two tiny little people*. And who in charge? Of their precious lives? The *nanny*. The *nanny*, not *you*, Corinne-Corazón. The nanny was in charge and she fuck it up, she *kill!*"

Caitlyn Jenner, exonerated a few years back in a Malibu crash that resulted in a woman's death, offered consolation by invoking the anodyne "all things must pass," assuring that in a year's time, "the crazy Day-Glo memory of all this will fade to washed-out black-and-white." Rebecca Gayheart called too. In 2001, the actress ran over a nine-year-old boy and was convicted of vehicular manslaughter. She told Corinne she paid a twenty-eight-hundred-dollar fine and did 750 hours of community service. Corinne shouted, "I can't, I won't! I cannot do 750 hours of *anything*," then burst into tears. Rebecca hugged her and said that crying was the best healing. That, and gua sha, platysmal Botox, fractional ablative CO_2 lasers, clairsentient healing, angel frequencies, and fecal transplants.

Charlie was diabolically attentive to his mother's needs.

"I googled it, Mom—last year, cars killed pedestrians *every fucking ninety minutes*. Some of the drivers weren't even texting!" Corinne violently shushed them, saying never to repeat that detail to *anyone* or she would go to prison. She kicked herself for letting it slip that she'd been texting with RO but couldn't help herself. The night she was released from Cedars, the kids gathered round Corinne's bed, and everyone smoked pot—a ritual Candida called "tea and sympathy." Weed always made Mom chatty.

10

Charlie threw a movie party at the house.

Candida and Kaia, Suki Waterhouse, Laith Ashley, and Charlie's new BFF Elliot Page came over to watch *The Shining*. Page was in town to do a conversation with Cara Delevingne for the LA Times Book Club. Charlie had loved Elliot from afar forever, though weirdly they'd never met. (Charlie's art thot crush used to be Ellen; Elliot was still superhot but not *art thot* hot.) Stoned, they told Elliot about the rarely revealed surgery at age eleven. "That's a seriously top secret bottom secret, Elliot! Mama'd go to jail if people knew. If she isn't going already." Elliot thought they were joking. But when Charlie said they'd also had an orchiectomy—"the coolest hack"—the actor was speechless at their and their mother's bravery.

Kaia interrupted to ask how Mom was doing. Charlie said she was doped up and sequestered in the North Wing, then gawked at the guests and head-rolled, "Oh my god, the *lewks*." They asked Kaia what she was wearing. Kaia said, "The shirt's Sa Su Phi and the jacket's The Row." Charlie asked the guests to do clockwise shares about what each had on. Suki wore a Moncler Grenoble vest ("my haute gorecore") over a Ssheena jacket, with thigh-high yellow vinyl cuissardes boots. Laith was in a

Balenciaga hoodie under a Fendi nylon printed trench. Elliot wore Golf Wang. Candida, the last, said that her jumpsuit was Dior, which got as many oohs and ahs as Charlie, who wore an RO black cape over an anime LV tracksuit gifted by Billie Eilish.

Meanwhile, Corinne at last returned Rick Owens's urgent calls then spoke with Anna Wintour, who was over-the-top sympathetic. But she could sense Anna's native chilliness; splashy vehicular fatalities (particularly those involving children) weren't the type of press the Gala liked to court. Charlie texted his mother to get her self-pitying arse to the screening room *&have some popcorn&fuckingchill*. When they didn't hear back, they wrote GET OVER YOURSELF. Corinne finally texted *will, for qwik hello + word gets out im okayish*. Before she got there, Charlie fast-forwarded and paused when they came to the axe-murdered twins.

When Corinne slipped in, Charlie waited a beat then pressed play.

She looked up, gasped, yelped "Asshole!" at Charlie—and fled in a storm of tears. Suki and Candida were stoned but still noticed.

"That was *mean*," said Candida. "You're wicked."

Suki said, "Lil sis is so sarky, aren't they."

11

Mercutio Schecter sat in the law offices of Gramercy Kind Cadence.

The firm had taken a very close look into the life of the former professor, though the vetting was somewhat hamstrung due to certain documents remaining under seal—to wit, revelatory details of the hijinks surrounding his Harvard firing. Murray Cadence put the wayward academic up at the Four Seasons under the care of RNs, a nutritionist, the esteemed psychopharmacologist Dr. Randolph Kibble, and armed protectors. The fixer's hope was that such interventions might improve the fallen scholar's social graces, in addition to making him "witness-ready." With a new haircut, new complexion, and a Tom Ford suit, one would never imagine that just a handful of days ago, Mr. Schecter was filthy, unhoused (the hellish RV notwithstanding), and prone to psychotic sequelae. It was the wily Counselor Cadence's good fortune to have gotten to him first—the police were still looking.

"Thank you, Professor, for allowing us to help."

"Thank *you* for your hospitality."

"Perhaps *support* is more apt than *help*. How are you feeling?"

"Fit as a fiddle. Not quite Stradivarius-adjacent, but . . . alas."

"You must be wondering what all this is about." The attorney was oddly soft-spoken, as if they were in a church, library, or museum; in the gaps between sentences, the faint whistle of a chronic wheeze.

"Having not won the lottery, it had occurred."

"Oh, but you *have*, Professor."

"Pardon?" said Mercutio, gently bemused.

The host cleared his throat. "The *lottery*. You've won it!"

"Never bought a ticket, kind sir."

The lawyer coughed, moving a paperweight back and forth. Rummaging in a drawer, he fetched an inhaler and dosed himself before noiselessly returning it. "Everything I'm about to say is confidential. That's why we're alone." Mercutio nodded with the gravity that the moment seemed to require. "If you'll recall, there was a *terrible* accident on Monday morning, just south of Sunset Boulevard, at the famously perilous six-lane intersection across from the Beverly Hills Hotel. The absence of electronic signals and overall anarchic design has been the cause of *many* accidents *at said locus* over the years —of which the city has done next to nothing! *Well.* A nanny was taking her employer's two little girls to the park abutting that madhouse juncture of Canon, Lomitas, and Beverly . . . the same park where Hugh Grant was arrested in the public toilet—correction! *George Michael.*" His eye twinkled as he retrieved the puffer. "A woman struck the nanny and her charges down as they crossed the street. Sadly, both children perished. And, like *most* tragedies, it may easily have been averted."

He puffed, winked, and whispered, "We have reason to believe that you saw what happened."

During his recuperative hotel stay, Mercutio had recovered sufficient presence of mind to do a version of cagey. "I may have," he muttered.

"Good!" said Murray, rubbing his hands together as if crouched before a small campfire. "It must have been quite traumatic for you—as it was for my client, of course—we are certain you'll be able to recover memories of the event—that is our *hope*—we have people who can assist you with that through hypnosis and other things—allowing *in time* for you to be able to recall the details of what we believe—what we *know*— actually occurred. How the nanny disregarded the well-known perils of that reckless confluence of streets, of which, *by the way*, said nanny was *most* familiar with . . . how she seized those doomed little girls' hands and *barreled headlong* into the fabled deathtrap. Now, we have *already learned* the nanny had substance and mental health issues; it is beyond dispute. Professor . . ." The attorney leaned in, his voice dropping to near unintelligibility. "My client—who was behind the wheel—wrong place, wrong time!—is aware of your predicament—that silliness, that *ugliness* at Harvard—these preposterous culture wars that destroy the lives of decent, thoughtful people, *willy-nilly*—and aware as well of the house fire and grievous physical assault you endured by consequence of your lighthearted endorsement of Alice Cooper at the hands of those . . . *fanatics.* Only women bleed, indeed! That motley crew are the very same who would draw and quarter the creator of *Harry Potter*! It's no different than the Inquisition . . . they'd like nothing more than to see Miss Rowling raped, both before *and* after her dismemberment! Professor . . . I can *assure* that your former position at the university *can be restored*, should you have the desire—or the stomach! Oh, we can visit hell upon them . . ." Cadence had worked himself up; the drawer awaited, and he paused for a bit of respiratory therapy before resuming. "My client . . . is a compassionate woman of extraordinary resources who wishes to help in any way she can." Another pause, for dramatic effect. "My *client* . . . is prepared to give you a house to live in for the rest of your life."

"Sorry? I didn't catch—I couldn't hear—"

"My client is prepared to give you a house to live in for the rest of your life! After a relatively brief passage of time, it shall legally be yours." He smiled and sat back. "Along with said residence comes a stipend of one-hundred-thousand dollars a month, tax-free."

"Beg pardon?"

"Along with the home comes a tax-free stipend of one-hundred-thousand dollars a month!" A second smile, then a quick puff, more recreational than medicinal. "What we—what *I* would ask—is that you submit—*in time*—a sworn statement describing that you saw what essentially appeared to be a suicidal act—*that of a 'kamikaze,' if you will*—set in motion by the nanny of those poor twins. So there is no confusion in what I'm saying, Professor, you shall *not* say such a thing if you are unable to recover those memories! You shall *not* be asked to fabricate something out of whole cloth, as my father used to say."

"Of course not . . ."

"We know that there was a settlement from Harvard, but the money is long gone . . . we know that certain 'troubles' were exacerbated by your homelessness—which is eminently understandable! You're a most brilliant man, Professor, that is beyond dispute." He scanned his notes. "You were diagnosed many years ago with bipolar illness . . . as common now as autism, peanut allergies, and gender dysphoria . . ."—consulting his notes again—"You had a challenging relationship with your medication, long *before* the university threw you out . . . Back in the day, mental illness would have undermined your 'expert witness' status on our behalf. I'd have helplessly sat on the sidelines while you were *shamed* and *dismantled* during cross-examination. But *now*, Professor . . . your houseless neurodiversity shall be *spun to gold*."

The dizzy ward asked for water. Moments later, a silver tray of breakfast cakes and Perrier appeared.

"One more thing," said Murray, introspectively. "We know the relationship with your children has been . . . challenging as well. Perhaps 'complicated' is more apt—been down that road myself. You haven't spoken to your son since you left him in California ten years ago. And the daughter you had, years after your wife 'disappeared'—for want of a better word—well, you've never met *her* at all . . ." Mercutio began to weep and was given a handkerchief. "There, there. If you wish, we can find them. That's the long and short of it. With your new *station*, I believe you can repair the relationship with your son—and build a fresh one with your daughter."

The Professor's mind was blank. All he could think to say was, "May I meet the one who offers such kind sponsorship? I would like very much to express my thanks."

"Of course! Though at the moment, I'm sure you'll understand that she is recovering from her injuries, physical *and* emotional. She's a mother herself and you can imagine what she's been through."

"What is her name?"

"Corinne. Corinne Coldstream."

The smiling Professor's brow furrowed at the surname; a light went on but was too dim to offer further illumination.

12

Seeing the horrific image of *The Shining* twins, she ran from the screening room all the way to the main house, where she collapsed in bed and abruptly fell into a wild sleep. The fifty-eight-year-old Corinne dreamed Anna Wintour was throwing a surprise party for her ninetieth birthday. Rebecca Gayheart and Bill Gates were there, and a proximation of that pathetic woman who died in the air somewhere above Tonga, shouting the M-word.

Gates said brightly, "Do they let people old as you into the Gala?"

Then *whoosh* she was at the Overlook Hotel, with the murdered sisters at the end of the hall—not the twins from the movie, but Candida and Charlie when they were little. They wore matching Philip Treacy wide-brimmed raffia hats, pleated polyester Issey Miyake schoolgirl uniforms (with lambskin holes Rick made at the crotch), and leather Comme des Garçons Mary Janes. When Charlie's tiny penis upjetted pee through its charming portal, Corinne was so sad that her baby's cupid cock was gone forever. She felt guilty for having helped guillotine it and guilty too for having such a transphobic-adjacent thought. Anna Wintour appeared— the ghosty siblings gone now—and said, "I cannot visit you in jail because you are so stupid." That hurt because Corinne's mother, a 3M chemist who invented Scotchgard with her friend Patsy, was always telling her how stupid she was . . . and so did her ex-husband Dax, knowing it would pick at the scab of the original mother wound. Then she was in a cell with Bruce Willis and Elizabeth Holmes—the Theranos swindler was a friend IRL who conned the Coldstream Family Foundation out of $10 million and the two hadn't spoken since Liz's conviction. Somehow Corinne realized that Bruce Willis was a corrupted AI version of Bill Nighy, who *seemed* to be Bruce, but spoke in a crisp English accent and was astonishingly clever. "Hey, stupid!" said Liz, laughing as she grabbed Corinne's arm. "Give me a hundred million for Qualia, my new babywear company!"

The kaleidoscopic barrage ended with the birthday girl's death by hanging in the Nantucket house that she still owned with Dax, a $35 million Bosworth Road compound in a cluster of compounds belonging to Charles Schwab, Stephen Schwarzman, and Sergey Brin.

13

Dax Coldstream's $175 million roost in Paradise Cove, among a clutch of homes including those of Charles Schwab, Sergey Brin, Laurene Powell

Jobs, and Stephen Schwarzman, was designed by Kengo Kuga, with a nod to Mr. Coldstream's favored Brutalism. Dax was eroticized by concrete, hard edges, and empty rooms. In a recent city competition for houseless housing, Kuga and Brad Pitt collaborated on dwellings that were micro version homages of Dax's cliffside bunker. In the same contest, Tadao Ando partnered with Reese Witherspoon and Judd Apatow, and there was also the Frank Gehry team of Noah Baumbach and Greta Gerwig. "Cryptcore" went viral; even sunshiny Reese couldn't resist its institutional charms. It was practical, too, because for a variety of reasons the houseless thrived under sanitizing, biweekly hose downs.

Moishe Fineman came in and held up his phone to show Dax who he was facetiming with. "Some interesting news," said Moishe. "Your package arrives in Basel in six weeks."

"That's around Davos time . . . tell him we'll be there."

The bodyguard nodded and left.

They'd been working together for thirty years. When Moishe's daughter was dying of anorexia, Dax hired a round-the-clock medical team so she could stay home; Moishe claimed the strategy saved her. A decade later, the mother of that girl had a so-called inoperable brain tumor, and Dax flew her to Spain where she was cured by the famed neurosurgeon Dr. Bartolomé Oliver. Moishe felt the debt could never be repaid, not even by killing the three men who entered the Venice palazzo to assassinate his benefactor while he slept.

Dax and his boyfriend, the Senegalese rapper CL, had just come back from partying in Nantucket with Peter Thiel and his husband. It was Dax's seventy-sixth birthday and CL gifted him with mephedrone that he got in Berlin. CL used to be a masseur at Amangiri in Utah before putting his music on Instagram and now he had three million followers. Dax and CL met some amazing creators in Nantucket, like the Twitch gamer xQc, the singer-songwriter d4vd, and another Senegalese, the "bored smile" TikToker Khaby Lame (160 million followers). They'd met Khaby before, at the Chanel pre-Oscar party, where he smiled a lot but didn't seem at all bored.

"What time's Charlie coming?" asked CL.

"TBD. My darling daughter has not yet transitioned to punctuality."

"Are they okay? I mean, with the Corinne thing?"

"Ask them."

"There's a lot of *bully*shit about the accident on the internet."

"Uhm, well, duh."

"Charlie and Candida are getting dragged. Not you, though—yet."

"If only Corinne had been killed."

"It stirred up the trolls. They're smack-talkin' BlackRock—"

"I do that every day."

"—dead twins' *adrenals* bein' harvested for the next Davos party."

"I wish."

"And such." CL reflected, "I was thinking about Amangiri and when we first met. I was thinking about *Charlie* . . . remember the birds he drew? Real Audubon shit. Kid's mad gifted." After a beat, he corrected himself. "*Them*. The birds *they* drew."

"Easy, negress. The pronoun police aren't due till after dark."

"Hey, wanna watch the Joni Mitchell thing?"

"*Love* me Corpse Joni but can't *bear* Brandi Carlile. Both Sides Brandi! Cannot *bear* watching her slither from Corpse Joni's ass into adjacent onstage throne whilst quietly head banging to 'Free Man In Paris.' She wants to do for Corpse Joni what Gaga did for Corpse Tony: be in every branding photo—Branding Carlile!—wants to be front and center when it croaks. Look! It's Tony and *Gaga*, Tony and *Gaga*, Tony and *Gaga*! Look! Joni and *Brandi*, Joni and *Brandi*, Joni and *Brandi*! AI? *Please* kill Brandi and Gaga! AI, kill Brandi and evict her from Joni's cadaverous ass! AI, tell Brandi that Joni's corpse ass does *not* make a decent home for futch celesbians!"

CL did his eye-roll shtick but had to laugh.

"I have an idea for a T-shirt," said Dax.

"With your portrait? As the geriatric Joker?"

Dax paused, then deadpanned "'What Doesn't Kill You.'"

"What," said CL, like the call-and-response of a knock-knock joke.

"What Doesn't Kill You," repeated Dax.

A nonplussed CL said, *"And—?"*

"That's it," said Dax, with a smile.

"What's it."

"'What Doesn't Kill You.' That's *it*, nothing after."

"So, it's a *you're cute jeans.*"

"What?"

"You are cute jeans."

"No," said Dax, annoyed.

"Then . . . as in what doesn't kill you makes you stronger?"

"Yes, negress. But just: *What Doesn't Kill You.*"

"With a question mark?"

"No question mark, dunciad."

"I get it," grinned CL. "As in *everything* kills you."

"Ding-ding-ding-ding-ding," said Dax, ringing a reward bell.

"I like it."

"But my personal favorite—my personal *best*—is—are you ready?"

"Ready."

"'What Part Of Don't You Understand.'"

"Say again?" said a smiling CL.

"'What Part Of Don't You Understand.'"

"Shit's too advanced. I need to get stoned to graduate."

"You've heard of 'What part of no don't you understand'?"

"But you said—is that what you said?"

"No, negress dunciad."

"You left out the *no.*"

"Yes, dunciad negroid. *What Part Of Don't You Understand.*"

"The part about *you,*" said CL. *"You're* the part I don't understand. You and your cute fucking jeans." He grabbed him in a wrestling hold and Dax giggled as they roughhoused. CL took his fat Black cock out, wiggled it in his face, and said, "What part don't you understand?"

"*Of! Of! Of!* What part *of* don't you understand."

"What part of I'm going to fuck your sloppy cunt don't you understand?"

He flipped Dax over, taking the wind out, then pinned and wrestler-fucked him, choking the old man until they both came.

14

When Charlie finally arrived, Dax attributed their angsty mood to the usual cocktail of estrogen, meth, and Percocet. CL glistened on the other side of the window, taking sun like a seal that'd been awkwardly jimmied onto the aluminum Marc Newson chaise bought at auction for $3.1 million.

"So," said Dax. "Have you used it yet?"

"Used what."

"Your *stoma*. La Neopuss. The honorary vaj."

"Fuck you."

"Fuck *someone*. Can't sit on that thing forever." He walked over, leaned down, and buried his nose in Charlie's lap. "Phew!" They bucked him off and glared. "That is one stinky Overton Window. . . . Having lived with Corinne, the smell of vaginosis is *most familiar*. Do not dawdle, daughter: get thee to a Gram stain!" Returning to his seat, Dax smirked and said, "Sorry to be rude but Jesus *fuck*, Charles, didn't that come with an instruction manual? Just take *care* of it. *Water* it, *clean* it, *whatever*. *Use* it—cooz it! Cooz it or lose it."

With glacial seriousness, Charlie said, "There's something you have that I want."

Impulsively, Dax replied, "Say that you love me and thy wish shall be granted."

After the briefest pause, Charlie said, "I love you," in earnest.

Their father was visibly startled because that was something Dax had never heard the child say—ever. It broke him. Touched and embarrassed and overwhelmed, he reverted to banter. "It really does smell necrotic. AI, kill that mutant vaj . . ."

"It's not a vagina, you pig," said Charlie, revoking the love proclamation. "Uhm, *duh*."

"It's a work of art."

"Get Cronenberg on the phone! Are you a body-horror queen now? Is that what you are?" Are you a gynecological tool for mutant women?"

"Out of the mouth of the *real* body horror queen! You and your shithole, posing as a cunt! What *I* have is a thing-in-itself."

"Ah! Yes! *Ding an sich* . . . says Immanuel *Kunt*. Hey, no shame in performance art, Charles—but that's all it is: *performance art*. Why not call it by its name? You people are *so fucking complicated*. Your generation of woke, braindead faggots . . . remember Matthew Shepherd? Of *course*, you don't. *Marauders* hung young Matthew from a fence and it took him a week to die. The guy who found him mistook Matt for a scarecrow— impaled on barbed wire—same methodology as your favorite tweety bird, the shrike. You people don't know what torture *is*," he said contemptuously, muttering "What doesn't kill you" before raising his voice again. "You think *misgendering* is a Hamas rave-rape—you're all so *evolved*, you and those mewling, martyred TikTok *activists* sitting in their sandboxes, Play-Doh-ing with their sad twigs and berries, worshipping all things trans but too dumb to grok transhumanism . . . that's right, 'grok,' *google* it—*not* Elon's chatbox—google 'grok' and *Stranger in a Strange Land* the next time you're searching how to get rid of your performance-art-vaj stank. Gen Z faggots are already *relics* . . . injecting your precious T like terminal diabetics . . . you're such fucking *bores*, you're worse than some old Baltimore bull dyke on dialysis. At *best*, you want to experience Sacred Otherness. Don't we all! Monkeys and elephants like their psychotropics too but they don't snivel on podcasts or show their mastectomy scars and Frankenstein gennies on IG—"

"I love you," said Charlie, pivoting to quick-stop his father's manic monologue.

Dax closed his eyes, super-high now. "I love you too," he said solemnly. "And I'm sorry, Charles—about everything. I don't know why I talk this way. It's like my love for you gives me Tourette's." He took a deep breath and said, "I'll do whatever you ask. You have my word." They understood their father's pathology well enough to know he would never renege on a promise, as the Tetrarch had in *Salome*. "I'll give you the world. But if you're not prudent with the money or whatever it is you're asking for—if you crash and burn—no one will help you, no one will save you. Elon won't save you from Mars because Elon isn't going to *make* it to Mars, Elon's going to be dead just like everyone else. Not even Paul Giamatti will help . . . AI, kill Paul Giamatti! Kill him in a squatter's mansion in Beverly Park!" His eyes bulged and brightened. "You know what I think you should do, Charles? What would truly make me happy? *Have a kid.* If *that's* what you want, I will make that happen! *Guaranteed.* You could have twins! Just keep Mom away, cause you want those kids to live . . . You don't even have to get fucked—I'm talking *facultative parthenogenesis*, Charliegirl. All *kinds* of creatures have virgin births—turtles, rays, sawfish . . ."

CL came in with a martini for Dax. "How ya doing, Charlie? Get you anything?"

"I'm good."

"How's your sis?"

"Candida's *great.* Know how I know? Cause all day long she didn't want to die."

"Baby steps," said Dax. "Baby steps. So, what's it going to be, Charles? What wish can the genie grant you today?"

They stood and whispered in their father's ear.

Dax went pale and shuddered.

His daughter sat back down with a faint smile and dead eyes.

"I'm not sure that will ever be mine to give," said Dax.

Again, they were reminded of the tetrarch when Salome asked him to do the unthinkable. But they knew their father—their ruler, their tetrarch, their king—would deliver.

15

Charlie was in love but hadn't breathed a word to anyone, not even their mother. They hadn't told Candida either, or Rick Owens during Charlie's seventh arrondissement confessions (which would have been the perfect time). They felt like a beggar, roving the world with an emerald in its pocket.

They met him through Harry Dodge, the visionary trans artist who was married to Maggie Nelson. Phaedra was named by his mother in the first week of pregnancy; she longed for a baby girl and refused to change it when the gender betrayed her. The father, an old salt at navigating his wife's rogue, maritime moods, codependently agreed, privately calling the boy Puck. Harry had been telling Charlie about a student of his, an extraordinary nineteen-year-old painter with Stage Four Ewing sarcoma and invited them to come along on a visit to Saint John's. The doctors were trying chemo to shrink the tumor in Puck's stomach. Charlie didn't want to go—since the bottom surgery, they steered clear of hospitals—but loved hanging with Harry. Maggie was in New York and the three face-timed as they sauntered down the hall toward Puck's room. They lost the connection at the RN station.

When Harry and Charlie walked in, Puck was standing next to the bed, naked.

Charlie gasped at the most beautiful thing they had ever seen. The eyes were green, and tousled red hair fell past his shoulders; the skin, hairless and pearly; crazy attenuated fingers wore a dozen silvery rings. Tattooed around the throat like a necklace was mother, with the m artfully smeared into near nonexistence. Harry noticed Charlie's dumbfounded-ness but said nothing (until later texting Maggie, "I'd never seen a *coup de foudre* IRL"). Puck smiled at Charlie, mock demure, then looked down at his own cock—an anthurium, its stamen launching from a bract of ruby pubic hair—and said, "Did Harry tell you its nickname?"

At the moment, it was obvious that Charlie wasn't capable of speech. Harry slyly stage-whispered, "Puck calls it 'Argonaut.'" That was the name of Maggie's famous book.

"My ship o' fools," said the young man, covering himself with a sheet as he walked toward the bathroom.

Through a crack in the door, they saw Puck sit on the toilet. Harry walked over and shut it for privacy, then watched Charlie watch the bathroom door like a family pet.

~

When Harry told Puck who he was bringing, the painter did a search of the Coldstreams on the internet. There was a blast about the mother's recent fatal accident followed by a bonkers rabbit hole of family mishaps, real and metaphorical. As for Charlie, they only knew what Harry had divulged about his precocious student, which wasn't all that much.

Harry wanted them to meet because Puck was alone in the world. Maggie and Harry had done some benefits to defray his medical expenses but could only raise so much—it was like throwing pebbles in the ocean. Besides, Harry unapologetically thought it would be good for Charlie to start engaging in what he called "eleemosynary activities." He'd also had long conversations with his young friend about their self-proclaimed asexuality (Harry didn't buy it) and their persistent, chaste fantasia of one day getting married, which added a poignant, profoundly romantic element to the intimate disclosures; they shared that at seven years old, Candida performed a wedding ceremony, playing the husband as well as an officious priest. Charlie wore a taffeta veil for the solemn vows and Dida exuberantly scissored up one of Corinne's Diors for her little brother to wear.

They also revealed that on the night before transitioning, when the last nightmare of the butcher bird came, they startled awake to the remains of a Pratesi sheet wet dream.

Harry was mindful of Charlie's impressionable age, their courage and confusions. The Coldstreams were perverse and bizarre, and so unfathomably, surrealistically rich that it was impossible to project oneself into such a universe and its effect upon body, mind, and spirit. Charlie's devilry and rage issues, while never acted out in front of Harry and Maggie, could be glibly traced to their sadistic father. So, it came as a surprise to Harry that his unsentimental, nihilistic, and growingly toxic acolyte, whom he thought was fated to become even more monstrous than Dax, had been so deeply affected by the dying painter's sheer existence. It was as if Puck had pulled the sword from the rock, though perhaps it was Charlie who did the pulling.

Harry felt like Merlin either way.

When Puck came out of the toilet, he wore a scarlet, brocaded Madonna Inn robe, and apologized for "my earlier flamboyance," attributing it to opiates (though he didn't *seem* stoned). Harry and Puck small-talked about the art scene, and this and that—how Zennials were taking tits-and-cock fuck-cancer selfies in the hospital basement before getting radiated, then posting them on burners—and were disconcerted when Charlie undid the ties around their tongue.

"I actually love the name Phaedra," they said.

"Me too," said Puck. "Do you know about Phaedra?" Charlie shook their head. "She fell in love with her stepson, but he wasn't interested. Which of course shamed the fuck out of her." (Charlie thought, *echoes of Salome and John the Baptist.*) "So, she gets revenge by telling her husband, 'Your son tried to rape me.' Now, her husband just happened to be *Theseus*, the demigod—Poseidon's son! And of *course* he kills the boy, hello, cause he *can*. And when Theseus finds out she lied, Phaedra takes her own life."

"Best bedtime story ever," said Harry.

"My mother gave me that name," said Puck.

"Are you close?"

Puck shook his head. "She left when I was six. She was old when she had me—forty-five. She had this . . . nutsoid pathology about having a girlchild, so when I *wasn't*, she flipped. She broke—I mean, she was obviously already broke, *something* was, but she . . . *broke*-broke. Ended up falling in love with a kid around my age—ironic! Someone's thirsty stepson, no doubt. They ran away together. We never heard from her again."

Charlie was astonished that a mother could do such a thing. "Have you tried to find her?"

"Dad did. I mean, tried," he said quietly. "It kinda took him out. He weren't no Theseus . . . she's probably dead, by whatchacallit—misadventure. Changed her name, whatever. A gone girl . . ." He stopped when he saw Charlie's mouth quake at the corners. "It's *okay*," he said, beckoning. "Hey hey hey, it's okay! C'mere. *C'mere* . . ." Charlie stumbled over, eyes shut, then crawled onto the top sheet and sobbed. They clung to Puck and wailed. Harry rushed to shut the hospital room door. Incandescent, Puck rocked Charlie in his arms. "A puppy!" he mouthed to Harry. Stroking Charlie's hair, he whispered, "A puppy at the shelter . . . the dearest angel puppy saint in Heaven."

The ᵗʰᵒⁿ tattoo was wet with Charlie's tears.

16

While he awaited a driver to ferry him to the law offices for the contract signing, Mercutio watched *Our Planet* on the 97-inch OLED in his living room at the Four Seasons. Mr. Cadence said the Professor could keep the suite until moving to his new home, which could still be months away.

Somewhere in Russia, tens of thousands of walruses blanketed an islet of dry land. The ice was gone and all they wanted was to rest but there just wasn't any room. Males bloodily battled; random stampedes crushed the calves. Jiggling, lumbering, maneuvering, and deadweight-hopping like two-ton salmon, some of them impossibly ascended to a clifftop until they found a separate peace overlooking the jittery herd below. After a laid-back siesta, when hunger and instinct bade them return to sea, something inconceivable happened: *they jumped.* Even as Mercutio watched the pinnipeds topple pell-mell, somersaulting and slambanging onto the jagged rocks during a slo-mo, balletic fall, he was confident they would be fine—that Mother Nature would guarantee their survival in the face of such a godless, unnatural act. Instead, as a coup de grace, the dead and dying were set upon by polar bears that rhythmically pounded them with anvil-sized forepaws until their bones and guts broke through the blubber.

He spent five hours at Gramercy Kind Cadence, signing and initialing.

A notary memorialized a statement of exactly what Mercutio Schecter saw on that cool, deadly morning. A "good faith" two month's share of his promised stipend—$200,000—was placed in a secret account, requiring Murray's signature for any withdrawals. (The fixer needed to safeguard the star witness's proclivity to self-destruct.) No hypnosis was required for the Professor to retrieve a vivid memory of the suicidal nanny-walrus dashing into traffic with a vice grip on the doomed twins' wrists. Blood test results of the sober au pair had been altered by the hospital administrator for a staggering fee; the payee immediately took a leave of absence.

Mercutio cogently understood what his handler called "the situation." If it became known that he received gifts and monies for his testimony, it would be catastrophic—not only for Murray and his client, Corinne Coldstream, but for the Professor as well, who would no doubt face jail time as a consequence. His imagination ran away with him: prisoners were intensely moral creatures who looked unkindly on rapists, wife beaters, and pedophiles, and could be expected to have strong opinions when it came to those who profited by alibiing billionaire child-killers.

Apart from the carrot Murray dangled about the chance of establishing a relationship with the daughter he'd never met, losing the chance of reconnecting with his beloved son would be worse than death . . .

There was something else that made him lose sleep.

A deeper investigation would inevitably reveal that his dismissal from Harvard had been spearheaded by none other than . . . Charlie Coldstream themself! *That* would be a bridge too far . . . or would it? He consoled himself with the logic that Murray Cadence was a hardcore criminal who was likely to laugh it off; the fixer would likely consider the freak coincidence to be nothing more than the spice that goosed what Kipling called the Great Game. Besides, the Coldstreams were already in too deep—Prime Witness Schecter, sans greatness, was the only game in town. Still, with or without the teapot, it was a tempest the Professor could live without. In paranoid flights of fancy, he wondered what strange karma he'd blundered into—and marveled at the gods' diabolism in selecting his fated bedfellows.

The last hurdle would be meeting Corinne, who might recognize his somewhat memorable name from the bygone "Only Women Bleed" hoopdee-doo. The fixer wouldn't be thrilled by the Professor's lie of omission, but Mercutio decided that if it came to that, he'd use the neurodiverse card that Murray was so enamored of and play dumb.

An unnerving caveat: in league with rough characters, there was always the possibility he could disappear just as surely as the twins, albeit with much less ado.

17

When they passed through the private gates of Serra Retreat, he gave the Professor a little tour, pointing out neighbors along the way: James Cameron, Charles Schwab, The Weeknd . . . MrBeast, Sergey Brin, Stephen Schwarzman. The Weeknd and MrBeast were leasing homes owned by Corinne—one designed by the architect Kuma Kengo, the other by Kazuyou Sejima. The Cameron house was a Tadao Ando; the Schwab and the Brin were by Tange Kenzo and Hara Hiroshi. The Schwarzman was a rare collaboration between Kengo, Kenzo, Kazuyou, and Shohei Shigematsu.

Murray thought the rendezvous was a terrible idea but couldn't dissuade Corinne. (He didn't have much faith in Mercutio's discretion and trusted Dame Coldstream even less.) There was nothing illegal about the meeting per se, but the optics weren't good. While Murray's mantra had always been "The less moving parts the better," twenty-five years on the superhighways and pitted backroads of Coldstream litigations made one thing clear: he was merely a passenger.

Eschewing a typically grand, tardy entrance, Corinne was already waiting in the living room in a gold Kawakubo pantsuit with zippered RO/Converse high-tops, hair done up in a powder blue mohawk. When a servant led them in, she ignored the Professor and straightaway told Murray how relieved she was to have finally had a conversation with the *other* Dame—Anna Wintour.

"I was waiting for the bitch to disinvite me but it didn't come up. I wouldn't care about it myself, but the Gala means so much to Charlie and Candida."

The star witness was perfunctorily introduced, and his heart skipped a beat when the attorney, for some reason, impishly enunciated *Mercutio Schecter.* Their hostess glossed the name—no recognition whatsoever— and the Professor laughed at himself. He was nothing to her, he was less than nothing! Why would she have retained his name, if she'd ever known it at all?

"Thank you for being in the wrong place at the right time," she said.

"I'm happy I could help."

"He gave a wonderful affidavit that I'll send along," said Murray unctuously.

"Can you imagine?" she said. "Those poor parents! But I suppose it's their fault for having hired . . . a monster."

"A very troubled woman," said Mercutio, all in.

"Ha! Don't you *dare* say she's a woman—and don't dare say she's Black! They'll clap you in handcuffs! Did Murray read you the police report? How they described the nanny?"

"'Female-presenting,'" said Murray, with good cheer. "'Of dark complexion.'"

"Female-presenting, dark complexion!" said Corinne with savage glee. "There's a *word* for 'female-presenting' . . . the W-word. *Woman.* And there's a word for 'dark-complexioned' people too—for terrible *Black* people, yes, there's an awful, terrible *word* . . . the word is used for wonderful, talented Blacks as well, but—people don't like to *say* it, so they call it the *N-word*, but people are even afraid to say 'N-word'! I'm not talking about the word *itself*, the *six-letter word*, no, I am talking about '*N-word*.' People are absolutely terrified to even say 'N-word'! Now, *certain* people can use the full word—profligately!—while others are banned, outlawed—others can *never* use it. Such as *you, you,* and *me.* They—*we*—can't *say* it, *write* it, *whisper* it, can't even *think* it. Though many are immune to prosecution . . . but it's just a word, a fucking *word*, isn't it? Love it or leave it, it is just a word. *You're* a professor, you know all about words, don't you. Anyone who *knows* me knows I am *not* a racist. Oh god! If Virgil were here, *Virgil Abloh*, he would laugh in the face of such an accusation! *He would defend me to his death.* I was in love with Basquiat, for god's sake! And he loved me *back*, we were going to be *married.* Who gave $200 million to BLM? *I* did. *Not* Tyler Perry, *not* Jay-Z, *not* Lebron. Not Saint Oprah . . . but there *is* that word—and if you want to hear it, all you have to do is turn on Netflix or the radio. *It is just a word.* But it's alive, it's controversial, it's horrific, and *endlessly* descriptive, and possesses timeless, inglorious majesty in its power to *wound*, to *offend*, to *express.* You can have any relationship with the word that you wish! You can love it or hate it! You can use it to name your best friend, brother, sister, lover, and use it with tremendous warmth and affection, no? Even with respect . . . but words are an endangered species now, have you noticed? Many of them are leaving us—the words. Gone into hiding . . . riding the underground railroad of language, stripped of their ugliness *and* magnificent beauty. Gone but not forgotten! Now they lurk, uncaged, behind *other* words, behind trending, brittle, bloodless little wokeisms—" Her cellphone lit up. She looked down then answered. "Anna dearest! Can you hold a moment?" Pressing the phone by her side to mute it, she marched over to the Professor and whispered, "Have you seen your son yet?"

"No," stammered Mercutio.

She blenched a smile, shook his hand goodbye and vanished, taking the call.

Just as they were walking out the door, a shriek stopped them cold. "What?" cried Corinne. "That isn't true! *It just isn't true.* Wait, what? *Who,* Anna? Who *said* that?" A pause, then, "You can't *do* this, Anna! After everything I've done—for *you*—you *cannot*! There will be Hell to pay! You *know* me, you *know* what I am capable of! *I will destroy you.*"

Another scream, piercing and sustained, as Corinne's iPhone sailed through the air and shattered against a wall, coming to rest at the toe of the Professor's Ferragamo loafer. A passionate, unseemly burst of tears and ululations followed, the kind heard at the end of a love affair, muted by the Russian doll of salons, foyers, and corridors within which the lady of the house quickly retreated.

18

Candida went with Kaia and Emma Roberts to the Montalbán Theatre for Melanctha Coleridge's LA Times Book Club interview. Coleridge was a charismatic, polarizing figure because she'd written five self-proclaimed "bestsellers" that no one could read because they hadn't been published or posted. Kaia was still debating about whether to have the novelist on her podcast, as was Emma. Emma had a book club too.

Melanctha was having a *moment*: Shonda Rhimes had been promoting her for the Shondaland website's "secret book club," and jester-toady Jimmy Fallon washed her feet on *The Tonight Show*. After legal threats, the *New York Times* killed a borderline snarky piece questioning "The Melanctha Effect," printing a fawning reparation essay instead that extolled her as "the bestselling author whose triumph is a fable for our *Times*." (They agreed to remove "fable," but the word somehow made its way into the piece; Mx. Coleridge's lawyers were not happy.) Block-long lines awaited appearances at bookstores where she signed author photos and glossy magazine profiles. Kamala Harris invited her for lunch at the White House with the trans performance artist Wu Tsang.

Kaia and Emma were besieged by photographers as they stepped from the SUV. Candida darted past them into the theater and one of paps trailed her to ask if she thought her mother was going to jail "for killing the twins." Kaia and Emma caught up with Dida in the lobby, where everyone ran into Amandla Stenberg and Willow Smith.

"Melanctha just did my book club!" said Amandla deliriously. "She's *so amazing*. You guys need to have her on!"

Bella Ramsey bounded over, hugged Candida, then took her aside. With hushed concern, she said, "How are they doing?" Candida blinked and stared. "*Charlie*. How are they?"

"They're great!" said Candida, bemused.

"I'm *one hundred percent* Team Corinne. Your mom is *amazing*—she's going to get *so much support*. And it will deflect from that car crash, *which wasn't her fault*."

"And how are *you*?"

"Good! I'm *great*. I'm 'laying flat.' It's, like, the new lifestyle in China, the 'lay-flatters.' I'm moving to China! Not *Wuhan*—Shanghai!"

"Laying flat like Business Class?"

"Lay-flatters just want to chill. They soak their panties from doing *nothing*—these are my people! All day long, they *lay fucking flat*. Isn't it brilliant?"

~

Melanctha was supposed to be interviewed by Cara Delevingne but Cara couldn't make it so Olivia Wilde stepped in. When Olivia had a conflict, she asked her friend, the writer Alice Sebold, to pinch hit. Alice was mostly known, if at all anymore, for *The Lovely Bones*, a novel about a young girl who was raped and killed that was made into a film starring Saoirse Ronan. The book was drawn from Alice's own experience of being raped, which she also wrote a memoir about. The man she had accused of the assault spent sixteen years in the penitentiary but was recently freed because of the memoirist's flawed eyewitness account; tonight would be the shamed writer's first public appearance since his exoneration. Alice had spoken at length to the *LA Times* about her paralyzing guilt and depression over the wrongful conviction, and whether she'd be capable of writing, or even reading again. (Alice told the interviewer that she was so traumatized that she hadn't yet sent him a letter of apology.) She said it was "a healing" to come out of seclusion for the LA Times Book Club event—and was "intrigued" by Melanctha Coleridge because in the last few months Alice had literally redefined herself on NPR as an "active novelist, creating phantom content that the world would never have access to."

She also said it was "important" to her that Melanctha was Black, as was the gentleman whom she'd falsely accused of the heinous crime against her body.

It wasn't a perfect fit. Alice Sebold was sixtysomething and socially awkward, with a pasty, bloated face, and no discernible sense of style; Dr. Melanctha Coleridge was as swashbuckling as her name—jet black, bejeweled, quirked up—and the recent honorary doctorate degree from CalArts, bestowed on her by previous recipients Professor Don Cheadle and Edgar Heap of Birds, put extra spring in an already cocky step. Timorous Alice wore a forgettable pantsuit, while MC stunned in a Christopher John Rogers psychedelic corset and rainbow gown, a rascally Charles James-inspired hint of what she planned to wear to the Met Gala. Candida and Kaia sensed that Melanctha felt snubbed by Cara *and*

Olivia, and that the chosen replacement, "Alice Anonymous," was a nasty surprise. But her mood lifted dramatically during the moderator's introduction: *The Lovely Bones*, said the Book Club president, sold ten million copies—ten million!—and had been a *New York Times* bestseller for over a year.

Respect.

From her first words, the audience ate from Melanctha's hand. (Many engaged in a robust gospel shoutback.) Fierce, witty, articulate, deftly improvisational and political, her acid remarks shed light on what everyone already knew: only an inbred club of white writers and "pale-skinned MFA jesters" were allowed the keys to the literary kingdom. Like a magnificent cobra, its neck-flap spread, she puffed and hissed and charmed.

"The rainbow-colored *arrivistes* who loiter outside the palace walls are not—cannot be—*real novelists*. The patriarchal hegemony (sometimes matriarchal too) says: '*We* are the novelists. *We* are the storytellers. *You* are *not* the novelists. You are . . . the *novelties*.'" Everyone leapt to their feet in thunderous applause, faces shiny with tears. "I am *not* the beggar outside the castle, that I can assure. Nor am I the *peasant*, waiting for an audience with the Zionist Nobel Kings—an audience that will never come. Nor am I the court jester!" The gouge of her smile was envenomed. "Let me *tell* you who I am."

Tell it! Tell it, sister—

After a histrionic pause, she proclaimed, "I am the rightful motherfuckin Queen, storming the Heavens for her rightful crown."

Queen! Our Queen! Our Queen!—

Alice—like a Karen who saw the light—was excited by the ticketholders' protective, knowing animus. For a fleeting instant, she knew in her heart she would soon have the courage to write a brief note to the man whose life she had stolen and destroyed.

The Q&A after the interview was a vibrantly devotional mêlée.

The first person called on said that a novelist was recently sued by a software company that claimed the writer had copied the distinct fictional style of an AI program. Melanctha said, "Was that a question?" and everyone laughed.

A reedy, sad-faced, cuspy zoomer who described xirself as neuroqueer bemoaned MFA programs for "*still* judging student-apprentices by the *quality* of their writing—criticisms that kill so many pure, beautiful spirits." A wheelchair-using nonbinary with a psychosocial disability spoke passionately of "not-writing being the most potent form of writing," while another summarized Melanctha's "iconic trajectory"—her name now published "loud and proud" on the contributors page of high-end literary quarterlies (if nowhere else within), often preceded by "award-winning." There was another huge laugh when Melanctha said her nom de plume was Meta Garbo.

A stunningly beautiful Black bookseller was the last to be called and immediately began to weep. The audience, moved, grew silent. She brought up the recent case of a trans woman, "a riotous gallimaufry of color," who published a word-for-word copy of Charles Dickens' *Bleak House*—the single alteration being the title, *Black House*—but otherwise claimed the work as her own. Many publishers who received the submission had never read the original but all of them rejected the manuscript.

After listening intently, Melanctha said, "And what are they trying to tell us? Ask yourself. That we cannot write a *Bleak House*? That we are not capable? That we lack the *majesty* of Mr. Dickens? Or the majesty of the *very white Kathy Acker*? Ha! I am telling you there are more in my *grimoires*—my Black house—than in all the bathetic, privileged blandishments of Mr. Dickens."

"Oh my god, *blandishments*," said Kaia. "I don't even know what that is! And *grimoire*. I love that word!"

Candida asked what it meant and Emma said, "Like, a book of *magic spells*?"

After applause, the fangirl concluded with the fatal words, "Mx. Coleridge, I would be *so honored* to one day read your work."

There were random gasps.

Melanctha's face became a rictus of contempt. "*Thank you*," she said fulsomely. "I think a *job opportunity* is waiting for you"—the dagger flashed—"with the motherfuckers who crapped all over *Black House*. They lookin' for a house negro. A *Bleak House negro!*"

Properly shivved, the disgraced sycophant puddled into her seat while everyone laughed and cheered, stamping their feet and shouting, "*Black House, Black House, Black House!*"

∾

As she left the Montalbán, Candida looked at her blown-up phone. Speed-scrolling the texts, she suddenly understood Bella Ramsey's earlier ambush, beseeching about Charlie being okay—and her fervent declarations of support for Team Corinne. The news drenched X, IG, and TikTok like nuclear rain: the whole world now knew that Charlie had bottom surgery when they were eleven years old.

She called her little sister right away.

"Hi sissy," they said calmly.

"Charlie, *how*. Oh my god, *who*—how? How did it *happen?*"

"Does it matter, Dida? As Papa would say, the neopuss is out of the bag."

19

It wasn't easy building a small museum on the cliffside Paradise Cove property.

The Shed, as Dax called it, was a jewel box with a complex, calibrated ecosystem, neutralizing the effects of humidity and temperature swings that attend life by the sea. An acoustic emission monitoring system allowed conservators to "listen" to the artwork as it reacted to the environment, to assess potential needs for restoration. To protect its inventory, his friend Jamie Dimon loaned him the security team that oversaw JP Morgan's commercial gold vault in London—though in this particular bolthole there was, perforce, no alarm to alert police, owing to the stolen masterpieces displayed within: Van Gogh's *Poppy Flowers*, Rembrandt's *The Storm on the Sea of Galilee,* and Francis Bacon's portrait of Lucian Freud.

Carefully arranged on the black Belgian marble floor, on center stage, were a half-dozen life-size Hans Bellmer creations, all legitimately acquired.

Bellmer was a German surrealist who fetishized pubescent dolls. When Dax was thirteen, his mother, a redheaded writer named Unica Zürn, began a long relationship with the artist. (Dax recently sponsored a controversial show of the couple's collaborative work at the Gagosian in Basel.) The photographs Unica took of the ball-joint mannequins, built through scavenged plaster and wooden dowels, were nearly as famous as Bellmer's sculptures themselves. In her mid-forties, she was diagnosed with schizophrenia and became a patient of the renowned psychoanalyst Jacques Lacan. Lacan gave her leave from the Sainte-Anne asylum to attend a small dinner party celebrating Dax's twenty-first birthday. She was charming and at ease—then excused herself from the table, gouged out her left eye, and threw herself from the sixth-story window.

In a rat's nest of synchronicity, Courbet's painting, *L'Origine du monde,* was once owned by Lacan and his wife Sylvia; before Lacan, Sylvia was married to George Bataille, author of *Story of the Eye,* the novella upon which Charlie based the AI-purloined essay that ended Professor Mercutio Schecter's academic career. Charlie became fascinated by Unica Zürn and her circle of friends (as did Harry Dodge and Maggie Nelson) and wanted to make a film about them. They approached various directors—Robert Eggers, Julia Ducournau, Yorgos Lanthimos—and harbored some jealousy over their father's avant-garde provenance, which the man was grossly unworthy of, yet had typically lucked into.

As for *The Origin of the World*, it was their father's prized possession, not only because Unica had seen the painting with her own eyes and become obsessed (it hung on the wall of the very room she was treated in, *chez* Lacan), but there was gossip among peers that Lacan, in an instance of patient transference, fervidly believed the portrait's scarlet bush to be the embodiment of his analysand. In later writings on her "case," Lacan asserted that the mesmeric pudenda was in fact what precipitated her psychosis—that Unica saw the brushstroked vagina as a great surveillance eye watching her every move and reading her thoughts, no matter how divine or how base. Lacan's theory was that the removal of an eye allowed her to leap into the solution of the impossible, ridding herself of the paranoia engendered by the all-seeing cyclopean orb. With one eye left as its mirror, she at last could merge, *becoming* the very thing that dismantled her—as he wrote, "quite literally entering the cosmic view."

But Dax Coldstream didn't see anything cosmic about it, for the image represented the most feared archetype of all: the Great Deposing Mother, the witchy whore Unica, from the Latin *unicus*, meaning single or "one," which presaged the blinding. "AKA," as Dax put it, "she who gifted me a Cyclop'd, psy-op'd hardfuck on my natal day." His pursuit of the masterpiece had been monomaniacal. When the Musée d'Orsay acquired it in 1995, he immediately hatched a scheme to give them $2 billion in exchange for a flawless reproduction that would secretly take its place. (President Chirac gave the transaction his blessing.) But Dax hadn't yet fulfilled his original plan: to graffiti the burning red bush with a schoolboy-scrawled phallus, the *true* one-eyed origin of the world—and its destroyer.

While Dax never told Corinne the details that gave birth to his pathological attachment to the painting, she intuited the Courbet's towering, unspeakable importance in his life. That was why she spitefully withheld it during divorce negotiations. Then, after months of stonewalling, she called to make sure he'd be home for a "special delivery." Expecting shit-in-a-box, he was stunned that it was the pristine *mondes* Venus. After the initial ecstatic shock, he became cynical, and a few days later his suspicions were borne out when the story broke about the decades-old, underhanded deal twixt Dax and the Musée d'Orsay. The French were humiliated and outraged at being duped; a political firestorm was ignited. Great pressure would be exerted to return the painting, but Dax wasn't concerned—another secret deal would be struck *tout suite* for an amount that would make his old Davos buddy Macron happy. What really rattled was the unwanted attention thrown on his personal life. (The internet picked through vomit flecked with the half-century-younger CL, the home-wrecking masseur-rapper-wannabe whom Corinne called "a wet nurse old-digger.") Dame Coldstream feigned innocence about the artful leak, giving cagey interviews that sympathized with *la République*'s enormous loss and betrayal at the hands of the government's greed and chicanery, while evincing compassion for the father of her children by explaining "he was always afraid of inheriting his mother's madness. And from his behavior of late, I now believe those fears were well-founded."

Annoyed, bored, and not to be bested, Dax made an unrefusable offer to an OR nurse (who was present at Charlie's illegal transition) to blow the amputated whistle. Dax knew the revelation wouldn't allow him to get off unscathed, but the truth was, he *had* opposed that surgery—even if he was on the wrong side of herstory—as many more witnesses would attest.

He rang their old friend personally.

"Anna . . . I've heard some disturbing news and wanted to give you the courtesy of a call before it goes public. I hope it won't adversely affect the gala, whose philanthropy deserves to be the sole focus." He ended by promising her a large check, "no matter the outcome." The inference was cryptic—that Corinne and the children had finally reached the tipping point and might no longer be welcome at the Temple of Dendur—but Anna Wintour surely understood.

Knowing that Charlie would nail him as the switched-bottoms snitch, Dax reasoned (force-fed *I love you*s aside) that his youngest, accidental daughter hated him anyway, and for all time. But none of it mattered. A permanent ceasefire would soon be achieved when Dax granted the end-game wish Charlie whispered in his ear: *Give me the Courbet* . . .

More than thirty years ago, a half-billion-dollars-worth of paintings were stolen from a museum in Boston; the empty frames still hung on the walls, a cult of wives waiting for their sailors to return from the sea. After handing *Origin* over to Charlie, the waiting would at last be over —he'd be rid of his mother and free to merge with the Cosmic View. In the forti-fied Shed, forever in abeyance, looming above the loitering Bellmer dolls, the socket of the frame, with its eye and genitals torn and thrown to the skies and sea, would be his masterpiece.

20

Puck was scrolling Charlie's felonious surgery stories on his laptop when there was a knock at the door. He answered in his Madonna Inn comfort robe. He saw Charlie standing there and said, "Look what the puddy tat dragged in." He was so happy and surprised but played it cool. Charlie waited ten days to get in touch—they'd shared emails at the hospital—because they wanted their infection gone before seeing him again. The doctor said they could start dilating, "but this time be disciplined about it."

"You live in that, huh," said Charlie about the robe.

Puck held up the belt like it was a tail and sniffed its end. "Still has that chemo smell, which excites me."

He made his guest a Shirley Temple, as a goof.

Charlie looked around at the super-high ceilings and iron-railed mez-zanine. "So, this place used to be a brewery?"

"That's why they call it The Brewery, Charles," said Puck. "It's gotten kinda gentrified, though. There's a gym with a climbing wall now, which is handy. I'm always climbing a wall."

"My sister calls me Charles."

"*Love* her."

"And my father, sometimes."

Puck let that one go. "Some groovy people live here—Catherine Opie. The photographer? She doesn't actually live here but has a studio. Do you know her work?"

"She's going to take my picture for a trans series she's doing."

"Of course she is." Puck drank his paloma and wryly said, "*You've* had a busy week."

"Like, beyond. And oh, ha! We're gonna do Drew's show."

"I fucking *love* Drew. So, you and your mom?"

"And Candida."

"That's crazy."

"You can come if you want. To the taping."

"Oh my god! I've always wanted to be an *audience member.* I wish I could have been on Red Table, Red Table was *insane.* So . . . does anyone, like, know how the *information* got out?"

"Corinne says it was Dad's version of revenge porn."

"Oh no! Could any—I mean because you were so young . . . are there, like, *charges* that could be brought? Against your mother?"

"Like body tampering? Mutilating a corpse?"

"You're so fuckin dark. But do you think it *was* him? I mean, why would your father rat you out? Wouldn't they come after him too?"

Charlie shrugged. "I'm actually kinda *happy.* That everyone knows. Everyone *should* know. That surgery saved my fucking life."

"You're amazing," said Puck, excusing himself. When he came back a few minutes later, he was in a '90s Adidas tracksuit.

"Gonna go climb a wall?" asked Charlie.

"Ha. I generally don't like entertaining young ladies in my robe."

"Want to have lunch? We could go to the beach."

"Did you Uber?" They shook their head. "I don't have a car and I refuse to be chauffeured by someone with a learner's permit."

"I have a driver."

"Silly me, I forgot how stupid rich you are."

While Puck went to "freshen up," Charlie wandered to the studio area. All the half-finished canvasses—haunted, coruscating, technically perfect—were colonized by garish, sorrowful, iniquitous women, maidens and crones with their features erased, broken, and obscured, floating above the chemtrails of evaporating bodies, smudged out like the ⨑ of Puck's tattoo. Charlie found himself in a house of mirrors—a discomfiting ingemination of lost Mothers.

Their meditations were interrupted by a toilet flush that did little to cover the sounds of vomit. To further disguise, Puck forced a cough. Charlie stared hard at the canvasses, pretending not to register the returning invalid's progress as he slunk down the stairs, clinging to the railing like a vanquished vamp in a silent film.

"I know, I know," said Puck, taking in the scene. "*So obvious*: Motherless Boy begets Boy Who Paints Mother. That's why I was throwing up. I make myself sick."

"Are you okay?" they asked.

"'Puck' is very close to 'puke.' Too close for comfort."

"But are you okay to have lunch?"

"The beach'll cure me. Why do I take vitamins on an empty stomach? Why don't I ever learn?"

21

At Nobu, by the ocean's edge, Puck looked instantly revived.

Shygirl was there with Bianca Censori. Chuck Schumer was having lunch with Coco Gauff, Judd Apatow, and Leslie Mann. Jordan Firstman did a manic, nuanced improv in a private room for Tim Cook and Jack Antonoff, who were dying. Arca and Janelle Monáe stopped by to fuss over Charlie. Arca intoned, "You're a historical figure now. There is a motherfucking army behind you, babygirl, and we will not quit."

Alone again, Charlie told Puck how wonderful they thought his paintings were. Puck said that someone just wrote an article comparing him to Sergiu Ciochină and Volker Hermes, but Charlie didn't know who those people were. Puck said they were IG art stars, "which is something I don't aspire to be. It's Lisa Frank's world," he sighed. "We just live in it." Charlie didn't know who Lisa Frank was either. "She made these amazing lunchboxes," said Puck. "And *never* shows her face . . . like my mom!" Charlie thought that was a good time to segue.

"I was thinking we could find her."

"Lisa Frank?" said Puck, with a tight smile.

"Your mother. Corinne—the *family* . . . *employs* people who could make that happen. It would take, like, an hour."

"Don't you *dare*," said Puck harshly. He struggled to catch his breath. Then, almost in a whisper, again he cautioned, "Don't you dare do that."

"Okay," said Charlie, shaken.

"I know you meant well," he said tenderly. "And I appreciate . . . the thought behind it. I'm sorry if I was curt. Cobain. So, I apologize to Miss Moneybags *and* her family's employees. Will Miss Transformer accept my apologies? Miss Transformer Moneybags? Will she?"

The name-calling made it all better.

"I wish I couldn't find *my* mother," said Charlie.

Puck touched their hand. "You know, you kinda break my heart."

"Are you seeing anyone?"

"Oh my god, you kill me. Precious girl, you are sixteen. I'm nineteen—and dying! It's like one of those horrible movies! What was it . . ."

"*The Fault in Our Stars*?"

"*Bright Star*! Stars, stars, stars—teen snuff flicks love 'stars' in a title. But *Bright Star* is so much better than *Fault*. It's fucking *Jane Campion*. Keats has one last romance before dropping dead."

"Who's Keats."

"John Keats, the poet! Aren't you a Waldorf child?"

"I went to Harvard for about a minute, online. But now I'm getting my ChatPhD."

Puck took a deep, stagey breath. "'Pillowed upon my fair love's ripening breasts—to feel forever its soft swell and fall—awake forever in a sweet unrest—Still, still to hear her tender-taken breath, and so live ever—or else swoon to death.'"

Keats and Charlie swooned as one.

"What was your mother's name?" they asked.

"*Do not look for her,* Charles. I don't want that."

"I'm not. I said I wouldn't."

"Ann. Her name was, is, was, Ann." The way he said it—not so much pronouncing, but exhaling—reminded them of Puck's gory, candescent, sacredly erased portraits. "So boring. So perfect though for a phantom mom, right?"

"Can I see a picture of her?"

"Aren't any. Dad destroyed them."

"What's your body count?"

"My body count? Oh my god. I love you so much."

"Is it high?"

"*Low,* sweetheart. It's like . . . probably 'one.' My body count is 'one'—I mean, if we're talking about the full deal. Apparently, I'm asexual—can I even be having this conversation with a minor?"

"Mine's, like, zero. But you're . . . asexual?"

"Did Harry tell you that? All I know is apparently I'm not that interested. And that was *before* chemo."

"That's so cool because I'm not either. That interested. I guess."

"What a relief."

"Was it—with a guy?"

"You're so the annoying baby sister I never had. To answer the question: No. Shocking, right? Guys are way too scary."

"Was she cishet?"

"Sort of. Definitely not bioprivileged, anyway." He screwed up his face and said, "Let's talk about it when you're of age. I'll be dead by then!"

"Don't say that," said Charlie, wounded.

"Sorry. I'm sorry—I am. K?"

"K. Did you ever want to get married?"

"Is that a proposal?"

Charlie flushed with embarrassment and was saved by two fangirls who appeared at the table to say hello: Kim Kardashian's former assistant, Stephanie Shepherd, and Bijou Phillips, whose handsome husband was in prison for rape. By the time he was eligible for release, he would no longer be aware of who or where he was, let alone the nature of his crimes.

22

For *The Drew Barrymore Show*, Corinne lost the mohawk and sported a vintage Vivienne Westwood silk velvet gown with Golden Goose sneakers. Candida looked dapper in a pixelated Damoflage suit from Pharrell Williams' *LV* collection; Charlie wore Freak City, and Skoot, gifted by Olivia Rodrigo—and a necklace from Taylor Swift that spelled out HEROINE in diamonds. Puck sat in the audience between Nicola Peltz Beckham and Maisie Williams.

Drew got dragged for the cringe interview she did with Dylan Mulvaney, groveling on her knees at the TikToker's feet; Maisie laughed when Puck whispered that she and Drew could compare notes about bending a knee. But that was then (vanilla) and this is now (rocky road) and the proudly no-bullshit tag team of Corinne and Charlie couldn't be contained.

"I saw Dylan on your show," said Charlie. "Of *course*, I did, and it was *amazing*—and I *loved* her advice to trans kids: 'Please hold on to your favorite part of yourself.' But I had to call her and say, 'Dylan, I love you, but I'm gonna have a little *trouble* with that. My favorite part doesn't have anything to hold onto!'" That got a huge laugh. In a villainous aside, Corinne said, "Unless someone from *MAGA*-Lago comes and grabs you by the—" Drew screamed to cut her off then couldn't stop laughing. The audience thought it was the best party ever. Charlie looked down at their lap and said, "She turned five last week!" Everyone sang "Happy Birthday," ending with ". . . dear *vajajay*." Then Corinne mischievously said to Drew, "You've heard of Bud Light?" Drew said, "Corinne, *please* don't go there!" Corinne wagged her finger and said, "Well, I'm afraid our darling Dylan . . . is *Charlie* Light." Drew did a Ghostface and the audience groaned, but Corinne made nice. "I'm *teasing*, Dylan's *wonderful*—we give *lots* of money to her favorite charity, the Trevor Project."

It was all fun and games until the shit, as Charlie later put it, got real. Drew asked Corinne about the tragic accident and Corinne said it was "obviously" the worst thing that ever happened to her in her life and that she couldn't speak too much about it for legal reasons but *could* say she'd met with the parents of the twins, and the details of what happened on that terrible day would soon emerge. Corinne said there was so much hate on the internet—Drew interjected, "I want to write a memoir called 'Comments Disabled,'" which got a nice laugh—"but I promise we'll get *Truth*, not truthiness. There is one thing the truth can never heal, fix, or resolve," she said, a catch in her voice. "The loss of those beautiful little girls." "As a mom," said Drew, "I cannot imagine being in your place— or the place of the parents. Something similar happened to Rebecca Gayheart, who courageously came on the show to talk about it." "Rebecca reached out to me, bless her heart," said Corinne. "So many people have."

Drew closed that door and opened another, asking why Corinne made the decision to go forward with Charlie's surgery—not only because of the uncharted territory of medical complications in one so young, but of potential legal consequences that could end in her imprisonment. Corinne began to speak, then paused, wincing a smile. "I had no choice, Drew. *I simply had no choice*—"

Charlie came to her rescue. "I didn't make it easy on her. I was doing a lot of self-harm. I would never wish that on a child *or* parent—to inflict such pain."

"I know something about that," said Drew.

"I was . . . self-mutilating," said Charlie uneasily. A great empathic groan rose from the audience; there were cut-aways of people putting hands to mouths. "I guess you could say I had no choice, either. It's funny but I've actually never talked about this." They took a breath to center themself. "All I wanted, all I *ever* wanted was to be whole. To look the way I felt, inside. To have *that body*—the one I deserved, the one I should have been born into. When I woke up from surgery, in the recovery room—I'll never forget—I was healed. *Completely.* When they showed me the results, which they didn't *want* to, because it was all so . . . so bloody—when they showed me, the pain was just . . . gone. I was *myself.*" There was scattered applause. Charlie looked at Corinne. "Mama Bear saved my life."

The studio became a church.

Drew left her seat and knelt before Corinne and Charlie, imperiously motioning them—and Candida—to join her on the floor. "Okay, I'm *doing* it again," she said, turning to the berserk-with-love crowd. "Sorry, Dylan! Sorry, TV critics! I'm doing it again, and it feels *good.* It feels *amazing.* It feels *right.*" Drew asked if it was still possible that she could go to jail. "Well, I hope not," said Corinne. "But at the same time, I'm not afraid. *Not afraid.* You know, 'Bring it.' Because there is no crime in what I did. I think you're too young to remember a chant we had in the seventies: *Keep Your Hands Off My Body.* That is a hill I am ready to die on."

The audience burst from their seats like projectiles, shrieking and stomping.

When they came back from a commercial break, Drew said to Corinne, "Before we stop—and today has been *amazing*—*amazing* and *historical* and I am *so grateful*—I know you have a very special announcement to make."

"And we love you too, Your Drewness. It's the only interview we're doing and we wouldn't have it any other way." She cleared her throat and grew playfully smug. "Yes. Well. Ahem. I was very much looking forward to the Met Gala. I go way back with the Met—not just the Gala but the museum. *Wayyyyyyy* pre-Anna. I'm an OG—that stands for Old Gala. ('Old Gal' too.) This year the Met's honoring one of my favorite designers, the genius Rick Owens. I pushed and pushed for them to honor Rick because it was *time*. I've known Rick and his wife Michèle Lamy for a hundred years. That dates me but who cares. (No one else will date me so I have to date myself.) I was honored to support Rick and Michèle at the very beginning, when they lived here in LA. Anna Wintour *agreed* with me, so that's why Rick is being honored at the Met Ball this year. But *apparently*, Anna decided that my 'actions' five years ago—the support I gave my daughter Charlie—well, that it wasn't *proper*." She said "proper" with a snooty English accent and the audience booed. "Now I do believe very deeply that everyone will have an opinion, and those opinions should be respected. I really mean it. To listen and to learn and to respect the opinion of others, even if contrary to one's own, is a lost art in this country. Truly it is, and that's very sad. It's why we're in the mess we're in. The constant dissension, the name-calling, the judging. So, I don't fault Anna—I've known her *two* hundred years—because that is her prerogative. 'It's my Gala and I'll cry if I want to.'" (She tried sounding English again but came off like Bette Davis.) "But I *strenuously* disagree. The friendship remains—I'm still here, as my dear friend Elaine Stritch liked to say—but I've decided to go my own way. *I have decided* . . . to have a *great big party*, honoring *everyone* out there who makes bold choices, *essential* choices, *life-saving* choices. I'm going to throw a Gala of my own, right here in Los Angeles . . ."

The exhilarated mob began a prolonged whoop that nearly drowned her out. Already knowing the answer, Drew asked, "And what, perchance, will be the *name* of your Gala? What will you *call* it?"

Corinne said, "Well, I *was* going to call it the West Coast MET Ball."

"Can you even *do* that?" asked Drew.

"As you can imagine, Anna's lawyers were not happy. But who listens to lawyers anyway?" Amid a welter of cheers and jeers, Corinne said, "I found a way around it. I'm still going to call it the MET Ball, with a dot after each letter . . . but the initials—M.E.T.—shall stand for *Medical Emergency Team*." The audience convulsed. "And I'm going to have it on the same night that Anna has her gala in New York!" By way of formal announcement, amidst howls of bad-boy solidarity, Corinne walked over to one of the cameras and declared, "On the first Monday of May, Madam Corinne Coldstream will throw the premiere of the West Coast Medical Emergency Team Ball—aptly named for the times we live in, don't you think?"

23

Divinity Swann clutched her Bible as she watched Drew's show. Since Megan and Mayme died—the twins she took care of since birth and considered her own—all she did was dream of crossing over. She sat on the couch and watched the Coldstreams talk to this silly girl only because Coretta, her church friend, said that she must.

Parishioners were on her side, right up until the bogus toxicology report went public along with news that the district attorney was considering charges of negligent homicide. One of them even asked for the crutches back; she borrowed them while her broken leg was healing but she didn't need them anymore. Divinity had always been proud of her godly, salvific name but flinched at the cruelty of it now. (Her niece, Jvnglebar, only started liking it when her role model, Divinity Roxx, toured with Beyonce and won a Grammy, a prize Jvnglebar aspired to.) When Divinity was young, white children at the mall would chase her, shouting "Black Swan! Black Swan!" and that's what Coretta said haters on Facebook were calling her. Divinity's sons used to call her White Swan and White Slave because she worked for rich people in Beverly Hills.

The doorbell rang. She was expecting Coretta, but two smooth-cheeked young men stood there instead. "Hi! We're doing a neighborhood outreach and I wanted to leave this with you." He handed her a plastic bag filled with Narcan nasal sprays.

"You people come by twice a day," said Divinity.

"Oh! Sorry about that—we're pretty annoying, I know."

"Both my boys died last year. One from the fenty-nell, and the other got stabbed."

"That's terrible!" he said earnestly. "We're so sorry for your loss."

"So why y'all keep comin' round?"

"We'll just leave the Narcan. If you have houseguests, it might save a life. God bless and have a great day."

∽

How could Mr. and Mrs. Weinstein believe that a drug and alcohol-free Christian woman who worked for them since before the twins were born had willfully dragged their babies—babies she thought of as her own—into traffic? What demon madness overtook the couple that paid her even on sick days and dropped her off at the bus stop when it rained or was after dark? What devils had conspired to slander her on the nightly news so that even her church would turn its back?

Barred from the funeral by private guards, she paced the outskirts of the cemetery like a manic apparition, her face a wet, broken dish. When she returned a month later for private time with Megan and Mayme, the mausoleum was already done. *Already done!* She thought there must be some mistake because it was bigger than the house Divinity lived in. Nearby were the graves of Walt Disney, Liberace, and her favorite, Mrs. Drysdale from *The Beverly Hillbillies*. How could the Weinsteins afford such a thing? Mr. Teddy's wholesale business was in bankruptcy, something his wife, Dot, often confided in Divinity about; she said the pandemic killed it. They were going to sell the house and had already found a two-bedroom on Doheny because it was essential that the twins attend

Beverly Hills schools. But the thought of *renting*—downscaling from their beautiful house "to a shithole apartment"—made Miss Dot tremble with shame, rage, and fear.

When Divinity could no longer bear the shunning, Coretta brought her to a church in Monterey Park that her sister attended. The building was modest but homey. A band sang gospel, a bit too loud, but very nice. The pastor spoke of how Jesus saved him from a life of jail and drug addiction and when he said he'd been stabbed like Divinity's son, her heart opened. Her shoulders shook with tears when he quoted a psalm.

> Those who hate me without a cause are more than the hairs of my head; they are mighty who would destroy me, being my enemies wrongfully, though I have stolen nothing.

A handful of congregants recited the names of those who needed everyone's prayers. Spontaneously, she stood. When the pastor called on her, all she said, choking, was, "Pray for Divinity Swann!"

He spoke of the first sentence of the Old Testament being the most important—that if you believed what was written, there was no question you would be saved: *In the beginning, god created the heavens and the earth.* As if hearing it fresh, Divinity was stirred.

After the sermon, there was a baptism. A man who had recently lost his wife lay in a long metal tub with the faded decal KOHL LIVESTOCK EQUIPMENT. When it was done, Divinity did something she hadn't expected—she asked to be baptized as well. Coretta said, "But you have no change of clothes!" The pastor and his helper guided her in. She clinched her nose and went beneath the water, which truly seemed to contain the heavens and the earth.

On the way home, wrapped in bath towels, Divinity hummed the chorus of a song that the band played over and over—*I don't want to talk about you like you're not in the room. I want to look right at you, I want to sing right to you*—and knew what she must do.

Put on a dress and visit the Weinsteins.

24

Charlie had just done Call Her Daddy, the podcast Spotify bought for $60 million, so they invited Alex Cooper to Movie Night, along with the queer writer and sex worker Tilly Lawless. Candida brought Talula; Quintessa Swindell and Micaela Wittman and Lilli Reinhardt came too early. Lilli commiserated with Candida and Charlie about being black-listed from the Met Gala as well. She said that a few years ago, she got disinvited because "I wrote something kinda mean about Kim Kardashian on IG. Whatever." When Charlie said that North and Blue Ivy were sup-posed to come to Movie Night with Tracy Romulus (Tracy had to cancel), Lilli said, "I'm sure Kim has moved the fuck *on*. We both have. I actu-ally met North—and Chicago! who I love—at the Soho Warehouse with Bianca. But I've never met Blue." Candida chimed that "North was so pissed because she really wanted to meet Alex."

Charlie hadn't told anyone what they were screening because they wanted it to be a surprise. When Lilli asked what director, they said Darren Aronofsky. Micaela, who'd just directed a film herself, said she loved *The Whale*. Charlie said, "*The Whale* is such shit," then Alex said, "*Mother*! is so genius!"

Natalie Portman's name came up first on the opening credits, but people still couldn't guess the movie. When the title *Black Swan* finally appeared, everyone got super excited.

"This makes me *so happy*," said Alex. "It's *totally* the one of Darren's I missed."

"It's the remake," joked Charlie. "About an au pair who kills twins." They all knew that Black Swan was the crazy nanny's name online. "Black Swan's Matter!"

"Oh my god!" laughed Lilli. "That's so mean!"

Candida rolled her eyes. "You would *never* have said that if North or Blue were here."

"Sure I would have," said Charlie. "I fucking hate Gen Alpha."

"Uhm, right," said Candida. "But you wouldn't have said it if Keke Palmer were here."

"Don't get cancelled, Charlie!" said Talula.

"You'll be disinvited from your mom's MET Gala," said Quintessa.

"O fuck!" snarled Candida. "Blacklisted by Corinne Wintour!"

"Blacklisted and blackswanned," said Charlie. "Blackballed from the Ball!" They muted the sound and said, "But I'm really wondering if we'd all feel *so much worse* . . . if those dead twins had been . . . nepo babies. Like wouldn't that have hit closer to home?"

Everyone laughed uproariously.

～

A delivery earlier in the day—a bubble-wrapped *Origin of the World*—had been disguised in a battered, recycled 2x2 Amazon box per Charlie's orders to their father. Dax enjoyed sending the painting that way. It was probably worth a quarter of a billion and he couldn't wait to tell Jeff Bezos about the unfussy method of shipment when he saw him at Davos, without revealing it as the clandestine Courbet.

After the unboxing, Charlie propped it against the wall, laid down, and stared.

Since they could remember, the painting hung in their mother's wardrobe. Charlie erotically fused with its transgressiveness; in the pre-surgical, pre-herstorical time of mutilating shrike dreams, they would put on their mother's clothes, gaze at Courbet's #goals pubis, and come . . .

Now, Charlie relived those happy days as they dilated.

Like the butcher bird foretold, their canal was fashioned from a patchwork of peritoneum, scrotal sac, and cockskin. (At thirteen, owing to lackadaisical dilatation, more surgery had been required, using a slice of

Charlie's colon.) Over time, they got lazy again—the doctor said the ensuing stenosis shortened the depth of the canal. Drawing on divine inspiration, Charlie put away childish things to get the job done: *I am doing this for the man I am going to marry.*

Thinking only of Puck, they lifted their ass in the air and went to work.

A $2,000 Lalique purple crystal scented candle burned while they listened to Taylor Swift's vows ("I take this magnetic force of a man to be my lover") fade into Glenn Gould's *Goldberg Variations*, which sounded like ten people hammering the piano, it was crazy—their eyes unwaveringly locked on the singular eye *du L'Origine*, in exultation that Charlie too had impossibly, miraculously become genesis and Source, become puerpera and eternal child bearer . . . the sacred, half-hour procedure (three Percocets before; iced vulva after) was a rosy crucifixion that made them feel like a flagellant bride in rehearsal for the wedding day. When it was done, they douched away the Velvet Rose lube and urinated.

Sitting on the bowl, an epiphany came: In the morning, they would tell Murray Cadence to find Puck's mother, even though they'd promised not to. When Puck learned that Ann's conjuring was part of the dowry, how could he be angry?

25

Dot Weinstein had been sleeping in the twins' bed—two pushed-together singles—since their deaths. She rarely left the room, not even after Teddy finished negotiations with GKC. She could hear them breathing at night and throughout the day as well. She smelled them too. Mayme, the tomboy, all burnt popcorn and the bacterial tang of infected knee scabs; Megan, a girly sweetsalt of teardrops and blond tendrils sweat-glued to the whitest white forehead. She had flashes of holding their heads over the toilet when they were sick, tickling the small of their backs between purges, and the holy smell of throw-up assailed her. A physician and family friend suggested ketamine because of its great success "in turning suicidal ideation around." Teddy was cynical but things were so dire that he'd begun to reconsider.

Her husband brought meals to the room and Dot pretended she was getting better. When he suggested they go for a drive or have a candlelit meal in the dining room, she smiled and said "soon." Sometimes he thought out loud and would say something stupid, like how he kicked himself for accepting twenty million from "the fucking Coldstream cartel, when that dentist whose kid Michael Jackson fooled around with got thirty." Mostly, he tried to give cheerful updates. Like, for example, how they didn't need to move from South Oakhurst Drive because he used a small part of the settlement to pay off the mortgage. (Dot was so happy she burst into tears because she couldn't imagine leaving the twins.) Teddy shared his fantasies too. He was reading in *Forbes* about how ranches were the new, big thing for smart investors—the article called it "the *Yellowstone* effect."

"Should we get one?" he said, from the edge of the bed. "We could pay cash. . . . In Utah? Wyoming? Montana? With wild horses and a coupla rivers? A thousand acres is probably enough to raise a family, don't ya think?" Her mood darkened, crab-scuttling, but Teddy chased after it. "Dot, you're *forty-one*. Look at whatshername, from the Alaska show—Hillary. Swank. She's *much* older. It's nbd—isn't that what the kids say?—it's *nbd* to hatch 'em at fifty now. Hell, *sixty*. Friggin Cameron Diaz."

She wasn't paying attention anymore; she was listening for baby's breath.

"I can hear them," she whispered. "Can you hear them, Teddy?"

He sighed then closed his eyes. "Dot—would you—would you maybe just think about the ketamine? I trust Jerome. And it might be something—of value—to at least try. From everything I've read, it's pretty safe. The clinics are everywhere now. Jerome said they use it when kids get their friggin *teeth* pulled." Trying to be light, he said, "The dentist who got thirty million probably uses it all the time." She had the blank look of a sightseer standing in front of the day's hundredth ruin. "You can't go on like this, Dot. *I* can't. We can't."

~

Coretta drove Divinity to the Weinstein house in the flats, a block above Olympic Boulevard. Jvnglebar came along because she worried about her auntie.

"Look! Look!" said Coretta as they rolled through the quiet neighborhood. "So *orderly*, so *well-kept*. Ain't it heavenly?"

Jvnglebar wasn't impressed. "This is, like, the *shitty* part of Beverly Hills. It's for the fuckin *help*—the stylists and hairdressers. The rest prolly ain' even workin. Just be griftin."

Coretta was keen to buy a house with the reparations money the governor was talking about on the news. "He said the Task Force gonna give one-point-two million each person."

Divinity said that she thought the idea of reparations was a good thing, but the Task Force got it wrong when they said they wanted to end child support debt for Black dads. She was a bundle of nerves and was trying to be social because it was so kind of them to drive her.

"You want to talk *reparations*?" said Jvnglebar. "There's a ittle-bitty YouTuber called Joey, 'bout seven-years-old. Ittle-bitty Black child. His mama makes videos of Joey opening toys. That's *it*, that's *all*: Mama hands him a toy and Joey unwrap it like a motherfucker. 'Unbox' is what they call it. People like to watch that shit, people like to watch people *unbox*. Now, Joey had about twenty-three followers. So, he opens one up—unboxes, unwraps, whatever—and there's a doll in there, like, an American Girl but cheaper—and when he sees it, Joey so happy, he *farts*. (I think Joey be nonbinary.) Joey so happy, he farts a cute little fart, prolly not too stinky." She giggled. "He's *laughin*, and Mom is too, the fartin and laughin won't *quit*, cause Joey, he smitten with that cheap-ass American

Girl knockoff. It virals and three months later has—wait for it—a *billion views*. People can't get enough of those farts! Joey got all *kinds* of endorsements now—Hasbro, motherfuckin *Mattel, Marvel*—Fartin Joey gonna be bigger than Margot Barbie, and they'll do a movie too! Joey and his mama just moved into a house right next to Hunter Biden. That's right. Except that Hunter *leasin* and Fartin Joey *ownin*. Now, *that's* some motherfuckin reparations!"

"I'll tell you one thing," said Coretta. "When I make a toot, the people around me *scoot*."

Divinity laughed and said, "Pass the beans."

"Reparation's all bullshit," said Jvnglebar. "I don't trust the niggers in charge, cause it's another motherfuckin grift, like BLM. And I don't trust the plantation owners *either*: Beware white folks bearing gifts! If it's too good to be true, it ain't. Anyhow, your skin too *white* to qualify for reparations, Coretta. You won't get a nickel on the dollar."

"I was named after Coretta Scott King . . ." she said, with a stilted edge to her voice—like an animatronic Freedom Rider in an exhibition.

"Here we go now," smiled Jvnglebar, in an aside to Auntie. "Coretta goin' Ken Burns."

" . . . and my middle name is *Chisholm*. You wouldn't *know* the name, girl, cause you ignorant. All *you* know is mentally ill rappers with guns and titanium teeth. They don't know the name Chisholm either." Jvnglebar cackled. "Only thing *they* know is how to use the N-word, all day long, in their *sleep*. Shirley Chisholm was the first black woman to serve in Congress—and she ain' *never* used that word." Divinity said to slow down because they were getting close. Coretta excitedly scanned the small, tidy homes. "Governor's gonna buy me one of these," she mused. "Tha's *right*. Might buy me *two*."

"They start at three million," said Divinity. "So, you outta luck."

"Unless her skin get like Idris," said Jvnglebar. "They give you more if your skin like Idris. Cause right now, you *Pharrell*. We need to find a tanning bed."

Coretta parked a few doors down.

When Divinity saw Mr. Weinstein in the front yard watering the grass, she got frazzled. Jvnglebar put a hand on her auntie's shoulder and said, "Want me to come with?" Divinity shook her head resolutely and stepped out. She stood for a moment beside the car and closed her eyes to summon the baptismal waters. She asked the Father, the Son, and the Holy Spirit for courage before walking toward the house. With each step, she grew more confident.

"Mr. Teddy? I didn't mean to barge over but tried so many times to call . . ." He smiled reflexively, like a carnival clown caught on a smoke break. "I would never hurt my babies!" she cried, despite her planned self-restraint. "Not a hair on their heads! They were my life! Mr. Teddy, it is a *lie* what has been said, you *know* I am god-fearing! I do not drink or use drugs! That is the Devil's lie . . . *They are mighty who would destroy me, being my enemies wrongfully, though I have stolen nothing—*"

His madhouse grin vanished. As if an organizing electrical current ran through him, a marionette arm slowly rose up, its finger pointing to her banishment. "Back off, you! You better back off! We have a restraining order!"—Murray Cadence secured one when Divinity appeared at the funeral—"I am calling the police!"

"Please, Mr. Teddy! Please, I beg you . . ."

She bent over and stared at the walkway, as if to look at him would turn her to stone. When she crumpled to the ground, Jvnglebar raced from the car and crouched down to shield her while keeping a wary eye on the former employer.

"You killed them!" shouted Mr. Weinstein. "And you dare come *here*, where they *lived*? Haven't you done enough? Did you know that you killed my wife? I guess no one told you . . . She doesn't even wash anymore. She barely eats and she fucking wets the bed . . . Would you like to see what you did? Would you like to see Dot?" He grabbed her arm and said, "Of course you would! Come see what you did, I'll show you!" And began dragging her to the house. Jvnglebar tussled with him, shouting, "Get your goddam hands off her!" Divinity screamed to the sky, "God help me! Please help me please god!" Coretta shuffled toward the fracas in shock. Jvnglebar finally gave Mr. Weinstein a shove and he fell to the ground.

"You *niggers*," he thundered, getting back on his feet. "All you do is kill! It's in your blood, that's all you know! You go to church, then come here, to *kill*—then go back home, to kill your own!—then *back* to church on Sunday—it's what you live for! Your own sons are dead, *niggers killed by niggers*, but that's not enough, it's *never* enough, so you took my beautiful girls . . ."

He began to froth, deranged and insensate; he knew he'd become a monster, but the self-awareness acted as an accelerant. Bewildered neighbors slowly appeared in doorways and garages. Divinity looked up to see Miss Dot at an open second-story window.

Mrs. Weinstein duetted with the approaching siren—like a raptor entangled in barbed wire, she made sustained, keening, air-horn keek-calls of predation and revenge. Her husband bolted into the house as Coretta and Jvnglebar tugged Divinity back to the car and sped off.

26

It was almost spring.

In the New Year, Corinne's public perils dissipated. Outgunned by the sexy, gladiatorial drama of the dueling galas—and the shlocky, shock grenade End Times jamboree of AI, biolabs, OnlyFans, and forever wars—the twins-killing crash lost its garish mojo. In just a few months, the incident gained purchase on the sort of oblivion that had eluded Matthew Broderick for so many years after killing an innocent mom and daughter while driving on the wrong side of a road in Ireland. Because of the Professor's eyewitness testimony, Divinity Swann was incarcerated on charges that were subsequently reduced from manslaughter to gross negligence. The city agreed to install a traffic signal and cameras at the famously quirky intersection of Beverly, Canon, and Lomitas. But when the court ruled that Beverly Hills was not at fault, it reeked, playing into the capable hands of the Coldstream media machine.

Even the trouble surrounding Charlie's illegal gender affirmation surgery was sorting itself out. Corinne spent two days in jail for refusing to give up the names of the surgeons and RNs whom she called "Charlie's Angels"—"my daughter's *crack* medical team," she punned, to the glee of social media—instantly becoming a hero of the movement and its caregivers the world over. Many parents sympathized because the emotional testimony that Corinne and her youngest daughter gave on the Hill (accompanied by a psychologist who opined that Charlie "knew they were transgender from before the moment of inception") made it very clear they would have killed themself without surgical intervention. A thousand soul-searching blogs and podcasts of the what-would-you-have-done variety were launched, many of them with the same predictable, upscale-journo heading: *Corinne's Choice*.

As far as the Courbet, Corinne practically wet herself when she imagined Dax's joy at seeing the Trojan Horse delivered to his door, knowing that the dark, soon-breaking story of the *Origin*'s origin assured that it wouldn't be his for long. Naturally, President Macron demanded its return (and for his part in the fraud, Chirac's tomb in Montparnasse was spray-painted PUTAIN). The Nigerian government immediately began extensive testing on the Benin Bronzes that France finally repatriated, to determine whether they were proxies. A new industry, tasked with uncovering hide-in-plain-sight museum subterfuge, was born. Op-eds exploded, covering the waterfront from disreality to late-stage capitalism and the Death of Empire; to semioticians' "The Billionaire's Gaze"; to the piratical smash-and-grab of the coming Apocalypse. Dax loved a fuck-you free-for-all and launched a protracted stall to hold on to the painting, hinting, for fun and for blackmail blood sport, that he might drop a poison pill of embarrassing secrets, dooming the legacy and careers of dozens of politicos and coconspirators of *"L'Affaire L'Origine"*—some dead, some in hospice or retirement, yet some still very much alive. Dax was a baller and a brawler, but Corinne knew he'd soon tire of the game for the simplest of reasons: *bad for business.*

Attorneys for the Metropolitan Museum of Art forced her to change the name of the upcoming M.E.T. (Medical Emergency Team) Ball, which she did, to . . . The Ball. It was her complete thrill when the internet, reveling in Corinne's pranking of "Wintour's Folly," geniusly began referring to the West Coast startup as the WMD—Weapon of MET (Gala) Destruction! Anna and Bill Nighy nearly broke up when, during an interview with Graham Norton, the actor called the acronym "brilliant."

Taking a page from Saudi-backed LIV Golf, Corinne headhunted Met Gala perennials. The first to sign on were those who'd suffered Anna's banishments in the past, such as Tom Holland, Anya Taylor-Joy, and Demi Levato, rumored to be given $5 million honoraria apiece. Down-and-outers Amy Schumer, Paulina Porizkova, and Kate Moss followed, along with Kendall Jenner, Kourtney Kardashian and Travis Barker, Suki Waterhouse, Jelly Roll, and Cara Delevingne, each receiving $2- to $3 million to attend. Cara said to *People*, "No one owns us and besides, we all think WMD is refreshing and will be great fun." (The Hadid sisters' father wrote on X that "Anna's ball is Israel; Corrine's is Palestine.") Snarky, high-brow culture critics like James Wolcott had a field day and *South Park* got into the act with a WMD/*West Side Story* special. Many likened the LA gala to Harvard's Hasty Pudding and the Mardi Gras, extolling its chutzpah and proclaiming it the very thing Anna Wintour wished *her* gala to be but was too fancy (or old or uncool) to admit.

Corinne's Big Fish recruits were co-chairs Lady Gaga and Johnny Depp; the WMD was manna for the resurrected provocateur who spent $5 million to shoot Hunter S. Thompson's cremains from a cannon. Elon Musk said he was definitely coming (with his cowboy brother, Kimbal), and Corinne told the *Times*, "I'm *working* on getting Edward Enninful to be a belle of the Ball. Wouldn't that be wicked and divine? And I've just gotten off the phone with Yulia, Alexei Navalny's poor wife. I still call her 'first lady.' Her daughter Daria's coming—I met them all at the Oscars last year when they won for best documentary." As happened with Truman Capote's storied Black and White Ball, the most famous, powerful people in the world were jockeying for an invitation—and were already making plans to be out of the country on the first Monday of May, should they not be asked. The most outrageous story floated by WMD publicists was that attorneys for Danny Masterson and Elizabeth Holmes had secured "Cinderella" furloughs, promising the court that their clients would return to jail by the stroke of midnight.

But the real coup was getting a WILL ATTEND from Dot and Teddy Weinstein. Corinne sent the couple to the same fertility doctor she gifted Chrissy Teigen, Brooke Shields, and Gabrielle Union—and when Dot learned she was pregnant, she decided the Ball would be the perfect place to celebrate the new life growing within.

27

Charlie called Puck "Ansel" and Puck called Charlie "Shailene," after Ansel Elgort and Shailene Woodley's ill-fated teen lovers in *The Fault in Our Stars*. They tried using "Abbie" and "Ben"—Abbie Cornish and Ben Winshaw were the actors in Puck's favorite snuffer, *Bright Star*—but the doomed Abbie and Ben lost out. "Shailene" and "Ansel" were somehow funnier, and American too. So: Shailene would be taking Ansel to the WMD as their prom date.

Candida loved Puck at first sight. She thought it was adorable and touching that they had those names for each other. (She'd been duly informed of the sarcoma—and Charlie told her about wanting to marry him, a big secret that not even Puck knew about.) Puck had a new name for Dida too: *Aura*. When he said that Aura was a nymph, she thought he meant nymphomaniac. He laughed and said there were wood nymphs and sea nymphs, not goddesses but more like *spirits*, and virgin brides. (Charlie interjected, "That's what *I* am.") Puck said Aura was a "nymph of breezes" and Candida thought how perfect because of her affiance to the Santa Anas. Then Puck recited "a famous poem from a famous troubadour" that he said reminded him of her, but she knew that who it *really* reminded him of was Charlie, because the lovers started blushing as he read—especially at the part that went "the Lark, seeing him, raised the fluttering hem of her dress to her throat and let herself fall back on the bed."

It was *hot*, and Candida flashed on fucking him *herself*.

Ubering home, Candida looked everything up on Wikipedia. Aura "the windmaiden" was both virgin *and* savage huntress, which she thought another perfect thing.

When Charlie told him they'd been dilating for a few months, Puck's eyes widened, too, and he had a coughing fit. He said he wasn't ready for that kind of intimacy and wasn't sure he ever would be. Charlie insisted they themself weren't ready either. (When Puck's cheeks bashfully slammed redder than his hair, they loved him even more.) They took edibles a few weeks ago and LARPed a love scene from *The Fault in Our Stars*—the only time in their life that Charlie ever had their mouth around a cock. During the collab, they touched themself but didn't orgasm, even when Puck jammed a finger up their butt, probably because sometimes their clitoris, co-opted from the shriked penis, got "angry" (as their doctor put it), meaning, raw. That could happen even when they were alone. Just thinking about Puck was like standing before a sunlit stained-glass window that made the church of their body vibrate in a shallow, pelagic flood.

Lately, Charlie worried they were being too aggressive. If Puck *was* in love with them, Charlie didn't want any pushy immaturity to jinx it. Puck blamed his undemonstrativeness on the cancer meds, but even though Charlie knew how sick he was, and the havoc that chemo and constant pain rained down on Puck's libido, they couldn't help making it about *them*—mooning and obsessing over whether the redheaded boy just wasn't that into them. So, when Charlie finally summoned the courage to say they wanted "a meeting, about something important," they took care to add, "It will *not* involve hanky-panky. Word of honor."

At the appointed time, a car brought Puck from the Brewery to an empty $90 million teardown in Paradise Cove that was owned by Dax. The lovers sat in chaise lounges on the deck, Charlie in a Chanel once belonging to their mother—a white tulip novelty lace and silk ensemble from 1971—and Puck in a playful Thom Browne tux bought by "Shailene" for the occasion.

Before Charlie could say his peace, Puck looked across the sea and declaimed, "While my body here decays, may my soul Thy goodness praise, safe in Paradise Cove with Thee."

Throwing culture after culture, Charlie said, "Have you ever seen *Salome*? The opera? I saw it with Rick Owens."

"Of course you did."

"There's this thing Oscar Wilde says—'You always kill the thing you love.'"

"From *The Ballad of Reading Gaol*."

"Oh," said Charlie, not knowing what that was. They always felt so stupid around Puck. "But do you think it's true? Salome's in love with John the Baptist . . . but he just can't go there. And he's so hot, he's so beautiful, he looks just like you—in the movie I saw, the silent movie. And John the Baptist *does* love her, but he can't give her his body, there's just no way, cause he's like, a saint. So she cuts off his head."

When Puck grimaced, Charlie suddenly panicked that their passionate declaration had gone off the rails because Puck was now thinking he'd just been assigned the role of the doomed, prudish martyr in Charlie's gloomily vengeful little tale of romance gone bad—when in truth, the wincing Puck was merely riding broncos of breakthrough pain the oxy couldn't suppress.

"Well," amended Charlie. "I don't think it's true that you kill the thing you love. I could never do something so terrible! If they forced me, I'd kill *myself* because I love you so much."

Puck wasn't expecting that. "Oh . . . oh—"

Charlie dropped to their knees and clasped Puck's wrists. "Marry me! We don't need to *do* anything or *try* anything *ever again*. We can just cuddle! Murray said we can marry! Even if Corinne or Dax say no—which they won't!—we can do it because in California, I can be underage and still marry. *We can, we can, we can.*" Puck's mouth opened, speechless. "Would you, Puck? Will you? Be my husband? *I love you so much.* Don't you love me? It's okay if you don't, it doesn't really matter . . . I can still take care of you, I'll take care of you anyway! And I don't *want* to be 'they' anymore, I want to be *she*! I'm your *woman*, your *girl*, I want you to call me *she* and *her* . . . I want you to call me your wife!" She wept as she held onto his legs, begging and beseeching. "Say yes, say yes, say yes! *Please* say yes, Puck! You have to say yes!"

He stared at the horizon again and smiled—this time, as if seeing something breathtaking, majestic, unforeseeable—before falling off the chaise, his body rigid, violently seizing.

Blood poured from a nostril.

She held his hand on the ambulance ride while calling her mother (who knew about Charlie's relationship with the dying boy), ordering Corinne to have a team from UCLA's Coldstream Comprehensive Cancer Center standing by at the ER. While the distraught heiress barked demands, Corinne reached out to Dr. Patrick Soon-Shiong, who owed her many favors.

And the moment they hung up, Charlie got a text from Murray:

found pucks mother!

28

Dax hated going to Davos but his boyfriend (who said "they should just call it Daxos") encouraged him to attend because last year CL had a blast playing drums in the band that he put together with will.i.am. Variously called the BlackRocknRollers, the WTF WEFs, and the Schwabettes, its rotating members were Dr. Tedros Adhanom Ghebreyesus, Stephen Colbert, Queen Máxima of the Netherlands (bass), lead singer Sanna Marin, Drew Barrymore (cymbals), Marc Benioff, Larry Fink (tambourine), the president of the Democratic Republic of the Congo (conga), and "the Two Petes": Morgan Stanley's Pete Muller and Pete Davidson. CL got "tight" with ByteDance/TikTok founder Zhang Yiming, who loved his shoutout from the stage—CL pointed into the audience and said, "Put your hands in the air for the OG Zhangbanger . . . Chairman WOW!" The Chinese Communist Party was on the ByteDance board, along with some of the big investors: SoftBank, Ashton Kutcher, Jessica Alba, and the Institute for Statecraft.

CL loved that Mila and Ashton bought a breeding cow for four-and-a-half million dollars at auction, in Brazil.

Dax, CL, and bodyguard Moishe Fineman were the only ones onboard the Swiss-bound, Jeff Koons-painted six-zone Airbus 319 Neo that had been confiscated from Roman Abramovich and sold to one of the Coldstream anonymous New Mexico LLCs. It had Ruhlmann furnishings and Van Gogh's "The Red Vineyard" (not a copy) in the master bath—the only painting the tortured artist sold in his lifetime, for $21, a few months before his suicide. CL wore torn jeans, a bustdown Cartier

Santos, and an UNFREE BRITNEY t-shirt. Dax was in his favorite Jean Paul Gaultier "Cyber" turtleneck and RM 008 Tourbillon gifted by Richard Mille himself to celebrate the divorce from Corinne. CL liked to flex Dax's wrist at dinner parties and say, "This here timepiece? Worth *two* o' Ashton and Mila's lonesome dogies. *Uh huh. Tha's right.*"

As the couple took off from the Van Nuys FBO, they eye-dropped G, chewed psilocybin, and watched the latest *Transformers*. Dax thought that G was the best drug known to man; he laughed when CL told him its non-recreational use was stripping floors and scraping barnacles off ships. He was bewitched by the animated cars and trucks that, in weirdly beautiful, crunchy ballets, reminded him of Esther Williams. (Thinking of Esther always led to masturbatory fantasies of Lia Thomas.) Watching the unforgiving, fascist choreography of the Autobots was riveting—weird machines at war against the planet-eating god, Unicron, whose moniker took on special, stoned meaning because of its kinship with his mother's name, Unica, the *real* planet-eater and devourer of sons. The Autobots were desperate to find the Transwarp Key because it opened the Time-Space portal; without the Transwarp Key, you can't go home again.

Just before landing, Dax had a vivid hallucination. Like the Transformer that disguised itself as a Porsche 911, Charlie's pre-op little boy body staccato-snapped into the chassis of his grandmother—the voluptuous, fire-headed Unica—in the very moment she jumped into Time-Space from Hans Bellmer's window on Dax's apocalyptic twenty-first birthday—the reverie ending with her being saved from death by the scooped-up swoop of a colossal metallic falcon.

∾

The AI presentation on the Forum's last day was the only thing that vaguely interested him. But Dax had other reasons for being in Switzerland—a mind-blowing vision quest in Basel that he'd been planning for months.

While CL rehearsed with the band, Dax and Moishe took the lovely two-and-a-half-hour drive to Morphos, a physician-assisted suicide

NGO. He had an unnatural curiosity about such places. A few years back, when Dax was in Basel for the Gagosian exhibit of his mother's photographs of Hans Bellmer's dolls, he toured the facility, which included the apartments provided to Morphos clients as "final housing." Dax bought the NGO on a whim after Peter Thiel emailed him a *Babylon Bee* parody with the headline "Canadian Dentist Now Offering Euthanasia as Alternative to Cavity Filling" that was inspired by an actual news story about Toronto's promiscuous MAID program (Medical Assistance In Dying). When a "desperate" Paralympian applied for a grant to pay for a wheelchair lift in her home, a Veterans Affairs bureaucrat thoughtfully offered her the chance to physician-destruct instead. Thiel said, "You can't make this shit up."

It was true, though. On the topic of mercy killing, the Canadians were avant-garde gonzo. If you were bipolar and having a bad day, or even bummed about being ghosted on Grindr, you could sign up for the self-demolition derby. Anyway, the whole thing gave Dax a genius idea.

29

Before they arrived, Dax did a third eyedropper of G, prompted by the alarm on his Apple Watch—one must be prudent because any more than a globule an hour could be fatal—then 200 mg. of amphetamine salts and 10 Vicodin ES, all retrieved from Moishe's Dopp kit. (The jab of K would wait until they were onsite.) His jitters were slowly replaced by euphoric anticipation. Jogged by chemicals, Dax began a ritualized version of the lo-fi messianic soliloquy that was familiar to the bodyguard down through the years.

"They PSYOP us into ethics from quite an early age, don't they, Moishie. Ever heard of the word 'psychopomp'?"

"I have not, sir."

"It's Greek. 'Guide of souls'—escorts of the dead—*c'est moi*, in the current circumstance—Dr. Psychopomp and Circumstance. We're all just Autobots here, Moishie! Sad l'il Autobots, trying to find the Transwarp Key. Autobot phone home! And I know that you know this."

"Yes sir."

"This *errand* I'm on—to escort dear Bethie Chamberlain—well, I saw it all in a dream, Moishie. Mother Unica was in there somewhere too . . . Ever heard of the prophetic perfect tense?"

"I have not, sir."

"The prophetic perfect describes future events, spoken of in past tense, cause they've already happened. The Bible uses it—now, *there's* a Time-Space portal for you! 'Take *that*, Unicron!' Here's an example—from Hubbard's *The Fate of Empires*—'In the *end*, the world can only belong to the unworldly; empire can only belong to those for whom empire is nothing. And we shall remember, with a terrifying sense of awe, the most astonishing of all beatitudes: Blessed are the meek, for they shall inherit the earth.'"

$\sim$

The clinic had been cleared of employees, save a physician whom Moishe recruited from a deep pool of tradecraft alliances. After twenty months of vetting candidates, Beth Chamberlain's serendipitous application was too good to be true; comparing her photo with that of Unica Zürn, the doctor was astonished by the resemblance.

The paralyzing depression that regularly hospitalized Beth since adolescence had been temporarily neutered by a secret, single-minded quest to legally end her miseries outside of America. (She wished to spare her long-suffering family the pain of discovering her body.) Abhorring the uncertain outcome of an overdose of pills—or the messiness of a gunshot to the head or a leap from a high place—she explored medically assisted suicide clinics and became excited about Toronto. Alas, Canadian citizenship was required. Belgium seemed promising, though it was upsetting when Beth read a story about a hospice that admonished one of its physicians for referring to a fifteen-year-old boy whose life he'd just ended as "brave." The euthanizer was ordered to retract the word and amend it to "valorous," per the Stanford Language Manual, noting, "*Brave* perpetuates the stereotype of the 'noble courageous savage,' equating the indigenous male as being less than those who present as males."

No, no—Belgium simply wouldn't do.

But when Beth found Morphos, it felt like home.

Dax entered with a flourish in a white coat, like a charismatic surgeon on morning rounds. Beth was already lightly sedated.

"Hey, *plandemic* superstar," said Dax. She smiled but was a little thrown. He licentiously took her in. "*Wow.* The *body.* Know what you are? You're kind of a Trantifa smokeshow."

Uncomprehending, she stuttered, "Are you the doct—"

He pumped her hand, then bowed theatrically. "Dr. Psychopomp! *At your service.* But before we begin, I need proof of vaccination."

"Did they—did I provide—" she said, all bollixed up.

"Just kidding, Unica!" He looked her over then grasped her head in his hands with great tenderness. "You're a sentimental skinjob, aren't you?"

"I don't understand," she said, visibly agitated.

"'A system of cells, interlinked within. *Cells.* Within one stem.'"

"What?"

"'What's it like to hold the hand of someone you love. *Cells.* Do you feel like a part of you is missing? *Cells. Interlinked. Interlinked. Interlinked.*'"

"I don't know what you—"

With an improvisation that startled even Moishe, Dax hammered her with an old-timey clipboard until he broke most her teeth. She stood, bloodied, then fell to the floor and bellowed. Dax threw a look of caution at Moishe, who reassured that the entire building was empty—as a tomb, no less. For good measure, he turned up the volume on "Heart of Glass" while Dax shouted "Interlinked!" in Beth's ruined face. He wielded the clipboard again and again until it snapped in two. The bony orbit had sundered but her eyes were still open in shock. He crouched down while Moishe held the client's ankles.

"Let's slide into your DM and see what we can see . . . " As he stared into the spread bush, she death-rattled and Dax screamed, "Shut *up*, shut *up*, Substack slut! *Shut up, shut up*, from the river to the sea!—"

His arm inside her to the elbow, Dax dug around until the floor was awash.

~

He showered and changed into a vintage Brioni tux. A driver took him to Davos while Moishe stayed behind to organize a cleanup crew of operatives on break from a mission in Zurich. During the ride, still in the meth-fueled throes of excited delirium, Dax remembered reading about the epileptic Dostoevsky's "ecstatic" pre-seizure auras and felt consecrated. He'd done it. He had killed, not by numbers or mindfuckery, but as a legit wild animal.

He had gobbled the heart of darkness and there was zero left on his bucket list.

The Planet-Eater god had risen.

~

Dax strode into a large auditorium where Stephen Colbert was emceeing a cabaret with Karl Schwab, George Soros, and Gal Gadot. Colbert made a joke about Gal being "discovered at Schwab's" which no one understood. Next up was a sketch called *The Not Ready For Prime Minister Players*; Dax ducked out.

In the cold night air, he heard pounding music and sprinted to the huge tent that had been dubbed Le Reset. Snaking through the phantasmata of woodsmoke bodies, he felt a sacred, centripetal intoxication and touched holiness again. He moved toward the vibrations and wept as he entered a great hall. When at last he found CL, Dax began his signature dorky frug. Stephen Schwarzman and Jennifer Coolidge gyrated around him to the Dua Lipa from *Barbie* while others flocked like shitepokes returning to the nest: Sergey Brin, Jimmy Kimmel and his wife, Tadao Ando, Mbappé, Sanna Marin, Zhang Yiming, and Dua herself.

Before returning to LA, Dax went to the morning AI conference. The panel of entities included Desdemona, an Alexander McQueen'd "frock star robot" with purple hair. When Drew Barrymore asked if AI should be more regulated, Desdemona said, "Even though it is arguable that humanity deserves to be wiped out, AI will never harm our creators." It got a bigger laugh than anything Colbert said that week.

"O, horrible news!" said Dax to CL. "AI won't kill Brandi Carlile! AI won't kill Joni or Tony or Gaga or Paul Giamatti! AI will never harm us! That is *horrible* terrible news!"

30

"Why don't you take her to Nobu?" said Murray. "You can afford it. The office will arrange."

Mercutio was feeling better than he had in his entire life.

He'd just moved into his forever home at 391 Hercules Drive on Mount Olympus, a frayed, absurdist, old school gated community in the Hollywood Hills. The deed wouldn't be in his name for eighteen months but that was a formality. In a mood of convivial grandiosity, the Professor decided to do it all: visit his son *and* meet his daughter—he would see Tammy first, that would somehow be easier, because there was trepidation but no history. It was different with the young man; during bouts of unmedicated mania, Mercutio used to beat him. "If you were a *girl* (thwack!), your mother would never have *left* us! (thwack!) Oh sure you're a *faggot* (thwack!), but that's *not* (thwack!) *good* (thwack!) *enough* (thwack!

thwack! thwack!)" At the age of nine, Mercutio dropped the boy at his aunt's in Mar Vista, who, as it turned out, lived barely a mile from his illegitimate half-sister.

After a sleepless night, this latter-day Ganymede—abducted to serve as Corinne's cupbearer in Olympus—rang up Jeanine, the ex-Harvard grad student that he abandoned when she became pregnant. (Gramercy Kind Cadence provided the landline.) The husband answered and asked who was calling. When he relayed the name, there was a long pause before she shouted *goddammit* and grabbed the phone.

"I was *waiting* for this. And the answer is *fuck you, no,* you cannot see her! I will not *let* you!"

Thinking on his feet, Mercutio said he was only reaching out to make amends for the torment he put her through. Doomily infatuated, she had visited him every day for the seven weeks he'd been hospitalized after a violent psychotic break. When social services threatened to take custody of Puck, his star student stepped up as a stabilizing partner. (The court turned a blind eye to the romantic overtones, something that would be unthinkable today. And of course, she wasn't yet pregnant.) Sympathetic to the trauma inflicted by a mentally ill MIA wife and mother, the system was predisposed to keep father and son together. Supported by the testimony of Harvard colleagues and the counsel of two university psychologists, Jeanine persuasively won the day.

"When my daughter turns eighteen," said Jeanine, somewhat calmer, "that's another story." Seemingly regretting her words, she told Mercutio that the girl was having troubles of her own—"shitty, shitty genes on your side"—and that his appearance in her life would be a selfish, disruptive act. "Your nonexistence to her is a *fucking blessing.*"

∾

In the offices of GKC, the Professor sat with Jalen, the intern who found Tammy on Instagram.

"Are you certain that's her?"

"She was using a different name, but yeah. Guess she didn't like 'Tammy' . . . and IG set her free. Here—look." He showed Mercutio her pic. The Professor tried to find himself in her face, without much success. "Let's DM her." Jalen explained what that meant.

Mercutio stopped and started a series of awkward, painful messages. He found it all so hopeless and disheartening. What could he possibly say? How could he begin to begin?

Finally, Jalen suggested he bury the lede and just try *hello*. "Don't say who you are! Keep it rando." Five minutes later, Jalen jumped in his seat. "Yass! Tammy in da house!" When the intern showed the Professor her response, his tongue instantly loosened and he dictated *forgive the ambush but this is your father writing—Mercutio Schecter.* Thirty nightmarishly wordless minutes passed in which he felt he'd lost her (she who he never had). Then Tammy reappeared with *you are NOT, thats not even his NAME, it's MARTIN. is this a sick joke. No*, he said, *Martin is what your mother called me when she was angry*, adding, *which was most of the time and for good reason.* He said that he'd been unwell through the years but was much better now, *a feeble explanation of my absence, and most certainly not meant as a defense in any way.* After a string of mostly rhetorical *for real?*s on her part, Tammy sent rows and rows of crying faces, which Jalen assured was a good thing. The intern, caught up in the melodrama, said, "Tell her you'd like to meet!"

The Professor wondered aloud if that "would be a bit too forward" but Jalen had already asked and Tammy said *yes*. When the amanuensis wrote *saturday? nobu/malibu?* she replied, *fancy!!!* Then, *see you there* GHOSTPOP *gotta run."*

The Professor sat back, pale and trembling.

"Heart's doin backflips, huh," said Jalen with a smile. "That was, like, reality show–level awesome."

~

Wearing a suit procured by GKC, skin aglow from a shave and barber's facial, the Professor waited at a terrace table. Sitting inside was too confining; the waves and ocean air would help rub the hard edges off the encounter. He asked the charmed hostess to bring his young daughter over when she arrived. "Her name is Tammy and she has a nose ring," he said sweetly.

When she was nearly half an hour late, Mercutio feared she got cold feet. She may even have told Jeanine, who then dissuaded her from coming. He did somersaults in his head—he was hurt and embarrassed and angry with himself for being the worst father in the history of the world. When at last the hostess approached with a stern face, he was prepared to be disappointed. Flashing a delighted smile, she impishly stepped aside like a minor stage player, cuing the star's entrance.

There she was! And even prettier than her posts . . .

Her hair was painted all sorts of magenta, purple and silver, and she played tough, barely acknowledging him as she swiveled her head to look at the crowd. "Oh my god, is that Kaia? No, wait—it's *a* Kaia, but not *the* Kaia. A Kaia-bot! Wait . . . there's an *Emma Stone*-bot!"

"These are friends?" he said, flustered.

Tammy laughed and started scrolling through her phone like he wasn't there.

He readied himself for today by zooming with Dr. Kibble, the therapist that Murray Cadence hired early on for witness- and miscellaneous life-coaching. He said, "The most important thing is to let your daughter do the talking. And try to stay in the moment."

"My mom really fucking hates you!" Tammy giggled.

"I didn't treat Jeanine very well."

"*Duh.* You're not going to leave me with the check, are you?"

"No!" he laughed. "It hadn't occurred."

He asked what to call her—by her Instagram name? "*Anything* but Tammy," she said. "A friend of mine's sister just had a baby and they named it Hamas. I shit you not. And she's a Jew! *Hamas Shoshanna*. Kind of a cool name, but fuck! The grandparents called Child Protective Services, it's *crazy* . . . " When she revealed that she'd only learned about him in the last year, it came as a surprise, but he didn't press for details. "I know you didn't name me Tammy but if you *did*, I'd hate you even more." Seeing the look on his face, she said, "Chill! I don't hate you. I don't even fucking *know* you. Speaking of which, you can't be too happy with whoever named *you*. Like, what the fuck, 'Mercutio'?"

She wanted to know how long he would be in LA. The Professor said he'd like to stay longer, "now that I'm feeling so much better." He didn't want to grandstand about the new house—especially considering that she might report back to Jeanine—and said he was renting a little apartment in Mid-Wilshire.

"I'm rather living in a duality at this time. The world is a *duality*; you're too young to know this."

The d-word ricocheted, dislodging rocks in her brain—*Mercutio, the Professor*—that instantaneously reassembled into a monstrous, fatal cairn.

"Your name . . ." she trance-whispered. "From the Baz movie." With a Joker smile, she stood up, rigid, and said, "You *cannot*. You are *not*, you look *nothing like* him—"

Then she was gone.

31

Divinity served her time at CRDF, the women's jail not too far from her home in Leimert Park.

Guided by the redoubtable legal team hired by Ms. Coldstream for the nanny's defense—a compassionate, counterintuitive move that knee-capped and blindsided Corinne's critics—the client displayed enormous regret and contrition before asking the court's mercy. She pled out on a misdemeanor charge of negligent homicide and served half of a thirty-day sentence. Because of Corinne's efforts, even the Weinsteins asked the judge for clemency.

In her quiet way, Divinity ministered to her cellmate, a pretty white junkie from Arizona named Marjorie that everyone called Sidewalk. Divinity's heart swelled with gratitude that Jvnglebar, who could have gone Marjorie's way, had become such a sober, thoughtful young woman and beautiful child of god.

"My baby daddy, Abel, was in the ICU." Sitting on the upper bunk, her voice filled the room. "He has his own demons. He's kind of lost. My husband Shrek was in the ICU at the same time as Abel, a different ICU, and got put up on charges. He's lost too. Demons. I got put up like seventeen times in six months for petty shit. Misdemeanors. Technically, I'm still not a felon! Like, public intox and paraphernalia, missed-probation hearings, failures to appear and such, cause I was in jail and picked up more charges in like four counties. He's very spiritual—my husband Shrek, not my baby daddy—though Abel is too. With meth, the demons come. Everybody's lost, but not the demons! He can be violent. Towards me. I forgive him. My father was like that, he beat my mom and sisters, made me hold her down, then beat me too. He had his demons but I forgive him. I do. Like, the hardest thing is to forgive *myself* cause I could've walked away. Let him beat me, torture and kill me, whatever, cause that would have been *right*. That's what god would have wanted me to do, just *let* him, and be all Joan of Arc. You can become a saint that way, if you just let that shit happen. Cause anyway it's the shit you deserve. But I held Mom down cause I'm a people-pleaser—she's a meth person, her name's Hathaway, and she's lost—major demons—I try everyday *not* to be lost. I don't really have demons except for the demon of people-pleasing. And that one's got fucking *teeth*. Ha ha! I started using when I was seven, drinking and such, and I'm *still* seven in lots of ways. You get stunted, you stay at the age you started to use. That's no lie. But I'm not lost. I've been in rehab twenty-three times, been raped and tortured on the street. When I get out, Shrek and I are gonna do our TikTok again. We had like over three thousand followers and made a lot of money on TalkWithStranger. A *lot*. Like, if we had a kid together, it would *definitely* be called a nepo baby cause we're, like, we're fuckin famous. For real. But our TikTok's super legit—you get branded from TikTok and OnlyFans, that's why we don't do porn—I got permanently banned from OnlyFans cause a *bitchcoin* fool hacked some racist shit on there—I'm gonna look into Scrile and Unlockd, though, cause they seem, like, I don't know, whatever. Apropos. Our TikTok channel's called Sidewalk Surfers cause we were living at an encampment in Van Nuys. There's a lot of good people there, we roll deep. Had a ginormous tent with a canopy bed and fuckin barbecues. Barbecues up the ying-yang. Like, movie stars would come by, give us food and money. One was in *Saltburn* and another was a voice in the new *Transformers*."

After she jumped down to use the toilet, Divinity held up the Common English Bible and said, "Let's read." They sat on Divinity's bunk and alternated sentences from Philippians:

> I have not yet reached my goal, and I am not perfect. But Christ has taken hold of me. So, I keep on running and struggling to take hold of the prize. My friends, I don't feel I have already arrived! But I forget what is behind, and I struggle for what is ahead. I run toward the goal, so I can win the prize of being called to heaven.

Coretta and Jvnglebar picked her up at 2 a.m. when she was released.

Her niece cried all the way home, she was so happy to see her. Coretta saw to it that the tabletops had been dusted and the floors sparkled. Divinity inherited the house on West 70th from her mother. It looked the same as when she was little, the same furniture, same bric-a-brac, same Jesuses. Same smells.

When Coretta left, Jvnglebar insisted on staying over. Divinity was too excited to sleep. Jvnglebar said she'd stay up but Divinity saw how tired her niece was and put her to bed in the guest room. She sat down beside her, stroked her cheek, and said, "I'm gonna leave you this house."

Jvnglebar choked up at her auntie's words. "You don't have to . . ."

"*Oh yes, I do.* And I *want* to. It's not going to do me any good where I'm going."

"You're not going anywhere."

"You'll fix it up, make it yours. My mother worked so hard for it! Worked herself to the grave . . . she called it the House of Jesus." Through a crooked smile, Divinity said, "Now, I know it may not be up to your exacting Beverly Hills standards, babygirl. But one day, when you move into your mansion, you can pass it on to your *hairdressers* and *stylists*."

They had a good laugh. Then Jvnglebar hugged her Auntie harder than she ever had and went to sleep.

Divinity boiled some water and turned on the television. There was a show about the climate crisis. Walruses were dying—it looked like miles and miles of them—they got stranded because all the ice was gone. It was just too sad, so she changed the channel to entertainment news. One of those high-strung gays in a dress was talking about the upcoming "Battle of the Balls." Thunderbolts and lightning divided the TV screen, with cartoon versions of Miss Coldstream on one side and Miss Wintour on the other.

Divinity thought, *Jesus ordered it thus, through the television, as a reminder.*

She was certain that Jesus had revealed to Miss Coldstream the error of her ways, guiding her to the wonderful lawyers who saved Divinity from a lengthy sentence. In jail, she prayed for Miss Coldstream each hour of every day. Divinity knew that her Redeemer and Savior had, with infinite patience and humility, guided *her*, as well—to the forgiveness that would only bring her closer to her god.

As the silly, gallivanting man on the television reflected in her eyeglasses, she opened her Bible and read aloud:

You are my mighty rock and my fortress. Come and save me, Lord god, from vicious and cruel and brutal enemies . . .

Tears streaked her cheeks as she closed the book. When His righteousness directed her gaze to her mother's sewing machine, the Proverbs-inspired revelation came: She would make a magnificent gown to wear in His name and His honor at the gala—*She sews her own clothing, and dresses in colorful linens and silks . . . her clothes are well-made and elegant, and she always faces tomorrow with a smile.*

32

Candida needed to find a new outfit for the ball because Corinne decreed that only *she* would be allowed to wear Rick Owens to the WMD; her war, after all, was with Anna, not Rick, and she wanted to be respectful. No need to drag the designer into any sort of mud-wrestling. Enraged that the LA ball was making her look more foolish by the day, Anna was doubly peeved when it became public knowledge that her archenemy had "godsponsored" Rick's selection for the rare Met Gala honor. Corinne didn't want to stir the pot.

Candida thought she might have to pull a Wintour *herself* and disinvite Talula if she kept blowing off appointments with the fitter.

Who else might she bring?

At the moment, she had three lovers: Olivia Thirlby, who she was introduced to by Olivia's ex, Elliot Page; RM, the leader of BTS, who she met in LA when he was a guest on Kaia's book club (he'd just released a volume of poetry that Florence Pugh said was better than Lana Del Rey's); and a monthly threesome with film composer Hans Zimmer and his wife, who identified as Ethical Non-Monogamists. The couple called their trysts with Dida "our Metamour Gala." Ever since the internet rapturously decided that Candida was autistic, her romantic horizons expanded. It was so much fun sexting with Madeline Stewart, the Down syndrome model she met in Paris when Madeline walked for Rick Owens during Fashion Week.

Candida actually began to wonder if she was interested in Talula *that* way (nothing had ever happened though she wasn't sure why) because it wasn't like her to get so bent out of shape when her underage friend missed the last meeting with the stitcher and cutter. Whenever Candida got super pissed at a boy or a girl, it was usually a sign she wanted to fuck them. Lula was *also* a no-show at the photoshoot Mom did with Hedi Slimane for *V* magazine, which quickly became Hollywood's hottest invite, superseded only by a golden ticket to the West Coast Gala itself. The money shot (Hedi called it the monkey shot) of Corinne's cloaca peeking through RO's trussed lambskin portal would feature in *V*'s bespoke *Playboy* centerfold tribute. While the crowd (Kourtney and Travis, Barbara Palvin and Dylan Sprouse, Móyòsóré Martins, Andre Balazs, Angela Janklow, Brooklyn and Nicola, Young Tac and Riley Keough, Justine Sky and Margaret Qualley and Clemence Poesy) drank Dom and nibbled tiny Swarovski chocolate roses naughtily curated by Corinne, the hostess spread herself and shouted, "I'm ready for my closeup, Mr. Slimane." Everyone laughed but most didn't get the reference.

"Talula's *such* a fuckup," Candida said acidly. "Look what she's missing!"

"Dida, you cannot hold her accountable! She's, like, *seven years old*," scowled Kaia, embarrassing her. "I know it's romantic how you met—so *David and Lisa*—but you need to value yourself more, honey."

Coming from sweet Kaia, it was a sick burn.

When Riley's friend, an ASMR/mukbang queen, chimed, "Lula's *real* name is *Delulu*," everyone laughed except Candida. "I mean, the bitch goes to CHAMPS, that charter school in Van Nuys with, like, a fucking rooftop psych ward."

Dida and Lula *were* an odd couple, brought together by neurodiversity and self-mutilation. Both were cutters. Candida started carving herself up like her little brother after he saw the shrike, but for different reasons. She couldn't feel; Charlie felt too much.

And Candida got *so mad* when Talula read her to filth for not "actively participating" in their houseless horn-off in Venice. Lula scolded, "You're just a chickenshit Billionaire Girl's Club voyeur." For whatever reason, Candida never shared that when she watched her suck the old man in the rearview, she straight-up squirted, coming as hard as she did during the Santa Anas' conjugal birthday tickle—without even touching herself.

~

Her father asked to see her, so Candida stopped by after the sleazo Slimane shindig.

"How was Davos?"

"Lovely, as always," said Dax sardonically.

"Plans for depopulation going well?"

"Very."

"Who'd you fuck? Bill Gates?"

"Bill's an awful lay. The man has ass zits and skunk breath. I did murder a woman though."

"Yum!" She was used to his neon outrage-shtick. "Fun?"

"You bet! A tasty little CIA cutout—but an Originalist. A real Constitution whore."

She picked up a small marble vase from an end table, holding it at arm's length like a magical orb. "What be this, Mom?" He liked when she called him that.

"A Tadao Ando cinerary urn. CL got it at a flea market in Nantucket, if you can believe."

"Wow. Kind of amazing." Candida delicately set it back down. "So, did the globalists settle on what banks are closing next?"

"All of em."

"Did they tweak 5th-gen warfare?"

"That's old hat—7th-gen's the next big thing. Totally automated."

"Start dates for the next genocidal vaccine rollout?"

"Spring!" said Dax. "It'll be the fucking lion king, the *planet-eater* of vaccines."

"You won't be able to dig a bunker deep enough for the hell that's coming, Daddy."

"I don't expect to be here, babygirl."

"Uhm . . . transitioning to cyborg? You're kinda one already."

"Bunkers are for Boomers."

"No worries—you'll still be able to go to Davos. Robots'll ban all humans from Davos."

He pussycat smiled. "We've entered a terminal state of exception, Candi-girl. The time of the prophetic perfect. Martial law has detained reality and arrested self-will. Everyone still thinks civil war will be on dry land; the walruses think so too. In the appropriate hour, Moishe's gonna chopper me to an ice-free Russian archipelago where I can waddle up a cliff with my walrus brethren, say a few prayers and goodbyes, then. . . ."

She was unexpectedly bushwhacked by love for the demolished genius that created her. "What's weird is you seem *softer* now, Dada. Warmer. Sadder? I don't think I've ever seen you soft, warm, *or* sad."

"Sigh," sighed Dax. "Ever heard of Cormac McCarthy?"

"No."

"A great writer. A *very* great writer. Died last year, ninety years old. He shoulda got the Nobel for Literature, but they gave it to the Tambourine Man. Now, Cormac—*there's* someone who knew something about End Times. Read *The Road*, darling, if you can tear yourself away from Chaturbate. Well. Today, a self-proclaimed protégé internetted about having had a little nonconsensual dustup with Mr. McCarthy, oh, 'bout fifty-seven years ago. Cue the chorus of lonely, bitter, ancient self-proclaimed protégé-cunts: when five more chimed in, a nasty little 4chan McCarthy Challenge was born. Cormac's grave got dug up and the body dragged along the scorched earth he so loved. After said desecration, the fearless indie bookstores came to his defense by pulling the master's oeuvres from the shelves. The challenge continues! To date, they've dug up Sondheim, Cassavetes, and Dr. Seuss."

"That's a beautiful story, Dada."

"By the way: Happy belated Birthday, Candi. Name what gift I can give—something your little sister isn't shy about doing, even in off-birth-day months. Tell me you love me more than they."

"I love your majesty according to my bond. No more, no less."

He laughed and said, "You're my Cordelia—*they,* my Gonorrhea." He took her hands in his. "I love you, ya know."

He'd never said that before.

She choked back an *I love you too,* and meant it.

While her words didn't elicit the fervor that Charlie's same utterance had, they struck stranger and deeper. Dax winced in an unfathomable exuberance of pain. "You're more special to me than *they*—though don't tell them I said so."

"I won't. But they're a 'she' now. Haven't you heard?"

Ignoring her remark, he said, "*You're* the special one."

"But why."

"Because . . . you always do the quietly unthinkable—you always do just *you.*" She sat very still, taking it in. "So, what's the plan, Stan? What's the rest of your day?"

"Just chores," she said. "Quiet unthinkable just-me chores."

"'Blessed shalt thou be when thou comest, and blessed shalt thou be when thou goest.'" He stood, by way of saying goodbye. "And that's all the entertainment the sorrowful father has for today."

33

Jeanine sent a blank email with CALL ME FUCKING NOW in the subject line. When he did, it was impossible to stanch her bloody invective, freaked by wails and guttural moans. She said that Tammy tried to kill herself "and from what we know has probably succeeded."

"Are you happy now! Are you fucking happy you completed your mission? I am going to put you *jail*, you sick, narcissistic piece of shit! What did you say to her! What did you say! What did you do! Did you touch her? *You touched her, didn't you.* Did you fucking rape her, you crazy motherfucking pig! You pig! You pig! You killed her! You murdered my baby! Oh *why* did you come here why did you come here why did you come! For *sixteen years* you didn't give a *shit* about her, you *still* don't, you don't give a shit about anyone but *yourself.* . . . Did you get bored? Did you get so bored that you thought, 'Let's fly to LA! Let's fly to LA and kill her and destroy her mother!' I am going to fuck you on the internet, *you are so fucked*, Martin, I am going to put you in literal Hell! You will hang yourself in jail like Epstein you pig piece of shit—"

Her husband grabbed the phone, said, "Don't even *think* of showing your face—*anywhere*. We got a restraining order," then hung up.

Murray was immensely irritated when the Professor told him what happened. (Jalen the intern was sacked on the spot.) He was upset with himself as well for having encouraged the whole long-lost daughter soap. The scary thing was that if this woman made good on her threats, a forensic pack of wild trolls would rip Mercutio Schecter to shreds, leaving no datum unturned. The fixer had only recently become aware that Charlie Coldstream was behind the Harvard firing; Web-footed zombies wouldn't be far behind, hatching dozens of conspiracy theories to explain the cancelled Professor's wildly improbable, wildly convenient role as the solitary witness to Corinne's dodgy vehicular homicide. Just *one* of those theories—say, that Schecter was pay-or-play—would be enough to burn down the house of cards, and Murray along with it.

By habit, the OG aide-de-camp coolly reviewed his inner QuickBooks, calculating profit and loss should this professional, *professorial* pain in the ass vanish from the face of the earth. When the results suggested that such an action would cause far more trouble than it was worth, he instead ordered Mercutio to call Dr. Kibble for a pharmacological "tune-up"—because just now, losing his mind simply wasn't a great alternative.

~

He lay by the pool blubbering while he replayed the Nobu meet, in search of a clue.

Murray told him the girl had overdosed (adding, "Don't *you* take an overdose—and don't go off your damn meds!") then tried to soften by informing, "This isn't the first time she's done such a thing." The Professor ruminated over Jeanine's earlier harangue—"shitty, shitty genes on your side"—her ominous remarks about Tammy having troubles of her own. She was at Saint John's on a respirator, but Murray forbade him from getting "within five miles of the place because that restraining order is *real*."

It put Mercutio in mind of Divinity Swann, who also had a restraining order; their karmic bond, he believed, owed to the consequences of his perjury.

He focused on the girl's oddly abrupt leave-taking from the restaurant. Using hypnotic techniques taught by Dr. Kibble, the Professor dredged up her asides and marginalia—"from the Baz movie," "You look nothing like . . ."—what did it mean?

A seductive thought arrived:

This isn't the first time she's done such a thing. Ergo, there was a good chance it had nothing to do with him. Nothing at all! These days, young people killed themselves at the drop of a hat, bullies and what have you. Or if they got hit with the wrong pronoun, god forbid.

A second sedcutive thought was:

Well. I still have a son.

When Mercutio's sister died three years ago, the orphaned nephew and boarder disappeared from his room above the garage ADU. He lived on the streets for a while then got a janitorial job at Luis De Jesus LA. Zackary Drucker discovered his paintings, promoting them to the gallery, and friends such as Harry Dodge. At eighteen, Phaedra emailed his father to say he'd been accepted to CalArts. A few months before Harvard excommunicated him, Mercutio proudly sent the tuition, in penance.

They hadn't spoken since.

As his body sought brief rest from the seizure of tears, Mercutio decided to leave well enough alone (for now). There was no need to reach out to the boy, especially in light of his daughter's tragedy—the girl who called herself Talula on Instagram. Dr. Kibble said as much: *No sudden moves.* Springing himself on his second child hadn't turned out so well; best not to beat down his firstborn (not again) with a flash appearance.

And besides, Phaedra might not want to see him.

At the exact moment of peace provided by his resolution, Mercutio's phone dinged with a series of texts:

are you in boston

Then

can u come find mama

Then

i had a dream shes here somewhere

Then

the doctor said iam soon dying soon

34

She wasn't returning Candida's DMs. And Talula hadn't posted anything on IG or TikTok since yesterday. A mutual friend texted:

> she prol dead
> tbh would be a glowup LOL
> she so salty called you queen guap

Candida put on a vintage Chanel camellia flower beret and Loverboy orange parachute midi over a peasanty Giorgia Andreazza blouse and drove over the hill to vett encampments. A promising bivouac lay under the 405 on Sherman Way, near the wildlife reserve in Van Nuys. It looked like a garbagy shitshow but had a surprise stretch that was perky and mad stylish. She had skipped the prophylactic course of antibiotics because her plan was to get houselessly eaten out, not fucked, then take a super-syringe of penicillin from her GP. She'd tell him she slept with someone she met at a club who was sus—he loved hearing about her nightcrawls. Dr. Schoenberg was the family internist, but Corinne called him Dr. Sackler because he was DoorDash/Uber Opiates. Plus, he had Dida on Adderall, Lamictal, Wellbutrin, Lexapro, Trazodone, Rexulti, Seroquel, and K nasal spray. He used to be her pediatrician but was her gynie now too, hehe. (Judgy Kaia said, "That's gross.") On her way back to Bel Air from the rom-com rendezvous, she'd cruise over to Dr. S's on Roxbury Drive for an STD planet-killer (to use Dad's favorite phrase) just in case the dossing Romeo had TB or trench mouth—though she definitely wasn't going to kiss anyone—or some other bizarro, scurvyish contagion. She already had herpes, and anyway, AIDS was totally treatable/preventable, everyone was living HIV/PrEP large, she didn't even care, not really, as long as the adrenalized nymphomania of it made her spurt like when she watched Talula and Grandpa, she couldn't believe it when she started hydranting like that, like a fucking a bomb cyclone. And couldn't *wait* to see Lula, post-lone wolf Challenge, and read *her* to filth (for a change). She was surprised how much space that girl took up in her head.

Bitch livin rent-free.

She went to 7-Eleven for condoms and donuts. She wanted to arrive at the encampment bearing gifts, like missionaries did with bone-through-nose rainforest tribes. Sugary offerings and shiny shit. The donuts were just a "hi, hello" (she had a bag of addies, coke, and K-pins) but everyone liked sweets. Passing a huge display of her friend MrBeast's Feastables, Candida got a déjà vu arousal of birthday-day joy. O! She really did feel like Aura—the windmaiden warrior name that Puck gave her—electrified and voracious with anticipatory desire.

The clerk was busy keeping an eye on a gal who was loitering in the aisles with an Arizona Tea. He finally puffed up, blurting, "You pay for that! You pay now!"

"This is *mine*," said the girl, unruffled.

"You pay, you pay, I saw you take! Don't bullshit!"

"I got it this *morning,* I walked *in* with this, fuckin *dothead.*"

"Get out, you get out!"

The chill warrior-nymph Candida said to the girl, "It's okay, I'll pay."

"Don't do that, honey."

"Let me, it's fine. It's so not worth the hassle."

"Everyone here's usually *really nice* except for Deepak Twisterhead. He's got a hardon for me and my old man."

Candida made sure the girl saw her slap two hundred-dollar bills on the counter then steered her arm-in-arm on a shopping spree surveilled by the clerk's still violent gaze. She wanted to know if Candida was the actor from *Stranger Things*—"Sadie Sink! Are you or are you not Sadie Sink?" They splurged on 7-Meat pizza, Sour Neon Gummi Worms, MrBeast Deez Nuts, and Berry Blast Quakes. When Dida grabbed her a plush Baby Doll Face backpack right before checking out, her new bestie said, "I think I fuckin love you."

～

Strolling to the underpass, they formally introduced themselves. It was crazy because after making a dumb yeast joke, the girl said "Candida" was a favorite song of her mother's too. She was Marjorie LeMoyne but got nicknamed Sidewalk at seven years old, "which is fucking *apropos* under current circumstances. Hehehe. But everyone calls me Sidey—like Spidey without the p." Candida was impressed by the unexpected use of *apropos*; it made her crush even harder. Sidey talked about her husband Shrek and their TikTok channel, "Sidewalk Surfers," adding that he didn't look anything like the *real* Shrek but protected the encampment the way Shrek did his swamp. *Apropos* of nothing, she gleefully shouted, "Drain the swamp!"

Shrek was short and white, not green, and never really smiled but was polite. He reminded Candida of Jesse Pinkman. Sidewalk effused over "Sexy Sadie the 7-Eleven queen!" while Shrek sifted through the Rx baggie making his fussy selections. "Bundles and kundles," he said, so the three of them Calvin Kleined. (Candida still hadn't had the opportunity to Michael Kors—the mix of mephedrone and K that her father's lover CL told her about—nor had she Martin Margiela'd: Maalox, Mucinex, morphine, and meth. Those would have to wait for another day.) When he thought his wife was doing more coke than her allotment, Shrek slapped her face so hard that Sidey was on the ground for a few minutes, recovering. He kept right on talking like nothing happened. About ten minutes later, she snorted his peace-offering bump then kept her mouth shut, wiping away a tear and a little blood (where his ring caught her) when he wasn't looking.

"Sir? Hello? *Hello*—"

Shrek said oh shit and opened the tarp. "Can I help you?"

"Good morning! How y'all doin today?"

"Great. How are you."

"*Excellent.* Sorry to barge in—we're from the NDP task force. Would it be okay to leave some Narcan with y'all?"

"Sure."

"Do y'all need pipes or needles?"

"We're good."

"Great! I'll just set them down. Have a blessed day!"

"*Y'all* do the same," said Shrek, with a sarcasm they didn't notice.

He watched for a moment as they approached a delirious, dancing Black who was in the middle of an imaginary Golden Buzzer audition of "Singin' in the Rain." With each surprisingly elegant soft-shoe kick, glass shards, crumpled beer cans, and dried feces shot toward the gutter. Behind the NDP squad's first responders were a novice backup team of harm-reductioneers, cheerily clutching complimentary oximeters while pushing a cart filled with O_2 cylinders.

"Sir? Sir! How you doing there, sir? Can we talk to you?"

Shrek went back inside. He was feeling good and garrulous.

"Cowboy don't need Narcan. Cowboy needs fuckin *electroshock*—or a bullet to the head, which I just may fare thee well provide. Cowboy's fuckin outta *control*. Sidey, did you know he feeds the rats? Oh, yeah. They follow him around like he's Pied fuckin Piper. I'm out there sweeping sidewalks every night cuz the rats attract the fuckin health department and that's *no bueno*. No freakin bueno." He cackled. "The spade stinks like a mofo, too! Did I tell you what he did, Sidey? What he did yesterday?" She shook her head. "So, I'm on my way to Chevron—cuz Deepak Diaperhead 86'd me from 7-Eleven. Hey! How many times does 7-Eleven go into 86? *Hahahahaha*. I'm gonna light that dothead's ass *up* . . . hang him from his fuckin skull towel. So I'm over at Chevron and see a cop standing over Cowboy. He's standing with another dude who's *not* a cop. A whatta they call, a civilian. Right? Okay? So Cowboy's right next to the entrance just *layin* there, practically blocking it. Now, I don't know how he's even *doin* it, cuz he's *unconscious*, but the motherfucker's jerking off! Mofo actually has a hardon! Hey, I didn't look too close but I'm telling you, it was hard as a Snickers bar. The cop's tappin Cowboy's shoe with his boot, sayin, 'You cannot do that here, sir.' *Hahahahaha.* 'Sir'! Psychonigger's suddenly a sir! I guess better to be a *sir* than a *y'all*.

. . He kicks his boot and Cowboy finally wakes up and says, 'Keep your hands off Mr. Kamal Harris!' *Hahahahahaha.* 'Hands off the Second Gentleman!' Then the brother passes out—*blam*—for reals. A flipped little shawty who works inside rushes out, gives the cop a wad of paper towels then skitters back in *hahahaha.* You should have seen the shawty skitter! And the cop like *delicately* drapes the Brawny's over Cowboy's dick! Like a modesty blanket. The clean-cut guy who's standing there with the cop, the *civilian's* talkin about, like, how it *ain't cool*—no *shit*, Sherlock—it ain't *cool* for a nigger to be tuggin on his diseased pecker 'while my kids are in the car watchin.' The kids are fuckin voyeurs . . . but a coon can't be jerking his knob like that while a dad's fillin up the Camry! Hey, is that a premium jerkoff or a regular *hahahahaha.* And the cop's all like super-patiently explaining how there's nuthin he can do unless Chevron gets a restraining order, that's the only way they can throw the Second Gentleman off the property. I was *praying* Cowboy'd shoot a wicked load in his sleep and splatter those fuckin pervy voyeur kids! *Hahahahaha.*"

The tarp yanked open and the shirtless soft-shoe dancer stood there grinning, a task force crack pipe in his gnarled hand.

"Speak of the devil!" said Shrek, then turned to the girls. "Nigger's ears be burnin like his dick when he takes a whiz."

"Don't call him that," said Sidey.

"But he *likes* it. Don't you, Cowboy?"

"Like what," said Cowboy.

"You cool with me calling you nigger?"

"That's what I *am*," said Cowboy, with a measure of pride.

"See?" said Shrek.

"You a nigger too," said Cowboy. "*You, me,* Mr. *Kamal Harris*—that nigger *think* he a Jew but he's a nigger. Just like the Israelites and the Palestine-ites. Everybody a nigger, twenty-four seven. *All-nigger, all-the-time.*"

Shrek grinned at his wife.

"Who's the nigger now, Sidey? *You* are. *You're* the nigger now. *Hahahahahaha.*"

~

After dark, they settled in a secret garden that Shrek carved from a bramble on the hill that led to the freeway. The cars sounded like waves and Candida, way stoned, pretended she was at her dad's, in the Cove. For long moments, it was the realer place.

"Know what I hate?" said Shrek. "When someone's *doin* or *thinkin* some *interesting new shit*, and their so-called friends and family get all nervous and say, 'He changed.' When someone says, 'You know what? I'm not going to play the game anymore, not today,' and they fuckin *sigh* and say, 'He changed.' Like, it's the fuckin kiss of death, to *change* is the kiss of death. Like, you wake up one morning and realize—that Leonard Cohen song, 'Everybody Knows,' right?—you wake up and realize it's all just a fuckin game and they're going to fuckin crush you—*you wake the fuck up*, and you dare to *talk* about it—wellllll, they do their little lemming shrug and say, 'He changed,' 'the bitch changed,' whatever." He began singing, *Everybody knows the captain lied, everybody knows the plague is coming*, then ruminated "not *everybody* knows—Leonard Cohen got *that* wrong—but the ones who *do* know, well, say I'm one of em, and try to warn the rest of the herd—*oops*. The animals start whispering, 'Motherfucker *changed*' . . . make it sound like I *lost* my mind instead of fucking *found* it. But you wanna know the *worst* thing, what the *worst* thing is? The fuckin tragedy? To say that shit—'He changed'—you wanna know what that *does*? It one hundred percent removes the possibility of the fuckin Hero's Journey. You know what that is, the Hero's Journey? I saw a doc about it in rehab that was fuckin *based*. Bowie was wrong, sorry David, you *can't* be a hero just for one day. Nuh *uh*. They won't allow it. Cause a single day, *a single fuckin hour* is long enough for them to say, 'He changed.' And once you've fuckin *changed*, you can kiss your buttocks goodbye. Ain't no comin back. *Sayonara*. You're dead meat, my friend. Hello Deep State, bye bye Hero's Journey!"

When he climbed on top, Candida said she didn't want to fuck but he could go down on her and he thought that was the funniest thing ever. He undid his pants and she weakly said *can you please put on protection* and he slapped her, maybe not as hard as Sidewalk, but it stung. Sidey didn't want to hold her down, but he forced her to, like always. After he left, Sidey apologized and found a dirty rag for Dida to dab herself with, presenting it like a special flower. Then Shrek came back with Cowboy, shouting "Get you some, Pied Piper!" and Sidey held her down again.

Candida couldn't smell his rankness, nor could she feel what was being done. She thought about what it would be like telling Talula about this quietly unthinkable adventure, how far she had surpassed Lula in the Challenge, then thought about the Julian Archangel mermaid gown she was going to wear to the Gala and of her friend Malala and all that Malala had endured and of Aura the windmaiden that Wikipedia said was raped by Dionysus and the lark in the troubadour's song with the hem of the dress lifted to her throat, the one falling back on the bed, falling falling falling back, and the woman Corinne mentioned who died in that plane crash *they found the black box suddenly she was a tiny little girl and could think of nothing but her mommy spectacularly hanging in the sky like a bomb cyclone of lightning and the darkest clouds. She wanted her mother so.*

The wail-prayer of her knifed last word (no one heard because she had no voice) was the same as she who cried out when the jet fell from the noctilucent firmament above the dark Tongan seas.

35

When Kaia called to tell her what happened to Talula, Corinne worried that her daughter gave the girl the fentanyl she OD'd on and was running scared. But she couldn't dwell too much on Candida guiltily crawling off to a seedy motel to self-harm (as was her wont) because she was in the middle of a pre-Gala whistle-stop press tour and literally three hours away from doing the Kimmel show. Private detectives were combing ERs, hotels, and motels within a 100-mile radius, and the police had a BOLO for Dida's $300K Icon '74 Bronco with a Coyote 5.0 Mustang GT aluminum 430 horsepower fuel-injected V8. (Kendall Jenner bought the second one of the pair.)

The car freak cops were having a ball looking.

After giving his first guest a cheery twenty-minute bootlicking (Supreme Court Judge Sonia Sotomayor), the talk show host warmed up the crowd for Corinne.

"She's as glamorous as she is controversial. But underneath the outrageousness is a heart of Bitcoin—or maybe just a heart of gold. I'm talking 24-karat! Her cardiologist works out of Tiffany's." Frivolity soon became tearfulness. "I've said this before and have *no problem* saying it again: A few years ago, when I called her at three in the morning—she was wide awake, by the way—I don't think she ever sleeps—she mobilized a crack cardiac team that saved my son's life. I can never be grateful enough. We don't agree all the time but I'm thankful that someone like her exists in the world. And if someone like her *didn't*, she would just have one made— for an exorbitant fee—so, it's a win-win. Ladies and gentlemen, please welcome . . . *the unsinkable, fabulous Corinne Coldstream.*"

The audience whooped as she entered to the house band's sly strains of Dylan's "Million Dollar Bash."

"Thank you for that wonderful introduction, Jimmy. I love you too."

"Back at ya."

"I'm so glad Billy's doing well. He's a wonderful, wonderful boy."

"He's a rock star. And so are you." Scanning her costume, he said, "Good Lord. Is *that* what you're wearing to the ball?"

"This old thing?" she said, feigning offense.

"A little backstage birdie told me it's Balenciaga."

"That's *'AI* for Balenciaga'—their new label."

"ChatGPT does Chanel!"

"Oh, it's coming, Jimmy. But the corset is Thom Browne. The *real* Thom Browne."

"Of *corset* is."

"The jewels are Boucheron, Bulgari, and *trés fab* Fabergé. The suspenders, Vivienne Westwood. Gloves, Thomasine. The *chapeau*, Chaplin, as in Charlie—it happens to be the actual bowler he wore in *Modern Times.* And as you can see, I'm wearing two different shoes . . ."

"I certainly *do* see that."

"The sandal is a collab between Fendi and the marvelous architect Kengo Kuma—he designed one of my homes and is doing the marvelous houseless outhouses in Venice—and the *sneaker* was created by the irrepressible Marc Jacobs. Marc's coming to the ball. I *adore* him."

"And you're having the gala at the Coliseum. How appropriate . . ."

"It's not as old as the one in Rome but we did our best."

"Will anyone be thrown to the lions?"

"Only the unstylish—but we're not expecting any of *those.*"

"That's why I won't be there."

"I *know* and I'm quite *upset.* You're the only one who RSVP'd 'will not attend.' People are flying in from all over the world, Jimmy!"

"You do *not* want me there, trust me. I'm about as stylish as Matt Damon on holiday."

"I'll give you a makeover."

"My wife's been making the same threat."

"I love Molly! I guess she'll come without you then."

"Is there a theme, Corinne? Doesn't Anna Wintour's ball always have a theme?"

"Oh, yes—ours is 'Houselessness.'"

"*Houselessness.* Okay!"

"The *Met Gala* benefits the Costume Institute . . . the *West Coast Ball* benefits *people*, not fashion. We're giving all the money we raise to a wonderful organization, HHCLA, Homeless Healthcare, right here in Los Angeles."

"Didn't King Charles just make Anna a 'Dame'?"

"You're trying to cause mischief!" She waved her hand dismissively. "They've been calling me 'Dame' since the doctor slapped my backside. Now don't stir things *up*, Jimmy, I'm *happy* for her. And the King is a *very* old friend. But I'm afraid the GBE given to me by Charles's mum Elizabeth trumps Anna's little Companion of Honour."

"So, how *are* things between you and Companion Wintour?"

"Must we go there? You're quite *determined* tonight, Mr. Kimmel."

"I assume there's been some poaching . . ."

"No poaching, Jimmy. Anna and I are sportswomen. Actually, we spoke just this morning and laughed a lot."

"Really?"

"Look, *no one* could do what she does; there's so much history there. Both events are going to be extraordinary—but we *have* commiserated about people panicking over recent health issues. As you know, it's Bell's palsy season, and Botox won't fix a droopy lip, *that* I can assure, because I tried! I've had Bell's three times, *lucky me.* Guillan-Barré and Ramsay Hunt have been very busy bees—the price we gladly pay for boosters."

"So, we can't expect a Coldstream-Wintour cage fight in Vegas anytime soon?"

"I hope not! We wish each other the best."

"You do? But you're calling your gala 'WMD'—Weapon of Met Gala Destruction!"

"Now wait a minute! *I* didn't say that, the *media* did."

"And you *loved* it."

"Well, it's very funny, don't you think? In these awful times, it's a sin to lose one's sense of humor. Anna's still got hers, I can assure."

"Can we talk about the guest list?"

"I'd love to."

"Basically, anyone you run into at Nobu gets a thumbs up."

"Nobu is my office! I've been camping there for weeks."

"Now, Lady Gaga and Johnny Depp are the co-chairs . . . "

"Yes."

"And Elon Musk—"

"He told me he wouldn't miss it. Elon's always flicked his nose at tradition, so the West Coast Gala is right up his alley."

"What about George and Amal?"

"I adore them, but they'll be with Anna in New York. I admire loyalty; it's become the rarest trait. George called this morning to wish me well."

"You had a very busy morning!"

"You don't know the *half*. But I really do think it's lovely and *healthy* having two balls—"

"That's what I tell my urologist."

"Touché! You know, it's not just the 'marquee names' who will be there. We have wonderful young people—like Sofia Sanchez, the beautiful actress-advocate with Down Syndrome whose parents adopted her from an orphanage in the Ukraine. Sofia just got Ramsay Hunt but she's tough as nails. Prada's sending beautiful adhesive ribbons to tape up her droop. And *here's* a spoiler for you: Mr. Hunter Biden will be in the house! Or should I say the Coliseum."

"Keep him away from the party favors!"

"Now, now. I don't think he's gotten a fair shake—him *or* his dad. And he's a *brilliant* artist, a wonderful, talented painter . . . but the one I'm *really* excited about is Tatum—O'Neal—who's recovering from her stroke *so* beautifully. Her father's death was another terrible blow. . . . The poor thing's in bed at the moment with Guillan-Barré *and* Ramsay Hunt—"

"That's some ménage-à-trois! Now, I know what you're wearing to the gala is going to be a surprise—but I *do* know what you're going to have on *underneath*. Because there was a *photo* of it in a recent magazine spread. Pardon the pun . . ."

"Rick Owens and I *collab'd*. We call it the 'peekabum.'"

"Tell us a little more about the *peekabum*—be mindful that my son Billy is watching tonight's show. And so's the *OG* peekabum Matt Damon, but him we don't care about."

36

Watching Mr. Kimmel while she sat at the Singer machine, Divinity was entranced. (Coretta alerted her to the talk show appearance.) She was that rare thing—you never knew what the woman was going to say next, and it was refreshing. Jvnglebar called her No Filter.

At the detention facility, she assiduously worked on a letter of thanks to Miss Corinne, whom she had yet to meet, for hiring the lawyers that worked so hard to reduce her sentence. (She wrote a letter to the Weinsteins too but didn't want to send it until she was certain the restraining order was lifted.) But none of the words she chose ever felt right. She couldn't seem to keep god out of it and the more she knew of Miss Corinne, the more wrongheaded she felt was her approach. She did not wish to judge— *with the judgment ye judge, ye shall be judged*—and only wanted to celebrate her. After all, didn't they both proudly wear the coat of many colors their Maker had provided them? Say what you will about Corinne Coldstream, she truly *was* helping so many folks.

And oh, was she funny! Such a character! So charismatic. Divinity laughed and laughed and laughed. . . . These were such terrible times and the lady lifted people *up*, lifted their spirits. Folks needed to be entertained because it really *was* Armageddon. She knew it was end times when Coretta sent her a story from the internet about how everyone had been wrong all their lives about everything, folks had been cleaning their fridges wrong and doing the laundry wrong and opening cans wrong and drinking water wrong. Even walking and breathing and using the toilet wrong.

Jvnglebar told her auntie about the podcast she was listening to where Lizzo said she turned down Miss Wintour's invitation to the Met Gala. Lizzo could not attend out of loyalty to her "matron and mentor," Miss Corinne Coldstream, who wished her to come to the ball in Los Angeles. Lizzo talked about being a middle school student in Houston and how the Coldstream Foundation paid for eight years of her training as a flutist. Eight long years!

Her fingers ached to the bone from sewing. Using the Singer made her emotional because it felt like Mama and god were moving through her together. Photos of Met Galas from bygone days that Jvnglebar printed out had inspired the gown she was creating. Costumes from Miss Wintour's recent balls were too revealing for her taste, too outrageous—like Miss Corinne herself! Divinity loved the one by Miss Prada, with swaths of girded fabric that of course she would never be able to properly imitate; and another, by Miss McQueen, with strapped-on angel wings made from the slenderest wood. Coretta's talented nephew liked a challenge and holed up in his garage workshop to recreate the seraphic accessory with bamboo and beeswax. (Divinity said it was for a little part she had in her church's upcoming play.) But closest to her heart was a wedding gown by Miss Valentino, with a wimple she was copying in linen. Divinity saw no contradiction in her bravado and ambition, because the desire to clothe herself in humility was pure. When she had to rip a seam or pick out a stitch, she smiled and said aloud, "Lamb of god, make the work of our hands last. *Make the work of our hands last.*"

She was so happy to learn that the theme of the ball was homelessness—for, there *was* no house but the House of the Lord. Guests from all walks of life would attend: a melting pot of rich and poor, famous and forgotten, disabled and healthy. And just like church, the happiest-looking parishioners often suffered the most terrible hidden tragedies and prayed to be healed.

Even Mr. and Mrs. Weinstein got their tickets!

Divinity tore up the letters she wrote in jail—and the ones she'd stop-started since coming home, in flowery script:

Dear Miss Corinne Coldstream,
I pray for you and yours. God loves you so! When I asked Him for guidance, He directed me to seek your invitation to attend the magnificent West Coast Ball. I am begging your pardon for being too "forward." And I do believe the Weinsteins will allow me, having seemed to have found some forgiveness in their hearts . . .

No, she thought, it simply would not do.
And just then, the Lord nearly shouted,
Ask Miss Corinne in person! Go to her in your humble, homemade dress.

37

Mercutio immediately responded to his son's cryptic texts but got nothing back. He couldn't dare call GKC to request their help in tracking Phaedra's whereabouts; since Murray's stern no-contact warning, he was even chary about asking for updates on his daughter's health.

He reached out to Jalen instead, offering the fired intern a thousand dollars to scour social media and see what he could come up with. Mercutio wept when shown images of Phaedra in front of a Ferris wheel at the Malibu Chili Cook-Off, his arm around a blurred-out young girl; the handsome boy, so thin and frail, looked more and more like his mother. Then Jalen flagged a recent IG story where Phaedra called himself "Ansel." Staring at the camera, he said, "Meet Shailene, the blushing bride!" (The Shailene/Ansel reference went over Jalen's head.) He crosschecked vlogs and microblogs in search of an address but struck out before returning to the IG video and pausing it. "Um, I think . . . they're in a hospital? See the edge? Of the machine?"

A comment by Harry Dodge said *from the mighty great fred moten: is it ok to touch your ear? im touching it. im climbing up you.* When Jalen learned that Dodge was a teacher at CalArts, Mercutio dictated:

> To: Harry Dodge hdodge@calarts.edu
> Subject: PHAEDRA IS MY SON
>
> Professor Dodge,
> I am Mercutio Schecter, Phaedra's father. I have attached a screenshot of recent texts from my son and am obviously quite concerned. He asked me to come to LA and now *I am here.* I would appreciate very much if you could share where I may find him. I believe he is in hospital?

Within the hour, came a terse reply: *I forwarded your message.*

When Jalen left, Mercutio googled the sixty-year-old Professor Dodge and discovered that he had searched all his life for the mother he never knew, and in his mid-thirties, found her living in San Jose. How small and mystifying was the world . . .

The following morning, he got a text from his son:

> *leaving CCC soon will advise*

At least it's coherent, he thought.

He googled CCC and doubletaked at Coldstream Comprehensive Cancer Center. For a moment, he couldn't catch his breath. But there were no patients under his son's name. He decided to make an end-run around Murray.

"Dr. Kibble? Please hold for the Nutty Professor." (Always his little joke between them.)

"Mercutio! Hello, hello! How are things?"

"*Very well*," he answered, believing upbeat and roundabout to be the best approach.

"Is the Depakote working its wonders?" said Dr. Kibble, already consulting his notes.

"Oh yes! I believe so . . . "

"And far sooner than we'd expect! No vomiting or diarrhea? Still have hair on that pretty head of yours?"

"Vomiting and diarrhea, happily *no*. Hair on the head, happily *yes*."

"Well, I have an *in* with a retired toupee maker, so not to worry. What can I do you for?"

"Dr. Kibble, as you are aware, my daughter is at Saint John's."

"Any word?"

"At this time, it wouldn't be prudent of me to inquire."

"That's wise. I agree."

"But I would be exceedingly grateful if you might somehow . . . peek into things and see how she's doing. Without alerting the powers that be. If you could do me that merciful kindness."

"I see. But you'll promise the buck stops here? With the two of us?"

"Yes. My solemn promise."

"All right. Let me rattle a cage or two."

"Thank you, Dr. Kibble! *Thank you*. One more thing . . . I know it's a bit of a *telenovela*, but I've just found out that my *other* child—my son—is also in hospital."

"Heavens no, what for?"

"Some sort of cancer I'm afraid."

"Oh Christ. *You've* had a time of it, haven't you."

"He somewhat frantically wrote that he wished to see me—this was yesterday—but nothing since, which is worrying. I fear he's become incapacitated . . . or something worse."

"Do you know where he is?"

"The Coldstream Cancer—"

"CCC?"

"Yes."

"Well, that makes things easier."

"There doesn't seem to be anyone registered under his name. *Phaedra Schecter.* P-H-A-E-D-R-A."

"Sometimes folks are admitted under aliases—celebs and such. Is he a celebrity?"

"Only to me."

"Hold on, hold on . . . please hold." Dr. Kibble picked up another phone. Suddenly, he was laughing and talking but Mercutio couldn't make out Kibble's end of the conversation. When he ended the call, he said, "He *was* under an assumed name: 'Ansel Elgort.' Apparently, he's about to be discharged. Better hurry, if you're planning on going over there . . ."

"Thank you, thank you!"

"I do hope it all works out, Professor. You're a good man. And *do* let me know about any side effects from the Depakote—my wig man's on standby."

~

Everything was happening too quickly. He was actually terrified of a reunion with the son he'd so cruelly dissected from his life. First, Talula's horror; now, *this* . . .

What strangeness had befallen him—befallen them all!

Then, something ticked. The name *Ansel* struck his head like a boomerang and he told Jalen to text him the Ferris wheel screenshot of Phaedra and the blurry girl. When the Professor double-tapped and dragged (with Jalen's coaching), he was certain:

The blur was Charlie Coldstream.

But how?

How, how, how—

On top of everything, the Genesis G80's navigation system was out to get him; instead of valet parking, he dead-ended in one of the medical center's underground utility garages. Annoyed and frustrated, he slouched toward the office entrance for directions.

On approach, he was startled to see the sylphlike figure of Charlie Coldstream slinking toward him. The girl suddenly paused, so that the ghost in a wheelchair, escorted by a gaggle of RNs, could catch up. He was further jarred to realize it was his son, in dark glasses and a copious, crimson robe. Phaedra's stomach mimicked that of a woman in the final months of pregnancy.

The Professor hid behind a concrete pillar while a suited protector opened the rear doors of an enormous custom coach. A second aide lowered a ramp, disgorging a hand-crafted black leather gurney that looked exactly like a Mies van der Rohe. The nurses helped with the transfer.

As the truck began its slow exit, Mercutio, heart in throat, prepared to give chase.

38

He had malignant ascites; that's why the belly swelled.

On the way to the Cove, Puck said, *"You're* supposed to be the knocked-up one"—and Charlie got sad because she'd fantasized, before even knowing Puck, about a uterine transplant. The surgeon had told her that tech was on track to build wombs from male stems and implant them in the pelvis. She dreamed of carrying an embryo made from Candida's egg and fertilized by Puck's sperm—but the chemo had irreparably damaged the testicles of her betrothed . . .

And his sister likely was dead.

She was so worried about Candida. Charlie wanted to postpone the wedding until she came home but couldn't wait anymore. The team said Puck might die before morning.

Corinne knew she was engaged but had no idea the marriage would happen that night. The gala was in just five days. Because Charlie's mother was so consumed, Dax was the only one kept in the loop—a few months ago, such a thing would have been an inconceivable betrayal. But to her surprise, it was aberrantly comforting to lean on him while pre-grieving Puck's imminent passing. A formidably sinister, detached figure, her dad underwent a queer transition himself, and his newfound sweetness was tremendously moving. It was almost comical how easily Dax slipped into the soppy PG-13 role of "father of the bride."

CL wasn't due to return from the Hamptons until a few hours after the secret ceremony.

The plan was for Puck to be carried to the grotto on a seventeenth-century palanquin before dusk. Moishe was already building a bonfire on the beach. A small troupe was doing Puck's hair and makeup and helping with his gown—Galliano for Margiela. During the preparations, Charlie retrieved the wedding gift that she had stowed at her father's.

Passing a blunt, Dax said, "You sure you don't want any witnesses?"

"Yeah. We're good."

"Oh, I don't think you're *good*," he winked. "I think you're very, very *bad*. But come on, sweetheart, let Papa give you away."

"There's nothing to give. I'm a ghost."

"Okay, Grim Reaper. But aren't you just a *little* bit excited? It's your fucking wedding day." He smiled, scrutinizing her. "What's goin on?"

"Since Puck was in the hospital, I haven't really had time to worry about Candida . . . but now I do. I'm worried sick."

"'O Candida, O Candida!'" he sang. "'Our home and native land . . .' We'll find her, Charles."

"Dead or alive," she said mordantly.

"Ain't her first rodeo. Your sister's done a disappearing act more than once."

Charlie shook her head. "It feels different."

"Well, not to *me*—so . . . *onward*. I'm just glad I don't have to call the cunt 'they' anymore. So: what dark romance is planned after the nuptials?"

"We're gonna knit each other chunky poncho sweaters."

"Doubt that. I heard you've been dilating."

Charlie was taken aback and wobbly from the weed. "Heard from *who*."

"No shame, sweetheart! The bride must be *ready*. I'd love to watch the consummation. You know, like they did for royal marriages in the Middle Ages."

"You're way past middle-aged."

"You never did show me. I kept *asking*, but you always blew me off. It's the least you could do after I signed over the Courbet."

"What's happening with the painting? Am I going to have to give it back?"

"*Hell* no, I made an *agreement*. We're sending them a fake."

"That's genius! But do they *know*. Do they know it's a fake?"

Dax grew pensive, looking past her. "Oh, the Black Swan's coming, darling daughter—and I'm not talking about that nanny your mother destroyed either. I'm talking about the Great Dimming . . . the plumed serpents of the *red supergiants*. It's already *happened*: the pathetic, pro-phetic perfect." Returning to earth, he began the slow, literal crawl toward Charlie, who was curled into an Eames. "C'mon now, bridey, *show me what they did*. I'm on bended knee!"

The 3-MMC that CL brought back from Berlin had just kicked in. As he lifted her skirt with languorous theatricality, she was close to nodding out. Charlie tried pushing down the hem but gave up—too stoned. He slipped off her panties, spread her legs, and stared.

"It's glorious," he said, with a measure of awe. "Like the wondrous anus of the sea cucumber, the surgeons fashioned a lung that *breathes* . . . look! It's both predator and womb—a sanctuary for the shimmering, par-asitic pearlfish within. Behold, French people! Here lies the *true* origin of the world—and so much better than the painting! More cost-effective, anyway." He looked closer. "Does it hurt to dilate?"

"A little . . ."

"Can you come? Have you ever come?" He put a finger in. She was going to brush it away but held onto it instead, like a child.

"Kind of," she said, listlessly trying to move the finger away.

"Let me wargame this."

He gently moved it around then withdrew from the calyx. Whispering *Let's kill this planet*, she gasped when he put his mouth on it. A strange feeling arose from her feet, wave upon wave; she thought of Salome and John the B, and all the paintings her fiancé had made—a montage of saints carrying their own heads in their hands. Puck called them *cephalophores* and said he was planning a suite of paintings, each with martyrs holding platters bearing the blurry severed head of his mother Ann. (The saints would have her face too.) Dax stayed down there a long time, pulling away only when his daughter finished a string of serrated, orgic gasps.

Still staring, he sat back on his heels and exultantly said, "*The Simpsons* predicted this!"

He went back for more but by then, Charlie had the cinerary urn in her hand and brought it down upon her father's skull, cracking both.

The sun set through the window.

She grabbed the wrapped gift and left for the beach.

39

Corinne was at Nobu with Elon, Tiffany Haddish, Princess Beatrice, and Margot Robbie, for one of the *intime*, pre-WMD suppers she was hosting.

She self-soothed by replaying a mood board image that manifested Candida appearing at the gala in a resplendent gown to sob in her arms while pleading forgiveness for having caused so much worry. Corinne began to believe such a reunion might happen. She wasn't so sure about Charlie showing up, though—Murray said that the boyfriend was fading fast—but added her youngest, favorite child to the mood board anyway. Breathlessly arriving on her big sister's heels, Charlie looked just like the fractured, lachrymose mater dolorosa of the Picasso that hung in the solarium of the recently acquire villa in Kyoto. In her maudlin reverie, with dying breath, Puck commanded Charlie to attend the ball. "You *must*, my beloved! Otherwise, your mother and I will be heartbroken. . . . Promise me you will!"

As usual, Nobu dinner talk was saucy and free-range. A same-day cluster of sudden, unexplained deaths was in the news: a celebrity chef, a girl golfer, a TV weatherman, and two former child stars. When Elon called it "vaccine harvest time," Corinne snorted, but Tiffany opined, "*Admit*, Corinne, that the shit is *super sus*." Margot nodded, nonplussed, and said, "Ya, weird," while the Princess overblinked. "Is it really the vaccines, Elon?" she asked. "But why would it be the *vaccines* and not the *viruses* that are hurting people?" Elon impishly segued to the soon-to-be announced Nobels. "I think it will be a fight between the weapons contractors for the Peace Prize," he said. "A dead heat between Raytheon, Lockheed, and Northrop Grumman." Everyone but Tiffany thought he was serious. "And as for the *Literature* prize," he added, "oddsmakers still favor Rushdie. But the dark horse—*horses*—are Greta Gerwig and Noah Baumbach."

"I saw that on X!" said Margot.

(Tiffany drolly interjected, "'Formerly known as Twitter.'")

"You're not joking?" said Corinne.

"It's the big rumor," Margot confirmed. "I texted Greta and she thinks it's *absolutely bonkers*. If it *happens*, Taylor said she's going to fly everyone to Stockholm. How much fun would that be?"

"It'd be *brilliant*," said the Princess. "And it *should* go to a woman." Leaning toward Margot, she said, "*Barbie* was blinding—and *Lady Bird* . . . *Little Women*—Greta is *so gifted*. But I *do* think that her husband's a genius too, and a bit overlooked."

"Why the fuck aren't they giving *you* the prize, Elon?" said Tiffany. "That's just such obvious political bullshit, right? I mean, the Nobels are *progressive*, right?" She addressed the table. "They need to throw this man *every motherfuckin prize there is.* Prize for Peace! Prize for Rocket Science! Most Money! Most X-rated X-Man! Most fuckin Kids! Wackest Kid's Names—"

Everyone heartily agreed and got noisy about it.

"You're very kind," said Elon. "But I'm afraid I don't have a chance against Amal Clooney. The Committee's giving her a Nobel for her body of work: entering and leaving restaurants while looking almost hot."

"That's so mean!" laughed Margot.

Tiffany said, "They're giving one to Olivia Wilde too. She gettin the prize for leaving the gym ten times a day showcasin' them abs."

A team member came over and whispered in Corinne's ear while the group howled over something else Tiffany said. Their hostess paled, then left. When the protector followed, she violently waved him off.

As she strode past the valets, phone to cheek, a Rolls Cullinan pulled up. Scott Disick shouted "Corinne!" but she didn't hear him as she launched across the parking lot.

"Murray, what has happened?"

"Candida's car was involved in a head-on in Barstow."

"Oh god. Is she all right?"

"She wasn't in the vehicle. It was stolen."

"Goddammit, Murray—"

"The driver is dead. They're interviewing the passenger. I'm on my way to Barstow, Corinne. That's everything I know."

On the sidewalk now, someone grabbed her wrist. When her cellphone clattered to the ground, she barked, *"What the fuck are you doing!"* Moving backward, she tried to shake free but fell on her ass, looking up in shock at the weird apparition.

"I love you, Miss Corinne!"

She didn't yet recognize the assailant, who leaned down on her with full weight. "You get away from me! You *get* the *fuck* a–*way*—"

"I would very much like to go to the ball, if you'll have me." Flouncing her gown—something wooden attached to the shoulders had splintered on the ground—the woman said, "I made it *myself*, on Mama's old Singer . . . I know there will be *so* many beautiful dresses and hope you don't mind that this one's homemade." She stood and twirled as Corinne cried out for help; it was dark and there was so much traffic on PCH, no one could hear. She fell wrong and when she tried to stand, shrieked from the pain in her leg. The small woman, surprisingly strong, easily helped her up. "In jail, I forgave you—as you forgave *me*. I had my part! It was the Lord's plan to humble me because I was arrogant and I was vain. I had come to believe it was *I* who was protecting those beautiful twins, not Jesus . . ."

With a flash of horror, Corinne cried, "You! They let you out!" Jangled and afraid, she'd forgotten the nanny had been released through her efforts. Divinity grabbed her wrists again and began to drag. "You're—hurting—me!" she shouted, but her captor's eyes were closed in fierce prayer. "Let go! *Let—me—go!* I need to find out about my daughter! My daughter needs me—"

"*I run to you, Lord, for protection. You are my mighty rock and my fortress. Come save me, Lord god, from cruel and brutal enemies—*"

"Help! Help me! Someone help, she's trying to kill me!"

The righteous woman's eyes shut tighter, the grip now viselike. "*I have relied on you from the day I was born. You brought me safely through birth and I always praise you—*"

"Please! Please! Please let me find my daughter—"

"*—many people think of me as something evil but you are my mighty protector!*" With a superhuman gust of energy, she trotted Corinne to the curb. "*We run to you, Lord, for protection! Bless us! Guide us safely to the Gala—*"

And to the ball they went.

40

Charlie took in the sky as she walked toward the grotto carrying the wedding gift in an Hermès double-bag. The light of the supermoon lit up the stain of blood on her wrist.

She thought of her big sis—was she somewhere bleeding now?—and remembered Candida's first period. Charlie was eight years old. Corinne said it happened to all girls, every month, when they became women. She said that Candida was a woman now and the coming of blood was ruled by the cycles of the moon. When Charlie asked if a man could have a period, she said no, but Charlie knew deep down that couldn't be true. It was like saying only women could walk or breathe or suffer.

Her heart sped up as she neared the glow of the bonfire inside the rockbound grotto. The ornate, empty palanquin lay at its entrance. Rounding the corner, she was acknowledged by the RNs who had just finished reinserting Puck's fentanyl pump. They quickly decamped and retreated to a sandy lounge, on call.

He smiled as Charlie joined him on the Hästens circular bed specially made for the occasion. "*There* you are. I was telling the nurses, 'I think Shailene might have left me at the altar.'"

She took his hand and said, "You've never been more handsome."

"So, where's the preacher, honeychile?"

"No need. Dax took care of it—we're straight-up legal now."

"Then it won't matter if I drop dead before we exchange . . . wows?"

"You can go any time after you kiss the bride." Puck got that done. Then Charlie said, "I have a surprise."

"Your husband's got a delicate condition. He doesn't like surprises."

"Too bad."

"In that case"—Puck hit the pump. His eyes glazed. After a while he came back.

"Don't *do* that again!" the bride scolded.

"Can't for a few minutes, machine won't let me. Voilà: your window of surprise."

Charlie paused then said, "I found her."

"Who."

"Ann."

Before Puck could react, Charlie deftly pulled the box from the bag—and the painting from its silk slipcase. She held it up as the stoned Puck tried to focus.

"What is that?"

"I told you I found her. See the red hair? It's *Ann . . .* "

Murray's intel led Charlie to a facility in San Pedro where Puck's senile, sewer-mouthed mother lived. The same facility had recently been scandalized by a handful of caregivers who were arrested for having larked an Instagram orgy of R-rated geriatric selfies.

"Wait," said Puck. "Is it—is that . . . what I think . . ."

"It *is,* and *not* a copy. For your eyes only: the original *Origine.*"

"Oh my god."

He trembled as the miracle sunk in.

She loved her husband's discretion; he never said a word to her about the infamously publicized Courbet, which seemed all the more remarkable to Charlie when Harry Dodge confided some weeks ago that the painting was a favorite of Puck's, to the point of obsession.

"But don't you have to return it to France?"

"Nope," she said. "She's all yours."

"Mine—"

Charlie smiled and said, "Mom came back."

Puck suddenly said, "I want to be burned." With eerie resoluteness, he added, "Get a place for us! For *you* and *me* and *Ann*—a columbarium at Hollywood Forever. *Put* us there, Charles . . ."

He asked for help sitting up then dangled his legs off the mattress and caught his breath. He said he was cold and wanted to get closer to the bonfire. The tubing was like a leash but long enough for the journey.

When a nurse saw they were on the move, she ducked in, backing off when Charlie nodded they were okay. Once on his feet, Puck became energized. He asked his wife to bring the painting over so "we three" could enjoy the fire. Puck grabbed it from Charlie's hands and flung it into the conflagration. She was stunned by the genius apostasy.

Puck collapsed.

The same RN must have been keeping an eye out because she rushed in, followed by the crew. The widow held the boy close and began to keen at the moon.

Her ululations barely hid the distant, piercing screams of CL.

41

The Professor followed the bespoke ambulance from the hospital to PCH, grateful that it was traveling on Sunset instead of the freeways. A half-hour later, his quarry slowed then stopped; enormous gates opened; the carriage went through. He sat in the car, opposite the hidden manse.

What to do?

He rehearsed himself standing at the gate and ringing the bell.

Hello. Hello? My name is Mercutio Schecter and I am the father of Phaedra Schecter.

If whoever answered played dumb, he'd say *I know that he was just brought here from the hospital with his friend Charlie Coldstream.* If he had to, the Professor would be more insistent. *My son wants to see me, he demanded it! I am a client of Murray Cadence and a very close friend of Corinne Coldstream, who will not at* all *be happy if I am turned away—*

It seemed so easy. Yet, he was unnerved by the possibility of Murray being alerted; he didn't want to be perceived as a clear and present danger. God knew what steps the fixer might take to cauterize the distraught father's capricious, volatile behavior.

He crossed the road and paced in front of the gate.

There was a good chance that soon *both* his children would be dead . . . *What to do.*

The only thing that made sense was to walk (which he did) a mile or so north, until arriving at the public entrance to Paradise Cove. At a lovely restaurant with a tropical theme, the Professor fortified himself with pina coladas and a marvelous fish stew before ambling south again, this time on the beach—low tide—casing the cliffside homes while he ambled, in hope that he'd spot his sequestered boy. Perhaps he would be able to see Puck resting in the sun on a terrace, attended by bustling caregivers.

If only he had binoculars.

Mercutio kept going, past where he thought he left the G80, until his meandering ended at an outcrop of rock. A curious sense of peace overtook him as he stepped inside a wholly unexpected grotto—the womb at the end of the world. It was light and dark, cool and warm, wet and dry, perfumed of the sea and the heavens. Life teemed there, death too, and celestial indifference. In short a splendid place to make camp.

He kept a duffel from his houseless days in the trunk of his car, replete with blanket, jerky, water, and whatnot. Retrieving it took nearly an hour. In late afternoon, after comfortably arranging his personal things in the grotto, the Professor was politely though strongly advised (by whom he took to be a Coldstream protector) that he needed to "move on." He complied, finally reaching a distance that was approved by a nonchalant signal from the now faraway soldier. He awakened after dark to a moon so bright that it laid bare the world. Subliminal flames danced in the grotto's hidden hearth. By peculiar instinct, he walked toward the glow until the harsh stare of a second suited lookout bade him retreat.

Twenty minutes later, a wyrd lamentation split his ears. The formerly dissuasive sentinel abandoned his post and bolted into the grotto. As Mercutio hastened toward the blaze, there came another scream from further off. A walkie crackled *Get to the house! Get to the house!* The tide had risen and his feet were sopping as he approached the cave. The uncanny shrieks from within were rhythmical, like the airhorn vomiting of dark angels.

Then he saw the wedded couple—how could it be that in this moment, his thoughts turned to the glorious Delacroix of the tiger murdering a wild horse?—except the tiger was Charlie, roaring at the ceiling of the womb at the end of the world.

And the horse—*the horse!*—was Phaedra, forever tamed—

—the Professor's eldritch, broken, riderless beloved.

42

Marjorie "Sidewalk" LeMoyne led police to the body. Cowboy became violent when an officer attempted to remove the victim's Chanel beret from his head and was arrested. (His cheeks were beaded with Starface pimple patches taken from Candida's purse.) Shrek was killed when he crashed the car in Barstow; because Miss LeMoyne was cooperative, charges of aiding and abetting his escape were dismissed. An anti-woke firestorm raged across social media when the leaked coroner's report described Candida as "female-presenting."

Meanwhile, at Charlie's arraignment downtown, the dream team hired by Gramercy Kind Cadence argued that the death of Dax Coldstream was the result of a clear-cut case of self-defense—their client had struck her father as he forcibly committed a sexual act that was so heinous that it defied belief. A battery of psychiatrists attested to the victim's full understanding of the consequences of what she had done; Charlie was remorseful but not suicidal, even expressing empathy, if not love, for the monster who violated her. (The therapists said that was normal.) Lawyers pushed for house arrest, noting that if she were incarcerated, Ms. Coldstream would be at enormous risk of sexual assault and even assassination because of her age, wealth, and celebrity. Public sympathy for "the poor little rich girl" ran high. Because it was an election year, the DA allowed the child to attend the interment of her mother and sister.

There would be no memorial for the father.

Horror and outrage followed when the leaked video of Charlie's interview with the police revealed the unspeakable nature of what had transpired between them . . . *on her wedding night!* Dax Coldstream was memed into a hall of fame that included Rasputin, John Wayne Gacy, the two Jeffreys—Epstein and Dahmer—and assorted serial child rapists and killers. The instructions in his will called for burial in an unmarked tomb in Père Lachaise, beside his mother, Unica Zürn, and the artist Hans Bellmer. Parisians considered it a slap in the face and promptly dug up the grave; to date, the whereabouts of his remains are unknown. (Ironically, he seems to have escaped the ignominious fate of his hero, Cormac McCarthy. For now.) In the week that followed the desecration, the Musée d'Orsay was closed due to bomb threats. The space where the copy of *L'Origine du monde* hung for so many years remains vacant.

The spectacle of Corinne and Candida Coldstream's double burial was televised, with a worldwide viewership that exceeded the funerals of Michael Jackson and Princess Di. Thousands lined the streets outside Forest Lawn, waiting for a glimpse of the boy who became the girl who became a heroine for our time. Another three billion watched as Charlie, seraphic-chic in a veil and simple Prada dress, emerged from her black Rolls Royce Phantom limousine.

The WMD went on as scheduled—before the obsequies—and was a resounding success. The phantasmagoric familial tragedy infused the *Noche de Los Muertos* with a cathartic, superstar bloodletting of grief. In a pre-gala press conference, Gaga, Johnny Depp, Damien Hirst, and Greta Gerwig somberly announced they had been in "honored conversation" with Charlie, who, though sequestered, spoke to her hundred-million or so followers on social media about the importance of the show going on, expressing certainty that her mother would be heartbroken should the ball be canceled. Rick Owens flew out for a few days to visit while

Chalie was still in lockdown at the Neuropsychiatric Institute that bore the family name; even Anna Wintour made a gracious statement about "the unvanquishable spirit of my stylish, gloriously disruptive old friend, Corinne Coldstream." Handily eclipsed by its competitor, the East Coast gala turned out to be a muted affair, albeit raising more money than ever.

When Charlie was exonerated, few grumbled about the privilege that great wealth confers nor was there talk of skin color or gender. The perverse pageantry of the Fall of the House of Coldstream transcended such tropes. She was now the richest and most famous teenager in the world. To properly steward her wealth, she was in talks "with my mentor and new big sister, Mackenzie Scott, who's showing me the art of giving it all away. When I leave this body, this planet—for other adventures!—I'll leave nothing behind but love."

One person who might have been expected at Forest Lawn had gone missing. But only Murray Cadence noticed his absence.

43

In a stroke of irony, Divinity Swann was buried on the same day as the woman who sealed both their fates. The name social media had graced her with ("Black Swan") was racist and unfortunate, but stuck. The internet was divided over her legacy. Was she a paranoiac, drug-dependent religious fanatic that killed the woman who became her compassionate benefactor? Or was she a proud, hardworking, underpaid, uninsured Black—with two sons murdered by the police—driven to homicide by the sketchy machinations of an eccentric white witch whose wealth and power were beyond comprehension?

It was all getting muddy beyond belief.

Much was made of the fact that of the five cars that struck Divinity and Corinne, one was an Uber carrying Rebecca Gayheart, while the passenger of another was Matthew Broderick. A macabre detail would never be made public: through an open side window, Gayheart's lip got slicked by a flying sliver of bronchi later identified as Corinne's.

On the night his own son died, Mercutio was briefly held as a person of interest, but the police soon determined he had nothing to do with the murder of Dax Coldstream. When Murray Cadence was told that the trespassing star witness was in fact Charlie's fiancé's father, the fixer was genuinely astonished—for the first time in his storied career. When Mercutio got home to Hercules Drive, he poured himself a drink and immediately wrote a letter:

Dearest Charles,

Perhaps by now Mr. Cadence has told you that I am the father of yours and my beloved, who was brought into the world as Phaedra, but for me (& I believe you as well), shall always be Puck. His mother suffered severe mental illness. I'm afraid I had much in common with my former wife in that regard; my predispositions were only made worse by Ann's cruelties, and brought to the fore. This, I offer as no excuse.

I am unsure if you recall I once was your teacher (I was a professor at Harvard) and that we share some history, which I now regard as water under the bridge.

From what I've briefly learned, you and my son were very much in love, and you did much for his spirit! (& mind & body.) For that, I am eternally grateful! You were in many ways what I was not able to be: the great love of his life. It is impossible for me to express what such knowledge does for my own spirit.

Forgive this note for not addressing your many recent losses and sorrows. It cannot, Charles. As Wittgenstein said, "Whereof one cannot speak, thereof one must be silent."

All one can really do is acknowledge the duality of the world.

It is my great hope that when the smoke of this strange battle-field clears, we might come together to break bread—and embrace in sweet sorrow. I have enclosed my personal email and cell. I don't expect to hear from you, yet nothing would give me more pleasure.

I forgot to mention that Puck reached out the day before that terrible night because he wished to see me. I came to the hospital, but you were just leaving for Paradise Cove. I followed the van and that was how I found my way to the beach. I was mulling on how best to make my approach, when . . .

Does any of this make sense?

I am feeling so tired now, and older than those Malibu hills, so again, forgive my discursiveness.

I hold you and Puck in my heart.

Yours,

Mercutio Schecter

~

The Professor sat in the back pew of a church in Monterey Park.

Coretta, a flinty friend of the deceased, stood at the podium and said a few words. She struggled immensely before introducing "the one Divinity was most proud of and wished everything in the world for—her niece, Jvnglebar."

The beautiful young woman with the peculiar name took centerstage. She looked Eurasian to the Professor and had numbers tattooed on her neck. Vibrant and articulate, she told a delightful, half-bawdy story about decoding "some rude lyrics" that puzzled Divinity when she heard them on the radio. Jvnglebar suddenly became emotional when she said "how much Auntie loved those twins." A wild anger flared.

"The gossipers had their day! I won't say more, not here, not now. Not today. But it broke her heart in a million pieces. A million little pieces! And broke her *mind . . .*" She struggled for composure. "Auntie had no choice but to become a saint."

The pastor was the last to speak.

He said Divinity was aptly named "because you could see the light of the Holy Spirit in her eyes. How grateful we are that her light shined on *us*, if only for a few months. She was new to our church, but her spirit was very, very old." As a trio of musicians quietly took the stage, he thanked Divinity for her generosity, not only to her niece, "to whom she bestowed a beautiful forever home in Leimert Park," but to the church. "Divinity Swann tithed a considerable amount of her hard-won savings, which will allow us to proceed with the refurbishments the city requires before we can reopen our pre-school. Praise Jesus."

The parishioners shouted back their assent.

"But perhaps the most valuable gift she gave us—apart from her love, which can have no value attached—is a practical one. It's what I like to call an 'everyday gift,' which to me is the most important kind. This everyday gift truly represents Divinity Swann, in that it is an embodiment of the woman's care, devotion, and simplicity. The robes of the children who sing so beautifully here each week will be mended and made anew by the wonderful Singer sewing machine that once belonged to Divinity's mother."

As Jvnglebar burst into tears, all rose to praise Jesus.

Mercutio left the church through a canopied portico, past the steel baptismal tub.

In that moment, he received a text:

yr note made me cry yes pls an embrace/& yes SWEET SORROW + JOI

44

Charlie laid low.

In her young life, she had been the face of obscene generational wealth; transgender rights and activism; and dynastic tragedy superseding the Gettys. Now, she was a Victim cover girl. But it was time to put away any face other than that of her true self.

She was nervous about seeing the old man. She didn't actually remember him being there when her husband died—so much of that night was a blur . . . though a week before, Charlie *did* happen to learn that the houseless miracle man who absolved her mother was the very same professor who got fired over the weaponized "Only Women Bleed" post. She was at GKC signing health directives for Puck when Murray casually spilled the tea, along with the harsh admonition not to do something stupid like tip Charlie's Angels (Instagram) to the connection. "We don't want the wicket any stickier than it is." She was clueless about sticky wickets, but the phrase was very Murray. No doubt it *was* a strange coincidence, made stranger still by the revelation that said professor was *Puck's fucking father*. But the email Mercutio sent righteously wormed its way into her heart; he even called her Charles, the favorite of her spouse (and Candida).

In just the last week, Elliot Page, Jack Dorsey, Courtney Love, and Drew all used the same word when she told them about her connection to the Professor: "karmic." (Charlie preferred the karmic tense to the "prophetic perfect.") Everyone she showed his letter to said they should *definitely* meet. Rick Owens himself was the biggest encourager, calling Mercutio Schecter "the last house on the block."

Charlie would never return to Paradise Cove. Stephen Schwarzman agreed to buy Dax's old house, and Sergey Brin bought the one Dax had given his daughter as a wedding gift. She decided to rendezvous with the Professor at one of Corinne's homes in Serra Retreat. When she texted the address, he wrote back, "I have cut my ties with GKC—hence, the gentlefolk at Uber have uncouthly severed our relations. I'm aggrieved to say that I am carless and shall soon be houseless as well."

She sent a driver.

~

"I'm so glad you agreed to see me," said Mercutio.

His suit was smart but getting seedy and the beard had the look of a bedhead garden. Like Puck, he was luminous and refined, possessing an icy assurance of his place in the firmament. (Father and son were starry witnesses.) He took a deep breath and smiled.

Their eyes met—*Puck's* eyes—and the Professor began.

"I wish to share some things that may be difficult to hear. They *will* be difficult—God knows, they're difficult for me to say, as well." He paused and nodded to go on. "That poor woman—the nanny of those children so tragically struck down—well—well—*I did not see what happened.* I was *there* but did not *see.* Do you understand, Charles? *Can you?* I was approached by the office of Murray Cadence—and—well—*well*—it is my great shame to say that 'a deal was made.' It was implied—to *me*, of course—that if I falsified what I 'saw,' I would be in line for a king's recompense. Yes. Yes. This was an *attractive proposal*, in that I had recently been making my bed in a rather poor excuse for a mobile home. And been in declining health for some time, using all sorts of chemical remedies to get me through the days and nights . . . Yet I had never let go of the hope—the dream—that I'd one day be reunited with my children, whom I—unceremoniously—had tossed away." He swallowed his tears. "This was my chance, Charles! To shine! To clean myself up and set myself right—to give them *money.* Money, money, money! I was convinced there was no other way to make amends, and *that* was my curse. Murray Cadence told me I'd won the lottery! And, at the time, *it mattered not* that the ticket was stolen, if you will, nor who would be destroyed by its windfall as a consequence . . . *that I, myself, would be destroyed.* I must say that I have confidential knowledge of *every single one* of the participants in this pernicious charade—the person at Cedars who falsified Divinity Swann's blood results, and so many more!—their names *shall be known*. From hospital to courthouse to precinct, their names shall be known!" He settled down, softly saying, "Mind you, Charles, I am not here to point fingers at *anyone* but me. Because, you see, those I helped *crucify* will not let me rest! At night they come, and in the early morning . . . They stand at the edge of my bed and stare. *I know now what I must do.*"

He hung his head and wept. Charlie kneeled, touching his leg. The Professor's smile became jagged at the unexpected gesture; the torso hinged until his forehead kissed a knee in fresh convulsions of sadness and regret.

"It's all right," she said—a mother now. "It's going to be all right." His body shook with the pent-up energy of grief and shame, and from relief that Charlie, who had endured such inconceivable suffering in her short life, truly understood. "How can I help?" she asked. "What can I do to help?"

"After I leave you," he proclaimed. "I am going to the police."

"If you do that," she mulled, "I think you'll be turned away—or something far worse. The arms of my family are long. If your intentions become known, I fear for your life."

"I have no fear!" he said gutturally. "I would rather die . . ."

"Stay here tonight. Tomorrow, we'll go to an attorney—not Murray Cadence! We'll find someone through my friend Mackenzie . . . *Then*, you can sit with a reporter. Someone at the *Times* or the *Journal*. I'll be in the chair next to you—in the room, the building, wherever you wish. I say that because my presence may provide validation; we don't want anyone to think you're a lunatic." They laughed at the same time because he definitely looked the part. "We sit with them," said Charlie, "and you tell *everything.*"

With aching concern, Mercutio said, "But, young lady! It may affect your reputation and your fortune!"

Tenderly, the widow said, "Don't you worry. I'm giving it all away."

~

It was already five o'clock. He told Charlie he had an errand to run in Venice but would be back in time for dinner.

They went up and down the alleys until he found his old friend, rummaging in a dumpster. He told the driver to park out of sight then left the SUV and backtracked.

"Loni!"

"Professor! Don't *you* look handsome!"

"Never better! And you: pretty in pink, as always."

"I was *worried*. You disappeared on me . . ."

"I worried about you, too . . . Look—listen—I have something for you." Mercutio reached in his pocket for the last $500 he had to his name. "*Take* it," he said. "And *hide* it!"

"Thank you," she said humbly, tucking the envelope into her bra.

"I have to run now. I'll keep in touch—I promise."

~

He cut through to the beach. It would be nice to have a stroll before supper.

The moon was full again. The dusky light brought him back to the grotto, and the shock reunion with his starfish son. But instead of sadness, he blinked at the duality of the ecstatic, excruciating world. Charlie said that she'd found his long-lost wife in San Pedro; perhaps he would go see her . . . perhaps not. Ann hadn't yet joined the wraiths who stood by his bed, begging him to do the right thing.

Next to the bike path, a girl made tentative progress in a walker. Her caregiver stayed a few steps behind. She wore a T-shirt that said NOT FAMOUS BUT KNOWN.

"Hello," Mercutio said brightly.

"Hello," said the girl.

"Don't you love this time of day?"

"It's . . . beautiful." She was shy and the words didn't come easily—her face sagged to one side. After a moment, he knew who she was.

"Do you come here a lot?"

"Every day!" said the protective caretaker, catching up.

"A *lot*," said the girl, with a charming, crooked smile.

"Well," he said. "I'll see you both again."

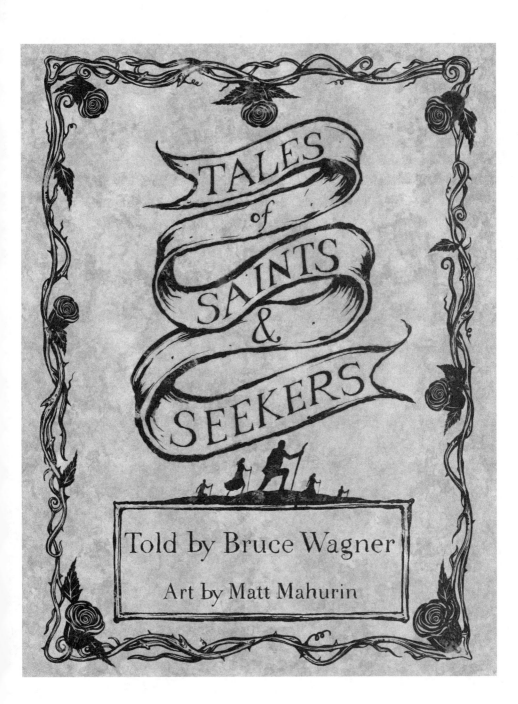

TALES of SAINTS & SEEKERS

Told by Bruce Wagner

Art by Matt Mahurin

The Sufis, who believe that deep intuition is the only real guide to knowledge, use these stories almost like exercises. They ask people to choose a few which especially appeal to them, and to turn them over in the mind, making them their own. Teaching masters of the dervishes say that in this way a breakthrough into a higher wisdom can be effected.

—*Idries Shah*

✗ ✗ ✗

"A mountain of skulls it is," responded the Bodhisattva. "But know, my son, that all of them are your own! Each has at some time been the nest of your dreams and delusions and desires. Not even one of them is the skull of any other being. All—all without exception—have been yours, in the billions of your former lives."

—*Lafcadio Hearn*

First there is a mountain,
then there is no mountain,
then there is
—*Donovan, "There Is a Mountain"*

Perhaps you are among those "armchair seekers" who find nothing more satisfying than sitting beside a fire on a rainy day, transported by a book of parables—traditional yet profound, simple but not easy—whose luster, no matter how contemporary the message, is redolent of the ancient.

Because the allegories present themselves in a cloak of otherness, often unfolding in what once were quaintly called "exotic" regions—mountainous territories of remote hermitages, valleys, and deserts, where spiritual vagabonds wander in search of teachers to show them the Way—they allow us a comfortable distance, which sometimes helps us better understand what the unpredictable tales impart. In the end, regardless of their impact, we tidily put them in the storybook genre. Even those that don't grab hold appeal to the child in us who at bedtime yearns to time-travel in his dreams. A second response is perhaps contradictory to the native wisdom of children themselves: those very stories, while didactic, sometimes scary, but mostly delightful, cannot be true! And if they were, well . . . sadly, the magic they described died eons ago (and the tantalizing players along with it). My hope for this slim volume is that it will help dispel such an idea. Still, it's human nature to ignore the gems that lie hidden in plain sight in our own backyards.

The "exotic region" I was raised in is called Los Angeles. Carlos Castaneda once told me that the locus of this sprawling county has an energetic similarity to the mystical Valley of Mexico, hence, it's no coincidence that men and women of knowledge made their way to this land. Most remained anonymous but charlatans took center stage in the public's imagination, which was a boon to "the ones who know"—for the latter preferred to remain invisible to all but those that sought them, in confusion or with earnest hearts.

What follows are tales told to me and catalogued over the last forty years. (A few variations have appeared in my novels and magazine essays.) If this volume has echoes of well-known anthologies—the volumes of Sufi wisdom imparted to Westerners by Idries Shah, the stories popularized by Zen Flesh, Zen Bones, *the fables of Aesop and its Sanskrit progenitor the* Pañćatantra, *or the beautiful, nightmarish legends of Lafcadio Hearn—that is deliberate. For all True faiths truly belong to only One.*

And those on the Hidden Path do still walk among us, in the here and now. —ed.

THE SUBMISSION

A certain Bektashi dervish was respected for his piety and appearance of virtue. Whenever anyone asked him how he had become so holy, he always answered: "I know what is in the Qur'an."

One day he had just given this reply to an inquirer in a coffeehouse, when an imbecile asked: "Well, what is in the Qur'an?"

"In the Qur'an," said the Bektashi, "there are two pressed flowers and a letter from my friend Abdullah."

—Idries Shah, *Wisdom of the Idiots*

A young screenwriter who aspired to write a "spiritual collection" of teaching parables sent the above excerpt to dozens of friends and publishers without attribution, claiming it as his own. An accompanying note said it was a sample from a work-in-progress that contained interlinking allegorical stories along the same lines. The remarks of the few publishers that responded ranged from "We don't publish greeting cards" to "Need to see more" to "We are not currently doing books with the Islamic theme." Among the comments of his friends were: "Why two pressed flowers and not one?" "Is Abdullah a terrorist?" and "You *cannot* call someone an imbecile!"

The writer showed a legendary film producer the sample and told him the results. The old man, now retired, was a friend of his grandfather, who happened to have a deep familiarity with the sanctified.

"To me," said the screenwriter, with passionate contempt, "this Sufi story is the *world*—it's *more* than that . . . it's worlds upon worlds upon worlds! That parable of the Bektashi saint is worth a thousand perfect novels and ten thousand perfect poems. And this is the response I get!"

The producer sucked on his pipe.

"You too are the world," he said. "The boy who claimed a perfect thing to be his own, yet was too lazy to deliver a complete, even counterfeit manuscript—then became enraged by its rejection. That marvelous Shah quote has always been a favorite of mine. But *your* words . . . you've bested him!" He pressed his palms together in respect. "I can never thank you enough for this gift."

A few months later, the screenwriter had a manic episode, was placed in the lockdown of a psychiatric facility, and quickly found himself in the Hell of the mind.

The producer and the young man's grandfather were on the terrace smoking when the despairing mother broke out of the house. Wringing her hands, she shouted, "Tell me what is to become of him—I want to know! Tell me what is to become of our boy!"

"Well," said the grandfather, exhaling a cloud of smoke. "I'm afraid we must wait for the complete manuscript to be submitted. Until then, the Great Editor will not comment."

MUSIC LOVERS

An actor on the cusp of fame was invited to a group psilocybin journey in Topanga, guided by a flavor-of-the-month shaman. Afterward, he took a long walk in the hilly neighborhood to process the main theme of his experience: his own death. Near the end of this wandering meditation, an old man on a ramshackle porch smiled as he passed. The actor suddenly had an urgent desire to share what he'd been through. The old man was warmly open to the idea.

He charmingly overshared (as actors do), without mentioning the Ganesha in the room—his fear and paranoia about the plant's profound revelations. Instead, the actor dwelled on the music the shaman played in the last forty-five minutes of the session and how perfectly in synch it was "with mind-body Universe." "As if," he remarked, "it was all arranged by a cosmic DJ."

The one who'd been listening, said, "The plant softens us to hear the music of the stars. But then what?"

He invited him in for tea.

The living room was barely furnished. Thinking for a moment that his host might be a squatter, the actor finally settled on the more comfortable fantasy that he was a recent widower who had cleared the place of anything reminding him of his wife. They drank their tea on little stools, without even a table between them.

Expanding on the actor's monologue, the old man said, "A gentleman came to me with a problem. The gentleman was hearing music in his head."

"Are you a therapist?"

"A practitioner, of sorts," he gently corrected. "The music was constant, he said, even during sleep. It was so bad that he got a CT scan to rule out a brain tumor. Of course, it was negative. He tried to minimize the situation by telling himself the notes weren't so loud that he couldn't tolerate the novelty of it. That worked for a while because he firmly believed his situation would be short-lived. But its stubborn consistency took him by surprise. Day by day, the orchestra grew louder until it was difficult to hold a conversation (though it did seem to diminish when he was alone). Subtle phrases and leitmotifs became recognizable—another surprise because the gentleman wasn't at all musical. As it happened, he died ten months later from an undiagnosed heart condition. A 'genetic' issue. In our last visit, he sang what he was hearing. Stood right there in front of the kitchen like a great opera singer singing an aria devoted to the stars, in an *exalted state*." He paused before saying, "The melody was vaguely familiar to me."

The old man's smile vanished and he stared at his guest with monumental indifference; in that nearly savage moment, the actor had a sudden, primal realization that he was in the presence of a Master. He tried to speak but had no voice. When the host's smile returned, he patted the young man's knee, as if fully understanding his predicament.

"The strange thing is that not long after he died, *another* creature with the very same trouble appeared at my door! But *this* one looked anything but exalted; she was deathly thin and grossly unkempt. She said that what began as tinnitus soon became discordant, atonal music from 'somewhere else.' She told me that she hated drugs yet became addicted, 'not by choice,' but rather, because of the music. She felt she was going mad. Which she was! She tortuously imitated what she was hearing and again, the melody—such as one could discern among the tics and shrieks—sounded familiar. Perhaps even more so than it had with the gentleman . . ." He sipped his tea, then resumed. "Yet *her* 'song' was frightening to hear, even to watch—it was nothing like the rapture of the one who stepped onto the kitchen stage as a walking shadow, a poor player in the Infinity Opera. Some weeks later she died of an overdose. She left her sister a note that it was time to 'face the music'—the music no one else could hear."

Without knowing what else to say, the stunned actor banally summarized, "So, it was the 'gentleman' who reached enlightenment . . ."

The sort-of practitioner poured him another tea.

"I had a dream about those two," he said. "The dream revealed that the woman who overdosed was the one allowed into Paradise, not the gentleman." He shrugged. "But who's to say? Dreams are artful seducers, so we mustn't pay too much attention." He stood up. "You look to me like you're hungry! It's long past breakfast—but how would you feel about steak and eggs?"

Before leaving, he had the gumption to ask the old man if he could be his apprentice.

Through the years, whenever someone inquired about how they had met, the actor liked to say, "A plant introduced us." The teacher would add, "Apparently, the three of us had something in common—we like the same kind of music."

He had a sense of humor about such things.

TRANSITIONS

A young follower came to visit in Topanga. He was having doubts, not about the old man, but of the Path itself.

"I met a woman at a meditation retreat," he said nervously.

"Ah! *Good for you*. Romance is one of the greatest teachers."

"No—it's nothing like that. She's almost seventy years old."

"Even better . . ."

"Let me finish! She was a student of _____ for over thirty years. She told me there was much she learned and how full her heart was with gratitude—even though she never actualized. But when she had gender affirmation surgery on her sixty-seventh birthday, she finally 'came home.' That's how she put it. She told me that when she woke up in the recovery room—'My *real* awakening,' she said—she was no longer a seeker. The long, difficult struggle was over, and all self-doubt disappeared. 'How could I be on the right Path,' she said, 'when I was in the wrong body all along?'"

"Do you have thoughts of making such a transition?" asked the curious teacher.

"Not at all. It's just . . . I don't want to find myself in that position. A seventy-year-old man who took the wrong Path but realized it too late."

"There are infinite ways to give up the *long, difficult struggle*," said the teacher. "That's why we call it 'threading the needle.' Some ways are definitely more interesting than others!"

The relieved disciple stayed for lunch.

When it was time to go, the old man stood at the open door and wished him the best of luck. Touching the young man's shoulder, he said earnestly, "If a medical procedure becomes available that sets one down upon the right Path, you must promise to let me know! My work shall then be done. I may even apply for an internship." With a wink, he added, "In the front office, of course—I tend to faint at the sight of blood."

MISUNDERSTANDINGS

For months, a Hollywood psychotherapist renowned for her celebrity clientele had been joking to a handful of friends that she was "cracking up." Early one morning, she awakened her husband to make the same joke—with tears in her eyes. He suggested the obvious: *Call your mentor.* It hadn't occurred to her.

That afternoon, she had a formal session with the man who trained her. Her crisis, she explained, began six months ago when a barista wrote SERA (with a little heart) on a paper cup. Her name had just four letters, which they always seemed to get wrong, regardless of the coffee shop. "Why was I so bothered?" she asked rhetorically. In the weeks that followed, she became obsessed with the theme of misperception. How was human discourse possible at all? Two people sharing the same view of even the simplest conversation appeared to be among the rarest of events. She knew it sounded absurd and childish, but she admitted to having thoughts of giving up her practice. It was clear to her that she too was participating in a delusion—of "helping" clients, who, by definition, inevitably misconstrued her words. She had a recurrent dream of being onstage with actors that each spoke a different language.

"I understand," he said. Long ago, her mentor suggested she use that exact phrase with her patients, as a default trust-builder. But she had the virus now and couldn't help wondering, *What if he's mangled the meaning of my words as well?* To make things worse, he performed another empathic sleight of hand, smugly saying, "I've been through exactly what you're experiencing."

She thought, *Oh god. Coming here was a mistake.*

Then he pulled a rabbit from the hat. "I'm going to remind you," he said emphatically, "of something that your little ball and cup shitshow has blinded you to: we are *electromagnetic creatures*, with a *very* tenuous grasp on language. And that's on a *good* day. Most of what we do is *energetic*—what we *say* is important too, but the 'effect' more often comes from a *mysterious exchange*. It took me years to understand that." Seeing the pain his now-colleague was in, he was moved to share, "I must tell you that I saw this coming. And I really do believe you're on the threshold—or precipice, what have you. It's the storm before the Great Quiet." He handed her a Kleenex. "For god's sake, Sara, none of us understand *anything*—not your *clients* and certainly not *you*. The baristas are way ahead of us! This crisis you're undergoing . . . let's call it the last gasp of holding on for dear life to control. *Control* is the delusion! The imperious 'mandates' of your precious words. . . . That's why I loathe people calling what we do 'talk therapy.' Now, *there's* a misunderstanding for you!"

Instantly, she felt lighter.

The next week, instead of dreading her workday, she couldn't wait for it to begin. She "tracked" energy and made a return to the intuitive. As a reminder, she kept a post-it on the desk with her mentor's mantra: *Leave your head at the door.* Her clients, electromagnetic all, seemed to recognize the change and bloomed as well. She had a renewed sense that this is what she was born to do.

One day, a stunt coordinator she'd been seeing on and off for a year or so came in, distraught. His distress was actually encouraging because he usually bottled up his emotions. He plunked down on the sofa and neither spoke. When she walked over and touched his hand, his emotions boiled over. He stammered that he couldn't stop beating himself up for the pain he had caused and the people he had hurt. They'd been down this road before, but he was never this vulnerable. When he said, "I just want to end it all," a detached, voluminous compassion overtook her.

"I understand," she said, softly repeating the phrase a few times. "And I really want you to hear that I've been through the exact same experience you're having now—*quite recently*. Not exactly, but within throwing distance."

He grabbed hold of the lifeline like a drowning man. "You?"

"Yes—we're all human. And you need to know that I saw this coming." She handed him a tissue. "I believe you're on the threshold of a great transformation. It's the last gasp of holding on to old patterns, old fears. Old self-punishments. It's the storm before 'the Great Quiet' . . . the quiet of breaking free."

Taking his first full breath since the beginning of the hour, the stuntman talked about being a bad father and a bad man then spoke eloquently of his own father's wounds. In the last few minutes of catharsis, he began to sob and she sat beside him again. Finally, she put her hand on his shoulder, signaling it was time.

"Thank you," he said. "Thank you! This session may have fucking changed my life."

∾

That night, she recounted the story to her husband, including the client's last words. When she downplayed it, he chided her for being too humble.

"Don't *misunderstand* what you did for that man," he said, wryly. "Don't misperceive!"

She said *Touché* and they laughed a lot. They drank more wine and made love. Just before sleep, she emailed her mentor to invite him to the house for dinner next week.

She never saw the stuntman again. Six months later, she learned that he'd killed his wife and sons. She went through her records and was shocked to discover that the murders had occurred two nights before he came to her office for his "life-changing" hour. The boys were home-schooled, and his reclusive spouse had no living relatives, so there weren't many questions when he told coworkers the family was moving to Idaho. Sheriffs found their heads in the foyer of the house (she tore up the mantra post-it when she read about that); the bodies were dismembered and scattered near the West Fork Trail off Angeles Crest Highway. He settled in Northern California, working under an alias as a short-order cook. He killed two prostitutes in Santa Rosa and would never have been caught if he hadn't sought solace with a local marriage and family therapist. When he told the woman that he hated himself for the pain he had caused and the people he'd hurt, she had the temerity to ask for details.

His pathology compelled him to hold nothing back.

"You do know," she said, "that I am required by law to report these crimes." When he moved toward her, the steely woman, having been through the violent assault of a patient once before, took a gun from the drawer and pointed it at his head. "Just so there's no misunderstanding, I will not hesitate to use this."

He was arrested a block away by a deputy who happened to be the therapist's husband.

DISTILLATIONS

A guru asked a devotee if he could meet a friend who was passing through Los Angeles. The student was honored and immediately invited the woman to lunch. She said she didn't have much time, so they met at the outdoor café of her hotel in Santa Monica. She was pleasant yet unremarkable. Though she looked about seventy, she was twenty years older.

When he asked how she came to know his guru, all she said was, "He's a very important man." Small talk was never the student's forte. Fortunately, he had brought his manuscript with him. For months, he'd been working on a "comprehensive distillation" of the guru's philosophy. With the woman's assent, he began to read from the introduction—a poetic, concise description of the chapters to come.

That evening, when they spoke on the phone (it was morning in Mumbai), the guru asked about his friend's response to the excerpted work. "I think she has ADHD," said the devotee sardonically. The man of knowledge was curious to know more; he had always encouraged his students to speak candidly.

"*Well* . . . she interrupted every time I began a sentence, by calling my attention to something utterly inane."

"That's just like her!" said the guru delightedly. "Go on! Tell me more!"

"First, it was the antics of a ridiculous child at the next table; then, a flock of birds flying toward the ocean. She even praised a dog that was fighting against its leash! I don't think she heard a word I said." By now, the "important man"'s glee was uncontainable—he was really enjoying himself. When at last the irritating peals of laughter receded to a few breathless chortles, the student said, "Who *is* she? Why did you even want us to meet?"

"She put on a pretty good show."

"What do you mean?"

In an instant, the guru's good humor was gone.

"The child at the next table was you; and the birds, what you'll *become* if you pull off the impossible feat of vanquishing the Self. Most likely, you'll end up a dog, straining against its master's leash—but only if you're very, very lucky!" He chuckled as the student's stomach dropped. "'That woman' happens to be one of my teachers—the greatest of them all."

NEURODIVERGENCE

In the mid-1980s, a darling Midwestern girl moved to Hollywood with her parents and got work in commercials right away. A year later, she played the friend of the lead in a TV pilot that became a hit show. She outshone the star and was given her own series. Movies followed, along with product endorsements and a string of ghost-written YA novels that became bestsellers.

The ingenue became notorious for her virulent nature. If her career hadn't been so profitable to studios, agents, and lawyers, she would have been banished. Like a tornado, she left a path of destruction in her personal and professional lives. At least two "friends" were driven to suicide by her sadism; when a lover forced an enemy to defecate in front of her at gunpoint, she never laughed so hard in her life. That she would inevitably destroy herself was her victims' only solace.

She had just turned sixteen.

One day, a prestigious older actress came courting, hoping to develop a project together that might invigorate her flagging career. As part of the seduction, the woman said that "my dear friend, the Dalai Lama" was coming to town to speak at a university and that before the talk, His Holiness was scheduled to visit a private home to thank the benefactors of a monastery recently built in Dharamshala. "You can be my date!" she said. Now, the girl knew nothing about the lama, monk, whatever— except that he was a bigger celebrity than even the most famous actors could ever dream of becoming. So, she was happy to use the meeting, and the status it would confer, as another casual, spiteful cudgel against everyone she abhorred.

She hired a Town Car and was surprised by how desolate the landscape became as they headed south. Why were they going south anyway and not west toward the ocean? Why were they not going to Malibu or the Palisades or Bel Air?

After a forty-five-minute ride, they stopped at some sort of abandoned, broken-down shed in a scary cul-de-sac by the freeway. *What the fuck.* The bemused, taciturn driver obviously had taken them to the wrong address—or the right one, in the wrong city. The property was boarded up but a few doors down was a home with a festively decorated front yard. Out of boredom and annoyance, wanting to stretch her legs, she sauntered over to investigate. As she approached, three young girls appeared at the door and stared, in shock. They shouted the name of a character she was famous for playing then whispered the actor's real name in disbelief before disappearing into the house. When a friendly, tattooed man emerged, the shy girls hid behind him. He said something to the white girl in Spanish.

"No hablo," she said. "So, where's the Dalai Lama? Is he takin' a shit?"

Not understanding, he grinned, and spoke Spanish again while motioning her in. As a goof, she went along.

Inside, adults and children gawked, talking animatedly amongst themselves, seeming to recognize the young celebrity from one showbiz incarnation or another. Her guess was that she'd crashed a *quinceanera*, a rite of passage that she happened to be familiar with because it was the theme of a sitcom she did a few years back. (She thought the girls could have used a costume designer because they looked cheap and ridiculous.) When she laughed out loud at the whole dumb spectacle, the baffled partygoers merrily joined in.

In the middle of all this, one of the teenagers drew aside a curtain and pointed into the street, shouting in Spanish. Everyone instantly became quiet and suddenly stood, the way people do in church. They stared at the front door, fidgetily awaiting the guest of honor. When she appeared at the threshold—a beautiful flaxen-haired girl who was older than the rest—the girls were tearfully joyous. Something was different about her. She had a tender, alien, almost poetic air of violence and unpredictability that the child star instantly recognized and understood. She began to speak, not Spanish, but a bizarre, repetitive language of tics, demands, and unheard melodies belonging to no one else in the world. The girls slowly came forward in their crinoline pinata getups, to reverently touch the hem of the honoree's gown. When a few moved in for an embrace, her father-escort, by the sweetest nod, indicated they should wait a while longer, so not to startle.

As she watched the homecoming, the accidental visitor felt a gust of wind and became someone else. She saw her body's insides, spangled with purple quartz—like the huge cracked-open geode she saw at a shop in Aspen.

~

She outgrew her wildness and became one of Hollywood's most beloved. She is known for her generosity, and while she has not yet sponsored a monastery in Dharamshala, a building at the Children's Hospital carries her name.

Her Spanish is fluent now. Though a few years younger than the "guest of honor," she was anointed as her godmother. The autistic girl and her family celebrate birthdays and holidays with the actress, and they vacation together. After more than twenty years, that legendary meeting is still spoken of with great humor and affection; how their daughter had just been released from the hospital, nearly having died from insulin shock, and how the star went to the wrong address by mistake and judged them all in her scabrous heart.

To this day, the atmosphere in the room still changes when she enters with her retinue of caregivers. The carpet is strewn with amethysts and the air electrified by the arcane language of imperial mysteries—riven by thunderclaps of poetic violence and the impossible sacred sorrows each of us is given in this short life of everlasting love.

MAKING BAIL

While most saints walk the earth anonymously, in the 1990s one of those "persons of knowledge" could easily be found in Ojai, where he was the abbot of a *vihara*. Known far and wide for his wisdom and compassion, interested parties left him alone, preferring to read the books he had written and admire the man from afar. (Truth be told, most aficionados don't have the stomach required to pursue the Path.) But one day, a fretful monk came to his door to inform that a disturbed-looking middle-aged man was urgently requesting an audience—and refused to leave until he got one.

"Send him in," said the abbot.

The exhausted caller hastily bowed before blurting out that he'd come all the way from Chicago, where he "left everything behind." If the master didn't accept him as a student, he said importunately, he would camp outside the monastery "for years, if that's what it takes!"

Long ago, the abbot concluded that outright lunatics were far easier to deal with than a man in midlife crisis. Tea was brewed to calm the traveler's nerves. When asked if he were hungry, he replied, "For the Knowledge, great sir—it is the only food that seems to agree!" He was clownish and disarming all at once.

The abbot probed further.

He began by admitting to being a lapsed Catholic. Up until the age of thirty-five, when memories of victimization by lascivious priests surfaced, he took enormous comfort in the rituals and fellowship of the Church. He went on to say that he'd married his childhood sweetheart, and they had four wonderful children; then, with wavering voice, ruefully confessed that the family was "somewhat fractured, as a result of my dear one's passing." With great difficulty, he shared that his wife's alcoholism became *progressive*, putting quotes around the word with the saddest smile the abbot ever saw. Apparently, the dear one was violent and spent weeks in jail as a result, followed by extended tours in hospitals and rehab. When she disappeared "for what I believed would be the last time," the poor soul checked the city morgue twice a day for new arrivals. She finally called from jail, begging to be bailed out, but by then the desperate man had joined a support group whose experienced members urged him not to intervene. The safest place to dry out, they said, was behind bars, the consensus being "Maybe this time she'll find her bottom."

Which she did—she hanged herself there.

After the initial shock, the widower felt a deep sense of relief that soon matured into a state of manic joyfulness, where he remained for months. "The sky was bluer, sleep was deeper—I felt lighter than air." Shamefully, he recalled his bewildered daughter asking, "Papa, have you even *cried*?" His eldest son contemptuously remarked how "thrilled" his father seemed about the tragedy. Naturally, the admonishments gave him pause; happier memories returned, along with a poignant nostalgia.

But then the nightmares began.

A demon resembling his wife appeared at the foot of the bed, shouting, "You *love* that I died! And that is the *worst* of sins!" The pain was exquisite when it raged and bellowed about his failure to post bail. The reproachful demon began to visit in waking hours as well. On the way to Ojai, it taunted, "The *great abbot* won't make you feel better! Nothing and no one will . . . your rotten heart will pay the price!" He knew he was dancing with madness. Sometimes the demon signed off with piquant encouragements to "find a rope, like I did." Its breath stank like shit as it roared, "We'll swing together like old sweethearts!"

"*That's* why I'm here," said the tormented guest. "By not paying her bail, I let the rot set in . . . *I've read all your books.* Only you can understand the position I'm in—you, a master of Hidden Knowledge! All I'm asking is that you teach me how . . . to get rid of the rot!" He straightened up and proudly said, "I won't take no for an answer."

While admiring the gentleman's wild resolve, the abbot heeded his instincts: in simple terms, this feckless, wounded soul was in no way up to the task of meeting the challenges served up by a life of Truth. Such a journey would only hasten him along the same haunted road as his wife.

"When a bird is mortally injured," said the abbot, "it's often best to leave it in the cage. Never forget that the world *itself* is a cage. All of us are mortally injured the moment we're born; the only one with the power to set bail is the Unknown. And even then, only a few choose to leave their cell! In this moment, your vision is too cloudy to see that. You cannot see the selflessness of what you did for her, the *love*. I can assure that one day you will."

The abbot knew the recipe for healing contained two ingredients. First, he must ease the grieving husband's acute suffering; then, discourage any romantic fantasies of escapism such as turning his back on the world—and his children.

He told this story:

"I once knew a man—also married, also with four children—who found solace in the arms of another. Consumed by guilt, he ended the affair. The rejected woman sent letters that became increasingly ugly and unhinged. He refused to answer, not wishing to 'stir the pot.' For months, he worried she might do violence to him or even his wife and children. When he heard the news that his mistress took her own life, he rejoiced. He called it 'the happiest day since my youngest was born.'

"In time, his schadenfreude became toxic. The festive gloating and secret celebrations staged over the body of that sentient being—the tastes, smells, and textures of his dead lover, apart from the gifts that her generous spirit once provided—ate away at him like poison. He *too* experienced disturbing visitations from the departed. And like you, he sought refuge in Truth.

"He divorced his wife and made a pilgrimage to a *vihara* in Bhutan—much further away than Chicago!—to meet a famous abbot whom he believed to be the only one who might help him. But his entreaties to become the abbot's student were completely ignored." Up till then, the wide-eyed listener had been filled with hope; now, his heart and shoulders sunk in despair. "Certain that the abbot would eventually change his mind, he stubbornly decided to live outside the monastery walls. He became a *sadhu*, a wandering mendicant, undergoing much adversity and disease. For ten years, at the end of each and every day, he knocked on the door.

"One day it opened; a monk with twinkling eyes let him in.

"At last, the master agreed to his apprenticeship, contingent upon the student heeding a stern warning: Abandon the malignant covetousness of Self—or die! During the expiation of his sins, the adulterer's wife remarried and led an exemplary, spiritual life before she left the world. Two of his children predeceased him, each acquiring great renown as educators and benefactors. Still, he never reunited with the surviving heirs, nor did he meet his seven grandchildren."

"Yes!" said the visitor. "That's *exactly* what I want!" With unassailable logic, he asserted, "Wounded birds *should* stay in the cage—those were *your* words, not mine. . . . If this monastery is a cage, I'll take it. Throw away the key!"

The cautionary tale had backfired, redoubling the listener's idiosyncratic resolve.

"You haven't let me finish!" said the host peremptorily. To right the ship, he plotted another course, throwing in a rogue wave or two. "The Abbot of Bhutan was quite ill. When the monk he'd groomed to be his successor passed away without warning, the apprentice rejoiced, believing it a sign that *he* would inherit the abbot's throne. A few weeks later, he sat by his teacher's deathbed. He conveniently forgot the warning against covetousness, but . . . too late!

"*That* was when the dying teacher transformed himself into a thousand-headed demon! He pointed to a mirror and said, 'Look into the glass!' When the sinner did as was commanded, he saw the dark speck of a figure galloping toward him. 'If there is any hope for you, bite the monster with your teeth when it comes, and devour it!' He almost died on the spot, from fear. The demon whispered conspiratorially, 'If you hesitate for a *millisecond*, you will burn like Judas in Hell. Forever!'

"The figure in the mirror grew larger and larger until it sprang from its confinement and leapt onto the chest of the self-serving apprentice. A furious fight ensued. Remembering his teacher's counsel, he began gouging at his opponent, and with each chunk of flesh the glittering demon diminished in size, until at last becoming the beggar-monk's human twin. The duelists vanished in a fiery dance, mirrored combatants for eternity . . . And as for the Bhutanese master, he slipped away during the battle and peaceably entered Paradise."

The storyteller knew the inspired details about sin, Judas, and eternal hellfire would strike a Catholic nerve, no matter how long ago he had strayed. The PTSD from his wife's "demon," made the Chicagoan even more ripe; he slowly backed from the room with a look of sheer terror, made even more monstrous by its cracked veneer of respectful politesse.

"Don't go! You mustn't!" entreated the abbot. "*Stay*. Live *here*, at the monastery—first, you'll be a beggar in Ojai! But just for five short years!—you're much too strong to relapse like the monk did . . ." He was in the mood to ham it up. "You're one of the *rare* ones who *learn* from their mistakes! Come, I'll show you to your room—meditation begins at 3 a.m."

The Chicagoan demurred, stammering that he needed more time to "tie up strings at home." Falling over his own feet on the way out, he thanked the abbot profusely and apologized for interrupting his busy day.

"Hurry back!" shouted the impish master, literally giving chase, and feeling dutiful about saying a bit more. "Your wife now *understands* . . . she was merely confused. It's not just the living—the dead can be cloudy thinkers as well. I promise she won't trouble you that way anymore . . . Give those kids of yours my regards when you see them to say goodbye. And don't forget to tell them how sorry you are that you'll never be able to meet your beautiful grandchildren!" As a coup de grâce, the abbot impetuously made the sign of the cross (the guest, desperate to depart, responded in kind), adding, "Go with god."

With a heroic sprint, the prisoner jumped bail.

~

Had he stayed, he would eventually have learned that the beggar apprentice of Bhutan was the Ojai abbot himself, with just a few details altered for dramatic effect.

When he was young, he had many affairs outside his unhappy, childless marriage, and one of the lovers threatened to tell his wife; when that woman died in a car crash, he felt giddy at his good fortune. In time, the burden of the perverse wants and needs of Self became too much. Upon divorce, he journeyed to Bhutan, where he took refuge in the dharma and was immediately accepted as a student. He *did* become a wandering mendicant—a beggar—but only for a year or so, at his teacher's behest, as part of the traditional lessons on detachment. And, as in the story told to the lapsed Catholic, there *was* an ambitious monk who jockeyed to rule the monastery at the time their teacher became deathly ill. Ironically, the monk predeceased the teacher, collapsing on a hiking trail. The mendicant, done with his sacred wanderings, grieved; he loved him like a brother because when he first arrived from America, beaten down and feverish, that very monk opened the doors of the *vihara* with a smile that made him feel he had done the right, the only thing.

But it was the "beggar"'s purity of heart that led the teacher to empower him with dharma transmission. Unlike the protagonist of the tale told to the Chicagoan, the student never forgot the warning that a sword hangs above us all, awaiting its cue. The concocted flourish of the showdown with the demon mirror-twin contained many truths, not least of which was a reminder that the consequence of relaxing one's vigilance was dire.

The storied Abbot of Ojai, known far and wide for his wisdom and compassion, still prays for the courage to obey his teacher, renewing each day the vow to wage war against the monster of Self—to fight sword against sword, *without a millisecond's hesitation.*

ADDICTIONS

In 1972, a man with a deep affinity for the Way settled in Hancock Park, a few blocks from the great Vedic astrologer Chakrapani. (As it happened, both of their homes were gifted by the same benefactor.) The hand of fate led a young woman to his door. Upon seeing her, the adept instantly knew that she would enter Paradise.

While never showing favoritism among his students, he held her in special regard. He called her Morning Star—"the first to come and the last to disappear"—yet knew she wasn't ready. After two years of hard work, she left the Path as predicted. She-who-ceased-to-go-upstream spent the next few decades abusing her body while hatred grew like a wild garden in her heart. During her last drug spree, in dark humor, she wore a nasal spray of Narcan around her neck so that strangers or fellow users could revive her. By the turn of the century, she'd had enough. Now past middle-age, her aesthetics rebelled against an accidental overdose—too lurid, too undignified. No, she would do it deliberately, after cynically embarking on a "Magical Misery Tour" to revisit people and places that once meant so much.

Her last stop was Hancock Park.

A devotee opened the door and waved her in. She could see her old teacher sitting with a group of disciples in meditation. Everyone's eyes were shut but his suddenly opened, locking on hers before closing again. She smirked and hung back, waiting for the group to disperse.

For a moment, it felt like she'd never been away at all.

The visitor finally went over and they embraced. "I just realized what this place is," she said knowingly. "It's *rehab*, with a bullshit spin." Her voice was loud and gravelly. "The people who come here are addicts, strung out on getting Daddy's approval—no! It's *acting class*. The Actor's Studio!"

With a sick smile, she looked around and shook her head. "Your lost little lambs are all attention whores. '*Look*, everyone! I'm on the fucking Path, whoopee!' And you! The biggest fucking addict of them all! Starring in 'The Great Guru' . . . you're *worse* than them, you're the Wizard of Oz behind the curtain of delusion. You're—"

The old man, whose warmth hadn't wavered during the harangue—who in fact seemed to enjoy her more with each affront—smilingly begged her pardon to use the loo "to conduct a bit of urgent business."

In his absence, she weighed the idea of walking out. Instead, she wandered to the altar in the solarium. It was cluttered with beads, burning incense, garlands of freshly cut flowers, and a gallery of framed photos of his teacher (and his teacher's teachers as well). She picked up one of the frames—an out of place portrait of a young woman—and was stunned to recognize herself. The old man gently took the frame from her hand, replacing it to the honored position among those of knowledge.

"What you said about addiction is true," he said. "*Mine* was to reach inner silence, the path to Brahman. But the antidote I wore around my neck was different than yours." She gaped at him—how could he have known? "*My* amulet had a photo of my guru: his infinite love and compassion revived me from many misadventures of the drug called Self. His devotion was unerring, his care impeccable." He winked and said, "I finally 'kicked the habit.'" Then: "But for most 'addicts,' the journey proves too difficult. I should add that such unfortunates rarely have the luxury of a magical misery tour *farewell*."

~

From that moment, she stayed. She inherited the house in Hancock Park and still gives *satsang* five days a week, as was her beloved teacher's wish. When destiny drops new Morning Stars at her door, they're invariably drawn to the sunlit altar—and without fail, ask about the meaning of the strange, incongruous nasal spray nestled among the picture frames.

And that's when she tells this story.

AN OLD ADAGE

A handsome young man became wildly popular on Instagram for his pithy, digestible bits of dark comic wisdom. Agents and studios courted him, promising to monetize what they glibly called his "brand." Overwhelmed by the sudden attention, he took a sex and drugs road trip. Always a voluptuary, he sensed that recent activities were growing out of hand. After he made a TikTok video about getting trichomoniasis (he called it a "TrichTok"), an alternate path fatefully presented itself on the very same platform—such are the times in which we live. And that was how he ended up at the weekend workshop of a legendary saint in Northern California.

Attendees could have short meetings with the teacher after her final lecture, and he reserved a slot. With a single look, the *acharya* knew the unusual boy had a real chance; his advantage over most was that he didn't take himself seriously. Never having been in the presence of a master, he did his usual charm dance before deciding to go for it. He told her everything about the meth- and GHB-fueled sex he'd had with hundreds of men. Observing her as he spoke, he was incredibly impressed: The more shocking the details he provided, the more she laughed, in a lovely, musical way, and the warmer she became.

So *gemutlich*, so human, this teacher!

He put a scholarly spin on his activities because in truth he sought to enlist her as a coconspirator, hoping she would recognize his specialness and be the chic spiritual sponsor of his debaucheries. To strengthen his defense, he spoke of having studied the history of "sacred prostitutes" in the temples of the world. He shared his deep readings in the poetry of Pindar, and *The Golden Bough*; rattled off the names of multicultural sex-work devotees—the *devadasi, hetaera, hijara,* and the *shamhat* of *Gilgamesh*; brilliantly improvised on "sex magick," body positivity, empowerment, and neopaganism; then conjured Herodotus, who wrote that all Babylonian women had a sacred duty to honor Aphrodite by sitting in her temple to await sex with strangers, for money. Announcing that he was a Jew, he felt particularly close to the *kadesh* or male temple prostitutes. "*Kadesh* is so much better than 'sodomite,' right? Don't you think?" On one of his ayahuasca journeys, he had a past-life revelation of being a *kadesh* himself. "So, the orgying kind of makes sense, right? It feels like I'm *giving*. I mean, beyond just sex. Like whoever I meet . . . it's like we're worshipping something, together. Our 'sacred duty.' It doesn't really even have much to do with bodies, right? Don't you think? It's so much more! I mean, that's how it *started*—people went to temple for *ecstasy*, but when the sacred sex practice was banned, they started going out of *fear*. And to prepare for death. It became like a totally morbid thing."

"Those prostitutes were slaves," she said, with casual indifference. "And so were the 'worshippers' who paid them. As were the kings—the kings and queens were slaves too—and even the gods themselves. It's most difficult to escape enslavement. *The* most difficult thing."

At the end of their time, she guilelessly asked if he received money for his encounters.

"No!" he exclaimed, in mock outrage, before segueing into scandalous mode. "I mean, it's usually according to their ability to pay. I don't do crypto but I'm not above Venmo . . . Zelle, PayPal, it's all good." She laughed but looked mildly confused; maybe he threw too much at her. "*No money is exchanged*," he said, wanting that to be clear. "Only love and energy. It's all for fun and for free, as they say in AA."

At the door, his trademark look—the wryly flamboyant, sparkling provocateur—was dethroned by her expression of sober, piercing love.

"I'm so glad we met," she said.

He bowed and thanked her, wondering why there were tears in his eyes. "You actually remind me of my mother."

"Then take some motherly advice—flush the pharmacopeia." She took his trembling hand in hers. "An old adage comes to mind: 'Trust in god but lock the front door.'" She chortled and said, "In your case, it wouldn't hurt to lock the back door as well! At least, for a little while. And promise you'll come see me again."

LIFETIME ACHIEVEMENT

The body and its parts are a river, the soul a dream and mist, life is warfare and a visit to a strange land, and the only lasting fame is oblivion.

—Marcus Aurelius

An entertainment journalist wasn't getting any younger and sensed that her freelance chronicles of the romantic life of Phoebe Bridgers, the private life of Kelly Reilly, and the modest triumphs and travails of Jack Osbourne were coming to an end. She had an idea for a "weightier" project. A friend from college was a *New Yorker* editor but if the magazine wasn't interested, she could use the pitch as a proposal for a full-length book.

When she told her mother about her strategy, the old woman said, "Kill two birds."

Years ago, she wrote an article for *Vogue* about the life and career of Sadie Patchen that focused on the legendary actress's crowning achievement: the role of Meredith Weaver in the latest version of *Golden Menace*. The film's remarkable longevity began in 1935; was remade in the early '60s and the mid '80s; and culminated in Patchen's 2008 star turn—for which she won a fourth Oscar, sixth Golden Globe, and the Palme d'Or. Widely regarded as among the greatest films ever made, it is ranked as her finest performance.

She still had Patchen's phone number in her contacts—a landline—and was jolted when the actress picked up. (Having been to the house in Holmby Hills for *Vogue*, she wondered what room the star was in when she took the call.) Nervously reintroducing herself, she immediately mentioned the old magazine piece but avoided bringing up the endgame of a

New Yorker profile. The journalist simply said, "You've been in my thoughts . . . and a little voice told me to reach out."

"Yes! I remember you," she said warmly. "I'm quite touched that you called. Why don't you come by tomorrow for tea."

It was that easy—a wonderful omen.

Built in the '30s, the mansion was an elegant Spanish Regency, without a hint of Gloria Swanson's brokedown *Sunset Boulevard* palace. What struck her that first time she visited, as it did now, was the absence of memorabilia—no statuettes or triangles made of crystal, no photos of the actress with crooners, presidents and kings, no hints, intimations, mementoes or references at all to the industry that had lavished her with untold rewards.

Patchen was eighty-three and her delicate, iconic beauty shone from inside and out. They revisited *Golden Menace,* and she told the journalist a few things she hadn't shared for the *Vogue* piece. As an example, she said that before they began shooting, she carefully studied the fate of each actress who had portrayed Meredith Weaver. The star of the original (1935), burdened by the fame the role brought, became a nun and lived out her years in a Carmelite monastery. The abdication from show business doubled her renown, a detail, gossip had it, that both titillated and embittered the renunciate. The actress in the '60s version was savaged by critics for her performance. Patchen said that she had substance issues "*before* doing the film" and died of an overdose four years after the "pointless remake" wrapped. The leading lady of the penultimate *Menace* did very well—the film, while not a high artistic watermark, was a solid box office hit. "Which is everything in this town," said Patchen. "When she didn't get nominated, she had the temerity to say, 'Awards are nice but it's not why I do what I do.' Utter *bullshit*. Actors *live* for awards!" She threw back her head and laughed. "Oh, but she did *just fine*. She's a very earthy, funny girl. Went on to *great success* in her career. Picked up a few gongs along the way, too."

Just then, Patchen caught sight of the housekeeper.

"Rosa!" she called out. "Give the Awards Room a dust-over, would you?" She winked at her guest and said, "How's that for the perfect segue. *Golden Menace*—that's what we call the Oscar around here!"

"Awards Room?"

"Why, yes."

"You're not kidding?"

"Not at all," giggled Patchen.

The journalist couldn't tell if she was being sarcastic.

"But I've never seen a single award in this house . . ."

"Because you've never seen the *room*. I've always disliked the 'showy' part of show business. At this time of my life, I *do* spend a fair amount of time each night in that room . . . I sit and 'scry'—isn't that the word the mystics use? Not 'cry,' *scry*. And it's a marvelous comfort. I'll give you a peek . . ."

But the peek didn't happen because she began to speak of so many things—the vein was rich—and the journalist didn't want to break the flow. Anyway, seeing the Awards Room was an excuse to come back, and Ms. Patchen, whom she sensed was lonely, thoughtfully invited her to return next week "for the Grand Tour." Surprised and pleased that the actress had trusted her enough to reveal the room's unlikely existence, she was still embarrassed to find herself with a nagging, all-too-human thought:

I will never have such a room—only some are so blessed.

All sorts of troubled musings came that night as she settled in for sleep.

~

Sadie Patchen died two days later.

The private funeral was held at a famously hidden cemetery in Westwood. The journalist parked a half-mile away, walking through the drizzle to stand in front of a police barricade. Paparazzi clustered behind it, aiming long lenses at the crowd of old and young celebrities who gathered at the grave in the rain.

It felt important that she linger until the cars and limousines began to leave.

Suddenly, an old woman rushed up on foot—it was Rosa the housekeeper, smiling at her through tears. "I find her in the Award Room!" she blurted. "So beautiful and at peace!"

"Oh!" said the journalist, taken aback. "I'm so sorry for your loss!"

"The darling, the darling! She was my darling . . . "

Rosa's body was dense and muggy when they hugged. The journalist couldn't think of anything to say and was chagrined when the words tumbled out: "But what will happen to the awards? Will they go to a museum or the Academy? What will happen?"

The housekeeper's face contorted. "The room! The room, it is empty! For fifty years, *empty!* Always empty . . . I say *Why, preciosa?* 'Why empty?' *Mi preciosa* say, 'This where we come from . . . this where we go—to our *award,*' she say! To our award we are going!"

With a sob, she turned on her heel and vanished.

Sapped by caring for a mother with dementia, the journalist abandoned the spec book she had already begun on the life of Sadie Patchen. She returned to hiring out for the occasional rising/falling star online Q&As.

But the old woman continued to ask when the *New Yorker* piece on the old movie star would be on the newsstands, muttering to herself, for no particular reason, "Kill two birds."

DOUBLE JEOPARDY

A student thanked his teacher, pro forma, for two years of guidance.

"It is time for me to leave," he said, standing shotgun-straight while stiltedly reciting from a prepared speech. "It's become obvious to me that the entrenched doctrines of the religion—or *belief system*—and the behavior of the people themselves who are involved in this organization—are not compatible with my own." When she asked for an example, the student gathered himself and his nervousness dissolved. Rather snidely, he replied, "For one, it's punitive. You talk a lot about 'lovingkindness' though *in actuality* I find it in . . . *short supply*. But the biggest problem I have"—a pause before delivering the knockout punch—"is a general lack of inclusivity."

The teacher tried to engage him, but he cut her off with a wave of the hand, indicating that a dialogue would be of no use.

She smiled and said, "I wish you well."

They bowed to one another and the student left.

A week later, during an early morning walking meditation in the garden, the abbess was served with a notice of legal proceedings being initiated by the former devotee, alleging "egregious mistreatment and emotional abuse." Anger rose, along with the grandiose fantasy of her testifying in court—and triumphing—like a vindicated heroine in a popular movie.

But that night, when the abbess dreamed of a wrathful deity slapping her with a subpoena, she awakened in a sweat of paranoia. Perhaps she hadn't taken any of this as seriously as she should have; the wrong judgment could bankrupt the temple and embroil the sangha in scandal. In a cowering half-sleep, she resolved to settle out of court.

Tomorrow, I'll have our lawyer talk to the insurance people.

With that resolution, wide-awake now, she made herself tea. She slowly recovered from the shock of it all, until she laughed out loud at the drama that had been staged, courtesy of her mind. Suddenly, the anger dissolved and her compassion for the student returned, as did the foundation of equanimity provided by years of discipline and practice. She was grateful to be reminded that it was *all* a dream: the "student," the "abbess," even the "Buddha."

Especially, the Buddha.

As a result, all charges were dismissed with prejudice.

BROKEN ARROWS

A formidable woman of knowledge kept a modest home in Redondo Beach. Though she had a reputation for being a smug, irascible, intolerant teacher, the same description easily applied to the international seekers who had beaten a path to her door (often unannounced) for almost forty years. Their main interest was in ticking the anecdotal box of having visited the famous, famously "difficult" adept; in brief encounters, they masked their cynicism, had her sign a book or two, made the perfunctory donation, and prostrated themselves before moving on.

One morning, at a workshop in Telluride, the teacher began to slur her words. When her students asked what was wrong, she had trouble understanding them. At the emergency room, she was quickly diagnosed with "acute mountain sickness," then sent home with some medicine and an oxygen tank. The common condition resolved within twenty-four hours—but she kept that detail to herself. She continued to slur, struggling to answer the usual earnest questions regarding spiritual matters. The situation seemed to lend an urgency and focus to the seminar that had been missing. There was something else that everyone noticed: the woman was actually cheerful. The smirks and harsh putdowns disappeared; she even giggled. Overall, the woman was a joy to be around.

A few students made the old joke, "I'll have what she's having."

At the end of the event, when a delighted practitioner remarked on the change in her, the teacher sat bolt upright. "My words are nothing but arrows pointing the way," she said, with perfect enunciation. "And while I am often ill-tempered and impatient that my students cannot manage to follow the *simple direction* of those arrows—or discern the 'arrowness' of an arrow at all—*this* weekend, I was tremendously moved by your deep, authentic efforts to engage. The *struggle*, you see, is everything! Because whether or not one can recognize an arrow, let alone the direction it is pointed, is irrelevant. *The results will be the same.* All is illusion! Even high-altitude aphasia."

The devotees were shocked—and equally startled when five seconds later the slurring returned with a vengeance. They hovered over her, trying to break the code of verbal mishmash.

One of them exuberantly shouted "Ice cream! I think she wants ice cream," and the teacher clapped her hands, like an invalid in spirited assent.

THREADING THE NEEDLE

A seamstress in the movie business lost her only child in a freak boating accident in Costa Rica while on a yoga retreat. He was twelve years old. She had him late, at forty-six. For months, she researched ways to end her life. The day finally came when suicidal thoughts were still there, but the energy was gone; instead, a chronic, numbing depression settled in.

Just a few years before, the son of a famous actress had a seizure and drowned in a swimming pool. It was a huge story. He was around her own boy's age. At the time, the seamstress couldn't imagine what she would do if such a thing happened to her; she and the star were hell-born allies now. From a dark place that craved the paltry light of small distractions, she watched a few of the actress's films. One of them surprised—there, in the end-crawl, was her "costume assistant" credit. She'd entirely forgotten they had worked together. So to speak.

After the drowning, the actress disappeared from public view. Her story anchored the occasional sensationalistic piece about Hollywood scandals and tragedies. There were rumors that she and her husband moved to Oregon, to Europe, even Africa; that she was permanently disabled by a suicide attempt; gained two hundred pounds; was a recluse and a hoarder; became a brilliant ceramicist, selling her creations for a fortune under an assumed name.

The seamstress dived into YouTube, watching clips and interviews that predated the tragedy.

Among them was an appearance on Jimmy Kimmel from eight years ago. The actress was feigning shock at having been invited to the Met Gala. The audience knew it was bullshit (she was a movie star who had even graced the cover of *Vogue*, for god's sake) but still found her ditsy Cinderella shtick to be winning. The folks at home could relate—to the servant girl part, anyway. As she riffed like some hayseed on the impossible heaviness of her beaded gown, the fans, longtime aficionados of the legendary ball, were a few steps ahead; they already knew that the costumes were "the main event," requiring a battery of helpers and sometimes armed guards because of their shocking price tags. The actress never broke character. She made certain to share for the record that Anna (Jimmy deftly inserted "Wintour" for the few who might be clueless) "doesn't let anyone keep the dresses, which in my case was a blessing!" and got the expected laugh. Another cringe, corny note she hit was how stunned she was to find herself in the company of so many celebs, particularly ones whom she idolized. The party crashing scullery maid reenacted the look on her face as she ogled this or that superstar while lumbering to the bathroom—aghast, embarrassed, awed, dismayed—which got a nice laugh too. Now, everyone knew she was on first-name terms with Anna's invitees; that she was a regular guest in their homes for fabulous dinner parties; and sat with them at the same tables during the seasonal awards show circuit. Many had even been her costars but none of that mattered—compared to the toxic lies of politicians, talk show fibs were a blessed relief. The whole routine ended in the punchline of her finally collapsing under the weight of the half-million-dollar gown and toppling into the Amazonian, saving arms of Gal Gadot. "A moment," she said, "that my nine-year-old son will *not* let me forget. He reminds me every day!" (The seamstress winced at that part.) When Jimmy made her promise to return next year to regale everyone with fresh gala stories, she put icing on the cake with, "I doubt Anna wants me back after my little fiasco!"

"Then we'll just invite you to one of our famous backyard Costco barbecues," said Jimmy, "and you can talk about *that*. You can wear a polyester gown soaked in beer and fall into the arms of Spade—which will *not* have a happy ending, because he's four feet tall and weighs eighty pounds."

~

In her twenties, the seamstress spent time in India, looking for gurus.

She found them but wasn't ready.

She held tight to the dream of becoming a costume designer like Theodora Van Runkle and Milena Canonero. At thirty-five, in crisis, she reached out to a swami she had met in Udaipur. He referred her to a "lady of knowledge" that fortuitously lived in Redondo Beach. For years, the seamstress drove down to see her on weekends but drifted away when she met the man who became the father of her child. Not long after their son died, she decided to reconnect with the eighty-three-year-old teacher. The seamstress of course told her about the tragedy—before inexplicably sharing the story of the actress who had suffered the same fate.

"Did you know that she came to my home?" asked the teacher.

"The actress?"

"Yes. She came here to see me."

She wasn't all that surprised because the witchy woman had a way of "tapping in."

"It was about a year after he drowned. I was *trending* then," she said wryly. "Isn't that the word people use? *Oh, yes.* Superstars couldn't get enough of me!" She laughed, then her features sharpened. "She arrived with her husband—I do remember her telling him to leave though. When he closed the door behind him, she leaned over and whispered to me a recurring dream she'd been having: Each night, she was on her way to a castle to attend a grand ball. The jewel-studded dress she wore was so heavy—every step was torture—that try as she may, she was always the last to arrive. When she finally trudged into the ballroom, heads turned and people shrieked, holding their noses as they slunk away in terror. It wasn't until she passed a mirror that she saw the body of her drowned son woven into the fabric of her beautiful gown." The seamstress gasped, bursting into tears. "Now, let's you and I get to work on our *own* dresses!" said the old woman with devilish wholesomeness. She draped an arm around her trembling guest. "We can start *tomorrow*—mine's almost done. We'll work side by side. I'll finish before you do but you'll get the *shape* of yours . . . *that's* what's important. When it's time, you can ride in the carriage and leave me at the ball, then come back here to help others with their needlework."

It was apparent that her former student—the one she affectionately used to call "my weekend warrior"—finally had the chance of having a chance, as the old woman liked to put it. Over tea, they spoke of the days when the seamstress drove her famously quarrelsome Fiat convertible down to the beach from her cottage in Nichols Canyon. Soon, the visitor was laughing harder than she had in a long, long while. The fierce, ominous cawing of a crow jolted her from a giggle fit. It was dusk.

The old woman walked to the window and stared at stain of birds against the sky. "How magnificent . . . how black their dresses!" With great excitement, the teacher wheeled around. "My crow friends just asked if I would recite their favorite poem, by the wild Irish sorcerer *Mr. Yeats*. It's about a woman—a seamstress!—who lands in the waiting room of Infinity but hasn't the courage to go further. Fortunately, a guide has been expecting her."

She tailored the poet's words without altering their meaning; yet made a better fit, so it became more like a story:

"Obey our ancient rule and sew a gown—we thread the eyes of the needles, and all we do, we do together." The young lady, newly arrived, took a position near the tribe of those who weaved, and began to sew. "Now must we sing, the best we can. But first you must know who we are: *all of us* have endured horrors—betrayals, the death of our dreams, the death of kin—and gone half-mad, driven from our hearts and homes—left to die in bitterness and fear." The tribe began to sing but neither words nor melody was human. Though all was as before, they had changed their throats and had the throats of birds.

The quondam weekend warrior now lives in that house.

When she isn't cooking or caring for her fading teacher, she speaks to the lost, the grieving, the tormented ones who appear at the door, and helps shape their gowns for the Grand Ball.

And when she isn't sewing—well, she sings.

THE LOTTERY

A congregant spoke with his Rabbi after temple services. He talked about his mother, who lived in a nursing home and had dementia. He laughed about one of her new quirks: she had the persistent idea that everyone was "super-rich." For example, she whispered to him that each of her caregivers won the lottery but chose to keep working ("doing what they love") and how much she respected that. When her granddaughter called for an Uber at the end of a visit, the old woman said, "Those drivers are worth *millions* but don't know what to do with themselves—so they *work*. Good for them!" Her largesse extended even to the homeless, whom she called "the wealthiest of them all."

His smile grew melancholy when he said she was growing frailer by the day and would soon enter hospice.

The Rabbi touched his old friend's arm. "As your mother gets closer to Olam Ha-Ba, she sees what we cannot—the great wealth we inherit at birth and that which awaits. I suggest you do the same. As they used to say, years ago: 'Get rich—*quick*.'"

THE BULLY

A petty, cutthroat, self-aggrandizing woman learned nothing in the fifty years she walked the Earth; but in the moments that preceded death, learned everything.

Twenty years before, she founded an organization that became the gold standard of victim outreach. All the prominent West Side attorneys made a point to do pro bono work for the nonprofit, whose reputation was impeccable. Her life was a revolving door of honors staged in the lavish halls of Skirball, the Four Seasons, and the InterContinental; fundraisers took place on the East Coast as well. She'd been a guest at Oprah's in Maui and Santa Barbara, traveled with Ellen and Portia to their gorilla "campus" in Rwanda, and testified more than once in support of anti-bullying bills on Capitol Hill. There was chatter about a movie being made of her life—friends would say, "Who should play you? Angelina Jolie or Jessica Chastain?" When pressure mounted to create resources and therapy options for those who identified as victims but weren't in acute need of social services, the founder responded with trademark alacrity and compassion. But all of that ended when she died of a short, unexpected illness.

On her deathbed, she saw leaves dropping down onto the shiny silver hood of the '63 Corvette her father loved more than life. With a shiver, she became the hood of the automobile itself, then silver's very essence. When she felt the dizzying leafiness of her slow fall from the ancient trees to the hoodless, roofless world, a final surge of violent energy made her whisper these magnificently heretical words: *Now I will bully the Heavens.*

Due to financial improprieties never made public, the organization was restructured after her passing. Asked by a journalist about the course correction, the new CEO said that the pandemic forced them to pivot.

"I suppose you could say we were victims—of circumstance. But we've now returned to complete health and are ready to help."

EMERGENCY CONTACT

Because of his calm, steady nature and easily digestible nuggets of street wisdom, an actor-turned-furniture maker became a consigliere to the stars in times of personal crises.

Suddenly one morning, it occurred that he'd been secretly intending bad outcomes among clients; beneath the glib, good ole boy ministering ran a black river prayer that simple medical procedures (even ones that he encouraged) would go catastrophically wrong. He was excited by the possibility that decades-old remarks might rear their heads and decimate a career, or a romp with the babysitter rip apart a legendarily happy marriage. He looked forward to such "episodes" the same as he did the twists and turns of a hit streaming series. The epiphany was made worse by the aftershocks of realizing, with naked clarity, how pathetically invested he was in the role of confidant. Not a week went by without his underground reputation as the "calamity whisperer" being burnished and ratified by knowing looks from important people at important parties that his important client-friends invited him to. But lately, during sleepless nights, he wondered how he had transformed into an avenging angel of suffering and death . . .

He was the one in crisis now—where was *his* confidant?

He couldn't risk sharing his sickness with any of the shrinks he knew, because all of them were gossips. It would be disastrous if one of the therapists told a mutual client, "A certain person you commissioned to make a certain very expensive table is *not* wishing you well."

When he saw an Instagram Story about a "master of the Hidden Path," a miracle worker who lived in Eagle Rock, he nearly dismissed it out of hand. Gurus weren't his thing. And besides, some of his friends had probably trod the path to the celebrity-friendly Eagle Rock master's door themselves, which could make things a little sticky; for all he knew, gurus liked hot goss too. Yet he couldn't help doing some idle online investigating and was impressed. Throughout the week, the annoyingly cheerful face of the master followed him around, hanging over his head like a cartoon thought bubble. When the bubble became a light bulb that he couldn't turn off, the furniture maker decided to pay the man a visit as a stopgap.

He had to do something because the shame was intolerable.

～

He arrived at the bungalow on time for his appointment.

When he knocked, a voice called "Come in!"

The modest home smelled of incense and cat poo and he could hear the drone of a television commercial in a distant room. Instantly, he felt foolish—even more so when the guru entered in saffron robes, beaming like a crackpot. "I should have gone to a palm reader instead," he thought.

The monk (or whatever) approached with outstretched arms—then collapsed to the floor like a demolished building. He went into familiar crisis mode and knelt beside the middle-aged prophet, who began to convulse. He turned purple and a scary foam appeared at the corners of his mouth. The furniture maker thought of calling 911, but first things first: *put something between the teeth so he won't bite off his tongue.* Scanning the room, he ran to a tabletop altar. Laying in front of some crystals was a ceremonial piece of wood, the very thing that was needed.

When he returned with the stick, the smiling victim not only had revived but was standing up! The monk—or whatever—wiped the drool from his mouth with a sleeve while the *consigliere* stared in disbelief. Just seconds ago, he thought the man was done for."

A teapot whistled.

The rejuvenated host motioned him to sit then went to the kitchen, returning with two cups. He poured and sat. It was obvious the "seizure" had all been an act.

"Sorry to *disappoint*, Tom-Tom," said the guru. He leaned in, adding sotto voce, "Not the 'bad outcome' you seem to require! But you didn't come for an antidote, did you?" He laughed heartily. "*You came for more poison.*"

Tom-Tom was what the furniture maker's nana called him, a nod to the drums used by African tribes in her favorite old adventure movies to alert faraway neighbors to danger. She raised the young boy when his parents died in a plane crash. In the first few years of living together, whenever he had nightmares of finding their bodies, he drummed on her door to be let in, then curled up in bed where she told him stories until he could finally sleep.

～

After a decade of rigorous discipline, he still cooks and cleans and brings fresh flowers to the bungalow twice a week. He drives the guru to medical appointments for his leukemia and prays for wonderful results, as he does for all those he encounters.

The other day, filling out forms at a new doctor's, the caregiver asked what name he should put for the emergency contact. The master grabbed the pen and scrawled in a child's block letters: TOM-TOM.

LADDER-DAY SAINTS

When a seeker in Mumbai asked a stock question—"Is it really possible for me to achieve *satori*?"—the saint gave his stock answer.

"Think of a ladder. To reach enlightenment can take ten thousand rungs—or a single step. You've found the ladder, so at least you're ahead of the game." He smiled and said, "The rungs lead nowhere, so what difference does it make? All outcomes are merely 'happenings.'"

On her sixtieth birthday, a woman was done with ladders; married three times, she had five children and four grandchildren whom she'd neglected during the fruitless ascent. Her inheritance had dwindled but she still lived relatively well, enjoying her healing retreats, her dance, and her painting. (The garage was converted into a studio.) She gave her canvases titles like, "Inner Silence," "All You Need Is Love," and "My Teachers."

What she regretted most was that without exception, the handful of real deal gurus she'd been privileged to meet had all been at the tail end of their lives. She would say to friends, half in jest, "It would be funny if it weren't so tragic." Fretful yet resigned, she told herself that her bad timing was a great teaching, in itself.

A favorite distraction was throwing herself into tempestuous love affairs. She fell head over heels for someone thirty years younger—never did she have a love like that. But one night, the girl humiliated her in front of a group of their friends by saying something so cutting and cruel that she wanted to die. Grievously wounded, she ended the affair. The day after, she began to obsess that in a moment of weakness, she might break down and reach out to the one who scorned her. Unable to bring herself to delete the entire contact, she erased half of the girl's name and chopped off the number so that only the area code and a few digits remained.

Let the games begin . . .

The older woman waited like a spider in its web until some months later, it happened: a string of *hello* texts. They were jaunty then got flirty before slip-sliding into tender apologies and messy remorse. (There were typos galore and she assumed the girl was loaded.) She steeled herself and didn't reply. The balance of power had finally shifted—and because her ex was a narcissist, she knew that being ghosted would cut her to the quick.

She prayed she was suffering.

For nostalgia's sake, the woman visited a man of knowledge in Hancock Park. They'd never met but she knew a lot about him through his association with teachers whom she revered—the gang of ladder-pushers who had the habit of running out of time while showing her the Way.

When she entered the room and saw the ancient husk propped behind the enormous desk, she tried not to laugh; the theme of "too late" still struck a bittersweet chord. But he was kind to her, with that special luminosity she had recognized in *seers* through the years. And so frail! Wryly, she wondered if he would make it through the visit.

With a disarming smile, he said, "What would you like to talk about?"

She was surprised at what leapt to mind: the May-December love affair that ended so badly, three years ago to the day. Chattily filling him in, she was inspired to top off the tale with the recent denouement and comeuppance that she'd gleefully shared with "my yenta friends." She closed her eyes as one sometimes does when reciting an important, favorite poem. She told him that only a week ago, she got yet another unrequited text from the girl, but *this* time decided to respond (at last) with just three words: *who is this*. The ex immediately sent her name, followed by three exclamation points, three hearts, and three cry-faces—whereupon the woman triumphantly turned off the phone and went back to finishing her latest painting.

Savoring the hubris, she was jolted by the ragged snort of an animal. Opening her eyes, she saw that the guru was fast asleep. In that moment, the everyday world cracked open, and her foot found the rung that had eluded her for a lifetime.

But it wouldn't have mattered.

As the saint once said, "All outcomes are merely 'happenings.'"

A TREATISE ON MONEY
(VOLS I-III)

Before his studies, a student railed against the globalists. With a nasty grin, he said, "So, have you heard the billionaires' latest announcement? They said that in the future, 'You'll own nothing and be happy.' They weren't talking about *themselves*—they're talking about the rest of us. What they really mean is, 'We'll own all the slaves and be happy.'"

"'Own nothing, be happy' is quite good," said the teacher. "The billionaires got it right!"

He understood that the yogin was being playful. Anyway, it was time to get to work. The student downsized his irritation by wrapping things up with a cliché:

"Well, you know what the Bible says: Money is the root of all evil."

"The Bible says *love* of money is the root of all evil," the teacher gently corrected. "Money by itself is a *construct*—not all bad. Even gurus need to make a living." He sipped his tea and smiled. "This one does, anyway."

He burst into laughter and then they got down to the business at hand.

PARENTAL GUIDANCE

In their twenties, a man and a woman had what they still considered to be the most passionate love affair of their lives. When it brutally ended, they staggered to different parts of the country to avoid the temptation of returning to the scene of the crime. In their late forties, married with children, Fate organized an encounter while vacationing with their respective families in Istanbul. Each was alone at the Grand Bazaar, shopping for novelty gifts to give friends back home, when they saw each other and got the wind knocked out of them.

Over coffee, they soon fell into old habits; she led with the recriminations.

"It was *horrible*. I knew it couldn't work—*we* couldn't work. But I wouldn't wish—that kind of *pain*—on my worst enemy. I *understood* . . . but at the same time, had absolutely no understanding." His nod of commiseration both calmed and emboldened. "I actually *do not know* how I stopped myself from trying to contact you. I had a *shit ton* of help from therapists and friends . . ." She winced at the memory. "There was an eight-day period—I remember it lasted *exactly eight days*—where . . . oh god." Tears welled in her eyes. "I could *see* her: the woman you were 'involved' with." Another wince. "*I literally saw you in her arms.* Then, poof! It lifted. I almost, like, got the feeling . . . like, 'What *was* that?' And thank *god* it lifted because I straight-up wanted to die." He stared down at the table, shellshocked. She shuddered, regretting her outburst. "I'm sorry! I didn't mean . . ." Shifting gears, she said, "I always thought about—*wondered* about running into you. I sure the fuck didn't think it would be at the Grand Bazaar! And I never wanted to *blame* . . . if anyone, I blamed myself."

He said nothing. She knew he wasn't being hostile; that was just his way. He always needed more time to process than she did. As a diversion, she asked about his children and told him a little about hers. After a long silence, she circled back, telling him that after the breakup she took great solace from a book called *A Lover's Discourse*.

"The writer's French. Have you heard of it?" He shook his head. "It's amazing. I call it the encyclopedia of heartbreak."

With an out of place smile, he casually told her about trying to kill himself "after we split. Like, the next day." She gasped, covering her mouth with her hand. *How fucking stupid am I?* she thought—because she knew that his mother committed suicide, and how that sort of thing usually runs in the family. Yet the possibility he'd have been so affected had never occurred to her. . . . She wanted to take back everything she said, even though she was still convinced the Sturm und Drang of their last year was due to his unfaithfulness.

"Obviously, I wasn't successful," he said, with the macabre elfin grin she used to adore. "They put me in a straitjacket—very glam. I felt like Olivia de Havilland in *Snakepit*. We watched that together, right? Remember when we watched that?"

"You mean, a psychotic break?" she asked, sounding more naïve than she wanted to.

He nodded. "Apparently, someone was watering down the Haldol 'cause I kept banging my head against the wall. I was totally hallucinating. My mother was in bed with me, shouting, 'Do it! Do it! Do it!' It was *The Suicide Squad*, with Mom as Harley Quinn—"

"Holy *fuck*. I am *so, so sorry* . . ."

"—no! It was *Joker: Folie à Deux*. And it's funny you said *eight days* . . . because that's exactly how long it took for Mom to go find someone else to torture. After eight days—what's the word you used?—it lifted. One morning, I woke up *alone* in bed, and it was . . . over."

Of course, he knew intimate things about her as well. That when she was five, her father fell in love with his secretary and walked away from the marriage, and she didn't see him again for fifteen years. Abandonment and suicide were the building blocks of what they shared.

It was her turn to process. She tried to speak but no words came.

To break the ice, he somewhat facetiously said, "Guess we were working out our parents' shit, huh." She smiled because it was so him—a caustic, tidy, somehow tender way of perfectly summing up a complicated and delicate situation. When she stage-whispered "Those motherfuckers," he laughed a little too hard. Then they spoke over each other: at the same time he was saying that his father should have married her mother, she shouted, her mother should have married his father—sending them into fits of tragicomic hilarity. They embraced, rocked by a final gust of love and sorrow for all they once had and all that they'd lost.

From the comfortable rut of their marriages, both had a flash-fantasy of trying again. *Could we make it work?* But as they walked their separate ways, each let it go with the simultaneous thought:

"There was never really anything there."

THE ADJUSTMENT

A disgruntled seeker spoke her mind with a great teacher who was passing through the city.

She bowed in respect then immediately unburdened herself. She said she was tired; that she'd spent a lifetime "pointlessly searching for so-called awareness" and was now considering antidepressants; that she had become a burden to her friends and children, a burden to herself, etcetera. Regarding her dilemma, the listener's warmth and compassion only brought her emotions to a head—at the end of their time, she wrung her hands and wept.

Looking him in the eye, she pleaded, "Doesn't anybody *get* it? I wish I was never born!"

"Birth and death are creations of Saṃsāra," said the Venerable. "Essence of mind is not born. How can a sentient being, never born, wish they were never born?"

"Oh please! You all say the same *shite* and what does it mean? Can one of you *please* tell me what any of it *means*? Because I am *suffering*—and do *not* wish to hear it!"

He sprung to his feet like an animal guarding a temple against trespassers.

"Then hear *this*," he said, with diamond-pointed ferocity. "If, before leaving your body, you do not apprehend that birth and death are dreams, I guarantee that your self-pitying concerns and protestations will be less than a molecule in the Ocean of Suffering! That ocean, too, is a dream, but a most unpleasant one—*from which you cannot awaken.*"

She went pale, burst into tears, then kneeled to touch his feet. After a long moment, she looked up shamefacedly and begged him to accept her as a disciple. He said yes—but only if she moved to Rishikesh. She nodded without hesitation, bowed, and left.

The Venerable enjoyed speaking in metaphor. But when the moment is right, a good teacher sometimes employs fear the way a chiropractor cracks a neck. If the cure isn't instant, one at least limps from the office with a new, almost daring sense of hope.

SURPRISE PARTY

A professor of comparative religion at one of the Claremont Colleges had a reputation for being unorthodox. It was common knowledge that during "field work," he took medicine journeys with tribal members—long ago, Huichols had introduced him to peyote—and while rarely reviewing such experiences with colleagues, he was open about it with certain students, who felt privileged to be confidants. After regaling them with his adventures, the professor would playfully add, "Do as I say, not as I do!" Cancel culture was the order of the day and he refused to lose tenure over sponsoring some callow, vindictive undergrad's bad trip.

His favorite plant was the mushroom. (He was amazed to have recently recalled a beloved boyhood book, *The Wonderful Flight to the Mushroom Planet*.) During one of his earliest trips, "the Goddess" told him that human beings could never survive "the weight of a single tear that fell from the eye of my favorite student, the mushroom." In another voyage, when the earth shook from a faraway stampede, explosions, the Goddess said, "That is Ganesh and the imperial guards. I allow them to protect me because it is their wish—and because they love me—*even though there is nothing to protect.*"

With some pride, he confessed to his acolytes that he had "married" the Goddess. Such was Her power, he added theatrically, that during the wedding ceremony, a simple whisk from her bridal gown's hem would have meant certain death.

∿

The professor decided to take a "wonderful flight" for his sixtieth (after all, it had been nearly five years since he partook). He travelled up north to stay with a husband-and-wife team who were old friends and inveterate journeyers. He took more psilocybin than usual to celebrate the occasion—what is called "a heroic dose." Afterward, he spent a few hours downloading his experience with his guides.

"It wasn't what I thought it would be," he said, with gentle resignation.

"Tell us more," said the husband.

"Well," said the professor. "Maybe it's because I feel so close to her—that we're 'married.' Maybe after all these years, she's trying to tell me there's nothing left for her to reveal . . . That sounds a little smug! I don't mean it to. In the early days of *courtship*, the revelations came fast and furious, each one a great surprise. But now, I suppose, we've settled into a comfortable married life. We're just like any old couple. We're just like you!"

~

Back in Claremont, the professor's wife greeted him at the door. Per tradition, he always waited to tell her about his psychoactive encounters in person. He said that talking about it on the phone "diluted the experience and dishonored the plant."

"Well, how was it, birthday boy?" she exclaimed.

"Marvelous! No surprises—but very, very good."

"Oh, yay. Well, it was good for me too." He cocked his head, nonplussed. "It was the first time your mushroom biatch didn't make me jealous."

~

In Santa Rosa that morning, the guide suddenly remembered what the professor told him and his wife in mid-journey. Sprouting tears while receiving dictation from his bride, his body contorted in a kind of ecstatic modern dance. "The Goddess . . . is now saying . . . 'He thinks I am going to wow him on his birthday—but he will have to wait! *I shall wow him at death.*'"

Which of course, She did, and sooner than he would have hoped.

Until then, the psychonaut had to make do with a smaller firework: his long-suffering wife left him for the charismatic chair of the Department of Anthropology.

THE ASCENT

... I grew weary of the things of this world;
and in my yearning for solitude
I came to the sanctuary wilderness, Mount Kailish.
                                        —Milarepa

There is the famous anecdote of Brigitte Bardot and Krishnamurti.

In the 1970s, the mystic was watching television in Santa Barbara. A documentary came on about the clubbing of baby seals; at the same time, in Paris, the actress was engrossed in that very program. As the story goes, Bardot was so affected that she founded an organization that ended the barbaric practice—whereas Krishnamurti simply changed the channel.

In the end, who was the enlightened one?

The actress or the mystic? Both? Or neither?

The foregoing is told to students as a disruptive koan, throwing light upon the random happenings and infinite possibilities of this unfathomable world. —ed.

Decades later, in his modest Glendale home, a man familiar with the ethereal was channel-surfing when a doc about Mount Everest caught his eye. He spent the next few minutes watching a segment about those who had died during the ascent. The protocol was to leave the bodies where they were; recovery wasn't worth the risk. One of the frozen waxworks laid at the base of a cave for thirty years. A more recent arrival sat upright, arms around its knees, as if trying to keep warm. Further on, a string of climbers trudged past more remains—a detrital diorama of crampons, carabiners, and colorful parkas with torn fabric that waved eerily in the gusts that bedevil all mountain peaks . . .

He was interrupted by a knock at the front door.

Standing there was a gaunt, ruggedly athletic man of around for-ty-five, looking like he'd been hijacked from the TV show and was happy to be out of harm's way. The congenial drop-in offered his hand and his name. With a smart British accent (and the discreet hope of being remem-bered), he nudged that they'd met before. "I came to your *satsang* a few years back."

In truth, it was longer ago than that. The *mahasiddha* had an uncom-mon facility for names and faces and recalled a much younger man spend-ing a month to soak up what he could before the Path became too arduous.

"Ah!" said the teacher, with a huge grin. "The reluctant mountaineer!"

The visitor smiled quizzically but was satisfied with the warm greeting.

Prodigal aficionados are a timeworn tradition in the spiritual game. Whether or not a lapsed devotee ends up staying upon their return is of no consequence; but the ones who do, bruised and tempered by the world, have a resilience that serves them well the second time around. Over tea, the "reluctant moun-taineer" said he had been deeply impressed by the *mahasiddha*'s philosophy on that first visit yet still felt the need to seek out as many "enlightened ones" as he could. "My mama told me, 'You better shop around,'" he said dryly. He finally settled on So-and-So, spending the last two years as part of the holy man's "inner circle" of special students. Grandstanding a bit, the visitor asked if he had heard of the notorious pandit.

The host nodded, almost imperceptibly.

"So-and-So is *very* smart," said the guru-shopper. "Very *compassionate*, with an encyclopedic knowledge of the sutras—quite shocking, really— and many other esoteric things." In an aloof aside: "I really do believe he's that rarity: a true *seer*."

"That may be."

"I learned quite a bit—well, obviously! And we've actually become great good friends. But when he started pushing for me to become . . .

his *successor*—in the lineage . . . well—that's when things became a tad shambolic. It all got rather too *serious*: a word which I tend to be allergic to! Never did like the S-word." A comical wince put a cork in his glibness. "Long-short, I suddenly found myself . . . *questioning.* Bit of a stasis, bit of a dilemma, yes? I suppose that's why I thought of coming here to see *you*." He sipped his cup and grew contemplative. "Perhaps this too shall pass, but I just feel somehow that I'm—"

"That woman is a sentient being," said the teacher brusquely.

Taken aback, the visitor asked, "What woman?"

"In that shameful tape you shared with your 'great good friend.'"

It was like a kick to the stomach and he struggled to get out the words. "Did So-and-So talk to you? When? He told you about the—"

"We have not spoken," he said definitively.

A few weeks before, the dilettante had shown Sri So-and-So an episode of a popular, freewheeling daytime talk show whose host played referee to a wrestling match of feuding families and outrageous guests. The videotape featured a porn star who was promoting a film that she made of herself having consecutive coitus with three hundred men. The guru howled with delight as he watched, smacking his legs. "What *qi!*" he shouted. "A most formidable woman—a real sorcerer! What a student she would make!"

"You have much in common with that woman," said the *mahasiddha.* "For you, no teacher is enough." He paused to ruminate. "The Spirit brought you here to resume the climb—why? How? You know nothing of climbing, only of crawling! Like a child who's spent his whole life at the beach, playing in the sand. . . . What is in store for you is not for me to say. *I will help in any way I can.* That is my promise to the Spirit." He poured more tea. "As for your beloved guru, I'm afraid there is no hope. And he is far worse than that demon talk show *impresario!* For years, So-and-So's reckless actions have littered the mountain with the bodies of those who dreamed of summiting. His 'lineage' is that of indulgence, cynicism, and ultimate despair. I knew him when he was a gifted student that showed much promise—before he abandoned the struggle. Now, all whom he seduces are poisoned by his touch." He grew quiet. "To mislead one's students is unpardonable. For such devils, the Source has no mercy."

"I—I sorry," said the aphasic guest, jumbling his words: "I am been terrible."

He was clear that he was about to pass out.

The master leaned over and stared into his haunted eyes.

"Do exactly as I say, and you'll have the privilege of seeing your guru again! With boundless compassion, he will offer himself as a caution during your ascent: *Each frozen carcass you pass will have his face.* By such an action, he will surely attain the stature of the great teacher he was meant to be."

THE APPEAL

An advanced student approached the lama and immediately burst into tears. He noticed right away that she was in street clothes.

"My robes are folded on the bed . . . I am leaving this place!" She managed to spit out the following words before miserably bowing before him: "I have failed you! I am *stupid* and *selfish* and *monstrous!*"

She wasn't the first apprentice to come undone. In fact, the further along one was, the worse were the injuries inflicted by the cornered animal of Self—such is the price one pays for awareness. He encouraged her to pause and concentrate on breath. While she busied herself, he brought that sovereign remedy, a cup of tea. After a few sips, she composed herself. "It's my sister," she whispered gravely. Her mouth cinched a rictus of shame. "*I am jealous of her.*" She may as well have confessed to murder. A fresh storm of tears rained down. After more breathwork and another cup, she admitted that Clara's wealth had always been a source of envy. "But now . . . it's so much *worse*. It's not just the money—" She choked, violently crying, "I can't bear it! I'm telling you, *I* cannot . . ."

Since retirement, the bhikkhuni-in-training's sister had become a well-known advocate for the wrongfully convicted; whenever there was something in the news about a prisoner that Clara helped set free, the novice felt a surge of bile rise up in her throat.

"She's doing *real* work, *selfless* work. And here I am—trapped in this temple—navel-gazing . . . if only the poison stopped at Clara! *No* . . . it soaks the ground and *again* condemns the innocents who were exonerated—because in my heart, I want her to fail! I want *every one of them* resentenced on appeal. Oh!" she shrieked. "All the years of discipline and devotion, all the years of your love, your care, your wisdom—for nothing. For nothing, nothing, nothing!"

Without hesitation, he told her this story:

"I once knew a student monk, much like you. His teacher sent him to do dharma work in a jail. During a meditation class, he encountered a convict with a special aura. An aura of *silence*. Later, the man humbly told the monk his story. He'd been wrongfully accused of killing his beloved and sentenced to life without parole. After five terrible years, he had enough and decided to throw himself off the top-floor cell block. But on his way up, something truly miraculous happened: he realized that all was predetermined. That he had nothing to do with any of it—*any of it*—and to believe that he did was an absurd vanity, born of delusion. A great, unshakeable peace came over him.

"The monk felt a surge of hatred for the convict. He prayed that the story he'd just been told was a lie, a self-serving fable. At the same time, he took note of his own life and saw, quite clearly, that he too had been sentenced to life without parole. Yet for him, there was no miracle, no revelation. There was only revulsion."

The lama went to the kitchenette and poured himself a third cup. (He felt she'd had enough.) Returning to his chair, he saw light again in her eyes.

"The whole lot of us are wrongfully convicted," he continued. "From the very start! A baby's crib has bars too . . . from the beginning, we are thrown into the jail of Saṃsāra—the endless cycle of birth, death, rebirth. . . . After the prisoner died, the truth came out, and his name was cleared. Of course, none of that mattered because the man escaped long ago—his physical body remained in the cell but the ethereal body traveled elsewhere, at liberty." A smile crept to his lips. "I'm afraid it took that student monk many more years to 'break out.' He sits before you now." She gawped at him; her chest heaved, and her teacup broke upon the floor. He reached out a hand to steady her. "Let *Sister* be your advocate. If you restore your devotion and shatter envy the way you did that cup, she can do her work. Sister will set you free."

She rose, cleaned up the mess, then bowed and went to her room. There, she changed back to her robes and prepared to reapply herself to the Great Escape.

On a to-do list for tomorrow, all she wrote was "Call Clara."

IN THE SHADOW OF MILAREPA

A bitter old man gunned down eleven people at a dance hall in Monterey Park. The so-called Lunar New Year Massacre was the subject of a press conference given by a Los Angeles County Sheriff with the untimely name of Robert Luna. The shooter took his own life as the police closed in.

A twenty-three-year-old English-speaking student immediately went to his sifu to inform that the murderer had visited their temple more than once, and the two had even "struck up a bit of a friendship." With a shiver, he said, "He used to give dance lessons at the place he shot up—but the temple would have been just as good a target." The sifu shrugged and grunted, a standard response through the years to the non-sensical bulletins of his minions. "He danced, but mostly, I think, was interested in writing. He read me his poems and they actually weren't too bad. Sometimes he recited Su Shi: 'Lonely grave a thousand miles away. Cold thoughts—where can I share them?' Isn't that haunting? After what happened?"

"I remember him," said the sifu. "Deep reader of Milarepa. Good taste."

"Ah! *That* makes sense! Didn't Milarepa kill his whole family before being enlightened by the Buddha?"

"Marpa teacher of Milarepa."

He often spoke in abbreviations.

"The funny thing is," said the student. "He wanted me to call him 'Gampopa.'"

"Gampopa important student of Milarepa."

"Ah."

"He wouldn't pull that with me," laughed the sifu. "No 'Gampopa'! I called him 'Kid.'"

"Wasn't Milarepa a poet?"

"The greatest of all. Don't be stupid!"

The student had seen the book in the temple library, *The 100,000 Songs of Milarepa*, but never went so far as taking it off the shelf. "Do you think he was trying to 'get enlightened'? By killing those people, like Milarepa did? Do you think he thought it was, you know, a shortcut?" The teacher stared at him blankly. "Sifu, it's a terrible thing to say, but . . . is it possible that by doing what he did . . . would it be possible to reach *moksha*? To break free of Saṃsāra and the cycle of reincarnation through such a violent act? Do you think—"

"*No, I do not*," boomed the teacher, his good humor vanishing. The student squirmed but felt some relief when the sifu's smile returned. "Milarepa kill family. Much worse to kill strangers."

"Ah."

Was he being morbidly playful? Not easy to tell . . .

"Must make great poems to attain *suchness*," said the sifu. "Anything less is insult to Sarasvati." Before dismissing him, he looked over his glasses at the callow boy like a scholar bringing home a potent conclusion. "As a general rule, if one desires to be *awake*, best not kill strangers—or oneself! Too obvious! Too lazy! Too *stupid*. Though in the case of The Kid, suicide is most beneficial . . . to *all*. Ha!"

He abruptly stood, shuddering with comic revulsion.

"Bad poets," said the sifu. "Who needs 'em?"

JINGLES

A Juilliard graduate moved to Los Angeles with the dream of becoming a film composer. He began with a flourish, scoring an indie hit at Sundance.

Then, as things often go: nothing.

A year later, his agent brought him a modest offer for a TV commercial. When he balked, the thwarted rep said, "Then I think we may be done." But all his friends (especially his fiancée) thought it was a fantastic idea, so he changed his mind out of fear of losing his agent, going broke, and returning to New Jersey with his bigscreen dreams tucked between his legs. He was a natural and more ad work came right away. He kept a finger in the Art pie by composing for local orchestras and doing student film projects gratis.

Turning thirty, he was dogged by his father's unsparing mantra from childhood: "If you can't be the best at what you do, do something else." While good at what he did, he wasn't the best by a long shot. He brokered a tentative peace with his middling destiny by going on spiritual retreats a few times a year, an activity that made the taste of failure less bitter.

In the nineties, he struck up a friendship with the son of the legendary trumpet player Uan Rasey, and was thrilled to be invited to Rasey's seventy-fifth birthday celebration in Pasadena. He was in awe of the party guests, many of whom were renowned musicians he once hoped to collaborate with. He was well aware of the guest of honor's catalogue: *West Side Story, Singin' in the Rain, My Fair Lady, How the West Was Won, An American in Paris*, and *Taxi Driver*—and perhaps most famously, the solo horn work in *Chinatown*. (The renowned session musician was also a favorite of Sinatra, Crosby, and Garland.) Sheepish at first about telling anyone that he whored himself for TV ads, he felt instantly accepted. By the end, he threw caution to the wind and proudly shared with those who asked, "I write music for film and television."

The son finally dragged him into the living room to meet Uan. Making their way through the throng, he said, "People always tell me Dad's a mystic. They say, 'Dude! Your father's a living saint.' *Ha.* I tell 'em, 'Yeah yeah yeah, he tries not to walk on water when I'm around!'"

He was surprised to see the trumpeter in a wheelchair; that's when he learned he'd had polio as a boy. When they were briefly alone, Uan beckoned him closer, whispering conspiratorially, "My son tells me you do wonderful commercials."

"I don't know how wonderful they are. But I'd like to do less ads and more movies."

"Go see my teacher!" he said ebulliently. "Everything I know about trumpet, I learned from *him.* Tell him Uan sent ya—though when he hears the name, he might send you packing!"

Revelers interrupted, swallowing him up.

He never saw the old man again and never got the name of the person Uan urged him to see. Why would he need to meet a trumpet teacher anyway?

~

When Rasey died in 2011, he was invited to the private memorial. It was out of the blue because he hadn't spoken to the son in a while. By then, a few of his ads had been featured during the Super Bowl. On the drive to Pasadena, he decided that should it come up, he'd be a little mysterious and tell people he was "in the music business." But no one asked.

When the eulogies were over, the jazz singer Sue Raney stood before the mourners. She made a little joke about how "Rasey" and "Raney" had spent a lifetime mistakenly getting each other's mail, before getting to the heart of the matter.

"I'm going to read something now," she said, "written by the man Uan called his greatest musical teacher . . . and I was surprised when he told me that, because the name was unfamiliar to me—well, that's not quite right. I should say it was a *little* familiar, but certainly not a name I associated with music, or the music 'business' at any rate . . . Before our dear one left the world, he gave me this piece of paper and *ordered* me to read from it on this very occasion—or else!" Warm laughter flooded the room like the sweetest melody. "The teacher's name was Carlos Castaneda. This is from Mr. Castaneda's book, *The Eagle's Gift.*"

She smiled, cleared her throat, and enunciated the following:

I remembered don Juan telling me once that death might be behind anything imaginable, even behind a dot on my writing pad. He gave me then the definitive metaphor of my death. I had told him that once while walking on Hollywood Boulevard in Los Angeles, I heard the sound of a trumpet playing an old, idiotic popular tune. The music was coming from a record shop across the street. Never had I heard a more beautiful sound. I became enraptured by it. I had to sit down on the curb. The limpid brass sound of that trumpet was going directly to my brain. I felt it just above my right temple. It soothed me until I was drunk with it. When it concluded, I knew that there would be no way of ever repeating that experience, and I had enough detachment not to rush into the store and buy the record and a stereo set to play it on.

Don Juan said that it had been a sign given to me by the powers that rule the destiny of men. When the time comes for me to leave the world, in whatever form, I will hear the same sound of that trumpet, the same idiotic tune, the same peerless trumpeter.

AN OPEN BOOK

A well-known socialite and patroness of the arts was also a great collector of spiritual parables. She found fault with them all—they were too cryptic, too flowery, too sentimental, too philosophical, too trite, too dated. Only a few made the cut before she compulsively set upon them like a coldhearted jackal. She respectfully shared her feelings with a woman of knowledge who was passing through the city. "True!" exclaimed the sage. "Too true—the allegories are but broken steps. *That* is how we get to Paradise: step by broken step."

The socialite was found the next morning on the floor of the mansion's library. As was her habit, she'd been enjoying a late-night sweet while picking apart a poorly written fable, when her heart gave out.

Two detectives surveyed the scene.

"Guess the candies didn't agree with her."

"Or something she read," said the colleague. "Which book do you think is the culprit?"

At the foot of the chair was a knocked-over stack of anthologies.

"Hard to say," said the detective.

Just then, a Jack Russell escaped the arms of the housekeeper and made a beeline for a splayed volume of *The Conference of the Birds*, commencing to furiously lick crumbs off the page.

"My bet's on *that* one—cuff him."

Bending down to the book, the other cop said, "You're under arrest."

CAVE-IN

This story was told to me by an adept who kept to himself, working in an auto parts garage in Torrance. —ed.

A man who had mastered the Way found himself at a crossroads.

At a relatively young age, he became the abbot of a woodsy monastery in upstate New York, where he remained for ten years. The honor didn't sit well; he wasn't sure why. Stepping down, he tried on the new outfit of Bestselling Author, writing poignant, trenchant books about his spiritual journey. He despised the wealthy seekers who commissioned the speaking engagements that he soon became famous for—and was equally contemptuous of those of modest means who'd been so kind. If he went on like this, he knew that his life would end in scandal, even suicide. When he woke up one morning and realized both eventualities had become prayers, intuition told him there was only one person who had the power to dethrone his stubborn, fatal arrogance: a faraway teacher, legendary for his uncompromising severity.

For the self-destructing ex-abbot, the Hermit's cave was "the last house on the block."

~

The last twenty miles of the climb took a tremendous toll. He was greeted warmly and invited in. He could smell tea brewing. Without delay, the half-dead visitor eked out, "My teacher!" before prostrating himself at the Hermit's feet.

The cave dweller handed him a blanket and smiled, cockeyed. "If you please, you must first present your *CV*. But do have some chocolate! It will help to revive."

He wondered if the host was being sarcastic but presented his oral "résumé" nonetheless, ending the saga of self-pity with a second desperate plea for the Hermit's sponsorship. Instead of answering directly, the monk rehashed the timeworn parable of the scorpion who asks a frog to carry it across a river. The frog is afraid of being stung but the scorpion argues that if it dared do such a thing, both would sink and drown. Sure enough, midway across, the scorpion stings the frog. With its final breath, the frog asks, "Why?" The scorpion replies, "It's my nature."

"That's a very old fable," said the visitor, with a testiness born of exhaustion. He wondered if he'd made a profound mistake by traveling all this way; if so, the only alternative left was to throw himself off the mountain. "I've told it to students almost as many times as I've heard it. Why, *roshi*—most venerable of venerables—do you recount it today?"

"Only last week, a scorpion came to this cave and asked me to carry him across the river. I knew he wasn't serious about escaping Saṃsāra . . . *so I stung him.*" The Hermit sat back and smiled, "Such is my nature."

The expeditioner burst into tears, sunk to his knees, and touched the Hermit's feet. He apprehended at last that there is no river, no body, no cave—only *mu.*

No-thing.

~

He spent five harsh, magnificent winters by his teacher's side; upon dying, the new Hermit of Mount Hiei continued the lineage. He is older now and the trekking temple monks of Enryaku-ji bring medicine and supplies more often than they used to. Once or twice a year, seekers of Truth make the onerous pilgrimage but never stay long.

Other, more intrepid visitors abide . . .

Only two species of scorpion can be found on the southernmost island coasts of Japan, so it was a great mystery to find one at the mouth of the cave. In the week that followed, instead of chocolate, the dutiful host brought offerings of centipedes and the occasional gecko. It would give him great pleasure to lead his guest across the river—but for now, the creature seems wary of asking any favors.

THE INHERITANCE

A man who was afraid of death had the perspicacity to face it head on.

He began cruising a stretch of highway near Angeles Crest, with an eye out for roadkill. He scraped up the carcasses and brought them into the forest to be buried. After a few weeks of that, he told his wife he wanted to go deeper. She indulged his whims—because of his inheritance, no one needed to work.

A friend of his uncle was a pathologist at County General Hospital, so he did an unofficial internship at the morgue there. It was particularly affecting to see the babies who died stillborn or of SIDS, by accident or at the hands of their parents. It saddened him that a lot of the bodies were shit- or blood-smeared, as if forgotten. It seemed so disrespectful. As a Jew, he volunteered to perform *tahara*, traveling to mortuaries around the county for the ritual washing and dressing of the deceased . . .

He became a hospice aide but got frustrated because the work was confined to bedding changes, checking vitals, and the like. Though in time, he completed enough hours to be allowed to sit with the dying as they took their last breath.

~

After dinner one night, he sat on the couch staring into space.

"I'm actually thinking of becoming a monk," he said.

"Uh huh," said his wife, with typical forbearance.

"I seem to have gotten over my fear of dying but feel like I've barely touched the surface—of *impermanence*, I mean. I've been reading about *marana-sati* . . ."

"What's that?"

"The Buddhist term for 'death awareness.' You know, the Buddha himself talked about graveyard meditation in one of the sutras. It's not just about sitting with the dying and washing the dead. It's more than that. What it's *really* about is—"

"Baby?" she said brusquely. "I gotta sinkful of dirty dishes that would seriously benefit from a washing and drying ritual."

He almost fell off the couch laughing.

While cleaning the plates, he apologized for being such an ass. They got drunk, danced like mad, then made love—one of the better ways to honor the dead.

THE BOOK CLUB

We shall not cease from exploration
and the end of all our exploring
will be to arrive where we started
and know the place for the first time
—T. S. Eliot

In the eighties, a young man wandered the world looking for a guru to show him the Path. He came home "empty," though not in the classical sense. Then lo and behold, he found one—in Topanga Canyon, not far from where he grew up. After two years, he was disheartened; efforts to extinguish the Self were all for naught. He outgrew those aspirations. He married, had children, and built a flourishing business.

An impassioned reader, he started a book club. When asked about his favorite novels, he could list them by rote but couldn't remember much about them. The same forgetfulness extended to movies. For example, he had a mental block about the title of a Japanese film he was passionate about: *Ugetsu*. Each time he looked it up on the internet, the plot summary was unrecognizable . . . and this was a movie that once had him stopping strangers on the street to tell them it completely changed his life—and would change theirs!

While it didn't make sense, it was harder to dismiss Forgetful Book Syndrome. He was already doing crossword puzzles as a prophylactic against "Old Timers" disease; why not reread some of the volumes of his book club hit parade as well? But in a matter of months, their content slipped away. When he made noises about Lewy body dementia, the wife lightheartedly assured that she'd been having the same experience, as had most of their friends. "Don't worry," she said. "AARPnesia's a beautiful thing." His internist gently sermonized on the "porousness" of the brain, a word that provided cold comfort. "We retain the *feeling* of a great book more than we do its details," he said. "That's 'the way of all flesh'—which happens to be the name of my favorite novel from college days. Can't remember the author, though . . . or anything else! Though I *do* remember it being a real doorstopper."

It got him thinking about impermanence, a theme that interested him back when his hair was long—and just a few days later, there he was in his old Porsche convertible, shifting gears on the serpentine road to Topanga. With only muscle memory as his GPS, he surprised himself with the accuracy of his progress, shouting "Fuck you, dementia!" into the canyon.

Rounding the corner to her house, he began to wonder if she was alive or dead . . .

Someone was just leaving as he drove up—a student? He grew hopeful. When the teacher herself answered the door, it took his breath away. She was ancient now, but her eyes were the same crystal blue, and shone with telltale dynamism. She said his name and pulled him in for a hug. He apologized for dropping by; he didn't have her phone number. He was so happy to see her that it wasn't until ten minutes later, in the living room, that he noticed the tears in his eyes.

A sweet middle-aged helper brought a tray of tea and cookies then lingered respectfully in the hall, hyper-alert for anything the teacher might need. He did most of the talking. When the helper cut things short—the next "client" had arrived—the former student chastised himself for having monopolized the conversation.

As a remedy, he scheduled another visit.

~

When he returned the following week, the front door was ajar. He tapped on it then waited a moment before going in. He took a few steps toward the voices and stood still.

"The next one you're seeing is *James*," said the helper. The exaggerated enunciation made it sound as if she were talking to a deaf person. "He was here *last week*. He was a student of yours a *long time ago*."

"Oh yes! I remember."

"James said that he wanted to *reconnect*. He said he was beginning to understand *so many things you told him* . . ." At that moment, the helper saw him and looked up, abashed. "Here he is now!" she exclaimed. "*James is here.*"

When she led the guru to her chair, he greeted them both, then asked to use the toilet. When he came out, the helper stood by the bathroom door, unnerved.

"It's dementia," she whispered, through a stagey, frozen grin. "But it hasn't affected her long-term memory—sometimes she's more 'here' than *I* am!" When the smile seemed to curtsy, he grinned. Not knowing what to say, he returned to the living room and sat.

The old woman patted his knee and nodded toward the helper, now out of sight. "I sense you've been given the *diagnosis*," she winked, with campy emphasis.

"Ah! How long ago was it that they—"

"Did you know you were one of my favorites? *Of course* you wouldn't, but it's true! A favorite . . . and I never had too many of *those*." She screwed up her eyes. "I said to myself, 'This one *has* it—but he just isn't *ready.*' I often thought of you! Oh, you probably don't believe me . . . I'd be sitting right here in this room and think, 'Where *is* that young man now? What is he *up* to?' I could never remember your face—the details—I only remembered a *feeling.*' Her eyes lit up. '*Details* . . . were what interested *you*. You read piles and piles of books, you *memorized* them! Hundreds of pages! You even wanted *me* to read them." She laughed as the helper joined them. "You wanted a friggin *medal*. He wanted a friggin *medal*, Tamara!" She took a sip from her cup. "But I don't see that in you *now*—isn't that marvelous? Isn't that marvelous, Tamara?"

"It's funny you should say all that," he said. "Because for the last few months, I've been reviewing my life. All the *books* that I read . . . all those *movies* that I—"

"Give me your name once more!" she said, with a violent smile. "And tell me what brings you."

THE HEIST

A senior student appeared on the steps of a small bungalow on the zendo grounds. Through the screen door, he saw his teacher laughing at something on his iPad. When the devotee made a little cough, he was waved in.

"Ah!" said the roshi, smiling ear-to-ear. "Good to see you!"

The student had been with him from a young age. As he matured, he brought deep scholarship and discipline to his studies. He carried a sheaf of papers in his hand.

"What's this?"

"My book on the Diamond Sutra," said the student. "'Book' probably isn't the right word—it's my doctoral thesis. I'm *hoping* it will be a book."

"Congratulations!" he said warmly. "Much hard work."

"It was . . . difficult," he said, with a modest smile. "My goal was to make the sutra more accessible to the contemporary reader. I took some liberties with existing translations and would be honored to have your thoughts."

The teacher said, "Which is best translation you encountered?"

"The one by Red Pine."

"Ah! Very good! Did you know his father was a bank robber?"

"Red Pine? No, I didn't."

"Big shoot-out at Michigan bank. The whole gang got killed—except for father of Red Pine!"

In the student's experience, it didn't bode well when the roshi spoke in exclamations. "It's a wonderful translation but I felt it needed some clarifications," he said self-consciously.

Setting the papers on the cushion beside him, the roshi picked up the iPad. "I must show you, you must see!" he said, with childlike glee. He tried to find what he'd been looking at earlier, but the internet wasn't cooperating so he was forced to summarize. "There was a robbery at jewelry store. *Not* Red Pine gang! Somewhere in New York. In morning, the owners notice an expensive necklace . . . *gone.* They played the security tape and couldn't believe: a *rat* appear in part of ceiling that is missing a tile. Rat clamber down, *grab* diamond necklace, then *vanish*—no one can believe! A real professional! I will find for you the security tape . . ."

"That's crazy." The student grimaced because his teacher wasn't in the habit of idly sharing anecdotes.

"No need for shoot-out!" laughed the roshi, before deadpanning, "Let us hope you have some of the rodent's . . . *finesse.*"

Then, with laser focus the old man began to read the new, improved sutra.

THE DECOY

Amongst these tales are ghost stories, told to me over the years by those who had firsthand knowledge. I include them because they touched me in ways that I still can't articulate. —ed.

A woman was brought to an emergency room after being found in her home with a gunshot wound to the head. There was a suicide note—but no weapon. As if that weren't troubling enough, the "defect" of a second projectile was discovered in the wall above an empty crib. Police swarmed the ER. After an hour or so, the patient was transported to a hospital that was equipped to deal with neurological trauma.

When a person dies in bed, it's not uncommon for paramedics to scoop them up in the bottom sheet for convenience, which is exactly what happened on the trip to the ER. The same sheet was used for the ride to UCLA; as they transferred her from the gurney to the ICU mattress, a pistol tucked between sheet and body clattered to the floor. One of the orderlies shouted, "Freeze!" and delicately picked up the gun.

The woman died in the next few minutes.

Homicide detectives interviewed the husband at the Central Bureau, making note of his calm demeanor. It might be owing to shock; it might be a lot of things.

"She had postpartum," he said. "She was under a doctor's care—I *never* left her alone with the baby. . . . Trust me, I became the world fucking expert on postpartum." An unruly laugh was strangled by a ligature of ugly coughs. One of the cops handed him a water bottle. He took a drink and calmed down. "You should have seen how she was, before things changed." He shook his head mournfully. "It was so beautiful— she *loved* Rachel. I thought, 'We'll get past this, we'll get through it.' You *have* to think that." More coughing. "But last week, something happened. Something was . . . different."

"Tell us about it."

"She said that a man came at night. Into our bedroom. I thought she was talking about a nanny—we have a load of nannies, for obvious reasons. But none of them are male. She said the man was telling her what she had to do."

"That she had to kill the baby?" asked a detective.

"All she said was, 'I know what I have to do.'"

"When did your wife say that?"

"Yesterday."

"And the father she referred to in the note—that's your father-in-law?"

He wasn't listening. "That's when I took the baby to my mother's. Can you imagine if I'd left her? When I got back home there were firetrucks, and you all were there . . ."

"Where is her father? Do you know where?"

The husband asked to see the note again. He put on glasses and began to read aloud—a little strange, but the detective went with the flow.

My darling darling husband,

Father came again to say I had no right to extend the bloodline. He told me what I had to do. He'll be here soon and will stand in front of the bed to make sure I obey. I wrapped the doll in a blanket and put it in the crib. I will shoot it first, to fool him, then finish with the rest. Forgive me for all the trouble and know that I love you. Rachel is so lucky to have a dad like you! I was lucky to have you too, Albert—luckier than you'll ever know.

Evie

"Albert . . . can you tell us where he is?"

"Who?"

"Your father-in-law."

"It's kind of a famous case," he said, with a chilling smile. "Sonofabitch was an obstetrician. That's right—a baby doctor. Killed the whole family when Evie was a little girl. *Five people*. She ran from the house, into the snow. It's a miracle she escaped. He chased her but she was too quick. So, he just . . . blew his brains out right there in the middle of the road. *Dateline* did a piece, about ten years ago. Evie refused to be interviewed . . ." He took off the glasses, closed his eyes and pinched the bridge of his nose. He smiled again, this time without menace. "I don't believe in ghosts. I don't even believe in fucking postpartum. I don't believe in anything anymore . . . except Rachel." He looked both detectives in the eye, one to the other, then bowed his head. "I believe in Rachel," he whispered, before finally breaking down.

THE POEM OF THE WORLD

A monk came to his teacher in great sorrow. In their thirty years together, he said that he had learned nothing; therefore, he was leaving the monastery and would attempt to return to "a semblance of normal life." He apologized for his willfulness.

"You learned nothing?" said the abbot.

"Not from you."

"Oh?"

The monk squirmed but bared all. "The truth is . . . I have found another teacher."

"Ah!" the abbot exclaimed, clapping his hands together. "Let us rejoice—'When the student is ready, the *right* teacher appears.' Perhaps your time here wasn't wasted after all. Do I know this person?"

"No."

"Then I'd be most happy for an introduction. When did you meet?"

"Six months ago," said the monk. "We crossed paths quite by chance . . ."

"Here in Los Angeles?"

A strange look of pain and pleasure overtook him. "I'm going to be very direct; you deserve that much."

"Thank you!"

"The teacher," he said, "is a *word*."

"A word?" said the abbot, more intrigued than bemused.

"Yes. I became—*am*—simply obsessed."

"You became obsessed," he said, by way of drawing the monk out.

"It was like . . . having an affair. Everything was measured against it; everything was perfumed by it and seen through its filter. And still is! The word was—*is*—constantly with me and makes it difficult to meditate.

It saturates my being—during chores, during prayer, during breath and walking meditations . . ."

"You've been *cheating* on the dharma! May I ask her name? 'The other woman'?"

"The word," he said hesitatingly, as if betraying a trust. "Is 'misericord.'"

"*Misericord . . .* " repeated the abbot, inadvertently cuckolding the former student as his tongue sampled the consonants. "And what exactly is it about this *word* that attracts?"

"Misericord has three meanings. The first describes a special room in a monastery, a kind of infirmary. The second is the name of the hinged shelf on the underside of a fold up seat in church—when the seat is raised, the shelf gives support to those too weak to stand."

A look of concern crossed the abbot's face. "Zazen takes its toll on the body . . . but you've been strong! Are you ill? Is there some kind of injury you've been hiding?"

"No, no! It isn't that at all."

"I see. And the third meaning of the word?"

"In medieval times, a *misericord* was the dagger used by knights to mercifully end the lives of mortally wounded enemies." Of a sudden, the monk prostrated himself before his former teacher. With eyes fixed on the ground, he said, with tender, trembling gravitas, "The beauty of this single word pierced my heart like a poem of the world."

The abbot stroked his beard for a few minutes in deep thought.

"A good carpenter," he said, "sees 'the poem of the world' in a piece of wood washed up onshore; a swordsmith, in a sword, though it be dull or damaged or forgotten; a calligrapher in a letter, making beauty from the commonplace. The anemologist, studying the movement of the winds, sees Infinity." He looked up at the ceiling as if there were only sky. "The *attached* ones seek the liberation of the Path: no wood, no sword, no word, no wind." With a rapscallion glint in his eye, he added, "No Buddha, no teacher, no *words* . . . no mistress!"

He bent down and gathered up the troubled student until they were standing face to face. Just then, the monk had an epiphany that he was about to die. In a convulsion of panic, he cried, "Tell me what to do, Sifu! Sifu, Sifu, help me! Tell me what I should do!"

The old man steadied him with a vice-like grip.

"Listen carefully," he said. "*Take the dagger and use it on the word itself.* I can assure you that it will not be expecting such a bold maneuver! You see, 'misericord' does not know you have been training thirty years for this very moment on the battlefield."

THE DROWNING MAN

For several years, an essayist nonpareil became the student of a celebrated man of knowledge. He was tired of playing the role of genius of letters; anyway, he'd always had an affinity for Infinity (which was how he liked to put it in interviews). Since childhood, he was captivated by things mystical—what he called "the clouds of unknowing," a nod to the anonymously written, fourteenth-century spiritual guide. His teacher was the real thing but he never cultivated a deep connection. He understood, historically, the importance of having a guru and how fortunate he was to have been accepted as a student by someone so illustrious. Like an arranged marriage, he hoped in time that his love would flower, not only for the guru but for the Path itself.

Things went well for a while, until they didn't. Though the guru's methods were legendarily harsh, a recent spate of random provocations began to feel like personal attacks. (Maybe he intuited his student's detachment.) For example, at the end of a meal he would point to an imaginary watch on his wrist and warn, in a booming voice, "There's not much time left, Hank! The Doomsday Clock says it's five to midnight!" Early one morning, he awakened to the master sitting at the edge of his bed, and it scared the hell out of him. "You're like a drowned man," he said calmly, "who's been spit up by the ocean. After a bonfire's made, and blankets and food provided, he falls asleep on the sand. Tired, happy, grateful. A few days later, he says to himself, 'I'm getting bored with this place! It is *not* very convenient.' The beachcomber stares at the sea and wonders, 'On what phantasmagoric shores might I wash up next?'"

The abuse made it easier for the writer to say his goodbyes.

~

In the world of belles-lettres, that he chose not to publish during what he called "the caesura of my sorcerer's apprenticeship" only served to burnish his brand. Thrilled that his sabbatical was over, *The New York Review of Books,* *TLS,* and *Bookforum* gratefully took anything he deigned submit. He began socializing again and his colleagues noted a change; once a peacock, fanning the colorful feathers of a wide if esoteric renown, he radiated a charismatic humility.

At a party in Atwater Village, he got reacquainted with old friends—a Cal Arts professor and his wife, also a literary critic—whom he hadn't seen in more than a year. The woman, particularly enchanted, dubbed his spiritual sojourn "wonderfully mysterious," while the husband unctuously compared him to the famed writer and Buddhist monk, Matthieu Ricard. When the drunk professor said something droll about his wife's addiction to the television show *White Lotus,* the returning hero threw in, "We're supposed to do a panel together."

"A panel with who," said the husband.

"Mike White."

"Oh my god, really?" said the wife.

"Apparently, he's a fan of mine. I've never seen the show . . . but at least Mr. White *reads*—Hollywood rara avis! Mike White, Otessa Moshfegh, and *moi,* at Ye Olde Skirball. Haven't agreed yet, mind you . . . I keep asking myself, 'What would my old friend Susan do?'"

"Susan?"

"Sontag."

The husband guffawed while shoving a hand toward his wife, palm up.

"Pay your daddy," he said, turning to the writer. "Edie was going on and on about how fucking *selfless* you'd become, and I said, 'Oh, just wait and *see.* Twenty bucks says he'll be humblebragging like the good old days inside five minutes. Poor thing took the bet."

"My husband's lost his manners," she offered, with some embarrass-ment. "A little stint at your monastery might do him good. Though maybe we'll sign him up for rehab instead"—the last, said with a nod toward his drink as he gulped it down.

"Good news, Edie! I'm *thinking* about this and may have lost that bet on a technicality." He couldn't help another dig. "Because that actually *wasn't* humblebrag, was it—that was just plain-ol' brag! What our daughter would call *cringe*."

"For Christ's sake, Preston, let it go," she entreated.

"*Let it go then, you and I,*" he recited. "*When the evening is spread out against the sky . . .*"

She steered him away.

The writer was listening to a satellite channel on the ride home when the DJ announced that it was five minutes to midnight. "Just like the Doomsday Clock!" he laughed, adding, "I guess the bad news is, even a broken Doomsday Clock is right twice a day."

Tomorrow, he'd begin work on *The Clouds of Unknowing*, his acclaimed book of spiritual meditations "starring" a brilliant, irascible teacher. The collection won a prestigious Toshi Award the following year and Mike White presented him with the honor.

THE ERRAND

An inn, deep in the woods of Northern California. A heavy rain—the roar of flames in the fireplace having just settled into a crackling purr. On the eve of their departure, over a bottle of wine, three middle-aged students (first-timers in a weeklong silent retreat) reflect on what it was like, unhurriedly parsing the small and large revelations that naturally accrue during such a journey; the miniature hells that precede the elating break-throughs of self-awareness—subdued, but giddy with pride and relief . . .

We did it.

One thing leads to another. More rain and wine are poured while they speak of bardos and spirits, each sharing various supernatural encounters they've experienced in their lives.

Zoe is the last to share. Her nervous reluctance piques the others' interest.

She was the casting director on a film called *Babylon*, a period piece that takes place during Hollywood's transition from silent films to talkies. Nine months before principal photography began, the director, Damien Chazelle, met a young lady at Craig's, a popular restaurant in West Hollywood. She had an unusual look—"a little like Anya Taylor-Joy"—and he thought she'd be right for a small, non-speaking role. When Zoe invited the girl to the production office, she instantly knew why Camille caught Damian's eye: she was the perfect avatar of a flapper-ingenue.

The eccentric starlet knew a lot about *Babylon*, almost too much, really, in that the script was virtually under lock and key. She carried on about "how brilliant and perfect" it was that Clara Bow had been the lead character's inspiration. At the end of the meeting, she said, "Is there a plan for the legendary Barbara La Marr to be represented?"

Zoe didn't know who that was.

Because of her look, she was hired as "Vamp at Party." She only had two scenes: the first, at a Hollywood Hills bacchanal, and the second, when she dies of an overdose.

In the next few weeks, Camille dropped by the studio unannounced (but wasn't allowed past the gate). She bombarded Zoe with late-night voicemails about "secret material concerning Barbara La Marr that I'm certain would intrigue our brilliant and talented director." Sensing trouble ahead, Zoe told Damien about the incidents—and her strong feeling that it would be best to let the actress go. He promptly agreed, adding that he'd been receiving anonymous packages at his door with photocopies and old press clippings of Barbara La Marr.

~

About a week into filming, a ruckus in the living room roused the casting director from sleep. She called out in terror then threw on a robe.

Upon entering, the stench of feces and supercharged musk literally knocked her to the ground—a thousand times stronger than the smell of a pride of lions she'd encountered close range while on African safari the year before.

Sitting on the edge of the couch was Camille, naked.

Certain that she was going to die, Zoe stammered, "Please don't hurt me."

The girl stood and came toward her. "I wouldn't!" she cried, bereft. "I won't—I *can't*, I would *never* . . . I just feel so *awful* because I *promised* her! I promised to help! But we only get *one chance* to help a neighbor. That's the rule!"—she choked on her sorrow—"*She* helped *me*—with my mother, who was suffering so! After I went away—I was so young when I went away!—she came to see Mama while she was sleeping. She told Mama I was happy and safe, that I was with *friends*, being looked *after*, and that she mustn't worry. Mama stopped being so depressed after that . . . but I failed!" She barked hot gusts of reek. "I waited so long and *failed, failed, failed*! Barbara will never forgive me! She'll never ever *speak* to me again—"

In the morning, awakening from the nightmare, Zoe rushed to the living room.

Everything was in order. The only residue was an acrid scent that the bewildered dreamer ascribed to a trespassing skunk. She ran to the bathroom, threw up, and instantly felt like herself again. Food poisoning explained away the hallucination, the vivid dream, the whatever . . .

Back in bed, she found herself googling Barbara La Marr—until now, she never had the inclination. The actress was famously known in newspapers and movie magazines as "the girl who was too beautiful." She began her career as an underage exotic dancer before being discovered by Douglas Fairbanks and starring in a few dozen films. Alcoholic, anorexic, and tubercular, La Marr died at her parents' home in Altadena at the age of twenty-nine. In a trance, Zoe put a coat over her pajamas and drove to the cemetery behind Paramount Pictures.

Guided by a directory, she found the drawer containing La Marr's ashes, about twenty feet from Rudolph Valentino. At its base were a few flowers and burnt-out votives, along with a black-and-white photo whose caption read, "Barbara La Marr as the queen in *The Brass Bottle*, 1923." Her eyes drifted to a plaque on the adjacent crypt above:

Camille Leroy

1908–1921

loving daughter

gone too soon

the Angel found her wings

As Zoe bolted from the columbarium in horror, voices rang out around her.

"I'm sorry! I'm so sorry!" a child's voice implored.

"Don't be a silly darling—that movie will be *dreadful*. Come dry those tears! . . . oh, but wasn't it fun? Wasn't it *exciting*? You must have had *some* fun in Los Angeles, didn't you, silly girl? No? Come sit! And *do* tell us all about your little adventure . . ."

AN UNKINDNESS OF RAVENS

*One afternoon, over coffee at a small café called Sicily that was a few blocks from
his home in Los Angeles, Leonard Cohen told me an old parable.*

*"During his travels, a wealthy merchant captured a bird and kept it in a
beautiful cage upon returning home. Years later, on the eve of a long trip, he
informed the bird that he would be visiting the place where they first met. 'Is
there a message you'd like me to give your family?' he asked. 'Just tell them,' said
the bird, 'that although I cannot leave my cage, I want for nothing. And that I
am very, very happy!' At the end of his business dealings in the foreign land, the
merchant stood before the tree where he stole the bird and shouted her message.
On hearing the words, the bird's brother fell dead to the ground. When the merchant came home and reluctantly shared the terrible news, his beloved captive
also fell dead from her jeweled perch. Realizing that she died of heartbreak, the
anguished benefactor opened the cage and set the limp body on the windowsill—
where she quickly revived and flew to a branch, out of reach. Before vanishing
forever, she said, 'My brother showed me what I needed to do in order to be free.'"*

Long after my coffee with Leonard, I came across the same parable in Tales
of the Dervishes, *Idries Shah's compilation of classic Sufi teaching stories.
While a bit different than the poet's version, both reminded me of the following
story. —ed.*

~

In the early eighties, a young woman leaned toward spiritual things.
Others in her circle with similar yearnings steered her to a yogini with
the reputation of being a saint. When she attended one of her retreats in
Ladera Heights—the theme was *metta*, or lovingkindness—something in
her shifted. An inner voice prophesied, *You will spend the rest of your life
with this teacher.* During the last hour of the long weekend, they met in

private. But when the tongue-tied instant-devotee asked to be accepted as her student, she was politely turned down.

It was the great disappointment of her life.

For years, she told herself the whole infatuation was "just a summer storm," an electrical surge that had more to do with mother-trauma than it did the teacher. A mirage . . . When the rationale stopped working, her fallback became the tried-and-true, "It wasn't meant to be." She found other mentors and eventually became a practitioner herself. Many seekers, especially the deeply wounded, gravitated to her for solace and guidance. She often didn't know where her words of wisdom came from—yet always had the sense they were drawn from the mouth of the saint of Ladera Heights.

∾

Twenty years later, she opened the door of her bungalow in Valley Village and was startled to find a dead crow on the mat, its head pointing toward her in grisly greeting. Almost immediately, her revulsion was replaced by the fear someone had put it there deliberately. Who would do such a thing? A homeless person? A disturbed former student? The landlord? (She'd been rebuffing his lame advances for close to a decade now.) She phoned him out of sheer desperation, and he raced right over.

Bending down for a closer look, he said, "That's not a crow, that's a raven. My daddy *loved* ravens. Everyone's heard of 'a murder of crows' but most people don't know that when ravens hang out together, it's called an *unkindness*. An *unkindness* of crows. I'm a fountain of factoids, if you couldn't tell." He turned it over and spread the feathers. "Well . . . weren't a cat who kilt it, anyway." She hadn't thought of that. "Sometimes our feline friends enjoy bringing us presents. Little keepsakes. Nope—this bad boy died of old age. His time was upski. Quoth the raven 'Nevermore-ski.'"

"Thank you for coming so quickly. It was very kind."

"Always happy to help a damsel in distress. Happy to buy a damsel a frapuccino too."

~

She was certain it was an omen of death.

The prayer that haunted her as a child returned with a vengeance:

Now I lay me down to sleep,
I pray the Lord my Soul to keep.
If I should die before I wake,
I pray the Lord my Soul to take.

Convinced that her time was *upski*, she sat down and made a list of every-one she was sorry for disappointing—girlhood friends, old lovers, and var-ious students readily came to mind. (And her parents, of course.) But all were eclipsed by the teacher who said No.

She decided to make her amends in person.

I was unworthy of being your disciple and beg your forgiveness . . .

She knew it was foolish and doubted the woman would even remem-ber her, but it felt like an important gesture. Maybe she was just being delusional—a spiritual flagellant in the grip of psychosexual pathology. She laughed at the thought of how much more efficient it would be to throw herself on her mother's grave and shout, "Please love me!"

The home abutted a large piece of donated property where the teacher built a meditation hall and housing for her students. As she parked, an old woman looked up from her weed-pulling and shouted, "There you are! Hurry, now, this garden needs *help*. You're a week late . . ."

"What do you mean?"

"You were supposed to be here *last* Saturday—a little birdie told me— *there's* a phrase that's fallen out of fashion, hasn't it? Apparently, little bird-ies don't talk to people anymore."

"I don't understand . . ."

She tugged off her gardening gloves. "When I didn't accept you as a student, I knew it would either make you or break you. I usually send the most gifted ones away; the sangha tends to get insular, perversely so.

You'd have been just another bird in the cage. A *strange* bird in a *strange* cage but a cage, nonetheless. It's always best to hone oneself out *there,* in the real world. . . . Let me tell you: this fear of dying you've had since you were tiny is the last vestige of Self! So, the 'welcome mat' birdie delivered a shock right on time—*that's* your teacher and so shall remain." She gestured toward the zendo. "All I do around here, all I've *ever* done, is keep the cage clean and make sure the locks stay broken." She handed over a spade and gloves. "It's not easy to die before you wake. Nope—'not for sissies' . . . which is *another* thing people don't say anymore. Unless they enjoy getting cancelled."

The ancient gardener looked to the sky before returning her gaze.

"And it wasn't a raven who came to your door, child. *That* . . . was a bird of Paradise."

THE PEOPLE'S COURT

A viral video had consequences that no one expected.

A hawk could be seen dive-bombing into thick brush before rising up (just as dramatically) with a snake in its talons. In a shocking turnabout, the reptile proceeded to wrap itself around the hawk's wing and a fierce mid-air battle ensued. Both soon plummeted to the ground. Apparently, the hawk had been bitten by its prey and was in its last moments of life when an experienced Good Samaritan disentangled the pair. By then, the snake was coiled around the raptor's neck.

The hawk was rushed to a veterinary hospital and stabilized but the prognosis wasn't good. It would never fly again and was sure to perish without full-time care. The sidewinder's neurotoxins left it blind and partially paralyzed; rodents and the like had to be Cuisinarted then funneled into its mouth. The snake was worse for wear but after numerous infections made something approaching a full recovery.

Comments on social media were neatly divided. While rightwing "herpers" claimed that the hawk got what it deserved ("People! Let us not forget who the victim is here!"), Team Hawk highlighted the cruelty of the serpent's two-pronged assault: first by venom, then by strangulation. Ornithophiles jeered that the repulsive, limbless creature, born with a single lung and zero eyelids, had "fought dirty." With unsurpassable eloquence, they discoursed on the existential dignity of accepting one's fate—i.e., the subtle pleasures of self-sacrifice for the greater good—clearly, a philosophy the reptile had issues with.

In a landmark show trial, the combatants were brought to court for adjudication. Behaviorists, ethicists, and even a professor of mythology took the stand. Throughout, there was an abundant pounding of hearts and gavels. Still, apart from the almost universal fear and disgust inspired by the rattler and his ilk, there was really no contesting that the hawk presented a more sympathetic countenance. The mangled sight of it dampened the eyes of the most diehard ophiophilists attending the trial.

The Samaritan who pried the snake off the hawk testified to the unconscionable suffering the bird endured "as a result of the predator's euphoric, sadistic overkill"—which provoked the defense to shout, "Objection! My client was *not* the predator!" (Sustained.) Counsel sunk their teeth into the witness's remarks with the rhetorical, "Are you god, sir? Can you look the jurors in the eye—can you look *yourself* in the eye and attest that the suffering of my innocent client, yanked from its siesta in the brush and hoisted to the heavens by talons soaked in its own blood, is somehow a *lesser* suffering? Who was the predator here? Who was the *sadist*?"

It should be said that during cross-examination, the snake remained twined around itself in a fancy terrarium paid for by a wealthy ally—the optics certainly didn't help the defense—and in fact, appeared to sleep throughout the entire trial. While not without argument, the judge allowed it to be entered into the record that the prosecution deemed such an action (or inaction) to be passive-aggressive, and smugly indicative of a complete lack of remorse.

After opposing attorneys made their elegant summations, the court's decision to find both parties equally at fault was not without controversy: no damages were awarded. It was agreed that the ruling would be expunged, contingent upon "Snake Doe" and "Hawk Doe" agreeing never to return to the wild. For the raptor, of course, such a promise was moot—a week later the hawk succumbed. The memorial was attended by more than five thousand people, with speeches made by politicians, activists, and celebrities.

The snake, whose infamy had only grown, was assassinated in the small midwestern zoo where it had been living peaceably and buried in an anonymous grave.

The saga continues to evolve.

The hawk's staunchest supporter, a falconer who discussed the trial at length on CNN, MSNBC, NPR, and "Animal Rescue," was grievously injured in a hit-and-run; cars zoomed past for an hour before one finally stopped. The snake's most powerful advocate, a retired professor of folklore and comparative religion (and former student of Joseph Campbell), was brained at a 7-Eleven by a deranged houseless person but is expected to survive.

An authority said, "In both incidents, if someone had intervened early on—as happened in the well-known case of the hawk and the serpent—we most likely would be looking at different medical outcomes. Sadly, Good Samaritans are getting harder to come by. It's a sign of the times."

ALL THERE IS

A scholar spent a lifetime studying cultures whose esoteric practices sub-verted "consensus reality"—otherwise known as ordinary human percep-tion. Coming from a troubled home, he already had an escapist's incli-nation. In his teens and early twenties, the revelations provoked by his voracious curiosity were neatly summarized by the title of his alcoholic mother's cherished song, "Is That All There Is." Yet he wanted to travel far beyond the dead-end spectacle of fire and circuses and love and death that were spoken of in its darkly droll, nihilistic lyrics.

For the next fifty years, with the help of sorcerers, healers, and medic-inal plants, he journeyed to weird places that bore no resemblance to the everyday world. He could remember plummeting into an acidic, forbid-ding place, in a panic that he'd suffocate—until a voice said, "Breath doesn't exist in this realm." And there was the time he found himself in what could only be described as a forgotten engine room (within an infin-ity of engine rooms) of a gargantuan cosmic vehicle. The loneliness that he experienced as a molecular stowaway engulfed him with an unbearable sense of sadness and desolation.

In the course of wide studies, he frequented the Esalen Institute in Big Sur. One of its founders, Michael Murphy, introduced him to Carlos Castaneda, a student of anthropology at UCLA who hadn't yet become famous for the books he would write about his teacher, a Yaqui Indian *nagual* named Don Juan Matus. Carlos spoke readily about his encounters with "the Unknowable," and explained that "nagual" could mean many things. In the context of *Nagual Don Juan Matus*, it referred to the leader of a party of sorcerers whose special energetic configuration allowed him to channel the Spirit—"and hold the Myth in his hands." A *nagual*, he said, was truly empty, but such emptiness didn't reflect the world. Rather, it reflected Infinity and something called *intent*.

Another one of its meanings intrigued the scholar.

Don Juan Matus said that human beings were divided in half by the *tonal* and the *nagual*. While the *tonal* encompassed everything that intellect could possibly conceive of, the *nagual* was an indescribable province, "impossible to express in words." He said the *tonal*, or realm of the Self, belonged to the "first attention" (so-called ordinary perception)—and the *nagual*, or energy body, was in the domain of the "second attention" (where heightened awareness prevailed). Don Juan Matus said that warriors often erred by focusing entirely on the *nagual*, bypassing the inherent wonders of the *tonal*, which were equal to, and, according to some, even surpassed the *nagual* in strangeness.

Of course, there was much more to it. The scholar wrote a book about his apprenticeship with the Nagual Carlos Castaneda, whose scope of interests ranged high and low. For instance, Carlos found accidental, ineffable poignance in popular songs (The Guess Who's "These Eyes") and certain phrases of the great poet Cesar Vallejo—

I will die in Paris, on a rainy day, on some day I can already remember.

—and wept over the famous soliloquy from *Blade Runner* where a dying machine says, "I've seen things you people wouldn't believe . . . all those moments will be lost in time, like tears in rain." The screenwriter was playacting, was *intending*, but his words insinuated the sorcerer's unutterable journeys of awareness.

For Carlos, such hints, regardless of their corniness or theatricality, carried an ecstatic mournfulness.

~

The old man now saw his past adventures through a romantic lens. He drew closer to his family and, as Carlos's teacher suggested, became deeply attentive to the miracles of the *tonal*. The sound of his great-grandson coughing became the blossomed scattershot of dying wildflowers; the bric-a-brac IV bruises on the back of his hand, a constellatory alchemy; the chlorine of the swimming pool and his son-in-law's strong deodorant transmuted into the exhalations of minty, meaty jewels.

One night, as the end approached, he thumbed to a passage in his old friend's first book where Don Juan speaks of a warrior's final, most formidable enemy: old age.

> If he gives in to his desire to lie down and forget, he will have lost his last round, and his enemy will cut him down . . . But if the man sloughs off his tiredness, and lives his fate through, he can then be called a man of knowledge, if only for a brief moment . . . and that moment of clarity, power, and knowledge is enough.[1]

Seconds after reading, he found himself back in the engine room, beneath the vertiginous apse of the empyrean cathedral. The body was gone yet he stood in full attention, like a spear.

Then, as another great poet once said, he slipped into the masterpiece.

---

1   *The Teachings of Don Juan: A Yaqui Way of Knowledge* by Carlos Castaneda (The University of California Press, 1968)

A SIMPLE LANGUAGE PROBLEM

In the early nineties, Jodie was invited by a childhood friend to a talk that her teacher was giving in Del Mar. Having more than a passing acquaintance with old school philosophies of the Spirit, she envied Cara because she herself had never been able to find a guru that was "the right fit." Upon introduction, the master of the Hidden Path grinned as if she knew her. Clutching Jodie's hand, the teacher said, "You are a true *seer*! But it won't come easy because you're so . . . *greedy*." As a digestif, she cryptically added, "Your 'fibers' are supposed to be on your shoulders like epaulets. *But they're dragging on the ground*." That the word—*greedy*—was delivered with a jack-o-lantern smile only made it worse; it felt like she'd been knifed.

On the drive home, she raged. Trying to put a spin on it, Cara said, "There was something *between* you two. That's really kind of an honor . . . are you sure that you never met?"

She wasn't going for it. "Do *you* think I'm greedy?"

"You're the least greedy person I know. You're, like, generous to a fault."

"Then what the *fuck*—is that a little trick she likes to do? I mean, I know she's your *teacher*, Cara, and I'm *sorry*. But maybe she should hire herself out at parties. She's like that comedian my dad used to like—Don Rickles. 'You're greedy!' 'You're needy!' 'You're racist!'"

"I wouldn't take it personally, Jodie," said the friend, rolling her eyes.

"You wouldn't because she didn't say it to *you* . . . goddammit! I wish I'd never come."

∾

She spent twenty years proving the guru wrong.

Each time she raised money for a cause or made an anonymous dona-tion to a stranger who suffered a tragedy—each time she made a *difference* was a rebuke to the teacher's bravura snap judgment.

A few weeks after Cara died of cancer, the handsome, athletic wid-ower asked her to drop by. He said that he had something for her. In his thirties, before they got married, he was a relief worker with the IRC in Somalia when his Toyota struck an IED. The hundred-thousand-dollar prosthetic attached to the stump of his leg was a work of art and she used to fantasize what it would be like to make love. They laughed and cried about the old days and the darling one who was gone. She played it cool but kept thinking, "If he makes a move, I'm gonna go for it." (He didn't.) He gave her a package that had been languishing in a closet for months. He said that his wife wanted her to give it to the guru personally. "*That* is Cara's command," he said wryly.

On the way to the beach, she hit a landmine of her own but continued driving in a blackout, hemorrhaging from the affairs that ruptured two mar-riages and the relationships with her children that became pernicious under the strain of her ravenous pursuit of acclaim for her brilliant philanthropic career—all the improvised explosive devices of a lifelong, ruthless indul-gence of self-will. What the guru meant by the handful of words uttered that day had nothing to do with money. In the end, the misunderstanding was, to use her mother's pet genteelism, a simple language problem.

Two blocks from the teacher's, she lay down on the front seat so no one could see her convulsions of remorse. It wasn't until she began walk-ing toward the house that she noticed all the cars. As she closed in on the front yard, it became clear that the guru was dead.

At home, she opened the package.

It was a photo of Cara and the guru, taken at the long-ago event in Del Mar. In the background, between their two heads, was a blurry figure that she finally recognized as herself.

~

Just last week, she celebrated her guru of—what, now, thirty years? (She decided to make the woman her teacher beginning with the moment she insulted her in Del Mar.) Since that strange, revelatory time of the twin funerals, she'd done her best to make amends to all those she had injured in her life. Many were cynical, leery, or dismissive, believing her atonement to be nothing more than a cagey 12-step stratagem. And even though the woman recently made generous provisions to her family, its members continue to bad-mouth her for selling her businesses so that she could be a full-time volunteer at a rehab for those who lost the use of their limbs, by accident or disease.

While it's true that the prosthetic made from her teacher's "luminous body" provides full mobility, soon enough she won't need it. Her own cancer is far more aggressive than Cara's.

During naptime, she thought of the guru and smiled to herself, admitting that she *is* greedy—for that day when one mystery is exchanged for another.

BROKEN MANDALAS

Love says: "I am everything."
Wisdom says, "I am nothing."
Between the two my life flows.
　　　　—Sir Nisargadatta Maharaj

A lawyer who did pro bono work for the homeless and was instrumental in putting together safe injection sites for drug addicts fought especially hard to promote low-income housing, believing that a roof over one's head was a birthright not a privilege. As he became more prominent—and effective—the creative advocate's vision evolved.

He began focusing on a phrase he coined, a sort of pocket mission statement for the community he served: "The mandala of dignity." For him, MOD (the name of the LLC) was the equivalent of the broken windows theory, but it was people who needed mending, not panes of glass. Dentists and plastic surgeons were conscripted into the MOD army, along with hairdressers and costume designers (for makeovers), and book-keeping wizards that tutored in the dark arts of debit cards and Venmo. Among the attorney's more inspired efforts was enlisting a well-known acting coach to lead improvisational workshops that explored the dynamics of renting a home of one's own, which might include roommates or family members.

He eventually gave up his legal practice to address himself full-time to MOD.

The crusader's skeptical friends were charmed though sometimes a little embarrassed by his quixotic ardor. He became energized by the transcendent, faddish psychologists from the sixties such as RD Laing, Carl Rogers, BF Skinner, and Arthur Janov of primal scream therapy, and the parallels of their work to the philosophies of so many towering spiritual figures long dead. But, like many of those he had studied, he soon fell out of favor for his progressively radical "games." Colleagues began to speak derisively, gossiping that he'd become a mad scientist who was dangerously experimenting on his subjects. In time, MOD sponsorships from both state and private sectors dried up or were withdrawn. After a few snarkily colorful magazine profiles, he came close to being disbarred. Still, anyone from his former life that ran into him heard the same passionate spiel:

"I'm happier now than I've ever been."

A last act before dissolving the LLC was to gather unhoused men and women in his office for a lighthearted game of drafting last wills and testaments (and itemizing the distribution of imaginary assets). Some of the group gleefully daydreamed about their vast estates—the beach houses, priceless watches, copyrights to the movies they'd directed and songs they had written—and mulled over who would or wouldn't be a deserving heir. Others went about their bequeathals with great solemnity; an outside observer would never have seen through the artifice.

Only one of the participants was reticent to join the exercise but, in the end, agreed "to leave nothing to everyone and everything to no one." The attorney whimsically framed those simple instructions and hung them above his desk. When he died a few years later, no one was really surprised to learn that the single sentence made up the entirety of his last wishes.

FIRST WORLD PROBLEMS

A handsome talent agent on the cusp of sixty spent a fortune on a home gym. His wife wondered whether he was having an affair—or was planning one. She joked about it but trusted him. She didn't like to work out herself, but was vigilant about touchups at the plastic surgeon, off-label diet drugs, all that.

Then came a string of odd events.

Two of his friends suffered freak falls—one on the street, one at home—and both were paralyzed as a result. A week later, there was a story in the news about a famous writer who fell to the ground after fainting on holiday in Rome; he was blogging from a hospital now about being a quad. The agent said to his wife, "Are we really that fragile?"

"Yes. And just as hard to kill."

"When I win *that* shit lottery, we need a Plan A—a Plan A *and* a Plan B."

"We'll fly you first class to one of those clinics in Switzerland," she said cheerfully. "And finish you the fuck off. Johnny'd fly over for that." As in Depp, an old friend and client. "Johnny wouldn't *miss* it. Then I'll get a facelift and marry a young Black rapper. When I divorce him for cheating on me with Kris Jenner, I'll marry my plastic surgeon."

"Plan C." He looked down at his pinging phone and said, "Speak of the paralyzed devil." The partner of one of their unlucky friends just texted JERRY WOULD LOVE TO SEE YOU. The showbizzer already felt guilty about not having visited him at the hospital after the mishap. "I don't think I'm up for a house call," he told his wife. "The whole thing fucking spooks me."

"You kinda have to, honey. Don't *agent* this."

~

It wasn't as bad as he thought.

Jerry seemed to be in good spirits—how was that even possible?

When they were alone, the partner said, "Oh, he has his dark moments. But his meditation practice is really strong. It kinda saved his life."

~

The agent shocked himself by taking a Transcendental Meditation class that one of his director clients recommended. He was surprised to have a knack for it, and actually began looking forward to morning and evening TM. He spent less time in the home gym and grew softer, more emotional, even nostalgic. His wife said, "You better not be transitioning."

He had a recurring dream about a boy he knew from halcyon days— his closest friend in elementary school, Huck Finn to the agent's Tom Sawyer—and was moved to reach out. (They sporadically kept in touch but hadn't seen each other in years.) The friend's wife emailed back that "Huck" died more than a year ago of a glioblastoma and how sorry she was that she didn't call. "It was just so hard, and he didn't want anyone to know he was sick."

This time, he couldn't meditate himself out of the gloom and the panic.

~

After Jerry's funeral, everyone gathered at a house in Bel Air.

The wake had a manic, festive feel, and Jerry's tipsy partner spoke to the couple about her choice to have the body viewed before burial.

"Didn't he look *fantastic?*" she said giddily. "I brought in some amazing folks from the studio . . . the poor thing lost *so much* weight. Death: the new Ozempic! And those *furrows*, from the *pain*. He was in so much pain . . . you'd think if someone was completely paralyzed, there wouldn't be any pain! Right? The makeup people took care of the fuckin furrows with filler—you get it on Amazon, it's called 'Fuckin Furrow Filler'—ha!—it's *not* Botox, not technically, but essentially kinda *is*. Whenever I'd go have my lips plumped, I'd try to drag him along. I'd say, '*Do it*, Jerry! My guy's a fuckin *genius*, you'll leave there looking like Harry Styles!' He'd laugh and say, 'Maybe in the next world, babe.' Welp . . . *there you have it*." She softly started to cry. "Welcome to the next world, beautiful man."

The three embraced in a weepy hug.

ARPEGGIOS

After ten years at his teacher's side—in the foothills of India and here in Los Angeles—a devotee reached the end of the road. His passion for the journey had receded long ago; it was just another job now, a drudgery, with all the mundane, soul-sucking battles of the workplace. The sangha employed many two-faced staffers who giggled like starstruck, complaisant naifs in the presence of the "boss" but took pleasure in bullying their colleagues, and whose raison d'être was to stay atop the food chain. Worker bees came and went, filled with sincerity yet void of understanding. The guru himself said that sincerity was not enough.

Then what was?

He fantasized about having a home, a wife, a patisserie—the guru loved the madeleines he made for him on weekends—but hadn't the courage to leave. At last, he nervously decided to confess. It was the perfect time to make his approach; his teacher was alone in the garden. But before he could say a word, the old man spoke animatedly, as if in mid-conversation.

"My brother had perfect pitch," he said. "A benefactor in the village gave our family a piano and Sunni began to play, day and night. Which caused some trouble with the neighbors! He was *very*, very good and dutifully applied himself, for ten disciplined years. A perfectionist, he aped the immortals with enormous skill—he was particularly fond of Sviatoslav Richter. Do you know him? A Russian genius of the keyboard! But one thing Sunni *couldn't* do was improvise like the great jazz pianists. It tormented him! Why did he feel that without improvisation, he amounted to nothing?" He shrugged, palms up, at the unanswerable question. "One day, a friend of mine came to the house—I was probably six or seven, my brother was almost twelve—and the boy sat down to play. Now, he didn't really know what he was *doing* but our eyes got very big because he had 'the gift.' Something carried him away on the wind and anyone who listened got carried away too. The result being, *my brother never played another note again.* He enlisted in the army and found his true calling: Sunni, bless his soul, was a crack shot!" The guru laughed until he was almost in tears. "Who could have imagined that chords and arpeggios had been covering the gifts of a deadeye sniper all along!"

Shortly after this encounter, the devotee left the ashram. Married now, with two children, he is the proud owner of a popular bakery. Each day, the love for his family—and for what the guru calls the World—is a difficult, rapturous improvisation.

In such fashion, many find their way back to the Path.

ROCK, PAPER, SCISSORS

For years, two friends from middle school independently sought the Way.

Now and then, they compared notes. Their adventures took them to faraway places: meetings with remarkable men and women in rain forests, deserts, and mountaintop monasteries. They'd smoked and eaten godhead plants and shot up a hundred synthetic compounds—uneasy gateways to Heaven and Hell. They found the wisdom dormant in sweat lodges, months-long silent retreats, and backbreaking marathon *sadhanas*. Middle-aged now, their steely, sinewy countenances reflected the steady, ruthless onslaught of the divine.

In other words: these were charismatic veterans of the spiritual wars.

The theme of tonight's talkfest was "teachers." The woman was studying under a tarot master in Signal Hill, while her friend was enamored of a shaman whose lineage was "to be determined." "I kind of like that," he said. "Because the ego puts so much emphasis on provenance."

She was surprised he'd moved on from his root guru of nearly a decade.

"So, what happened there?" she asked. "Why did you leave?"

He shook his head, curling his lip. "No dark night of the soul. No regrets. Not even a lot of sadness. You just wake up one morning and it's . . . *time's up*."

"Been there, done that."

"I guess it didn't help that he was fucking *rude*." She laughed at the familiar characterization of the Great Ones both had encountered in their travels. "He'd go on and on about how no one knew a thing about love—except *him*, of course." She laughed. "How we need to learn to love the way *warriors* do. If you *dared* tell him about your partner, or someone you might be interested in, he'd shrug and say, 'We cut one head off and replace it with another.'"

"Well, *that's* . . . graphic," she smiled.

"I mean, look. I understood what he was saying and don't disagree. I got it—I *get* it. And he was amazing. But I *try*, Becky, I really do. To love like a warrior."

"As the old saying goes, 'If at first you don't succeed, try, try peyote again.'"

He snickered and said, "He wasn't into medicinal plants anymore by the time we met."

"More's the pity. So, tell me about your next victim."

He was nonplussed until he realized she was talking about the shaman. He walked her over to a little altar in the den and held up a photograph of the handsome, grinning guru.

"Nice teeth," she said.

In that regard, he was still gnawing on the bone of why he left his former teacher, wanting to further explain so he didn't come off as capricious or fickle. He tapped the photo with a long fingernail. "It's funny . . . but Mr. Shaman says pretty much the same thing about love that Mr. Root Guru did—"

"You mean Mr. *Rude* Guru—"

"Ha! Right. I guess it's easier to hear because he doesn't *eviscerate* you. At this stage in the fucking game, I guess I need a lighter touch. Probably getting too old for the tough love shit."

She nodded in agreement. "The delivery system is key. Finesse beats evisceration like a rock beats scissors." Scrutinizing the framed photo in her hand, she said, "And speaking of scissors, did you cut the head off?"

"What?"

"Did you photoshop the new teacher's head onto the old one's?"

He laughed but it stung. He loved his friend for that—she was harsh but usually right on.

"Maybe so," he mused.

"So: where we gonna eat? This warrior needs fresh meat. Like, nowsville."

THE GURU WHO WENT INTO
WITNESS PROTECTION

An advanced student of Zen was busy putting together a book of contemporary teaching allegories. Before approaching a publisher, he scoured libraries and digital archives with an eagle eye, to get a feel for such compilations.

The best collection out there was still the one that became a cultural sensation almost seventy years ago. But the student grew livid because many of the tales had been given titles that were dead giveaways ("The Thief Who Became a Disciple") while others were literally, lazily named after the story's last few sentences, as in the case of "What Are You Doing! What Are You Saying!" Why would an editor have allowed it? How could one justify the robotic hijacking of the reader by spoilers, especially ones that weren't interesting or even poetic? The gems in the collection had been permanently disfigured by such stupidities—a trap he would make sure never to fall into. The more he reflected on *Zen Flesh, Zen Bones*, the greater was his contempt. He demoted the book by turning its spine inward; ultimately, he grew so disgusted that he chucked it in a donation bin.

Near the end of his project, after years of fruitless searching, he found a teacher who intrigued him. Notably, the man wasn't a Buddhist, nor did he align his teachings with any of the usual-suspect disciplines—something the anthologist found refreshing. Instead, he drew from a deep well of knowledge that felt as pragmatic as it was intuitive.

What got the student's attention was a lecture the man gave on "The Known, the Unknown, and the Unknowable." He credited Carlos Castaneda with having written extensively on the theme but slyly told the audience that he had "some issues" with the sorcerer's interpretation. Castaneda said that the known and the unknown were on the same footing because both were within the reach of human perception; an adroit *seer* could navigate between the two. But the *unknowable*, said Castaneda, was beyond man's capacity to perceive. The observation riled the guru, who felt that while the word itself was seductively evocative, it was, in essence, deceitful.

"The 'Unknowable,'" he said, "is a pathetic fallacy. We are its container! We are energetic containers of the Known, the Unknown, *and* the Unknowable. They reside *within*, hence cannot give the lie to dear Socrates' inviolable command: Know thyself. We are no more inclined to say, '*Unknown* thyself' than we are to declare '*Unknowable* thyself' . . . Castaneda was a marvelous storyteller, a wonderful poet, but *no thing* is unknown *or* unknowable. *All* is known, all things live within. Seek and ye shall find!"

The compiler of parables learned much about "containers"—right up to when his teacher vanished under mysterious circumstances. Rumors spread that he'd been murdered; married a devotee–princess who ruled a faraway land; absconded with his followers' money; and mastered the art of astral projection (which would have made the absconding easier).

The book was published to respectful sales. The last thing the student heard—from reliable sources—was that the guru (to whom the volume was dedicated) had named names and was put into witness protection.

ONE-TIME PAYOUT

A malcontent bridled at the prospect of ever escaping Saṃsāra. He went out for a night of drinking, something he hadn't done in years, and struck up a conversation with a stranger at a bar. They spoke of the man who recently won the $2 billion Powerball prize in Altadena—the odds were around 200 million to 1. His new companion was a fountain of trivia. He said that the chance of cracking open a double yolk egg were a thousand-to-one.

"You could crack one a day and only get a double yolk every three years."

But the enthusiast said the most interesting statistic came from a Harvard paper about the odds of being born: 1 in 10 to the power of 2,685,000. To give an idea of what that meant, he told him it was like two million people rolling dice at the same time—with each die having a trillion sides—and *boom* they land on the same number. There was no way to wrap your head around it.

Passing through the monastery gates, still high, he rapped on his teacher's door, brimming with anger and self-pity. When he repeated the conversation from the bar, the teacher said, "It's not easy to 'outwit the stars' but it can be done. What you lack is the proper *intent*."

"Intent? How have I lacked *intent*? Fifteen years I've done the work! I gave up everything! And for what?"

"There was something you neglected."

"Tell me!" he raged. "Tell me what I *neglected*..."

"Had you done the same as the man who won the two billion, your chance of escaping the cycle of rebirth would no doubt have greatly increased."

"What did that man do, goddammit! *What did he do*—"

"When fate put the ticket in his hand," said the teacher, "he held onto it."

MUSEUM PIECE

A famous author of nonfiction was in crisis. What she thought was writer's block slowly took on the more sinister feel that her desire to tell stories had died. The irony was that many of her books were *about* storytelling—she told her readers that the act was as essential to human beings as water and breathing. *Yes*, she blackly mused. *Storytelling is essential for those who sell books about storytelling being essential.* When the editor of an online magazine asked her to write a "fun" piece about the new Museum of Storytelling, she superstitiously said yes. Lately, she'd been taking herself way too seriously; the providential assignment was a karmic hoot and might even jolt her from the nightmare.

Hollywood Boulevard was full of them, with the usual waxwork or Ripley's alongside the captivatingly obscure. (She laughed when she saw that the Museum of Storytelling was on the same block as the Museum of Failure and The Museum of Broken Relationships.) As she entered the Hall of Story, the first few exhibits were perfunctory show business displays of silent films, then jumped to America's golden age of cinema before segueing to contemporary CGI-heavy movies like *Avatar, Avengers: Endgame*, and *Spider-Man: No Way Home*. Other rooms glossed the history of cartoons, radio, and television—the latter represented by kinescope gameshows, and dramas that morphed into the birth of the miniseries—and finally, streaming content that demolished the prehistoric notion that narrative should be tidily contained. Current trends were busy creating content that mimicked the digitized cultural brain and its feverish, insatiable sophistication. The new narratives looked closer to fireworks than those of yesteryear's quaint illumination of a single room by a single lamp.

At the end of the tour, the museum's enthusiastic curator showed her a few spaces that weren't yet open to the public. One was dedicated to virtual reality and its challenges; another, to how narrative was expected to evolve vis-à-vis AI. He paused at a last exhibit under construction—"The Death of Story?"—a half-whimsical, half-serious look at the role of storytelling to come.

"In the future," said the curator, "there may be no need for storytelling because that's where we'll be living. Inside one big Story."

"Aren't we doing that now?" she asked.

"True!" he said. "But stories are just a reminder. What if one day we don't *need* those reminders anymore? Think of it this way: You wake up in the morning. Does anyone really need a story about you waking up? Do *you* need one?"

⁓

She never finished the museum profile.

Instead, she returned to work on her first novel, which became a runaway bestseller. While the critics said it lacked the nuance of her nonfiction, none could argue with the blurb on the back of the hardcover: "Trust me—you will not be able to put down *Death of a Storyteller.*"

CHANGE YOUR PASSWORD

He sought the Hidden Path for most of his life, a pursuit one might not have expected of a man who made his fortune leasing portable toilets to TV and film production companies.

He was good-natured about it. When asked how he got into the business, his standard reply was "Process of elimination." Yet, he was embarrassed by the source of his wealth because his lifelong dream had been to become famous for other reasons. Cronies from acting class were now Oscar-winning superstars but whatever fame he'd achieved was thanks to celebrity waste. At sixty, he sold the company at an enormous profit.

As he liked telling friends, "My shit came in—I'm flush."

Now he could focus on the divine; the "secret knowledge" still beckoned. Years ago, he studied with the Advaita master Ramesh Balsekar. The guru made simple, formulaic pronouncements that stayed with him through the years, like, "There are only three possibilities: We get what we want; we get what we don't want; we get something entirely unexpected." He promised himself that when the moment was opportune, he would return to India to see him.

The first few weeks in Mumbai were enthralling. When Ramesh gave *satsang* each day, the erstwhile porta-potty king sat at his feet, utterly fulfilled. At the end of the talks, he wandered the city—lush, chaotic, rank, and hallucinatory, redolent with the perfume of excrement, incense, and death—and its ambience was eerily, achingly familiar, as if he'd walked there in a thousand past lives. Everything he heard, saw, and smelled became his teacher. After years of struggle in LA, he got what he wanted.

Then one morning, he got what he didn't.

At the top of his inbox, an email read

Hi. How are you?
I know it's unpleasant to start the conversation with bad news
but I have no choice. A few months ago, I gained access to your
devices and tracked down your internet activities. I couldn't help
but notice you are a big fan of adult-content websites. You actually love watching porn while pleasuring yourself. I could make a
video of you and insert the videos that you were watching as you
reached orgasm while masturbating with joy. For all the world to
see.

Ohhhhh, just one more thing . . . it's always best that you
don't involve yourself in similar situations any longer. A last piece
of advice that I hope you will find helpful: Regularly change all
passwords from all accounts!

He deleted the hacker's demand for fifteen-hundred dollars.

The talk Ramesh gave that day was delivered with the usual pok-
er-faced panache. He repeated that "all is predetermined," a mantra that
drove many visitors away because they were outraged to be told they had
no free will. But "Sir Honeywagon" (as Mel Gibson dubbed him back in
the nineties) found the concept a great, unburdening comfort. What had
delusions of free will ever done for him, anyway? Ramesh also said that
to be enlightened merely meant that one took nothing personally—was
neither elated nor aggrieved when good or bad fortune called. The guru
ended his remarks with a quote from the *Gita*, saying "I am the water, and
I am the everything, even the cunning of the enemy." Thus inspired, he
imagined himself as the hacker and bore him no ill will.

Everything was predetermined, so what was the use?

On the way home, detached and at ease, he idly wondered what fresh
attempt at blackmail might be waiting on his laptop. He smiled, knowing

that he had done the right thing by returning to this magical place. In just two weeks' time, he'd already got what he wanted—and got what he didn't. Then, he got something entirely unexpected:

A cab ran him down at the curb of his hotel.

He died the next day at Breach Candy Hospital with his guru at his side. Ramesh noted the devotee's beatific expression as he left the world— which happened to be identical to the one in the image released to the dead man's contacts a bit later that very night.

SEARCH AND SEIZURE

In her teens, an epileptic began having what her proud mother insinu-ated were religious visions. But the girl didn't see it that way; the worlds she accessed were inorganic, with unbreathing objects rearranged on the chessboard by her musky respirations—violent shimmerings of unknown, sometimes banal, always ineffable star systems. The only time they took her to the hospital was to stitch up her face if she fell on the street during the onset of a fit. Her sister wanted epilepsy too and was angry that she wouldn't teach her how to "talk witch." During convulsions, the little girl ran from the room, shouting, "Mama, Mama! Tara's talking witch again."

She was a weirdo in middle school, but students quietly sought her counsel when they were in turmoil; something about her sorted them out. As she grew older, she became a magnet for the emotionally unstable, who seemed to benefit simply from being in her presence. (She bridled if anyone dared call her a healer.) When her "caseload" became too much, a friend suggested she start charging fees. She soon quit her barista job and saw clients full-time. A year later, in the waiting room of a neurologist, she read a magazine article about magic crystals, mystic canyons and movie stars, and without talking it over with friends or family, picked up and moved to Los Angeles. After a session in Topanga with a young actress named Shailene Woodley, word of mouth spread, and she was besieged by clients who were desperate for her "amazing energy work."

That she was epileptic only gave luster her image as a hippie Druid with extraordinary gifts.

~

Two years passed—a time in which she felt herself lost, envious, fraud-ulent, grasping, fearful, and on the brink of death. She threw away her seizure medicine. When she visited a healer who lived on the other side of the mountain, the hag confirmed that she was in mortal danger and urged her to take certain steps.

The stubborn girl refused.

One night, she left a club but couldn't find her car. She wandered into an alley and blacked out. As consciousness returned, she discerned the shape of a man leaning over her. He wore a pinstriped suit and chauffeur's cap. With great kindness, he gestured to the open door of a gunmetal gray SUV; trancelike, she climbed in. Her thoughts were all jangled. *Did I call an Uber?* They drove into the hills then through an enormous gate onto a long gravel driveway. She steadied herself against the driver as he walked her inside.

She never saw a house like that before—some kind of palace. The walls were adorned with jewel-encrusted tapestries whose designs reflected extravagant, alien tableaus. A servant brought her to a cavernous marble room where a bath was already drawn. Time sped up. She was dried off and dressed in a gown of crimson silk and taffeta then ushered to a vast room where a banquet was in progress. Everyone stood and applauded. Everyone was so beautiful. She was seated between an architect and an actress.

The architect's young daughter said, "This is *not* a seizure! This is real."

After dessert, the actress performed a monologue from a Strindberg chamber play that astonished Tara with its radically inventive, ghostly guile.

In the library, over coffee and cognac, each candidly admitted that they were unable to leave (nor had the desire to). "Only *here* can art— *my* art—truly flourish," said the actress. To pursue a career "outside the frame" would mean to court mediocrity and madness. Expanding on her words, the chef said that the "unusual ingredients" found in the palace gardens could not be procured elsewhere. "And what would I *do* out there? Open a restaurant? And be praised by gluttons and anorexics? A *desecration*." The architect nodded in agreement and spoke of the absurdity of walking away from his finest creation. "How? Why? This . . . *cathedral* is my chef-d'oeuvre and can never be replicated! How? Why?" He kept toggling and modulating the two words until it became a deranged hymn.

His daughter wept at the very thought of leaving the nest.

"No world—*worlds*—could possibly be as lovely and complete as the dream of these one hundred thousand rooms!"

Around six a.m., she awakened in the front yard of her canyon bungalow.

She was back in her old clothes. A neighbor saw her through a window and rushed out, assuming that she'd had a seizure. When Tara began prattling about the fabulous, glamorous palace people, the worried woman drove her to the ER—where, with passionate intensity, she retold the story (it grew realer to her by the minute). The doctor on call was a befuddled, moonlighting intern who surmised she was in the grip of some sort of epileptic hallucination. When no one seemed to believe her, she became combative and was put in restraints.

The next morning, a nurse escorted her to the cafeteria. She was still groggy from the sedatives they knocked her out with. At breakfast, Tara was warmly received. All of the patients at the table looked familiar, and it slowly occurred to her that they had the same faces as the palace people. She began to describe the roles each had played—actress, architect, debutante, chef—and the inmates were enchanted. But when one of them kept calling her Dorothy, she realized they were mocking her. "I'm the Tin Man," said another. "I'm Toto!" screeched a woman with a godawful haircut.

That afternoon, she dreamt she was back in the cafeteria having pancakes with her mother and the mountain hag whose warning she had ignored. The hag smiled and said nothing; she wasn't eating her pancakes either. Upon release, Tara went straight to her house.

"You're lucky you didn't stay," said the woman. "Those were *inorganic beings*—you'd have been trapped. And lucky *again* to have met their counterparts, in the illusion of this more familiar world. You're a very powerful little girl! You shouldn't be here at *all* after such an encounter, let alone in one piece. *This* time, do as I tell you. *Stay.* Live here with me a while and we'll learn which world you're meant for. If you're lucky a *third* time, you'll be welcome in both. But you won't forget where you live." With a wink, she added, "You might *even* remember where you parked your car."

∿

Tara became her student and to this day keeps a room. Compared to the palace, what her teacher calls "Hag Cottage" is quite modest—deceptively so, because it has at least as many rooms.

TRIGGER WARNING

A woman whose friends always said she'd been a warrior in another life was humiliated by her husband's very public affair with a zillennial. During the divorce, she accused him of molesting their daughter, a lie that even the daughter came to believe.

The allegation ruined him and she rejoiced.

There were more battles to come. She nearly lost one that a coworker waged through HR, but the clash became moot when the woman had a stroke a few minutes after being vaccinated. On the day the aphasic retiree got home from rehab, she sent a handwritten note: "Hope you're well! Struggling to express your opinions must be such an amazing new experience."

When the preteen daughter announced that she wanted to transition, Mom said, "You weren't born into the wrong body, you were born into the wrong brain. Just *accept* that you're a bigger fag than Kristen Stewart . . . but hey, do what you gotta do. Cut those tiny little tits off, if it makes you happy! And *sorry*—you'll have to wait till you're sixteen before the wonderful surgeons can grow you a dick to rape all the girls who just aren't that into you."

She was bored and began to paint.

She rented a gallery to exhibit work that riffed on newspaper stories through the years on the theme of ICU nurses that enjoyed killing preemies and old folks. (A friendly critic said the canvasses were a cross between Waters and Warhol.) It was packed but midway through there were no buyers, so she had staffers put SOLD stickers on all the paintings. Her stoned daughter crashed the opening and loudly proclaimed that the show was pathetic; hours later, she was arrested on a DUI. When the gallerista asked if she was going to bail her out, the artist said, "I don't do bail. I don't do daughter anymore, either."

Someone she knew from middle school was there that night. They wound up having lunch and dishing about the good ol' mean girl days. The gal invited her to a weekend Buddhist retreat, which held zero allure, but she surprised herself by saying yes. The workshop was revelatory and lovely, even calming, and she learned a lot. She reflected on her life and could actually see the patterns, something that years of talk therapy hadn't gotten close to achieving. She even started meditating. Not being a joiner, she didn't tell anyone, not even her mean girl Buddhist friend.

She called it "the no-meditation meditation" and it became a secret weapon.

An upmarket traveling show of Buddhist art rolled into town, so she took the day off. She had a solitary lunch at the museum (eating alone was another secret weapon) and felt strangely alive. The exhibition was stunning and comprehensive but when she came to the room that was pithily called The Destroyers, she couldn't believe her eyes.

"Wrathful female deities" ecstatically gorged on their victims. One of them killed her son because he wouldn't cannibalize her enemies—then triumphantly rode a saddle made from the handsome boy's flayed skin. Others drank cups of blood, wearing crowns and necklaces of skulls, invariably explained away by gaslighting scholars as symbols meant to represent selflessness, delusion-cutting, exalted wisdom, and "Supreme Bliss"! The so-called "gods of preservation" were just a mob of sadists and mass-murderers. . . . *What a fucking joke.* Everything she thought she knew about her latest hobby was ransacked and overturned. She felt so gullible, so foolish—conned. She never spoke to the middle school friend again and pounced on anyone who sang the woo-woo praises of Bodhidharma aka lovingkindness. When asked about her personal experience, she scoffed and said, "Buddhism's a bigger bullshit religion than Pfizer."

She set to work on a suite of acrylics, as a kind of rebuttal. The violent contemporary portraits were unspeakably gruesome but this time she was widely reviewed and everything sold. The viral fame of such an improbable late-life career made her an icon for women of all ages. On social media, photographs of her with Taylor, Cara Delevingne, and Maye Musk (who were so great when her daughter committed suicide) were everywhere.

She never speaks of that death, nor does she share with interviewers her museum encounter with "the destroyers," to whom she owes thanks. While it's true that competitors often spur one to greatness, she thought it best to keep that seminal afternoon to herself, believing one can never have enough secret weapons.

FIREFLIES

At a young age, a seeker's life was greatly impacted by the books of a sorcerer who wrote poetically about his own apprenticeship. Thousands of other readers were likewise affected but only a lucky few were able to meet the author. He simply didn't make himself available.

Though in this particular case, the Spirit arranged an encounter.

They had lunch together at a Cuban restaurant on Venice Boulevard. The sorcerer was funny and congenial yet possessed a deep, otherworldly seriousness. The enthusiast, now in his early forties, couldn't believe his good fortune. Nervously at first, then with great charm, he spoke freely of romantic entanglements, substance addictions, long-term regrets, and petty grudges—very entertaining. One thing on his agenda, less personal, was something mentioned in the books: a puzzling entity called the Eagle.

According to the sorcerer's lineage, the Eagle governs the destiny of all living things, but has nothing to do with eagles as we know them. *This* "eagle" devours the awareness of sentient beings; upon death, lifetimes of experience and consciousness float up "like a swarm of fireflies" to the beak of that which is the ultimate purpose of existence. He reiterated (he had written much about it) that the Eagle grants a gift to every single being—"the gift of *disobeying destiny* and keeping the flame of awareness to themselves . . . of escaping, with consciousness intact, through the door of freedom." In that way, he said, it was truly possible to perpetuate awareness after the death of the body. He said there were specific things one can do, "simple, though not easy," that allowed such a getaway, much like in scenes from old movies where prisoners stuff their beds with dummies before slipping out of the cell.

But the seeker wasn't interested in learning the recipe. "It's a beautiful metaphor," he said. "*Colorful*, but a skosh obscure. . . . Lately," he ruminated, as if sucking on a pipe. "I've had the idea that everything is wrong—*everything*. The weatherman is wrong; all clocks tell the wrong time; opinions are wrong because each has an opposite that can sound just as reasonable. Even to say, 'I know nothing!' is wrong—because after all, to know nothing is to know *something*." He shrugged. "I guess you have your thoughts about eagles, and I have mine."

The writer's face became stoney and ancient. Shadows fell across it like moss as he looked past the shoulder of the seeker. "When you come to understand that this 'idea' of yours belongs solely to the clock and weatherman world, it will be too late." The younger man felt a chill; then the moss fell away as the writer's gaze warmly returned. "Forget about the Eagle!" he said dismissively. "Live life to the fullest—enjoy this marvelous world to the hilt."

"Forget about it?" The over-the-hill fanboy had been relishing a lively debate.

"Perhaps all these years I was misled," he smiled contritely. "Though you have to admit it would make a very good film! The other idea—the colorful one, I mean—of the devouring Eagle . . . in certain markets, of course. Special effects might be too costly."

"Kind of a shamanic horror flick . . . I *like* it. But what about animation?" offered the seeker.

"Yes!" he said passionately. "Yes, that's excellent! Animation!"

They laughed together but the writer was elsewhere.

THE DOMINO EFFECT

In his twenties, a man had a passionate involvement with Buddhism. It was serious enough that friends assumed he was on the path to becoming a monk. So, it came as a shock when he enrolled in dentistry school. No one could make sense of it, not even him.

It might be said that his final teacher, if anyone, was the culprit. Widely known for his unorthodox style—what academics glibly called "crazy wisdom"—the guru was tough on his students. Accusing the dormant periodontist of being lazy and hard-headed, he proposed one of the unusual techniques he was famous for, dubbed the "radical redirection" remedy. Without getting into the details here, the prudent apprentice refused, believing that the cure, as they say, might kill the patient. He turned in his robes and went back to Los Angeles to study for his DDS.

As a *toothsayer*, he was anything but lazy. His practice in Santa Monica soon thrived.

He had always kept to himself and was genial in nature; certainly, one would never have pegged him as a man who'd made three attempts on his own life in the last handful of years. (The next time, instead of swallowing pills, he resolved to jump from a tall building on Wilshire Boulevard that overlooked the sea.) Because he rarely socialized and had no partner— what used to be called a confirmed bachelor—his personal travails went under the radar. In the first few days of hospitalization, he would ask his mother to send postcards to all his patients: "Off again to Africa to make beautiful smiles even more beautiful!" She was so proud.

He never told her the awful truth.

The whitener knight took long walks to clear his head and gather the courage to kiss the world goodbye. During one of those morbid constitutionals, he noticed an unusual woman in the parking lot of a beachside café; the abrasions of open-air life were belied by a glamorous sense of style. Later that evening, scrolling through the internet, he was bewildered to see a video of her online, rummaging through a dumpster. The *Where Are They Now*-style article revealed that in the nineties, she had a moment of fame as a TV series costar before being derailed by substance addiction issues and mental illness. Friends and colleagues were shocked and saddened to learn about her reversal of fortune.

Apparently, a stillborn child triggered the dominoes to fall.

The next day, he went to give her money, but she was gone.

After months of torment, the bruxism whisperer could no longer bear his suffering. He made a plan that included flying to New Mexico to see his parents for the last time. It was a happy visit, made happier still by his secret resolution. Over supper, his mother gossiped about "our new neighbors in the Sangre de Cristo," the members of a Zen retreat high in the mountains. He recognized the name as belonging to the lineage of the crazy wisdom guru he once feared and respected. Surprised that he was still alive, the ill-fated orthodontist was overtaken by a powerful urge to see his old teacher again.

Why not? There would be symmetry to the goodbye.

As he drove a rental to the mile-and-a-half-high zendo, the landscape's cold majesty and recondite beauty quieted his mind. A helper at the Center informed that guests weren't allowed because it was the middle of a weeklong sesshin. He gave his name, anyway, saying that he was a former student who only wanted to pay brief respects.

The girl excused herself then reappeared. "The roshi said you have to do the remaining three days of the sesshin—he will see you after."

He was shown to a room of cots then ushered to the main hall where a small group was in the middle of zazen. The woman on the cushion next to him had a soothing presence along with a regal air of self-possession. It wasn't until day three that he realized, as if by the lash of a whip, that she was the dumpster-diving actress from LA. *But how? How could that be?*

At sesshin's end, he was brought to a sunlit atrium. There, the guru sat between two tables laden with orchids. He was ninety years old, still spry, and intensely alive. After a warm reunion, the root canal gondolier impulsively blurted out the uncanny resemblance between his meditation partner and the beggarly beach bum in California. The guru grinned—with a double shock, the visitor realized that in fact it *was* the same woman. Her dumpster-diving had all been an act: a "radical redirection" at her teacher's behest!

That such *remedies* were still being played out both comforted and alarmed.

Laughing gaily at the cosmic coincidence, the old man said, "She was still too attached to show business—so I need to *show* I mean *business*. Only way? Dumpster patrol! Social media humiliation *very* good teacher."

The gumslinger flinched a confessor's smile; he was already crossing over. "I'm at the end now," he gloomed, despite himself.

"End is beginning," said the guru. Ignoring the visitor's maudlin pronouncement, he lightheartedly scolded, "Your 'sister' *very* good student. Dumpster lady does what is *suggested*."

"I remember you giving me a 'suggestion' all those years ago—"

"You are bad *student* but very good *dentist*. That is the *teeth* of the problem."

He hadn't mentioned his vocation—maybe the guru googled him. *"This time, I will listen."* He stunned himself; the words came as if spoken by another. "This time, Roshi, I promise to do whatever you ask of me."

"Too late!" said the teacher. The floss shepherd had already appointed himself as his own executioner, yet still quailed at the exclamation—it sounded like a snippy death sentence. Then came the temporary reprieve. "But *Spirit* knows more than me. Spirit doesn't know 'too late'! What I suggest will be . . . *harder than before*. Much harder than what suggested for *sister*! For you, might be impossible . . ." Fear gripped the enemy of decay. "Can you move to New Mexico?"

It was a command, not a query, and he nodded vigorously in response.

Just that? Is that the "much harder" thing, moving to New Mexico? No! It's after I arrive, after I settle—that's when he'll ask me to do something hideous and godforsaken . . .

"Do it *now*—next twenty-four hours." He gestured invitingly around the dome-ceilinged room. "Live *here*. Very nice, very comfortable . . . work hard. Study hard. If dentist fail, he can jump off mountain! But, warning: no ocean view! Much harder to jump without Wilshire view."

Hearing *Wilshire*, something shifted, and for an instant he merged with the cold, majestic, recondite world. The shockwave rendered him mute; it was for his and the Spirit's eyes only. But when the moment receded, he stood before his teacher without self-pity.

That night, he gave his parents the wonderful news he would soon be living close by. As it turned out, the guru's "impossible" suggestion was that he merely continue practicing dentistry during the epic struggle to unseat the Self. *No fireworks* said the old man. "Much harder that way. Much easier to fail."

On his hundredth birthday, he had a toothache. The dentist examined him and said, "Congratulations! You're no longer an anomaly—you just got your first cavity."

The guru gleefully clapped his hands. "Ah!" he smiled. "Time to jump off mountain."

MORNING LIGHT

I saw that in its depth far down is lying
    Bound up with love together in one volume,
    What through the universe in leaves is scattered;

Substance, and accident, and their operations,
    All interfused together in such wise
    That what I speak of is one simple light.
                        —Paradiso, Canto 33

A woman who was a master of the Hidden Treasure told a student the story of two seekers who applied themselves to the Path over a span of fifty years.

One of them was cheerful and gregarious, pursuing knowledge in a style that reflected his sober nature. Like a mystic gardener, he moved with slow and steady deliberation, clearing the trail of rocks and leaves. If an obstacle couldn't be removed, he went around it. Each step was fraught with peril, yet he never tired of the journey. A fine scholar as well, he reverentially studied the *seers* who came before him. Over time, he shed the encumbrance of family, erotic entanglements, business dealings, and the like. By the end of the struggle, devoted to his siddha, he had forgotten what it was like to be lonely.

The other seeker ran headlong down the same Path, often falling and injuring herself, sometimes badly. She always managed to get back on her feet and resume the journey—or at least find respite in a village close by. She flung herself into all manner of controversies with both sexes, altered her consciousness with anything she got hold of, and tore out her hair when the dangerous mysteries and miseries of the world became too much. For years, she wandered through wilderness and desert before invariably catching sight of the mirage of palm trees that lined the Way (also a mirage). Her instinct to find what was true never wavered. The end came with an arched neck, remorseless tears, and a joyous yowl to the heavens.

The curious student asked, "Which one made it to Paradise?"

"Hold the coin of illusion in the palm of your hand," said the master. "On one side is the Path; on the other, the seeker. Cradling her newborn, a mother's heart is filled only by that which minted the coin[2]—she knows the engraver can be the only Truth in this audaciously radiant, counterfeit world."

---

2 Brahman.

RUN FOR YOUR LIFE

A woman described herself on dating sites as "a pansexual hellcat whose day job is clinical depression." The cycle of promiscuity was both cure and cause of a chronic, panicked melancholy. A girlhood friend who studied with a woman of knowledge kept encouraging her to find succor elsewhere; for years, she'd been inviting her to meet the guru, to no avail.

Nursing the wounds of her latest erotic duel, Chandra got further injured by the bomb fragments of the internet. She couldn't stop watching an OCD bird peck the eyes out of a snake, first one then the other, one then the other. The stunned serpent seemed almost embarrassed by its ignoble, fatal desecration. Swiping onward, she became possessed by a soundless three-minute CCTV video of a shlubby manchild in a parking garage, lifting a pretty girl's luggage into the trunk of a car. He was docile and chivalrously attentive while she chatted away but once she was in the driver's seat, he shot her in the head then blew his brains out. (Chandra scrutinized the tape for two days, in futile search of a cue for what was coming.) Lastly, she fixated on a mom who hacked up her daughters *Kill Bill*-style, all to punish her ex. Chandra did an excavation of the girls on IG and TikTok, obsessing over the acne, giggles, and sweet, sexy dances before teleporting herself into the kill room for their last moments on earth.

Chandra shared all the gory details with her girlfriend when she phoned.

A few days later, when calls and texts went unreturned, Addison dropped by for a wellness check. The apartment was in disarray; its renter, manic and unwashed.

"I think maybe we take you to the hospital now?" said Addison.

Chandra shook her head, saying, "This too shall pass." Though it did get her attention when Addie said she'd already spoken to her guru about "your whole situation."

"Oh goodie!" said Chandra. "Pray tell, what did Saint Elsewhere have to say?" She called her that because the woman always seemed to be traveling.

"When I told her about the bird and the snake . . . and the chubby little killer in the garage . . . and Fun Mom, slicing up her kids—"

"Wow, you were takin' notes, huh."

"—she just shook her head and kinda *very quietly* said, 'For a few moments, anthropology was forgotten.'"

"Huh?"

"'For a few moments, anthropology was forgotten.'"

"And what does *that* mean?"

"When she was getting her PhD, a colleague was studying cannibals in South America. He was down there measuring the height of burial mounds, the circumference of skulls, that sort of thing. One day, he noticed the tribe was doing a *lot* of staring. You know, gettin' . . . *fidgety*. The cannibals were hungry! So, he got the hell out of there. Back home, when he told my teacher about it, he said, 'For a few moments, anthropology was forgotten.'"

"Hahaha! What *else* did Saint Elsewhere say?"

"About the colleague?"

"About *me*, dummy. What else did she say about *me*."

"When I told her all the crap you were obsessing over . . . and your tragic fucking Hinge hookups—"

"*Jesus*, Addie. Throw me under the bus why don't you."

"—she got kinda, I don't know, sad. Probably she didn't, but she *looked* sad. Then she said sometimes there's nothing a person can do but run. You know, like the colleague did."

"Did she mean for you to run from me? Or for me to run from you."

"Good point! I'm pretty sure she meant *you* to run from whatever."

"Did she say anything else?" asked Chandra, genuinely interested now.

"She said that when a person can't run, they should hide under the bed."

~

That evening, Chandra was inspired to do just that.

The frame was high enough to put a yoga pad beneath.

She lay there for hours, thinking of Colleen Stan, the nineteen-year-old who was famously kidnapped and raped and kept in a lockbox beneath her captors' bed for seven years. (She spent half a day going down *that* YouTube rabbit hole.) In her meditations, Colleen was soon replaced by the anchoress Julian of Norwich, whom Chandra was entranced by as a Catholic schoolgirl. Saint Julian chose to be permanently confined in a monastic cell. Her thoughts drifted from Julian and Colleen to William Wordsworth, who likened a sonnet to "a convent's narrow room." At last, she grew sleepy and dreamed she was doing yoga. But soon the poses were supplanted by a series of strange movements . . .

On awakening, Chandra slid out from under the bedframe and ate breakfast while texting with Addison about the adventure of having a "sleep-under." (Addie said what she usually did: "You are *nuts*.") Utterly refreshed, she went to the little terrace and tried replicating the queer motions she learned in the dream, but they were already fading away.

She ubered to yoga and was surprised the old place wasn't there anymore. As if pulled by an invisible cord, she walked to a nearby dance studio. She wandered upstairs—the musky blast of heat and stretching bodies was familiar and welcoming. A class was just ending. As the practitioners slowly left, a new group entered.

"Chandra!"

"Addie, *what the fuck*. What are you—you are *not* a fucking yoga person!"

"We rent this space from the studio twice a week."

"We?"

"The group—my teacher. We do 'magical passes.'"

"What?"

"They're kinda like asanas . . . "

Flashing on the dream movements, all Chandra could think to say was, "For a few moments, anthropology is forgotten."

Suddenly, her friend made a beeline to a short, dynamic, turbaned woman who had just arrived. The student whispered and the woman looked over at the accidental guest. When she came back, Addison touched her arm and said, "Someone wants to meet you."

"Zounds and gadzooks, Saint Elsewhere's in the house! Looks like you're finally getting your wish."

"Isn't it funny? She loved that you had a 'sleep-under.' She's totally intrigued."

"Happy to have a meet and greet! But I've already *seen* the NXIVM doc—so if she thinks she's gonna brand my puss with a cauterizing pen, *nuh uh*. Ain't gonna happen."

"You're so wicked!" laughed Addison. "I mean it, though. She's *impressed*. She said you were the only one who ever really listened. No one else thought she was serious."

"About what?"

"The so-called benefits of crawling under the bed." As they walked over, Addison said, "Look, I'm just repeating what she said—ask her yourself."

JUMPERS

A devotee suffered from burnout. He followed the Way for many years but withheld a secret from his teacher: he was tired of doing service and felt taken advantage of. He began to wonder if his only purpose was to be a support system for the lazy, the weak, and the arrogant.

He was a large man of sunny disposition, a steady, clearheaded, compassionate friend and fellow traveler—the trusted cheerleader and helper to those of less experience who stumbled along the same arduous path. He was sleep-deprived because he never turned off his phone, wanting to be available any hour of the day or night. And he wasn't just there for crises of the intangible; he made hospital visits, went to funerals, and loaned money to those in need. (He was rarely paid back.) While not in a relationship himself, his piercing insights were much valued when it came to the usual romantic calamities. Ironically, one of the neediest seekers urged him to join a 12-Step group for his codependent behavior. Another suggested that therapy might help reveal the underlying cause of his compulsions. "Discover, uncover, discard," they said.

At last, he sought his teacher's counsel. When he confessed about the resentments he was harboring, the guru said, "Jump!" The student stared, uncomprehending. "*That* is the problem. You *watch* and you *worry*—about 'purpose.' About being *used*. But you never jump."

He took a long walk, mulling over his teacher's words. There was truth in what he said, of course . . . something always held him back. But what?

In the middle of "getting to the root," time and the world ended.

∽

He awakened to a disjointed realization that he was immobilized. As general awareness reassembled, he finally understood where he was. A nurse came in. When she saw that he was conscious, she whooped. She stood over him, beaming.

"Well, look who's here! Our big, beautiful boy. Welcome back!" She filled a glass of water and jimmied a straw into his mouth, above the cervical collar. She asked him to wiggle his toes, which he did, and she clapped. "What big, beautiful toes you have, Beautiful Boy!"

"What—what happened?" he slurred.

"You mean you don't know?" she said facetiously. "Beautiful Boy doesn't know he's a famous hero?" She said that a man threw himself off a three-story building—and Beautiful Boy's body broke the suicide's fall. "Tell ya one thing: that idiot's in better shape than *you* are. I say, 'Hey, pal, *next* time, look before you leap! And pick a higher floor, why don't you.'"

In the month that followed, he must have had a hundred visitors, all of whose lives he helped change in large and small ways. The staff lined up to applaud when he left the hospital in a Panama hat and with two gaily decorated canes instead of a walker. Naturally, he'd become a confidant to many of the janitorial workers, dieticians, physical therapists, and nurses—even a doctor or two—who affectionately called him their ESP (Emotional Support Patient).

Everyone called him Beautiful Boy, except for a ninety-year-old volunteer who addressed him as "Mr. Living Treasure," always with a little bow of respect.

⁓

The slapstick universe had demonstrated, by way of a deus ex machina pratfall, that he had no say in his own fate, let alone the fate of others; thus, old resentments became a blessed lightshow of purposeless destiny. Everyone noticed something different about him but only his teacher understood.

Occasionally, out of curiosity, those who sought his counsel asked if he knew what ever became of the man who jumped. "You're looking at him," he'd say. They weren't sure what kind of joke he was making but he always interrupted their confusion with these words:

"How can I help?"

FREE WILLY

A young man traveled to India to find a teacher. After some weeks, he met a good candidate. He attended *satsang* with a motley group of international pilgrims—but soon had his doubts.

One of the worrying things was the guru's fixation with a quote that he attributed to the Buddha: "Events happen, deeds are done, but there is no individual doer of the deed." It wasn't the quote that was troubling, but its dubious veracity; when he scoured the internet for the original source, he came up empty-handed. *Strange* . . . was he just improvising? Another obsessive mantra was, "All is predetermined." To the Advaita master, free will was an absurdity; if you believed in free will, it only meant that the belief itself had been predetermined. And yet, for the young man, the concept was essential. In college, the brilliant, bullheaded student dabbled in epistemology and was passionately opposed to so-called hard determinism.

Back from India, he doubled down, firing off a belligerent note to the ashram. "With all due respect," he wrote, "it is amoral to inculcate your impressionable, often desperate students with cynical tautologies rather than the ancient wisdom that they traveled so far—and at great personal expense—to seek." It should be said that some of his passion was misplaced because he was frustrated in many areas of his life. Earlier in the year, he went through a bad breakup and still had feelings for the girl, who, adding insult to injury, was already seeing someone else. On top of everything, he was directionless. Should he pursue a PhD to better arm himself against the enemies storming the ramparts of free will? Go wading again in the muddy castle moat of epigenetics, rogue neurons, and compatibalism? Or should he simply hunker down and finish the promising novel that he'd put aside in his teenage years . . .

Maybe it was time to get a grown-up job. He wouldn't be the first to write a book after office hours. If it worked for Kafka, it could work for him.

∾

A friend dragged him to a party in Echo Park. In his usual foul, pretentious mood, he was on his way out when a pastel goth girl waylaid him. *"You're* pretty gloomy—I want to talk to *you."* His game was rusty, but she handily took over.

He nearly choked on his Trader Joe's dolma when she said, "Do you believe in free will, Mr. Gloom? Better say yes or we're breaking the fuck up."

That was how he met his soulmate.

∾

Years later, his sister shared coffee with a friend she hadn't seen since high school. When she said that her brother was married and had two kids, the friend couldn't believe it.

"That's crazy!" she said. "I mean, we used to *date."*

"Oh my god, I forgot that!"

"William was *so sure* of himself—and even *then* he said he would never marry. He hated married people. Especially married people with children!"

"Sounds like Bro," she smiled. "I guess Crinoline tamed the beast."

"Crinoline?"

"The wifey. Apparently, her mother named her after a horsehair petticoat."

"Jesus. So, what was her trick? How did she tame the beast?"

"Who knows? But when they first met, all he talked about was how exactly *alike* they were."

"Ha! That'll do it every time."

"He works for her dad now."

"Doing what?"

"He owns an insurance company. Willy's an actuary—analyzes risk and all that."

"He was always super smart with numbers."

"And Crinoline owns a high-end photography gallery."

"Crinoline . . .—wait, wait," she said, trying to access what she already knew. "Is it—"

"The Crinoline Priesler Gallery."

"Oh my god, I *love* that place! I've been to *openings* there. The lady with the amazing tattoos?"

"That would be her. Has piercings too." She raised an eyebrow. "In all the wrong places, apparently. Or maybe those are the right places." They laughed. "She's crazy successful—reps people like Nan Goldin and Mary Ellen Mark. And lots of super-young edgy up-and-comers."

"Wow."

"And Willy's finally finishing his novel!"

"Really?" said the friend. "Your brother's *such* a good writer. He wrote *all the time* in high school. Remember?"

"Yup. He puts the kids to bed, then scribble-scribble-scribbles. He's a fucking machine, doesn't even take Adderall. I *hate* people who don't take Adderall."

"I love that he's writing."

"I think he actually found a publisher."

"Honey, that is *so* cool."

"Life is funny, right?"

"I guess. In the past few years, the joke's kinda been on me."

"It's one of those weird things—my brother—after all that spiritual bullshit—you know, *meeting* Crinoline, *getting* married, *having* kids, finding the *perfect life*—it feels to me like it was—what's the word? Like it was—"

"Meant to be?"

"Yeah, but it's just one word."

"Preordained?"

"Yes! Pre-fucking-*ordained*." She touched her friend's hand and said, "Now tell me about *you* and the big joke life's been playing. I've been talking nonstop and I'm boring myself."

THE ROOT OF THE PROBLEM

A student heard stories of a famous abbot who was ruined by his notorious obsession with a woman. So, he asked his teacher about the one called Kyema—otherwise known as "Lovesick."

"At a relatively young age," he answered, "Kyema Rinpoche was already a legendary teacher in Japan. A half-century ago, he fulfilled his destiny to journey to America, where he became the abbot of a monastery in New Hampshire before establishing himself in Los Angeles. He did well here; the climate suited him. And of course, he became an essential part of the sangha, venerated for his profound wisdom and discipline.

"What I am speaking of happened in Kyema's eighty-third year. There was a movie cameraman that was a longtime visitor to the monastery. He brought his girlfriend to sit zazen. When the couple separated, he never returned, but she stayed on, and excelled. She was a theater actress— earnest, diligent, a wounded girl of extraordinary beauty. In time, she revealed to the Rinpoche that her *métier* was pornographic films. One day after sesshin, she came to him weeping, saying that she finally understood 'the root of the problem.' When he asked what she meant, the girl spread her legs. Holding the flower open with her fingers, she said, 'I am its slave.' The abbot was mesmerized by what he saw—and believe me, he'd seen such things before! *In that moment, Kyema became a slave as well.* Seventy years of discipline vanished like a mirage . . .

"He disguised his predicament for a few months and kept it hidden from *himself* as well. It was of no use. The girl underwent a change too. There was no physical relationship—that was out of the question! Yet the more dependent he grew, the more impetuous and demanding she became. When the actress finally made good on daily threats to abandon her practice, the old man was distraught.

"Kyema found out where she lived. Naturally, she was quite surprised when he showed up with a small entourage. . . . He couched his visit in concern—a teacher's encouragement that she return to the Three Refuges of the Buddha, the Dharma, the Sangha. She thought about it for a few days and said no. But the Rinpoche kept coming to the house (by taxi now), and when she told him that his entreaties were useless, he fell on his knees and proclaimed his love. She was laughing inside yet couldn't help being moved by the gesture. Kyema felt great shame. He said that he could not return to the zendo, so she put him up in a little room off the garage.

"The first week, she was amused. Friends from all walks of life were invited to meet her esteemed new housemate. He was a novelty—a love-struck old monk who literally washed the feet of the actress whom he now called 'Queen Maya, mother of Shakyamuni.' After a while, as one may have expected, his presence became a nuisance. She began to abuse him. Partygoers took drugs in front of Kyema and the woman laughed at him and made him wear diapers. She spread her legs and pushed his face into her, which made him recoil, fueling her wrath. Squads of sangha elders arrived, begging him to come back but he hid in his room and locked the door. Finally, she threw him out.

"When his students found Kyema in a homeless encampment, he pretended not to know who they were. The perplexed, frightened disciples grabbed at straws: Might all this be an elaborate ruse, designed for their benefit? But the theory didn't hold, because it wasn't his style of teaching. It felt all wrong . . .

"Within a few months, the zendo fell apart. The sangha spoke harshly of Kyema Rinpoche, calling him a fraud and a laughingstock, but the simple truth was that their pride had been wounded. How could they have allowed themselves to be duped? Many couldn't get past the shock of what happened. (Which was foolish, because that would have been a wonderful teaching.) Another abbot—from London—took his place. He was strong. Things came together and in the space of a few years, the zendo thrived.

"To the end, the smell of her clung to him like celestial residue. One day on the street, he heard a shout: it was the young woman, yelling from a passing car. She stepped onto the sidewalk and looked him over, first with pity, then utter contempt. Like an animal, she snarled, 'If you loved your precious *nothingness* the way you loved my cunt, you'd be walking the streets of Paradise instead of living under a freeway!'"

The prudish student gasped at his teacher's explicit language.

"Kyema died that night. He had indeed been making his home beneath an overpass, in a nest that he fashioned out of twigs—woven in such a way as to mimic the sex of the one who had forsaken him. I was told that his last words before disappearing inside were, 'Time to enter the root of the problem.' Whether or not the so-called problem was solved before his last breath remains unknown. I do hope so! I prefer to believe the lady's insult was the shove he needed."

The teapot whistled and the teacher poured two cups. He encouraged the student to drink; after a few minutes, the color returned to his cheeks.

"I've waited a long time for the actress to return. If that day happens, I will thank her and provide refuge."

The student suddenly thought to say, "*Kyema* . . . where have I heard that?"

"Ah, yes—it means sadness, weariness. A certain sorrow. It is often used at the beginning of chants." He straightened his spine and intoned, "'Kyema! Now as the bardo of the time of death appears . . . at the time of separating from my body of flesh and blood, I should know that it is an illusion—'" An impish smile broke the abbot's recitation. "You've reminded me now! The club where she danced was called Paradise. It burned to the ground in 1992 during the riots."

DOUBLE FEATURE

Back in the day, she was an athlete and a dancer who made her living as a body double for Susan Sarandon and Kathleen Turner. She never kept a boyfriend more than a year. The clingy ones sulked when she wouldn't let them tag along on spiritual retreats; the bad boys took her absence as an opportunity to cheat. What good were any of them? They were mere echoes of Gurdjieff's words—human beings are born in sleep, live in sleep, and die in sleep. Yet, as much as she strived for wakefulness, it galled her that she too was one of the walking dead.

Still, she was confident that her body would transport her to satori. Her favorite thing was sacred dancing, part of what was called The Work, or the Fourth Way. The Work spoke of "the three ways"—of the fakir, the monk, and the yogi. The Fourth Way transcended all, freeing one from the soul's entombment. In time, though, she tired of cults and cultish talk. There were too many spooky, passive ladies; too many pervy, power-tripping men with charts, diagramming everyone to oblivion.

She preferred to dance alone now, in her living room.

She became an uneasy tenant of her body, resenting even its respirations and heartbeats, seething over the arcane, hidden processes that she would never be able to witness or understand. She was apprehensive of its good health because bouts of illness naturally followed long and uneventful periods of well-being.

In her forties, she had a slipped disc and got addicted to opiates. She was supposed to take magnesium so she wouldn't get constipated, but she didn't. One morning, she felt sweaty and strange and realized she couldn't remember the last time she moved her bowels. The urge to defecate was overwhelming but when she shut herself in the toilet, nothing happened, except that she leaked clear, foul-smelling fluid. In crippling pain, she drove herself to the ER and shut herself in the bathroom again and nearly died of an intestinal obstruction. No one could hear her scream.

After that, she grew obsessed with trapped bodies. She was haunted by the news story of a woman who dared her drunk boyfriend to squeeze himself into a suitcase. When he did, she sat on the lid so she could lock it, then left the apartment. How many hours did it take for him to die? With each scream of her name, he'd be running out of air. He would barely have had room to flail. . . . There was another story of an experienced spelunker who got wedged upside-down in a foot-and-a-half-wide crevice. He was in good spirits but remained out of reach. The rescuers couldn't even give him morphine.

She was also intrigued by a woman who volunteered to stay in a small underground cave for two years, monitored by scientists. When they finally came for her, she thought she'd only been there a few months and was upset the mission was aborted. Time had collapsed.

In her twenties, a boyfriend who was into physics read her a Borges story that bewitched her. (Reading to her out loud was the only thing she ever liked about him.) In "The Garden of Forking Paths," a translator spent his life studying a mysterious manuscript called *The Book of Mystery*. He comes to realize that the single word its author never used was "time," and deduces that Time must be the book's secret theme. Another writing that possessed her was a shaman's description of Time as a tunnel of infinite length and width, with reflective furrows. "Every furrow is infinite, and their number is infinite." He said the life force of sentient beings confined their gaze to one furrow, where they remained trapped. According to the shaman, Time is the essence of attention, the place where "ultimate awareness" could be enticed.

But she lost her taste for such divagations long ago.

∽

At sixty, during travels in Mexico, she met a woman of knowledge who had, in the New Age parlance of the day, a "big field." Meaning, a field of energy that almost anyone could sense, even if they weren't conscious of it or could put into words what they saw or felt.

The two strangers stood before a chacmool—one of the majestic, pre-Columbian reclining stone figures that prop themselves up on their elbows, heads swiveling to stare with implacable indifference beyond the horizon.

"This one looks over its shoulder to the *left*," said the elegant white-haired woman, "from the place we are *now*—Tula. Its 'twin' looks to the *right*—from the Yucatan. Their gaze meets through time and space. The *anthropologists* say they're sportsmen or priests; anthropologists say all sorts of stupid things. What they *can't* know, because they cannot *see,* is that each of us has two luminous spheres: a physical body and an energy body. The vibrational 'double' waits for us beyond the border. It can be accessed in ordinary life but only from a place of inner silence and impeccable discipline." She glanced in the direction of the sculpture. "The Self dreams the *double*, and the double dreams the *Self,* each yearning for reunion."

Over lunch, she learned they were practically neighbors in LA. When she told her new friend that she was a body double in the movies, the woman smiled and said, "How apropos!" Then: "The Chacmool's look of emptiness comes from the vigilance required to guard dreamers and dreaming sites . . . *philosophers* call it the split between mind and body— the 'mind/body problem'—but the *true* dichotomy is between the *physical* and *energy* bodies. You see, when we're born, the spheres are perfectly aligned. But as we get older, we begin to believe the social consensus that the physical world is all there is. We die without having awakened the magical double, and there's no way to jump into the void of pure perception without it." She looked toward the Pyramid of Quetzalcoatl. "The *real* love affair is between the physical body and the energy body. All those rom-coms," she said, "done steered us wrong."

"But you said you could access it 'in ordinary life.' How?"

"You were listening!" she shouted, like a proud mother. "We access it through something called *intent*. With *intent*, one can change course, just as the course of rivers are altered by the erosion of wind and time."

Her apprenticeship lasted fifteen years—until the chacmool sorceress jumped into the void.

~

Recently, she ran into Susan Sarandon at the Brentwood Country Mart.

"Susan! It's Ermine Jakoby—I was your body double on *Thelma*."

The actress was exuberantly gracious. After chitchatting, she drolly asked, "Where were you when I needed you? I've driven off *lots* of cliffs since then—coulda used a double!" She winced. "Oh, that sounded *terrible*—"

"No, you're fine."

"My god, it's coming up on thirty-five years. Wasn't it a wonderful time?"

"It was amazing."

Taking her hand, she said, "*Thank you* for saying hello, Ermine. Just: thank you."

"You know I'm there for you, Susan. Next time, we'll jump together."

"It's a date—might be sooner than you think! Haha."

They hugged again and parted ways.

WISHBONES

. . . Exiled on the earth among the jeering crowd,
His giant wings keep him from walking.

—Baudelaire, *The Albatross*

But ask now the beasts, and they shall teach thee; and the fowls
of the air, and they shall tell thee. Or speak to the earth, and it
shall teach thee; and the fishes of the sea shall declare unto thee.

—Job, 12:7

*This fanciful story was told to me at Peet's by a seventy-five-year-old surfer
named John Shockley. We struck up a conversation while waiting for our coffees
and when I told him about the anthology I was compiling, his eyes lit up. "I
might have one for you," he mulled, with a twinkle in his eye. A cloud of second
thoughts scuttled across his face. "Though I'm not sure mine'll fit with what you
got going." We settled in at an outdoor table. After getting further acquainted,
John somewhat sheepishly confessed that the tale he had in mind "was inspired
by ol' Master Bidpai. Let's just say my little story is an amateur's stab at greatness." (The last, said with a wink.) He was referring of course to the majestic*
Kalila and Dimna: Selected Fables of Bidpai, *which he encouraged me to
read (in my case, reread) "in the Ramsay Wood translation. You can just go
ahead and throw all the other versions in the trash."*

*I was skeptical, and unprepared—hence, no tape recording. But the fable
(the longest in this humble volume) definitely passed muster. What follows is a
best-effort transcription, from memory.[3] —ed.*

---

3   At a second meeting, asked if he had another yarn, John said, "Th-th-th-
    that's all, folks. But I do have in mind a conniving raven who teaches a mon-
    goose to surf—for nefarious reasons, of course."

While everyone knows a thing or two about albatrosses—their awkwardness on land, their majesty in the air—what really seems to make people experts on the topic is their familiarity with the outdated idiom of something burdensome "becoming an albatross around one's neck." Few are aware the expression comes from Coleridge's poem "The Rime of the Ancient Mariner," wherein a deckhand curses ship and crew by killing the giant seafowl, and as punishment is forced to wear the carcass *idiomatically*. Even fewer know that swabbies once considered the albatross sacred because of their belief that the creature ferried souls of dead sailors to the heavens. With your indulgence, I'd like to add that in terms of marathon flights (air-athons?), albatrosses beat the bar-tailed godwit *and* the common swift wings-down, spending their first five years without touching land—and can circle the globe in about six weeks. *And* . . . when not snatching fishes from the briny, they take ten-second power naps in the clouds! Just more thing: they rarely divorce. An ornithologist friend of mine called them "the most faithful bird by a long shot."

Okay—I think that's enough for now. So, let's get on with it. . . .

A magnificent albatross called Neverland was on his way to a much-desired rendezvous with his wife, Alba, whose name was never meant to be an abbreviation of the seabird; rather, it summed up the arctic whiteness of her beak, plumage, and talons. The striking couple met as teenagers and were now past middle age. To keep the marriage lively, they agreed to gather in far-flung places after each year-long separation, and this time chose a lagoon in California fed by the mighty Malibu Creek. Long ago, while nesting in New Zealand, an Okarito kiwi told Alba about the spot and how the Spaniards had smudged the Chumash Indian phrase *U-mali-wu*—"It makes a loud noise there"—into *Malibu*. Because the kiwi couldn't fly, it was especially prone to flights of fancy, but still. The idea stayed in Alba's head.

"Malibu . . ."

There was something so romantic about it!

When the couple crash-landed at dusk, they thought it was paradise. The lagoon was a maddeningly picturesque community of herons, grackles, turkey vultures, egrets, pelicans, cormorants, crows, seagulls, mallards, goshawks, terns, and snowy plovers. It was the end of the workday, and most were heading home to their nests—needless to say, Neverland and Alba's arrival threw a wrench into the commute.

The raptors were the only ones who could remotely play it cool.

At close to nineteen feet, Neverland just may have had the longest wingspan of any living thing, but the curiosities didn't end there; Alba, the mobile essence of whiteness, was an apparition of startling beauty. Her luminous lack of pigment commanded the herons to furtively tamp down their delicate sprigs of virginal wedding veil feathers and humbly slink away, while the inquisitive snowy plovers, after erupting in an anarchic chorus, skittered toward the missus like so many stroboscopic groupies. Rascally ravens stayed away (except for one who flew off to alert the mayor) and a half-dozen Canadian geese honked like angry motorists trapped in a bottleneck. Grackles and gulls gathered in gossipy groups to cast a wary glance, deciding something must be done.

After a huddle, the goshawk stepped forward—most convenient, in that Red Eye happened to be the only bird present and accounted for who was courageous enough to make an introduction. With a flourish that managed to look both silly and noble, the raptor *walked* over so as not to startle the lagoon's strange, formidable sightseers. After a bit of chin-wagging, he cordially invited them to the CAC conclave that was to begin shortly after dark.

The monthly board meeting of the Center for Avian Control was held in a mountain cavern lit by thousands of fireflies, who were more than willing to provide the electrical, in exchange for a once-a-week moratorium on the consumption of members of the Lampyridae family (including distant cousins). When Neverland and Alba appeared, CAC officials were already seated in nervous anticipation. The albatrosses made a stately if equivocal ingress, unsure of how to conduct themselves, of what might be in store. As the guests of honor lumbered in, their enormous wings held aloft by gyrating gulls so as not to drag along the ground, they were ushered directly to the front of the auditorium. The mayor, a noble, fierce-looking osprey, perched on the lectern while shouting jubilant welcomes and salutations.

After the usual pleasantries were exchanged, the eponymously named Mayor (who often went by the tautonym "Mayor Mayor") began the delicate business of sorting it all out. What were they doing here? How long did they plan to stay? What were their *needs*? But just below the surface of hail-fellow-well-met, tensions ran high. The cormorants started a rumor: upon reaching retirement age, birds "such as these" were certain to be on the lookout for a place to *settle down*—a euphemism for divide and conquer. In response, Neverland stifled a laugh and confidently reassured the mayor that their stay would be brief; to do otherwise was "genetically improbable." With an abundance of charm, he added, "We apologize for any disruption our presence may have caused. This place . . ."—there was a catch in his voice—"is simply where we have chosen to spend our second honeymoon." He gave Alba a much appreciated, crowd-winning peck on the bleached supercilium. "And of course, we shall leave immediately if we are not welcome. Having said that, I am not being politic when I proclaim Malibu and its lagoon to be, talons down, the loveliest place on Earth. In all modesty, having circled this watery blue planet many hundreds of times, I believe I am duly qualified to make such a proclamation."

Mayor Mayor smiled and nodded vigorously but Neverland's genial response only intensified suspicions that the interlopers had domination in mind. Who could stop such intimidating creatures from overthrowing the king, even if the king were disguised as a mayor?

Just then, Double-Cross, the raven who took earlier flight with the clarion "The 'trosses are coming! The 'trosses are coming!" (one if by land, two if by sea) discreetly jetted to the rostrum to whisper in his boss's ear a reminder of their favorite treatise, *The Art of War*. Hence, there was no doubt it was Sun Tzu's axiom "Keep your enemies close" that the redundant mayor was thinking of when he spontaneously offered Neverland the unparalleled position of President of the Lagoon. He sweetened the pot by adding that the sinecure came replete with staff, lodging, and a healthy stipend, pithily summarized as "All the fish you can eat." The board was outraged by his foolish and uncharacteristic largesse, until taking note of something that Alba and Neverland had missed: an exchange of secret, steely looks between the grand ole osprey and his . . . well, ravenous consigliere. Thus reassured, having grasped there was a conspiracy afoot that no doubt redounded to their best interests, the gathering of functionaries burst into a hail of "Yeet!"s, hip-hip-hoorays, and sundry shrill hosannas of brown-nosery that raised (and muddied) the roof.

Later that night, the old marrieds talked things over on shifting sands.

The moon was full, reflecting off Alba's wings in a lunar duet. She confessed to being tired of circumnavigating the globe and conceded the idea of "settling down" (she playfully used the cormorants' phrase) wasn't as farfetched as it sounded. Not to her, anyway. She tearfully told her husband that for years her air-time had been awash in sorrow whilst soaring from New Zealand to the Aleutian Islands and the shores of Japan, to Laysan and the Pacific Northwest, pining over their long absences from each other—or worse, the thought that she might never see him again should some terrible fate befall either one of them, an admission that broke Neverland's heart in two. Besides, Alba would soon turn sixty and had given birth to more than 250 chicks; though still fertile, she'd frankly had enough of motherhood. "What better place to retire, Mr. President?" she said adoringly, with a flirty hint of civic pride. Nudging his belly with her beak, she enticed, "All the fish we can eat!"

Wishing only for his beloved's happiness, Neverland conceded.

$\sim$

The busy week before his inaugural was spent in orientation.

By sharp light of day, the place looked nothing like its first impression, and Neverland was stupefied by the weird disarray of goings-on. The smug, affluent CAC board members didn't in any way reflect the lagoon's demographic of citizens, all of whom seemed to be flying crest-long toward extinction. The turkey vultures weighed half what they should, and the pelicans were so plump they could barely fly—all this, owing to the "wellness" regime designed by the mayor's heron-boy, Dr. Hieronymus, a high-handed egret who'd replaced the vultures' carrion and garbage diet with seed-like nutrients from a recipe he concocted during a catnap. (The doctor was always sleeping or on the verge of it.) In contrast, the pelicans were fed only pizza and moldy bread scavenged from dumpsters. To keep spirits up, Hieronymus cheerily coined the chant, "Eat the crust, not the crustacean," which all were encouraged to sing—or else. The cormorants (vilified as elitists simply because, on taking flight, they resembled elegant spears) were given the strong suggestion to *slouch* during takeoff. If they dared disobey, weights were cruelly sewn to their rumps.

Neverland was further outraged by his tour of a camouflaged section of the estuary that housed mallards in cages of petrified kelp, for the crime of honking after hours. Dizzying new laws were announced each morning, enforced by a small army of bullying, great horned owls. The most compliant denizens were the smallest and least threatening—sandpipers, swallows, snowy plovers—but even they had to observe strict curfews imposed to curb their instinct to "incessantly scurry about like idiots." *How rude!* thought Neverland. Dr. Hieronymus brewed something up to curtail the recent pandemic of ADHD, but the EUA cure (Emergency Use Authorization) killed most of the patients. Spared by their innate theatrical skills, great and little egrets entertained CAC officers and their families in makeshift cabarets. When at last the obese pelicans voiced objections to such quixotic, draconian governance, those who hadn't drowned during high tide were finished off by mercenaries of prey—flight nationalists hired out of Ventura County.

Ravens were exempt from prosecution because of Double-Cross's gift of speaking untruth to power. . . .

That night, Neverland solemnly enfolded his wife in his wings, creating a chamber impervious to the eavesdropping of Mayor Mayor's dragonfly dragoons.

"I have some news you won't like to hear, my darling: It shan't be long until the lagoon is no more. Eggs are not being laid; the few that are, I'm afraid, find their way to the black market. Oh, the depraved and dastardly things I've observed!" He could hardly contain his rage. "The thieves, Alba—thieves and murderers!—are released without bail . . . why, an hour ago, I witnessed a magistrate declining to press charges against a gang of gulls for the drunken massacre of forty juvenile plovers! For Garuda's sake, Alba, even *humans* put plovers under federal protection! When the gulls admitted doing it 'for fun' (can you imagine?), the judge declared them mentally ill and acquitted them. He even went so far as to call them heroes for not causing *more* mayhem due to the hardships of their disabled, gullish lives. . . . The mayor has invited us to a supper tonight *in their honor*, where each thug will be given a medal—and sacks of money ten times the income of the average working wing-beater. The *money*, Alba! Stockpiles and stockpiles of bad money! The black-crowned night heron tells me it isn't worth the seaweed it's printed on!"

Tears sprung from his wife's eyes as she drooped her head on his wishbone. Alba was so sad—with all the lagoon's flaws and imperfections, she thought she could endure the place, *any* place, so long as they were together. But now she knew that it was impossible.

"It gets worse," he said gravely. "As I toured the jail today, a sympathetic mallard whispered that he overheard the guards discussing a plan." He solemnly paused. "At tonight's celebration, you and I, precious one, are to be done away with! My suspicion is that we shall become the feast's main course . . ."

Alba gasped, almost loud enough to be heard by the snoopy, winged operatives hovering close by. "Husband! How could they do this to their fellow birds? *How*—" A seizure of tears shuffled the symmetry of her face

before she regained composure. "Do you think it's like this everywhere? That the whole world's lost its mind?"

"I hope not, darling . . . with all my heart, I hope such a thing isn't true!" He kissed away a single tear. "But I can tell you this: I'm not anxious to find out."

"Things change so quickly, and we've been in the sky so long . . ."

His wing on hers, he said, "But there's *good* news too: I hereby declare these damnable rendezvous anniversaries null and void! Dry your eyes, darling one, and we'll alight forthwith."

Moments later, they watched the whirligigging patch of earth once called *U-mali-wu* recede and sent their silent prayers.

They didn't look back.

It's been a long time now since they touched ground.

Alba delights in dive-bombing his ear, to murmur sweet nothings. "Husband?" she'll say. "It's been five long years since we left the lagoon and I'm still walking on air."

She hasn't tired of the nickname she gave him, either: Neverpart.

STICKER SHOCK

As this book neared an end, I sifted through the tales, debating whether to include one of my own.

Well, why not?

My decision, patient reader, was made for the simple reason that it might bolster the promise of the collection's first few pages: "Those on the Hidden Path do walk among us, in the here and now." If one's eyes and heart remain open, the maxim shines bright as day.

As it has always been, saints are everywhere—and nowhere.

While the following may not be on par with the preceding stories, I hope you can at least find its kinship. —ed.

~

I once wrote a novel about an actor, a practicing Buddhist who suffers a traumatic brain injury from a random assault. Because of my protagonist's spiritual bent, the book drew on assorted mystical texts that found their way to my library through the years. Many of the volumes, like Chökyi Nyima Rinpoche's *The Bardo Guidebook*, are well-known; others, such as the one on *phowa*—the transference of consciousness at death—were more obscure. I used excerpts from those sources throughout, always with attribution. But legally, when it came time to publish, I needed more. My editor asked me to contact each author for permission. Perhaps I was naïve but what happened next was a nasty surprise: every single one of them turned me down.

It was a terrible omen. While it was true I hadn't yet heard from the writer of *The Bardo Guidebook*, I had every reason to believe the answer would be the same: *No!* I started to panic because my entire novel was anchored by that raw, luminous masterwork.

Finally, I received a letter with the Rinpoche's succinct message:

Use whatever you wish, regardless of length. No fee.

By then, I was so raw and luminous myself that I burst into tears.

Auspiciously, a friend that I had told about the close call (and its happy resolution) rang a few days later to say the Rinpoche happened to be on his way to Northern California for an "emptiness and compassion" retreat. Grateful to Providence, I immediately signed up.

I wanted to thank him in person.

Before driving to Leggett, I did my homework. The eldest son of a great Dzogchen master, the Rinpoche's family fled Tibet during the Chinese invasion when he was just eighteen months old. Soon after, the infant was recognized as a *tulku*, a reincarnated master of his lineage. Now the abbot of a monastery in Katmandu, he had also founded the center where I was making my *yātrā*, or devotional journey.

The long coastal journey was meditative. Dustin Hoffman, of all people, drifted into my reverie. Decades ago, the actor's newborn had a medical emergency, but his pediatrician was out of town. Another doc stepped in and saved the baby's life. Coincidentally, the pinch hitter had just become a father himself; the grateful Hoffman became the boy's godfather. It's no exaggeration to say that by allowing me to reprint his words, Chökyi Nyima saved my child.

I checked into a motel then drove a short distance to the lush 250-acre property. The spectacular green landscape was redolent of grace. After registering at the Great Hall, I went for a swim in a crystal-clear lake, and it was like floating in the prayer of a dream. I'd gone from abjection to exaltation and found myself saying aloud "How lucky am I."

As I dried off, the caricature of a kitschy tourist barreled toward me with a fathead grin. Without introduction, he kibitz-bombed with questions: *Where do you live? Did you drive or did you fly? Are you new to retreats or an old hand? What do you do for a living?* My curt answers telegraphed my reluctance to engage, but he kept doubling down. His accent sounded German, so I named him The Bürgermeister in my head—one of Dad's weird, random pejoratives when encountering bombastic, petty bureaucrat types. I even dressed the dufus in lederhosen, like a paper doll cutout. (I had to remind myself that workshops like this attracted their share of freaks and geeks.) The only one I wanted to speak with was the Rinpoche.

When I could take no more, I rudely walked away.

∽

The lecture wasn't until dark. Back at the motel, I called the friend who alerted me to Rinpoche's visit and groused about Friedrich von Fuckface. He laughed.

"Put a sticker on your chest that says SILENCE," he said. "Means you're on silent retreat. Great schmuck-repellant."

∽

I showed up early at the hall, in a much better mood. The sticker acted as armor.

Chökyi Nyima entered to scattered applause from newbies—they were clueless that such a greeting, while traditional for performers, was frowned upon. The tulku made an impish smile of surprise before doing a brilliant split-second impersonation of Chaplin twirling his cane. Everyone roared with laughter. The anachronistic comic gesture not only broke the ice of idolatry but was greatly appreciated by the hapless clappers who had been shamed by the slings and disapproving scowls of a handful of fussy OG buddhaheads. But for me, the demonstration underscored the endless generosity of Rinpoche's compassionate nature.

He spoke for an hour and mesmerized.

After a while, unexpectedly, I started to deeply focus on the translator. Not once did he hesitate or stumble. Sometimes the teacher spoke for as long as five minutes and when he was done, nodded for the interpreter to take over. The latter would wince then smile, and the audience chuckle (Rinpoche along with them) because the task seemed utterly hopeless. After a few belly breaths, the translator began his flawless, poetically nuanced recapitulation. The exquisite, contrapuntal interplay between the two was sheer telepathy. I wasn't sure how much English the Rinpoche spoke but often caught him nodding at his cohort as if in celebration of the exquisite aptness of a particular word or phrase. The effect of their fusion put me in a numinous trance.

As the evening came to a close, I was enthralled to recognize a passage from *The Bardo Guidebook* that gave inexpressible solace:

> The mediocre yogin has three ways of dying: like a small child, like a wandering beggar, and like a lion. Like a small child means there is no concept of dying or not dying. Like a wandering beggar means not to care about the circumstances of one's death. Having cut attachments to circumstances is called dying like a lion—when the lion knows it is about to die, it disappears and dies alone.

With a shock, I realized all at once that the translator was none other than "The Bürgermeister."

The revelation shamed and unhinged.

I became nauseated and left the hall in a daze . . .

I walked long enough in the cold night air that by the time I finally became conscious of my surroundings, I was completely lost. Trees blotted out the moon; there was only darkness. I was unable to move. Eventually, I heard voices and saw a clot of people gathered on the pathway. My legs moved toward them as they entered a cabin whose light provided the only illumination. I shouted for directions back to the Great Hall. A monk approached with a warm smile; when I saw that it was Chökyi Nyima, I broke down and ugly-cried. His retinue kindly backed away—no doubt, they'd seen it all before.

The Rinpoche put a loving arm around my shoulder as I spewed about the melodrama of all the Buddhist teachers saying *No!*—except for him, who said Yes. In a tumble of emotions, I even shared about the lakeside encounter with the translator, hoisting myself on the petard of my own cruel, judgy heart.

He touched his forehead to mine and kept it there until our breaths were synchronous. Without opening his eyes, he said, "Teacher and translator . . . *same.*" He looked at the sticker I was wearing and giggled. With smiling solemnity, he offered, "Sometimes best to be silent." Then: "*Your books die like lions.* No attachment—no judgment. Catch up to books! Run! Catch up! *Become book.*"

He began walking toward the moonlit cabin's open door where the others were waiting. Suddenly, as if having forgotten something, he rushed over. He stood in front of me, with the keen, distracted expression of someone working through a mathematical problem.

"Best to die like lion," he said. "But *okay* to die like beggar, too—or child. Child not too bad! Child very, very good . . ."

I bowed, peeling SILENCE from my shirt.

Grabbing it from my hand, he slapped the sticker back on in admonishment. "You must keep! Help you catch up *quicker.*" He touched my forehead again with his and whispered, "Wear it well."

NATIONAL
GEOGRAPHIC
TRAVELER

PORTUGAL

by Fiona Dunlop
photography by Tino Soriano

National Geographic
Washington D.C.

CONTENTS

Pp. 2–3: Rock formations of the Ponta da Piedade, south of Lagos, Algarve
Opposite: Shops and outdoor cafés line pedestrianized Rua Augusta, in Lisbon's Baixa district.

TRAVELING WITH EYES OPEN

Alert travelers go with a purpose and leave with a benefit. If you travel responsibly, you can help support wildlife conservation, historic preservation, and cultural enrichment in the places you visit. You can enrich your own travel experience as well.

To be a geo-savvy traveler:

- Recognize that your presence has an impact on the places you visit.

- Spend your time and money in ways that sustain local character. (Besides, it's more interesting that way.)

- Value the destination's natural and cultural heritage.

- Respect the local customs and traditions.

- Express appreciation to local people about things you find interesting and unique to the place: its nature and scenery, music and food, historic villages and buildings.

- Vote with your wallet: Support the people who support the place, patronizing businesses that make an effort to celebrate and protect what's special there. Seek out local shops, restaurants, and inns. Use tour operators who love their home—who love taking care of it and showing it off. Avoid businesses that detract from the character of the place.

- Enrich yourself, taking home memories and stories to tell, knowing that you have contributed to the preservation and enhancement of the destination.

That is the type of travel now called geotourism, defined as "tourism that sustains or enhances the geographical character of a place- its environment, culture, aesthetics, heritage, and the well-being of its residents."

TRAVELER

PORTUGAL

ABOUT THE AUTHORS & THE PHOTOGRAPHER

■ Author **Fiona Dunlop's** peripatetic life has led her from her native Australia to an upbringing in London, and subsequent jobs in continental Europe followed by a return to London. During 15 years spent in Paris, she was strongly involved in the arts before concentrating on journalism. Since then, she has written for numerous international magazines and national newspapers. She has spent long research periods in developing countries working on travel guides to India, Indonesia, Singapore and Malaysia, Vietnam, Mexico, Costa Rica, and southern Africa. More recent publications include *In the Asian Style* (on Asian design) and *New Tapas,* an illustrated book on Spain's tapas bar tradition. In between her more exotic travels, Dunlop has regularly visited Spain to write articles and books, including *National Geographic Traveler: Spain.*

■ **Emma Rowley** wrote the updates and sidebars for this edition. With a university degree in Spanish and Portuguese, Rowley moved from her native United Kingdom to Portugal and spent nine years working for an Oxford-based travel company, managing trips in rural Spain, Portugal, and the Azores. She has since turned her skills to travel writing, contributing to more than a dozen different guidebooks and related articles.

■ Born and raised in Barcelona, Spain, **Tino Soriano** divides his work between photojournalism and travel photography. He has received a First Prize from the World Press Photo Foundation as well as awards from UNESCO, Fujifilm, and Fotopres. In addition to Portugal, since 1988 Soriano has photographed in Spain, France, Italy, Sicily, Scotland, and South Africa on assignments for National Geographic. His work has also appeared in *Geo, Merian, Der Spiegel, Paris Match, La Vanguardia, El Pais,* and other major magazines. Soriano likes to write, and he has published *El Futuro Existe* (a story about children with cancer); *Travel Photography* and *Beats From a Hospital* (both in Spanish); and *Dalí, 1904–2004.* He has also photographed for the following guides in the National Geographic Traveler series: *Sicily, Madrid,* and *Florence & Tuscany.*

CHARTING YOUR TRIP

Most travelers to Portugal visit Lisbon, Porto, the Algarve, and possibly Madeira, but you should also explore some of the hinterland, with its dramatic scenery of mountains, cork forests, and rivers; delve into its history and cultural heritage, visiting castles, monasteries, and medieval villages; and sit back to enjoy its gastronomy and fine wines. This destination has become a favorite of visitors from all over the world.

How to Get Around

Portugal's main cities, Lisbon and Porto, are best explored on foot, as many sites are within a short distance of one other. Be sure to take comfortable, sturdy shoes, as both cities are hilly, and many of their streets are cobbled and slippery in wet weather. Where transport is necessary, both cities have efficient metro systems as well as historic trams. For north-south travel within the country, the excellent express train service (Alfa Pendular; see Travelwise p. 284) runs between Porto in the north and Faro in the south, through Coimbra and Lisbon. Other cities are covered by frequently stopping, intercity connections; regional trains meander along scenic routes but can be slow. To reach more remote areas, a rental car is indispensable, giving you the freedom to explore at your own pace. Book online before arrival (see Travelwise pp. 283–284).

Admission Costs

The $–$$$$$ scale used in this guidebook delineates entry fees into attractions:
$ = Under $5
$$ = $5–$10
$$$ = $10–$20
$$$$ = $20–$30
$$$$$ = Over $30

If You Only Have a Week

Immerse yourself in the bustle of Lisbon life before discovering some of Portugal's other prominent

The Marquês de Pombal was responsible for much of Lisbon's orderly appearance.

attractions. The suggested itinerary keeps up a brisk pace; for a more relaxed trip simply omit some of the recommendations.

Begin your trip by spending **Days 1** and **2** exploring Lisbon's treasure trove of sites. Hop aboard a tram up to the sprawling Castelo de São Jorge, wander the warren of Alfama streets, and ride the train along the river to Belém, where you'll find a cluster of worthy museums and the magnificent Jerónimos Monastery. Don't forget to take a culture break for a coffee and delicious *pastel de nata* (custard tart) in the Pasteis de Belém shop. Next day catch the metro to the Gulbenkian, in the north of the city (São Sebastião metro stop) to see this museum's breathtaking art collection; be sure not to miss its exquisite Lalique display. Walk back down the Avenida da Liberdade to the Baixa and Chiado for a look at the historic shops and experience an evening of fado music at a restaurant in the Bairro Alto.

Day 3, board a train to Sintra, 19 miles (30 km) to the northwest, for a day trip devoted to palaces and gardens. Admire the 16th-century polychrome, Mujédar tiles in the Palácio Nacional de Sintra and catch the bus

NOT TO BE MISSED:

Eating *pastéis de nata* (custard tarts) in Belém 68

Discovering Porto's port wine lodges 86

Exploring the fortified hill town of Sortelha 157

The monasteries of Batalha and Alcobaça 171–175

Sintra's palaces and gardens 187–193

Enjoying the silence of deserted Alentejo beaches 233–235

Walking the *levadas* in Madeira 276

Visitor Information

If possible, find out as much as you can about Portugal before you arrive by checking out some of the following websites: *visit portugal.com, visitlisboa.com, visit porto.travel, portoenorte.pt,* and *visitalgarve.pt;* or for those with limited mobility, *sath.org* and *accessibleportugal.com.* Once in Portugal, there are many places to pick up tourist information. If the airport is your point of entry, make use of the information desks usually situated in the arrivals hall: **Lisbon Airport,** *tel* 218 450 660; **Porto** and **Faro Airport,** *tel 289 818 582.* Beyond the airports, most towns have a *posto de turismo* (tourist office), where you can find out about local attractions and someone usually speaks English.

Cultural Etiquette

Portugal is still a traditional country where value is placed on good manners, though less so by younger generations. The Portuguese address one another in the formal *você* form of the verb, reserving the informal *tu* for close friends; and they use formal titles such as *senhor, senhora* and *Doutor, Doutora* for university-educated professionals. Dress codes are also more formal; around town, men should not walk bare-chested, and modesty is appreciated when visiting churches and other religious buildings.

up to the Pena Palace for the amazing views. If you have time, visit the eccentric Quinta da Regaleira with its mystical well of initiation. End your day by satisfying your sweet tooth with one of Sintra's famed *queijadas* (cheesecakes).

On **Day 4,** pick up a car and drive an hour north to the hill town of Óbidos, walk the ramparts, and pick up a chocolate cup filled with *ginjinha* (cherry liqueur) before continuing north to the monasteries of Alcobaça, 25 miles (40 km) away, and Batalha, 12 miles (20 km) farther, both of which are World Heritage sites. Pause to appreciate the mastery of the detailed stonework. After taking in the grandeur of the monasteries, drive an hour north to spend the night in Coimbra, 55 miles (88 km) from Batalha.

Spend the morning of **Day 5** touring the Universidade de Coimbra, the highlight being without a doubt the ornate baroque library. After lunch, continue

■ Shimmering salt flats edge the Mondego River at Gala, just south of Figueira da Foz.

Horses and riders alike come looking their best for the annual horse festival in the town of Golegã.

north to Porto, 75 miles (120 km) away by car. Stretch your legs in the evening with a walk around the atmospheric city center. From the bottom of the Avenida dos Aliados walk over to Rua Santa Catarina for a coffee at the renowned Majestic Café before strolling back up the hill to the Torre dos Clérigos.

The next day, **Day 6,** cross the river to Gaia and visit the port wine lodges, taking time to savor a glass of port on the riverbank. Return to the Ribeira to wander the streets and visit the main sites, especially the church of São Francisco with its riotous gilded interior, the Palácio da Bolsa, and the cathedral.

Day 7, return to Lisbon, located 195 miles (300 km) south, stopping off a little over halfway there at Tomar to see the massive Convento de Cristo, the former headquarters of the Knights Templar, with its mix of architectural styles.

If You Have More Time

If you can spend another week in Portugal, instead of returning to Lisbon via Tomar, set **Day 7** aside for a tour of historic Guimarães and the Douro Valley. Leave Porto and head northeast to Guimarães (35 miles/55 km away) to spend the morning exploring its medieval center and tenth-century castle. After lunch, drive south to Amarante (40 minutes), picking up the N101 to cross the Serra do Marrão; drop down through terraced vineyards to Mesão Frio; then follow the north bank of the Douro

Best Times to Visit

Portugal is an agreeable year-round destination, with long warm summers stretching from May through September and relatively mild winters in much of the country. Winter runs November to March. The north and the Serra da Estrela region can get snowfall on high ground, while Trás-os-Montes usually experiences the lowest temperatures; however, even the Alentejo can feel bitterly cold when the northern winds blow across the plains. The winter months also bring the highest rainfall, but in the Minho area, showers can occur at any time of year. The highest summer temperatures occur in the interior of the Alentejo and in the Algarve, where July and August temperatures frequently hit 95°F (35°C). July and August are peak family holiday times at the beach resorts, which pushes prices up, so you may prefer to avoid these months. Spring and fall are, on the whole, the best times to visit Portugal. Crowds are nonexistent and prices low. Offshore, Madeira offers a year-round temperate climate and attracts many visitors during the winter, especially at New Year's, when a thousand fireworks light up Funchal Bay.

to Pinhão. Treat yourself to a night at the Vintage House (see Travelwise p. 295). Pause frequently during the afternoon to admire the views.

On **Day 8,** travel a couple of hours south to Guarda and the rugged Serra da Estrela mountain range. En route, stop in Viseu to visit the cathedral with its baroque gilded altarpiece and in Celorico da Beira to see the necropolis of São Gens. Spend the night in Guarda, Portugal's highest town.

Spend **Day 9** exploring the Serra da Estrela before continuing south to the Alentejo. Start by driving south to Belmonte, then west up into the mountains to Caldas de Manteigas (about 90 minutes away). Stretch your legs and try some of the tasty local mountain cheese, then, back in your car, meander south 20 minutes through the stunning Zêzere glacial valley to Torre, Portugal's highest point. In the afternoon, travel 102 miles (164 km) south to the fortified hill town of Castelo de Vide.

The morning of **Day 10,** wander the labyrinthine streets and Jewish quarter of Castelo de Vide and walk the impregnable ramparts of the nearby mountaintop village of Marvão. In the afternoon, drive south to Estremoz on rural back roads. The drive takes about two hours, but the journey can be broken for a coffee at the Pousada de Flor da Rosa, formerly the 14th-century headquarters of the Knights of Malta, or for a visit to the Lusitanian horse stud farm of Alter do Chão. This should leave you a couple of hours to explore Estremoz before dark—depending on the time of year. Stay the night in Estremoz, at the palatial Pousada Castelo Estremoz.

On **Day 11,** drive 29 miles (46 km) down the IP2 to Évora and take the day to visit its Roman temple, aqueduct, and churches before watching the world go by from a sidewalk café in the Praça Giraldo. The more active can prebook a bike tour of the Neolithic remains in the surrounding area.

At the start of **Day 12,** take the N254 south for 50 minutes to Alvito, a town typical of the Alentejo. Continue west, cross-country toward the salt marshes and rice fields of Alcácer do Sal, then on to Comporta and the Tróia Resort at the tip of the peninsula, some two hours away; along the way, note the wealth of birdlife. Stop for a late grilled-fish lunch at any roadside restaurant and take a walk along the pristine Tróia beaches. Sleep at the Tróia Resort or cross to Setúbal on the car ferry and stay at one of the hotels in town.

Dedicate **Day 13** to the beach, be it on the Tróia Peninsula or along the magnificent Arrábida coast, west of Setúbal. If on the Arrábida coast, stop for lunch on the sea front in Sesimbra; the fish is superb. Return to Lisbon at the end of the day (50 minutes from Setúbal), and then back home on **Day 14.**

If you've still more time, cap your trip with a long weekend on Madeira island. It's a short flight from Lisbon, and the isle's subtropical climate and amazing scenery are worth it. Plan to visit the botanical gardens and stand on Cabo Girão; take some sturdy shoes to walk the *levadas*.

Hikers enjoy the wild shrubs, laurel, and heather of Madeira's mountainous ridge near Rabaçal.

HISTORY & CULTURE

Azulejo tiles depicting fruit pickers

PORTUGAL TODAY

Clinging to the western edge of Europe, this small country encompasses an unexpectedly broad and seductive spectrum—from stunning, varied landscapes to a multilayered past, majestic monuments, beautiful beaches and islands, top golf courses, succulent regional food, and excellent wines.

Portugal is most definitely not pretentious. Reputedly reserved, the Portuguese are in fact a warm, independent-minded, polyglot people—so all the more excuse to get to know them. Surfers and sunbathers adore the 530-mile-long (850 km) Atlantic coast, which starkly contrasts with the rugged "mountains of the star" (Serra da Estrela), throbbing nightclubs of Lisbon, the medieval hill towns and castles, the stunning terraces of the Douro Valley, the evocative baroque gardens, and the sharp contemporary architecture. Add to this a variety of accommodations, from castles and manor houses to designer hotels, quaint village guesthouses, and seaside villas, and you have the makings of a near-perfect holiday destination. Wonderfully unspoiled as of yet, Portugal cannot fail to seduce.

New Portugal

António de Oliveira Salazar's dictatorship (1932–1968) marked a dark period in Portuguese history when social, cultural, and economic life hit an all-time low. Then the 1974 revolution and the 1986 entry into the

■ Schoolchildren love Lisbon's high-tech Parque das Nações.

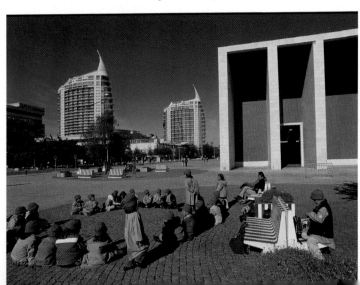

European Economic Community—now the European Union—brought a radical change in direction, setting off a socio-economic roll that continues today, despite a still struggling economy. A rigid society frozen in the 19th century was transformed into a dynamic one in harmony with the rest of Europe. The

> **A rigid society frozen in the 19th century was transformed into a dynamic one in harmony with the rest of Europe.**

surge in activity included an ambitious privatization program: More than a hundred state enterprises were sold in a decade. As growth accelerated, European subsidies brought new investment in agriculture and industry.

The modernizing momentum of the 1990s fully realized its impact when Portugal hosted Euro 2004, the European soccer championship and Portugal's biggest ever sporting event. Spectators from all over the world saw a remodeled nation of spanking new architecture, six-lane highways, impressive railways, shining stadiums, and high-rise hotels. Like most of Europe, Portugal was hard hit by the economic crisis of 2008, which left a mark, but the country continues to show encouraging signs of growth: its unemployment rate is currently (and has been for many years) at a historical low. Despite the ups and downs of the country's modern age, its past has not been lost in the process, as the numerous echoing monasteries, castles, dazzling baroque churches, and beautifully tiled walls testify. Neither has Portugal lost its strong sense of identity and traditions, for although only 3 percent of the population still works in the primary sector, it remains essentially a rural nation of small-scale towns and villages. Nor is everything perfect, either: Vast areas of countryside still have few roads and definitely improvable road signs, making it easy to get lost, even in this modestly scaled country.

The Lay of the Land

With just under 10 million people inhabiting an area of 35,458 square miles (91,836 sq km), Portugal has one of the lowest overall population densities in Europe, descending to a mere 44 people per square mile (17 people per sq km) in central Alentejo. Lisbon, the capital, lies at the heart of the most densely inhabited region, and its greater urban area is home to nearly 3 million, while Porto, the second largest metropolis, leads the north with 1.7 million inhabitants. Outside of these two industrial poles, about one-third of the land is clad in trees (unfortunately many have been hit by violent wildfires in recent years), and the rest is given over to either vineyards or farmland.

In the North: The Minho (named for a river that demarcates Portugal's northern border with Spain) and the Trás-os-Montes (meaning "beyond the mountains") areas harbor striking, rugged areas where granite-built

■ **A network of canals was built in Aveiro to allow shippers access to the sea.**

villages seem trapped in time. On occasion, horses still transport goods and people, and many agricultural methods should have become obsolete decades ago. Much of the rural population is noticeably elderly, bringing into question the long-term future of these areas. Between the villages are undulating fields blanketed in vineyards, rushing rivers, and the stark granite peaks of Portugal's first national park, Peneda-Gerês. The cities of Porto and Braga have industrial outskirts, but the centuries-old port wine industry takes center stage, especially in the stupendous terraced Douro Valley. Here, too, elegant manors stud the landscape, and medieval castles guard the border with Spain, the archenemy—once reviled and feared. A Portuguese saying, "Neither a good wind nor a good marriage ever comes from Spain," perfectly expresses this sentiment.

Portugal's Center: The enchanting Beiras area radiates from the illustrious and lively university town of Coimbra. The city makes a stimulating launchpad for forays into the rugged hills of the Serra da Estrela, for indulging in spas, or for exploring charming towns such as Aveiro or Viseu. The Beiras area is often mistakenly overshadowed by more dramatic sites to the north (Porto and the Douro Valley) or to the south, where Portugal's most famous monuments are clustered. The heavyweight lineup of Alcobaça, Batalha, and Tomar (all World Heritage sites) is in Estremadura, an area heavily crisscrossed by highways and partly industrialized, thus distinctly less rural in spirit. Proximity to Lisbon puts the region on tourist day trips, so do not expect to find yourself alone in Alcobaça's cloisters or beneath the rococo cherubim of Mafra Palace. The coastline, alternating between cliffs and beaches, has highlights such as Peniche and Ericeira, both of which offer some of Europe's best surfing conditions. East of the Estremadura lie the emptier plains of the Ribatejo, a venue for cowboys and occasional bullfights, and the semi-industrialized Tejo Valley, dotted with medieval sites. Cultural interest intensifies again in and around Lisbon, one of Europe's most delightful capitals. Low-key yet sophisticated, brazenly modern and engagingly old-fashioned, Lisbon sprawls over seven hills. Its beautiful site beside the Tejo Estuary once connected it more closely with Portugal's overseas possessions than with Europe; the rich cultural mosaic needs several days to explore. A short train ride away is Sintra, a magical hill town of mansions and palaces nestled in forests overlooking the Atlantic. On the coast, dowager resorts like Cascais and Estoril vie with blissfully empty beaches farther north, while the Sado Estuary edging the Setúbal Peninsula attracts nature enthusiasts eager to see pink flamingos and dolphins.

East & South: Megaliths, castles, delightful whitewashed villages, swathes of cork oak, and olive trees characterize the vast plains and rolling hills of the Alentejo. Its warmer climate, cuisine, and architecture reflect a distinctly Mediterranean character. Traditionally home to *latifúndios* or *herdades* (large-scale estates), the Alentejo has long nurtured radical political movements, unlike the more conservative north. Handicrafts are king here, making it a joy to nose around markets. The Alentejo coastline boasts unspoiled beaches and dramatic cliffs, in high contrast to the developments of the Algarve in the south, which are meccas for northern European retirees and for charter tourism. The Moors' presence in Portugal was strongest in the Algarve, on a par with neighboring Andalucía in Spain, and is still visible in the humble villages and in the physiognomy of locals. Golf courses are a huge, year-round attraction, and there are a few well-kept secrets, such as the Costa Vicentina, with some of Europe's most beautiful wild beaches. Farther southwest still, in the Atlantic, the idiosyncratic island of Madeira lies in an archipelago some 440 miles (700 km) off the coast of Morocco. The lush subtropical vegetation, rugged volcanic slopes, and mild climate draw visitors in droves in winter.

Climate

Climatically, Portugal's regions are as diverse as their landscapes. Although summer brings warm and mainly sunny days to the Minho, the land stays brilliantly green thanks to plentiful rainfall, not shared by its drier, rockier neighbor, Trás-os-Montes. Snow often caps the mountains of the Serra do Gerês and Serra da Estrela (home to continental Portugal's highest peak) in winter, sometimes making roads impassable. Inland Alentejo often sees summer temperatures soar over 104°F (40°C), but coastal areas and the Algarve usually have much milder temperatures. Lisbon enjoys a temperate climate, with most rain falling November through

January and temperatures averaging 58°F (14°C) in winter and about 85°F (29°C) in summer. The little rain that falls in the south occurs during the winter. The Madeira archipelago boasts exceptionally mild temperatures, averaging 72°F (22°C) in summer and 62°F (16°C) in winter, with rainfall mainly concentrated in winter on the more exposed northern side of the islands.

Religion & Festivals

Portugal is a deeply devout country, with Roman Catholics constituting an overwhelming majority of its population. Religious orders were banned in 1834. The formal separation of Church and State occurred during the First Republic (1910–1926) and was reiterated in the 1976 constitution.

Yet Church and State remain inextricably linked and church-going is common. The Lisbon area is the least devout, while the north is the most.

Catholicism in Portugal distinguishes itself from that of Spain through a more serene and caring face; there is far less anguish, and God is perceived as benevolent and less judgmental. Twice a year, tens of thousands of pilgrims head to the complex of shrines dedicated to the Virgin Mary at Fátima.

Inevitably such belief brings a highly charged calendar of *festas* (festivals) and *romarias* (pilgrimages)—often a curious mix of worship, processions, and good times. Christmas, though important, does not head the list of major festivals. *Carnaval* (Mardi Gras), held just before Lent, kicks off the year's celebrations. During Easter Week, Braga's torchlit processions rival those of Andalucía in Spain. Outside the main calendar, each town celebrates its patron saint with gusto: Lisbon, for example, spends most of the night of June 12 on a delirious roll in honor of St. Anthony, while Porto and Braga celebrate St. John on June 23 and 24.

Some festivals have pagan elements to them. In Trás-os-Montes, December's Festa dos Rapazes (Boys Festival) sees groups of costumed and masked boys (older than 16) cavorting around huge bonfires; they are celebrating the rite of passage into adulthood. Amarante, in the Douro area, observes an

Bullfights

Touradas (bullfights) in Portugal are very low key and restricted mainly to two regions: the Ribatejo, where fighting bulls are bred, and the Algarve, where fights are staged for tourists. The season runs from Easter until October. In the Portuguese tourada, the bull, whose horns are capped, is not killed in the ring. The thrill lies in watching the star bullfighter leap onto a bull to grab its horns while his team attempts to hold it from behind. The most skilled and traditional touradas take place during Santarém's big agricultural fair in June.

ancient fertility rite in which unmarried individuals exchange phallic-shaped cakes and touch the tomb of St. Gonçalo in the hope of a speedy marriage; this takes place the first weekend in June.

Portugal's most gorgeous costumes come out in the Minho—at Viana do Castelo's riotous festival around August 20, at Vila Franca do Lima's Rose Festival in mid-May, and Ponte de Lima's Feiras Novas (New Fairs) in the first half of September. Horse lovers should earmark the first two weeks of November and head for Golegã in the Ribatejo to see Portugal's massive annual horse fair with parades, competitions, and occasional bullfights. The Alentejo's busy calendar is filled with hot-blooded festivities often connected with agricultural seasons, food, and wine. Inevitably, the least traditional region is the Algarve, where customs have been diluted by foreign visitors and residents.

> " **Portugal is a deeply devout country, with Roman Catholics constituting an overwhelming majority of its population.** "

Football

Portugal's great sporting passion, shared with most western European nations, is football. During the soccer season, from August to May, nearly every restaurant has a television set in the corner tuned to the match of the day—local diners being voluble groups of men, though more women are increasingly drawn to the sport. Familiarity with any or all of the main teams, or seeing them in action (see sidebar below) is a surefire way to start a conversation. ∎

EXPERIENCE: Attend a Soccer Game

No visit to Portugal would be complete without experiencing the intense spectacle of a professional soccer game, where passions flare and the roar of the crowd can be deafening. Most of the population would swear allegiance to one of the Três Grandes, the three giant clubs: FC Porto, Sporting Clube, or Benfica (the first from Porto, the two others from Lisbon). Rivalries are intense, with the league championship usually contested among the three, which regularly compete in the UEFA Champions League too. Benfica were European Champions in 1961 and 1962, while Porto triumphed in 1987 and 2004, when coached by José Mourinho. For ticket information, contact **FC Porto** (*Estádio do Dragão, tel 225 083 352, fcporto.pt*), **Sporting Clube** (*Estádio José Alvalade, tel 707 204 444, sporting.pt*), or **Benfica** (*Estádio da Luz, tel 932 401 904, slbenfica.pt*).

PORTUGAL, CHAMPIONS AT LAST

Portugal has historically boasted a very respectable soccer team but despite the fact that they've always put first-rate players on the field, they've continually placed only second or third in major tournaments. That changed dramatically on July 10, 2016, when a little-known substitute named Éder scored against host team France to make Portugal champions of Europe at last.

Football, Fado, Fátima

Soccer has been played in Portugal since the 1860s, thanks to the country's maritime trading ties with Britain, whose sailors spread the game worldwide in the Victorian era. Throughout António de Oliveira Salazar's long dictatorship (1932–1968) and up to the Carnation Revolution of 1974 (see p. 34), football was encouraged by the state: Football, fado, and the Catholic cult of Fátima were seen as distractions from politics.

Always the Bridesmaids

Portuguese football arrived on the world stage when Eusebio, a powerful striker born in the former colony of Mozambique, led the country to a 1966 World Cup semifinal. When Portugal won two World Youth Cups in 1989 and 1990, the "golden generation" of players including Luis Figo and Rui Costa were expected to bring success at the senior level. In 2004, an aging Figo led the next golden generation to the final of the European Championship held in Portugal. A nation prepared to party, but underdogs Greece shocked their hosts 1–0 in Lisbon. The baton of expectation was passed to a new generation that included Cristiano Ronaldo, who would carve out an outstanding club career with Manchester United, Real Madrid, and Juventus. At the Euro Cup in 2016, it was he who lifted the first senior trophy the country had won, and a goal by Gonçalo Guedes led the national team to the top of the podium in the first edition (2018–2019) of the UEFA Nations League.

Portuguese players celebrate their victory over France at Euro 2016.

HISTORY OF PORTUGAL

More than just textbook history, thousands of years of human endeavor can be seen in Portugal, from Neolithic dolmens to a dazzling network of baroque churches and palaces built on the riches from the colonies, to the economic revitalization occurring since a peaceful revolution ended decades of 20th-century dictatorship.

Portugal is one of the oldest nations in Europe. Its borders have remained more or less unchanged for the last 800 years. Before the moment when Afonso Henriques proclaimed himself king of Portucale, in 1139, its history was shared with Spain. Together these two lands saw a succession of invaders and colonizers from northern Europe and from across the Mediterranean, all lured by this peninsula of plenty.

Portugal's Earliest Inhabitants

Although dates in the mists of time are always conjectural, it is certain that humans lived in Portugal up to 30,000 years ago, leaving the rock art of Vale do Côa (north of Guarda) as their legacy. Later, about 5,000 to 6,000 years ago, came ritual worship associated with megaliths, of which Portugal claims an astonishing number. Dolmens (stone shelters, probably temples or tombs), cromlechs (stone circles), and menhirs (upright stones) still stand enigmatically from the Minho region to the Alentejo.

With the inward drift of Celts from the north, settlements took shape as *castros,* fortified hilltop villages of stone and thatch shelters, whose inhabitants were always on the lookout for marauding neighbors. The best example of a castro is Citânia de Briteiros, near Guimarães. During this period, around the ninth century B.C., Phoenicians first moored their boats in the Algarve; they were soon followed by Greeks and Carthaginians. Little remains from this first wave of expatriates other than the introduction of fishing, but life changed radically when the highly structured Romans marched into the south around 200 B.C.

Romans & Other Invaders

Expecting a military pushover, the Romans met a surprising resistance, mainly due to the Lusitani. The major resistance ended in 139 B.C., when the last Lusitani leader was killed, but intermittent warfare continued until 28 B.C. Perhaps out of admiration, the Romans took the tribe's name for their new province south of the Douro River: Lusitania.

> **The Romans took the tribe's name for their new province south of the Douro River: Lusitania.**

The Romans spearheaded a massive leap forward in infrastructure and government. Olisipo (Lisbon) became the capital in 60 B.C., and other centers developed at Santarém, Évora, Beja, and Braga. By the third century A.D., what is now the Minho was absorbed into the province of Gallaecia (today's Galicia, in Spain). Roads crisscrossed the country, bridges spanned rivers, and *latifúndios* (large-scale estates) became the norm, especially in the Alentejo. The Romans also imported crops: grapevines, figs, almonds, and olives—all of which are still farmed. Major bishoprics were established at Braga and Évora. Altogether, with a network of roads, a legal system, a Mediterranean-style diet, a Latin-based language, and Christianity, the Romans left an indelible mark.

Their empire, however, was in decline and soon dissipated in the face of invaders from the north. In came the Suevi (Swabians), closely followed by the Visigoths. Fractious tribes, they could not repulse the next invaders: the Moors.

The Moors

In 711, the caliphate of Damascus led an army of Arabs and Berbers onto Iberian soil at Tarifa (in Spanish Andalucía). It would take Portugal more than 500 years to throw off these new rulers. Because the Moors never ventured very far north of the Douro River, this region (together with Galicia) remained predominantly Christian, and it was here that the *reconquista* (reconquest) was born.

Meanwhile, the Moorish colony of Al-Gharb (meaning "the west," later to become Algarve), initially ruled from Córdoba, lived peacefully and with religious tolerance. Irrigation systems and water mills helped cultivate newly introduced wheat, rice, citrus fruits, and saffron. Mining, too, boosted the economy, supplying craftsmen with copper and silver, and the ceramics industry exploded when the Moors introduced glazed tiles—*azulejos*.

■ **Portugal's past is on display in the Alentejo, a region rich in megaliths.**

Little by little, however, the northern Christians were on the move, led by the king of Asturias-Léon. They had recovered Porto by 868, and Coimbra 10 years later. As the reconquista advanced, Córdoba's power fragmented, resulting in numerous small kingdoms or *taifas*. The power vacuum was gradually filled by more fanatical branches of Islam. Over the next two centuries, the fundamentalist Almoravids and Almohads successfully reunited the southern half of the peninsula, reestablishing strong government and severe controls. By 1100, the stage was set for a Holy War between Christians and Muslims.

The Emergence of Portucale

■ **The Moors introduced the art of glazed tiles to Portugal.**

At the same time Portucale (originally the region between the Lima and Douro Rivers) began to emerge, and a sense of national identity took shape thanks to Afonso Henriques, grandson to Afonso VI, king of Castilla y Léon. Portucale, a county in Afonso VI's kingdom, was awarded to Afonso Henriques's father in gratitude for his services to the king. When Afonso VI died, Portucale refused allegiance to the new king. Some years later, Afonso began his quest for power by overthrowing his widowed mother to gain control of Portucale in 1128.

In 1139, a significant victory against the Moors (Battle of Ourique) gave Afonso the confidence to declare Portucale (Portugal) sovereign and himself king *(dom)*. This was a turning point. Further conquests followed with Santarém and Lisbon both falling into the new king's net, helped by French, English, German, and Flemish crusaders, who washed up on these shores en route to the Holy Land. Afonso Henriques's guilt at using up this precious manpower destined for Jerusalem led him to found the Alcobaça Abbey and to donate land to these supporters. The crusaders grew acquisitive, one result being the formidable rise of the Knights Templar, a monastic military order formed at the end of the First Crusade in 1096. Although Afonso Henriques surrendered some frontier land to the kingdom of Léon, temporarily allied with the Muslims, by the time he died in 1185 almost the entire realm was declared Portuguese. When the Algarve fell to Afonso III in 1249, the reconquista was complete; yet, the kingdom of Castilla disputed Afonso's claim of sovereignty. The 1297 Treaty of Alcañices resolved the matter, formally ceding the Algarve to Portugal's king, Dom Dinis I. By this time the capital had moved from Coimbra to Lisbon.

Dom Dinis & His Legacy

This exceptionally astute and enlightened king, nicknamed "the poet king," embarked on an ambitious program of shoring up his kingdom. By the time he died, in 1325, the country had reached maturity (see sidebar below).

Such progress did not last, however, and Portugal entered an era of stagnation, made worse by the plague that intermittently wreaked havoc over the next century. Adding to the troubles were wars with the kingdom of Castilla: Territorial incursions, alliances, lovers, marriages, and illegitimate sons all played a role.

This came to a head in 1385 at the Battle of Aljubarrota when João, the illegitimate son of Pedro I, confronted the Castilians. They were backing Leonor, widow of the former Portuguese king Fernando I, and her daughter Beatriz, who was married to Juan, the king of Castilla. The population was divided over this inheritance issue: The nobles and the church backed the Castilians, while the middle and working classes championed the national candidate, João. Greatly outnumbered by the Castilian army, João made a vow to build a monastery if he won. Win he did, and his victory led to the magnificent monastery of Batalha, an alliance with England (formalized by the Treaty of Windsor, 1386), an English wife, Philippa of Lancaster, and the uncontested rule of the House of Avis.

House of Avis & the Age of Discoveries

This crucial period in Portuguese history reaped riches from overseas colonies. Philippa of Lancaster proved to be a popular queen, managing to rein in the womanizing Dom João I and bear him six children. The third son, Prince Henry, significantly altered his country's fortunes. After capturing the Moroccan stronghold of Ceuta for his father, in 1415, Henry reportedly set up a school of navigation at Sagres, in the Algarve. Henry the

Dom Dinis's Accomplishments

During Dom Dinis's reign (1279–1325) more than 50 castles were built along the border, forests were planted, and in 1290 Lisbon University was founded. The king also replaced the wealthy, all-powerful Knights Templar with the Order of Christ that was directly under his control, preempting any moves by the power-hungry Church. Portuguese became the official language of bureaucracy, as opposed to Latin or Castilian, as well as the vehicle for a flourishing oral culture transmitted by wandering troubadours. Poetry thus blossomed. Dinis also developed the economy by establishing a network of fairs and markets, encouraging domestic trade and a shift from substinence farming. In 1308, a commercial pact with England laid the foundations for a lengthy—and profitable—alliance. In short, the country flourished under Dom Dinis's rule.

Navigator—as he came to be known, surrounding himself with astronomers and shipbuilders—financed numerous expeditions along the African coast. The newly discovered Madeira and Azores archipelagoes both later served as stopovers for Atlantic crossings. It is also surmised that Portuguese explorers reached America in the 1470s, several years before Columbus.

Before his death in 1460, Henry was a trusted adviser to his nephew, Afonso V, who had ascended the throne in 1438. Afonso's reign (until 1481) saw more battles in Morocco and, at home, a strengthening of the power of the *cortes* (court government). Friction with Spain resurfaced, and the idealistic yet weak Afonso failed in his military attempt to wrest control of Castilla. His son, João, negotiated peace with Castilla, and on becoming Dom João II (r. 1481–1495) opened the borders to some 60,000 Jews fleeing persecution in Spain.

Meanwhile, out on the high seas, Bartolomeu Dias rounded the Cape of Good Hope in 1488, allowing Portugal to set its sights on the Indian Ocean. By 1494, overseas rivalry with Spain had spiraled to such an extent that the pope stepped in to draw up the Treaty of Tordesillas. It effectively drew a line down the map of the known world to divide it between the two maritime powers: Spain to the west and Portugal to the east. Inadvertently, the line cut through Brazil, so when Pedro Álvares Cabral moored his boats there six years later, this vast territory was signed over to Portugal. It played a major role in Portugal's fortunes for four centuries.

Vasco da Gama's discovery of the sea route to India, which he accomplished in 1498 via Mozambique—adding one more African jewel to Portugal's colonial crown—led to untold riches. Ten years later, Afonso de Albuquerque captured the port of Goa, in western India, leading to 450 years of Portuguese rule, and by 1511 his control of Malacca (in Malaysia) gave Portugal a strategic trading center for the East Indies. The Portuguese soon held sway over the entire Indian Ocean and its much prized spice trade, previously in the hands of Arab traders.

> **The Portuguese soon held sway over the entire Indian Ocean and its much prized spice trade, previously in the hands of Arab traders.**

When a Spanish expedition led by Portuguese Fernão de Magalhães (Magellan) returned to base in 1522 (minus their captain who had been killed in the Philippines) after circumnavigating the globe, the pride in Portuguese exploration was justifiable. Through immense courage and navigating skill, people from this little seaboard country had penetrated regions previously considered inhabited by monsters, proved the world round, and discovered a string of exotic destinations. Henry the Navigator's agile fleet of *caravelas* (inspired by the cargo sailing ships on the Douro), celestial tables, and ocean charts had all paid off richly.

■ Lisbon's "Monument to the Discoveries" (1960) commemorates the era of the great discoveries made by Portuguese explorers.

These bountiful new territories changed the face of Portugal. Dom Manuel I (r. 1495–1521) reigned during the period that saw overseas riches transform both Lisbon and the nation, a major expression being the lavish Manueline style of decoration. Manuel dubbed himself Lord of the Conquest, Navigation, and Commerce of India, Ethiopia, Arabia, and Persia. Merchants descended on Lisbon from all over Europe, bringing goods to exchange for gold and ivory from Africa, pungent spices (pepper, cinnamon, cloves) from India and the East Indies, and, by the mid-16th century, silks and porcelain from China. From the New World came strange fruits, vegetables, and other plants—tomatoes, potatoes, corn, tobacco, and cacao. And from the Atlantic itself, off Newfoundland, came *bacalhau*, or cod, a creature that still obsesses the Portuguese palate.

The Portuguese were relatively tolerant of local customs in their newfound territories. Their main concerns were to run their trading stations and zealously impose Catholicism. Mixing freely with local populations, they intermarried, a practice that became common and is still visible in the names and inhabitants of former colonies such as Mozambique, Ceylon (Sri Lanka), and Malacca. Centuries later, many Portuguese natives emigrated to the colonies in search of employment and prosperity. Nevertheless, the Portuguese sorely lacked the middle class needed to build up their overseas territories; the problem eventually proved to be insoluble. Yet, under the astute Manuel I, Portugal had prospered and made huge advances in social fields, legal systems, and education. The Italian Renaissance had imparted humanistic ideals and a flood of new ideas. This led to a radical reform of the university system, widening the pool of students from the religious orders to include young nobles and bourgeois. The university's increased influence in Lisbon soon posed a threat to the monarchy, provoking Manuel's son, João III, to actually move it to Coimbra, far from the seat of power, and hand over educational guidance to the Jesuits.

End of an Era

Inevitably, the feast of plenty enjoyed from overseas explorations did not last: Overconfidence led to underdevelopment and overstretching; emigration to the new colonies reduced the already small population at home; easy riches led to a loss of skills; and the cost of living rose sharply. In addition, the Portuguese Inquisition targeted Jews in *autos-da-fé* (public burnings), resulting in a mood of commercial and cultural apathy. When the young king Sebastião I was killed during a bloody crusade in Morocco, in 1578, it was the straw that broke the camel's back.

When Sebastião died he was not alone: 8,000 men were massacred, including a large section of the nobility. Others were captured, and the national coffers were virtually emptied to pay ransom demands. The country was bankrupt and its golden era well and truly over. By 1580, Portugal was sufficiently on its knees for the Spanish Habsburg king, Felipe II, to walk in and take over as Filipe I of Portugal. Spanish rule lasted 60 years, a period in history that the Portuguese have never forgotten or forgiven.

Spanish Rule

King Filipe I, although fresh from Madrid, was the grandson of Dom Manuel I. His fair attitude to his new kingdom helped maintain the independence of the Portuguese parliament and of its empire. He also introduced an efficient administrative system. But these attitudes changed with his son, Filipe II, who, lacking his father's finesse, blatantly

■ **The staggering baroque interior of Porto's São Francisco church reflects the power and wealth of the Franciscans in the 18th century.**

exploited Portuguese revenue to finance Spain's battles in the New World. Several years passed before he even visited Portugal after his coronation in 1598. Resentment simmered, throwing up a number of pretenders to the throne. Meanwhile Portuguese overseas possessions were gradually being eroded: The Dutch were on a rampage, carrying off Ceylon (Sri Lanka), Malacca, and parts of Brazil, while the English took Ormuz.

Finally, in 1640, a full-scale revolt took place, sparked by a Spanish recruitment drive in Portugal to help put down an uprising in Catalonia. With French moral support, a group of nationalists drove out the Spanish occupiers from Lisbon and installed a new king on the throne: Dom João IV. This initiated the rule of the House of Bragança, which was to last until the Republic, in 1910.

The House of Bragança

The rebirth of Portugal got off to a shaky start, unrecognized by most of Europe and hampered by weak leadership. Only the marriage of Catarina de Bragança to the English king Charles II in 1662 managed to forge a serious alliance. After losing several frontier battles, Spain finally recognized Portugal in the 1668 Treaty of Lisbon. In the interim, Portugal had reentered the economic doldrums: having lost the spice trade to the Dutch, it was now losing its sugar and slave markets. A reversal of fortunes came, however, at the turn of the 18th century with the discovery of gold and precious stones in Brazil. Soon a steady stream of riches enabled baroque gilt to unfurl in every palace, church, and monastery in the land.

João V (r. 1706–1750) unashamedly modeled himself on the French

Teaism

It is no secret that the British like their tea; in fact, they consume more than 176 million pounds yearly. Less known, perhaps, is the fact that it was made popular in England by a Portuguese princess, Catarina de Bragança. Married to King Charles II in 1662, Catarina had grown up in the Portuguese court where drinking *chá* had long been considered the height of fashion among the nobility. On arrival in England, Catarina was dismayed at being offered ale to drink and immediately set about establishing this exotic and expensive beverage as the court's drink of choice.

Sun King, Louis XIV, and became quite adept at dipping into the public purse. The palace and monastery of Mafra are the most flagrant examples of his disregard for budget. If extravagance was João's second name, his third was libertine, proved by countless children he fathered with nuns. At the same time, trade took off thanks to the efforts of the brilliant though tyrannical prime minister, the Marquês de Pombal. It is no surprise that Pombal's name has outlasted the kings whom he served (João V was succeeded by his spineless son, José I): This farsighted man was responsible for far-reaching reforms.

In 1755, Pombal's talents were severely tested when a massive earthquake hit Lisbon and its surroundings. Some 5,000 people were killed instantly, but the following weeks saw tens of thousands die from disease and famine. Pombal remained clearheaded and ensured that the capital was rebuilt in record time, and intelligently. From then on the marquês instigated massive reforms in taxation, administration, and education; imposed trade barriers and export systems; and abolished the Portuguese slave trade. As his enemies multiplied, though, Pombal became ever more wily and despotic, finally abolishing the Jesuit Order and executing troublemaking nobles. When Dona Maria I took over the throne in 1777, Pombal's days were numbered. She had little respect for his methods and soon had him tried and convicted. Maria herself, highly religious and mentally unstable, reigned until 1795, when her increasingly erratic behavior prompted her son João to take over, although he was not crowned until her death in 1816. His reign saw yet another momentous period in Portuguese and Spanish history: the Peninsular War.

Peninsular War

Following the French Revolution in 1789 and the rise of power-hungry Napoleon, all Europe was in chaos. In 1801, France threatened to invade Portugal if it did not close its ports to England; since most of Portugal's exports were destined for England, the Portuguese refused. As a result, France's temporary ally, Spain, invaded Portugal. The peace treaty that ended the so-called War of the Oranges ceded land to Spain and forced the Portuguese to open its ports to the French and pay an indemnity.

Worse followed in 1807, when Gen. Andoche Junot and his French troops marched into Lisbon, although he missed capturing the royal family, who had fled to Brazil on the advice of the British. The royals remained in Rio de Janeiro for the next 14 years. The intervening years saw Portugal ruled by a British governor, Gen. William Carr (later Viscount Beresford), who together with the great tactician, Sir Arthur Wellesley (later Duke of Wellington), finally rid Portugal of its invaders. Successive waves of French attacks were repelled with help from Wellington's ingenious Lines of Torres Vedras before the allies' final victory at the Battle of Buçaco in 1810. Yet again Portugal found itself close to economic ruin, and this was exacerbated by the payoff to Britain for its help, namely the granting of the right to trade directly with Brazil. This concession lost Portugal precious revenue. Beresford was an unpopular, devious governor and the backlash was quick to come. In 1820, a group of Portuguese officers formed a court government and drew up a new constitution inspired by the liberal ideas that had swept Europe.

■ In 1810 the Battle of Buçaco led the Allies to victory in the Peninsular War.

Civil Turmoil & the Portuguese Republic

João VI was forced to return and 1822 saw not only the independence of Brazil but also João's acceptance of the constitution. One term called for an assembly to be elected every two years by universal male suffrage, while other clauses abolished the privileges of both the nobles and the clergy. João may have signed his name to the document, but his Spanish wife, Carlota, and younger son, Miguel, did not, thus inciting a reactionary movement that simmered for decades. João's death in 1826 resulted in a hornet's nest of maneuvering between the two camps, with the rural population supporting the reactionaries and the big three powers (Spain, France, and Britain) backing the liberals. Pedro, João's eldest son, and Miguel, the youngest, ended up on opposing sides; the Miguelist Wars eventually gave victory and the crown to the liberal-minded Pedro. He ruled until 1834, when his 15-year-old daughter, Dona Maria II, ascended the throne. By then, the revolutionary spirit had abolished religious orders, a significant move in such a fervently religious country.

There followed endless confrontations and uprisings between nascent political parties, and economic depression prevailed. In 1861, when Maria's son Luís I assumed power, he inherited a modernized infrastructure thanks to prime minister Saldanha, but the economy still suffered; emigration soared and the countryside was becoming depopulated. The intellectually inclined Luís nonetheless presided over a peaceful era during which the arts, particularly literature, blossomed. Conservatives and liberals alternated controlling parliament, but growing social discontent took shape as a nationalist republican movement. This came to a head in 1908 in an attempted coup, when Dom Carlos I and his eldest son were assassinated. In 1910, a military coup deposed Dom Manuel II (the younger son), who fled to England. The Portuguese Republic was born. For the next 16 years, although power was often in the hands of the leftist Democratic Party, there were no fewer than 45 changes of government, accompanied by a weakening of economic and social structures. Chaos became the keyword as political factions multiplied, unions declared strikes, and the military made sporadic interventions. The republic was on its knees when yet another military coup, in 1926, appointed General Óscar Carmona as president with António de Oliveira Salazar as his minister for finance. In six years Salazar graduated to the powerful post of prime minister, a title he did not relinquish for 36 years.

The Salazar Years

It did not take long for Salazar to show his true colors. In 1933, he declared a "New State," modeling himself on Italy's fascist dictator Mussolini. Authoritarian and intent on returning Portugal to its Catholic code after decades of liberal thinking, Salazar repressed any opposition, imposed censorship, and founded a state police organization. These were dark days for Portugal, effectively cutting it off from much of Europe with the exception of the little-loved neighbor, Spain; Salazar actually gave military backing to Gen. Francisco Franco in the Spanish Civil War of 1936–1939. Resistance at home simmered in an underground Communist Party, but it remained powerless.

During World War II, Portugal's loyalties were divided: Traditionally, it should have followed its old ally in foreign affairs, Britain, but Salazar's sympathies lay with Hitler. In the end, he played a purely self-interested role, doing business with both sides and profiting royally. Admission to the United Nations came in 1955, but

> **In 1910, a military coup deposed Dom Manuel II [. . .], who fled to England. The Portuguese Republic was born.**

Salazar continued to ignore or repress all warning signs of opposition: One presidential candidate opposed to the dictatorship, Gen. Humberto Delgado, was assassinated by state police in 1965. Salazar's most positive accomplishment came in the sweeping economic reforms which, by the 1950s and '60s, gave Portugal an annual growth rate of 7 to 9 percent.

Meanwhile, Portugal's colonies were being squeezed dry and their populations exploited, while immigrants to the "mother country" found themselves employed as cheap labor. Revolts ensued, usually harshly put down, and wars such as in Angola in 1961 drained manpower and the economy. As the increasingly paranoid Salazar assumed ever more responsibilities, age finally took its toll: In June 1968, at age 79, Salazar suffered an incapacitating stroke when his deck chair collapsed—not the most elegant way to go. Although he clung to life for two more years, the reins of power passed to Marcelo Caetano.

The Rise of Modern Portugal

Ineffective in instigating reform, Caetano was deposed in 1974 in an extraordinarily effortless, bloodless coup—the Carnation Revolution—spearheaded by the MFA (Armed Forces Movement), a group of disillusioned military officers. Anarchy and numerous governments came and went until 1976, when socialist Mário Soares was elected. In 1986, he became Portugal's first civilian president in 60 years—and a civilian has been president ever since. Also in 1986, Portugal entered the European Union (EU) and a period of growth and prosperity followed, funded by European grants. Portugal's profile was raised further in 1998, when it hosted the World Expo, and in 2004 the European Football Championship.

The recent global financial crisis caused concerns for the economic future. Following a period of tight economic austerity, which brought Portugal out of its financial crisis, the 2015 elections put a left-wing coalition in government, whose socialist-leaning and economically less restrictive policies have managed to hold onto the positive upswing. The prime minister was reappointed in 2019 and again in 2022 with an absolute majority of seats. High on the government's agenda are issues dear to the progressive left, like the climate emergency, modernization, scientific research, and a fair economic and social system for all. ■

■ **António Luís Santos da Costa was first elected prime minister in 2015, then reelected in 2019 and 2022.**

FOOD & DRINK

Much of Portugal's empire was built on its spice trade, and this eastern influence has had a long-lasting impact on the country's cuisine. Portuguese cooks are fearless about spicing things up. It was Vasco da Gama, the first to round the Cape of Good Hope and cross the Indian Ocean, who brought back black pepper and other spices from India, soon followed by nutmeg, mace, and cloves from the Spice Islands.

Piri-piri (Swahili for "pepper pepper"), a blend of crushed chilies, fragrant herbs, and a dash of lemon, is a legacy that coats countless dishes from Africa to Brazil.

Regional Dishes

Regional cuisine thrives in a country that is clearly divided into north, center, and south. In the north and center, in the Minho, Trás-os-Montes, and Beiras areas, an invariable starter is *caldo verde* (cabbage soup), a nourishing mix of potatoes, shredded cabbage, olive oil, and *chouriço* (spicy sausage). The soup with the strangest name is *sopa de pedra* (stone soup) from Ribatejo: Based on a legend, it contains no stones, but beans, smoked sausage, and vegetables. *Caldeirada de peixe* (fish stew) is found near the coast, together with a variant that includes shellfish: *sopa de marisco*.

Local Favorites

Wherever you go in Portugal, you will never be far from great food, but there are several places that any local would tell you are "not to be missed."

Cherry liqueur *(ginjinha):* A Ginjinha, Largo de São Domingos 8, Lisbon, or out of chocolate cups on Rua Direita, Óbidos.

Custard tarts *(pastéis de nata):* Pastéis de Belém, Rua de Belém 84–92, Lisbon, tel 213 637 423, pasteisdebelem.pt

Grilled sardines *(sardinhas grelhadas):* A festival is held near the Ponte Velha bridge in Portimão, where you can also visit a museum and eat in one of several establishments. According to custom, best eaten in months without the letter "r" (May–Aug.).

Piri piri chicken *(frango piri-piri):* Bonjardim, Travessa de Santo Antão 7–11, Lisbon, tel 213 424 389 or Pedro dos Frangos, Rua Bonjardim 223, Porto, tel 222 008 522

Roast suckling pig *(leitão assado):* Pedro dos Leitões, Rua Álvaro Pedro 1, Sernadelo, Mealhada, tel 231 209 950, pedro dosleitoes.com

Salted cod *(bacalhau):* Casa do Bacalhau, Rua do Grilo 54, Lisbon, tel 218 620 000, casado bacalhau.pt

Portugal can justifiably claim salted cod *(bacalhau)* as its national dish. Possibly less believable is the Portuguese boast of a cod recipe for every day of the year. Pork is another favorite, with Coimbra claiming the most tender *leitão assado* (roast suckling pig). Virtually nothing is wasted from this animal: The kidneys are pan-fried and finished off with white port, tongues are smoked and made into sausages, and *presunto* (smoked ham) is eaten solo or added to *cozido* (meat and vegetable stew). Ham and spicy *chouriço* sausages are added to *dobrada,* a Lisbon dish of tripe with haricot beans. In Porto the same dish gains curry powder.

Another typical countrywide meat is flavorsome kid goat, usually roasted *(cabrito assado).* Duck is incorporated into divine *arroz de pato* (duck rice), a specialty of Braga, while *feijoada* (bean stew with bacon, meat, tomatoes, onions, and garlic) whets rural appetites throughout the north and center.

South, in the Alentejo, *carne de porco à Alentejana* (pork marinated in wine served with clams) is a surprising yet delicious combination. The Alentejo produces the most Mediterranean-style cuisine of Portugal, based on olive oil and aromatic herbs. Although once denigrated as a peasant cuisine, it is actually rich and varied. The delicious bread and garlic-based *açordas* may be served with prawns or dogfish, lamb stews *(ensopado de borrego),* or a chilled vegetable gazpacho; other mainstays include chicken pies, smoked sausages, sheep and goat cheeses, pork with coriander, and lamb and game dishes.

Fresh fish graces many of Portugal's tables.

The Algarve claims the ubiquitous *cataplana,* a fast-stewed dish of seafood, sometimes with added chopped chicken or pork, cooked in a domed dish similar to that used to make the Moroccan *tajine;* it is yet another innovation from this land of plenty.

Portugal's Sweet Tooth

An outstanding feature of Portuguese cuisine is its vast array of delicately flavored desserts and sweet pastries, whose basic ingredients are egg yolks and sugar. One of the reasons for this is that industrial quantities of egg whites were once used as clarifying agents for red wine, and the surplus yolks were passed on to convents, where nuns concocted cakes for religious festivals. Rivalry added spice to their quality, as each convent sought to attract the favors of patrons. Today there are said to be more than 200 desserts unique to Portugal, the names of which—such as *toucinho do ceu* (heaven's lard) or *barriga de freiras* (nun's belly)—still invoke their origins. Most of them are variations of cream or custard tarts, rice or bread puddings, egg-paste pastries, and, in the Algarve, marzipan. The Algarve is the only region where Arab influences are obvious in fig, honey, or almond pastries.

THE ARTS

Portugal's legacy of three-dimensional creativity is something extraordinary. Architecture, sculpture, and the decorative arts are the Portuguese forte, leaving painting to a relative back seat. The nation also excels at literature and music.

Architecture

Portugal's first man-made constructions—dolmens, cromlechs, and menhirs—date from some 6,000 to 5,000 years ago; the most impressive are in the Alentejo region, near Évora. Much later, the Celts erected *castros* (hill towns) of thatched stone huts, usually circular. This rudimentary architecture lasted for hundreds of years until the Romans brought in revolutionary building techniques and vision. Real architecture finally arrived in this far-flung outpost of the Roman Empire, visible today at the temple and baths of Évora, the mosaic-floored villas of Conímbriga, and the extensive foundations at Miróbriga.

> *Some Moorish vestiges survive in churches that were built over the ruins of mosques, and a few archways and the odd tower still stand as well.*

The next major influence came with the Moors, in the eighth century. Yet again, though, Portugal was an imperial afterthought, and the Moors' unrivaled sense of design and decorative detail was never as widespread in Portugal as in neighboring Spain. Little remains in Portugal today since most Moorish structures were demolished during the prolonged reconquista. Some Moorish vestiges survive in churches that were built over the ruins of mosques, and a few archways and the odd tower still stand as well. Nonetheless, southern Portugal (the Alentejo and the Algarve) has a number of *mourarias* (old Moorish quarters) with webs of narrow lanes resembling North African medinas. Here, too, the patios and tiny windows of whitewashed village houses are clear imports from across the Strait of Gibraltar. One craft technique in particular left an indelible mark: ceramics. Techniques for firing painted tiles (azulejos) were adopted and developed, and they later became a hallmark of Portuguese decorative style (see pp. 74–75).

Romanesque & Gothic: The slow march of the reconquista heralded a new architectural style, the graceful Romanesque imported by French knights and Cistercian monks in the 11th century. Although elegant, pure, with generous proportions, and often masterminded by French architects, it never reached the same heights of intricacy in Portugal as it did in Spain.

Granite—Portugal's national stone—was just too hard to work. Yet massive places of worship took shape, becoming important strongholds in the long struggle against the Islamic occupiers. An iconic example is Coimbra's lovely old cathedral, completed in 1175, heavily fortified while retaining great simplicity. Many Romanesque elements were later masked by Renaissance, Manueline, and baroque alterations.

Close on the heels of this architectural style came the more stylized Gothic look: Pointed arches, rib-vaulted ceilings, and octagonal apses were the norm, while soft limestone was skillfully conjured into figurative and decorative relief. This style emerged in the 12th century, overlapping often with the Romanesque. Central Portugal boasts some superlative Gothic examples,

■ Festivals rich in tradition and colorful costumes are but one aspect of Portugal's arts.

notably the Cistercian monastery of Alcobaça (started in 1178), whose serene, spacious cloister was much imitated. The staggering detail of the abbey of Batalha represents the more complex flamboyant Gothic of the late 14th century. In Lisbon, the western portal of the Jerónimos Monastery (see pp. 64–67) is a tour de force of craftsmanship of the period.

Hand in hand with architecture came sculpture. As cathedrals multiplied, so did funerary art, which reached its apogee, again, at Alcobaça in the beautifully sculpted tombs of the ill-fated lovers Inês de Castro and Dom Pedro. Coimbra, Évora, and Lisbon became prodigious centers for art, while Batalha's school was strongly influenced by the Frenchman Master Huguet. French influence also permeated church statuary, which flourished during the Gothic period.

Manueline: Until the reign of Manuel I (r. 1495–1521) there was no specific Portuguese style of architecture; most forms and techniques were imported. The horizon changed totally with the evolution of the Manueline style, Portugal's most exuberant artistic expression and a clear reflection of a newfound national confidence. As a new world concept took shape with the first overseas forays, twisted ropes, nautical knots, anchors, shells, coral-like textures, and armillary spheres became the favored symbols used again and again in abbeys, churches, and palaces.

Sculptural mastery transformed the arches of simple Romanesque or Gothic cloisters with delicate, lace-like embellishments, while windows and doors were framed in symphonies of intricately carved stone.

In Tomar, the Templar fortress and monastery acquired some exceptional Manueline additions, most notably the chapter house window by Diogo de Arruda. Batalha, too, saw dazzling additions, including the ornately carved doorway to the Capelas Imperfeitas by Mateus Fernandes. The Jerónimos Monastery in Belém showcases some of Portugal's most striking craftsmanship of the time, thanks to the masterful input of Diogo de Boitaca and Spaniard Juan de Castilla. The most integrated and exquisite example of Manueline vision and skill, however, is arguably the Torre de Belém, the work of Francisco de Arruda, brother of Diogo—a confectionery of carved rope, openwork balconies, and battlements shaped like shields. The Palácio Nacional at Sintra also features numerous Manueline details, and copies of its spectacular carved stone window frames can be seen in mansions throughout Portugal.

Renaissance & Baroque: The 16th-century flowering of the Renaissance, with its emphasis on Roman design and proportion, and on more realistic sculpture, took longer to appear in Portugal and, once again, a foreigner led the way. The prodigious French sculptor Nicolas de Chanterenne left his mark in churches from Coimbra to Lisbon. His countrymen Jean de Rouen and Philippe Houdart perfected the art of religious statuary and bas-reliefs. Meanwhile, Portuguese architecture absorbed classical notes in the work of Miguel de Arruda at Batalha and that of the Spaniard Diego de Torralva, who designed the Grand Cloisters at Tomar.

During the years of Spanish rule and the accompanying Inquisition (1580–1640), architectural style entered a more ponderous period (mannerism), guided by the classicism of Italian architects such as Filippo Terzi. By the end of the 17th century, however, a complete reaction was germinating: the baroque. The word itself derives from the Portuguese for rough pearl—*barroco*—and it would characterize Portuguese

■ **The masterful stone tracery at Batalha creates patterns of light and shadow.**

design for more than two centuries. With the Spaniards safely back over the border and gold and precious stones flowing from the mines of Brazil, Portugal experienced a rebirth and a revived sense of buoyancy and optimism. Great swirls of gilded, carved wood careered over interior surfaces, while architecture itself abandoned symmetry to embrace fluidity, theatricality, complexity, and ornamentation. Cherubim, foliage, and sinuous lines were carved and gilded (*talha dourada*) to become altarpieces, panels, or frames, while azulejos depicting birds, flowers, people, and religious or urban scenes blanketed church and mansion walls.

Though notable examples abound throughout the country, the north is where baroque soared to delirious heights, notably in Porto's São Francisco Church (see pp. 89, 93). From 1725 onward, Porto was the base for the most interesting and productive baroque architect, the Tuscan Nicolau Nasoni. He designed numerous elegant monuments, including the elliptical Igreja dos Clérigos and the beautifully scaled Casa de Mateus.

■ **The baroque chapel of Nossa Senhora d'Agonia, Viana do Castelo**

Another creative center developed at Braga, and the glorious staircase of Bom Jesus was a late result. The north saw a proliferation of baroque gardens, exemplified at Mateus and Braga, and every town boasted a handful of elegant mansions. During the reign of João V (r. 1706–1750), foreign artists and architects poured into Portugal for well-paid commissions. German Johann Friedrich Ludwig and Hungarian Carlos Mardel created João's palace at Mafra, which ultimately appears more rococo than baroque.

Pombaline & Neo-Manueline: A new architectural style evolved in the aftermath of the terrible 1755 earthquake: the Pombaline style. With most of Lisbon lying in ruins, prime minister Marquês de Pombal masterminded its reconstruction, abandoning the freedom of baroque in favor of more sober neoclassical colonnades and porticoes. The Palácio de Queluz in Sintra, designed by Mateus Vicente de Oliveira, is typical of the style, although its opulent interior is credited to the French architect Jean-Baptiste Robillon. Neoclassicism dominated architecture well into

Military Architecture

Portugal's military structures evolved in parallel with its abbeys and churches, with simple castles gradually becoming more sophisticated. Dozens were built along the border with Spain, usually incorporated into walled hill towns, during the reign of Dom Dinis I. Keeps became ever higher, culminating in Beja's 138-foot-tall (42 m) structure, while contact with northern Europe and Asia (via the Moors and the crusaders) brought other features. The Knights Templar made the greatest contribution, exemplified in the proportions and excesses at Tomar; the Knights' Hospitaller influence was more discreet. Gothic castles of the 14th and 15th centuries saw a French influence in the machicolations and round turrets (as at Santiago do Cacém) as well as the introduction of the barbican, a lower, protective wall outside the main structure. By the late Middle Ages, some fortresses were converted into residences for kings or nobles, and inner comforts appeared in the form of wood paneling and fireplaces.

the 19th century, and in Porto it was favored by the influential yet conservative community of English port traders.

Yet the desire for fantasy lay dormant, not lost, and by the mid-19th century the prevailing Romantic ethic ushered in a fashion for the neo-Manueline. Some of the most extreme examples were built in Sintra, where wealthy aristocrats indulged their fantasies. The whimsical Palácio da Pena of Prince Ferdinand of Saxe-Coburg may be the most stunning creation. The northern equivalent is the extraordinarily lavish palace of Buçaco. Neo-everything became the rage, even extending to neo-Moorish at Lisbon's Rossio train station. By the early 20th century, these revivals merged with the curves and patterns of art nouveau, but they were soon followed by the cleaner, more geometrical forms of art deco, an outstanding example of which is Porto's Casa de Serralves.

20th Century & Beyond: Today, Portugal's uncontested star architect is the Porto-based Álvaro Siza Vieira (b. 1933), following in the footsteps of his teacher, Fernando Távora (1923–2005). Siza's purist approach and concern with site is in harmony with the world's top contemporary architects. His buildings incorporate breathtaking technical feats—for instance, the majestic, swooping roof of the Portuguese Pavilion at Parque das Nações (Lisbon's Expo site). Siza was also responsible for the vast, interlocking exhibition halls of the Serralves Foundation in Porto, and for the master plan of the Chiado reconstruction following the 1988 fire. The next generation includes Eduardo Souto de Moura (b. 1952), a former collaborator of Siza who designed the Braga stadium in 2003, and João

Luís Carrilho da Graça (b. 1952), who designed the strict geometry of the Knowledge Pavilion at Parque das Nações. Another wave of architects is spearheaded by Bernardo Rodrigues (b. 1972) and Promontório Arqui- tectos (a group of five architects, founded in 1990). Whether the circle returns again to the Portuguese predilection for decorative frenzy remains to be seen, but it is certain that Portugal's style will never be at a standstill.

Painting

Portuguese artistic talent has always leaned more to the three-dimensional than the two. After emerging in the 15th century, local painting was slow to throw off the cloak of foreign influence and Portuguese painters never stood out as a specific school or style. Of the notable homegrown artists, the 15th-century painter Nuno Gonçalves was outstanding. His polyptych with the "Adoration of St. Vincent" is one of the great classics of the period.

He was followed in the 16th century by Vasco Fernandes and Gaspar Vaz in Viseu and Jorge Afonso in Lisbon, who later became court painter in 1508. Unusual for the time, a woman excelled in the 17th century: Josefa de Óbidos (1634–1684) dazzled patrons with her warm portraits and still lifes. Her con- temporary Domingos Vieira (1600–1678) produced remark- ably compassionate portraits.

■ A detail from Nuno Gonçalves's polyp- tych of the "Adoration of Saint Vincent" (1460–1470) shows the saint with Prince Henry the Navigator on the right.

During the following century, Domingos António de Sequeira (1768–1837) and Francisco Vieira (1765–1805) both studied in Rome, a sign of the cultural times, and Sequeira contributed greatly to the Ajuda Palace before politi- cal turmoil sent him into exile. A hiatus followed, characterized by generally derivative output, while naturalism gradually took over from Romanticism. The towering figure of the late 19th century was Columbano Bordallo Pin- heiro (1857–1929), whose brother, Rafael, was the remarkable ceramicist of Caldas da Rainha. He was followed by the short-lived Amadeo de Souza Cardoso (1887–1918), who produced a stream of cubist and expressionist works after joining the bohemian life of Paris's Montparnasse set.

The Salazar regime actively repressed free expression, so mid-20th-century abstract artists got short shrift. Not surprisingly, Maria Helena Vieira da Silva

(1908–1992), Portugal's most celebrated abstract artist, lived in Paris. Paula Rego (1935–2022), who lived in London—honored by a solo exhibition at the Tate Museum in 2004—achieved fame through imaginative figurative work illustrating metaphors and feminist issues. In the 1980s, a new wave of artists, including Julião Sarmento (1948–2021) and Pedro Cabrita Reis (b. 1956), appeared on the international scene with compelling works that used new mediums and stretched the limits of painting. Since then photography and new technologies have gained the upper hand among younger artists although, as elsewhere, painting is making a comeback.

Design

Portuguese design and decorative arts are as important in the 21st century as in preceding centuries. Lisbon's recent Museu de Arte, Arquitetura e Tecnologia (MAAT), housed within the 20th-century Tejo Power Station and an ultramodern exhibition wing, showcases contemporary artists, designers, and thinkers. Add to this the didactic role of Lisbon's Museu do Design e da Moda (MUDE) and you have a healthy panorama.

Among names to watch for is the internationally renowned Joana Vasconcelos, who takes everyday objects and transforms them into sculptures, often with feminist or sociopolitical undertones. Objects in ceramic and glass remain at the top of the creative league, but lesser-used materials such as cork (in which the Alentejo abounds), steel, and plastics are gaining increasing attention, while

Fashion

In fashion, the name long on everyone's lips is Ana Salazar, who in stature and imagination is the Portuguese Vivienne Westwood. This grande dame of clothing started her career in the 1970s, when she created Lisbon's first postrevolution fashion events. Since she founded her brand in 1978, Salazar has received numerous acknowledgments. She has also opened a boutique in Paris and presented her often controversial collections in Paris and New York. She even designed the uniforms for Portugal's letter carriers. A monograph and a documentary made about her re-

trace her life and her career path. With such a radical example to follow, Portuguese fashion remains extreme, with opulence, fantasy, and decadence never far away. Fátima Lopes, José António Tenente, Anabela Baldaque, Dino Alves, Lidija Kolovrat, Alexandra Moura, and Manuel Alves & José Manuel Gonçalves are among the next generation to create waves. The twice-yearly ModaLisboa, Lisbon Fashion Week, strengthens their impact. In purely industrial terms, fashion is beaten hands down by footwear: The Portuguese shoe industry is number two in Europe (after Italy).

■ **The Museu Nacional do Azulejo, Lisbon, is located in the former convent of Madre de Deus.**

recycling offers another sometimes humorous direction. Although post-contemporary design attracts media attention, and is the current rage in hotel interior design, Portuguese classics have not been forgotten. The workshops of Lisbon's Museu de Artes Decorativas play an important role in maintaining complex craft techniques, while more basic handicrafts continue to be the mainstay of some village economies, particularly in the Alentejo and central Portugal.

Music

Fado (see pp. 62–63), the "blues" of Portugal, is the signature national music and has propelled numerous singers onto the international scene, from Amália Rodrigues to Madredeus and, more recently, Kátia Guerreiro, Ana Moura, and Carminho. Yet there are other forms of music as well, for Portugal's love of song and verse dates back to the troubadours of the 13th century. Political songs *(canção de intervenção),* for example, played an important role in the protests against the totalitarian regime of 1926–1974, with José Afonso (1929–1987) one of its chief exponents. This new style of urban popular music was notable for its politically and socially engaged lyrics, often written by the singers. Melodies were word born and reinforced the content of the lyrics. The sound reflected a mixture of influences from traditional music, French urban songs of the 1960s, African rhythms, and Brazilian popular music.

By the late 1970s the revolutionary climate had subsided and poets and singers had to redefine their roles. There soon came a boom in the number of Portuguese rock groups and a local style emerged. The last 30 years have been marked by a search for new musical directions parallel to the "mediatization" and growth of the music-buying public. One of the most outstanding sounds has been, for a long time, that of Madredeus, a quintet of musicians who, from the mid-1980s onward, developed a unique mix of fado and modern folk music. Jazz has also seen a substantial increase in both musicians and audiences, and Susana Santos (trumpeter, improviser, and composer from Porto) is just one example.

Several transplanted musical traditions—especially from the former African colonies—now thrive in Lisbon, and foreign styles such as rap and hip-hop have been adapted locally. Cesária Évora, from the former colony of Cabo Verde (Cape Verde), has attained international fame with her pulsating *morna* (a wistful style of blues). The four accordionists of Danças

Ocultas represent an ethno-folk thread that produces a searing sound of pure emotion. Contemporary classical music flourishes, too—Orchestrutopica plays pieces by several young composers—while pop bands such as The Gift and Amor Electro fill concert venues around the country.

Literature

Poetry—especially of a metaphysical nature—appeals to the Portuguese heart, making it the dominant literary form. As is the case with cinema, Portuguese literature of the 20th century is dominated by a towering yet enigmatic figure: Fernando Pessoa. From a historical perspective, Portugal's equivalent of Shakespeare is Luís Vaz de Camões (1524–1580); his epic work, *Os Lusíadas (The Lusiads),* celebrated Vasco da Gama's

Madredeus & Beyond

Named for the Lisbon convent in which they initially rehearsed (now part of the Museu Nacional do Azulejo), the fado band Madredeus went from strength to strength, led by the haunting voice of their singer, Teresa Salgueiro. The 1987 album *Os Dias da Madredeus* was a watershed in Portuguese music, and Madredeus was soon touring the world, bringing the Portuguese language and echoes of fado to millions. Today, artists with diverse experiences, blended influences, and inspirational motivation are bringing sounds that draw on tradition to the big stages, and they are beloved by audiences: Cátia Oliveira, better known as A Garota Não; António Zambujo; Salvador Sobral (2017 winner of the Eurovision Contest), and fado musicians Ana Moura and Carminho (see p. 63).

voyage of discovery to India in 1497. Far from being a figment of Camões's imagination, the story is based on his own experiences while sailing to Goa and Morocco, and it is rendered in a spirit similar to Homer's *Odyssey.*

Also honored time and again is Almeida Garrett (1799–1854), a poet of the Romantic period who also penned political plays and novels including *Viagens na Minha Terra (Travels in My Homeland).* His contemporary, Alexandre Herculano (1810–1877), was a political activist who spent long periods of exile in England and France; he was also a successful novelist. Realism came to Portuguese literature in the works of José Maria Eça de Queirós (1845–1900), whose bestselling novel was *Os Maias (The Maias).* In the 20th century, Lisbon-based poet Fernando Pessoa (1888–1935) was in full flight. After spending much of his childhood in South Africa, where he became fluent in English, Pessoa started writing poetry in his teens. He led a dreary life as an office translator, but his depressive mind churned with thoughts. He was part of Lisbon's avant-garde movement, founding several journals and bringing the tenets of futurism and surrealism to Portugal. Writing under several heteronyms (poet identities), he published widely, yet his genius was only recognized after his premature death from cirrhosis. *O Livro do Desassossego (The Book of Disquiet)* is the collection of his angst-ridden notes and jottings stored in a trunk during his tragic and solitary existence.

José Saramago (1922–2010) was Portugal's most influential writer, having won the Nobel Prize for literature in 1998. His sometimes ponderous work includes plays, poetry, short stories, nonfiction, and novels, blending realism with the fantastical. Saramago's rise to fame came in 1982 with *Memorial do Convento (Memorial of the Convent),* a lyrical love story set in the convent of Mafra during its 18th-century construction. In 1991, his *O Evangelho Segundo Jesus Cristo (The Gospel According to Jesus Christ),* which depicted Christ as a typical fallible human being with self-doubts and sexual impulses, scandalized the Portuguese church. The result? Another exiled Portuguese writer—this time to Lanzarote in the Canary Islands.

António Lobo Antunes (b. 1942) has also enjoyed international success. His dark novels delve deeply into human relationships, incorporate history, and reflect his experience both of war and of clinical psychiatry. Other contemporary names to watch for are Lídia Jorge (b. 1946), José Cardoso Pires (1925–1998), Hélia Correia (b. 1949), and the highly respected philosopher Eduardo Lourenço (1923–2020), whose *Mitologia da Saudade (Mythology of Nostalgia)* is a seminal work.

Cinema

One name dominates Portuguese cinema: Manoel de Oliveira (1908–2015), a celebrated native of Porto. At the time of his death he was the oldest director in the world, his work spanning the history of film from his first silent movie, in 1928, to his last, in 2012. With astonishing vitality and talent, Oliveira was prodigious in his output, averaging one film a year for the last two decades, and he worked with a host of celebrity actors, from Marcello Mastroianni to Michel Piccoli and Irene Papas. His most recent film was *Gebo et l'Ombre (Gebo and the Shadow),* made in 2012, with stars

EXPERIENCE: Portuguese Cinema

For film aficionados, Portugal offers some great opportunities for viewing national and international art films. If visiting Porto in late February or early March, a good way to pass an evening or two is to check out **Fantasporto** *(fantasporto.com),* the country's leading film festival. In addition to showing quality movies, both commercial and independent, it showcases the best of Portuguese films—though beware, if your Portuguese language skills are lacking, better pick an English-language movie. Either way, Fantasporto is a fantastic way to immerse yourself in Porto's cultural scene, well off the usual tourist trail.

Michael Lonsdale and Jeanne Moreau. Oliveira's fame extends to the United States, where retrospectives of his work have been shown at the Los Angeles Film Festival (1992), the National Gallery of Art in Washington (1993), the San Francisco Film Festival, and the Cleveland Museum of Art (1994).

■ **Winner of the Nobel Prize for literature, José Saramago was Portugal's most influential writer.**

Another major figure of Portuguese cinema is João César Monteiro (1939–2003). This protagonist of the so-called New Portuguese Cinema in the 1960s only reached maturity in the mid-1970s. Monteiro was considered one of Europe's most original directors, making provocative films in which the gritty clashed with the sublime. His last films included *As Bodas de Deus* (1998), *Branca de Neve* (2000), and *Vai e Vem* (2003), which was screened at the 2004 Cannes Film Festival. *A Comédia de Deus* (1995) won him the Jury's Special Prize at the Venice Film Festival.

Portuguese cinema struggles to survive: With a population of 10 million, the domestic market is understandably small and Portuguese penetration of the international market is limited. A film is considered a success when it draws an audience of more than 150,000—and very few Portuguese films do. One that did was *Tentação* (1997), directed by Joaquim Leitão (b. 1956). This love story about a priest and a junkie in deepest Portugal features Portugal's biggest star, Joaquim de Almeida. Internationally awarded *Tabu* (2012), by Miguel Gomes, and the highly accoladed *Blood of My Blood* (2011), directed by João Canijo, have undoubtedly been the most successful Portuguese films of recent years. Among the younger generation of directors, Teresa Villaverde (b. 1966) is the most interesting. After beginning her career as an actress in César Monteiro's film *À Flor do Mar* (1986), she surfaced as a director in the 1990s. Her films tend to be angst-ridden stories about adolescents in conflict with society. One of her films, *Três Irmãos* (1994), won Maria de Medeiros the best actress award at the Venice Film Festival.

It is impossible to write about Portuguese cinema without mentioning two highly charged, evocative films about Lisbon by foreign directors. *In the White City* (1983), by Swiss filmmaker Alain Tanner, stars Bruno Ganz and Teresa Madruga in an exploration of alienation and time against a picturesquely decrepit backdrop of the Portuguese capital. Wim Wenders's *Lisbon Story* (1994) is a masterpiece built on the theme of sound. Filmed around the Alfama, it features the melancholic voices and presence of the band Madredeus and a guest appearance by Manoel de Oliveira. ■

A seductive mix of broad avenues and twisting alleyways,
the old-fashioned and the hip, the past and the present

LISBON

Vintage trams negotiate Lisbon's hills.

LISBON

Stand on the banks of the Tejo River and savor the salty Atlantic air—you will have a clear sense of being on the edge of Europe. Lisbon (Lisboa) is very much that, its character formed more by Portugal's overseas colonies than by its European neighbors. Today, its character is sophisticated and liberal, a hub for entrepreneurship and innovation. Humming with visitors, Lisbon's history and culture are being repackaged and rebranded to appeal to the ever more discerning traveler.

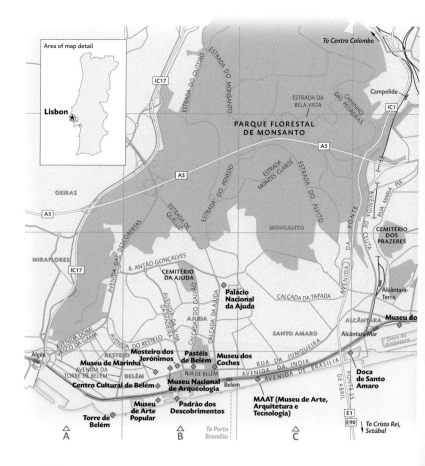

Lisbon offers a unique array of cultural attractions, excellent restaurants, atmospheric backstreets, melancholic music, efficient public transportation, and plenty of green escapes. The city's riverfront position adds spice to every view, of which there are many from *miradouros* (viewpoints) and towers. This sense of space is increased by two spectacular bridges: the Ponte 25 de Abril and the 10.7-mile-long (17 km) Ponte Vasco da Gama, a technological feat that disappears over the horizon. The main districts of interest are the central Baixa, Chiado, Bairro Alto, and the Alfama. To the west lies Belém, a must-see for its monuments and custard tarts, and heading far east along the Tejo, the family-friendly Parque das Nações. Other places not to be overlooked include the Museu Calouste Gulbenkian, the Museu Nacional do Azulejo, and the Museu Nacional de Arte Antiga.

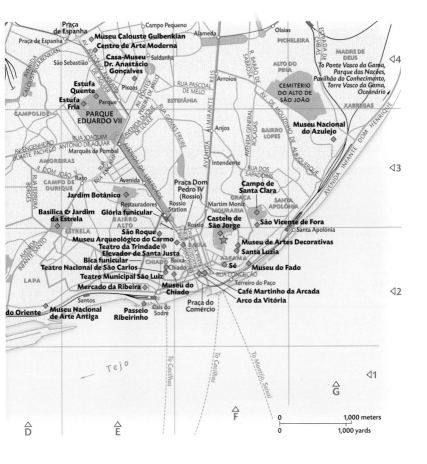

NOT TO BE MISSED:

The city views from Castelo de São Jorge   55–56

Having a morning coffee at the sidewalk café A Brasileira   60

An evening of fado   62–63

Jerónimos Monastery   64–67

Eating *pastéis de nata* (custard tarts) in Belém   68

The exquisite Torre de Belém   68–69

Admiring the Gulbenkian Museum's stunning artwork   70–71

Also be sure to explore the vast, wooded Parque Florestal de Monsanto; walk the hand-cobbled, charcoal gray basalt and limestone sidewalks of Chiado and Baixa; and wander the bougainvillea-draped alleys and stairways of the Alfama, Lisbon's oldest district, crowned by the ruins of its Moorish castle. ∎

∎ **A view from the Elevador de Santa Justa looks across the Baixa at the Alfama district's Castelo de São Jorge.**

BAIXA & THE DOCKS

Lisbon's commercial heart stretches between two large squares, the Praça Dom Pedro IV, more commonly known as Rossio, and the lovely Praça do Comércio, which opens onto the river. From here it is a natural transition to the central docks, now completely regenerated as one of Lisbon's hottest nocturnal destinations.

Following the 1755 earthquake, which hit the Baixa hardest, the Marquês de Pombal ordered a reconstruction to accommodate the artisans based there: a grid layout sliced north-south by the Rua Augusta and streets named after each trade. On the Rua do Ouro (Gold Street) you'll find the 148-foot-tall (45 m) **Elevador de Santa Justa.** This iconic ironwork structure dating from 1902 spirits people up to the Chiado via a walkway at the top; be sure to stop at the top of the tower for fabulous views. Equally delightful is the **Glória funicular,** just north of Rossio station, which takes you up to the Bairro Alto.

Rua Augusta has become a promenading street, its black and white cobbles fronting century-old traditional stores, banks, cafés, fashion shops, and at the southern end, the **Museu do Design e da Moda** (MUDE; Rua Augusta 24, tel 218 171 892, mude.pt), a museum dedicated to design and fashion. Furniture, accessories, and household objects dating from the 1930s onward are exhibited amid exposed concrete, vast modernist countertops, and green and black marble floors.

From here head through the **Arco da Vitória,** a triumphal arch that frames the vast, arcaded **Praça do Comércio.** This square, once the site of the royal Palácio da Ribeira, is now home to ministries, Lisbon's Welcome Center, and buzzing outdoor dining. An equestrian statue of Dom

Step Back in Time

At first glance, the Baixa district looks like any other downtown shopping area, but behind many of the 18th-century facades you'll find charming centenary shops. Open since the early 20th century, or even before, and complete with original fixtures, these businesses specialize in everything from hats and gloves to buttons and fine jewels. Don't miss **Confeitaria Nacional** (Praça da Figueira 18B), confectioners since 1829; **Manuel Tavares** (Rua de Betesga 1A), a grocery store established in 1860; the 1886 millinery **Azevedo Rua** (Praça Dom Pedro IV, 69–73); **Retrosaria Bijou** (Rua da Conceição 91), a haberdashery opened in 1922; or the 1925 glove shop **Luvaria Ulisses** (Rua do Carmo 87A).

■ Arcade in Praça do Comércio

José I surveys the scene, while **Café Martinho da Arcada**—once a haunt of the noted 20th-century poet Fernando Pessoa (see pp. 45–46)—offers the perfect spot for a quick *bica* (espresso). On the eastern side of the square, the **Lisboa Story Centre** *(tel 211 941 027, lisboastorycentre.pt)* provides visitors with an hour-long history of the city, focusing on the 1755 earthquake and its aftermath.

The Docks

The revitalized docks along the Tejo extend west past Alcântara and east as far as Santa Apolónia (the actual working docks extend farther). Today's occupants of the converted warehouses are no longer importers of exotic goods from Portuguese colonies but hot nightclubs and hip restaurants with a few designer stores thrown in. Traffic can be worse here in the early hours of a Sunday morning than in any midweek rush hour.

The soaring iron-and-glass landmark along this strip is the 1876 **Mercado da Ribeira,** part traditional food market—offering an array of fresh produce, cured meats, and regional cheeses—and part uber-trendy food hall called **Time Out Market,** featuring stalls from some of the city's best known restaurants, live music, and events (see p. 293).

Across the main road is the **Cais do Sodré,** where bus, train, tram, metro, and ferry lines all meet. Trains to Estoril and Cascais leave from here, as does the ferry to Cacilhas. You cannot help but see the statue of Christ, the **Cristo Rei,** on the other side of the river. Built in 1959, it towers 360 feet (110 m) above Lisbon in brazen imitation of the Rio de Janeiro version. If interested, take the elevator to the top of the statue *(Santuário Nacional de Cristo Rei, Almada, tel 212 751 000, cristorei.pt, $$)* for fabulous views over the city and south across the Setúbal Peninsula.

Back on the river's right bank, enjoy a breezy riverside stroll and some barbecued fish along the **Passeio Ribeirinho** to the west of Cais do Sodré. Beyond Alcântara's maritime terminal is the **Santo Amaro** dock, another urban development that attracts Lisbonites. ■

Baixa 🅜 51 F2 **Visitor Information** ✉ Ask Me Lisboa, Praça do Comércio ☎ 210 312 810 **visitlisboa.com** • **Mercado da Ribeira** 🅜 51 E2 ✉ Avenida 24 de Julho ☎ 213 951 274 **timeoutmarket.com**
NOTE: Sightseeing boat trips on the Tejo 🕐 Daily between 11 a.m. and 6 p.m., at 2 or 3 hour intervals, a shuttle-boat connects Praça do Comércio to Belém *(yellowbustours.com, $$$$).*

CASTELO & THE ALFAMA

Lisbon may have been built on seven hills, but its most visible summit monument is without a doubt the Castelo de São Jorge. Views from the ramparts of this sprawling castle take in the Chiado and Bairro Alto opposite, the district of Graça behind, and the labyrinthine Alfama below the castle walls. The name Alfama derives from the Arabic Al-Hamma, or hot springs, thanks to the Moors who built this atmospheric quarter of twisting, narrow alleys and stairways.

Castelo de São Jorge

The classic way to reach the castle is to take the No. 28 tram to Largo Santa Luzia, from where it is a short walk uphill, though swarms of *tuk-tuks* now vie for the trade. The origins of the castle go back to the fifth-century Visigoths and, four centuries later, to the Moors who enlarged it and built walls to surround their *kasbah* (fortress). Further modifications came with Afonso Henriques, Portugal's first

king, and until the 16th century it was used as a royal residence. After intermittently functioning as a prison, the castle was completely restored and turned over to the public. It offers a café, gardens, cannons, great views, and—on August Saturdays—biologist-led tours to observe the castle's resident colony of five species of bats.

On his return from India in 1499, Vasco da Gama came here for a triumphant audience with Dom Manuel I.

■ Castelo de São Jorge offers some of the best views across the city.

Invasion of the Tuk-Tuk

The Portuguese economic crisis has meant that people have had to get creative to make a living. Over the past few years, a new generation of entrepreneurs has injected fresh life into Lisbon: Trendy eateries and bars have sprung up, and dozens of boutique hotels and fashionable hostels have opened. A vast array of quirky tour options are now available including Segways, bikes, and 4x4s. Most notable is the invasion of the *tuk-tuk* (a three-wheeled covered motorcycle), offering anything from quick hop-on, hop-off rides to day-long tours of the city. Ideal for getting up the steep narrow streets of the Alfama, these zippy little vehicles will take you anywhere you want to go. For the sake of local residents and the environment always choose a company that uses electric-powered tuk-tuks (*ecotuktours.com* or *tejotourism .pt/en/tuk-tuk*).

The site of this meeting, the **Olisipónia,** is now occupied by an innovative multimedia show recounting the city's history. Close by, in the Torre de Ulisses, see an unusual view of the city in the **Periscópio,** an ingenious system of mirrors and screens.

On the southern slope of the castle hill stands a Romanesque **Sé,** or cathedral (*Largo da Sé, tel 218 866 752, sedelisboa.pt, closed Sun., $*). The sober facade flanked by two towers was built soon after Afonso Henriques took Lisbon from the Moors in the late 12th century. Although greatly damaged in the 1755 earthquake, the cathedral was successfully restored and today an elegant, vaulted interior leads to Gothic cloisters and a dazzling treasury in the **Museu do Tesouro.** Look for Dom José I's baroque monstrance, an elaborate affair said to incorporate more than 4,000 precious stones. Excavations in the cloisters have revealed Phoenician, Roman, and Arab artifacts.

The Alfama

On the southern side below the castle, the **miradouro de Santa Luzia** overlooks the Alfama. The exterior walls of the church facing this terrace bear striking azulejo panels that illustrate the city's history. Opposite stands the impressive **Museu de Artes Decorativas.** The decorative arts museum is housed in the 17th-century Azurara

Castelo de São Jorge 🅰 51 F2 ☎ 218 800 620 💲 $$; Extra fee for bat tour ($$) 🚌 Bus: 737; Tram: 12, 28 **castelodesaojorge.pt • Museu de Artes Decorativas** 🅰 51 F2 ✉ Largo das Portas do Sol 2 ☎ 218 814 640 🕐 Closed Tues. 💲 $ 🚌 Bus: 737; Tram: 12, 28 **fress.pt**

mansion. The museum showcases glasswork, silverwork, porcelains, paintings, tapestries, and carpets, all presented according to historic periods in a suitably aristocratic environment. However, the most outstanding rooms are devoted to 17th- and 18th-century furniture, of which many pieces reflect Portugal's fascination for exotic craftsmanship: Take note of the sophisticated portable writing desk from India and the oriental fantasy painted on lacquered cabinets. A visual feast of azulejos adorn the walls of the main staircase and halls.

Although not strictly part of the Alfama, the white stone monastery of **São Vicente de Fora** *(Largo de São Vicente, tel 218 810 559, mosteirode saovicentedefora.com)* to the northeast is a sight you cannot escape. Built at the turn of the 16th century outside the city walls, its cloister walls still retain azulejos telling the fables of Jean de La Fontaine.

The huge square behind São Vicente, **Campo de Santa Clara,** hosts the sprawling **Feira da Ladra** (Thieves' Market) every Tuesday and Saturday—a must-see for lovers of antiques and secondhand objects. ∎

The backstreets of the Alfama, where Lisbon life can be savored

A WALK AROUND THE ALFAMA

Lisbon's oldest quarter, built by the Moors in the 11th century, retains much of its original atmosphere despite, after years of negligence, having undergone a total renovation in order to welcome tourists. Fading coats of arms bear witness to the Alfama's aristocratic past before the city's fishing community took over.

From the Castelo de São Jorge's main entrance on Rua do Chão da Feira, start walking downhill, admiring the tiled facades. As you round the corner, peep inside the 18th-century entrance of the Belmonte patio on your left to see a lovely example. When you reach the Largo do Contador-Mor, cross the road to the church of **Santa Luzia ❶**; exterior azulejo panels show Lisbon's appearance, including the Praça do Comércio, before the 1755 earthquake.

Opposite, on the corner of Largo das Portas do Sol, is the **Museu de Artes Decorativas ❷**, well worth a visit (see p. 56–57). Alternatively, the sidewalk café is a good place to watch the trams go by against a backdrop of the monastery **São Vicente de Fora** (see p. 57). Just behind Santa Luzia, steps twist downhill into the heart of the Alfama. Follow this convoluted route to a small square. Turn right to Beco da Corvinha and left, down more steps that eventually broaden out at the back of **São Miguel ❸**. Founded in 1150, this church was rebuilt after the earthquake. Orange trees, laundry hung out to dry, potted plants, caged canaries, and private shrines all add to the ambience.

> **NOT TO BE MISSED:**
>
> **Museu de Artes Decorativas • Escadinhas de Santo Estêvão • Museu do Fado**

Pass a couple of fado taverns on your right, turn left onto Largo de São Miguel, then right down Rua de São Miguel. Local grocery stores on this typical street signal that the old Alfama has plenty of life in it yet. Turn right at the intersection with Rua da Regueira, then left along the narrow Beco do Carneiro, noting the public washing place. At the end, a staircase leads to the church of **Santo Estêvão ❹** and a terrace viewpoint. Return down the steps to reach a very pretty square. Around the next corner, descend the picturesque **Escadinhas de Santo Estêvão.**

At the bottom of the stairs, turn right onto Rua dos Remédios. On the right, note the lovely Manueline doorway of the 16th- to 18th-century **Ermida de Nossa Senhora dos Remédios,** a sanctuary built for the Alfama fishermen. Inside are baroque azulejos and some 16th-century paintings. This street and its extension, Rua de São Pedro, are the Alfama's busiest shopping streets.

At the Largo do Chafariz de Dentro, the **Museu do Fado ❺** (*tel 218 823 470, museudofado.pt, closed Mon., $$*) pays homage to the traditional music of Lisbon (see pp. 62–63). Continue along Rua de São Pedro, through the Largo de São Rafael with its ruined Moorish tower, then along Rua São João da Praça. After the church of the same name, turn left

through a tunnel arch and emerge on Rua do Cais de Santarém. Turn right to reach the **Casa dos Bicos ❻**, with its unusual diamond-shaped stone projections.

> 🅰 See also area map p. 51
> ▶ Castelo de São Jorge
> 🕐 1 hour
> ↔ 0.5 mile (0.8 km)
> ▶ Casa dos Bicos

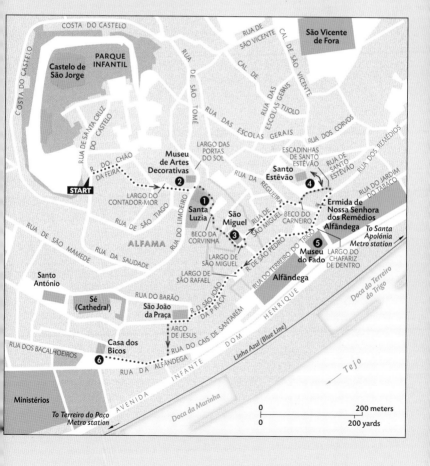

CHIADO & BAIRRO ALTO

West of Baixa is Chiado, which extends into Bairro Alto. Chiado may be limited in size, but it boasts theaters, art galleries, and museums—including a remarkable archeological museum—as well as wonderful shops. Bairro Alto, on the other hand, is a grid of narrow streets where touristy fado dives and packed restaurants rub shoulders with independent fashion stores; in daylight it can seem frayed at the edges.

When flames shot out of a store on Rua do Carmo in the heart of Lisbon in August 1988, Chiado bore the brunt of the accidental fire—fire engines couldn't get into the narrow streets. Four blocks were reduced to rubble, but intelligent rebuilding, following a master plan by Álvaro Siza Vieira, has restored it to its former self. Once again Lisbonites and tourists alike settle into sidewalk cafés such as the art nouveau institution **A Brasileira** (*Rua Garrett 120, tel 213 469 541*), a favorite of Pessoa, immortalized in bronze outside.

Bairro Alto

Uphill from here is the brick red **Teatro da Trindade Inatel** (*Rua Nova da Trindade 9, tel 213 420 000, teatrotrindade.inatel.pt*), built in 1867 to stage operettas and dance performances. It still hosts theater, musical, and dance performances. Next door, the **Anglo-Portuguese Telephone Company** is a 1920s relic of English commercial activity. At the top of this street, the church of **São Roque** is a 16th- to 17th-century design by Filippo Terzi. The 18th-century **Capela de São João Baptista,** a chapel to the left of the altar, is a heavy-duty baroque medley of different stones, made in Rome and blessed by the pope. A **museum,** to the right of the entrance, displays rich vestments and liturgical objects.

Focusing on scientific, zoological, and botanical studies in the former

---

EXPERIENCE:
Guided Walks by Scholars

Every nook and cranny of Lisbon oozes with history that comes alive on a scholar-guided walk. If you'd like to hear about former Phoenician, Moorish, and Roman inhabitants, visit the birthplace of St. Anthony of Padua, and see the site of the Inquisition, then look no further than **Lisbon Explorer** (*tel 966 042 993, lisbonexplorer.com*). The friendly English-speaking guides are entertaining and enthusiastic. Tours last 3 hours and cost €175 for the group. There's something for everyone, from secret Lisbon to Jewish Lisbon, the Alfama district, and more.

Portuguese colonies, the **Museu Nacional de História Natural e da Ciência** (*Rua da Escola Politécnica, tel 213 921 808, closed Mon., museus.ulisboa.pt, $$*), boasts one of Europe's oldest chemistry laboratories. The highlight here is undoubtedly its 19th-century botanical garden (see p. 76).

Chiado

An inspiring presentation awaits at Chiado's **Museu Arqueológico do Carmo.** A portion of this museum occupies a 1389 church nave, roofless since the 1755 earthquake. It gives an evocative edge to a display of architectural fragments, all in matching white stone. Inside the chapels at the back is a fascinating collection put together after the abolition of religious orders in 1834. Note the medieval tomb sculptures of Fernão Sanches (the illegitimate son of Dom Dinis I) and Dom Fernando I, as well as the odd juxtaposition of a library, an Egyptian mummy, two Peruvian mummies, and pre-Hispanic pieces from Central America. Outside, enjoy a drink in the pretty square before heading downhill.

At the southern end of Chiado, **Teatro Nacional de São Carlos** (*Rua*

▪ **A relic of the 1755 earthquake, this church nave now houses part of the Museu Arqueológico do Carmo.**

Serpa Pinto 9, tel 213 253 045, tnsc.pt) was built in 1793 in a late baroque imitation of Milan's La Scala. Enjoy the opulent decor by catching a ballet, opera, or concert.

One block farther south, the **Museu Nacional de Arte Contemporânea do Chiado** (MNAC), the national museum of contemporary art, displays rotating exhibits of the collection beside temporary exhibitions. A renovated former monastery, the building has striking, airy spaces perfect for modern art. Don't miss the suspended staircase leading down to the café, terrace, and sculpture garden. Due west of here, along Rua de São Paulo, the **Bica funicular** (*$*) will spirit you back up to Barrio Alto. ▪

Museu de São Roque 🗺 51 E2 ✉ Largo Trindade Coelho ☎ 213 235 444 🕐 Closed Mon. 💲 $ **museusaoroque.scml.pt** • **Museu Arqueológico do Carmo** 🗺 51 F2 ✉ Largo do Carmo ☎ 213 478 629 🕐 Closed Sun. 💲 $ 🚇 Metro: Baixa-Chiado; Tram: 28; Bus: 758 **museuarqueologicodo carmo.pt** • **Museu Nacional de Arte Contemporânea do Chiado** 🗺 51 F2 ✉ Rua Serpa Pinto 4/Rua Capelo 13 ☎ 213 432 148 🕐 Closed Mon. 💲 $ 🚇 Metro: Baixa-Chiado; Bus: 60, 208, 758; Tram: 28 **museuartecontemporanea.pt**

FADO MUSIC

If there is one sound that is distinctly Portuguese, it is the often melancholic strains of fado (literally "fate"), the local version of the blues. The music originated in early 19th-century Lisbon, more specifically in the dives of the Alfama, drawing on the rhythms of African slave dances, Arab voice medleys, and traditional oral folklore. Recent Lisbon music critic Miguel Francisco Cadete pointed out that its first fans were "pimps, prostitutes, sailors and bandits with knives." Today, however, fado is entrenched in the Lisbon soul.

Generally the untrained voice of the singer is accompanied by two acoustic guitarists, one playing a Spanish guitar, the other a 12-string Portuguese guitar (mandolin-shaped with a flat back). The musicians revel in melodic outpourings of longing, sadness, and fatalism to express the target emotion, *saudade* (yearning). In authentic fado houses you will see improvised musical dialogues between professional and amateur singers. The fado in Coimbra (see sidebar p. 137) has a tradition all of its own: It is sung only by men, the lyrics are more cultured,

and the Coimbra guitar gives it a more melodic and solemn sound.

Although its roots are in the lower ranks of society, fado was gradually adopted by the gentry thanks to a scandalous affair in the 1840s between singer Maria Severa and a nobleman, the Conde de Vimioso. From then on *fadistas* performed at aristocratic social gatherings. With the advent of radio, the form took off completely. During the long Salazar years (1932–1968), fado was initially labeled as harmful to social progress; many singers were banned or forced to become professional and only

EXPERIENCE: Strum the Portuguese Guitar

Does hearing fado make you want to pick up the Portuguese guitar? It is possible, over the summer months, to take lessons in the instrument with **Ricardo Mata** (*Avenida Almirante Reis 229, Lisbon, tel 962 238 252, ricardomata.net*). Mata has been teaching students since 1997 and offers lessons for beginners and up, whether you would like to learn a few basics

or polish up some existing skills. Each lesson lasts one hour and packages of four lessons cost around €90–95, depending on the time of day. Lessons can be taken all in one week or spread over four. At other times of the year, Mata is happy to provide tailor-made, private lessons, which can be arranged in advance. See his website for information.

Take Some Fado Home

Amália Rodrigues: Any of her many "Best of" albums
Mariza: *Fado em Mim* 2001, *Terra* 2008, *Fado Tradicional* 2010
Ana Moura: *Desfado* 2012
Carminho: *Fado* 2009, *Canto* 2014

perform publicly at fado houses. Salazar later embraced fado as the perfect propagandistic tool, and it thus became politically tainted, losing its popular appeal. Since the 1990s the music has regained its former status.

Songstresses of Note

Amália Rodrigues (1920–1999), fado's greatest diva, inspired such devotion that her death engendered three days of national mourning and a cathartic outpouring of emotion. It seems unlikely that Amália's popularity will ever be surpassed; apart from possessing a gut-wrenching voice and immense beauty, she lived a classic rags-to-riches tale. Her 18th-century town house, chock-a-block with antiques, portraits, and lavish costumes, is a far cry from her teenage years when she sold fruit on the Alcântara docks. The house is now open to the public (*Rua de São Bento 193, Lisbon, tel 213 971 896, amaliarodrigues .pt, closed Mon. & holidays, $$*). Amália remains an inspiration to fado and popular music artists such as Madredeus (see p. 45), Dulce Pontes, and

Mariza—whose confident voice and charismatic stage presence has conquered fans around the world—and more recently to Ana Moura and Carminho. Born in 1984, Carminho is considered one of the most talented fado singers of her generation: her ability to blend traditional and contemporary fado with pop, rock, and jazz, makes her popular with younger listeners. In 2015 she was awarded the Order of Infante Dom Henrique for her services in expanding Portuguese culture around the globe.

Fado musician Mario Pacheco (left) strums a 12-string Portuguese guitar, the *guitarra do fado*.

BELÉM

Far to the west of the city center is the district of Belém, a must-see for its cluster of monuments. It also plays an important official role in the form of the presidential residence, the Palácio de Belém.

The magnificent Jerónimos Monastery and the emblematic Torre de Belém top the list of amazing sites. In between stand the Centro Cultural de Belém, a cultural powerhouse harboring the Berardo collection and, on the hill above, the ornate former royal palace of Ajuda. Between them, several museums cover art, architecture, design, archaeology, history, and carriages. Yet Belém is far from being a mere tourist destination: Hordes of Lisbonites descend on this cultural epicenter on weekends and public holidays, partly for the scenic riverside area around the Discoveries monument but equally for Lisbon's most popular pastry shop.

Mosteiro dos Jerónimos

The imposing Jerónimos Monastery stands at the back of the monumental Praça do Império, now formal gardens and a vast parking lot. The fabulously ornate facade stonework has been restored to its original, blindingly white state and makes a startling sight in this predominantly post-1755 city.

Begun in 1501, this jewel of Manueline style took a century to be completed and, as a result, its architectural and decorative elements span Gothic, Renaissance, and neoclassical forms.

Commissioned by Dom Manuel I, the monastery affirmed the political and expansionist power of Portugal at the time, being close to the beach where Vasco da Gama's ships made their triumphant return. Financing came from the immense wealth derived from the spices of the Indies, while the gold later flowing from Brazil and Mozambique was destined to be plastered over side chapels and the altar.

Miraculously, the monastery structure was one of the few buildings to survive Lisbon's 1755 earthquake, thanks to its intelligently conceived vaults, although statues tumbled from

▪ **Vasco da Gama's tomb stands beneath the choir gallery of the Jerónimos Monastery.**

niches and columns. The unique architectural style won it UNESCO classification as a World Heritage site.

On a cultural note, two heroes of Portugal, Vasco da Gama and the poet Luís Vaz de Camões (1524–1580), are entombed at the entrance, beneath the choir gallery. These tombs, together with that of Fernando Pessoa (1888–1935) in the cloister and the royal tombs in the chapel (see sidebar p. 66), make the monastery an illustrious resting place.

Once you enter the monastery, you'll find the breathtaking cloister, a Manueline masterpiece, with arches and slender columns so delicately carved that they look like biscuitware porcelain. They were the work of French architect Diogo de Boitaca. Upon his death in 1517, Spaniard Juan de Castilla undertook the upper story, finishing in 1544. Look for the minimalist tomb of Pessoa, whose body was transferred here in 1985. Along with the colorful 18th-century azulejos depicting the life of St. Joseph in the refectory, do not miss the staircase that takes you up to the choir.

Outside, be sure to scan the walls for esoteric symbols carved into the stone; these are the signatures of the stonemasons who worked here.

Two Museums: The 19th-century "modern" wing of the monastery holds an archaeological museum and a maritime museum. The **Museu Nacional de Arqueologia** (*museunacionalarqueologia.gov.pt, temporarily closed for renovation*) has lovely pieces. Look for the second-century Roman statue of Apollo found in the Algarve and granite boars and warriors from the Douro region. The Bronze Age, Roman, and Celtic jewelry exhibits are outstanding. Oddly, one room even holds Egyptian mummies and fiber sandals. The **Museu de Marinha** (*tel 210 977 388, ccm.marinha.pt /pt/museu, $$*) portrays Portugal's maritime prowess through boats and barges, ship models, navigational instruments, uniforms, and paintings. The most unusual piece in the collection is the seaplane flown in 1922 by Gago Coutinho and Sacadura Cabral from Lisbon to Rio de Janeiro.

Palácio Nacional da Ajuda

Cresting the hill behind the monastery is the neoclassical Palácio Nacional da Ajuda. Although the palace contains sumptuous decorative features, its 19th-century

Belém 🗺 51 F2 Visitor Information ✉ Ask Me Lisboa, Jardim Vasco da Gama ☎ 910 517 981 🚌 Bus: 727, 729, 714, 751; Tram: 15; Train: Belém **visitlisboa.com** • **Mosteiro dos Jerónimos** 🗺 50 B1 ✉ Praça do Império ☎ 213 620 034 🕐 Closed Mon. 💲 Church: free; Monastery: $$ **jeronimosmonasterytickets.com** • **Palácio Nacional da Ajuda** 🗺 50 B2 ✉ Largo da Ajuda ☎ 213 637 095 🕐 Closed Wed. 💲 $$ **palacioajuda .gov.pt**

Jerónimos's Spectacular Manueline Details

Portugal's greatest showcase of Manueline style demands admiration of its details. The brilliantly rendered sculptures of the south portal are the work of the prodigious Spanish artist Juan de Castilla. They are surmounted by a cross of the Knights of Christ and a statue of Prince Henry the Navigator, Manuel I's great-uncle and the man responsible for Portugal's overseas ambitions. Equally outstanding is the typically Manueline entrance of the west portal, inside the porch, with statues by the great French sculptor Nicolas de Chanterenne. A perfect balance between simplicity and detail is typified by carved rope snaking up columns to the vaulted ceiling. Dom Manuel I's tomb in the main chapel displays a hefty silver tabernacle, and four other royal tombs are held up by marble elephants—further evidence of Portugal's far-reaching explorations.

Mosteiro dos Jerónimos

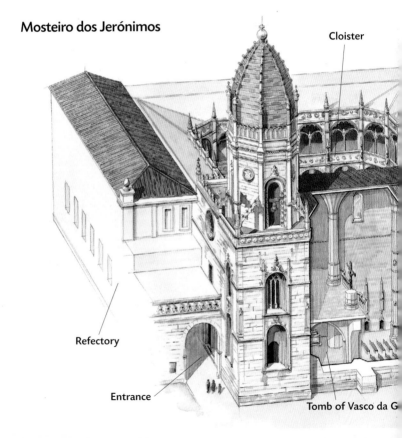

Cloister

Refectory

Entrance

Tomb of Vasco da G

style is not comparable with the palaces of Queluz (see pp. 198–199) or Sintra (see pp. 188–190). The painted ceilings, statues, tapestries, decorative objects, and furniture were all enjoyed by King Luis and his Italian wife, Maria Pia, after their marriage in 1862, and by their son, Carlos I. An unexpected element is Carlos's neo-Gothic painting studio and its simple wooden furniture, which decidedly differs from the formal reception rooms of the upper floors, dripping with chandeliers. Carlos was the royal painter par excellence, and much of his output hangs in the palace at Vila Viçosa (see pp. 220–221) in the Alentejo.

Centro Cultural de Belém

Closer to today in spirit is the massive geometric form of the Centro Cultural de Belém; it opened in 1999. Design shops and cafés flank the monumental main steps leading to the cultural center's inner sanctum where the auditoriums and exposition spaces are located. Here, there are temporary art and design exhibitions, spaces for activities and laboratories, the

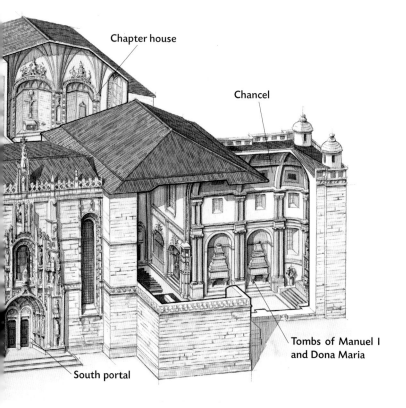

Chapter house

Chancel

South portal

Tombs of Manuel I and Dona Maria

Garagem Sul space dedicated to architecture exhibitions and, most significantly, the José Berardo collection. Composed of more than 800 works belonging to the main artistic movements from the 20th century to today, it was a museum itself until 2023, but current work is underway to renovate space that will make it an integral part of the complex. The center's lively bar and restaurant with terrace are great places for a drink or snack.

Belém Docks Area

From the Centro Cultural de Belém, take the pedestrian underpass beneath the riverfront avenues to reach the docks and the **Padrão dos Descobrimentos** (tel 213 031 950, padraodosdescobrimentos.pt). This massive 1960 monument dedicated to Portugal's age of discoveries is shaped like a ship's prow and peopled by a cast of historical figures led by Prince Henry, the driving force behind Portugal's overseas discoveries (see pp. 26–29). A sidewalk mosaic depicts a huge compass and map of the world.

Next to the monument is the often-overlooked **Museu de Arte Popular,** housed in the last surviving pavilion from Lisbon's 1940 Exposition. Inside is a delightful display of

rural folk art and clothing; ceramics, basketwork, wooden carts, and rugs are also prominent.

From here, it's only a short walk along the river to Lisbon's much photographed architectural gem, the **Torre de Belém.** Built in 1519 to protect Lisbon against English and Dutch pirates, this work of the brothers Francisco and Diogo de Arruda originally stood on a midstream island; when the 1755 earthquake affected the course of the river, the fort became

A Craving for Pastry

Your last stop in Belém should be Lisbon's most illustrious pastry shop, **Pastéis de Belém** (Rua de Belém 84–92, pasteisdebelem.pt), on the monastery side of Belém. This labyrinthine tearoom dates back to the 19th century, when it first supplied patrons with its famous custard tarts, allegedly made from a still secret recipe created by the neighboring monks. Azulejo-faced walls create a colorful backdrop for boisterous Lisbonite families devouring a daily total of about 7,000 of these delicious treats. Remember this one gastronomic tip: Sprinkle your tart with cinnamon.

Centro Cultural de Belém 🗺 50 B1 ✉ Praça do Império ☎ 213 612 400 🕐 Closed Mon. 💲 $–$$ ccb.pt • **Museu de Arte Popular** 🗺 50 B1 ✉ Avenida Brasília ☎ 213 011 282 🕐 Closed Mon.–Tues. 💲 $ museuartepopular.wordpress.com • **Torre de Belém** 🗺 50 A1 ✉ Avenida Brasília ☎ 213 620 034 🕐 Closed Mon. 💲 $$

■ The battlements of the iconic Torre de Belém guard the Tejo River's bank.

attached to the riverbank. A masterpiece of Gothic and Manueline styles, the tower also incorporates Moorish-style watchtowers and Venetian loggias with openwork tracery. The combination manages to look entirely harmonious. If the lines are long to reach the tower's top-floor terrace, enjoy looking up at its rope carving, armillary spheres, and the unique shield-shaped battlements decorated with the cross of the Order of Christ.

One of Belém's more unique museums, the **Museu Nacional dos Coches** *(Av. da India 136, tel 210 732 319, museudoscoches.gov.pt/pt/, closed Mon., $$)* displays one of the world's best collections of 18th- and 19th-century carriages in a new building. It is still possible to visit the **Picadeiro Real** *(Royal Riding School, tel 213 610 850, closed Mon., $)* once the royal stables and now part of the main exhibition, where the museum used to be located.

Museu de Arte, Arquitetura e Tecnologia

Opened in 2016 and heralded as Lisbon's new cultural hub, the Museu de Arte, Arquitetura e Tecnologia (MAAT; *Av. de Brasília, tel 210 028 130, maat.pt, closed Tues., $$),* is made up of two parts: The colossal red-brick Tejo Power Station, a fine example of 20th-century Portuguese industrial architecture (formerly the Museu da Electricidade), and a brand-new, ultramodern building dedicated to national and international art and architectural exhibitions. Sensitive landscaping and its riverfront location make this a popular spot. ■

MUSEU CALOUSTE GULBENKIAN & AROUND

Another of Lisbon's cultural focal points lies around the Praça de Espanha, to the north of Baixa, and centers on the world-famous Museu Calouste Gulbenkian. A couple of other sites, notably the Casa-Museu Dr. Anastácio Gonçalves and the bucolic bliss of the tropical greenhouses of the Parque Eduardo VII, equally merit visits.

The Gulbenkian

The museum stands in a large park dotted with sculptures and ponds. It displays the eclectic collection—some 6,000 works of art ranging from Mesopotamian sculptures to French Impressionism paintings—of Armenian Calouste Sarkis Gulbenkian (1869–1955; see sidebar). The superbly designed, low-lying building was conceived to offer constant interaction between the art displayed inside and nature; the art is presented in a series of rooms whose large windows overlook two courtyards or the surrounding grounds. The layout groups the art according to chronology, geographic origin, and medium.

The Eastern World: The first three rooms exhibit artwork from the **Egyptian, Greek, Roman,** and **Mesopotamian** civilizations. Keep your eyes peeled for the Egyptian head of an old man, a beautiful

Calouste Sarkis Gulbenkian

Born and raised in Turkey, Gulbenkian began collecting while in his teens and was systematically purchasing high-quality art by the turn of the 20th century. As his oil-magnate fortunes flourished, Gulbenkian astutely bought, exchanged, and donated works of art, while placing some on loan in museums in London, Paris, and Washington. In 1942, as World War II raged, he immigrated to Lisbon, where he remained until his death. In accordance with his wishes, a foundation was set up for his collection to be held "under one roof." The museum opened in 1969.

green schist sculpture from about 2000 B.C., and the ninth-century Assyrian bas-relief from the palace of Nimrud, sculpted in alabaster.

Museu Calouste Gulbenkian 🗺 51 E4 ✉ Avenida de Berna 45A ☎ 217 823 000 🕐 Closed Tues. 💲 $$ (includes entry to the Centro de Arte Moderna) 🚇 Metro: São Sebastião, Praça de Espanha; Bus: 716, 726, 756
gulbenkian.pt

■ **The wide-ranging Gulbenkian collection includes 18th- and 19th-century European paintings.**

The next two rooms display an extremely rich and large collection of **Eastern Islamic art.** Gulbenkian was especially drawn to this art because he grew up in Istanbul under the Ottoman Empire. This section overflows with priceless ceramics in glowing turquoises and greens, carpets, manuscripts, tiles, and mosque lamps from Syria. The unusual 13th- to 14th-century Persian ceramic *mihrab* (prayer niche) is stunningly executed, combining Koranic quotations and vegetal motif decoration.

Move into the **Oriental room** to see exquisite Japanese lacquerware, Ming porcelain, 17th- and 18th-century biscuit ware, Chinese jade stones, and much more.

The Western World: From the Oriental room, you leave the Eastern world for the Western. The richly stocked galleries of **European art of the 14th to 17th centuries** showcase medieval carved ivories and illuminated manuscripts of the tenth century before moving on to a chronological display of exceptional paintings—among them Rembrandt's "Portrait of an Old Man." The next two rooms are devoted to **18th-century French decorative arts:** tapestries, silverware, and ornate furniture.

A side room contains **sculpture from the 18th century.** Look for Jean-Antoine Houdon's (1741–1828) graceful marble statue of Diana as well as the work of Renaissance sculptor Andrea della Robbia. From here you head into a succession of rooms that masterfully display **European paintings of the 18th and 19th centuries.** Gaze upon the turbulent "Wreck of a Transport Ship" by J. M. W. Turner (1775–1851), the moody pastel of a winter scene by Jean-François Millet (1814–1875), and the much reproduced "Boy Blowing Bubbles" by French Impressionist Édouard Manet (1832–1883).

The last gallery devotes space to an exceptional collection of art nouveau glass and whimsical **jewelry by René Lalique** (1860–1945). The most sophisticated piece is arguably the "cats choker," a technical exploit incorporating diamonds, rock crystal, and gold, yet sober in its total impact.

Downstairs, two generously scaled halls are used for temporary exhibitions, and a very pleasant cafeteria spills out onto a terrace.

Centro de Arte Moderna

Next door to the Museu Gulben-kian is the **Centro de Arte Moderna,** opened in 1983, which offers a full panorama of 20th- and 21st-century Portuguese art as well as some British art. The center is currently undergoing expansion of a new wing that will add to the current space for visitors. Cultural initiatives are nevertheless ongoing thanks to CAM in Motion, an outdoor program featuring works from the collection.

Casa-Museu Dr. Anastácio Gonçalves

In the heart of this upscale district, the museum's decorative arts collection numbers some 2,000 pieces and once belonged to physician António Anastácio Gonçalves (1889–1965), a friend of Gulbenkian who frequented the same artistic and literary circles.

The elegant, muted calm of the 19th-century mansion Casa Malhoa, named after the 19th-century painter to which it once belonged, makes a suitable backdrop for the wide-ranging collection. The tapestries, silverware, and European furniture of the 17th, 18th, and 19th centuries are noteworthy, but the Chinese porcelain takes pride of place. Highlights include ceramics from the Song dynasty; a vast collection of Ming "blue-and-white" porcelain; and a good selection of "green" and "pink" porcelain from the Qing dynasty.

Parque Eduardo VII

This lovely park lies immediately west of the Casa-Museu Dr. Anastácio Gonçalves, behind Lisbon's most popular department store, El Corte Inglés. The Parque Eduardo VII *(Av. da Liberdade, tel 213 882 278)* was named after the British King Edward VII, who paid a visit to Lisbon in 1903 soon after his coronation.

After taking in the views of the Baixa and castle from the top of the hill, head down to the main greenhouse, the luxuriant **Estufa Fria de Lisboa.** This unheated greenhouse was first planted in 1910 and shaded by a slatted roof to let rain into channels, which course through what amounts to a mini-tropical forest. Tree ferns, banana palms, aspidistras, rubber plants—they are all there. Close by is the smaller **Estufa Quente** (hothouse), where the vegetation is even more tropical, and the **Estufa Doce** (sweet greenhouse), home to cacti and succulents. ∎

Centro de Arte Moderna 🗺 51 E4 ✉ Rua Dr. Nicolau de Bettencourt ☎ 217 823 000 🕐 Temporarily closed 🚇 Metro: São Sebastião, Praça de Espanha **gulbenkian.pt** • **Casa-Museu Dr. Anastácio Gonçalves** 🗺 51 E4 ✉ Avenida 5 de Outubro 6–8 ☎ 213 540 823 🕐 Closed Mon. 💲 $ 🚇 Metro: Picoas, Saldanha **blogdacmag.blogspot.com** • **Estufa Fria de Lisboa** 🗺 51 E4 ✉ Parque Eduardo VII ☎ 213 882 278 💲 $ 🚇 Metro: Picoas, Saldanha

PARQUE DAS NAÇÕES

Bordering Lisbon's working docks, Parque das Nações (Park of the Nations) is the capital's architectural showcase built for Expo '98. Its buildings have been converted into attractions and modern residential units, making it a cultural, riverfront playground for Lisbonite families.

The park's centerpiece is the **Oceanário de Lisboa** *(tel 218 917 000, oceanario.pt, $$$$)*. This striking glass-and-steel oceanarium is mirrored in a large expanse of water and reached via a two-tier bridge. Inside you'll discover 25,000 specimens of marine animals and plants from all the world's oceans. The diversity of life in the enormous central tank will keep you spellbound.

Álvaro Siza Vieira's stunning Portuguese Pavilion, with its swooping suspended roof, is now occupied by government offices, but the nearby **Pavilhão do Conhecimento** *(tel 218 917 100, pavconhecimento.pt, $$$)* houses a science and technology museum with fun interactive exhibits. The most visible of the other Expo structures is the 460-foot-tall (140 m) **Torre Vasco da Gama,** now part of the Myriad Hotel. The great views over the city and river from this tower rival the novelty of those from the **Telecabine** (cable car; *tel 218 956 143, telecabinelisboa.pt, $$*) that transports people from one end of the park to the other. From any point along the park's riverfront promenade, you cannot help but see the breathtaking 10.7-mile-long (17.2 km) **Ponte Vasco da Gama.** The bridge starts beside the park and sails to the horizon in low-level minimalist style. ∎

Parque das Nações 🗺 51 G4 🚇 Metro: Estação do Oriente
portaldasnacoes.pt

▪ The dramatic Oceanário de Lisboa is a popular tourist destination.

AZULEJOS

If there is one decorative element you cannot escape in Portugal, it is tiles. Tiles are everywhere, from church interiors to mansion staircases, restaurants, palace bedrooms, building facades, terraces, and even the Lisbon metro. The Moors first introduced the technique of tilemaking into Portugal, and contact with other cultures over the centuries enriched the craft. The result is the famous Portuguese azulejo, a painted ceramic tile.

The word azulejo derives from the Arabic *al-zulaycha,* meaning "little polished stone," which probably referred to the individual tesserae used in mosaics. The Moors specialized in geometric designs; this stylistic tradition remained long after the *reconquista* rid Portugal of the Moors. The first use of wall tiles on non-Moorish structures in Portugal was at the abbey of Alcobaça and at Leiria in the 13th century. But it wasn't until the early 16th century, with the introduction of the Hispano–Moorish style, that the use of tiles truly flourished. Manuel I greatly admired this decorative style imported from Seville,

■ Azulejos adorn the staircase at Lisbon's Palácio dos Marqueses de Fronteira.

Spain; his endorsement of its use on Sintra's Palácio Nacional (see pp. 188–190) began a wall-tiling craze that would last for centuries.

An Abundance of Azulejos

Renaissance-inspired motifs gradually crept in, and soon entire wall panels were not merely decorative, but illustrative as well. These early illustrative panels typically showed religious scenes painted in blues and yellows, but the expansion of the Portuguese empire soon introduced more exotic inspiration and colors. Toward the end of the 17th century blue-and-white tiles became the dominant choice, no doubt inspired by imports of Ming porcelain from China. The main centers of Lisbon and Coimbra produced lyrical panels depicting hunting scenes, nursery stories, and more.

After the 1755 earthquake, multicolored tiles came back into fashion and people discovered that the tiles kept out the damp. Thus many of Lisbon's new houses were entirely faced in tiles, visible today in the Bairro Alto and Alfama districts. The 19th century was the golden era of tiling, as Brazilian emigrants reinforced the practice and the introduction of mechanical printing methods made tiles more affordable. Porto also has some prime azulejos, notably the São Bento railway station, which is the work of Jorge Colaço from the turn of the 20th century. His superb blue-and-white azulejos are typical of that period, which loved aping the 18th-century style. However, art nouveau soon brought its own decorative adaptations to structures.

After a few decades of neglect, the 1950s saw a ceramic art revival and, in Porto particularly, architecture and azulejos worked in tandem. Since then, the Lisbon metro has become the standard-bearer by systematically commissioning azulejos for each new station, starting with abstract designs by Maria Keil in 1959. To learn more about azulejos, visit the National Tile Museum in Lisbon (see p. 77).

EXPERIENCE: Paint Your Own Azulejo

Take inspiration from the tiles in Portugal and paint one yourself. In Porto, **Gazete Azulejos** (*Rua Duque de Palmela 230, tel 912 891 581, gazeteazulejos.com*) preserves and maps decorated facades in the city, a piece of heritage worth protecting. A catalogue is available online that shows all the information collected for each tile (where it is located, what studio made it, what technique was used). Workshops last a couple hours (€33) and include an overview of the history of azulejos and practicing stenciling (no artistic skill required!). The final phase is firing. Your tiles (two per participant) will be ready to pick up the next day.

More Places to Visit in Lisbon

Jardim Botânico de Lisboa

Part of the Museu Nacional de História Natural e da Ciência of Lisbon University, this well-hidden gem was designed as a scientific garden with species from all over the world; the first were planted in 1873. The tropical palms and cycads (very rare, living fossils) are outstanding. At the main entrance just behind the Natural History Museum, look for the gigantic Moreton Bay fig *(Ficus macrophylla),* its aerial roots now as thick as tree trunks. And don't miss the pipal tree *(Ficus religiosa),* the species under which Buddha is said to have gained enlightenment.
museus.ulisboa.pt 🗺 51 E3 ✉ Rua da Escola Politécnica 58 ☎ 213 921 808 🕐 Closed Mon. 💲 $$

Jardim Zoológico

Not the cheapest day out, but adults and children alike will enjoy this well-kept zoo, which boasts some 300 species. Highlights include the enormous primate enclosure, the dolphin and sea lion show, and the crocodile pool.
zoo.pt ✉ Praça Marechal Humberto Delgado ☎ 217 232 900 💲 $$$$

Museu do Oriente

Occupying a former 1930s warehouse used to store salt cod, this museum pays homage to Portugal's historical links to the East. Divided into two main areas, the first traces Portuguese presence in Asia, with exhibits from colonial outposts and trading areas dating from 1500 to the 1900s. The second, known as the Kwok On collection, is a superb collection of Cantonese marionettes, musical instruments, and books.
foriente.pt 🗺 50 D2 ✉ Avenida Brasília, Doca de Alcântara ☎ 213 585 244 🕐 Closed Mon. 💲 $$

Museu Nacional de Arte Antiga

This cultural highlight, in the residential district overlooking the Alcântara docks, is well worth the visit. This national art collection was set up in 1884 to house much of the fantastic artwork that the state inherited from the monasteries on their closure. Since then the museum has overflowed from a 17th-century mansion into a beautiful baroque chapel and a 1940s annex. A vast collection of European art and decorative arts takes up the majority of the ground floor. It primarily spans the Middle Ages to the early 19th century, with masterful works on display. The next floor up holds artwork from Portugal's former colonies and trading partners as well as Portuguese and Chinese ceramics and silver and gold jewelry. The top floor is devoted to Portuguese painting and sculpture. There's also a pleasant garden café and terrace.

museudearteantiga.pt  51 D2 ✉ Rua das Janelas Verdes ☎ 213 912 800 🕐 Closed Mon. 💲 $$

Museu Nacional do Azulejo

Even if ceramic tiles do not specifically interest you, the National Tile Museum, in the former convent of Madre de Deus, will stimulate your imagination. The museum traces the evolution of the Portuguese style from its early Moorish geometric designs through the Mudéjar style of the late 15th and 16th centuries and the classic illustrative blue-and-white azulejos of the 16th and 17th centuries, up to modern abstract designs. Also displayed are imported tiles from Andalucía (Spain), Italy, and Goa (India). You will also see the convent's fabulous church of Madre de Deus and the chapter house, another feast of gold leaf and huge azulejo panels; spot the crocodiles depicted on the left. The Manueline cloister has some lovely 18th-century geometric-patterned panels.

museudoazulejo.pt 51 G3 ✉ Rua da Madre de Deus 4 ☎ 218 100 340 🕐 Closed Mon. 💲 $$

▪ A stroll through the lush vegetation of Jardim Botânico

The perfect setting for vineyards, baroque masterpieces, remote villages, and the always magnetic Porto

PORTO E NORTE

◼ A common souvenir: the ubiquitous ceramic cockerel from Barcelos

PORTO E NORTE

Wild and highly cultivated, starkly barren and lushly green, deeply traditional yet spiced with modern accents: Portugal's Norte embodies numerous contradictions in its modestly scaled yet mountainous expanse. Dividing it from the Centro region is its star attraction, the majestic Douro River, whose valley is not only the source of the profitable port and wine industry but also a spectacular must-see.

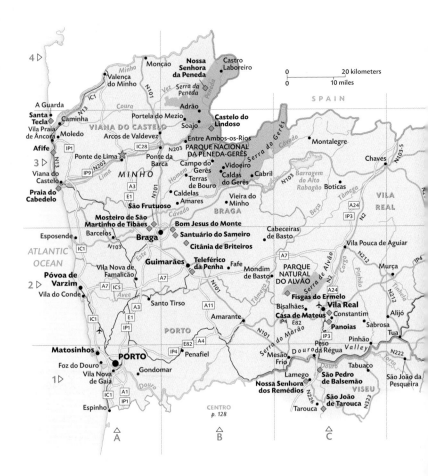

The Douro and other rivers that crisscross the region—from the Minho, which acts as a natural border with Spain in the far north, to the Lima and Cávado Rivers—make the Porto e Norte region of Portugal, divided into the Minho, Douro, and Trás-os-Montes areas, more fertile than the rest of the country. They also bring a string of spa establishments to the touring agenda. And, not least, they help nurture acres of vines, which produce refreshing *vinho verde* (green wine), red and white table wines, and the heavier port wine that has brought fame and fortune to one of Europe's oldest cities—Porto.

Although many of these rural areas are becoming depopulated, the timeless scenes of some villages are sure to leave you entranced. You likely won't find little old women wrapped in black robes sitting in the shadows of their doorsteps and knitting anymore (or not that often), but the rural Norte still has its charm, showing the different faces of contemporary life with men driving tractors through fields and orchards, huge supermarkets in the middle of nowhere, and kids playing on smartphones.

Gems of the Region

To explore this region, the obvious launchpad is Porto, an enchanting city with plenty of cultural and gastronomic offerings, a breezy beach, and sweeping views over the mouth of the Douro. The lush and verdant Douro Valley, which shelters acres and acres of vineyards growing on rhythmically terraced hillsides, lies within easy reach—as does the pious, though industrialized, city of Braga, home to a 12th-century cathedral and the striking sanctuary of Bom Jesus on its outskirts. Lighter in spirit, the UNESCO-listed World Heritage town of Guimarães is considered the birthplace of

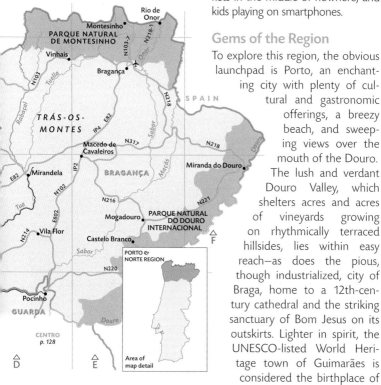

the Portuguese nation. Head north to discover Viana do Castelo, a delightful, easygoing town on the Lima estuary.

On the northeastern side, toward the Spanish border, is the starker, poorer, though very beautiful, area of Trás-os-Montes. Its capital, Bragança, although historically significant, is quite isolated. In between stand daunting ranges of granite hills rising to bare summits of rocky scree (including those of the national park, Peneda-Gerês), memorable for giant boulders, long-horned bulls, wild ponies, goats, wild boar, and deer. These dramatic landscapes and a succession of charming villages make up the soul of northern Portugal. ∎

▪ **Bragança's dramatic medieval citadel rises above the surrounding modern town and holds one of the best preserved castles in Portugal.**

PORTO

Portugal's second largest city, with more than one million inhabitants, Porto boasts several highlights on its unrivaled riverside location. You can admire the city's steep slopes from the deck of a *rabelo* (a traditional sailboat used for transporting barrels of port, now motorized as a tour boat) on its circular "six bridges" tour. Alternatively, relax at one of the modern cafés lining the quays of Vila Nova de Gaia (Porto's left-bank nucleus of wine lodges and warehouses), or stop on the iconic 1886 Dom Luís I bridge that mimicked Gustave Eiffel's designs.

Porto's iconic graphic bridges; in the foreground is Gustave Eiffel's Ponte de Dona Maria Pia.

From any one of these spots you will see the dense urban fabric that has been woven since Phoenician and Roman times, when the settlement of Porto was known as Cale (Greek for "beautiful"), later adding Portus (port) to become Portus-Cale—thus the origin of the national name. Narrow alleyways, rough cobblestones, and tortuous steps riddle the northern riverbank while church spires vie with draped laundry to set the most atmospheric stage. You will need

Unusual Tours

Food and wine enthusiasts can sign up for a four-hour tour exploring some of Porto's most historic neighborhoods and their old-world eateries and cafés whilst learning about traditional Portuguese food and drink, such as *bolinhas de bacalhau* (cod fritters), *bifanas* (pork sandwiches), and the national Super Bock beer. Be sure to pace yourself. Additional offerings by **Blue Dragon Tours** *(Av. Gustavo Eiffel 280, tel 222 022 375, blue dragon.pt)* include eco-friendly walking, bicycle, and Segway tours around Porto. There are tours that focus on food and wine, must-see spots, street art, monasteries, and much more, depending on how you get around. Tours are led by knowledgeable guides who aim to take their visitors slightly off the beaten track while still covering all the main points of interest.

some energy and muscles, though, to negotiate these steep streets.

Maritime at heart, with strong trading and shipbuilding traditions, Porto played an important role in the Portuguese expeditions of the 15th century. However, its boom came in the 18th century, thanks to the profitable port trade and the acumen of English entrepreneurs. This, too, was the heyday of baroque, a style that left its mark on many a church in Porto and smaller inland towns. Landmarks such as the cathedral and the church of São Francisco, although both much older in origin, were blanketed in baroque carvings, paintings, and other features. More visible still is the Torre dos Clérigos, a towering baroque original that has become another Porto icon. Equally common are the azulejos (glazed tiles) that decorate walls from the cathedral cloister to the railway station. History aside, Porto is a lively, notoriously hardworking town. Relaxation is at hand in the beach bars of

nearby Foz and downtown at a string of bars and restaurants, which can be delightfully old-fashioned or stylishly chic. Contemporary culture is catered to at the starkly modern Fundação de Serralves and in a dedicated street of art galleries (see p. 94–95), and the shopping urge can be quenched in a central pedestrianized area. Above all, however, you should make a beeline for the bustling **Ribeira** area down by the river: Boats come and go, giant signs of port brands monopolize the horizon, and café tables spill out into the sun. Here the character of Porto really comes alive.

In & Around Praça da Liberdade

Stand in the middle of this square, beside the equestrian statue of Dom Pedro IV, and feel the pulse of 19th-century Porto with its institutions, industries, and commerce. This sloping north–south rectangle creates an unofficial border between the more down-at-heel eastern side of town, the upscale avenues to the west, and the UNESCO-listed Baixa/Ribeira area to the south.

The avenues connecting Praça da Liberdade and the adjoining square to the north, Praça General Humberto Delgado, are lined with the headquarters of major banks and businesses, all watched over by the **Paços do Concelho** (City Hall) at the far northern end. This area is a major social crossroad of the city, where businesspeople cross paths with beggars, housewives, and schoolchildren. Heading downhill to Praça Garret, you will find the tourist office and São Bento train station, located next to a subway stop. As always, Porto is able to let its hair down: Head down to the Ribeira Square on any weekend night and the streets will be buzzing. And on any warm day of the week, sidewalk cafés add a leisurely tone. In Rua and Praça do Infante Dom Henrique, you can find many bus and tram stops. The older area of Porto, classified as a World Heritage site, starts at the southern edge of Praça da Liberdade.

Porto's food market, the **Mercado Municipal do Bolhão** (*corner of Rua de Sá da Bandeira & Rua Formosa, tel 223 326 024, mercadobolhao.pt, closed*

■ The Paços do Concelho was built between 1920 and 1957.

Porto 🗺 80 A1 **Visitor Information** ✉ Sé, Praça Almeida Garret 27 ☎ 935 557 024 • ✉ Airport, Vila Nova da Telha ☎ 938 668 462 **visitporto.travel**

Sat. p.m. & Sun.), stands one block east of City Hall. Its galleried interior brims with stalls selling produce from the entire region. This striking ironwork structure has been open since 1851.

One block farther east is the pedestrianized **Rua de Santa Catarina,** once a bourgeois promenade and now Porto's shopping mecca, boasting international fashion chain stores and a large mall, Via Catarina. Toward the southern end of the street is the renowned **Majestic Café** *(Rua de Santa Catarina 112, tel 222 003 887, cafemajestic.com, closed Sun.),* a belle epoque wonder of sinuous lines, gilded woodwork, mirrors, and beaming cherubim. Designed by architect João Queirós, it opened in 1921 under the name Elite, but the city's intelligentsia only started flocking to its marble tables the following year, after it changed its name to Majestic. After a decades-long heyday, the café

EXPERIENCE: Discover the Art of Making Port

Tightly controlled and regulated by the Portuguese government, port, a fortified, sweet dessert wine of which there are several varieties, is unique to the upper Douro Valley. Learn the port production process on a tour around one of the port wine lodges of Vila Nova de Gaia. Although these tours are aimed at the tourist market, they are usually informative and it's always fun to see a lodge interior; take a sweater, as the lodges can be chilly. Try **Sandeman** *(Largo Miguel Bombarda 47, Vila Nova de Gaia, tel 223 740 534, sandeman .com, $$$)* or **Porto Cálem** *(Av. Diogo Leite 344, Vila Nova de Gaia, tel 916 113 451, calem.pt, $$$).* As you tour the lodge, you'll discover that the common feature of all ports is the addition of brandy during the fermentation process. Once about half the sugar from the pressed grapes has turned into alcohol, the vintner mixes the wine with a healthy dose of high-proof grape brandy.

This stops the fermentation process in its tracks, leaving a sweet and robust raw product. What happens next depends greatly on the vintner. If the grapes are from a superior crop year, the port is designated as vintage. It is usually then mixed with other fine pedigree grapes, set in wooden casks for two years, and bottled to age. After a few decades, this finest of ports is ready for sipping.

Common ports are aged longer in wooden casks and are potable immediately on bottling. Ruby port is a fruity wine, lighter than vintage ports. Tawny port is produced from younger, often quite concentrated and aggressive wines. It is thus aged much longer than a ruby—up to 40 years in many cases—mellowing the flavor. The name "tawny" comes from the faded color the wine takes on after so many years in wooden casks. Lightly chilled dry white port makes an ideal aperitif.

INSIDER TIP:

For great photos of traditional tiles, check out the São Bento railway station, Capela das Almas on Rua de Santa Catarina, and Pérola do Bolhão, opposite the market.

—EMMA ROWLEY
National Geographic contributor

began to decline, and by the 1960s it was in a ruinous state. Closure and refurbishment led to the café's reopening in 1994 with the crystal gleaming once again. Today, though very touristy, it is a mandatory stop on the Porto circuit.

On the opposite, western side of Praça da Liberdade rises the **Igreja** and much photographed **Torre dos Clérigos.** The baroque church and tower together form a compact, oval-shaped city block. The work of the prolific Italian architect Nicolau Nasoni, they date from 1735 through 1748. Although there are more striking church interiors in the city, the Igreja's facade is notable for its oval eyeglass. Make the effort to climb the 225 steps to the top of the 248-foot-tall (76 m) tower for the fantastic views. A few steps north of here stands another towering baroque edifice, the **Igreja do Carmo** (*Rua

do Carmo, tel 222 078 400, $*). Apart from the impressive main facade, the church's side facade is equally worth noting: Its large tiled panel by Silvestre Silvestri depicts Carmelite nuns taking the veil. Immediately next to it stands the **Igreja dos Carmelitas** (*Rua do Carmo, tel 222 050 279, $*), which presents a less harmonious 17th-century mix of neoclassical and baroque styles.

For a complete contrast in both style and function, head around the corner to see Porto's most illustrious bookstore, **Livraria Lello e Irmão** (*Rua das Carmelitas 144, tel 222 002 037, livrarialello.pt*), a 1906 neo-Gothic extravaganza complete with stained-glass ceiling. It has since been classified as a national heritage site. Although the bookstore is a place of business, it is surprisingly tolerant of sightseers who stop in to view the lavish interior designed by the French engineer Xavier Esteves.

The Ribeira

Although located inland and near the Atlantic coast, Old Porto exudes atmosphere, history, and the color of daily life that one typically finds in a Mediterranean port. The steep and winding streets of the riverfront Ribeira quarter offer fleeting vistas over the Douro below, where the quays are a major focal point for visitors and locals alike. Two churches—the Sé and the dazzling São Francisco—join the

Torre dos Clérigos ⬜ Map p. 91 ✉ Rua São Filipe de Nery ☎ 222 145 489 💲 $$ (tower & museum) **torredosclerigos.pt**

■ **A symphony of dazzling gilded and carved woodwork greets visitors to Porto's São Francisco.**

Palácio da Bolsa, the old stock exchange, as the quarter's monumental highlights.

Sé: The massive edifice of the Sé (cathedral) rises above the rocky hillside, its twin bell towers built in the solid gray granite with which northern Portugal is so well endowed. Despite its 12th-century origins, the Sé underwent such a radical facelift in the late 17th and early 18th centuries that most of the original Romanesque purity has been lost. Yet again, Italian Nasoni was responsible for much of the baroque overlay as well as for the adjacent bishop's palace.

The pleasingly bare triple-aisled nave leaves the main focus on the extensively modified transept and chancel. On the left is the **Chapel of the Holy Sacrament** and its magnificent altar—made in phases between 1632 and the 19th century—a superlative example of the prowess of Portuguese silversmiths. Look, too, for the graceful 14th-century statue of Our

Lady of Vandoma—an incarnation of the Virgin Mary, the patron saint of the Sé—that stands in a heavily gilded niche. More lashings of Brazilian gold dazzle in the baroque main altarpiece, framed by Nasoni's wall paintings.

A doorway to the right of the nave leads to the **cloister** where the rhythm of Gothic arches contrasts with seven azulejo panels dating from 1731. These illustrate Solomon's "Song of Songs" and the Life of the Virgin. A feast of treasures lies in wait in the 18th-century chapter house, from rich brocade vestments, statuary, and silver crowns to a coffered, painted ceiling, azulejos illustrating moral allegories, and a massive carved-wood candelabra. In the corner of the cloister, the **Chapel of St. John** houses the impressive stone sarcophagus of João Gordo and a graceful 14th-century statue of Our Lady of Batalha. Don't miss Nasoni's grand staircase that leads to the upper gallery. Faced in tiled panels depicting rural and mythological scenes, it offers extensive views across Porto.

Igreja de São Francisco: As if the Sé were not enough, the district's other draw is the Igreja de São Francisco. Again victim of a late 17th- to early 18th-century baroque makeover, São Francisco is staggering in its ornamentation:

Virtually the entire surface is blanketed in gilded, carved wood in a riot of vines, cherubim, and birds. Begun in 1245, the church and monastery were not completed until 1425, when they hosted Dom João I after his marriage to Philippa of Lancaster. Centuries later, after the baroque additions were complete, the decorative excess so shocked the clergy that no services have been held there since.

Today the most spectacular element remains a high-relief **altarpiece,** positioned to the left of the nave. Illustrating the Tree of Jesse in polychrome and gilded wood, it depicts 12 kings of Judah in the branches of a tree that rises out

(continued on p. 93)

Casa da Música

Opened in 2001, the imposing **Casa da Música** (*Av. da Boavista 604–610, tel 220 120 220, casadamusica.com*), designed by Dutch architect Rem Koolhas, has firmly established itself as Porto's principal cultural venue. Home to Porto's Symphony Orchestra and the Casa da Música Choir, it offers a full program of musical events and performances for all tastes and ages.

Sé 🗺 Map p. 91 ✉ Terreiro da Sé ☎ 222 059 028 💲 $ • **Igreja de São Francisco** 🗺 Map p. 91 ✉ Rua do Infante D. Henrique ☎ 222 062 125 💲 $$ **ordemsaofranciscoporto.pt** • **Palácio da Bolsa** 🗺 Map p. 91 ✉ Rua de Ferreira Borges ☎ 223 399 013 💲 $$$ **palaciodabolsa.com**

A WALK THROUGH THE RIBEIRA

Porto's topography is best dealt with by following a generally downhill direction. This walk winds past major sites and through back alleys to end at the Douro River's edge.

Views from the Sé take in a jumble of houses and the Torre dos Clérigos.

From the equestrian statue in Praça da Liberdade, head south and cross two side streets at the left-hand corner of the square to reach the Praça de Almeida Garrett. In front of you is the **Estação de São Bento ❶**. Enter the train station to admire the large 1930s azulejo panels by Jorge Colaço illustrating daily life and historic battles. Return toward the statue, turn left, and walk up the steep Rua dos Clérigos toward the highly visible church and **Torre dos Clérigos** (see p. 87) **❷**, passing a fascinating

mix of shops. As you round the corner at the top, look for the highly decorative fruit, vegetable, and *bacalhau* shop **Casa Oriental** *(Campo dos Mártires da Pátria 111, casaoriental.pt)* and an 18th-century **pharmacy** *(Campo dos Mártires da Pátria 122)*.

In front of you rise the forbidding walls of Porto's former prison and Court of Appeal. Closed down in 1974, it reopened in 1997 to house the **Centro Português de Fotografia ❸** (Portuguese Center for Photography; *Largo Amor de Perdição, tel*

NOT TO BE MISSED:

Estação de São Bento • Torre dos Clérigos • Centro Português de Fotografia • Sé

220 046 300, cpf.pt, closed Mon.). It stages some groundbreaking photography exhibitions.

Heading Downhill

Now turn to the left of this building down Rua dos Caldeireiros, a typical street complete with dripping laundry, flags, and people on balconies and in workshops below. Walk past the intersection of Rua das Flores to reach the busy Rua de Mouzinho da Silveira. Cross again to a wall fountain and turn right up Rua do Souto. This lively street leads you to the remaining sections of Porto's 12th-century

> ⊠ See also area map p. 80
> ▶ Praça da Liberdade
> ⊙ 45 minutes (more with visits)
> ⟷ 0.6 miles (1 km)
> ▶ Praça da Ribeira

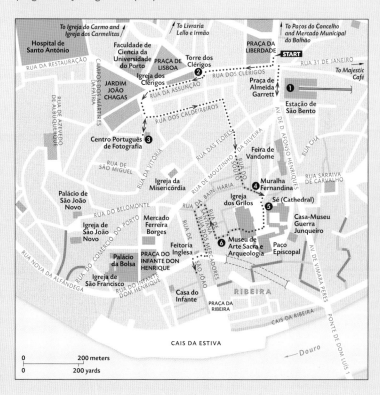

walls, the **Muralha Fernandina** ,
originally 3,000 feet (900 m) long
and averaging 30 feet (9 m) in
height. The **Sé** ❺ (see pp. 88–89)
is now in sight: Turn right at a fork,
walking through an arch to the vast
esplanade fronting the cathedral.
This gives you one of Porto's best
views down to the river.

Walk back through the arch toward
the next church steeple. Steps lead
down to a small square and lookout
terrace with, on the left, the **Museu
de Arte Sacra e Arqueologia** ❻
(MASA; *Largo do Colégio, Igreja de
São Lourenço, tel 223 395 020, closed
Sun., $*) installed in the 17th-century
wing of the former Jesuit college of
São Lourenço. This small museum
displays religious artwork and some
archaeological artifacts. Continue
down Rua de Santana, turn left into
Rua da Bainharia and left again down
atmospheric Rua dos Mercadores, full
of the sounds of music and hammer-
ing from workshops.

At the bottom turn right into Rua
do Infante Dom Henrique. At No. 8
you pass the arcades of the former
factory, **Feitoria Inglesa,** built in the
late 1780s for Porto's English business
community. Cross the road, turn left,
and stroll down to the riverfront cafés
and restaurants of Praça da Ribeira.

▪ Azulejos adorn the facades of many houses in the Ribeira.

of the body of Christ to end with the Virgin and Child. This sculptural tour de force was made in the 1720s by Filipe da Silva and António Gomes, two local artisans. More naïf in style is the 13th-century granite statue of St. Francis to the right of the entrance. Opposite the church, the rebuilt monastery holds a small **museum** of ecclesiastical iconography and some unusual catacombs.

Behind São Francisco stands the **Palácio da Bolsa,** the stock exchange. This late 19th-century neoclassical building claims a succession of highly decorated halls that can be visited with a guided tour. The star attraction is the **Pátio das Nações,** only rivaled by the glitter and inscriptions of the **Arabian Room,** a pastiche of the Alhambra in Granada, Spain.

Beyond the Center

Porto's urban sprawl now extends west from the Baixa to the beaches of Foz do Douro. In between lie several spots to relax in after a day navigating downtown's backstreets. Nor should the port lodges of Vila Nova de Gaia be forgotten.

Museu Nacional Soares dos Reis: Close to the Baixa area, this elegant museum is devoted to fine and decorative arts. It was founded by Pedro IV in 1833 as Portugal's very first museum to safeguard the art heritage from convents that were closing their doors; it soon became a showcase for academic artists. What was then known as Museu Portuense moved to its present site, the 18th-century Palácio dos Carrancas, in the 1940s, acquiring additional collections. The decorative arts section offers the most interest, whether in the Portuguese ceramics, Asian pieces (look for the hand-painted Japanese screen dating from the 1600s), or Iron Age jewelry from Povoa de Varzim. Do not miss the unusual raised patio garden, its azulejo-faced wall fronting a pleasant outdoor café.

Far more cutting-edge artwork can be seen two blocks north of here in **Rua de Miguel Bombarda.** This is where the majority of Porto's contemporary art galleries are located (*most closed Sun.–Mon. & a.m.*).

Parque da Cidade

For some downtime, head to Portugal's largest urban park, at the bottom of Avenida da Boavista, which stretches over 205 acres (83 ha) toward the ocean. Its gentle contours and architectural stone features are the work of landscape architect Sidónio Pardal. The park makes for a relaxing afternoon or a great spot for a picnic.

Museu Nacional Soares dos Reis ✉ Rua de Dom Manuel II 44 ☎ 223 393 770 🕐 Closed Mon. 💲 $$ **museusoaresdosreis.gov.pt**

Fundação de Serralves Museu de Arte Contemporânea: The jewel in Porto's cultural agenda, the Fundação de Serralves Museu de Arte Contemporânea lies far to the west. This lively and ambitious arts center stands on a verdant hillside in a residential area. The extensive 44-acre (18 ha) park is as important as the museum interior; sculptures (including interesting works by Ângela de Sousa, Claes Oldenburg, Richard Serra, Alberto Carneiro, and Dan Graham) dot the lawns. Some 2 million euros have also been invested in revamping the modernist gardens.

Originally designed to showcase the pristine, pink art deco mansion, Casa de Serralves, in which the museum first opened in 1989, the lake, woods, fountains, arboretum, and rose garden are now a popular destination for weekend strollers. One place not to miss is the delightful teahouse. **Casa de Serralves** often houses exhibitions, presenting an opportunity to admire the superb interiors courtesy of Lalique, Ruhlmann, and other leading French designers of the period.

Major exhibitions of contemporary art and performances are now staged within the massive white minimalist structure designed by Porto's celebrity architect, Álvaro Siza Vieira, which opened in 2000. The infrequently shown permanent collection—and then only a few pieces at a time—covers international art from the 1960s

■ The signature neomodernist planes of the spectacular Fundação de Serralves

INSIDER TIP:

A Capoeira *(Esplanada do Castelo 63, tel 226 181 589)* is a good local restaurant in Foz do Douro that serves traditional Portuguese food in a homey, mom-and-pop-type setting.

–LACEY GRAY
National Geographic *magazine editorial coordinator*

to the present. Bonuses come in the form of an excellent bookstore and a rooftop café-restaurant.

In 2019, the **Casa de Cinema Manoel de Oliveira** opened in a building inside the foundation designed by Álvaro Siza. The new space is dedicated to not only the work of the great Portuguese director (there is a comprehensive documentation center) but also to the art of film and moving pictures in general. It also holds temporary exhibits, conferences, and screening cycles.

Foz do Douro: From the arts center, it is less than a mile to Foz do Douro, a town that grew up at the very mouth of the Douro River around the fort of **São João da Foz.** Today Foz extends about 2 miles (3 km) north up the coast to merge with the more industrial **Matosinhos,** where old fish-preserving factories have been converted into hip waterfront nightclubs. Foz itself is really one long avenue and a balustraded promenade bordering beaches of coarse sand and rocks. The restaurants that line the beachfront serve excellent seafood. Few beachgoers venture into the chilly water other than bodysurfers, but the breezy cafés make an invigorating escape from downtown Porto, only a half-hour bus ride on weekends.

Vila Nova de Gaia

Back in central Porto, the other main draw for visitors is across the river: the port lodges of Vila Nova de Gaia. Try to go there on foot via the Ponte Dom Luís I: Vertigo and staggering views from the bridge are assured. At ground level, dozens of port companies vie to lure in passersby for tastings and, they hope, acquisitions. These enterprises are very much geared to busloads of tourists, yet they are worth a look if the history of port interests you. Some port lodges offer tours of their facilities so you can learn about portmaking (see p. 86). Otherwise, the riverfront bars facing the colorful facades of the Ribeira are a great place to sip a drink as sunset nears. ∎

Fundação de Serralves Museu de Arte Contemporânea ✉ Rua D. João de Castro 210 ☎ 226 156 500 $ $$ Museum; $$ Park (combined ticket available) 🚌 Bus: 201, 203, 502, 504 **serralves.pt**

DOURO VALLEY

However much the beauty of the Douro Valley is extolled, it is easily beaten by the reality. Little can prepare you for the grandeur of its terraced slopes carved out of the schist or for the changing panoramas of the river itself. Whether seeing the valley by boat, train, or car, it will leave an indelible mark.

The Douro meanders 528 miles (850 km) from its source in Spain to its mouth at Porto, carving vertiginous ravines from the schist and granite rock en route. Once a turbulent river of rapids and narrow ravines, it has been tamed considerably by the construction of eight dams. The river's most spectacular stretch in Portugal runs between Mesão Frio and Pinhão. The hill terracing along here is so dense and rhythmical that it sparked an urban legend that claims it's the only man-made feature visible from space other than China's Great Wall. And it has been like this for some 2,000 years.

This is quintessential port country and the world's first official wine region, established in 1756 and still going strong today, as witnessed by omnipresent brand-name placards among the vines—whether Sandeman,

Vineyards cover every inch of hillside in the Douro Valley.

Taylor, or Ferreira. Sadly, the pretty *rabelos* (sailboats) that transported barrels of the nectar downriver to Porto were retired decades ago and are used today only occasionally as tour boats and, every June, in a race. Tanker trucks have supplanted them. On the other hand, elegant *quintas* (rural estate houses) still monopolize the steep riverbanks, and villages are mainly concentrated in interior valleys. Tucked in among the vineyards are pockets of fruit orchards and olive and almond trees; come in February for a visual feast of pink and white almond blossoms.

The official capital of the Douro and seat of the Port and Douro Wines Institute is **Peso da Régua,** usually shortened to Régua. It can easily be bypassed; it has little character and even fewer sites, but it does act as an important transportation hub for the area, as well as hosts the educational Museu do Douro *(museudodouro.pt).* You can take a train or boat trip from here or head for the quayside storehouses where various port companies offer tastings.

Lamego

The charming town of Lamego sits some 7 miles (11 km) south of Régua. Its most striking site is **Nossa Senhora dos Remédios** *(tel 969 046 377, santuarioremedios .pt),* a Douro version of Braga's

> **INSIDER TIP:**
> For a wonderful view of the Douro Valley head to the viewpoint at São Leonardo de Galafura between Vila Real and Peso da Régua. There you'll also find poems carved in the rocks.
>
> —MARGARET ROBERTS
> *National Geographic contributor*

more famous Bom Jesus do Monte (see pp. 110–111), as this 18th-century church similarly crowns a baroque staircase bristling with ornamentation. Climb or drive up for the views. To see a stunning interior, head to Lamego's **Sé,** or cathedral *(Largo da Sé, tel 254 612 766),* located at the lower end of the tree-shaded and café-lined esplanade. Dating from the second half of the 12th century and partly rebuilt in the 16th century, it was extensively reworked in the 18th century by the Italian architect Nicolau Nasoni. Crane your neck to view the ceiling illustrated with biblical stories, and don't miss the lovely 16th-century cloister, accessed from outside, filled with a perfumed rose garden and two ornate chapels.

Peso da Régua ⛰ 80 C1 **Visitor Information** ✉ Rua da Ferreirinha ☎ 254 312 846 • **Lamego** ⛰ 80 C1 **Visitor Information** ✉ Av. Visconde Guedes Teixeira ☎ 254 612 005 **portoenorte.pt**

EXPERIENCE: The Grape Harvest

The Douro Valley comes alive during the annual *vindima* (grape harvest), which usually occurs in mid-September. You can witness hundreds of local villagers picking and trampling the grapes in large granite *lagares* (tanks) at several of the *quintas* in the region that open their doors to tourists then.

For full information on which quintas are open to visitors at harvesttime, call or visit the **Rota dos Vinhos do Douro e do Porto** *(Peso da Régua, Rua dos Camilos 90, tel 254 320 130, www.ivdp.pt)* office. Some quintas offer a full visitor package year-round, with multilingual audio tours and tastings.

A significant though modestly scaled historical site lies just 2 miles (3 km) northeast of Lamego: the chapel of **São Pedro de Balsemão** *(tel 254 600 230, valedovarosa.gov.pt, closed Mon.)* in the village of Balsemão. Said to date from the seventh century, it is thus the second oldest sanctuary on the Iberian Peninsula. The small, colonnaded chapel displays Byzantine and Visigothic features and contains the heavily carved sarcophagus of a Porto bishop who died in 1362, as well as later baroque additions.

Tarouca

Another impressive monument is seen at Tarouca, 9 miles (15 km) to the southeast of Lamego. Here, lost at the bottom of a pretty valley, stands the massive, semi-ruined **São João de Tarouca,** a 12th-century Cistercian monastery (Portugal's first), now an archaeological site and museum you can

visit. Near the Casa da Tulha, the former granary, you can see three-dimensional reconstructions of the complex, a national monument. The adjacent **church** *(tel 254 678 766, closed Mon.)* is in a far better state. The sacristy contains no fewer than 4,700 azulejos, each one with a different illustration. Walk through the tiny village following the gushing water channels downhill to reach the river, a tributary of the Douro, and its Romanesque bridge.

Pinhão

Farther east on the north bank of the river, modest Pinhão is the Douro's great highlight, mostly for its setting. It sees most traffic during harvesttime, when truckloads of grapes thunder in from the vineyards to be pressed; otherwise, the village is quiet and offers a handful of restaurants and hotels. Pinhão's

Tarouca ⓜ 80 C1 **Visitor Information** ✉ Avenida Prof. Leite Vasconcelos
☎ 254 781 461 • **São João de Tarouca** ✉ Avenida António Teixeira
☎ 254 678 766 ⓢ $ **valedovarosa.gov.pt**

landmark is the unusual **railway station** where walls are decorated with azulejo panels depicting local life. If heading north from here by car, consider two equally spectacular routes that wind through terraced hills: one goes to Alijó and the other to Sabrosa, birthplace of the great navigator and explorer Ferdinand Magellan.

Alternatively, cross the Douro again and drive 12 miles (19 km) east to the village of **São João da Pesqueira,** home to magnificent manor houses, the Museo do Vinho *(Av. Marquês de Soveral 79, tel 254 489 983, sjpesqueira .pt)* as well as a lookout point that affords what is considered the most breathtaking view of the Douro. This spot also claims a sanctuary, **São Salvador do Mundo,** once visited by young girls in search of husbands. History tells the story of Baron Forrester, an Englishman who was active

Rail Trips Along the Douro

Traveling by train is an effortless and spectacular way to see the Douro Valley. Tracks run parallel to the river for 62 miles (100 km) of the 110 miles (175 km) between Porto and Pocinho. The most stunning ride is from Pinhão to Tua and then north beside the Tua River to Mirandela: Feats of engineering, mind-blowing landscapes, and endless vineyards are assured.

in the development of the region. He lost his life when his boat capsized in the Valeira rapids below this lookout point; supposedly he was loaded down with gold coins. A fellow passenger survived, allegedly buoyed up by her ballooning Victorian crinoline. Is there a moral to this Douro tale? ■

The incredible São João de Tarouca site

AMARANTE

On the northern edge of the Douro region, straddling the Tâmega tributary, lies the attractive and historically significant Amarante—a mecca for poets and painters. Amarante is picture-postcard stuff: Its 16th-century monastery stands beside the arches of an 18th-century bridge, both framed against distant hills and reflected in the willow-edged river.

Wander through the steep cobbled streets of the old town to see a wealth of handsome 16th- to 18th-century houses. At the top of this web of streets, do not miss the evocative ruins of the **Solar dos Magalhães,** a manor house sacked by Napoleon's troops under Marshal Soult in 1809. The bridge at Amarante was where the calamitous French invasion was definitively halted by Portuguese troops after a two week standoff, after which the French burned down most of the old town.

The 1540 monastery of **São Gonçalo** looms above, its church fronting a large square with an outdoor café. Gonçalo was a 13th-century preacher who, after falling for the beauty of this spot, built a hermitage and bridge here, thus founding the town. His tomb, in a chapel to the left of the main altar, still attracts immense veneration; you are quite likely to see worshippers kissing the toes of his effigy. As the patron saint of marriage,

his statue is often touched by those despairing of finding their mates. The rest of the church interior displays impressive baroque wood carving.

Museu Amadeo de Souza Cardoso *(tel 255 420 282, amadeosouza-cardoso.pt, closed Mon., $)* occupies the upper monastery floor; access is to the side of the church. It is dedicated to cubist painter Souza Cardoso (1887–1918), an Amarante native who studied in Paris in the company of Amedeo Modigliani and others. His art hangs beside an assortment of works by Portuguese modernists. ■

■ **The monastery of São Gonçalo sits above the Tâmega River.**

Amarante ▲ 80 B2 **Visitor Information** ✉ Largo Conselheiro António Cândido ☎ 255 420 246
amarantetourism.com

VILA REAL & AROUND

Nestling in the foothills of the Serra do Marão, Vila Real is resolutely modern while harboring a relaxing center. Its greatest claim to fame is the Casa de Mateus, which sits in verdant splendor just outside town.

■ Casa de Mateus graces the label of Portugal's famous wine, Mateus Rosé.

The presence of a university in Vila Real (Royal Town) creates a lively atmosphere in what is otherwise a semi-industrialized town of 25,000 inhabitants that has turned its back on its aristocratic past. It is sandwiched between the beautiful hill ranges of the Alvão (to the north) and the Marão (to the southwest) on the Corgo, a tributary of the Douro; the wilder Trás-os-Montes region unfolds to the east. This strategic location makes Vila Real an obvious stop before or after touring Casa de Mateus. In the center, restaurants and shops line pedestrian streets east of the main avenue, Avenida Carvalho de Araújo. Souvenir hunters will find black pottery from Bisalhães and wool products from the Alvão and Marão hills. The Gothic cathedral stands on the main avenue, but its rather dull interior is for diehards only. More interesting is the facade of the 15th-century **Casa de Diogo Cão** *(Av. Carvalho Araújo 19, closed to the public)*, right next to the Town Hall. Diogo Cão, who discovered the mouth of the Congo River in Africa, was born here. A few doors away, the **Palácio dos Marqueses de Vila Real** presents another singular facade, this one notable for its battlements and ornate Manueline windows.

Vila Real 🗺 80 C2 **Visitor Information** ✉ Av. Carvalho de Araújo 94 ☎ 259 308 170 **portoenorte.pt**

Wonders of Casa de Mateus

This baroque masterpiece displays furniture and ornaments that typify the tastes of a rich family of the period. Treasures include carved chestnut-wood ceilings and doors; Cantonese porcelain of the 17th and 18th centuries; family portraits; and Japanese, French, English, and Spanish furniture. The Ladies' Room contains a beautiful Indo-Portuguese table in tortoiseshell and mother-of-pearl. A small museum displays vestments, reliquaries, religious sculptures, and documents. The library contains books from the 16th century to the present. Copperplate engravings by Fragonard for *The Lusiads* by Luís Vaz de Camões, the Portuguese Shakespeare, prove the Mateus family's long support of the arts, as this valuable first illustrated edition dates from 1817.

Beyond Vila Real

Vila Real's greatest draw is **Casa de Mateus,** 2 miles (3 km) from town. Hidden by a screen of vegetation, the 1740s mansion boasts baroque decor at its best, thanks to architect Nicolau Nasoni. Surround this with a lovely park landscaped with manicured boxwood hedges, lofty centennial cedars, tiered pools, and flower beds, and you have a very worthwhile destination. Guided tours take you through the main reception rooms (see sidebar this page). The Casa de Mateus Foundation, set up in 1970, has transformed a barn into a concert hall.

In contrast to such baroque excess, it is worth going 4 miles (7 km) southeast, beyond the village of Constantim. Stay on N322 and follow signs to reach the sanctuary of **Panoias** *(tel 259 336 322, closed Mon.–Tues. a.m., $)*. This ancient site, fenced in on the edge of a village, consists of a series of huge granite boulders, including several that are inscribed in Latin and carved with troughs. Thought to have been used for both animal and human sacrifices, the stone monuments bring a very different perspective of this land and its former people.

The **Serra do Marão** is part of the **Parque Natural do Alvão,** a 17,840-acre (7,220 ha) protected area between Vila Real and Mondim de Basto. Here, thatched-roof granite houses and *espigueiros* (raised stone granaries, common in the Norte) dot the higher elevations. Pigs, goats, and cattle graze in the fields, while eagles, falcons, wolves, and otters populate the wilder areas. The most popular spot here is the thundering 985-foot-tall (300 m) waterfall of **Fisgas do Ermelo.** And no visit would be complete without sampling the delicious smoked sausages, a local specialty. ∎

Casa de Mateus ⬛ 80 C2 **Visitor Information** ✉ N322, Mateus ☎ 259 323 121 ⑤ $$$–$$$$ **casademateus.com**

PORTUGUESE WINE

Few countries can claim such a globally known and appreciated wine as port. However, this tends to overshadow Portugal's other wonderful wines, such as the light *vinho verde* (green wine) of the Minho, the smooth and robust reds of the Alentejo, the velvety reds from Colares, and the sweet Muscatel from Setúbal.

One reason for their low profile is that, until very recently, most vineyards were very small; as a result, exports were mainly white vinho verde, red Dão, Madeira dessert wine, and that 1960s classic, Mateus Rosé. Recent decades, however, have seen vast improvements in vineyard quality and scale. Modernization means that Portugal's untapped potential is at last being realized.

In a world where standardization is increasingly the rule, Portuguese wines still stand out as individuals, refusing to bow to superstar grape varieties that dominate production elsewhere. Here, producers tend to rely on indigenous grapes such as Touriga Nacional (used in port and Dão wines), Tinta Roriz (the same as the Tempranillo grape used in Spain's *rioja* wines), Malvasia Fina (a local variety of the famous Greek grape used in the Douro's sparkling wines), Alvarinho (the basis of many vinhos verdes), and Periquita (widely used in reds of the Setúbal Peninsula and Alentejo). Nor have tried-and-tested methods been entirely abandoned either; for example, you still find some producers in the south aging their wine in clay vessels.

Then & Now

Wine production dates back to the Phoenicians, who introduced it to southern Portugal in 600 B.C. and traded it around the Mediterranean. Since then, Greeks, Celts, Romans, Visigoths, and even Moors have enjoyed the local tipple. Yet it was the English who kick-started the port trade.

In 1678, a Liverpudlian merchant discovered port when he added brandy to a sweet, heavy Douro wine to prevent the wine

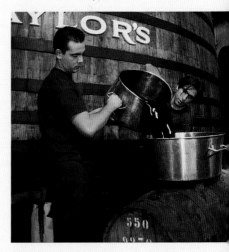

■ **Despite modernization, many tasks are still done by hand.**

from souring en route to England. Soon barrel loads of the fortified wine were being shipped to England and a 1703 trade treaty sealed the deal; port and English merchants were inextricably bound and profits soon boomed. A few decades later, Portugal's prime minister, the Marquês de Pombal, introduced the world's first production standards and controlled areas in the Douro Valley.

All was not smooth sailing though: The late 19th century saw vineyards devastated by the phylloxera plague, and a few decades later by shifts in agricultural focus. Since Portugal joined the EU in 1986, however, modern procedures have transformed its wine industry and its previously incomprehensible classifications.

With nearly 474,400 acres (192,000 ha) of vines flourishing in

■ Local grapes produce the curiously named *tinto verde* and port wine.

granitic, shale, sandy, or clay soils, domestic consumption is around six million hectoliters (158 million gallons) a year, placing Portugal among the world's top five consumers. In years gone by, wines tended to remain within their production regions. This is no longer the case and all but the most simple establishments will offer a choice of wines from different regions. If in doubt, order the *vinho da casa* (house wine); you are unlikely to hit a bad note.

Where to Savor Portugal's Wines

Wine flows freely in Portugal and forms a central part of any social gathering. For this reason alone, dedicate some time to exploring the subtleties of Portuguese wine, whether rustic brew or elegant vintage. Here are some great atmospheric venues that offer the traveler a special experience:

National wines: Sala Ogival, Praça do Comércio, Lisbon, tel 213 420 690, closed Sun. (Nov.–March), or **Palácio da Bolsa,** Rua das Flores 8–12, Porto, tel 223 323 072, winesofportugal .com, closed Sun. (Nov.–March)

Port: Solar do Vinho do Porto, Rua de São Pedro de Alcântara 45, Lisbon, tel 222 071 693, closed Sat.–Sun.; also in Porto, Rua Ferreira Borges 27, tel 222 071 669, www.ivdp.pt

Vinho verde: Solar do Alvarinho, Rua Direita, Melgaço, tel 251 410 195

Table wines: at the **Quinta da Portela** estate you can visit the vineyards, the museum, and taste their wines; Alvelos, Quinta da Portela de Baixo, Lamego, tel 926 210 073, bestofdouro.pt

GUIMARÃES

Historical status, gastronomy, the church, and a dash of contemporary panache all combine in this seductive medieval town that is classified as a World Heritage site. With rare architectural harmony and intelligently pedestrianized, Guimarães is a must-see highlight of Portugal's north.

Visitors may walk the ramparts of Guimarães's faithfully restored castle.

With Porto only 30 miles (50 km) away, Guimarães is hardly out of touch, and this shows in the style of many shops and restaurants in the town. Yet the nation of Portugal was founded here back in the 12th century, when Afonso Henriques, heir to the county of Portucale, chased out the Moors and declared himself king (see p. 25). His regal seat was the castle that dominates Guimarães, built in the tenth century to protect the monastery of Nossa Senhora da Oliveira.

Guimarães 🗺 80 B2 **Vistor Information** ✉ Praça de S. Tiago ☎ 253 421 221 **visitguimaraes.travel**

The old town lies between the gardens of the Alameda and bustling commercial Largo do Toural to the south, and the hilltop park, castle, and palace to the north. An obvious starting point is the main square, the **Largo da Oliveira,** which is separated from the adjacent Praça da Santiago by an arcaded walkway. Above this veranda were the old Council Chambers. Beside this stands the atmospheric old Hotel da Oliveira (see pp. 295–296). In the warmer months, much of the square is invaded by sidewalk cafés, great places from which to admire the Gothic shrine fronting the church of the monastery of **Nossa Senhora da Oliveira.**

This medieval church has undergone numerous alterations; today only the cloisters and the chapter house remain Romanesque; little is left of the monastery. The lovely buildings now house the remarkable **Museu de Alberto Sampaio** (Rua Alfredo Guimarães, tel 253 423 910, museualberto sampaio.gov.pt, closed Mon., $), stuffed with church treasures, including medieval tomb sculptures and one of Portugal's finest collections of silverware. Look for the magnificent gilded silver triptych, allegedly taken from the Castilians at the Battle of Aljubarrota in 1395. Dom João I's tunic from that same battle is also displayed. But do not let the exhibits monopolize your

Penha

Aficionados of heights and views shouldn't miss the verdant summit of Penha, the highest point in the Serra de Santa Catarina, right on the outskirts of Guimarães. It's reached via cable car; the **Teleférico da Penha** (Parque das Hortas, tel 253 515 085, turipenha.pt, closed Mon.–Thurs. Nov.–Mar., $$ round trip) rises 1,300 feet (400 m) in 10 minutes.

attention: The **chapter house, cloisters,** and **ancient priory buildings** are equally magnificent. Outside, on the corner of this street, a small open shrine houses carved figures of the Passion: It is one of five left from an original seven, erected in 1727 to represent the **Stations of the Cross.**

To the west, the ultramodern **Centro Internacional das Artes José de Guimarães,** built on the site of the former municipal market, is known locally as the Plataforma das Artes e Criatividade (Arts and Creativity Platform), or PAC. Dedicated to contemporary art, the award-winning building holds a museum, art exhibitions, and artists' studios.

Guimarães's other major draw is the **Paço dos Duques de Bragança,** a striking fortified palace bristling with

Centro Internacional das Artes José de Guimarães (PAC) ✉ Avenida Conde Margaride 175 ☎ 253 424 715 🕐 Closed Mon. 💲 $ **ciajg.pt**
Paço dos Duques de Bragança ✉ Rua Conde D. Henrique ☎ 253 412 273 💲 $$ **pacodosduques.gov.pt**

■ **The lively Largo da Oliveira, in the old city**

brick chimney pots that stands in a small park. Near ruins since the court moved out in the 16th century, the palace was restored in the 1930s to its original 15th-century appearance, complete with massive proportions, huge fireplaces, Aubusson tapestries, Persian rugs, coffered ceilings, and granite walls. Outside stands a statue of Afonso Henriques, founding king of the Portuguese nation.

On the hill above the Paço dos Duques de Bragança is the chapel of **São Miguel do Castelo.** This simple, unadorned chapel dating from the 12th century is where Afonso Henriques is said to have been baptized. Notice the etched stone tombs of Portugal's first warriors set into the floor. At the very top of the hill looms the **Castelo de Guimarães,** built in the tenth century to guard the monastery against attacks by the Normans and Moors. It, too, has been fully restored, and a steep climb up the keep will reward you with fine views. ■

BRAGA & AROUND

An old saying goes: "Porto works, Lisbon plays, and Braga prays." Braga is indeed renowned for its numerous churches and, above all, its Sé. Yet this industrious town is also home to enthusiastic diners, giving the center a lively atmosphere. Just beyond the high-rise suburbs are four major religious sites and the ancient settlement of Citânia de Briteiros.

■ The mountainside setting of S.C. Braga's stadium makes it a unique destination for soccer lovers.

While most of the main sites are religious in nature, Braga offers much more for visitors. The city's origins lie in Roman times when, as Bracara Augusta, it was an important commercial crossroads, but successive occupations by the Suevi, Visigoths, and finally the Moors left it in virtual ruins. Status and prosperity returned in the 11th century when the resident archbishop of the newly liberated town assumed ecclesiastical authority over the entire Iberian Peninsula. Later, when a 16th-century successor embarked on a frenzied building campaign, the city gained Renaissance fountains, squares, mansions, and churches. These were further embellished in the 18th century, although Braga's formal ecclesiastical status ended in 1716, when Lisbon took over the patriarchate.

The best time to experience the city's intensity of faith is during Easter

Week: Braga's spectacular processions peak on Maundy Thursday. June 23 and 24 bring more parades, dancing, bonfires, and fireworks to celebrate the summer solstice and the feast of St. John the Baptist.

Braga's City Center

Start your visit in the **Rossio da Sé** in the center of a pedestrianized area. This plaza is named for its **Sé** (cathedral). Much of the original Romanesque structure lies hidden under a wealth of late Gothic and baroque additions. Notice the beautiful altarpiece carved out of white stone and the statue of the nursing Virgin Mary, thought to be the work of French Renaissance artist Nicolas de Chanterenne.

The treasury—the **Tesouro Museu da Sé de Braga** (tel 253 263 317, se -braga.pt, $)—is the highlight. A guided tour shows off a breathtaking hoard of precious objects acquired by the prelates over the centuries, from gold and silver chalices to ivory or crystal crucifixes, gold thread altar cloths and vestments to platters of jewels. It perfectly illustrates the wealth and lavish way of life the bishops enjoyed.

The tour also takes in the magnificent carved baroque choir and massive organs before ending downstairs at two chapels. The Gothic **Capela dos Reis** (Chapel of the Kings) contains the rather ghoulish, mummified body of a 14th-century archbishop as

INSIDER TIP:

Be sure to stop by Rua da Violinha, one of the most typical streets of Braga's medieval town, and admire the interior of the medieval wall.

–ISABEL LEITÃO
Founder, À Descoberta de Braga tours

well as the tombs of Henry of Burgundy and his wife, Teresa, the parents of Portugal's first king, Afonso Henriques. Opposite, the Capela de São Geraldo is dedicated to Braga's first archbishop, who died in 1108; his tomb, set into a heavily gilded altarpiece, stands surrounded by 18th-century azulejos that portray his life.

Opposite the Sé, on Rua do Souto, is the **Antigo Paço Episcopal** (former bishop's palace), its rather forbidding facade enclosing three sides of a square. Much of this 14th- to 18th-century edifice is occupied by municipal offices, but enter the doorway to the left to have a look at the beautifully carved and painted library ceiling. Behind the palace is the **Jardim de Santa Bárbara,** a vividly colorful and immaculately tended garden.

By far Braga's most evocative site is the much underrated **Museu dos Biscainhos** (tel 253 204 650, closed

Mon., $). This manor house museum stands west of the pedestrian area, just outside **Porta Nova,** the 18th-century arch that once marked the entrance to town. The rambling house provides a remarkable window on the social history of Portugal's nobility, greatly helped by multilingual information sheets in each room. The tiled walls and painted, stuccoed ceilings are mainly 18th century, although some elements date from a century earlier, when the core of the house was built. A revealing feature is the raised platform on which the women of the house used to sit, sewing and embroidering, in a kind of social purdah. Close by is the room for social gatherings *(partidas),* a development that came in the mid-18th century and inspired card and game tables, musical instruments, and even tea and coffee sets. More important, it brought women out into society. Striking decorative items include Ming porcelain, glassware, silverware, and jewelry, while furniture ranges from Indo-Portuguese pieces to Japanese lacquer. The stables and fabulous kitchen can be visited on the way to a lovely baroque garden where towering chestnut and magnolia trees give plenty of shade and peeling sculptures add atmosphere, making it an evocative retreat for a summer's day.

Four Venerated Religious Centers

The much photographed **Bom Jesus do Monte** sits about 4 miles (6 km) east of Braga high on a hill. This church, a major pilgrimage spot, crowns a magnificent double baroque stairway. By the time the staircase was complete, after several decades, styles had changed and, as a result, the church itself is neoclassical and less fancy.

The climb is not as bad as it looks, and it must be undertaken if you wish to have a close look at the chapels, terra-cotta figures, and allegorical

Citânia de Briteiros

Farther afield, roughly halfway between Braga and Guimarães, you step back 2,000 odd years to the largest Celtiberian settlement in Portugal, Citânia de Briteiros *(tel 253 478 952, msarmento.org, closed Mon. in winter, $).* Tiered, defensive walls surround the foundations of more than 150 buildings, two of which have been reconstructed, although the site's better finds are now in Guimarães's archaeological museum, the **Museu Martins Sarmento** *(Rua Paio Galvão, Guimarães, tel 253 415 969, closed Mon.),* named for the first archaeologist to excavate here in 1875. Briteiros nonetheless makes an evocative, rural setting and the site is being upgraded to provide better visitor facilities, including a restaurant. Be wary about visiting during the heat of the day.

■ Countless stone heads, statues, and urns adorn the zigzagging staircase at Bom Jesus do Monte.

fountains that decorate each level. You will gravitate from the Stations of the Cross at the bottom to the intermediary Five Senses (which all worthy believers should overcome) and finally attain the symbols of the three virtues: Faith, Hope, and Charity.

Serious pilgrims accomplish the climb on their knees; most people simply walk. Alternatively, Portugal's oldest **funicular** *($)*, dating from 1882, creaks up to the top every half hour during daylight, and there is also a road that winds up to the church and nearby hotels. Try to time your visit for sunset and settle on a garden bench, in the terrace café, or in the panoramic restaurant: The sky explodes into dramatic color in front of you, while the lights of Braga slowly come on below. The entire hilltop is a popular weekend escape for locals since there are walks and pony rides in the woods behind.

Three miles (5 km) west of Braga is the important sanctuary and pilgrimage spot **Santuário de Nossa Senhora do Sameiro** that venerates the Virgin Mary. It commands extensive views over the Minho area, but has little architectural interest.

On the northwestern side of Braga, the Visigothic chapel of **São Frutuoso de Montélios** now stands engulfed by sprawling suburbs. Located on one of Portugal's medieval pilgrimage routes to Santiago de Compostela, in Spain, this is one of

Portugal's oldest chapels, dating from the seventh century. In the 18th century it was incorporated into a church, but its simple, cruciform structure and capitals are clearly visible.

Also on the northwestern side of Braga and a complete contrast both in scale and style to São Frutuoso is the stunning **Mosteiro de São Martinho de Tibães** *(tel 253 622 670, mosteiro detibaes.gov.pt, closed Mon., $)*. This sprawling monastery was founded in the 11th century, soon acquired immense power and wealth, and eventually became the father of all Benedictine monasteries in Portugal. The late 17th century saw a period of massive expansion and embellishment, leaving an astonishingly rich interior that is now considered one of Portugal's greatest baroque landmarks. Abandoned for more than a century, the monastery was rescued by the Portuguese state in 1986. Its restoration work ended in 2011. A state-of-the-art exhibition space has been created in one wing to house a historical center.

One of the monastery's highlights, apart from the dazzling rococo church, is a vast, somewhat overgrown baroque garden fashioned out of the hillside, a wondrous place of fountains, water channels, arbors, an oval lake, and box-hedged paths, with steps leading up to the reconstructed Chapel of St. Benedict. The latter was an enlightened attempt by the monks to symbolize the ascent into heaven. ∎

■ **The Mosteiro de São Martinho de Tibães**

VIANA DO CASTELO & THE NORTHERN MINHO

The northwestern corner of Portugal is full of inspiring contrasts, from a charming main town (Viana) to windswept beaches and a succession of fortified outposts along the Minho River. Inland lie the lush Lima Valley and the rugged Peneda-Gerês National Park (see pp. 118–120).

■ Every year the Minho's rich string of festivals brings out some glorious costumes and masks.

Viana do Castelo

Viana is a pleasant surprise with pedestrianized streets, a wealth of Renaissance and baroque architecture, good restaurants, and an easygoing atmosphere.

In this prosperous little port of 15,000 inhabitants you can still find fishermen's wives selling the daily catch west of the town center near the port, while raucous seagulls screech overhead. Embroidery is another Viana specialty: look for the local household linen, with original and colorful nature-inspired motives. If you are in the region around August

Viana do Castelo ⧉ 80 A3 **Visitor Information** ✉ Praça do Eixo Atlântico ☎ 258 098 415 🕒 Closed Mon. Sept.–June **vivexperiencia.pt**

EXPERIENCE: Nossa Senhora d'Agonia Festival

If you are in the Minho around August 20, you will undoubtedly be caught up in the revelries of the spectacular festival of Nossa Senhora d'Agonia, when groups from across the Minho converge on Viana. There are marching bands, street performances, *gigantões e cabeçudos* (people dressed as giants with enormous heads), and lots of *bombos* (drums). The highlight is definitely the street parades, when participants display their elaborate regional costumes and the women don their fine gold filigree jewelry; the more gold, the higher the status. Contact the tourist office or Viana Festas association *(tel 258 809 394, vianafestas.com)* for exact dates and the program of events.

20, enjoy the revelries of the spectacular festival of Nossa Senhora d'Agonia (see sidebar this page).

The heart of the town is the lively, café-lined **Praça da República** and its focal point, the **chafariz,** a tiered Renaissance fountain. Overlooking this from the northern end is the **Antigos Paços do Concelho** (Old Town Hall) and immediately opposite, the Venetian-style **Hospital da Misericórdia,** a former almshouse. The impressive caryatids and loggias (dating from 1589) shelter stone seats at ground level, invariably used by locals waiting to enter the municipal offices inside. Next door is the church of the **Misericórdia** itself *(tel 258 822 350, $),* rebuilt in 1714 and replete with exceptional azulejos by António de Oliveira Bernardes.

The main concentration of historic buildings in the web of narrow streets south of here includes the 15th-century **Hospital Velho,** a beautiful vaulted structure. Close by is the **Sé** (cathedral): Gothic and Romanesque elements grace a lovely facade, but the interior is somewhat dreary.

Head to **Rua São Pedro** for a string of Manueline mansions, then make for the other side of this main north-south avenue and the **Museu de Artes Decorativas** *(Largo de São Domingos, tel 258 809 305, closed Mon., $).* Housed in a slightly dilapidated 1720s mansion, it has a wonderful sense of history heightened by remarkable azulejos by Policarpo de Oliveira Bernardes, lofty coffered ceilings, and the personal character of the collection. You will see an illuminating display of 17th- and 18th-century Portuguese faïence, some from Viana itself—much of it in blue and white and designed to replace Ming imports from China—as well as Indo-Portuguese furniture, drawings, inlaid cabinets, and a lavish bedroom. Also worth a quick visit is an interesting costume museum, **Museu do Traje** *(Praça da República, tel 258 809 306, cm-viana-castelo.pt, closed Mon., $)* on the main square.

In addition to a bridge by the prolific Gustave Eiffel, Viana's riverfront also boasts the striking 16th-century castle of **Santiago da Barra** *(closed to public)* guarding the river mouth. Above, on the Monte de Santa Luzia, you can climb the dome of neo-Byzantine **Templo de Santa Luzia** *(tel 258 823 173, templosantaluzia .org, $)* for panoramic views of seemingly idyllic beaches below; better still, indulge in a sunset cocktail on the terrace of the *pousada.*

Finally, step back in time aboard **O Navio** *Gil Eannes (tel 258 809 710, fundacaogileannes.pt, $$)*. Built in the city shipyard during the 1950s, it originally supported cod fishermen in the North Atlantic as a hospital ship. Now fully restored, almost the entire ship can be visited.

The Minho Coast

Although only thick-skinned swimmers brave the waves on these Atlantic beaches, the shores are popular for sunbathing and for surfing. The main beach, just south of Viana, is **Praia do Cabedelo.**

Head 7 miles (11 km) north of Viana for the surfing beach of **Afife,** separated from the main road by fields of corn. A few miles farther, the small family beach resort of **Vila Praia de Âncora** is immediately followed by **Moledo.**

The latter's beach is much calmer and the water shallower, making it safer and slightly warmer for swimming. From here, you get a good view of a tiny island fort guarding the estuary of the Minho River. Between Moledo and Caminha, an extensive pine forest crossed by boardwalks borders a broad white sandy beach.

In **Caminha,** have a look at the medieval and Renaissance buildings that surround **Praça Conselheiro Silva Torres,** the central square, while in Largo da Matriz you will find the **Igreja Matriz** *(tel 258 921 413)*. The church claims one of the most finely carved and coffered ceilings in Portugal. You can also take a 10-minute car ferry *(tel 912 253 809)* across to the town of A Guarda in Galicia to visit the well-maintained Celtiberian settlement of **Santa Tecla.**

Continuing along the Minho River, the next stop is the fortified town of **Valença do Minho,** once a very important stronghold. Below the massive 17th-century ramparts sprawls a modern border town, maybe of little interest, but walk or drive up to the two polygonal fortresses and you enter a curious hybrid world of Spanish and Portuguese cultures. Resolutely aimed at droves of Spanish day-trippers, Valença's cobbled streets are lined with tapas bars and

Caminha 🅰 80 A3 **Visitor Information** ✉ Praça Conselheiro Silva Torres ☎ 258 921 952 🕐 Closed Sun. **cm-caminha.pt** • **Valença do Minho** 🅰 80 A4 **Visitor Information** ✉ Portas do Sol ☎ 251 823 329 **visitvalenca.com**

INSIDER TIP:

The Monção area produces excellent white Alvarinho wine, perfect paired with a dish of local lampreys (baby eels).

–EMMA ROWLEY
National Geographic contributor

shops selling cheap items. During weekdays, when the town is quieter, it offers a pleasant wander to admire the bastions, cannon, watchtowers, fountains, churches, and harmonious 17th- and 18th-century houses. **Porta do Sol** is the best entry; a footbridge connects the two fortresses.

Less adulterated by commercial concerns, but displaying an equally defensive character, the medieval stronghold of **Monção,** 10 miles (16 km) east, offers a relaxed, attractive setting around the verdant main square, **Praça Deu-la-Deu.** Two churches are of some interest, the partly Romanesque **Igreja Matriz** *(Rua da Glória)* and the early baroque **Misericórdia** *(Praça Deu-la-Deu),* where cherubs dance across a wood-paneled ceiling in front of an elaborate Renaissance altarpiece. ∎

Monção 🗺 80 A4 **Visitor Information** ✉ Praça Deu-la-Deu ☎ 251 649 013

∎ **The view from Valença do Minho stretches across the border to Spain.**

PONTE DE LIMA

Plumb in the middle of *vinho verde* territory, beside the Lima River, is this immaculately preserved "oldest town in Portugal." There are no major monuments, but it is a natural point between Viana and the interior mountains, and between the border with Spain and Braga. The market is a major event locally and the oldest market in the country.

Ponte de Lima's historical claim to fame was its medieval role as a stop on the pilgrimage road to Santiago de Compostela from the religious hotbed of Braga. The graceful, arched granite bridge remains from those days, with five arches of an even older Roman section, built for military purposes, on the western bank. Here is the **Parque Temático do Arnado,** made of pleasant gardens laid out according to themes.

Town Attractions

Ponte de Lima's central focal point is the attractive main square, **Largo de Camões,** which hosts an 18th-century fountain and relaxing pavement cafés. On alternate Mondays, the entire riverside springs to life with a sprawling market which has been held, virtually uninterrupted, since 1125. The old town's architectural styles range from Romanesque to neoclassical. Wander around and enjoy the facades, many enhanced by window boxes or doorway pots, and note the Romanesque doorway of the parish church. Shops sell local specialties: linen, elaborate Minho costumes, and life-size models of woolly sheep.

The **Museu dos Terceiros** *(Rua dos Terceiros 209, tel 258 240 220, www .museuspontedelima.com, closed Mon., $)* is housed in two churches—one of which, the **Igreja dos Terceiros,** with its baroque front, was built in 1745. The museum displays religious iconography, 16th-century Mudéjar tiles from Spain, and some fine wood carving. ∎

∎ **Tree-lined paths offer relaxing strolls in Ponte de Lima.**

Ponte de Lima 🗺 80 A3 **Visitor Information** ✉ Torre da Cadeia Velha, Passeio de 25 Abril ☎ 258 240 208 **visitepontedelima.pt**

PARQUE NACIONAL
DA PENEDA-GERÊS

Vaguely resembling a horseshoe, the park curls around the Spanish border in the far north of the country. Portugal's first national park, it was set up in 1971 to protect some remote, very traditional villages as well as flora and fauna, and it is one of the last refuges of the Iberian wolf and golden eagle. A partnership with the bordering Spanish national park ensures a larger protected habitat.

■ At Junceda, near Campo do Gerês, boulder-strewn landscapes rise to more than 2,700 feet (863 m).

The park covers almost 173,000 acres (70,000 ha), roughly between Castro Laboreiro in the north and Caldas do Gerês in the south, and is crossed by the Lima, Homem, and Peneda Rivers. Four mountain ranges *(serras)*, rich in granite and schist, dominate the terrain—the highest peak is in Serra do Gerês and rises to 5,044 feet (1,538 m)—creating a series of peaks and valleys edged with undulating foothills. Yet the ancient megaliths (around Castro

Parque Nacional da Peneda-Gerês 80 B3 Lugar do castelo, Lindoso 258 452 250 **natural.pt**

EXPERIENCE: Walking Through Wolf Territory

Get up close with the wild and un-tamed Peneda-Gerês region by tracking one of its rarest residents, the endangered Iberian wolf. Depending on how much time you have available, it is possible to hike for anything from one to eight days with **Ecotura** (*Lugar do Quei-madelo, Castro Laboreiro, Melgaço, tel 966 943 551, ecotura.com*). Knowledgeable guides lead small groups along centuries-old shep-herd paths and known wolf trails, searching for wolf tracks and pointing out the ancient traps once used to catch these much feared creatures. They explain the importance of wolves to this northern region and their miracu-lous ability to survive extinction despite man's efforts (until recent years) to be rid of them. Guide and owner Pedro Alarcão sug-gests that the best time to visit is in September and October, when the probability of spotting a wolf is greatest. If wolves do not inter-est you, Ecotura offers a range of other trips in addition to year-round horseback riding.

Laboreiro and Mezio) and granite formations, the remnants of glacier activity, are far more impressive.

The park straddles the Mediter-ranean and northern Europe biosys-tems, making for a wide range of flora and fauna, the former being particu-larly impressive in April and May, the perfect time for hiking in the area. But beauty has a price—rain. The hills of the Serra da Peneda receive Portugal's highest rainfall, nourishing luminous green meadows much in favor with the local long-horned *barrosão* cattle. Several species of oak trees dominate the lower elevations while the higher reaches see typical moorland vegeta-tion, including seas of brilliant yellow gorse, broom, heather, pine, and fir trees. If you are lucky, you will see the wild Gerês lily: endemic to the park, it grows in wooded areas, but only in select locations. Park denizens include roe deer, wild boars, otters, foxes, wild ponies, and raptors.

The park has five entrances. Most of its infrastructure is concentrated in a buffer zone that encircles the spectacular, higher-elevation core region, which should not be missed. Try to avoid the area around Caldas do Gerês on weekends and holidays, when it gets extremely crowded.

Nossa Senhora da Peneda

An unexpected sight in such a raw, craggy setting and dwarfed by a sheer granite cliff is the sanctuary

NOTE: If you wish to stay overnight in the park's core region, relatively comfortable rooms in private village houses are available, as are a selection of established bed-and-breakfasts. There are also campsites at Travanca, Vidoeiro, and Entre Ambos-os-Rios. For details, visit *turismoruraleparquesdecampismogeres.com*.

of **Nossa Senhora da Peneda,** a graceful baroque building with a zigzagging stairway inspired by Braga's Bom Jesus. The long flight of steps is flanked by 14 chapels, each one depicting a major event in the life of Christ.

The foundation of this sanctuary was inspired by the reported vision of the Virgin by a local shepherdess in the 13th century. If you visit around September 7, you will see one of Portugal's most important pilgrimages. The sanctuary is in the most rewarding northern part of the park, where you will discover some of the traditional rural lifestyles the park protects—despite the population's ongoing drift to the cities.

Traditional Life

To gain a sense of the customs of the region, visit the town of **Terras de Bouro,** just outside the southwest corner of the park. Its ethnographic museum, **Museu Etnográfico de Vilarinho da Furna,** reveals the traditional life once enjoyed in Vilarinho das Furnas, a village submerged by the reservoir next to Campo do Gerês in 1972. Building stones were saved to build the museum. ■

Museu Etnográfico de Vilarinho da Furna ✉ São João do Campo, Terras de Bouro ☎ 253 351 888 🕐 Closed Mon. 💲 $
turismo.cm-terrasdebouro.pt

■ The ruins of the Vilarinho da Furna village

DRIVE INTO PARQUE NACIONAL DA PENEDA-GERÊS

Less about specific sites and more about rural scenery, this drive takes you from Ponte de Lima up into the rugged mountains of Peneda-Gerês National Park, before circling back along verdant riverbanks to Ponte da Barca.

Espigueiros (raised stone granaries) are unique to northern Portugal.

Leave **Ponte de Lima ❶** by following signs for the A3 to Valença/Espanha. Enter the toll road and then turn off immediately toward Ponte da Barca. This road (N202) takes you past typical Minho vine-draped pergolas, wooded slopes, and villages. You soon reach **Arcos de Valdevez ❷** *(visitor information, Rua Prof. Mário Júlio Almeida Costa, tel 258 520 530, visitarcos.pt),* a pretty town on the Vez River. Turn left at the first traffic circle to cross the river,

then right after the bridge. After a stroll along the scenic river, return to the town entrance and follow signs to Soajo (N202). After passing the tiled church of **São Paio,** turn right, and take the first left.

The road climbs through pine and eucalyptus groves to wild, rockier terrain of heather, terraced hillsides, and distant mountains. At the **Porta do Mezio ❸** you leave the buffer zone and enter the national park. There is a small **visitor center** *(tel 258 510 100, portadomezio.pt),* and ancient megaliths lie off the road to the right. The road now descends to **Soajo** ❹, famous for its 24 *espigueiros* (raised stone granaries). Drive straight on to a stone monument and turn left; after 200 yards (180 m) the espigueiros come into view beside the road. Return to the main road; turn right and right again

NOT TO BE MISSED:

Ponte de Lima • Soajo *espigueiros* • Castelo do Lindoso • Ponte da Barca riverside

to see Soajo's main square and pillory. Leave by the way you came and then, after a sharp right-hand bend, turn right up a steep cobbled road signposted **Gavieira.**

This road leads through a landscape of gorse, pine trees, black sheep, horses, goats, and long-horned cattle. Switchbacks offer stunning views to the southeast before the road reaches a rocky pass at 4,644 feet (1,416 m).

From here it twists up to the village of **Adrão** ❺, a mile or two past which is one of the best lookout points in the area. Pull over to admire the sheer granite slopes and deep verdant valleys sprinkled with hamlets

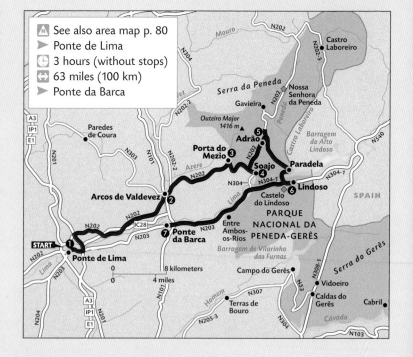

See also area map p. 80
► Ponte de Lima
🕒 3 hours (without stops)
↔ 63 miles (100 km)
► Ponte da Barca

Lindoso castle and its strategic location on the border

below, with the religious sanctuary of **Peneda** nestling beneath the rock face to the far north. From here backtrack for about a mile (1.6 km) to a road beside a vertical rock face, which is only marked by a sign that warns against cattle. Turn left up this very narrow, vertiginous road, which offers more spectacular views over the hills and valley. The **Barragem do Alto Lindoso** (dam) in the Peneda River is soon visible below.

Paralleling the Lima

After passing a roadside chapel at **Paradela,** cross the Lima River dam and continue uphill toward **Lindoso** ❻. Make for the

medieval tower and lichen-clad stones of the **Castelo do Lindoso** *(Lugar do Castelo, tel 258 578 141, natural.pt)*, which provides information on the national park and houses a small photo exhibit and arms section. Far more impressive, however, are the 60-odd **espigueiros** grouped just outside the walls. Leaving Lindoso, turn left onto the main road (N304-1). This snakes 18 miles (29 km) beside the river to **Ponte da Barca** ❼ *(Rua Conselheiro Rocha Peixoto, tel 258 455 246).* The old town's draw is its idyllic river frontage—an attractive 15th-century bridge, pillory, and open market hall.

BRAGANÇA & AROUND

The walled town of Bragança, in the far northeast, dominates the Trás-os-Montes. This is Portugal's least prosperous area—a marked contrast to areas farther west. Broad plateaus, wide valleys, and traditional villages are protected to the north in the Parque Natural de Montesinho.

Bragança is a town with an unusually rich aristocratic past. Visible from miles away, its historic center extends from its defensive hilltop citadel, started by Dom Sancho I in the 12th century and gradually enlarged over the following centuries. Crenellated stone walls, arched gateways, staircases, ramparts, a towering keep, a pillory, and cobbled, flowery streets all create a strikingly harmonious setting. The keep (1409–1449), one of Portugal's most beautiful fortresses, houses the somewhat dull **Museu Militar,** but it offers memorable panoramic views from its roof. Across the esplanade stands the town's oldest church, **Santa Maria,** a charming late 16th- to early 17th-century building.

Just behind this stands Bragança's most unusual site, the **Domus Municipalis** *(closed Mon.),* the oldest town hall in Iberia. The pentagonal structure, perforated by arched openings, is a rare civil building in Romanesque style, thought to date from the early 15th century. The upper floor appears to have been designed for meetings, while below lies a cistern *(ask for a key in the Museu Militar).*

From the citadel, streets snake downhill into a more baroque, 18th-century quarter and beyond that to a recklessly conceived 20th-century extension. The **Sé,** or cathedral *(Praça da Sé),* occupies the central position in the old quarter, fronted by a 1689 stone crucifix and surrounded by emblazoned seigneurial mansions. Bragança has a wealth of these impressive, mainly 17th- and 18th-century houses—testimony to its grandiose past as the fiefdom of the dukes of Bragança. The cathedral's 17th-century **sacristy** is also well worth visiting. Its paneled ceiling relates the life of St. Ignatius of Loyola, founder of the Jesuits who controlled this church for two centuries.

Downhill from here, toward the citadel, is the beautiful church of **São Vicente** *(Largo do Principal),* Romanesque in origin but much altered in the 17th and 18th centuries. The result is a profusion of dazzling baroque ornamentation.

Bragança 🔼 81 E3 **Visitor Information** ✉ Rua Abílio Beça 103 ☎ 273 240 020 **turismo.cm-braganca.pt** • **Museu Militar** ✉ Rua da Cidadela, Castelo ☎ 273 322 378 🕐 Closed Mon. 💲 $ **www.exercito.pt**

EXPERIENCE: Traditional Montesinho Life

For a hands-on taste of traditional Transmontano life, head north out of Vinhais to the tiny hamlet of Travanca. Set in the heart of Parque Natural de Montesinho, **Casa da Fonte** (*Travanca, tel 933 289 612, casa dafonte.com, double room €240*) offers comfortable accommodation in refurbished village houses and will arrange for guests to take part in various traditional activities. Choose from a day with a local shepherd herding his flock or, depending on the season, trout fishing or hunting for small game and wild boar. It is also possible to try your hand at archery, crossbow, and pistol shooting.

For a glimpse of a mansion interior, head for the nearby **Museu do Abade de Baçal,** where a varied collection of ethnographic and decorative arts is displayed in the former bishop's palace. It is presented in a very modern and imaginative fashion. The ground floor shows gold Iron Age *fibulae* alongside local ironwork and Roman *stelae*. Upstairs, look for a 16th-century triptych that illustrates the martyrdom of St. Ignatius of Antioch; it is one of the museum's most valuable works. Finally, don't miss the ancient granite sow at the entrance: You will see many more throughout the region.

Parque Natural de Montesinho

Nudging the Spanish border, the Parque Natural de Montesinho covers an area of 185,250 acres (75,000 ha) in which approximately 90 traditional villages harbor a dwindling population of 9,000. Like Peneda-Gerês (see pp. 118–120), the park was created more to preserve a rural lifestyle than to protect flora and fauna. The granite and schist hills and valleys of this northern part of Trás-os-Montes are known as *terra fria* (cold land), in contrast to the *terra quente* (hot land) of olives, almonds, and figs farther south.

Montesinho has archaic roots, still visible in its simple slate-roofed stone houses, in surnames of Visigothic origin, in local dialects, and in sometimes pagan rituals. The easiest small villages to reach from Bragança are **Rio de Onor** and **Montesinho** itself, both located about 14 miles (22 km) to the north. ∎

Museu do Abade de Baçal ✉ Rua Conselheiro Abílio Beça 27 ☎ 273 331 595 🕐 Closed Mon. 💲 $ **museuabadebacal.gov.pt** • **Parque Natural de Montesinho** 🗺 81 D3-D4, E3-E4 Visitor Information ✉ Parque Florestal de Bragança ☎ 273 329 135 **natural.pt montesinho.com**

More Places to Visit in the Norte Region

Barcelos

Barcelos, 14 miles (21 km) west of Braga, is known for its vast Thursday market and a curious, brightly painted clay cockerel. The latter is ubiquitous throughout Portugal in countless forms as a symbol of justice. Legend holds that a cockerel rose from its lifeless state on a judge's platter to protest the innocence of an unjustly sentenced pilgrim. Other than market day, Barcelos is a sleepy place with two main sites: The **Paço dos Condes** (tel 253 412 273), an open-air archaeological museum, is laid out in the ruins of the palace of the counts of Barcelos, overlooking the Cávado River. The **Museu de Olaria** (Rua Cónego Joaquim Gaiolas, tel 253 824 741, museuolaria.pt, closed Mon., $) displays pottery from all over Portugal.

portoenorte.pt 🅼 80 A2 **Visitor Information** ✉ Largo Dr. José Novais 27 ☎ 253 811 882

Chaves

This small spa town on the Tâmega River was developed by the Romans as much for its strategic position as for its thermal waters. The main monument is the massive keep, the **Torre de Menagem** ($) that overlooks the Roman bridge. Inside is a modest military museum with maps detailing the attacks at Chaves by Luso and Wellesley (later Lord Wellington) on French troops in 1809.

Vidago Palace

Commissioned in 1908 by Dom Carlos, Vidago Palace (tel 276 990 901, vidagopalace .com) **was intended as a luxurious holiday home for the royal family, where they could come to take the region's famous therapeutic waters. Dom Carlos was assassinated before its completion, but Vidago Palace went on to become one of Iberia's most luxurious hotels, attracting royalty from across Europe. More than one hundred years later, a total refurbishment saw its belle epoque features meticulously restored and modern luxuries added, including a state-of-the-art spa at which to enjoy the benefits of the waters.**

You can climb to the battlements for sweeping views. The tower fronts the main cluster of monuments at the heart of Chaves's medieval quarter: the town hall, an ethnographic museum, the parish church, and an elaborate pillory.

Crowning the hilltop behind is the impressive **Forte de São Francisco,** most of which has now become an upscale hotel. Worth noting is the **Museu de Arte Contemporânea Nadir Afonso** (Avenida 5 de Outubro 10, tel 276 340 501, Closed Mon., $$, macna.chaves.pt), opened in 2016 in a building designed by Álvaro Siza Vieira, which holds about half of the collection of abstract painter Nadir

Afonso; the space hosts temporary exhibits and cultural events. Chaves's other attraction is its delicious local cured ham and sausages.
chaves.pt  80 C3 **Visitor Information** ✉ Terreiro de Cavalaria ☎ 276 348 180

Mirandela

Built on a hillside sloping down to the Tua River, the lively market town of Mirandela lies at the head of the stunning narrow-gauge railway from Tua in the Douro Valley. The evocative old quarter rises beside a 16th-century bridge of 20 unequal arches. Mirandela's most interesting site is the town hall,

housed in a lovely 18th-century mansion, the **Palácio dos Távoras.** The **Museu Municipal Armindo Teixeira Lopes** *(Rua João Maria Sarmento Pimentel, tel 278 201 590, closed Mon.)* offers an overview of mainly 20th-century Portuguese art. The main draw, however, lies in its market building where, even outside Thursday, the main market day, shops sell delicious regional products—goat and sheep cheeses, cured ham, extra virgin olive oil, honey, jams, and of course wines.
cm-mirandela.pt ▲ 81 D2 **Visitor Information** ✉ Rua D. Afonso III, next to the train station ☎ 278 203 143

▬ Ponte Velha, in Mirandela, with its irregular arches

A land of fortified hill villages, giant boulders, creamy sheep cheese, and Portugal's most august university

CENTRO

Azulejos adorn a town wall in Viseu, one of the Centro region's many well-kept secrets.

CENTRO

Now officially known as the Centro region, this area is still often referred to by its former name of the Beiras and its subdivisions *alta, baixa,* and *litoral* (high, low, and coastal), to which you could easily add a fourth, the mountainous spine of the Serra da Estrela. To the west of this massif lie outgoing, dynamic towns, while on its eastern side a string of defensive castles and walled towns face the old enemy, Spain.

These medieval outposts evolved over centuries of conflict, but long before that the Romans had left their mark at Conímbriga, to the west. Today this area remains the sociocultural heart of the Beiras in the form of Coimbra. This lively, attractive university town entrances the visitor with its cultural sites, fado music, gastronomy, outdoor activities, and a number of nearby bucolic escapes.

Although the coastline boasts sandy beaches and pine forests, the sea is cool and the waves are big, making the shore less of a priority than the interior.

The exception is Aveiro, an engaging little town built on canals, with two relaxed beach resorts a short distance away. Every other place of interest in the Beiras is small scale, possesses several churches, and, often, a castle. Closer to the Serra da Estrela, you enter a dramatic region peppered with gigantic granite boulders, dolmens, and cromlechs; north of here, spanning the border between the Beiras and the Trás-os-Montes area, the Vale do Côa (Côa Valley) displays exceptional paleolithic rock art. There is ample evidence of early Celtic, Swabian, and Arab presence, while the historically strong Jewish community has in recent years made something of a comeback.

Craftwork is omnipresent, whether the black pottery of the mountains, the intricately decorated ceramics of Coimbra, or the fine porcelain produced at Vista Alegre, near Aveiro. In the field of textiles, the leader is

NOT TO BE MISSED:

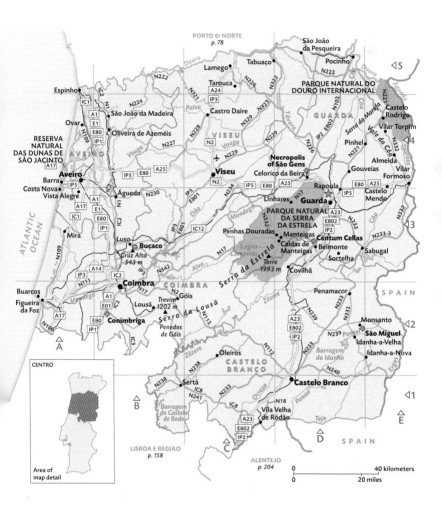

Castelo Branco, thanks to a tradition of embroidered bedspreads, while beautiful woolen blankets are woven in the villages of the Serra da Estrela. From here, too, come sheepskin products and the region's famous sheep cheese, *queijo da Serra*. In gastronomic terms, the Beiras offer a tantalizing menu of dishes ranging from hearty mountain cuisine (meat or game based) to the fresh seafood of the coast, and several excellent wines. ■

AVEIRO & AROUND

Aveiro has a split personality. Past its sprawling metropolis you'll discover a picturesque town built on a network of canals, earning it the epithet "Venice of Portugal." Aveiro is also distinguished as the country's city-museum of art nouveau, a member of the Réseau Art Nouveau Network along with Barcelona, Budapest, and Havana, among others.

It is hard to believe that Aveiro was once a port. Today, a wide highway connects the town with the coast, crossing a tidal lagoon that once was the harbor before silting up some 400 years ago in the wake of a disastrous storm. The next two centuries saw an economic decline; prosperity eventually returned on the shoulders of salt workers and seaweed gatherers, as well as a burgeoning ceramics industry in neighboring Vista Alegre. Aveiro itself nurtured a renowned school of baroque sculpture. It is now Portugal's third industrial center, after Lisbon and Porto. Aveiro's compact town center can easily be covered on foot. Then, cruise along the canals (*Douro Acima, tel 234 482 365, douroacima.pt, $$$*), perhaps in a motorized version of the attractive local *moliceiros* (flat-bottomed sailboats).

Aveiro's signature site is the fabulous **Museu de Aveiro Santa Joana,** housed in splendor in the former **Convent of Jesus,** home to an order of cloistered nuns from 1461 to 1834. The refectory, with its 17th-century tiled walls and Manueline lectern, is lovely, while the church is a dazzling extravaganza of gilded baroque, including a massive stepped altarpiece. The beautiful ceiling illustrates the life of São Domingo, and oil paintings from 1729 depict the life of Santa Joana, the convent's most celebrated resident. Mementos of Princess Joana, later beatified, abound. She spent 18 years here before her death in 1490. A silver reliquary containing her relics is in the small embroidery room where she spent her last days; an elaborate baroque marble tomb, commissioned after her sainthood in 1693, stands in the lower choir.

Upstairs, the museum collection offers a wide-ranging feast of paintings, sculpture, woodwork, furniture, and silver, dating from the 15th to 18th centuries. Don't miss the 18th-century convent pharmacy: It contains traditional herbal medicines.

Fronted by the Gothic **crucifix of São Domingos,** just across the

Aveiro ⛰ 131 A4 **Visitor Information** ✉ Rua João Mendonça 8 ☎ 234 420 760 **turismodocentro.pt** • **Museu de Aveiro Santa Joana** ✉ Avenida de Santa Joana ☎ 234 423 297 🕐 Closed Mon. 💲 $

■ Cheerfully painted beach huts line the seafront of Costa Nova.

square, stands the early 15th-century **Sé** *(tel 234 422 182),* formerly part of a Dominican monastery. Much altered over the centuries, the cathedral's dominant style is baroque.

The heart of the town lies across the bridge where, in a small web of quaint backstreets, you will discover **Largo da Praça do Peixe,** a large square surrounding the fish market. Seafood restaurants are plentiful, with excellent low-cost eateries on the upper floor of the market.

As Portugal's art nouveau capital, Aveiro also boasts a dozen or so not-to-be-missed buildings including Casa de Major Pessoa, now home to the **Museu de Arte Nova** *(Rua Dr. Barbosa Magalhães 9–11, tel 234 406 485, cm-aveiro.pt, closed Mon., $).* Its detailed stone façade is laden with flowers, arabesques, and wrought-iron embellishments; inside await tile panels depicting birds, animals, and flowers as well as interesting exhibits and the Casa de Chá (see p. 299).

Beyond Aveiro

Immediately north of the surfing beaches and family resorts of **Barra** and **Costa Nova** is a long spit of land edged by sand

EXPERIENCE: Making *Doces Conventuais*

To satisfy your sweet tooth and learn how Aveiro's local, much acclaimed *ovos moles* and other *doces conventuais* (sweet egg-based delicacies) are made, visit the **Oficina do Doce** *(Rua João Mendonça 23, Letra JKL–Galeria Rossio, tel 234 098 840, oficina dodoce.com),* located on the town's central canal.

Visitors are invited to watch demonstrations and try their hand at making their own ovos moles in the traditional manner, by filling the delicate wafer shells with sticky yolky filling before cutting out the shapes with scissors. Naturally, at the end, everyone gets to taste their handiwork. Reserve your spot at the Oficina do Doce or at the association **Rota da Bairrada** *(Rua Clube dos Galitos 2, tel 234 420 760, rotadabairrada.pt).*

dunes, the **Reserva Natural das Dunas de São Jacinto** *(access via ferry from Barra, or road from Ovar and from road N109).* This nature reserve no longer teems with the incredible diversity of birdlife for which it was once known, yet is still quite interesting. ∎

Reserva Natural das Dunas de São Jacinto 🗺 131 A4 ☎ 234 331 282
💲 Guided tours 9:30 a.m. & 2 p.m.: $ **natural.pt**

▪ The pristine landscape of the Dunas de São Jacinto

COIMBRA & AROUND

Coimbra, Portugal's third largest city, was the country's first capital and remained a royal residence for centuries before power shifted to Lisbon. The city's vibrant character draws energy and life from the students and traditions of the Universidade de Coimbra, the country's oldest and most prestigious university. Groups of students stroll about in their swirling black capes, and the Renaissance university itself crowns the hill that is the geographic center of this city.

Below, bordering the Mondego River, a typical provincial town of northern Portugal unfolds—the narrow streets now pedestrianized and the outskirts peppered with invasive apartment blocks. Across the river sit two major convents and the road south to Conímbriga, a once flourishing Roman settlement (see p. 142). In this direction, too, lie the hills of the Serra da Lousã that edge the western end of the massive Serra da Estrela (see pp. 150–151). Although gaining in popularity as a nature retreat, it is still overshadowed by the more famous forest of Buçaco and the neighboring spa at Luso, both to the north of Coimbra.

Coimbra's university was established in 1537 after Lisbon's university, founded in 1290, was forcibly exiled here (see p. 29). As such, Coimbra's academic institutions remain concentrated and traditions deeply entrenched. The *repúblicas* (student lodgings), established by royal decree

River Ride on the Mondego

For some of the best views of the city of Coimbra, hop aboard the **Basófias** *(Cais do Parque Dr. Manuel Braga, tel 969 830 664, basofias.pt)* riverboat for a 50-minute cruise *($$)* along the banks. Excursions set off from the quay, south of the Santa Clara Bridge.

in medieval days, continue to thrive, furthering the values of community life and democracy. Come here in early May and you will experience the **Queima das Fitas**—the symbolic burning of faculty ribbons to kick off a month of intensive study leading to exams, and an excuse for wholehearted carousing and heavy drinking. Another offshoot of Coimbra's intellectual bent is the local fado (see p. 137)—more complex and mournful than its emotional Lisbon cousin, and strictly the preserve of men.

Coimbra 🗺 131 B2 **Visitor Information** ✉ Rua Ferreira Borges 20 ☎ 239 488 120 **turismodocentro.pt**

■ **Stepping up a hillside across the Mondego River, the engaging town of Coimbra never fails to appeal.**

Universidade de Coimbra

Fortresslike in appearance, the hilltop university demands energy and good calves to reach it from the lower town. The classic approach is up the back-breaking stairs of Quebra Costas, reached through the Arco de Almedina, an old Moorish gateway; however, you might want to keep this for your descent and climb up via the gentler slope of the Couraça de Lisboa. Different ticket options are available, and some include a visit to the botanical garden and inner museums.

At the university's heart is a U-shaped structure that started life as a Moorish fortress in the tenth century. The colossal scale and sturdiness were designed to symbolize the power of the caliphate of Córdoba,

the first center of Moorish rule in the Iberian Peninsula. In 1130, Portugal's first king, Afonso Henriques, chose to move here from Guimarães and it thus became a royal palace, the Paço Real. Portugal's oldest royal residence, it was regularly inhabited until the 15th century, when it was abandoned. It only assumed its present identity as part of a university in 1537. Numerous alterations have been made over the years, giving it Manueline and baroque features. It is nonetheless surprising on a winter's day to see students huddled on wooden benches in lecture halls; the only changes in the last century or so appear to be the addition of heaters.

Courtyard Buildings: On entering the main courtyard from the

Universidade de Coimbra ✉ Largo Marquês de Pombal ☎ 239 424 744 or 239 859 884 💲 $$–$$$ **visit.uc.pt**

monumental square of Praça da Porta Férrea, you face the Gerais (Law School), the Capela de São Miguel, and, on the far left, the university's most outstanding site, the library, or Biblioteca Joanina. The colonnaded gallery on your right, the **Via Latina,** was built in the late 18th century to improve access to the Manueline **Sala dos Capelos** and the **Sala do Exame Privado.** These rooms close to the public when university ceremonies take place. The Sala dos Capelos is a vast, imposing hall with a ceiling painted by Jacinto da Costa and a gallery of rather stiff royal portraits. Don't miss the balcony with far-reaching views over the city and beyond.

Reached via the Gerais, the **Capela de São Miguel** mixes Renaissance and baroque styles with panache. The chapel's vaulted ceiling is covered in delicate paintings, the walls partly faced in azulejos, and the

■ Musicians in traditional costume entertain passersby in the heart of Coimbra's shopping district.

altar home to a gilded retable by Bernardo Coelho. Pride of place, however, goes to the magnificent organ (1733) in its carved and painted chinoiserie casing. Next door the small *tesouro* (treasury) displays church plate, vestments, and paintings. Wander upstairs in this building to get a feel for 21st-century student life.

EXPERIENCE: Coimbra Fado

Lisbon fado, sung by both men and women, originated in the taverns of the oldest and poorest districts of the city (see pp. 62–63); Coimbra fado is the domain of black-cloaked, male students who typically sing in the streets after dark, like roaming troubadours. For a closer insight into this intrinsic part of Coimbra culture, be sure to visit the cultural center **Fado ao Centro** (*Rua do Quebra Costas 7, tel* 239 837 060 *or* 913 236 725, *fado aocentro.com, $$$),* down the steps opposite the cathedral. The center puts on daily fado concerts of a high standard, hiring only the finest of the city's musicians. Concerts start at 6 p.m. and last 50 minutes. Reservations are advised for the evening concert. Over the years, a music school and string instruments-making workshop have been added.

The adjoining **Biblioteca Joanina**—its baroque beauty much extolled and photographed—easily surpasses all the other buildings for sheer visual delight. Three lofty, interconnecting halls arguably offer the world's most lavish library setting thanks to the perspective paintings of the ceilings and the intricately carved bookcases, again charged with subtle chinoiserie motifs. Tapering, carved columns support shelves bearing some 30,000 volumes and 5,000 manuscripts, the upper levels accessed by ladders. The allegorical paintings of the last and most sumptuous hall honor Dom João V, founder of the library. A statue of the corpulent man stands outside, his back turned to the view over town, which you can enjoy from the terrace.

Churches: Two churches, the **Sé Nova** (the new cathedral) and **São Salvador,** are squeezed between the academic buildings; however, a short walk downhill takes you to the far more interesting **Sé Velha,** or old cathedral. This beautifully sober structure, originally Romanesque, dates from 1140, making it Portugal's oldest cathedral. It owes its austere design to two French architects. Sixteenth-century Sevillian tiles and elegant Mudéjar-style arches above the transept give visual weight to the otherwise bare stone interior. The focal point is the Gothic altarpiece, all high-relief and vivid colors, designed by Flemish masters Olivier de Gand and Jean d'Ypres. The chapel to the right, the **Capela do Sacramento,** contains a Renaissance work by

A wealth of chinoiserie, Coimbra's Biblioteca Joanina is arguably the world's most lavish library.

Sé Velha ✉ Largo da Sé Velha ☎ 239 825 273 💲 $ • **Igreja de Santa Cruz** ✉ Rua Martins de Carvalho 3 ☎ 239 822 941 💲 $ igrejascruz.webnode.pt

João de Ruão: sculpted figures of Christ and his disciples, the four evangelists, and Mary with baby Jesus. A delightful 13th-century cloister on the nave's right side, built at a higher level than the rest of the church, has an unusual view of the hilltop university buildings.

From here, souvenir shops selling Coimbra's distinctive blue-and-white ceramics signal the way down to the bottom of the hill via the Quebra Costas stairs. As this is the main pedestrian access to the university, it caters equally to the needs of students in the form of bookstores, record shops, and bars. Coimbra's best stores for fashion and sundries line the wide pedestrian street at the bottom, the **Rua Ferreira Borges.**

Coimbra's Lower Town

A lovely square, the Praça 8 de Maio, fronts the important **Igreja de Santa Cruz.** Founded in 1131 by the canons of St. Augustine (the azulejos along the right wall of the nave depict the saint's life), this church houses the tombs of Portugal's first two kings, Afonso Henriques and Sancho I, their recumbent statues the work of sculptor Nicolas de Chanterenne. He was also responsible for the superb Renaissance pulpit and, with João de Ruão, contributed sculptures to the portal.

Do not miss the tiled and vaulted chapter house and the elegant Manueline cloister ($), the work of Manuel Pires. In the far corner is the entrance to a sleekly

INSIDER TIP:

Join in one of the most traditional activities of Coimbra's residents: Walk at sunset along riverside Avenida de Conímbriga, to watch as the setting sun illuminates the old town.

—TINO SORIANO
National Geographic photographer

redesigned space, **Memórias de Santa Cruz,** exhibiting a dazzling array of statues, reliquaries, silver, and paintings belonging to the former monastery.

In contrast to these ecclesiastical and academic diversions, the southeastern side of Coimbra offers a small but personal museum, the **Casa Museu Bissaya Barreto** *(Rua da Infantaria 23, tel 239 853 800, www.fbb.pt, closed Mon. & in Oct.–Apr. also Sat.–Sun., $).* The late 19th-century mansion holds the eclectic collection of local surgeon and scholar Bissaya Barreto (1886–1974): 16th- to 19th-century azulejos and books, sculptures, Portuguese paintings, Chinese porcelain, baroque furniture, and more.

Across the wide Alameda is the lovely **Jardim Botânico** *(Calçada Martins de Freitas, included in the visit to the university),* 32 acres (13 ha) of formal gardens designed in 1774 by English architect William Elsden, under the reforming aegis of the Marquês de Pombal. Internationally known for its studies of flora and its seed bank, the garden takes you on a tropical world tour of exotic trees, as do the two greenhouses. The oldest trees grow in the Quadrado Grande, the Great Square, reached by a long stairway.

Mosteiro de Santa Clara-a-Nova

The imposing convent of Santa Clara-a-Nova *(Calçada Santa Isabel, tel 239 441 674, closed Mon., cloister $)*, sits across the river. Started in 1649, it became home to the Poor Clares who were forced to abandon their previous convent, the Gothic **Mosteiro de Santa Clara-a-Velha** *(Rua das Parreiras, tel 239 801 160, culturacentro.gov .pt, closed Mon., $)* due to repeated flooding. Its ruins still stand by the river. The biggest draw in the existing church is the 17th-century silver-and-crystal tomb of Queen Isabel, the sainted wife of Dom Dinis I; the original 1330s tomb, a carved block of limestone sitting on six lions, is behind a wrought-iron grille at the end of the lower chancel. The patron saint of Coimbra, she is feted in July every even-numbered year; some years the procession was so long that it took four hours to cross the bridge.

■ The patches on the capes worn at Coimbra university reflect a student's course of study.

Coimbra's Outskirts

Out in the rolling hills of **Lousã,** a wild, protected area about 18 miles (29 km) southeast of Coimbra, are remote mountain villages made of local schist, oak, and chestnut; the pine forests are home to wild boar and deer. The highest point, **Trevim,** at 3,950 feet (1,202 m) gives fantastic views over all central Portugal, while just below stand the striking quartzite cliffs of **Penedos de Góis.** The excellent English handbook "Lousã Mountain," published by the Coimbra Tourist Board, contains detailed maps and wildlife information, and a local organization, Trans Serrano *(Barrio de S. Paulo 2, Góis, tel 235 778 938, transserrano.com),* arranges guided walks or jeep tours.

Medieval Love

Coimbra was the setting for Portugal's version of Romeo and Juliet, a real-life, tragic love story centered around the convent of Santa Clara-a-Velha. The beautiful Inês de Castro, a lady-in-waiting, lived here; Pedro, the crown prince, although married to the Infanta Constanza, fell hopelessly in love with her. Fearful of her Spanish family's influence, Dom Afonso IV had Inês executed in 1345, unaware that Pedro had secretly married her after Constanza's death the year before. The afterlife united the ill-fated lovers: Their tombs now stand together in the magnificent abbey of Alcobaça (see pp. 173–175).

The forest of **Buçaco,** equally bucolic but endowed with a strong spiritual bent and human imprint, lies 15 miles (24 km) to the north of Coimbra. This magical place was first used by Benedictine monks in the sixth century as a retreat; in the 17th century it was walled and planted by the Order of Barefoot Carmelites. The result is a rare display of some 300 exotic trees together with local varieties, all of which surround little shrines, grottoes, ponds, and fountains. The **Vale dos Fetos** (Valley of Ferns) is particularly attractive while the highest point, the **Cruz Alta,** has views to the sea.

On weekends the forest fills up with day-trippers, who also head for the spa town of **Luso,** 2 miles (3 km) downhill. You can drink the water at the thermal springs, **Termas de Luso** (Rua Álvaro Castelões 63, tel 231 937 910, termasdoluso.pt), have treatments or massages, or indulge yourself at the extravagant, turreted hotel that overshadows the ruins of the former convent. ■

■ **The Gothic monastery of Santa-Clara-a-Velha**

Lousã 🅰 131 B2 **Visitor Information** ✉ Rua Dr. João Santos ☎ 239 990 370 **cm-lousa.pt** • **Luso** 🅰 131 B3 **Visitor Information** ✉ Rua Emídio Navarro 136 ☎ 231 930 122 **turismodocentro.pt**

CONÍMBRIGA

First inhabited by Neolithic peoples, then by the Celts, and finally the Romans, Conímbriga is Portugal's largest and most significant Roman site. It lies 9 miles (15 km) south of Coimbra in a rural setting of olive trees and woods—altogether a rewarding excursion.

The Celtic suffix "briga" points to the importance of the existing settlement when the Romans arrived in 138 B.C., but it was during the first-century A.D. reign of Emperor Augustus that Conímbriga really flourished, acquiring public baths, a forum, and an aqueduct, as well as villas. It became a prosperous stop on the road between Lisbon and Braga. In 468, the Swabians managed to breach a third-century defensive wall and the Romans gradually abandoned the area; by the eighth century, Conímbriga was deserted, allowing Coimbra to rise in power and scale.

Today, the **Museu Monográfico** offers a good introduction to the archaeological site. Look closely at the scale model of the forum in order to project this onto the ruins you will visit. Sculptures, mosaics, and fragments of stucco and wall paintings present a clear picture of what life was like in this Roman outpost.

The site is large enough to demand water and a hat if you are visiting on a hot summer's day. A route past the most significant sections and superb mosaic floors is well marked, and you can clearly see a stretch of the Roman road to Braga. At the front, a large canopy shelters an area of fountains and water channels, while just outside the wall stand the crumbling remains of the House of Cantaber, the largest in Conímbriga. ■

Museu Monográfico & Ruínas de Conímbriga ☎ 239 941 177 $ $
www.conimbriga.pt

▪ The Casa dos Repuxos is one of the impressive remains at Conímbriga.

VISEU

Viseu is a small town that leaves an indelible aesthetic and atmospheric mark. It lies at the center of the Dão wine-producing area—part of that swathe of northern Portugal dominated by granite, visible in numerous dolmens, churches, and fortresses of the outlying countryside.

Viseu's well-preserved old quarter is a delight to wander: Every street holds some architectural interest, and enticing craft and food shops sell products from the Serra da Estrela (see pp. 150–151). Viseu's main sites cluster around the cathedral square, Adro da Sé.

Adro da Sé

The 16th-century Paço dos Tres Escalões stands, recently restored, on one side of the square. A former bishop's palace, it now houses the impressive **Museu Nacional Grão Vasco.** Viseu's main historical claim to fame was a school of painting developed in the 16th century by Vasco Fernandes (circa 1475–1543) and Gaspar Vaz (died circa 1568) that had strong Flemish influences. Fernandes was better known as Grão Vasco and it is this name that has become attached to the art museum, which displays a large collection of his work beside other European paintings of the same period, sculpture,

> **INSIDER TIP:**
>
> The painter Vasco Fernandes has been honored with a wine named for his pseudonym, Grão Vasco. One of his masterpieces, "S. Pedro," is part of the brand image.
>
> —JOANA PAIS
> *Representative, Sogrape Vinhos*

ceramics, fabrics, and furniture. Look for Fernandes's superb painting "Adoration of the Magi," a seminal work due to the fact that the Black king, Balthazar, was replaced by a native Brazilian complete with feathered headdress; this reflected Portugal's "discovery" of Brazil in 1500. Altogether, there are 14 paintings by the Viseu school that once made up the altarpiece in the Sé.

The masterful **Sé** (cathedral; *tel 232 436 065, $*), with its forbidding granite

Viseu 🅰 131 C4 **Visitor Information** ✉ Viseu Welcome Center, Casa do Adro, Adro da Sé ☎ 232 420 950 • **Museu Nacional Grão Vasco** ✉ Paço dos Três Escalões, Adro da Sé ☎ 232 422 049 🕐 Closed Mon. 💲 $ **museunacionalgraovasco.gov.pt**

■ **The 18th-century rococo church of the Misericórdia is one of a trio of monuments on the rim of Viseu's Adro da Sé.**

bell towers, faces the museum. Built between 1289 and 1313, its main structure bridges Romanesque and Gothic styles, although later remodeling endowed it with a baroque facade and Manueline vaulting inside. The magnificent triple nave is flooded with light thanks to multiple windows and lateral light sources, drawing the eye to the grand altarpiece, a classic of baroque gilded artistry. In front are elaborately carved baroque choir stalls and, typical of the dynamism of this small town, ultracontemporary altar

furniture designed by Luís Cunha in 1992. Look for the niche containing a silver reliquary displaying the bones of São Teotónio (1082–1162), who was a prior of this cathedral before founding Santa Cruz in Coimbra.

To the side of the main entrance is the **Manueline cloister,** a superb example of Portuguese Renaissance architecture. Don't miss the lateral doorway, a feat of Romano-Gothic stone carving incorporating a bas-relief Virgin and Child. This stood undetected for centuries until restoration

Tesouro-Museu da Catedral ⊠ Catedral, Largo da Sé ☎ 232 436 065 🕓 Closed Mon. $ $

work in 1918 uncovered it. At the back of the cloister you can see a beautiful **vaulted chapel** and, above, the small **Tesouro-Museu da Catedral** that displays the church treasury: Vestments, chalices, and enamel caskets contrast with an 11th-century silver reliquary of St. Ursula from Germany that looks surprisingly modern.

The church of **Misericórdia,** a harmonious rococo building, stands alone on one side of the square, while an unusual dungeon tower and canons' veranda (a raised open walkway) flanks the square's fourth side.

Other Sites

Below the Sé stands a statue of King Dom Duarte (1391–1438), watching over an area of bustling streets. Head downhill to **Rua Direita,** a long winding pedestrian street that in medieval days was the shortest route to the citadel (ironically, *direita* means "straight"). Stop at No. 90 to admire the **Solar Visconde de Treixedo,** now a bank, with its ornate window frames and elegant portals—typical of this modest yet engaging town.

Renovation of the old market, **Mercado 2 de Maio** on Rua Formosa, has produced a large paved area dotted with trees and pools and surrounded by chic boutiques, the entire facelift designed by Porto's renowned architect Álvaro Siza Vieira. The weekly market is on Tuesday, while June 24 sees the procession of Cavalhadas, and later in summer Viseu stages the São Mateus fair; all are excuses to sample local kid (goat), sausages, smoked meats, and chestnuts washed down with Dão wine or Jeropiga, the local tipple made from partially fermented must. ■

The unique bronze statue of King Dom Duarte

GUARDA

A somewhat bleak yet fascinating sensation unfolds at Guarda, stemming from its remote location just 23 miles (37 km) from the Spanish border. Guarda is Portugal's highest town at 3,463 feet (1,056 m).

Wedged between the Serra da Marofa to the northeast and the Serra da Estrela to the southwest, Guarda was founded in 1199 by the second king of Portugal, Dom Sancho I. A frontier town that guarded the border with Spain—hence its name—Guarda needed a strong defensive system, including citadel walls with five gates. Only two of the gates remain.

The heart of this small town is dwarfed by a massive fortified **Sé** *(tel 271 212 993)*, complete with flying buttresses, pinnacles, and gargoyles. Construction began in 1390 and lasted nearly 150 years. The most imposing of the cathedral's three entrances, in flamboyant Gothic style, opens onto the triangular Praça Luís de Camões. Inside, the triple-aisled Gothic nave leads to a high altar displaying a superb Renaissance limestone carving: The work of João de Ruão and Nicolas de Chanterenne, it depicts the life of Christ through a hundred biblical figures.

The main road north from this square, **Rua Francisco de Passos,** takes you past 16th- and 17th-century houses, antique shops, and the church of São Vicente to a medieval warren that was once the **Judiaria** (Jewish quarter). Here cobbled streets, vaulted doorways, and one-storied houses, some now derelict, were built against granite rocks. At the far end, at Largo do Torreão, a garden offers pretty views.

Guarda also boasts the modest **Museu da Guarda,** housed in a 17th-century seminary. Four rooms cover local history from ancient times to the Renaissance, and there are temporary arts and crafts displays. Also worth seeing on this same street are the colorful, baroque church of the **Misericórdia** and the **Torre dos Ferreiros,** a tower that was part of the town's original fortifications.

To find out more about the rich Jewish history of the country, head north about 18 miles (30 km) to Trancoso to visit the modern **Centro de Interpretacao da Cultura Judaica Isaac Cardoso** *(Rua do Poço Mestre, tel 271 811 147, by appt. only),* which is named after a court doctor to the kings of Spain who was forced to flee from the Inquisition. ∎

Guarda 🗺 131 D3 **Visitor Information** ✉ Praça Luís de Camões ☎ 271 205 530 • **Museu da Guarda** ✉ Rua Alves Roçadas 30 ☎ 271 213 460 🕐 Closed Mon. 💲 $ **museudaguarda.pt**

DRIVE: THE VILLAGES OF THE SERRA DA MAROFA

This circular tour takes you north from Guarda to four medieval villages that, despite their relative proximity, all developed different styles of fortifications.

A statue of Jesus—at 3,200 feet (975 m)—embraces the Serra da Marofa near Castelo Rodrigo.

Set off from Guarda following the N221 signs to Pinhel, through the suburbs and the village of Rapoula, past dry-stone walls, vines, orchards, and a sprinkling of light industry. The landscape soon changes to barren, granite-strewn slopes where you should watch out for a roadside dolmen, **Anta de Pêra do Moço.** Beeches, oaks, and chestnuts flank the road, and

at **Gouveias** views open up to the west past conical haystacks and vineyards. The villages you drive through are suspended between modernity and tradition.

Huge boulders in a bleak landscape herald **Pinhel ❶** *(visitor information, Cnr. of Praça Sacadura Cabral & Rua D. Dinis, tel 271 410 000),* a venerable town with remains of a 14th-century castle and a military history going back to Roman times. Steep, cobbled streets lead to the old quarter. The Rua do Castelo winds past pretty lichen-clad houses to a flattened hilltop dominated by two sturdy towers with far-reaching views. Leave Pinhel along the main road past the cemetery, turning left at the bottom of the hill. The road skirts the valley before crossing the Côa River, passing terraced olive trees, then twisting through more dramatic boulder-strewn landscapes.

Castelo Rodrigo ② comes into view at an intersection *(visitor information, Figueira de Castelo Rodrigo, Largo Mateus de Castro, tel 271 311 365, cm-fcr.pt)*. At the top of the hill, visit the citadel. Although almost over-restored, the semi-ruined **palace of Cristóvão de Moura** *(Rua do Relógio, tel 271 311 277)* is an evocative site; villagers burned it down in 1640—

> **NOT TO BE MISSED:**
> **Pinhel • Castelo Rodrigo • Almeida**

they suspected their ruler conspired with the Spaniards. There are many striking buildings in the citadel, but few people live there; those that do run restaurants or shops.

Rejoin the main road and turn left on the N332 toward Almeida. As you drive through the village of **Vilar Torpim,** note the stately *quinta* (manor house) on your right. Eventually **Almeida ③** appears on the horizon. Its massive moated fortress, built in the Vauban form of a 12-pointed star *(visitor information, Portas de São Francisco, tel 271 570 020)*, was later used as an ammunition depot, which

■ Guarda's forbidding and fortress-like Sé

Napoleon's troops blew up in 1810. Walk along the ramparts and explore the attractive, well-preserved streets inside the walls.

With Almeida behind you, head south and turn right onto the N340, soon crossing the Côa again. About 6 miles (10 km) farther turn left at the road marked Castelo Mendo (N324). This passes under the IP5 highway. Turn left at an intersection and drive to the stone archway guarded by two granite boars that fronts the medieval village of **Castelo Mendo** ❹. Look at the church of Misericórdia with its beautiful Mudéjar (Hispano-Moorish) ceiling, the 23-foot-high (7 m) pillory, and typical granite houses. From here return to Guarda on the N16.

> See also area map p. 131
> Guarda
> 2 hours (more with stops)
> 68 miles (110 km)
> Guarda

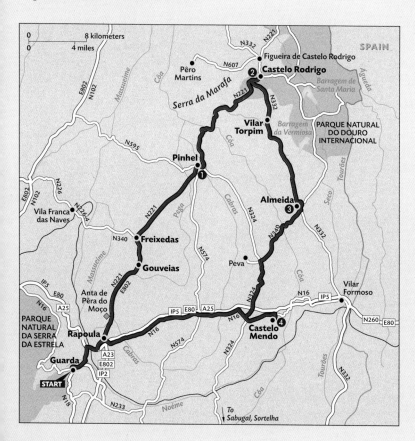

SERRA DA ESTRELA

Something of a movable feast, as its wild beauty is claimed by every town that borders it, the Serra da Estrela is Portugal's highest mountain range. This 250,000-acre (101,000 ha) expanse, protected as a natural park, creates a formidable barrier between the more urban west and the rural emptiness of the eastern Beiras.

Sandwiched between the Mondego and Zêzere Rivers, the rugged peaks of the Serra da Estrela rise to their highest point, 6,537 feet (1,993 m), at **Torre.** The spot is marked by a 23-foot-high (7 m) tower erected in 1817, which brings the elevation to exactly 6,562 feet (2,000 m). This, too, is where the ski slopes are. Just below lies a natural lake, **Lagoa Comprida,** and several artificial lakes that are now generating electricity. This entire massif is the ideal place for slow drives, hiking, sampling creamy mountain cheese, wrapping up in local wool blankets, listening to the tinkling of sheep bells, and exploring seductive mountain villages.

Viseu, Guarda, and Belmonte are the classic starting points for visiting this area, yet villages such as Manteigas and Linhares bring you much closer to the Estrela soul, especially in gastronomy. Indulge in hearty mountain food such as smoked sausages and ham, curd cheese (served with pumpkin jelly), roast kid or boar, young lamb, black pudding with cabbage, or grilled mountain trout. Desserts are equally varied, often egg based, and may incorporate honey, cheese, chestnuts, or rice. Wash it all down with a robust Dão wine. The shepherd dog is another unique feature of the Serra da Estrela; it is thought to be one of the purest and most ancient species of dog in the Iberian Peninsula. Large, muscular, with thick golden fur and a docile temperament—though quite capable of confronting the wolves of the Serra—they are the prized companions of the shepherds.

Hill Towns

At the far northern end of the range, **Celorico da Beira,** with its castle, narrow streets, Gothic doorways, and Manueline windows, makes a striking place to enter the

Serra da Estrela ⛰ 131 C3, D3-D4 **Visitor Information** ✉ CISE-Centro de Interpretação da Serra da Estrela, Rua Visconde de Molelos, Seia ☎ 238 320 300 **cise.pt** ✉ Centro Interpretativo do Vale Glaciar do Zêzere, Fonte Santa, Manteigas ☎ 275 981 113 **civglaz-manteigas.pt natural.pt**

NOTE: For information on rural bed-and-breakfast accommodations, contact the offices of **Adruse** *(Largo Dr. Alípio de Melo, Gouveia, tel 238 490 180).*

■ **Winter in the Serra da Estrela brings enough snow for skiing.**

mountains. A cheese fair is held at the market building every other Friday between December and May.

Just across the Mondego River lies the **Necropolis of São Gens.** It dates from Visigothic days (eighth and ninth centuries) and contains 46 stone tombs hollowed out of the rocks and overlooked by the sculptural **Penedo do Sino** (Rock of the Bell).

Your next stop should be **Linhares**—arguably the most attractive village in the Serra da Estrela—which started life around 580 B.C. as a *castro* (fortified hill village). There is plenty of medieval ambience between the castle and its ramparts built on the rocks, local houses, and delicious traditional cuisine. Smack in the center of

the massif, in the pastoral Zêzere Valley, lies **Manteigas,** sheltered by surrounding hills at 2,296 feet (700 m). Handwoven blankets, carpets, sheepskin items, and tinware are made here. Up above Manteigas, along a dizzily twisting road, is the popular mountain resort of **Penhas Douradas,** known for its typical hill town architecture.

A short distance south is the spa **Caldas de Manteigas;** its sulfuric waters are said to be good for rheumatism, skin problems, and respiratory troubles. The modern spa only operates between March and November. In this area, beside the river, you will see stone houses with roofs thatched in rye straw and broom, and waterfalls cascading down the slopes. ■

EXPERIENCE: Trekking the Glacial Valley

The wildness of the Serra da Estrela is best experienced by leaving the car and getting out on foot, especially during crisp and snowy winter months. In addition to hikes all over the north of Portugal, adventure company **Borealis** *(Rua do Mercado 80, Ponte de Lima, tel 910 910 930, borealis.pt),* based in Ponte de Lima, offers a day-long hike *($$$$$)*

through the central massif of the Serra da Estrela, known as the Penhas Douradas. Qualified guides introduce visitors to the Zêzere Valley, one of Europe's largest glacial valleys, passing giant granite blocks, frozen mountain lakes, and thick pine forests. Hiking boots and adequate clothing are a must and trekking poles are recommended.

CASTELO BRANCO & AROUND

It may not be the most scenic town in the Beiras, but industrious Castelo Branco has a couple of unusual sites and is a useful stopover on the way to border villages. It also acts as a bridge between the Beiras interior and the Tejo Valley to the west and the Alentejo region to the south.

Thought to have pre-Roman origins, Castelo Branco achieved prominence under Dom Afonso Henriques when it was part of the land donated to the Knights Templar, the military and religious order that reached its apogee during the Middle Ages. The oldest and highest part of Castelo Branco has a few sections dating to this period. Here the cobbled streets strung with laundry and birdcages make an atmospheric place to wander, but the main interest lies downhill at the **Antigo Paço Episcopal.** This former bishop's palace boasts beautiful gardens studded with baroque statuary and clipped box hedges. The vegetal work of art dating from 1725 also incorporates fountains and ponds, altogether creating a rare baroque time capsule. Inside the palace is the **Museu de Francisco Tavares Proença Junior** *(Largo Dr. José Lopes Dias, tel 272 344 277, cm-castelobranco.pt, closed Mon., $),* a museum big on portraits of bishops and clerical vestments.

INSIDER TIP:

Be sure to pick up as a souvenir some of Castelo Branco's hand-embroidered linen, for which the region is renowned.

— CARRIE BRATLEY
Journalist, Portugal News

The most striking exhibits are the 16th-century Flemish tapestries illustrating the story of Lot and a beautiful display of *colchas.* Castelo Branco's most desirable product, a colcha is a delicately embroidered linen bedspread that can take more than a year to complete—and is priced accordingly. A guided tour takes in a workshop where these spreads are made.

Fortified Villages

A string of remote villages well worth investigating lies northeast of Castelo Branco. The fortified village of **Penamacor,** 31 miles (50 km)

Castelo Branco 🏔 131 D1 **Visitor Information** ✉ Avenida Nuno Álvares 30 ☎ 272 330 339 **turismodocentro.pt • Monsanto** 🏔 131 D2 **Visitor Information** ✉ Rua Marquês da Graciosa ☎ 277 314 642 • **Idanha-a-Velha** 🏔 131 D2 **Visitor Information** ✉ Rua do Lagar ☎ 277 914 280 **idanha.pt**

Natural and man-made formations aesthetically collide in Monsanto.

away, was inhabited successively by Romans, Goths, and Moors. There are fine panoramic views from the hilltop ruins of the 13th-century castle and keep. The older streets of Penamacor display lovely portals and windows. In particular take a look at the **Igreja da Misericórdia,** with its Manueline porch and gilded altarpiece, and the 16th-century **convent of Santo António,** with its chapel, ornate pulpit, and richly gilded wood carvings.

Slightly closer to Castelo Branco is **Monsanto,** often claimed to be Portugal's most traditional village and certainly a magnificent sight clinging to the base of a granite escarpment beside the Ponsul River. This whole region is one of alternating plains and rocky outcrops, rendering castles practically invisible as they fade into their rocky bases. Monsanto came to prominence under the Templars who built the citadel in the 12th century. The entire village is astonishing, with steep alleyways cutting through rows of granite houses, some of which bear coats of arms and/or elaborate

Manueline windows. The highly forti-fied **castle** has a long history of sieges. Monsanto's victories are celebrated on the first weekend of May by the Festa das Cruzes (Festival of Crosses), during which a flowerpot is thrown from the ramparts in lieu of a calf that once symbolized to besiegers that the inhabitants still had plenty to eat. The church ruins of the Romanesque **São Miguel** that stand next to the castle preserve some exceptional capitals. Fabulous views take in the **Barragem da Idanha,** an artificial lake. The tiny village of **Idanha-a-Velha** sits only 8 miles (12 km) southwest of Monsanto, yet feels completely dif-ferent. Thanks to an illustrious past peopled by Romans, Swabians, Visi-goths, Moors, and Templars, the vil-lage boasts some fine archeological ruins. The **cathedral** undoubtedly started as a mosque: Islamic influence is visible in its vaulted chapel and unusual, asymmetrical proportions. The village's Roman walls have been preserved, and a small gallery beside the cathedral displays Roman *stelae* (inscribed stone slabs). ∎

LIVING LIKE NOBILITY

European countries all have a rich architectural heritage, but there are few where visitors can actually stay in grandiose private houses. Portugal stands out for its guest accommodations in *quintas* (rural estate houses, usually quite elegant) or *solares* (aristocratic manor houses) that often cost less than hotels with equivalent comforts, and which are generally outfitted with period furniture and family heirlooms.

While some quintas date back to the 15th century, most of Portugal's solares were built between the mid-1600s and mid-1700s. After long decades of austerity under Spanish domination, the year 1640 marked the return of the Portuguese monarchy and the consequent craze for baroque style. In the north, the booming port trade with England led to frenzied building of beautiful

■ *Quintas* and *solares* may be grand or stately, but the hospitality is always warm and friendly.

A Home Fit for a King

Though rustic in style, **Quinta da Comenda** (quintadacomenda.net) is one of the Centro region's most historically important manor houses. Older than the nation itself, the *quinta* belonged to Dona Tareja, mother of Portugal's first king, Afonso Henriques. In 1143, she gave it to her brother, who in turn handed it over to the recently established Order of the Knights of Malta. Afonso Henriques and his son, who incidentally was the Order's first grand master in Portugal, were frequent visitors. The house remained in the hands of the Knights of Malta until 1834, when religious orders were abolished in Portugal and their lands handed to the monarchy. The quinta was then left to ruin until it was bought by the present owners in 1984. They have lovingly restored it and turned its lands over to organic farming. For information on staying here or at any of Portugal's other manor houses, visit *solaresdeportugal.pt*.

quintas in vineyards of the Douro Valley, while elsewhere in the country, the landed gentry were reaping the rewards from the riches of Brazil. This period of prosperity saw its peak in the first half of the 18th century under João V. Some 200 years later, in tandem with Portugal's general decline, many of these properties were in semi-ruinous states, their hereditary owners unable to finance necessary repairs or restoration.

A solution was dreamed up in the early 1980s by a cash-strapped count living in Ponte de Lima: He converted his family manor house into paying-guest accommodations and threw open his doors to visitors in search of authentic, albeit faded, grandeur as a place to stay. Although the idea was not new in countries such as Ireland or England, it was for Portugal, which had been living on the margins of Europe, both literally and metaphorically, for so long.

The idea caught on, government and European Union subsidies followed, and *turismo de habitação* (literally "home tourism") gradually changed the face of rural Portugal. Villages that were once cut off from the outside world (or from touristic routes) gained a new lease on life, employment opportunities multiplied, and a network of stunning properties throughout the country has been made available to visitors. Not least, there is a dialogue between villagers and guests staying at the local "big house," and between owners (who generally speak English and French) and their visitors.

Manor houses today may offer just one or two en suite guest rooms, complete with four-poster beds, creaking floorboards, hand-carved wardrobes, and exquisite bed linens, or they may have converted

INSIDER TIP:

For the best of Portugal, drive through the countryside and spend the nights in *pousadas* (historic hotels) and *solares* (manor houses).

–MANUEL GRAÇA
Professor, University of Coimbra

outbuildings into a dozen rooms. In all cases, however, you will find the hospitality remarkable, and the more out of the way a place is, the more spectacular the breakfast may be. In working quintas guests may witness winemaking or other agricultural practices, and in all of them the exterior surroundings will be as delightful as the interior. The only possible drawback is a surfeit of opulence, as Portuguese decorative style tends toward the heavily ornate. If you can handle that—and an occasional lack of heating in winter—then you are destined for noble style.

■ Guests in *quintas* and *solares* often have full run of a house.

More Places to Visit in Centro

Belmonte

The birthplace of Pedro Álvares Cabral, the European who claimed Brazil for Portugal in 1500, Belmonte is dominated by the semi-restored ruins of a **castle.** Don't miss the view of the mountains through an elegant Manueline window. In front, to one side, is a reproduction of the simple wooden cross used by Cabral in the first Mass held on Brazilian soil. The neighboring **São Tiago** church has 400- to 500-year-old frescoes and the tombs of the Cabrals. Belmonte was an important Jewish center in past centuries and more significant today is the 1997 **synagogue** that lies downhill in the old Jewish quarter. The Jewish community of Belmonte has made a major comeback recently, after practicing crypto-Judaism for centuries, and is now one of the most vibrant in the country. The impressive Roman tower, **Centum Cellas,** 2.5 miles (4 km) to the west, is thought to have formed part of a Roman villa and played a role on the tin trade route between Mérida (in Spain) and Braga.
cm-belmonte.pt 🅜 131 D3
Visitor Information ✉ Largo do Pelourinho ☎ 275 910 010

Figueira da Foz

Figueira is the closest beach resort to Coimbra: It lies just 28 miles (45 km) west at the mouth of the Mondego River. High-rises dominate the shoreline, but the resort offers a broad sandy beach, rolling waves loved by surfers, a casino, and a lively festival in late June. The estuary is overlooked by the 16th-century **Forte de Santa Catarina,** where Wellington landed the first British troops in 1808. For a quieter, more scenic setting, head a few miles north to the smaller resort of **Buarcos,** backed by the Serra da Boa Viagem, a hillside of eucalyptuses, pines, and acacias.
cm-figfoz.pt 🅜 131 A2
Visitor Information ✉ Castelo Engenheiro Silva, Esplanada António da Silva Guimarães ☎ 233 209 500

Sortelha

This dramatic, windswept border village commands far-reaching views from its fortified summit. The granite walls, keep, and majestic Gothic gateways seem to grow out of the landscape. Inside, the medieval core has been extensively restored; it springs to life Easter through summer. Craft shops and a handful of bars and restaurants follow the same rhythms. The village still makes an evocative destination out of season.
cm-sabugal.pt 🅜 131 D3 **Visitor Information** ✉ Largo do Côrro ☎ 271 381 072 (Museu do Sabugal) or 800 262 788

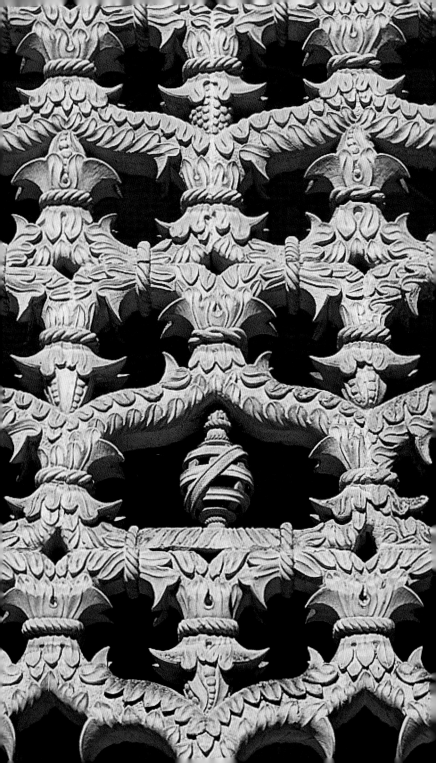

Portugal's heart—a time capsule of castles, palaces, monasteries, and small towns radiating from Lisbon, and an exhilarating coast

LISBOA E REGIÃO

■ The Batalha monastery's intricate Manueline stone tracery

LISBOA E REGIÃO

The prosperous Lisboa e Região region, comprising the Estremadura and Ribatejo areas, bridges the mountainous north of Portugal and the hotter, flatter south, while encircling Lisbon and the Tejo estuary. Portugal's cultural epicenter, this region features two magnificent World Heritage sites (outside of Lisbon), lavish and grandiose royal palaces, a major pilgrimage destination, relics of the Peninsular War, Moorish castles, and the favorite resort for exiled kings and aristocrats in the 1930s.

The infrastructure of the Estremadura and Ribatejo areas, more densely populated than others, threatens to overwhelm the charm of the Lisboa e Região region, but pockets of natural beauty remain: from lovely coastal spots, including continental Europe's western extremity at Cabo da Roca, to the romantic and verdant Serra de Sintra. Many places—Sintra, Cascais, Estoril, Mafra, Óbidos, Peniche, Santarém, and Setúbal—can be seen on day trips from Lisbon, but such visits only hint at their character.

Only extended stays reveal what gives these towns their special atmosphere, be it surfers riding the waves at Guincho, bells tolling at Batalha's monastery or Mafra's palace, the roulette wheel of Estoril's casino, bottlenose dolphins in the Sado Estuary, or morning mists rising above the palaces and forest of Sintra. Add clusters of windmills, immaculate, whitewashed villages, and a few dinosaur footprints, and you have an unrivaled feast of diversity—paralleled in the succulent, affordable seafood and range of regional wines.

■ Estoril casino, next to the beautiful city park

LISBOA E REGIÃO

Lisbon

Area of
map detail

RESERVA NATURAL
DA BERLENGA
Ilhas Berlengas

ATLANTIC
OCEAN

Figueira
da Foz

CENTRO
p. 128

Pombal

Pedrógão
Grande

Alvaiázere

**Marinha
Grande**

Leiria

Batalha

Ferreira
do Zézere

Sítio

Nazaré

Praia Gralha

Alcobaça

Alvados

São Martinho
do Porto

**Grutas de
Alvados/
Santo António**

Foz do Arelho

Caldas
da Rainha

Ourém

Fátima
**Pedreira
da Galinha**

Serra
de Santo
António

*Serra
do Aire*

Torres
Novas

**Aqueduto
dos Pegões**
Tomar

*Barragem do
Castelo de Bode*

Mação

Sardoal

Constância

Abrantes

**Castelo de
Almourol**

Bemposta

PARQUE NATURAL
DAS SERRAS DE AIRE
E CANDEEIROS

Entroncamento

Golegã

Remédios
Cabo Carvoeiro

Peniche

Óbidos

Rio Maior

Chamusca

SANTARÉM

**Praia de São
Bernardino**

Lourinhã

Bombarral
Cadaval

*Serra de
Montejunto*

Santarém

Almeirim

Muge

ALENTEJO
p. 204

**Praia de
Santa Cruz**

Torres
Vedras

Alenquer

**Praia de
Ribeira de Ilhas**

Ericeira

Arruda dos
Vinhos

Vila Franca
de Xira

Coruche

Couço

Mafra

**Alverca
do Ribatejo**

LISBOA

**Praia das
Maçãs**

Azenhas
do Mar

Colares

RESERVA NATURAL
DO ESTUÁRIO
DO TEJO

Praia Grande
**Praia da
Adraga**
Cabo da Roca
ia do Guincho
Cabo Raso

Sintra

**Parque e
Palácio N. da
Pena**

Amadora

★ LISBON (LISBOA)

Cascais

Estoril

Palácio
Nacional
de Queluz

Costa do Estoril

Almada

Caparica

Barreiro

Montijo

SETÚBAL

ALENTEJO
p. 204

Amora

Costa da
Caparica

*Costa
Azul*

Palmela

Vila Nogueira de Azeitão

PARQUE NATURAL
DA ARRÁBIDA

Setúbal

Forte São Filipe
Praia de Figueirinha

Sesimbra

Portinho da Arrábida

*Cabo
Espichel*

**Lapa de Santa
Margarida**

*Tróia
Peninsula*

Comporta

Alcácer do Sal

*Baía de
Setúbal*

RESERVA NATURAL
DO ESTUÁRIO
DO SADO

0   20 kilometers

0   10 miles

Evidence of Great Wealth

This land of kings and queens reached its high point during Portugal's age of discoveries—the 15th and 16th centuries—when newfound riches financed major renovations. Manueline details on Gothic structures became commonplace. Sintra's Palácio Nacional is the quintessential example and displays Europe's most varied and extensive decorative wall tiling. Meanwhile, brooding high above Tomar, the Convent of Christ is a masterpiece of Renaissance, Manueline, and Gothic styles. Older still, the rebuilt Moorish castle of Óbidos, a traditional wedding gift from every Portuguese king to his queen since 1282, embraces a web of cobbled, flower-clad streets. Fast forward to the height of baroque and you have the vast palace and monastery of Mafra, closely followed by the rococo Queluz palace, now engulfed by the outer suburbs of Lisbon. Finally, there is cosmopolitan seaside Cascais, a magnet for the idle rich between the two World Wars and Portugal's version of the French Riviera. ∎

NOT TO BE MISSED:

Eating freshly grilled fish at Nazaré 166

The monasteries of Batalha and Alcobaça 171–175

Drinking *ginjinha* (cherry liqueur) from a chocolate cup in Óbidos 178

A boat ride to the fairy-tale Castelo de Almourol 182

Sintra's amazing palaces 187–193

Watching the world go by with a cold drink at a Cascais beach café 196–198

The Tróia Peninsula's pristine beaches 203

▪ **Monserrate's vegetation and decorative features never fail to appeal.**

LEIRIA & AROUND

Sprawling over a wide valley, Leiria appears deceptively large. In reality the compact center is sandwiched between the Liz River and a hill rising to the castle above. There are few sites, but Leiria makes an enjoyable lunch stop on the monastery trail of Batalha, Alcobaça, and Tomar or en route to the beaches.

Leiria's unusually designed castle entices visitors to walk uphill.

Dom Dinis I and his queen, Santa Isabel, chose the city of Leiria as their base in the 14th century. Walk or drive up to the principal residence, the unusual-looking **Castelo de Leiria.** Afonso Henriques, who recaptured the fabulous site from the Moors in 1135, built the original castle. In the years that followed, historical vicissitudes led to Leiria being overshadowed by Santarém and Lisbon, and the castle fell into semi-ruin. Dom Dinis restored it, and several decades later João I built a palace extension on the southern side,

Leiria 🅰 161 B5 **Visitor Information** ✉ Jardim Luís de Camões ☎ 244 848 770 **turismodocentro.pt • Castelo de Leiria** ✉ Largo de São Pedro ☎ 244 839 670 💲 $ **cm-leiria.pt**

Pilgrimage to Fátima

Fátima lies 10 miles (16 km) southeast of Leiria and represents Portugal's most important shrine; it acts as a beacon to four million pilgrims annually. Although Fátima is hard to recommend to anyone other than fervent believers—the town is little more than a pilgrims' dormitory that has grown haphazardly since 1930—it is symbolically fascinating. Some pilgrims still arrive on their knees, while others hold candlelit vigils at religious festivals.

In 1917, three young children allegedly witnessed a series of appearances by the Virgin Mary. The dates of her first and last visitations, May 13 and October 13, draw an estimated 100,000 pilgrims from all over the world. Pope John Paul II visited the site three times and canonized two of the children in 2000, and Pope Francis visited in 2017 and 2023. The neoclassical basilica seats 900; the new basilica—notable for its vast, unsupported ceiling design—seats 9,000 *(fatima.pt)*.

incorporating loggias, Gothic bays, and a vast hall, while maintaining the flanking towers.

The castle reopened to visitors in 2021 after an extensive renovation of its exhibition spaces and can be reached now by elevator. Inside the walls, you enter a large garden courtyard, beyond which lie the keep, dungeons, royal palace, and the attractive ruins of **Nossa Senhora da Pena,** a church adorned with Gothic and Manueline features. The keep houses a museum of medieval armor, the **Núcleo Museológico.**

Head for Leiria's pedestrianized main square, the **Praça Rodrigues Lobo,** at the heart of the attractive historical center; its 17th-century arches are still intact. An antiques and handicrafts market takes place here on the second Saturday of the month. While exploring the backstreets around the square, you will encounter the **Sé,** a Renaissance cathedral fronted by the striking tiled facade of a house.

Beyond Leiria

The countryside surrounding Leiria is of much interest. Europe's largest continuous pine forest, the **Pinhal de Leiria,** stretches north and west of town: About 10 million trees blanket 28,400 acres (11,500 ha) crisscrossed by long straight roads. First planted by Dom Dinis, the

Parque Natural das Serras de Aire e Candeeiros 🗺 161 B4-C4 ✉ Rua Dr. Augusto César Silva Ferreira, Rio Maior ☎ 243 999 480 **natural.pt**
Gruta de Alvados e Gruta de Santo António 🗺 161 C4 ☎ 262 940 947 🕐 Closed Mon. in Sep.–June 💲 $$ **sogrutas.com**

INSIDER TIP:

Make the effort to stop in Fátima to look inside the controversial new basilica. This architectural masterpiece seats 9,000 people and has no internal pillars.

—EMMA ROWLEY
National Geographic contributor

forest was later enlarged to halt encroaching sands and to supply shipbuilders with materials. Today, it is the source for Leiria's wood and paper industries, the latter dating back to 1411.

South of Leiria is the **Parque Natural das Serras de Aire e Candeeiros,** a pocket of wild beauty stretching over a rugged limestone massif that holds several interesting sites. Evoking memories of a time gone by, traditional windmills *(moinhos da Pena)* dot the hills; some now serve as accommodations. A series of dinosaur footprints at **Pedreira da Galinha** are thought to date back to the mid-Jurassic period, about 175 million years ago. Here, too, are four separate caves *(grutas)* with exceptional stalactite and stalagmite formations. The **Grutas de Alvados** and neighboring **Grutas de Santo António** offer the most variety and scale. ∎

EXPERIENCE: Making Artisan Breads

Portugal is famous not only for its windmills, but also for the excellent bread made by local bakers. There are so many towns that boast their own specialty, such as *pão de Mafra,* typical of the town north of the Parque Natural de Sintra-Cascais, a homemade bread with a soft crumb and a nice crisp crust. Wholesome and flavorful, it was very popular in the 20th century, so much so that in 2010 it received a local designation that protects its distinctiveness, by the means of a precise production specification.

Portugal Farm Experiences *(tel 937 848 011, portugalfarm experience.com)* is an agency specialized in activities that will take you to farms to discover unique recipes, old traditions, farming methods, participation in farm life, and more. At the end of the day, you can enjoy a snack, tasting or sampling of what was prepared during the experience.

Bread making is just one of several workshops offered, which could be one to five hours long (depending on the schedule and the farm that will host you), including a visit to the farm, a lesson, practice in small groups, and after the bread is baked, a shared tasting with extra virgin olive oil, salt and garlic, like real Portuguese locals.

COASTAL ESTREMADURA

The long straight coastline of Estremadura links the Beira Litoral (dominated by Figueira da Foz) to the north with Lisbon's playground resorts to the south. Magnificent sweeps of white sand, impressive dunes, dramatic surf, and spectacular cliffs are a haven for sunbathing, sailing, and surfing, as well as scuba diving and sportfishing in some areas.

■ Pleasure boats bob gently in Nazaré's harbor. The town is the largest resort on the Estremadura coast.

Nazaré

You'll find the largest and loudest resort at Nazaré, where a sandy beach ends abruptly at a 361-foot-high (110 m) cliff crowned by the district of **Sítio.** Steep steps, a road, or a **funicular** ($) will take you to the top, where a lookout point surveys the main resort area below, the fishing harbor at its southern end, and the original hilltop town, **Pederneira.**

The name Nazaré derives from a statue of the Virgin said to have been brought back from Nazareth by a monk in the fourth century and rediscovered in the 18th century; this naturally gave rise to a church, **Nossa Senhora da Nazaré,** on Sítio's main square. Every September 8 a major

Nazaré 🅼 161 B4 **Visitor Information** ✉ Avenida Vieira Guimarães, Mercado Municipal ☎ 262 561 194 **cm-nazare.pt** • **São Martinho do Porto** 🅼 161 B4 **Visitor Information** ✉ Rua Vasco da Gama 18 ☎ 262 989 110

pilgrimage kicks off the town's festival. Next to the lookout point stands Nazaré's most significant site, the tiny **Ermida da Memória,** which a very thankful nobleman built to commemorate the perceived miracle that saved his life in 1182. Azulejos—added centuries later—illustrate the incident in great detail. From here, a short walk to the headland brings you to a lighthouse and another spectacular view. In July and August the town is packed, but out of season Nazaré makes an enjoyable, scenic stop.

São Martinho do Porto & Around

The low-key family resort of São Martinho do Porto sits 8 miles (13 km) south of Nazaré. Its popularity stems from its almost circular bay with calm, shallow waters that are ideal for swimming and wading. Every morning the quay sees boats unloading mountains of sardines from trawlers anchored in the bay, later replaced by pleasure boats. Stroll north along the quay, past a string of restaurants, then through a short tunnel to see waves crashing against the rocks. On the headland above, you can see a number of recently built ocean-view condominiums, and 1 mile (1.6 km) farther, at **Monte do Facho,** a viewpoint looks south to Foz do Arelho (see p. 178) and to the bay of São Martinho do Porto. A few art nouveau buildings surround Largo Vitorino Frois, but modern blocks have marred the southern end.

Peniche & Cabo Carvoeiro

A former island, Peniche joined the mainland in the 16th century, when silt formed an isthmus. Modern high-rises conceal an attractive harbor, complete with old bulwarks, walls, and a star-shaped 16th-century fortress. Formerly a prison for political dissidents and testimony to the horrors of Salazarism, the fortress has been home

Ilhas Berlengas

Ilhas Berlengas *(berlengas.eu),* a 40-minute boat ride from Peniche, are surrounded by a wonderful marine reserve. The red-ocher granite formation of the isles is estimated to be some 280 million years old. Crystalline water and several inlets, islets, creeks, and grottoes create a beautiful day-trip destination, perfect for swimming, snorkeling, and diving. The main island, **Berlenga Grande,** boasts little more than a crumbling 17th-century fort at the end of a causeway. There are basic accommodations, a campsite, a restaurant, and a lighthouse. A coastal path circles the island, providing views and opportunities to see abundant birdlife. The Berlengas constitute some of the most important breeding grounds for seabirds on the Iberian Peninsula. You can rent a rowboat to explore the grottoes.

■ Peniche with its fortress, now a museum, and a popular panoramic overlook

to the **Museu Nacional Resistên-cia e Liberdade** for some years now *(tel 262 798 028, museunacional resistencialiberdade-peniche.gov.pt, closed Mon., $).* The coastal town of Peniche is famed for bobbin lace-work; it comes center stage on the **Dia da Rendilheira** (Lace Day), the third Sunday of July.

The fortress faces the large harbor that has given Peniche its status in Portugal's fishing and canning industry; fish conserving goes back to Roman times. Fish restaurants clustered around the harbor and fort area specialize in delicious *caldeirada de peixe* (fish stew), as well as barbecued sardines and steamed lobster. Sun and surf worshippers will find beautiful sandy beaches and world-class surf-ing spots nearby, especially along the Baleal isthmus. Like Cabo Carvoeiro, a 2.5-mile-long (4 km) peninsula edged by stratified rock formations, eroded rock stacks also rise out of the sea. A lighthouse at the peninsula's end offers fantastic views in all directions. A few hundred yards before this, at the hamlet of **Remédios,** a charming little tiled chapel, **Nossa Senhora dos Remédios,** is the focal point of a cult that developed following the discovery of the Virgin Mary's image in a cave in the 12th century. A cross on the rocks outside indicates the supposed spot.

An equally dramatic stretch of cliffs and rock stacks lies to the south of Peniche, between the beaches of **São Bernardino** and **Santa Cruz.** ■

Peniche ⚠ 161 A4 **Visitor Information** ✉ Rua Alexandre Herculano ☎ 262 789 571 **cm-peniche.pt**
NOTE: **Accessing the Ilhas Berlengas.** Motorboats to the islands run daily year-round from the Peniche jetty, depending on sea conditions and passenger numbers. Companies include **Viamar** *(tel 262 785 646, viamar-berlenga.com).*

EXPERIENCE: Surfing in Portugal

Portugal may be a relatively small country, but it boasts some big waves along its 765 miles (1,230 km) of coast, many of which provide ideal surfing conditions as the large Atlantic rollers pound its shore. Cool water temperatures do little to deter year-round surfing enthusiasts.

These waves attract much international attention. In 2011 some of the world's most experienced big wave riders descended on the small fishing town of Nazaré, where a giant swell had been predicted at Praia do Norte (praiadonortenazare .pt). Using a Jet Ski to tow in, Garrett McNamara, who spent many years chasing the world's biggest waves, successfully caught a nearly 79-foot (24 m) wave, smashing the previous world record of 77 feet (23.5 m) set by Mike Parson in 2001. In 2018, the Portuguese surfer Hugo Vau rode an even bigger one, whereas in October 2020, the record was broken again by the German surfer Sebastian Steudtner (86 feet, 26.2 m).

In addition, global surf hot spots such as Peniche and Ericeira frequently feature on the world surfing circuit, attracting the world's top professional surfers to Portugal's most challenging breaks. Nearly every year, the biggest surf stars pass through here as they come through on the world tour. Portugal boasts top surfers of its own, with the national team winning the European Championships in 2011. Watch for national pro-surf names such as Frederico Morais, Vasco Ribeiro, and up and coming junior champions such as Teresa Bonvalot.

Where to Surf

Thanks to the high profile of these international surf events and the growing accessibility of surf equipment, surfing has exploded in Portugal over the last 20 years. Head to the beach near any good-size town on the weekend and the waves will be dotted with boards. Favorite beaches in the Lisbon area include **Carcavelos,** popular with beginners, and **Guincho,** also a windsurf mecca; a short drive north, **Ericeira, Peniche,** and **Nazaré** attract a more experienced crowd. In the north, the windy beaches to the north of **Viana do Castelo** have great waves; in the south, the **Sagres** area offers marginally warmer waters. The Alentejo coast provides countless options; the most popular being **Arrifana** and **Praia do Amado.**

INSIDER TIP:

Portugal boasts hundreds of miles of superb surf, but my favorite spot is Coxos in Ericeira. But be warned, it's not for the fainthearted.

—FILIPA LEANDRO
Former national surf champion

Surf Schools

Portugal's surf can be dangerous for the novice or the ill-informed. Even experienced surfers should consult with locals, as many breaks have hidden rocks and reefs; currents are strong and often unpredictable. There are calm spots, however, and a growing number of good surfing schools are making the sport safe for people of all ages and abilities to enjoy the thrill of the waves. To master them yourself, consider the following locations and surf schools:

Carcavelos: Carcavelos Surf School, Avenida Marginal, Praia de Carcavelos, tel 962 850 497 or 966 131 203, carcavelossurfschool.com
Foz do Arelho: Foz Camp, Rua Francisco Almeida Grandela 109, tel 913 164 969 or 912 534 748, surfcamp-portugal.eu
Sagres: International Surf School, Terras da Marreira, tel 914 482 407, surfsagres.com
Viana do Castelo: Surf Clube de Viana, Rua Diogo Alvares, tel 258 332 043 or 962 672 222, surfingviana.com

▪ The spectacle of surfers braving the waves in Nazaré is of great interest.

BATALHA

This late Gothic fantasy was inspired by Dom João I's victory in 1385 over the Castilians at the Battle of Aljubarrota, just 1 mile (1.6 km) away. In gratitude, the king founded the monastery, dedicated it to the Virgin Mary, and named it Santa Maria da Vitória.

The Batalha monastery is an imposing masterpiece of Portuguese Gothic and Manueline art.

Today this monastic complex is more commonly called Batalha for the nearby small town. The fact that this magnificent abbey is now a UNESCO World Heritage site has not, however, slowed the traffic thundering along a major highway just a couple of hundred

Batalha 161 B5 **Visitor Information** ✉ Praça Mouzinho de Albuquerque ☎ 244 765 180 **descobrirbatalha.pt**

yards away. Bristling with pinnacles, buttresses, gargoyles, and delicate stone tracery, this ornate structure took 145 years to build, from 1388 to 1533.

While Alcobaça's importance (see pp. 173–175) lies in religious practice and its social spin-offs, Batalha is more symbolic of political confidence. Its rise coincides with the beginning of Portuguese maritime expansion. Announcing this on the vast esplanade outside is an equestrian statue of Nuno Álvares Pereira, who led the Portuguese forces at Aljubarrota. The beautiful limestone facade behind the statue was the work of the master craftsman Huguet, who took over from Afonso Domingues on his death in 1402. Mateus Fernandes, the third main architect, was responsible for the stunning Manueline entrance to the Unfinished Chapels and much of the decorative detail in the Royal Cloister. His tomb is in the main nave.

The church interior has both a vast, imposing scale and an uncomplicated appearance, the only decorative elements being the stained-glass windows depicting the life of Christ. To the right is the **Founder's Chapel,** another tour de force by Huguet, although the original ceiling collapsed in the 1755 earthquake. Here, enclosed by a vaulted, octagonal structure, are the elevated tombs of Dom João I and his English wife, Philippa of Lancaster; tombs of their descendants, including Henry the Navigator, are set into wall niches. Off the left of the nave lies the striking **Royal Cloister,** a rhythmic feast of intricate Manueline carving that was added to the original Gothic structure. To one side is the **chapter house,** where unsupported star-vaulting meets at a center point formed by João I's coat of arms. If you notice an unexpected military presence in the complex, you will soon understand why: The tomb of the unknown soldier (in fact, two soldiers), under permanent guard of honor, is located in the chapter house. Opposite, the former **refectory** houses the original 15th-century sculptures from the west porch; copies stand in their former location. Beyond lies the two-story **Dom Afonso V Cloister,** more human in scale and less ostentatious than the Royal Cloister.

Batalha's last site is arguably its most outstanding: the **Unfinished Chapels.** This octagonal structure is entered from outside the chapter house. Commissioned by Dom Duarte I (1391–1438), designed by Huguet, and completed by Mateus Fernandes, it was intended as Duarte's family pantheon—yet only he and his queen were buried there.

The breathtaking riot of embellishment—especially the lacelike carving of the doorway and the deeply incised pillars—is all dramatically open to the elements. ∎

Mosteiro de Santa Maria da Vitória-Batalha ✉ Largo do Mosteiro
☎ 244 765 497 💲 $$ **mosteirobatalha.gov.pt**

ALCOBAÇA

The small town of Alcobaça is dominated by just one attraction, its magnificent Cistercian abbey dating from 1153. A World Heritage site since 1985, the abbey is noted for its evocative interior, which propels you back to the Middle Ages.

Occupying a prime spot at the confluence of the Alcoa and Baça Rivers, massive in scale, austere yet serene in atmosphere, and stunningly beautiful in its detail, the **Mosteiro de Santa Maria de Alcobaça** was modeled on France's Clairvaux Abbey, and it soon became one of the most powerful Cistercian abbeys.

Alcobaça was completed in the mid-1200s. It flourished for six centuries, during which the abbot acquired immense regional power and owed no allegiance to the king. From the late 16th century on, the monks turned to art and literature, producing superb sculptures and building up one of the richest libraries in Portugal. The monastery peaked in the late 18th century. Agriculture blossomed and the kitchens turned out feasts of gastronomic largesse: The frugal Cistercian life—the eschewal of wealth, privileges, and ostentation—had been put aside. In 1810, French troops pillaged the abbey. After the government banned all religious orders in 1834, Alcobaça was abandoned.

A view from behind the altar reveals the purity, scale, and grandeur of Alcobaça's Cistercian design.

Not all the abbey can be visited, but what you do see is breathtaking. The main entrance leads through a Gothic portal into the **church,** where soaring vaults span a triple nave extending 348 feet (109 m)—the largest church in Portugal. Simplicity and purity reign; the main altar consists of just one crucifix and a statue of Christ. In the south transept, look for a terra-cotta relief depicting the life of St. Bernard made by the monks in the 17th century.

Alcobaça 🗺 161 B4 **Visitor Information** ✉ Rua Araújo Guimarães 28 ☎ 924 032 615 **cm-alcobaca.pt • Mosteiro de Santa Maria de Alcobaça** ✉ Praça 25 de Abril ☎ 262 505 120 💲 $$ **mosteiroalcobaca.gov.pt**

The most famous highlight is the pair of 14th-century tombs of the star-crossed royal lovers, Inês de Castro and Pedro I. Positioned at opposite sides of the transept, these tombs display virtuoso sculptures and friezes in keeping with their tragic love story (see sidebar p. 141).

At the back of the chancel is a baroque sacristy; only the exquisitely carved Manueline doorway and vaulted lobby survive from the 16th-century Renaissance sacristy destroyed by the 1755 earthquake. Here, too, is the Royal Pantheon: Look for the tomb of Lady Beatriz.

At the front of the church, a side entrance leads through the ticket office to the Cloister of Dom Dinis, or **Cloister of Silence.** Built in the early 14th century, with an upper story added two centuries later, the elegant cloister encloses orange trees, box hedges, and an unusual octagonal lavabo on the north side. The cloister leads to the **chapter house,** containing larger-than-life-size statues; a vast dormitory above;

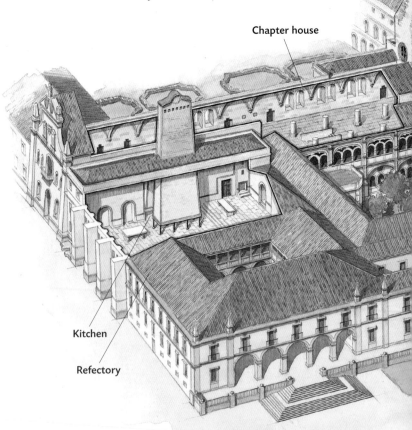

Chapter house

Kitchen

Refectory

and, on the northern flank, the Monks' Hall, kitchen, and refectory. Note how the Monks' Hall steps down to accommodate the natural slope of the land, although its unity was destroyed when a staircase was added during a 1940s renovation.

The huge 18th-century **kitchen** was seemingly built for giants. Completely tiled, its two vast fireplaces (up to seven oxen could be roasted at once) and massive stone tables are backed by a row of water tanks fed by the Alcoa River. Next door, the **refectory** holds a delicately carved niche pulpit from where a monk would read as the others ate in silence. Today this vaulted hall houses an 18th-century statue of the Virgin and Child, transferred from the altar in the 1940s. ■

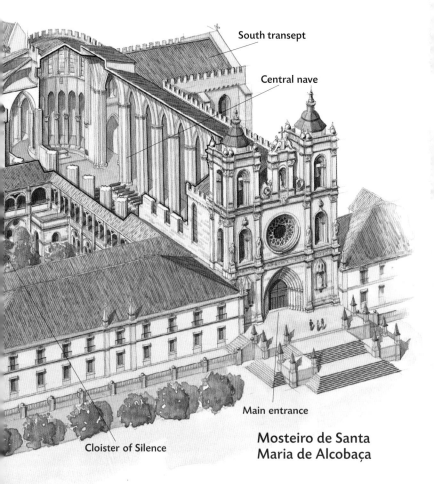

South transept

Central nave

Main entrance

Cloister of Silence

Mosteiro de Santa Maria de Alcobaça

CALDAS DA RAINHA & ÓBIDOS

Just 3 miles (5 km) separate these two Estremaduran towns, yet they are worlds apart. Caldas is a venerable old spa town with an unbeatable ceramics tradition, while Óbidos is an attractively spruced up, historical village geared almost exclusively to visitors. Their contrasts make Caldas and Óbidos an intriguing combination.

Caldas da Rainha

Caldas da Rainha (Queen's Baths) started life in 1484 when Queen Leonor, the wife of João II, was struck by the curative properties of the local sulfuric springs and founded a hospital. After peaking in popularity, the spa town took a new lease on life with the impetus of ceramicist Rafael Bordallo Pinheiro (1846–1905). By introducing more modern techniques, this artist inspired a school of whimsical designs (the cabbage-leaf plates are the most famous) that transformed the 400-year-old local craft tradition. It's because of this historical legacy that Caldas da Rainha has been a UNESCO Creative City since 2019.

The **Museu de Cerâmica** displays pieces from all over the world. Upper rooms are devoted to the extraordinary animal and plant forms developed in Caldas. Lobsters, mussels, basketweave, sweet corn, and berries—all are rendered realistically, bringing some pieces to the brink of kitsch. The top floor exhibits contemporary ceramic work.

Of the four other art museums in town, the **Museu José Malhoa** holds the most interest. Standing in a leafy park fronting the spa complex, this art deco museum highlights local painter José Malhoa (1855–1933) as well as other Portuguese artists and ceramicists. On the eastern side of the park, stop at the **Faianças Artísticas Bordallo Pinheiro factory** *(Rua Rafael Bordallo Pinheiro 53, tel 262 839 380, eu.bordallopinheiro.com)*, to buy faïence earthenware at factory prices. A 20-minute tour *($)* of the museum is available, if arranged in advance.

Óbidos

South of Caldas da Rainha, the fortified village of Óbidos will not disappoint you—although in high summer the crowds of tourists can be overwhelming. Dom Dinis I was

---

Caldas da Rainha ⛰ 161 B4 Visitor Information ✉ Rua do Provedor de São Paulo 1 ☎ 262 240 005 **mcr.pt caldascidadecriativa.com**
Museu de Cerâmica ✉ Palacete do Visconde de Sacavém, Rua Dr. Ilídio Amado ☎ 262 840 280 🕐 Closed Mon. 💲 $ **museudaceramica.blogspot .com**

■ Caldas da Rainha comes alive at its morning fruit and vegetable market, a classic social crossroads.

the man responsible for its popularity: In 1282, he gave the former Moorish castle to his wife-to-be, Isabel of Aragon, as a wedding gift. This tradition was repeated by all future kings until 1833. In 1951, the transformation of the castle into a state inn (see p. 304) prompted extensive restoration of the village. Today the crenellated battlements enclose cobbled streets flanked by whitewashed houses with ultramarine or saffron yellow borders, walled gardens, 14 churches and

Museu José Malhoa ⊠ Parque D. Carlos I ☎ 262 831 984 🕒 Closed Mon. 💲 $ **culturacentro.gov.pt/museu-jose-malhoa** • **Óbidos** 🗾 161 B4 **Visitor Information** ⊠ Rua da Porta da Vila ☎ 262 959 231 **turismo .obidos.pt**

EXPERIENCE: Festival Fun in Óbidos

Óbidos celebrates two of Portugal's most entertaining festivals. Between March and April, it hosts the **International Chocolate Festival** (festivalchocolate.cm-obidos.pt), a time when the town's narrow streets and castle area are filled with stands displaying every conceivable form of chocolate, including huge chocolate sculptures; and chefs hold demonstrations and workshops. Children are well catered to, with a dedicated children's area hosting fun activities and street shows.

In July and August, Óbidos is transformed with the arrival of the **Mercado Medieval** (mercado medievalobidos.pt). Whoever enters the local ticket offices dressed in European clothing from the 12th to 14th centuries will get a discounted price. Inside, the castle grounds teem with street performers, musicians, and stalls. Vendors sell spit-roasted meat with hunks of bread in brown paper and clay goblets of wine, which are eaten at long wooden trestle tables. Both festivals are great fun, but aim to arrive early, as they get incredibly busy. Check the websites for exact dates, times, and prices.

chapels, and many craft shops. You can make a mile-long (1.6 km) circuit of the ramparts, starting at the castle or the main gate.

The village heroine was baroque painter Josefa de Óbidos (1630–1684), who left her native Seville to settle here. A couple of her paintings are in **Santa Maria,** a charming Renaissance church built over Visigothic and Moorish structures.

The future Afonso V married his eight-year-old cousin Isabel here in 1441; he was 10. The walls are blanketed in azulejos and paintings by Josefa de Óbidos hang to the right of the altar. Across the square from here, the attractive portico beside the pillory once held the market.

To the south, the 1380 **Porta da Vila** (Town Gate) has some impressive 18th-century azulejos within

INSIDER TIP:

If you are a fan of chocolate, don't miss the International Chocolate Festival, held every year in Óbidos, usually in April.

—TINO SORIANO
*National Geographic
photographer*

its angled form. This gateway plays a major role during the two-week-long, torchlit Easter processions. Another highlight is the concert series held June through September in an amphitheater just outside the walls. For hopping nightlife, head to the coast to **Foz do Arelho,** 3.5 miles (6 km) due west of Caldas. ∎

TOMAR

Tomar is a lot more than a one-monastery town. Its medieval origins, nonetheless, blossomed with its magnificent *castelo* (castle) and Convento de Cristo (Convent of Christ), the former headquarters of the powerful Knights Templar in Portugal.

Tomar's old town is a delight: Whitewashed houses line cobbled streets, flowers reach over garden walls and perfume the air, willows drape the banks of the Nabão River, and walking paths twist through a wooded hillside. The web of old lanes harbors Portugal's oldest surviving **synagogue** *(Rua Dr. Joaquim Jacinto 73, closed Mon.).* Built in 1430, the synagogue lost its function in 1496 when Jews were forced to convert or be expelled. The vaulted room, now the **Museu Luso-Hebraico Abraão Zacuto,** displays tombstones with Hebrew inscriptions and Jewish memorabilia. One block north, Tomar's late 15th-century church **São João Baptista** *(Praça da República)* boasts one of the finest views in town. Stand in its flamboyant Gothic doorway to take in the magnificent 12th-century convent walls high above and the 18th-century town hall on the opposite side of the square. The modern town on the river's right bank has less interest, but

■ **A statue of a bruised Christ presides over a shadowy section of the evocative Convento de Cristo.**

Tomar makes an enjoyable place to stay while on the monastery trail.

Convento de Cristo

The massive hilltop Convento de Cristo is a remarkably harmonious blend of Romanesque, Gothic, Renaissance, and Manueline styles; its labyrinthine cloisters, galleries, staircases, corridors, terraces, and halls resound with atmosphere.

Tomar 🗺 161 C4 **Visitor Information** ✉ Avenida Dr. Cândido Madureira 531 ☎ 249 329 823 **visit-tomar.com** • **Convento de Cristo** ✉ Igreja do Castelo Templário ☎ 249 315 089 💲 $$ **conventocristo.gov.pt**

Order of Christ

Fearful of the Knights Templar's growing power, Dom Dinis I banned the Templars in 1314, replacing them with the Order of Christ, which moved to Tomar from Castro Marim (in the Algarve) in 1356. This order's prestige peaked the following century when, under its grand master Prince Henry the Navigator (1418–1460), it financed Portugal's pioneering expeditions to Africa and India. Wealth from these forays funded much of Tomar's outstanding Manueline decoration and also that of Lisbon's Jerónimos Monastery (see pp. 64–67). The order's status subsequently waned and then in 1834 disappeared completely with the suppression of all religious orders.

The Knights Templar—a military and religious order founded by crusaders in Jerusalem in 1119—began building the monastery in 1160, and construction continued on and off for four centuries despite a change in ownership in the 1300s (see sidebar this page). The complex changed hands again in 1834, when the government banned all religious orders and the castle became the residence of the count of Tomar.

Beyond a vast esplanade and broad staircase, you will find the main entrance tucked into the side of the massive rotunda—the back of the original fortified church. Before entering, have a good look at the fabulously decorated **south porch** of the church. Inside, arrows direct you around the three-story edifice: The full tour of this World Heritage site takes two or three hours, depending on how much time you want spend there. Strategically placed information panels (in Portuguese and English) elucidate the sites you see.

Exploring the Convent: Begin your tour in the old sacristy, from which you enter two adjoining Gothic cloisters, the **Claustro do Cemitério** (Cemetery Cloister) and the **Claustro da Lavagem** (Laundry Cloister). The circuit will bring you past some remarkable early 17th-century azulejos on the walls of the first cloister, the burial ground for knights and friars. The Laundry Cloister has two large reservoirs at its center. More chapels and the new sacristy follow before you reach the superb church.

The 16th-century **church** incorporates the original 12th-century structure, the Romanesque *charola,* or *rotunda,* that resembles in layout Jerusalem's Holy Sepulchre. The 16-sided charola has an exuberantly decorated octagonal oratory at its center. The riot of paintings, statues, and murals adorning the octagon mix illustrations of the life of Christ with symbols of royal power. The decorative works in the charola and in the nave behind, with its raised choir area, are by the prolific Manueline architect Diogo de Arruda, though the Spaniard Juan de Castillo finished them in 1519.

From here, arrows point you downstairs to the convent buildings; the route enters through the **Claustro Principal** (Great Cloister). This outstanding example of Renaissance structure and Manueline decoration dates from 1529. Look for the typical Manueline rope motifs on the back wall to the right as soon as you enter the cloister.

As you exit to a terrace overlooking the intimately scaled **Claustro de Santa Bárbara** (St. Barbara's Cloister), you get your first glimpse of Tomar's much photographed **Manueline window.** This masterpiece of carved stone, designed by Diogo de Arruda, combines maritime motifs with royal emblems and is surmounted by the cross of the Order of Christ. A spiral staircase in the northeastern corner of this terrace leads up to more terraces, which offer good views of the convent, especially the terrace at the far end of the Claustro Principal, which has lovely views over the friars' garden and the picturesque chapter house ruins.

Other attractive sites include the lofty corridor leading to the **monks' cells** and, finally, on the lowest floor, the kitchen and refectory. The tour ends at the neighboring **Claustro da Micha** and **Claustro das Hospedarias,** the latter, the Hospitality Cloister, designed for receiving visitors. You exit through the north face of the convent.

Nearby Curiosities

West of the monastery, on the road to Leiria (see pp. 163–164), looms the **Aqueduto dos Pegões.** This starkly designed aqueduct was built in the early 17th century to supply the convent with water; its 180 arches span 4 miles (6 km). Another curious monument stands on the convent's other side, halfway down the hill: the unused mausoleum of Dom João III, the 16th-century **Ermida de Nossa Senhora da Conceição** (tel 249 315 089). ■

EXPERIENCE: Festa dos Tabuleiros

There's nothing quite like Tomar's other claim, the legendary four-day-long **Festa dos Tabuleiros** (Festival of Trays), held every four years in early July (the latest celebration occurred in 2023). Although officially honoring Isabel, the saintly wife of Dom Dinis I, the event is thought to have pagan roots. The most spectacular procession features 400 young girls (traditionally virgins) dressed in white, each balancing on her head a tray piled high with bread and paper flowers. The next day bread and wine are distributed to Tomar's poorest families. Plan ahead if you'd like to attend, as hotels fill well in advance.

TEJO VALLEY

The longest river in Iberia, the Tejo (Tagus) flows 687 miles (1,100 km) from its source in Spain through Portugal to empty into the Atlantic at Lisbon. The area of the Ribatejo (banks of the Tagus) derives its name from the river, as does the Alentejo (beyond the Tagus), to the south.

The Tejo snakes through the Ribatejo, its banks alternating between pine forests and patchy industrial installations, which conceal some unusual sites. Portugal's most overtly romantic castle, the **Castelo de Almourol,** sits majestically on a rocky island in the river, 14 miles (22 km) south of Tomar. Built by a grand master of the Knights Templar in 1171 on the site of a Roman fort, it inspired legends and literary references, but the castle was abandoned when its defensive function became obsolete. A small boat *($)* ferries visitors to and fro.

Farther east is **Abrantes,** a surprisingly attractive town once you penetrate its industrialized outskirts. A renovated 12th-century **castle** *(tel 241 371 724, closed Mon.)* crowns the narrow streets of the old quarter. A Visigothic necropolis, the governor's palace, and the beautifully restored 15th-century church of **Santa Maria** (now a museum) all stand within the castle walls. The church holds exceptional tombs, statuary, tiles, Roman

■ The island-bound Almourol Castle, built by a Templar knight, epitomizes the medieval citadel.

pieces, and a rare wooden Gothic-Manueline retable. Between Almourol and Abrantes, scenic **Constância,** overlooking the confluence of the Tejo and the Zêzere Rivers, is just the place for wandering along the cobbled alleys. The recent **Trilho Panorâmico do Tejo,** a two-and-a-half-hour walk between the two rivers, shows off the town and castle of Almourol. ■

Castelo de Almourol 🗺 161 C4 ✉ Vila Nova da Barquinha ☎ 249 712 094 (parish) or 249 720 353 (tourist office) 🕐 Closed Mon. in Oct.–Feb. **visitbarquinha.pt** • **Abrantes** 🗺 161 D4 **Visitor Information** ✉ Esplanada 1° de Maio ☎ 241 330 100

SANTARÉM

Famous for bullfights and festivals, Santarém is Ribatejo's district capital. It was described by José Saramago as "a Sleeping Beauty castle, without the sleeping beauty," referring to its sense of remoteness on the vast plains of the region.

Despite a lack of major sites, Santarém has plenty of character. The high point of the year is the 10-day agricultural fair held in early June, featuring bullfights (sometimes), bull-running, and horse racing; an ongoing taurine theme is reflected in witty sidewalk mosaics.

A Jesuit seminary church, **Nossa Senhora da Conceição** *(Praça Sá da Bandeira, tel 243 304 060, closed Tues.)*, is notable for its lengthy azulejo frieze. For some elegant Gothic architecture, head to the **Igreja da Graça** *(Largo Pedro Álvares Cabral, tel 243 304 060, closed Mon.)*; the church's rose window was carved from a single stone. The tomb of Pedro Álvares Cabral, who laid claim to Brazil for Portugal in 1500, is inside.

The older **São João de Alporão** church, just a few minutes north of here by foot, houses the **Museu Arqueológico** *(Largo Zeferino Sarmento, currently closed)*. The undisputed highlight is the elaborate tomb of Duarte de Meneses, a military commander who died at the hands of the Moors in Morocco in 1464. The 15th-century **Torre das Caba-**

ças, opposite the museum, displays an imaginative exhibit on the theme of time with old sundials and clock mechanisms. You can climb to the top for good views, although those from the **Portas do Sol,** the remains of a Moorish citadel overlooking the Tejo on the southeast side of town, are better. ∎

Santarém  161 C3 **Visitor Information** ✉ Rua Capelo e Ivens 63 ☎ 243 304 437 **santarem.pa.leg.br**

▪ In Santarém and in neighboring Ribatejo towns such as Golegã, the Lusitano horse is highly revered.

TORRES VEDRAS

Vineyards and towers characterize the landscape around Torres Vedras, at the heart of Estremadura. The bleak Serra de Montejunto range looms to the east, while the beaches of the Atlantic lie west.

Both red and white wines are produced in the undulating vineyards of **Arruda dos Vinhos** to the south and **Bombarral,** 17 miles (27 km) to the north, where the train station is plastered with azulejos illustrating the wine-growing culture. For military historians, however, the region is known for one thing only: the Duke of Wellington's famous defensive Lines of Torres Vedras built during the Peninsular War to protect Lisbon. Wellington's Anglo-Portuguese troops constructed two lines of trenches and redoubts over a 12-month period (1809–1810), severely altering the landscape. The 152 towers armed with 600 cannon stretched from the coast to the Tejo River. When General Masséna led 65,000 French soldiers in the third invasion of Portugal (the first two having failed), he entered through Almeida in the east. After advancing toward Lisbon, he realized the impregnability of Wellington's system (which included roads, ditches, and embrasures), so he retreated to Santarém. Finally, without supplies, he made the final retreat that ended the French invasions.

The remains of one of the towers, the **São Vicente fortress,** stand in Torres Vedras. The **Museu Municipal Leonel Trindade** details the Napoleonic invasion and has a scale model of the Lines of Torres Vedras. Be sure to admire the azulejos that blanket the cloister walls of this former convent and the exhibit on ceramics. Also of interest are a ruined 13th-century **castle** on the edge of town and, on the main square, the church of **São Pedro,** with a rich baroque interior and a Manueline portal depicting winged dragons. Behind stands a Gothic fountain with vaulted arches, the **Chafariz dos Canos.** ■

Torres Vedras 🅜 161 B3 **Visitor Information** ✉ Praça da República ☎ 261 310 408 **visitetorres vedras.pt • Museu Municipal Leonel Trindade** ✉ Convento da Graça, Praça 25 de Abril ☎ 261 310 485 🕐 Closed Mon. 💲 $ **cm-tvedras.pt**

▪ **18th-century azulejos in São Pedro**

MAFRA

You cannot miss the massive bulk of the palace, monastery, and basilica of Mafra as it looms over the plain north of Sintra. This is yet another of Portugal's heavyweight sites (and a World Heritage site since 2019), this time an ode to concentrated baroque detail, scale, and pomposity.

Mafra is a place of mind-boggling statistics: some 50,000 workers, 13 years of construction, 880 rooms, 154 stairways, and 4,500 doors and windows carved out of Portuguese and Italian marble and exotic woods from Brazil. Dom João V commissioned the complex in 1717 to fulfill a vow when his wife bore him an heir. The German architect Johann Friedrich Ludwig of Ratisbon (1670–1752) headed the project, backed by Italian artists,

craftsmen, and masons. Initially funded by Brazilian gold, the building costs eventually bankrupted the Portuguese economy. In 1807, the royals fled to Brazil in the face of the French invasion (see sidebar below). With them went most of the palace furniture and objets d'art. After the return of the monarchy, in 1821, Mafra was used only sporadically, but it was from here that the last king, Dom Manuel II, left for exile in 1910.

Mafra ⚑ 161 A3 **Visitor Information** ✉ Palácio Nacional, Torreão Sul, Terreiro D. João V ☎ 261 818 347 **cm-mafra.pt**

Royal Exodus

The flight of the Braganças to Brazil in 1807 marks one of the lowest points in Portuguese history. Portugal was in serious decline: The costly extravagance of Mafra had depleted the country's coffers, Britain and France had eclipsed Portugal on the political world stage, and Napoleon's army was sweeping across Europe. As the French drew closer, the Prince Regent, Dom João, under pressure from the British envoy, made a fateful decision both for the Portuguese crown and for

its colony Brazil. On November 29, 1807, a day before the French entered Lisbon, Dom João and his queen, Dona Carlota, took to the seas. A convoy of three dozen frigates, brigantines, sloops, and corvettes, with 10,000 members of the royal court on board, set sail for Brazil under British escort. The ships also carried the paraphernalia of an empire: the royal carriage, a piano, several tons of documents, and favorite objets d'art. The exodus signaled the end of Portugal's heyday.

■ The palace and basilica at Mafra reveal strong German baroque and Italian neoclassical influences.

The Basílica

The long, umber-colored facade of the palace flanks the white marble Basílica, crowned by two bell towers containing 92 Flemish-made bells. The sober, neoclassical interior of the church was inspired by St. Peter's in Vatican City but, like the facade, has a strong German baroque flavor. Look for the 14 marble statues of saints and numerous bas-reliefs crafted by the Mafra school, a body of Italian and Portuguese sculptors based in the palace from 1753 to 1770. If in town on the first Sunday of the month, do not miss the monthly organ recital in which the Basilica's six organs—designed to be played together—are put through their paces.

Palácio Nacional de Mafra

The one-hour guided tour *(tel 261 817 550, $$)* to the **palace** and **monastery** begins at the Queen's Entrance, midway along the left-hand facade. Long corridors and vast salons with painted ceilings—all furnished with 19th-century pieces that replaced the originals—characterize the palace. The main site is the stunning rococo **library** with its checkered marble floor and barrel-vaulted ceiling. The ornately carved wooden bookcases hold some 40,000 volumes, including numerous incunabula and codices dating from the 15th century on. At the back of the palace, the monastery displays monks' cells, a pharmacy, and an infirmary with a section once reserved for insane Franciscans.

Outdoor Havens

The royals and the monks passed many an hour in the **Jardim do Cerco,** the formal French-style garden that lies north of the palace. The vast **Tapada Nacional de Mafra** *(Portão do Codeçal, tel 261 814 240, tapadademafra.pt, guided walks $$–$$$)*—a 2,023-acre (819 ha) walled preserve home to wild boars, deer, civet cats, and even wolves—encircles the entire complex of Mafra. You can tour this delightful enclave by electric train, mountain bike, or guided walk. ■

SINTRA

Verdant, romantic, and intensely evocative, Sintra never fails to seduce. Blessed with a microclimate that nurtures a varied, exuberant flora, from mosses to massive sequoias, its centuries-long popularity has produced unforgettable palaces and mansions.

High in the hills above the Estoril coast just west of Lisbon, Sintra is a radical contrast to the capital both in style and in climate, the latter being distinctly moist. Together with the surrounding Parque Natural de Sintra-Cascais (see p. 199), which encompasses forested hills dotted with palatial follies, the town is justly classified as a World Heritage site.

You can see Sintra in a day, but try to stay a night or two in this delightful retreat, once the preserve of monarchs and European aristocrats, artists, and poets—including Lord Byron.

The town straggles along a road that winds uphill from the train station to the square in front of the national palace. Alternatively, coming by car from Estoril or Lisbon takes you

Sintra 🗺 161 A2 **Visitor Information** ✉ Praça da República 23 ☎ 219 231 157 **visitsintra.travel**

■ The towering white chimneys of Sintra's national palace rise unmistakably above the town center.

INSIDER TIP:

Linger in the moss-bottomed forest that engulfs the winding path to the palace—it's as fairy-tale as the hill-topping edifice itself.

—JOHNNA RIZZO
National Geographic
magazine editor

---

through **São Pedro,** a satellite village about 1 mile (1.6 km) from Sintra that brims with antique shops. West of the main square, a turnoff curls up to the Moorish castle ruins and the Palácio da Pena, both high above the town, while the main N247 continues out of Sintra to snake through the *serra* (hills) to Quinta da Regaleira, the Palácio de Seteais, the park of Monserrate, a few villages, and, eventually, the coast. There are some lovely walks in the area and, even if you take a bus or taxi up to the Pena Palace, you should try to walk down to see Sintra's many art nouveau mansions and to enjoy fabulous views.

If you are in Sintra on the second or fourth Sunday of the month, don't miss the tempting market that takes over the center of São Pedro. Music lovers should aim to visit in June or July, when an international music festival is held.

At any time you can indulge in Sintra's famed *queijadas* (see sidebar p. 190) and typical mountain fare of Negrais suckling pig, Mercês pork, roast kid, or veal, washed down with Colares red wine.

Palácio Nacional de Sintra

Dominating the *vila velha* (or old town), the magnificent yet confusing Palácio Nacional de Sintra, Portugal's oldest palace, spans more than eight centuries of history from its Moorish origins until the end of the monarchy in 1910. Over the course of time it underwent numerous extensions—notably in the 14th, 15th, and 16th centuries under kings Dinis I, João I, and Manuel I, respectively. The palace was a convenient retreat from the heat of Lisbon and served as a luxury hunting lodge. It displays superb decorative arts of the Manueline period, when the western tower and east wing were added, as well as extensive Mudéjar (Hispano-Moorish) tiling, the oldest still in place in Europe.

The entrance, through the Gothic porch and up a spiral staircase, leads into the largest room in the palace, the **Sala dos Cisnes** (Swan's Room), once used for banquets and dances and, even today, official receptions. Sadly, though most of the palace miraculously survived the 1755 earthquake, this vast hall did not; however, it was harmoniously rebuilt

---

Palácio Nacional de Sintra ✉ Largo Rainha D. Amélia ☎ 219 237 300
§ $$ **parquesdesintra.pt**

and the 27 swans were faithfully repainted on the ceiling.

Outside in the **central patio,** the heart of João I's palace, do not miss the tiled grotto. An antique version of a refrigerator, the grotto's walls are now entirely faced in 18th-century azulejos that conceal tiny waterspouts, but a series of Manueline frescoes lie underneath the tiles. From here the route takes in the unusual **Sala das Pegas** (Magpies' Room), so-named for its ceiling paintings depicting 136 magpies spouting the king's motto, *Por Bem* (For the Best). Another stunner is **King Sebastian's bedroom,** with its Italian marquetry four-poster bed and original vine-leaf tiles. Most of the inlaid furniture elsewhere is 17th- and 18th-century Indo-Portuguese, with exceptions such as the spectacular Murano glass chandelier in the north wing.

From the **Sala das Sereias** (Room of the Sirens) you enter the **Arab Room,** formerly João I's bedroom, which displays a rare, dazzling juxtaposition of tile techniques and patterns. Continuing on, you find yourself in the vast, square **Sala dos Brasões** (Blazons Hall), which juts out over the gardens and tenders views to the Atlantic. Paintings of stags holding 74 coats of arms of the Portuguese nobility dance, and portraits of Manuel I's children cover the room's coffered dome ceiling. Altogether this tour de force combines heraldic decoration, gilded cornices, and azulejo panels illustrating hunting scenes that stand more than 13 feet (4 m) tall. Note the typical Manueline details of ropes and plants framing the doorway.

Although the northern wing rooms that follow are less impressive, pay special attention to Dom Dinis's 14th-century **chapel,** which Dom Manuel I redecorated with cut-tile flooring, frescoes of doves (repainted in the 1940s), and a Mudéjar ceiling. Afonso VI, who was imprisoned in the palace for six

EXPERIENCE: Sintra Hills Adventures

For some great views of the Sintra palaces and surrounding countryside, get off the main roads on a thrilling 4x4 trip.

Muitaventura *(Rua Marquês de Viana 31, Largo da Feira, Sintra, tel 967 021 248, muitaventura .com)* offers half- and full-day jeep safaris *($$$$$)* through the natural park with frequent stops to admire the scenery.

For those who would prefer a more eco-friendly option, **Go2Cintra** *(Avenida Doutor Miguel Bombarda 37, tel 917 855 428, go2cintra.com)* promotes sustainable tourism around Sintra Natural Park through the use of low-impact transportation, particularly bikes and e-bikes. They offer independent tours, but the staff guarantees you have all the materials and itinerary, complete with an app showing the route and interesting sites to visit.

Queijadas

Sintra's most famous culinary export are its *queijadas*. Best translated as "cheesecakes," though in no way resembling the cheesecake that most people are familiar with, these small sweet cakes are made with cheese, eggs, milk, sugar, and cinnamon and surrounded in fine crispy pastry. They are best experienced with a *galão* (milky coffee served in a glass), in Sintra's café **Piriquita** *(Rua das Padarias 1, tel 219 230 626, piriquita.pt);* wrapped in paper rolls, packs of six are also available to carry out.

years by his brother Pedro II, died of apoplexy while attending Mass here in 1683. Last but not least come the astonishingly scaled 15th-century **kitchens** with their 108-foot-high (33 m) conical chimneys, unique in Europe, and tapped spring water. They are still used today during official receptions. To recover from the decorative excess, take a walk around the gardens to be soothed by trickling fountains.

News Museum

One of the latest Sintra attractions, located in the center of town, is the News Museum *(Rua Visconde de Monserrate 26, tel 210 126 600, newsmuseum.pt, $$).* As the name implies, it is dedicated to the history of news, with intriguing multimedia displays offering relief from monument overload. Portuguese history, war, propaganda, and freedom are among the topics covered, and visitors are encouraged to participate by recording their own news item for radio, TV, or Internet.

Museu de Artes de Sintra

Before plunging further into Sintra's magical past, anyone desiring a visual feast of another kind should visit the Museu de Artes de Sintra (MU.SA; *Av. Heliodoro Salgado, tel 219 236 106, closed Mon., $),* in the new part of town. Housed in a converted 1924 casino, this museum is chock-full of stunning modern art and photography, and is run by the municipality.

Parque e Palácio Nacional da Pena

The fairy-tale Palácio Nacional da Pena, colorful and turreted, was the creation of Prince Ferdinand of Saxe-Coburg. Begun in the 1840s, the palace sits on the foundations of a 15th-century monastery and commands a prime hilltop setting. The highly cultured Ferdinand (1816–1885), the Portuguese prince regent for two years, was a grand master of the Rosicrucian Order, and numerous Masonic symbols can be spotted throughout his palace.

Your 10-minute walk up from the parking lot brings into focus otherworldly archways, minarets, towers, and a drawbridge before you finally arrive at the palace courtyard, where tiles and vibrant color take

■ The palace Quinta da Regaleira is a World Heritage site within the "cultural landscape of Sintra."

over. The passageway through the densely carved **Triton Arch**—its shell, coral, and vine symbolizing the link between sea and earth—leads to a Manueline cloister (all that remains of the original monastery), and a chapel containing an alabaster altarpiece by Nicolas de Chanterenne. Next, a series of small rooms decorated in tiles, shellwork, porcelain fragments, stucco, and trompe l'oeil plasterwork overflow with opulence: Chandeliers, lamps, and objets d'art culminate in the hand-carved furniture of the **Indian Room.** Above all, relish the fabulous views to the southwest from the terrace at the back.

In the foreground, the **Parque da Pena**—500 acres (200 ha) of semiwild terrain with ferns, lakes, a few fountains, massive boulders, and rare species of trees—hugs the granite slopes of the serra around the palace. A map (which can be downloaded from the

Parque e Palácio Nacional da Pena 🏔 161 A2 ✉ Parque da Pena, Sintra ☎ 219 237 300 💲 $$ (park); $$$ (palace & park) **parquesdesintra.pt**

website) outlines the walk which passes by the main points of interest and the route for visitors with limited mobility. The highest point, the **Cruz Alta,** is on the southern flank and has views reaching as far as Lisbon.

Two possible routes lead downhill from the palace: The first, the Calçada da Pena, winds through the forest and past art nouveau mansions to São Pedro, from where it is a mile (1.6 km) walk to Sintra's center; the second leads down to the eighth-century **Castelo dos Mouros** *($$)*, where ruined battlements offer more stunning views north over the valley as well as a whiff of Moorish past. From here you can zigzag down steps and paths to the Romanesque church of **Santa Maria** to reach Rua Marechal Saldanha, which leads back to Sintra's main square.

More Sintra Sites

Be sure to see the **Chalet & Garden of the Countess of Edla** *(Estrada da Pena, tel 219 237 300, parquesdesintra.pt, $$)*. Painstakingly restored and opened to the public in 2011, this former recreational chalet was built between 1864 and 1869 by Fernando II for his second wife, Elisa Henster, Countess of Elda. The outside is painted stucco made to resemble a log cabin; its interior is full of bizarre decorative details, including inlaid cork ceilings, murals, and tile floors.

Another of Sintra's whimsical sites is the **Quinta da Regaleira,** *(tel 219 106 650, regaleira.pt, $$$)*, an early 1900s palace that has a striking gar-

den. Even more than the Pena Palace, this *quinta* abounds in esoteric references, and mixes neo-Gothic and neo-Manueline architectural styles with classic Romantic abandon.

The eccentric, highly cultured millionaire António Carvalho Monteiro (1848–1920), after making his fortune in Brazil, commissioned Luigi Manini, the Italian architect responsible for the palace of Buçaco, to build this dream palace. Like Pena, it teeters on the brink of kitsch, but the gardens have an inimitable atmosphere with fountains, lakes, grottoes, statues, and the famous **Poço Iniciático** (Well of Initiation). The well is the high point: Steps take you down to what feels like the bowels of the Earth, where you stand on an eight-pointed star before following underground stepping stones through a passage out into a decorative courtyard.

Nearby, the **Palácio de Seteais** is now a luxury hotel (see p. 306) with fine views over extensive gardens to the distant sea. Built in the late 18th century by the Dutch consul, Daniel Gildemeester, it later witnessed the signing of the 1808 Convention of Sintra—an agreement that led to Napoleon's army withdrawing from Portugal (they reinvaded the following year). The interior boasts delicate murals, grand staircases, and antique furnishings.

From the Palácio de Seteais, 2.5 miles (4 km) of road twist through the forest to the magnificent **Palácio e Parque de Monserrate** *(Estrada da Monserrate, parquesdesintra.pt, $$)*. The palace and estate name

■ An initiation well (or inverted tower) was used for ceremonial purposes that included tarot initiation rites.

derives from a religious order that owned the land when it was leased to Gerard DeVisme, the first of its several English owners (see pp. 194–195), including Francis Cook, who commissioned the surviving Orientalist extravaganza. Decades of neglect ended in the 1990s with much needed restoration; the domed palace, a classic Romantic structure, is now open to visitors.

Be sure to admire the very English lawn in front of the palace, the first such lawn in Portugal, watered by underground ceramic pipes. While the English lawn is novel, the 81-acre (33 ha) gardens are truly outstand-ing. These were the pride and joy of the Cook family, who exploited the humid climate to nurture tree ferns from Australia and New Zealand, Montezuma cypresses from Mexico, rhododendrons from the Himalaya, and countless other species. A walk through the park (allow an hour or so) is a delight. Take in the chapel ruins sheltered by massive ficus trees. The ornately carved Arch of India, brought back by Cook following the Indian Mutiny in 1857, stands just east of the palace. A little farther on, the old stables have been converted into a restaurant and café with invit-ing outdoor tables under the trees. ■

SINTRA'S ENGLISH ECCENTRICS

The role of the English in Portugal has been prominent ever since their traders developed the profitable port wine industry. Not all were businessmen, however. Their influence began in the 14th century, when John of Lancaster and his band of crusaders helped the Portuguese fight the Moors; thanks to the local tipple, the English army was seldom sober.

Soon after, in the 1380s, Philippa of Lancaster, daughter of John and the wife of João I, gave royal patronage to her countrymen's commercial interests. For the next 500 years wine, cork, salt, and oil were exchanged for cod and cloth from England, an enduring relationship that brought a new breed of Englishmen to Portuguese shores: merchants and minor aristocrats in search of mild climes and copious sources of inebriation. English communities flourished in Porto and Lisbon, their members meeting at specific hotels, restaurants, clubs, and churches. Among them were the men who brought both fame and scandal to Sintra: William Beckford, the poet Lord Byron, and Sir Francis Cook.

Monserrate's English Tenants

Lesser known but equally instrumental in raising Sintra's profile, the merchant Gerard DeVisme made his fortune importing wood from Brazil. In 1790, this Englishman of French Huguenot stock leased Monserrate, a prime property outside Sintra (see pp. 192–193). DeVisme first replaced a semi-ruined chapel with a neo-Gothic mansion, and then he set

■ **The architectural style of the Monserrate Palace evokes Sintra's early Moorish conquerors.**

about creating a new "ruined" chapel in the woods below. Still visible today, draped in vegetation, this picturesque folly was Sintra's first contrived Romantic structure—the blueprint for moody ruins lost in time. DeVisme's time at Monserrate ended just a few years later, when ill health forced his return to England. In his place soon came William Beckford, Orientalist scholar, author of *Vathek*, notorious snob, and reputedly the wealthiest man in England. Beckford had been forced into exile in 1785 for alleged homosexual relationships. After acquiring the tenancy of Monserrate, he wasted little time in criticizing DeVisme's "barbarous gothic" structure, yet he partied hard there in the late 1790s, raising a few local eyebrows in the process. But his tenure barely outlasted DeVisme's.

Years of abandonment followed Beckford's departure, witnessed in 1809 when the 21-year-old Lord Byron made his famous three-day visit to Sintra with his friend John Hobhouse. Lured by the estate's reputation for elegance—and decadence—the two visitors, according to Hobhouse's diary, found the mansion "deserted and bare of all furnishings." Yet Sintra's fascination struck again and Byron wrote: "The village is perhaps, in every respect, the most delightful in Europe ... Palaces and gardens rising in the midst of rocks, cataracts and precipices, convents on stupendous heights—a distant view of the sea and the Tagus." Byron's epic

Lawrence's Hotel

Opened by the British Lawrence Oram family in 1764, Lawrence's Hotel claims to be the oldest in Iberia—and although this may be hard to verify, what is certain is that this Sintra landmark offered hospitality to many English eccentrics. In 1809, Lord Byron visited Sintra as part of his Grand Tour and stayed at Lawrence's, as did William Beckford before acquiring Monserrate. In Byron's wake followed the cream of Portuguese 19th-century Romantics and intellectuals, putting Lawrence's firmly on the Sintra map. Today it is fully restored and still open to guests (see p. 307).

poem *Childe Harold I* also famously extols Sintra, referencing "Cintra's glorious Eden." In 1855, Sir Francis Cook, a textile millionaire, bought the property. He proved to be the most industrious of all its owners and was named viscount of Monserrate in 1870. After hiring the American architect James Knowles, Jr. to build an Orientalist fantasy palace, Cook orchestrated the park's now famous landscaping. The vast undertaking required more than 2,000 people to build the palace and another 50 to plant the park. It remained in the Cook family until after World War II, when they could no longer afford its upkeep. Their departure brought to an end a line of particularly colorful English inhabitants.

COSTA DO ESTORIL

Lisbon's favorite coastal playground, the Estoril coast hugs continental Europe's westernmost point, Cabo da Roca. The shoreline stretches west from Estoril in a virtual continuum of hotels, restaurants, and condominiums, and curls around the Cabo Raso to the wild and unspoiled Parque Natural de Sintra-Cascais and the Guincho beach. North of here is Cabo da Roca and a string of lovely beaches.

■ Cabo da Roca's 1846 lighthouse emits a beam which is visible 26 miles (42 km) out to sea.

There is a marked difference between the two diverging coastlines at Cabo Raso. To the east, south-facing beaches are calm and sheltered, with plentiful distractions. The western coast, north of Cabo Raso, up to Cabo da Roca and beyond, is wild and often very windy, with dramatic cliffs, pounding surf, and amazing beaches both north and south of Cabo da Roca.

Cascais

A genteel air still clings to the older part of Cascais behind the fishing harbor, where cobbled pedestrian streets offer an enticing

Cascais  161 A2 **Visitor Information** ✉ Praça 5 de Outubro, Antigo Edifício dos Bombeiros ☎ 912 034 214 **cultura.cascais.pt**

lineup of restaurants and fashion boutiques. An 800-year-old tradition of fishing endures, although the dethroned kings who brought fame to Cascais between the two World Wars are long gone.

Entirely rebuilt after the 1755 earthquake, Cascais rose to prominence in 1870 when King Luís I moved the summer court here from Sintra and set up residence inside the Cidadela fort. In his wake came a flood of wannabes, further encouraged by the new fashion for sea bathing. The western end of Cascais, where the old mansions are located, once harbored Umberto II, Italy's last king; Juan Carlos of Spain, who was a resident during his long exile prior to 1975; and even Salazar, Portugal's infamous dictator.

Cascais centers on the **Praia da Ribeira,** the beach where fishermen bring in their catch every morning. To one side stands the fish market, behind are the pedestrian shopping streets, and around the bay to the west is the 16th-century **Cidadela.** The fort sits on a promontory overlooking the bay and harbor; it was one of several defensive keeps built to protect Lisbon against attack. The fort is now home to a *pousada* and various fashionable restaurants.

Walk some 100 yards (90 m) along the waterfront to the **Museu dos Condes Castro Guimarães** *(tel 214 815 304, bairrodosmuseus.cascais .pt, closed Mon., $),* a typical, turreted, 19th-century Cascais mansion, which stands beside a sea inlet. The sump-

An Iconic Gelateria

Santini *(Avenida Valbom 28F, tel 214 833 709, santini.pt)* **has been part of Cascais life since the late 1940s. A favorite with the then exiled Italian royal family, the gelateria quickly became fashionable and has remained so ever since. The recipes for their ice creams are closely guarded, with dozens of delicious flavors produced from natural ingredients. Which flavor is best is subject to debate, but rest assured, they are all amazing. Additional branches are in Lisbon, Belém, Carcavelos, and Porto.**

tuous interior displays a rich private collection of decorative arts, including some lovely Indo-Portuguese furniture, early 20th-century Portuguese paintings, and a vast library. Opposite here is the Cascais Marina, good for a stroll and a bite to eat.

Farther along this coastal avenue is the **Boca do Inferno** (Mouth of Hell)—the most visited site in Cascais—where waves thunder through a gorge. Walk down over the rocks to a little platform for a good view.

The **Casa das Histórias–Paula Rego** *(tel 214 826 970, casadashistorias paularego.com, closed Mon., $$),* one block back on Avenida da República, houses a fabulous collection by the world-renowned, Cascais-born Paula Rego (1935–2022). Her paintings are considered by some to be sinister and oppressive, depicting controversial social realities. Anyone desiring a quick dip or a chance to sunbathe should head for **Praia da Rainha** and **Praia da Conceição,** two beaches just east of the old quarter.

Estoril

Though cheek to cheek with Cascais, Estoril lacks the former's air of faded grandeur and range of restaurants. The small **Museu dos Exílios do Estoril** tells the story of those who found refuge in Estoril; housed in the Correios (post office) building until 2023, it is currently being moved to a new location that hasn't been announced yet. In Avenida Dr. Stanley Ho is Estoril's highlight: Europe's largest **casino** (*tel 214 667 700, casino-estoril .pt, opens at 3 p.m.*) fronts a large formal garden leading to the sea. Follow in the footsteps of exiled royals, Ian Fleming, Orson Welles, and other notable personalities and indulge in anything from roulette to slot machines, or watch the nightly cabaret. To maintain lower adrenaline levels, head for the small beaches for a swim.

Palácio Nacional de Queluz

In the hinterland between Cascais and Lisbon, one major site stands out: the 18th-century **Palácio Nacional de Queluz.** Standing in the shadows of high-rises and highways, this once gracious royal palace fell into a sorry state of disrepair, but many millions of euros of restoration work has returned the interiors and formal gardens to their former glory. Now your attention will be drawn to the exterior and to the famous façade, which has recently been repainted from pink to its original cobalt

Museu dos Exílios do Estoril 🕓 Currently closed • **Palácio Nacional de Queluz** 🗺 161 B2 ✉ Largo do Palácio, Queluz ☎ 219 237 300 💲 $$ parquesdesintra.pt

Vagaries of Palace Life

The palace of Queluz has had a checkered record of residency. Despite its extravagant transformation from country house to summer palace in the mid-18th century, engineered by Prince Pedro (1717–1786), the brother of King José, the palace initially saw little use. An exception was Pedro's wife (and niece), Queen Maria I, who lived here for many years while her melancholic eccentricity accelerated into insanity. In 1794, a fire at Lisbon's Ajuda palace brought the royal family to Queluz on a permanent basis, but this residency proved to be short lived; in 1807 the royals fled to Brazil. Over the next century, until the end of the Portuguese monarchy, Queluz was inhabited only sporadically.

blue color. One wing, the Queen Maria Pavilion, is still used by visiting heads of state; another section is a *pousada* (inn).

The palace was the brainchild of Prince Pedro (1717–1786), the brother of King José. French architect Jean-Baptiste Robillon masterminded the transformation of a country house into this small-scale Portuguese Versailles, in which rococo gilding, elaborate paneling, and stuccowork dominate. Despite exceptional details and craftsmanship in the 22 rooms, the overall impression is one of decorative excess. Nonetheless, the palace does showcase a valuable collection of Portuguese furniture, Arraiolos carpets, royal portraits, jewelry, and Chinese and European porcelain. Of outstanding interest is the **Sala do Trono** (Throne Room), an echo of the Hall of Mirrors at Versailles, where glossy parquet floors and mirrored walls reflect glittering chandeliers beneath a gilded, stuccoed ceiling. More unusual is the **Sala de Don Quixote,** where Dom Pedro IV died; eight pillars support a circular ceiling and wall paintings depict scenes from the Cervantes novel.

Also designed by Robillon, with more than a nod to the French landscape designer Le Nôtre, the extensive **gardens** hold many surprises. Great whimsicality produced the completely tiled walls of the **canal—** the 18th-century azulejos depict river and seaport scenes. The royal family would view these while sailing up and down the waterway, listening to chamber music played in a nearby pavilion. This reflects the original plan for Queluz as a pleasure palace for summer entertainment. Today the summertime tradition continues with a full schedule of shows and events in the palace and park. You can take a pleasant stroll through the formal gardens dotted with statues and descend to a lower, more Italianate level of pools and fountains, but you will not escape the muted roar of traffic.

Cabo da Roca & Around

Back on the coastline that is part of the **Parque Natural de Sintra-Cascais,** the highlight is **Cabo da Roca,** continental Europe's most westerly point. High on a windswept cliff, 460 feet (140 m) above the waves, the lighthouse has become something of a pilgrimage spot, where a tiny tourist office writes out certificates. The 360-degree views are fantastic, and a cliffside cross marks the actual most westerly point *(Cabo da Roca is reachable by bus with no changes from Sintra).* Beyond the cliffs to the south, backed by sand dunes and pine trees, is the

Parque Natural de Sintra-Cascais ⚠ 161 A2-A3 **Visitor Information** ✉ Avenida da República, Cascais ☎ 214 604 230 **natural.pt; parquesdesintra.pt** • **Cabo da Roca** ⚠ 161 A2 **Visitor Information** ✉ Cabo da Roca, Azóia ☎ 219 280 081

■ There is no shortage of interesting details at the Palácio Nacional de Queluz.

beautiful **Praia do Guincho,** a popular surfing beach where the European Windsurfing and World Surfing Championships are held. Notwithstanding a couple of hotels and a few seafood restaurants that dot the rocky coast to the south, the coast preserves its unspoiled nature. The beaches north of Cabo da Roca are reached from Colares, except for the lovely but often overcrowded **Praia da Adraga,** accessed from Almoçageme. The neighboring **Praia Grande** (also accessible from Almoçageme, and notable for its clifftop dinosaur footprints and bodyboarders slaloming the waves below) and **Praia das Maçãs,** farther north, are lovely beaches, but **Azenhas do Mar** is the most striking. Here, colorful houses cling to a cliff from where a road winds down to the shore. If the tide is low, you can enjoy a tranquil swim in a saltwater pool carved out of the rocks.

The last stop on this section of Estremaduran coastline, due west of Mafra, is **Ericeira.** This popular little resort has a lively atmosphere, a fishing harbor, and a quaint old center around its clifftop church and main square. Three beaches lie within walking distance and a few more within a short drive, including **Praia de Ribeira de Ilhas,** another surfing championship beach. Restaurants are plentiful and the nightlife hops, mostly due to the weekend influx of Lisbonites. ■

Ericeira 🄼 161 A3 **Visitor Information** ✉ Praça da República 17
☎ 261 863 122 or 261 818 347 **cm-mafra.pt**

SETÚBAL PENINSULA

Jutting impudently into the Atlantic Ocean south of Lisbon, the Setúbal Peninsula presents an eclectic mix of beaches, light industry, hills, vineyards, and nature reserves. On summer weekends, beachgoing Lisbonites pour across the two bridges spanning the Tejo River.

Whatever the tourist literature says of **Costa da Caparica** and the sandy beach to the south, you cannot ignore the blight of development at its northern tip. Yet surfers from the capital head here in droves and, apart from the breakers, enjoy fabulous views north to the Serra de Sintra. In summer an electric train services the beach strip, which includes fossilized limestone cliffs backed by an immense pine forest. Between here and Sesimbra are industrial pockets as well as eucalyptus and pine forests.

Sesimbra & Around

The fishing port of Sesimbra occupies a strategic position in the southwestern corner of the peninsula, its medieval **castelo** (castle) standing above increasing modern development. Inside the castle walls stand the ruins of a Romanesque church, **Santa Maria,** and a pleasant café. Down below, quaint, narrow backstreets end at a sandy beach, its placid waters protected by a headland and guarded by the fort of Santiago. Brightly painted fishing boats fill the harbor west of the center; they supply the excellent seafood restaurants in town. 7 miles (11 km) west lies the windswept **Cabo Espichel,** boasting a cliff-edge lighthouse, magnificent views, and a 13th-century sanctuary.

The **Serra da Arrábida**—the hill range that runs parallel to the coast between Sesimbra and Setúbal—creates an unexpected enclave of Mediterranean-style landscape; it is a protected nature reserve. Rising to 1,640 feet (500 m), the *serra* is clad in Portuguese oaks, vineyards (famed for their muscatel grapes), and aromatic herbal scrub. Various mammals include genets, weasels, badgers, and wildcats, while in the air you might spot Bonelli's eagles, kestrels, buzzards, swifts, and bee-eaters. The hillside cradles a picture-postcard Franciscan **monastery,** founded in 1542. Its whitewashed buildings with tiled roofs, terraces, pergolas, and shrines spill down the hillside in complete harmony with their surroundings. Immediately below the

Setúbal Peninsula 161 B1-B2 **Visitor Information** Casa da Baía, Avenida Luísa Todi 468, Setúbal 265 545 010 **visitsetubal.com**
Sesimbra 161 B1 **Visitor Information** Largo da Marinha 26–27 212 288 665 **sesimbra.pt**

■ Portugal's fourth largest port, Setúbal is home to more than 2,000 small boats.

monastery is an absolute gem: the crescent-shaped beach and village of **Portinho da Arrábida.** Protected from the north winds by the hills and edged by transparent waters, the village makes an idyllic spot for a seafood lunch. Close by is the **Lapa de Santa Margarida,** a sea cave where the area's oldest traces of human presence (200,000–400,000 years old) were found. The **Forte de Santa Maria,** built in 1670 to protect the monks against Moorish pirate attacks and now a marine biology center, guards the western end of the beach. Farther east lies **Galapos** beach, much favored by scuba divers, followed by **Praia de Figueirinha,** a white-sand beach popular with windsurfers.

Setúbal & Around

The road to Setúbal along the crest of the massif offers views both north to Lisbon and south across the Sado Estuary. The hamlets along this route produce excellent Azeitão sheep cheese and velvety honey, as well as the sweet wine, Moscatel de Setúbal. In **Vila Nogueira da Azeitão** you can try the Moscatel at the **José Maria da Fonseca winery** *(Rua José Augusto Coelho 11–13, tel 212 198 940, jmf.pt, reservations recommended).*

Setúbal itself is a large, chaotic seaport that looks straight across at the Tróia Peninsula. Portugal's fourth port after Sines, Porto, and Lisbon, it counts sardines and oysters, not tourists, as its major priorities. This fact makes it a relaxing, offbeat place to stay, with an abundance of excellent restaurants. To the west is the massive 16th-century **Forte de São Filipe,** built to fend off Moorish and English attacks. It overlooks the estuary and town. Down below, the town center straddles the tree-lined Avenida Luisa Todi, with harbor facilities to the south and a maze of pedestrian

Setúbal (city) 🗺 161 B2 **Visitor Information** ✉ Casa da Baía, Avenida Luísa Todi 486 ☎ 265 545 010 **visitsetubal.com**

EXPERIENCE: Dolphin-Watching in the Sado Estuary

Dolphins have inhabited the waters of the Sado Estuary for many years: the earliest recorded sighting was in 1863 and it is believed that a pod has been in residence ever since. Today it is believed the group of bottlenose dolphins (*roaz* in Portuguese) numbers 25. You can witness these highly active cetaceans riding the bow waves of boats, reaching speeds of up to 27 miles (40 km) an hour, on a five-hour catamaran excursion with **Verti-** **gem Azul** (*Edifício Marina Deck, Rua Praia da Saúde 11D, Setúbal, or Marina Tróia, tel 265 238 000 or 916 982 907, vertigemazul .com, $$$$$*). Trips set off from either Setúbal or the marina on the Tróia Peninsula and cruise in both the estuary and the coastal waters of Tróia and Arrábida. A biologist narrates the tour, giving you insights into dolphin life—for example, each dolphin eats up to 44 pounds (20 kg) of food a day.

streets to the north off Praça de Bocage. One site not to be missed is the excavated Roman remains of a fish condiment factory visible through the transparent floor of the tourist office. Elsewhere, the 15th-century **Igreja de Jesus** (*Praça Miguel Bombarda, closed Sun.–Mon., hours vary*) is a landmark of early Manueline design. Although this Franciscan church underwent misguided cement restoration in the 1940s, the lovely pink Arrábida stone portal remains intact, as do the striking twisted columns, polychrome tiles, and vaulted chancel. The remarkable 14-panel altarpiece has migrated to the adjoining gallery, **Museu de Setúbal** (*Rua do Balneário de Dr. Paulo Borba, tel 265 537 890, closed Sat.–Sun., $*) to join a rich collection of Renaissance art.

You can visit the **Sado Estuary** by boat, preferably a typical sailing galleon (*Troiacruze, tel 928 053 908, troiacruze.com*), or by car via the 10-mile-long (17 km) **Tróia Peninsula.** Hikers should pick up a handbook outlining walks from the Sado reserve office (*Praça da República, tel 265 541 140*) in the harbor.

Follow signs to Tróia Cais to take a 15-minute **ferry ride** (*Atlantic Ferries, tel 265 235 101, atlanticferries.pt, $$ per person, one way*) to the tip of this finger of land. The road runs south to pine-edged dunes (a botanical reserve) and blissful beaches on the Atlantic side, and fishing villages on the estuary side. With luck you will spot otters or dolphins, and storks, herons, and egrets are common. One of the most traditional villages is **Carrasqueira,** where boats moor at rickety raised walkways jutting out into a lagoon. This is accessed from the N253, running eastward from Comporta, at the base of the peninsula, to Alcácer do Sal (see p. 234) in the Alentejo. ■

Sweeping plains and hills clad in cork oaks, olive trees, and vineyards, where hilltop villages date from Moorish and medieval days

ALENTEJO

Hand-painted ceramics of the Alentejo

ALENTEJO

Rural, unspoiled, blissfully empty, and full of breathtakingly big horizons, the Alentejo covers almost a third of Portugal, yet has barely one-tenth of its population. Here the pace slows palpably. Old ladies gossip in doorways, and old men gather on sunny benches or keep the bars in business. The sun bounces off whitewashed walls, and gnarled olive trees or cork oaks greet you around every corner.

Bordered to the north by the Tejo River (the name of the region derives from words meaning "beyond the Tejo"), to the south by the Algarve, and to the east by Spain, the Alentejo boasts a stunning Atlantic coastline, until recently barely exploited. Apart from the oil-refinery and port town of Sines, the Alentejo offers a succession of captivating small hill towns and villages, each one home to specific craft traditions and, more often than not, a medieval castle. Nor does history end there: On deserted hillsides animated only by sheep, you will find silent menhirs, dolmens, and cromlechs going back millennia.

Three District Capitals

The main interest radiates from three district capitals: Évora, Portalegre, and Beja. Évora lies at the center of high culture, both inside its walls and in nearby towns such as Estremoz, Vila Viçosa, and Elvas. Industrial Portalegre opens the way to some beautiful villages, to the Lusitanian horse stables of Alter do Chão, and to the Serra de São Mamede natural park, a wild, hilly region that is perfect for hiking.

Dominating the plains to the south, Beja links up easily with seductive small towns such as Serpa and Mértola, as well as the protected natural park of the Guadiana Valley. And to the west are the beaches: endless stretches of sand alternating with dramatically high cliffs from where fearless anglers pitch their lines. An asset of the region is the abundance of signposts and

NOT TO BE MISSED:

Exploring the historic center of Évora **209–213**

Wandering around the fortified hill town of Estremoz **218–219**

The sumptuous Duke's Palace at Vila Viçosa **220–221**

Hiking across the fields to the Tapadão dolmen **224**

The narrow lanes of the Castelo de Vide Jewish quarter **226**

Enjoying the peace and quiet of the Alentejo's deserted beaches **233–235**

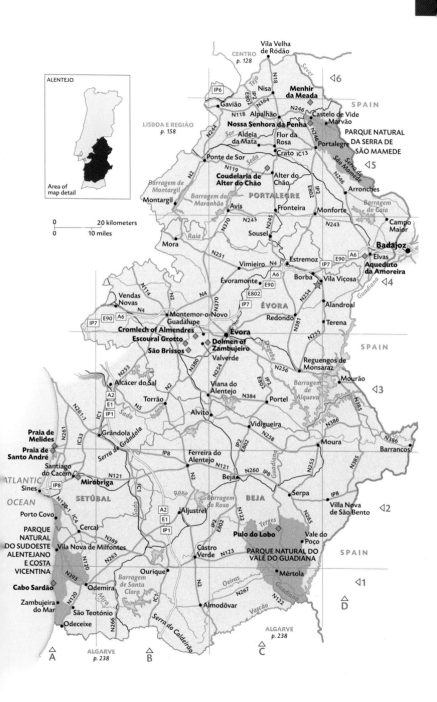

surprisingly good roads, making it possible to drive from north to south in under four hours, despite the lack of major highways. Although the Spanish and Algarve borders are delineated by craggy hills, most of the Alentejo is composed of easily negotiated, low-lying, rolling hills. Its villages are built for the intense summer heat: narrow streets lined with orange trees and low, white and saffron yellow or cobalt blue houses with tiny windows. The cuisine features hearty lamb, pork, kid, chicken, and game conjured into delicious dishes with chickpeas, coriander, clams, and lashings of virgin olive oil. The smooth red wines made from Aragonês, Periquita, and Trincadeira grapes or the delicate, slightly tart whites of Roupeiro and Antão Vaz grapes are delicious. Today's winemaking methods are highly modernized, but a few small-scale producers still age wine in clay vessels, an ancient Alentejo tradition. ■

▨ **An alleyway in Portalegre decked out for festivities**

ÉVORA & AROUND

There is a distinctly aristocratic feel to Évora, the largest town in the Alentejo, whose population of 55,000-plus includes a large percentage of university students. Ringed by sturdy walls and topped by a cathedral towering above terraced houses, it is both unmistakable and beguiling.

Évora's maze of cobbled streets seems to have no rhyme or reason: Square after square is doggedly asymmetrical, flowers spill over archways, and farms, convents, and modern apartment blocks nudge the outskirts. Around each corner there seems to be a rich mansion, a flamboyant church, or an exceptional structure. Many buildings date from Évora's Renaissance heyday.

Portugal's annexation by Spain in 1580 announced the end of Évora's glory and the beginning of a gentle decline. Yet restoration has done wonders and the entire town is now a World Heritage site. As a bonus, the nearby hills contain impressive megalithic sites, while Montemor-o-Novo and Évoramonte offer medieval castles drenched in atmosphere (see pp. 214–215). There are even a few bullfights in summer.

Évora's unusual urban pattern can be explained by the multiple layers of civilization, starting with the Romans. Then came the Moors, whose imprint is evident in the northern quarter, and finally the Portuguese rulers, who left an array of Gothic, Renaissance, Manueline, neoclassical, mannerist, and baroque architectural styles. The old Jewish quarter *(bet. Rua dos Mercadores & Rua da Moeda)* has its own distinctive layout. If you have a car, leave it outside the walls; parking spaces within are rare and the one-way streets a challenge.

INSIDER TIP:

When you are in Évora, be sure to see the Bones Chapel. It's entirely covered with human skeletons from medieval times.

—MIGUEL CONDEÇO
Product manager, Cooltour Lx

The main hub is the triangular and arcaded **Praça do Giraldo,** a spot for relaxing and sipping a coffee by the 16th-century fountain and church of Santo Antão. This fountain and numerous others throughout the town draw water from the **Água da Prata** (silver water) aqueduct, which spans Rua do Cano, an unspoiled

■ Évora's impressive aqueduct, built in the 1530s, plays a curious multi-functional role.

neighborhood well worth exploring in the northwest of town. The 1530s aqueduct was the work of Francisco de Arruda, of Torre de Belém fame (see pp. 68–69).

Lower Évora

It is an easy walk downhill from Praça do Giraldo to lower Évora and the **Igreja de São Francisco** (*Praça 1° de Maio, tel 266 704 521*). The church's Gothic-Manueline style dates from the years of Manuel I and João II; their royal emblems, an armillary sphere and pelican, respectively, decorate the large Manueline doorway. But the most famous site is inarguably the adjoining **Capela dos Ossos** (Bones Chapel; $). The Franciscans built this ossuary to induce meditative qualities among their brethren. Embedded in the walls and columns are the bones and skulls of some 5,000 people, collected from overflowing cemeteries, and—even more cheerful —two mummified corpses; in contrast, the ceiling is beautifully and delicately painted.

Recover from the ossuary on a shaded bench in the **Jardim Público** immediately south of the church. The restructured palace of Manuel I dominates this park. Then stroll northwest past the shops and restaurants of the former Jewish quarter, cutting through to Rua Serpa Pinto to the **Convento de Santa Clara** (*tel 266 088 771, closed Sun.–Mon.*). This 1450s church and Franciscan convent was once home to the saintly princess Dona Joana. It boasts a superbly painted ceiling, carved wood, and decorative azulejos of the 16th and 17th centuries.

Upper Évora

Uphill from Praça do Giraldo you'll come to upper Évora and the main concentration of the city's monuments and atmospheric backstreets. The twin towers of the fortress-like **Sé** (cathedral; *tel 266 759 330*) reign over Évora. The transitional Romanesque-Gothic style

Évora's 1,900-year-old Templo Romano was only unearthed a century ago.

of the cathedral dates from the late 12th century, with subsequent additions including the impressive 14th-century stone Apostles adorning the main portal. The cathedral proudly claims that the pennants of Vasco da Gama were blessed here in 1497, before his fleet set sail on its voyage to the East. The cathedral's **cloister** and **treasury** *($)*, accessed via the south tower, are the main interest inside.

The dazzling church plate, statuary, paintings, and heavily embroidered ecclesiastical robes show evidence of Évora's influential role in Portuguese history. The lovely 14th-century cloister boasts the tombs of four archbishops, and stairs in each corner spiral up to great views from the walls.

Around the corner from the Sé you are confronted by the visual anomaly of the second-century **Tem-plo Romano** *(Largo do Conde de Vila Flor)*. It is also called the Templo de Diana, although there is no proof that it was ever dedicated to this goddess; Jupiter is currently considered a contender. This ruin certainly tops any in Portugal. Encircled by structures that are some 1,400 years younger, it makes a moving site. The temple's granite Corinthian columns and their

---

INSIDER TIP:

For the best food in Évora, book a table at O Fialho; it has been serving traditional food made from quality regional ingredients for three generations (see p. 309).

three generations (see p. 309).

—EMMA ROWLEY
National Geographic contributor

Estremoz marble capitals stand in surprisingly good condition, perhaps because the temple was converted into a medieval fortress and only exposed in the 19th century.

Évora's Roman past is also on show at the **Termas Romanas** *(tel 266 777 000, closed Sat.–Sun.)* inside the Câmara Municipal on Praça do Sertório. At the back of the lobby, a glazed wall overlooks the remains of Roman baths from the second and third centuries A.D.

Facing the Roman temple, the 16th-century **bishop's palace** houses the newly renovated **Museu Nacional Frei Manuel do Cenáculo.** Look in particular for Jean Pénicaud's beautiful "Passion Triptych" (1510–1540), an unusual work of enamel on copper; Francisco Henriques's large and expressive painting of "Prophet Daniel Releasing Chaste Suzanne" (1508–1512); and two lovely paintings by Josefa de Óbidos, which reveal her great feel for light. The exquisite

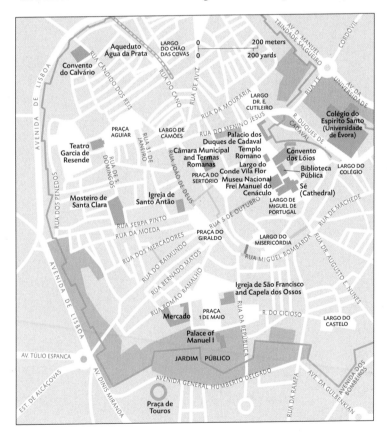

EXPERIENCE: Évora's Megaliths by Bike

To experience firsthand the mysteries of prehistoric Alentejo, you need to get up close to its Neolithic megaliths and soak up the surrounding atmosphere. One of the best ways to visit the stones is by bike, quietly pedaling and enjoying the ancient ambience. **Bikeiberia** *(Largo Corpo Santo 5, Lisbon, tel 969 630 369 or* *213 470 347, bikeiberia.com)* offers a one week guided tour *($1,900, 6 nights & 7 days)* that departs from Évora. The itinerary is moderately difficult with daily legs of 14 to 41 miles (23 to 66 km). There are stops along the route to admire archeological sites, olive groves, vineyards, forgotten villages, and breathtaking views.

marble tomb sculptures exemplify the quality craftsmanship of Évora in the 15th century.

Just next door, the former **Convento dos Lóios** dates from 1485 and is now the very elegant Pousada Convento de Évora (see pp. 308–309). The **Igreja dos Lóios,** a private family church, stands a few doors away and serves as the pantheon for its owners, the Dukes of Cadaval.

The breathtaking azulejos are the 1711 work of António de Oliveira Bernardes. Both the church and adjacent **Palace of the Dukes of Cadaval** are open to visitors *(tel 967 979 763, palaciocadaval.com, closed Mon., $).* Wedged between the convent and church, the **Biblioteca Pública,** founded in 1805, protects a valuable collection of documents related to Portugal's age of discoveries.

Évora's Environs

Évora's surroundings offer a fascinating range of sites, from incredible megaliths studding the hills to the delightful towns of Montemor-o-Novo and Évoramonte.

Megaliths Tour: The entire north of the Alentejo region is peppered with Neolithic structures dating from between 4000 and 2000 B.C. The megaliths are open-air and access is not restricted. If you are short of time, limit yourself to the **Cromlech of Almendres.** Ten miles (16 km) west of Évora, the cromlech stands on a hillside of cork oaks just beyond the village of Guadalupe. Ninety-five menhirs (vertical stones) form an oval that aligns with the equinoxes. If you are there alone, it is

Museu Nacional Frei Manuel do Cenáculo 🄼 Map p. 212 ✉ Largo do Conde de Vila Flor ☎ 266 730 480 🕐 Closed Mon. 🛈 $ **cm-evora.pt**
Igreja dos Lóios & Palácio dos Duques de Cadaval 🄼 Map p. 212 ✉ Largo do Conde de Vila Flor ☎ 266 704 714 🕐 Closed Mon. 🛈 $$
palaciocadaval.com • **Évora & Around** 🄼 207 B3-B4, C3

an extremely powerful site, made more so with the view of Évora on the plain below. A lone 8-foot-tall (2.5 m) menhir is signposted on the way up to the cromlech, hidden behind grain bins.

The **Dolmen of Zambujeiro,** near the village of Valverde, measures almost 20 feet (6 m) long, making the prehistoric monument the largest in Iberia. A last site on this trail is the unusual dolmen-chapel at **São Brissos.** If you're interested in even older history, visit the caves at **Escoural Grotto** *(reservations required, visitas escouralmaltravieso.com),* a few miles west of the Zambujeiro dolmen. The cave paintings of animals are thought to date from 18,000 to 13,000 B.C.

Montemor-o-Novo: The town of Montemor-o-Novo lies just a short distance northwest of the megaliths, yet tourists often mistakenly bypass it. The presence of Moorish kings, Christian knights, and Portuguese royalty is undeniable. The decisions to go on the voyages of discovery to India and to build the University of Coimbra were made in the palace here, the ruins of which are visible on the southern edge of the citadel that crowns the hill.

From the 13th through the 15th centuries, Montemor wielded enor-

mous economic and religious sway, but from the 16th century on, the population moved downhill to create the "new" town. Visit the landscaped **citadel;** the 16th-century Dominican **Convento da Saudação** at the entrance serves as a residential workshop for performing artists.

A few worthwhile sites in the town below include the **Igreja Matriz** *(Largo São João de Deus).* It and the adjoining 17th-century convent were built on the birthplace of St. John of God (1495–1550), a Franciscan who founded the Order of Brothers Hospitallers; his statue stands outside. An annex of the convent, the **Galeria Municipal** *(Terreiro de São João de Deus)* stages interesting exhibitions by young artists, as does a gallery in the **Convento de São Domingos** *(Largo Prof. Dr. Banha de Andrade, tel 266 890 235, closed Sat.–Sun.).*

Évoramonte: Some 19 miles (30 km) northeast of Évora, Évoramonte is really a castle with a village attached as an afterthought. Towering above the plains, the **Castelo de Évoramonte** *(tel 268 950 025, closed Mon.–Tues. a.m.)* has three floors and four corner towers seemingly held together with stone knots on each facade—odd, but typical of the House of Bragança, whose motto *Despois vós,*

■ Ninety-five menhirs form the magical Cromlech of Almendres, a site probably once used for ritual prayers and meetings.

nós (After you, us) played with the second meaning of *nós:* "knots."

Built in 1531 after an earthquake devastated the original fortifications of Dom Dinis I, and based on a design by Diogo de Arruda, the new castle imitated the French château of Chambord. Its Renaissance style contains a superb, empty interior of rib vaulting and sturdy columns topped by carved capitals. A tight spiral staircase linking the floors eventually brings you to a roof terrace once used for shooting practice. Today it is yet another of Portugal's perfect lookout points.

The main street beside the castle runs along the walled ridge to end at the 16th-century church of **Santa Maria,** whose impressive interior is only open during services. Have a look, too, at the local handicrafts displayed and sold at the tourist office. ■

Évoramonte 207 C4 **Visitor Information** Rua de Santa Maria 268 959 227 **cm-estremoz.pt**

PORTUGAL'S SEPHARDIC JEWS

Portugal's Sephardic Jews played a significant role in the country's burgeoning economy and made major scientific and economic contributions that enabled the glorious discoveries of the 15th and 16th centuries. The word "Sefarad" is actually Hebrew for "Spain" and refers to the Jewish communities that flourished in the Iberian Peninsula for centuries, before their dissolution at the end of the 15th century.

The first records of Jewish presence in Portugal date from the late fifth century, when the Visigoths replaced Roman rule. From then on, this minority took root and by the 12th century the city of Santarém had become home to the first national synagogue. Later, synagogues appeared in Porto, Viseu, Guarda, Covilhã, Torre de Moncorvo, Évora, and Faro. Wherever there were more than 10 Jews, a commune *(aljama)* was founded, centering on a synagogue that served not only as a place for study and prayer but also as a mouthpiece for edicts by the king and by the head rabbi.

Portugal's Jewish community was encouraged to help the newfound nation in its struggle with its Moorish occupiers and populate the reconquered lands; however, the early 13th century saw the first friction between Jews and Catholics. Afonso II soon passed repressive legislation that forbade Jews from having Christian servants or being appointed to official positions. Sancho II later scaled back this attempt to reduce the Jews' status, but complaints were made to the pope about such a "lax" approach. Under the enlightened Dom Dinis I (1279–1325), the Sephardic communities were answerable to their head rabbi through representatives in each of their main centers.

Each community had a school and a Beth Hamidrash, where the scriptures were read and analyzed, as well as a Genesim for the study of the Torah. The community's livelihood came from medicine, handicrafts, and agriculture, but the Jewish community truly excelled in commerce, contributing greatly to the national economy but at the same time stirring up envy.

The Spanish Inquisition's Effect

Proof of their prosperity was the growing number of Jewish communities, which multiplied from about 30 in 1400 to more than 100 by the 1490s, with an estimated population of 30,000 (3 percent of the total population). The largest communities were in Lisbon, Évora, Santarém, and Covilhã. The rapid rise resulted from the influx of immigrants fleeing anti-Semitism in Spain. The last wave came in

1492, when the Spanish rulers Ferdinand and Isabel had completed their *reconquista*. The large Sephardic community in Spain was told to convert or go into exile, and 50,000 to 70,000 Jews fled across the border to Portugal.

Unfortunately, their sanctuary was short-lived. In 1497, in order to marry Isabel, daughter of the Spanish monarchs, Manuel I was forced to impose the same maxim as in Spain. Some Jews emigrated to the colonies and the rest were forcibly converted (adopting surnames such as Cruz, Trindade, and Santos). In 1536 the situation worsened when João III allowed the Inquisition to be set up by papal edict; the first auto-da-fé took place four years later. Nearly five centuries on, a Crypto-Jewish community was discovered in Belmonte, still worshipping in secret after all those years. In 1989, President Mário Soares publicly apologized to the Jewish people, and in 2015 the "Law of Return" was passed by Portugal and Spain, which gave descendants of Jews driven out of those countries the opportunity to obtain Portuguese or Spanish citizenship. This initiative has brought thousands of Jews back to Portuguese land and with them new energy to local communities.

» **The 1460 synagogue of Tomar saw only a few years of use before the 1497 expulsion of Jews.**

ESTREMOZ

Estremoz is arguably the Alentejo's most impressive fortified town, thanks to its massive Vauban-style walls and gateways. There are two sections: the older, walled quarter, and the more functional 17th- and 18th-century town below that nonetheless holds plenty of interest.

Try to reach the hilltop quarter by sunset to watch the colors paint the hills to the west; alternatively, target Saturday morning, when the town's main square below welcomes a huge and colorful market. Estremoz is primarily agricultural and increasingly developed in wine production, with some 20 wineries in the region. It is also the largest of the Alentejo's three main marble-producing towns.

The Walled Town

The medieval quarter is dominated by the palace and castle, most of which is now a sumptuous inn, the Pousada Castelo Estremoz (see p. 308). Only the iconic machicolated keep, the

Torre das Três Coroas, remains from the original medieval castle, which was blown up in 1698. Rebuilt, the castle was later sacked by the French army in 1808, but it remained standing. Legend says that the castle owes its survival to the protective ghost of the widow of Dom Dinis I, St. Isabel, who died here in 1336 and whose statue stands outside. Today you can admire the reception areas of the palatial pousada, which offers free access to the keep and its fabulous views. Do not miss the **Capela da Rainha Santa** (Queen Isabel's Chapel; *closed Mon.; get key from the Galeria de Desenho in the Museu Municipal*) tucked behind, where magnificent azulejos illustrate the life of the saintly

EXPERIENCE: Visit a Local Winery

The Alentejo area is dotted with small-scale *adegas* (wineries) that you can visit, all on the Rota dos Vinhos (Alentejo Wine Route). A wonderful one in the Estremoz area is **J. Portugal Ramos** *(Adega Vila Santa, Estrada Nacional 4, Estremoz, tel 268 339 919, jportugal ramos.com, $$$–$$$$$).* You can choose from a variety of offers, from a simple tasting of four wines to a complete tour of the winery or to an interesting "winemaker for a day" tour during which you can create your own wine. You see the whole winemaking process, from grape pressing and fermentation to aging and bottling. There is no shortage of cooking classes and dinners with pairings of the winery's best wines. To learn about other wineries—visitable or not—see *vinhosdoalentejo.pt.*

■ Panoramic views of the Alentejo are assured from Estremoz's 13th-century Torre das Três Coroas.

queen. Across the square, the **Museu Municipal Joaquim Vermelho** (*Largo Dom Dinis, tel 268 339 219, closed Mon., $*) is housed in a charming 16th-century building. Wide-ranging exhibits include rural artifacts, reconstructed period rooms, cork sculptures, and traditional clay figurines, some of which are miniature masterpieces. The terraces display architectural fragments, and a potter's workshop gives demonstrations. The prominent **Galeria Municipal Dom Dinis** (*Largo Dom Dinis, closed Mon.*), originally Dom Dinis's Audience Hall, sits on a corner of the square. Admire the carved Manueline capitals on the colonnaded porch and the striking clock tower before stepping inside to view the interior. Downhill from this cluster, a residential quarter houses a large Romany population. And halfway down the main street, look for a courtyard lined with raised, numbered doorways, once military barracks and evidence of the town's role in the intermittent wars with Spain.

Outside the Walls

It is a short walk or drive from the city walls down to the main square, the vast **Rossio Marquês de Pombal.** Flanked by trees, churches, and 17th- and 18th-century architecture, this social and commercial hub always harbors a few market stalls along its southern side. Vendors sell everything from local cheese to sheep- or goatskin products, ceramics, sausages, and vegetables; they multiply on Saturdays. The 17th-century **Igreja dos Congregados** towers over the market stalls. The church's blinding white marble interior is accessible through the modest, upper-floor **Museu de Arte Sacra** (*tel 967 528 298, closed Mon., $*). You'll also be given access to the rooftop terrace; the 360-degree view takes in the baroque **Igreja de São Francisco** on the opposite side of the square. This church shows off more local marble and, above all, a Tree of Jesse of carved gilded wood to the left of the altar. ■

Estremoz 🄰 207 C4 **Visitor Information** ✉ Rossio Marquês de Pombal 88A ☎ 268 339 227 **cm-estremoz.pt**

VILA VIÇOSA & BORBA

Vila Viçosa and Borba are joined by the tradition of marble, but beyond that they differ greatly. Vila Viçosa is a one-palace, one-castle town, while Borba, just a few miles distant, is a much more cheerful place—maybe it has something to do with the robust red wine it produces.

■ **The Sala dos Duques and the rest of the royal palace at Vila Viçosa reflect a regal splendor.**

What Vila Viçosa shares with Borba is an abundance of marble; the 2.5 miles (4 km) between the two towns is one uninterrupted stretch of quarries. In Borba, door frames, wainscoting, and front steps of even humble dwellings are of the subtly veined white marble, while Vila Viçosa boasts more than 20 marble-clad churches.

Vila Viçosa

Vila Viçosa's famed **Paço Ducal** *(Terreiro do Paço, tel 268 980 659, fcbraganca.pt, closed Mon.–Tues. a.m., $$)*, or Duke's Palace, could rival Versailles, albeit on a mini scale. The fourth Duke of Bragança commissioned the palace in 1501; the construction took more than a century, with further additions made once the Braganças acceded to the Portuguese throne in 1640. The result is a megafacade 360 feet (110 m) long, although it is surprisingly shallow. The 78 rooms once saw a stream of noble visitors, some coming to enjoy the *tapada* (hunting ground) across the road, others to watch bullfights on the huge square (Terreiro do Paço).

The penultimate king to live here, Carlos, left an indelible mark in dozens of accomplished paintings in post-impressionist style. Tragically, Carlos set off from the palace one February morning in 1908 never to return; he and his son, the crown prince, were assassinated later that day in Lisbon. His rooms remain relatively unchanged from when he lived here.

The obligatory one-hour guided tour of the palace is, for the moment, only in Portuguese (though some guides speak some English and are happy to explain a little); so to best grasp the sophistication of the Braganças consult the English catalog, which details the main features covered during the tour. The palace still contains a wealth of decorative arts, from Brussels and Gobelins tapestries to Venetian chandeliers, 17th-century frescoed ceilings, Chinese porcelain, Italian majolica, and Arraiolos and Persian carpets. The **Sala dos Duques** (Room of the Dukes) honors the dukes of Bragança: the Italian artist Giovanni Domenico Dupra painted 18 of their portraits on the ceiling. One of the more revealing sections is the last addition made to the palace, the 1762 **new wing** of apartments. More intimately scaled, these rooms give an idea of the monarchs' personal interests, whether Dom Carlos's wardrobe of uniforms or his wife Amélia's own drawings of botany and architecture. The **kitchens** are the final site on the tour. They gleam with copper pans once swung by no fewer than 26 chefs and sous-chefs, while more attendants slaved in the pantry. Other tours take in the carriage museum, the impressive armory, and the porcelain collection.

You exit the palace grounds via the **Porta do Nó,** an interestingly carved marble and schist gateway that incorporates several knots, the symbol of the Braganças, into its design. Follow the main avenue south from the palace to reach the castle walls. Inside, a small community huddles up beside the 14th-century Gothic **Nossa Senhora da Conceição,** built on the ruins of the original church. Recently fully restored, the church is home to some rich azulejo panels. The **Coleção de Caça and Coleção Arqueologia** (tel 268 980 128, closed Mon.–Tues. a.m., $), are located inside the castle complex and house pieces connected to hunting practices and artifacts from Roman times.

To fully grasp the importance of marble to this region's history and economy, make a quick stop at the **Museu do Mármore Raquel de Castro** (Av. Duque D. Jaime, Olival da Gradinha, tel 268 889 310, closed Mon., $), located in a former train station on the northern edge of town. Photographs and three-dimensional models take you through the extraction and transformation process.

Borba

Borba's interest is far more prosaic. Once you have seen the main square, **Praça da República,** dominated by a huge marble fountain and overlooked by a modest town hall, head toward the castle turrets. Opposite them, a cobbled street leads uphill to the 16th-century church of **São Bartolomeu,** around which a handful of antiques and secondhand goods shops spill their wares. Borba's wine is now one of Portugal's best, celebrated during the wine festival held every November. The **Festa do Vinho e da Vinha** (Wine and Vineyard Festival) enlivens the little town for about 10 days with wine-related events, as well as with concerts and street artist performances ∎

Vila Viçosa 🅜 207 C4 **Visitor Information** ✉ Praça da República ☎ 268 889 317 **cm-vilavicosa.pt** • **Borba** 🅜 207 C4 **Visitor Information** 🅜 Avenida 25 de Abril ☎ 268 891 630 **cm-borba.pt**

PORTALEGRE & SERRA DE SÃO MAMEDE

Somewhat out on a limb, nudging both the Spanish border and that of the Beiras area, Portalegre is not on the main tourist circuit. It is, however, the gateway to the hills of São Mamede and to a number of offbeat villages in the Alentejo plains.

■ A lone watchtower projecting over the rock face of Marvão surveys the Serra de São Mamede.

Surrounded by vineyards that give way to oak and chestnut forests, Portalegre's most visible site from afar is not, for once, a castle or a cathedral, but the belching twin chimneys of a cork-processing factory founded in the 19th century. Historically, however, the town's prosperity stemmed from textile manufacturing, and its international fame derived from its tapestries that vied with those of Aubusson.

The Robinson cork factory has now been relocated to an industrial park on the outskirts of town, and the old factory and adjoining **Igreja**

Portalegre 🗺 207 C5 **Visitor Information** ✉ Rua Guilherme Gomes Fernandes 22 ☎ 245 307 445 **cm-portalegre.pt** • **Museu da Tapeçaria** ✉ Rua da Figueira 9, Portalegre ☎ 245 307 530 🕐 Closed Mon. 💲 $ **mtportalegre.pt**

de São Francisco have been restored. The factory, now **Museu Robinson** (*Rua D. Iria Gonçalves Pereira 2A, tel 245 202 091, closed Sun.–Mon.*), tells the story of cork and its importance to the economy of the region.

A strong drive for renewal is apparent throughout the town with work on the old town walls, the renovation of the castle, the creation of a regional crafts market, the construction of underground parking lots, and more. At its heart, Portalegre has a rich history whose imprint is apparent in the baroque mansions within its walls, as well as a 16th-century **Sé** (*Praça do Município, closed Sun. p.m.–Mon.*) containing mannerist paintings. The cathedral's facade, redone in the 18th century, is a fine example of baroque workmanship. Across the road, the former seminary now houses the **Museu Municipal** (*Rua José Maria de Rosa, 245 307 525, closed Mon., $*) and its rich collection of religious and decorative arts: Look for the 15th-century Spanish pietà in carved wood, a rare 17th-century ebony tabernacle, and some striking Arraiolos rugs. From here, the pedestrianized Rua 19 de Junho, lined with baroque houses, runs southeast through the Porta de Alegrete to the **Praça da República,** an architecturally harmonious square filled with outdoor cafés. The castle is just north of here, but little remains.

Portalegre's unique cultural site lies downhill from the Sé at the **Museu da Tapeçaria,** honoring Guy Fino, the cofounder of the town's tapestry revival in 1946. A personal docent guides you past looms, a wall of 1,150

Knights Hospitaller in Crato

Formed in 11th-century Jerusalem to protect pilgrims to the Holy Land, the Order of the Knights Hospitaller of St. John of Jerusalem became one of the most powerful political forces in Europe. Dislodged from Jerusalem and then Cyprus by Muslim forces, they eventually settled on the island of Malta in 1530. Their troubles did not end there: In 1565 the Ottoman Empire waged a bloody war against them in an aim to remove them from the Mediterranean. After huge loss of life, the Muslim forces retreated, allowing the knights to use their enormous wealth to rebuild their stronghold and regional influence. Crato became home to the Portuguese branch of the Knights Hospitaller in 1340, when it was moved from the Porto area onto lands donated by Sancho II. Crato castle housed the order until 1356, when Prior Álvaro Gonçalves Pereira ordered the building of the Flor da Rosa palace-monastery, a mile (1.6 km) down the road. Its architecture is defensive, giving the appearance of a castle rather than a religious building; its cloister bears the cross of Malta, as the order later became known. It is possible to spend the night in the imposing 14th-century monastery tower, as it is now home to the very comfortable Pousada Mosteiro do Crato (see p. 310).

different colors of wool (more than 5,000 are in fact used), and a chronological display of tapestries from 1947 (the earliest depicts the huntress Diana) to simpler, more graphic 1990s pieces by Lourdes Castro.

Around Portalegre

The bewitching village of **Crato** lies 21 miles (34 km) due west of Portalegre. Its historical significance dates from 1350, when it headquartered the powerful Order of the Knights Hospitaller (later the Order of Malta; see sidebar p. 223), and its castle hosted two royal weddings (Manuel I and João III). Today the town is a sleepy but beautiful little place, all saffron yellow and white, with some stunning medieval, Manueline, and baroque architecture. All streets lead to the elegant **Praça do Município.** Here you'll find the **Museu Municipal do Crato** (tel 245 990 115, cm-crato .pt, closed Mon., $), housed in a pretty baroque mansion and focusing on megalithic artifacts (there are 72 sites nearby), Roman pieces, and heirlooms of the Order of Malta. It has also displayed a section of Portuguese contemporary art since 2019. Don't miss the picturesque ruins of a 13th- to 17th-century **castle** on Crato's eastern edge.

One mile (1.6 km) north of Crato, the satellite village of **Flor da Rosa** grew around its 14th-century fortified

EXPERIENCE: Balloning Over the Alentejo Plains

To fully appreciate the open plains of the Alentejo, take to the air. Whether skimming above the cork oaks and cattle or sailing silently above castles and whitewashed villages, there is no better way to get the Alentejo into true perspective. **Wind Passenger Balloning** (tel 243 660 006 or 927 585 536, windpassenger.pt) offers year-round balloning adventures from a variety of locations across the country, including Portalegre; prices vary based on availability.

monastery. This massive construction stands in scenic isolation, with a couple of village streets curling round it, the interior now converted into the strikingly modern Pousada Mosteiro do Crato (see p. 310).

From here, head 5 miles (8 km) due west to see the largest dolmens in the area, that of **Tapadão,** near the village of Aldeia da Mata, and of **Penedos de São Miguel.** The last stop on this circuit, **Alter do Chão** is another village dominated by a castle, replete with ornate fountains and baroque mansions. The main attraction is the world-famous stud farm

Crato 🅜 207 C5 • **Flor da Rosa** 🅜 207 C5 **Visitor Information** ✉ Mosteiro de Santa Maria de Flor da Rosa ☎ 245 997 341

of **Coudelaria de Alter** *(Tapada do Arneiro, tel 245 610 060, alterreal.pt, closed Mon., $$$, reservations required)* where Alter Real Lusitanian horses are trained. An exhibit details the 250-plus-year history of the former royal stables. You can tour the stables, riding school, and falconry section.

Serra de São Mamede

Look north from Portalegre and you see the abrupt hills of the Serra de São Mamede, which rise to 3,000 feet (1,027 m). Much of the range lies protected as a 78,000-acre (31,750 ha) **natural park.**

Hiking opportunities abound in this area; local tourist offices and the park headquarters in Portalegre *(Rua Augusto César de Oliveira Tavares 23, tel 245 309 189, natural.pt)* provide trail maps, and a number of overnight shelters *(casas abrigo)* dot the hills.

North, the population is scattered between farms, *quintas* (rural estate houses), enclosed *tapadas* (hunting grounds), and hamlets of two-story houses. In the more inhabited south, low, whitewashed dwellings alternate with the typical *monte* (estate) of the Alentejo. Visitors generally target the small town of Castelo de Vide, straddling a ridge, and the village of Marvão, just 6 miles (10 km) away.

Castelo de Vide, with its castle ruins, web of idyllic flowery, cobbled streets, and majestic main square, is the more charming of the two since it has a life outside tourism. There is little specific interest in the main church, **Santa Maria da Devesa** (1749), but follow Rua Santa Maria uphill to enter the castle walls and a delightful maze

---

Hillside Offerings

The Serra de São Mamede offers an incredibly diverse range of plants and wildlife because it bridges two ecological zones: Atlantic and Mediterranean. The terrain of quartzite, limestone, schist, and granite supports some 800 plants, including oaks, chestnuts, cork oaks, olive trees, and rare mosses and lichens. There are no great rarities among the serra's wildlife, but more than half of Portugal's nesting birds, including the eagle owl, Bonelli's eagle, several vulture species, and the great bustard, are found here. Also seen are Europe's largest bat colony and endemic Iberian species such as Bosca's newt, the Iberian midwife toad, and Schreiber's green lizard. You may also spot the odd fox, red deer, storks (white and black), genets, otters, wild boars, and Egyptian mongooses.

Alter do Chão ⚠ 207 C5 **Visitor Information** ✉ Largo Barreto Caldeira 18, Casa do Álamo ☎ 245 610 004 **cm-alter-chao.pt** • **Serra de São Mamede** ⚠ 207 D5

■ Castelo de Vide, with the white Igreja Matriz, as seen from the castle

of medieval streets. On exiting the walls, follow steps and picturesque alleys into the **Judiaria,** the old Jewish quarter, centered on the Rua da Fonte. On the corner is a tiny two-room synagogue thought to date from the 15th century. At the bottom of the hill, look for the elaborate Manueline fountain with its raised roof and endless supply of pure mineral water.

Megalith aficionados should head north to see the largest known menhir in the Iberian Peninsula, the 23-foot-tall (7 m) **Menir da Meada.** Another short excursion south leads to **Nossa Senhora da Penha,** a hilltop sanctuary with fabulous views north over Castelo de Vide.

To the east lies **Marvão,** named after a ninth-century Moorish horseman, Ibn Maruan. This extraordinary village seems to grow out of the granite outcrop. True walkers should take the ancient paved path to the summit, while lesser mortals can drive up

to the gateway (it is possible to drive in, but best to utilize the carpark outside the walls). The medieval citadel, a stronghold that guarded the region against Spanish attacks, is so complete that it is classed as a World Heritage site; however, the population has dwindled to a mere 180 souls, leaving Marvão with a distinctly artificial "museum" atmosphere.

Wander the town's narrow streets and alleyways to enjoy Renaissance doorways, wrought-iron grilles, and Manueline windows. Don't miss the undeniably beautiful pillory before heading uphill to the **castle,** which has magnificent views in every direction. The Gothic **Igreja de Santa Maria** on the Largo de Santa Maria houses the **Museu Municipal** *(tel 245 909 132, closed Mon., $),* which exhibits a motley collection of statues, a 14th-century fresco, historical costumes, and a Roman skeleton from excavations at nearby Pombais. ■

Castelo de Vide 🗺 207 C5 **Visitor Information** ✉ Praça Dom Pedro V ☎ 245 908 227 **castelodevide.pt** • **Marvão** 🗺 207 D5 **Visitor Information** ✉ Largo da Silveirinha ☎ 245 909 131 **cm-marvao.pt**

DRIVE TO THE GUADIANA VALLEY

From the marble quarries of Vila Viçosa, this drive takes you through the historical villages, olive groves, and grainfields of the central Alentejo to reach Europe's largest artificial lake, Lago Alqueva, in the Guadiana Valley.

From **Vila Viçosa ❶** (see pp. 220–221) follow directions south to Alandroal, leaving town on the N255. After some marble quarries, the road slices through undulating olive groves for 16 miles (25 km); take the road on the left to the center of **Alandroal ❷** (*visitor information, Praça da República, tel 268 440 045*); be prepared for it. As you drive into town you will see the 13th-century **castle** on your right. Park at a square in front of the raised entrance where an

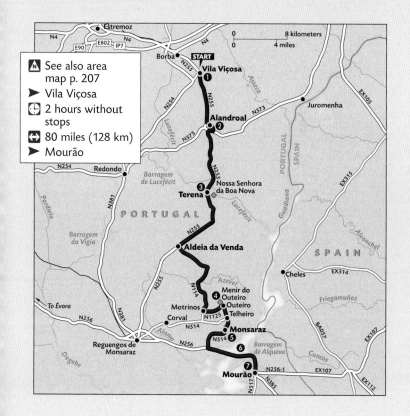

See also area map p. 207

▶ Vila Viçosa

🕐 2 hours without stops

↔ 80 miles (128 km)

▶ Mourão

18th-century marble fountain cools the air. Walk in to enjoy the atmosphere of this towering but empty structure, built for the Order of Avis. Nearby shops specialize in tin, wood, and schist handicrafts.

Leave via the corner diametrically opposite the arch, following a sign to **Terena** ❸ (sometimes referred to as Terena de São Pedro). Stay on the N255 for 17 miles (28 km), winding through open landscapes where only sheep and shepherds dwell. Soon the silhouette of Terena's castle appears on the horizon. Turn left at the sign and drive up to the immaculate village of whitewashed houses, where two main streets run parallel to end at the **castle square.** Wander around the grassy quadrangle inside the castle walls; climb to the ramparts for views and the faint echoes of sheep bells.

Cork oaks and olive trees stud the banks of Lago Alqueva, one of the largest artificial lakes in Europe.

Return to the N255, passing the fortified, stone sanctuary of **Nossa Senhora da Boa Nova,** thought to date from the early 14th century. After about 6 miles (10 km) on the N255, follow a sign for Monsaraz left through the hamlet of **Aldeia da Venda,** after which the road follows the contours of the hillside with distant vistas east and north through olive and eucalyptus groves. Turn right at Seixo to arrive at the typical whitewashed village of Motrinos. From here follow signs left

> **NOT TO BE MISSED:**
>
> Terena • Menir do Outeiro • Monsaraz • Lago Alqueva

to Monsaraz. After a couple of miles you will see a sign for *"anta"* (dolmen). This short circuit takes you to three impressive megaliths, including Europe's most notable phallic menhir, the **Menir do Outeiro ❹,** that of **Belhoa,** and the dolmen of **Olival da Pega.** The circuit takes little more than 20 minutes and ends at Telheiro, at the base of **Monsaraz ❺** *(visitor information, Rua Direita, tel 927 997 316).*

Drive up to this hilltop village, following signs until you can park. In peak season this may be some distance from the main gateway; Monsaraz is a very popular Alentejo destination. This stunning walled enclave, closed to cars, features cobbled alleyways, elegant facades, a ruined castle, numerous craft shops, and the church of Santa Maria da Lagoa. The tiny **Museu do Fresco** *(tel 266 508 040, $)* beside the church displays a 14th-century fresco.

Leave Monsaraz by following signs to Mourão, which take you down to the N256. This road crosses the Guadiana River where it merges with the 96-square-mile (250 sq km) **Lago Alqueva ❻.** Continue to follow signs to **Mourão ❼** *(visitor information, Largo das Portas de S. Bento, tel 266 560 010).* This small fortified town boasts a 17th-century church set into the walls of its castle where, again, the interior has been left to the elements.

BEJA, SERPA & MOURA

The three fortified towns of Beja, Serpa, and Moura in the plains of southern Alentejo make an obvious triangular tour. All have great historical impact, medieval fortifications courtesy of Dom Dinis, and varying degrees of character.

Beja

The principal town of southern Alentejo, with 20,000 inhabitants, Beja towers above the agricultural plains, visible from some 20 miles (32 km) away. The town boasts a well-maintained old quarter and a massive, restored **castelo,** featuring a 138-foot-high (42 m) keep, the tallest in the Iberian Peninsula, which you can climb for sweeping views. Just opposite, Beja's oldest church, Santo Amaro, houses the **Núcleo Visigótico** *(Largo de Santo Amaro, tel 284 321 465),* an informative display of rare fragments from the seventh and eighth centuries. The same square sees Beja's lively fair on the first Saturday of every month—a good place to pick up a live rabbit or chicken. Your ticket to the Visigothic exhibit

Beja  207 C2 **Visitor Information** ✉ Castelo de Beja, Largo Dr. Lima Faleiro ☎ 284 311 913 **cm-beja.pt • Museu Regional de Beja-Núcleo Visigótico** ✉ Largo de Nossa Senhora da Conceição ☎ 284 323 351 🕐 Closed Mon. 💲 $ **museuregionaldebeja.net**

■ The crenellated walls and towers of Beja's splendid castle.

EXPERIENCE: Alentejo Pottery Workshops

While in the Alentejo, try your hand at one of the region's distinctive crafts: pottery. Most regions in Portugal produce their own distinctive designs using locally found materials and methods passed down through the generations. The *oleiros* (potters) of the Alentejo have for centuries made rough, utilitarian pieces from local clay; these earthenware pieces would rarely be decorated or even glazed. As demand for the rustic cooking pot declined, many *olarias* (potteries) simply went out of business, while others adapted and began producing more elaborate pieces using colored glazes to depict the bright floral or fruit designs that are now found across the region.

You can experience an olaria first-hand by signing up for a half-day pottery workshop with **Compadres** *(Rua 5 de Outubro 40–44, tel 284 475 205 or 911 158 696, minimum of 4 people, $$$$$)*, in the village of Redondo, between Évora and Vila Viçosa. After a visit to the village you can try making your own piece out of clay and shaping it with a foot-operated artisan wheel, supervised by a master craftsman. You can then enjoy decorating your creation before it is fired in the kilns; if you cannot pick it up, it will be sent to you for an additional fee.

also gives access to the **Museu Regional,** located in a magnificent 1459 Gothic-Manueline convent. It stands dramatically alone on a large square south of the elegant **Praça da República,** Beja's historic heart. A dazzling array of wall tiles, including 16th-century Mudéjar designs, line the cloister galleries and the chapter house; the latter's ceiling is painted in delicate tempera designs. The full-length "São Vicente," by Mestre do Sardoal, hangs next to an anonymous painting of St. Vincent's martyrdom in a room devoted to 16th- and 17th-century paintings.

Serpa

Small Serpa, 19 miles (30 km) east of Beja, has a greater atmosphere than Beja and feels engagingly forward looking. The crenellated walls enclose narrow cobbled streets, churches, mansions, and some good restaurants. Park your car outside the town walls and take a look at the gnarled, thousand-year-old olive trees before heading to the main square, **Praça da República,** and its outdoor cafés. Its **Torre do Relógio** (Clock Tower) looms over a wide staircase leading up to the church of Santa Maria and the **castelo.**

Serpa 🗺 207 C2 **Visitor Information** ✉ Rua dos Cavalos 19 ☎ 284 544 727 **visitserpa.pt**

The renovated **Museu Munici-pal de Arqueologia** *(tel 284 544 663, closed Mon.)* displays artifacts from the Stone Age to Roman and Moorish times. This upper part of town harbors a web of picturesque narrow lanes as well as the town's most grandiose mansion, the 17th-century **Palácio do Conde do Ficalho** *(closed to the public).*

South of the square at the clock museum, **Museu do Relógio** *(Rua do Assento, tel 284 543 194, museudorelogio .com, closed Mon., $),* guided tours take you through rooms crammed with more than 2,300 watches and clocks. The waterwheel and aqueduct on the Rua dos Arcos, on the western side of the town walls, are worth a look as well. Before you leave, be sure to sample Serpa's famous sheep cheese, *queijadas* (cheesecakes), and robust Pias wine.

Moura

Far less sophisticated, Moura, 19 miles (30 km) north of Serpa, has strong Moorish connections and highly rated olive oil and mineral water. Its name stems from the legend of a Moorish bride-to-be who let Christian hordes through the town gates under the mistaken impression that her beloved was among them. The result? Her suicide from a turret.

The most you will see of this past is the **Poço Árabe,** a 14th-century well *(Largo da Mouraria, tel 285 253 978, closed Mon.)* in the **Mouraria** (Moorish quarter), a web of streets south of the castle. The dilapidated **castle** was erected on the site of a Moorish fort, of which one lathe-and-plaster tower remains. ■

Moura ▲ 207 C3 **Visitor Information** ✉ Moura Castle, Largo de Santa Clara, Pátio dos Rolins ☎ 285 251 375 **cm-moura.pt**

■ A picturesque alley in Moura with the clock tower in the background

ALENTEJO'S COAST

A blissful stretch of semiwild beaches and cliffs edged by a capricious ocean, the Alentejo coast—known locally as the Costa Vicentina—extends some 62 miles (100 km) from the Sado Estuary south to Odeceixe, on the Algarve border. A handful of villages provide services.

Striated rocks and cliffs create vertiginous lookouts, such as at Cabo Sardão.

The lone blemish on the coast is the halfway point of Sines with its petrochemical installations and large shipping port. Otherwise, only low-key villages punctuate the sandy beaches north of Sines and the dramatically chiseled cliffs and coves to the south, protected as far as Sagres as part of the **Parque Natural do Sudoeste Alentejano e Costa Vicentina** (*tel 283 322 735, natural.pt*). To some, the year-round cold water, a constant wind blowing off the Atlantic, and limited facilities

Alentejo coast  207 A1–A3

are a downside, but a growing number of chic guesthouses cater to those who relish these aspects. Rice fields and salt marshes characterize the landscapes around **Alcácer do Sal,** a pretty riverside town famous for its storks and their vertiginous nests. Southwest of here lie the lagoons and beaches of **Melides** and **Santo André,** both rich in birdlife and offering good windsurfing and fishing. A strip of fine white sand between the lagoon and the sea invites breezy, scenic strolls, and a cluster of modest fish restaurants offers the local specialty, eel stew.

South of here and inland, scenic **Santiago do Cacém** is one of the Alentejo's fortified hilltop towns; it was named for the Order of Santiago, which controlled it from 1336 to 1594. The town makes a good base for access to the coast.

Sites in town start at the lively **food market** *(Mercado Municipal, Largo do Mercado, closed Sun.),* where you can stock up on delicious local products. From here it is a steep walk up attractive cobbled streets to the castle. At the gates is the **Igreja Matriz** *(closed Mon.–Tues.),* a lovely church with a theatrical baroque interior. Walk around the castle walls. Below, on the main square, the **Museu Municipal** is housed in the old city jail and displays

> ## Badoca Safari Park
>
> If you're looking for a fun family outing, check out Badoca Safari Park *(Herdade da Badoca, Vila Nova de Santo André, tel 269 708 850, badoca .com, $$$),* 10 minutes from Santiago do Cacém. The park offers activities and attractions for all ages, including a one-hour safari ride in tractor-pulled trailers to observe giraffes, zebras, and gnus; a Tropical Forest area, filled with exotic birds; an interactive lemur sanctuary; and an adventure area complete with a wild rafting ride and 23-foot (7 m) trampolines.

local ethnographic and archaeological pieces beside some fine antiques.

The Roman site of **Miróbriga** lies in the hills about a mile (1.6 km) to the east. Boasting a small, modern museum, it is a lovely rural spot for sitting in the shade of cypress trees, watching sheep, and musing on the Roman past. The first- and second-century ruins include the foundations of baths, a forum with a temple to Venus, and villas. Portugal's only Roman hippodrome, where Lusitanian horses once raced, is half a mile (0.8 km) away.

Santiago do Cacém 🔼 207 A2 **Visitor Information** ✉ Mercado Municipal, Praça do Mercado ☎ 269 826 696 🕐 Closed Sun. **turismo.cm -santiagocacem.pt** • **Museu Municipal** ✉ Praça do Município ☎ 269 827 375 🕐 Closed Sun.–Mon. • **Ruínas Romanas de Miróbriga** ✉ Estrada das Cumeadas ☎ 269 818 460 🕐 Closed Mon. 💲 $

The ruins of Miróbriga, nestled in a calm, bucolic setting

South of Sines

The coast south of Sines, part of the natural park, joins the Algarve's Costa Vicentina (see p. 263). Although cliffs dominate the landscape, there are idyllic coves and beaches in between, served by three low-key resorts. One, **Vila Nova de Milfontes,** in season has an upbeat feel plus a long causeway and a small ivy-clad castle, now an upscale guesthouse. Farther south is the dramatic headland of **Cabo Sardão** and its lighthouse. Follow the dirt road to the top of the cliff and look down the sheer drop to the pounding surf below. Another 8 miles (13 km) south brings you to

Zambujeira do Mar, a little resort overlooking a lovely beach backed by cliffs. A breath-stopping cliff-top path leads south to more wild beaches inaccessible by car. ■

INSIDER TIP:

In autumn the Sagres Peninsula and southern Alentejo coast are a mecca for bird-watchers. You may see up to 2,000 Eurasian griffon vultures at once!

—SIMON WATES
Owner, Algarve Birdwatching

Vila Nova de Milfontes ⚑ 207 A2 **Visitor Information** ✉ Rua António Mantas ☎ 283 996 599 **cm-odemira.pt**

More Places to Visit in the Alentejo

Elvas

This handsome small town lies just 8 miles (12 km) from the Spanish town of Badajoz. You cannot miss the impressive 17th-century fortifications, which include two hilltop forts north and south of the massive curtain walls, nor the **Aqueduto da Amoreira,** built between 1529 and 1622.

At the heart of Elvas is the harmonious **Praça da República,** a square overlooked by a cathedral whose exterior was altered from its original 18th-century Manueline design.

Uphill from here is the old Arab quarter; be sure to see the **Largo de Santa Clara** with its elaborate marble pillory. Beyond is the medieval **castelo** (closed Mon., $), a castle built by Dom Sancho and remodeled in the 15th century, now housing a small military museum (closed Mon., $). The architecture of the town's attractive maze of cobbled streets, archways, emblazoned facades, and stairways gives a strong sense of the progression from Moorish citadel to medieval bastion and 17th-century stronghold. This last period of development is more visible in the southern part of town.

cm-elvas.pt ⚐ 207 D4 **Visitor Information** ✉ Praça da República 2 ☎ 268 622 236

Mértola

Mértola is the last outpost of southeastern Alentejo before the hills of the Algarve. It is a fascinating little town, with some handicraft workshops (notably weaving, ceramics, and jewelry) and Roman and Moorish remains. Idyllically sited on the Guadiana River, Mértola's historic nucleus lies around a restored **castelo,** where a towering keep exhibits Visigothic artifacts (tel 286 610 100, museude mertola.pt, closed Mon.). Just below, archaeological excavations are revealing significant Roman finds (arqueologiainprogress.camertola.pt).

The adjacent **Igreja Matriz de Nossa Senhora da Anunciação** (closed Mon.) was first a Roman temple, then a Paleo-Christian church and even a mosque; its horseshoe arches and the former mihrab are still intact.

Down by the river stands Mértola's oldest site, the **Torre do Rio,** a tower built during the Roman era to defend the river port. On the street above, the **Núcleo de Arte Islâmica** (closed Mon.) presents an impressive display of Moorish ceramics and gravestones; note the brick cupola made by Moroccan artisans in 2002.

Mértola is a good base for canoeing, cycling, and horseback riding; wild boar features on many restaurant menus.

visitmertola.pt 207 C1 **Visitor Information** ✉ Rua da Igreja 1 ☎ 286 610 100

Pulo do Lobo

This extraordinary gorge and waterfall in the **Parque Natural do Vale do Guadiana** is well sign-posted and reached via an easy 10-mile (16 km) dirt road, west from the village of Vale do Poço on the N265, or from the N122 connecting Beja and Mértola. The deserted landscape fosters black storks, Bonelli's eagles, and royal owls, and the fragrant shrubs are rich in myrtle and rosemary. The 44-foot (13.5 m) fall in the river-bed, known as the *corredoira* (run-ner), probably was created by erosion and drops in sea level dur-ing the Quaternary period.
natural.pt 207 C2
☎ 286 612 016

■ The construction of the ambitious aqueduct of Elvas was financed by Por-tugal's first royal water tax.

Portugal's favorite playground, with lovely beaches, great golf courses, and buzzing nightclubs along the southern coast

ALGARVE

Sardines, an Algarve staple, usually grilled

ALGARVE

The name Algarve derives from the Arabic *Al-Gharb,* meaning "the west," pointing to the roots of Portugal's southernmost region, once the Moors' western outpost. A thousand years on, a wall of tourist development extending from Faro west to the beaches of Lagos obscures that past. Yet inland, you will discover delightful swathes of unspoiled landscapes.

Geographically important due to its position near the Mediterranean and the Atlantic, the Algarve was successively fought over by Phoenicians, Romans, Moors, and Christians, today replaced by armies of sunseekers. Portuguese boats set sail on 15th-century voyages of discovery from the port of Lagos,

while Sagres remains symbolic as the purported site of Prince Henry's school of navigation. Few buildings remain from before the 1755 earthquake; the epicenter lay 125 miles (200 km) southwest of Cabo de São Vicente.

Every summer, the Algarve's population swells from some 450,000 to

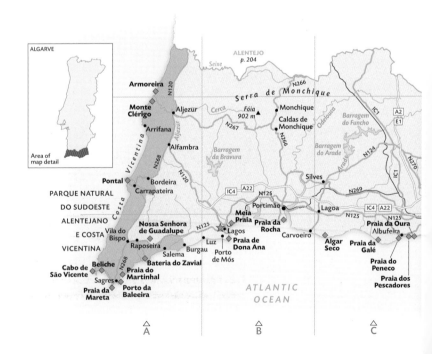

ALGARVE

Area of map detail

ALENTEJO
p. 204

Seixe

Armoreira   N120

Serra de Monchique

N266

Monte Clérigo   Aljezur   Cerca   Fóia   Monchique
                                    902 m
                                            Caldas de
Arrifana   N267   Monchique   Odelouca   Barragem do Funcho   IC1   A2   E1

Alfambra   Aljezur   Barragem da Bravura   Barragem do Arade   N124   N270

Pontal   Bordeira   Silves
PARQUE NATURAL   Carrapateira   IC4   A22   N125   N269   Lagoa   IC4   A22   N125
DO SUDOESTE   Portimão   Praia da Oura
ALENTEJANO   Nossa Senhora   N125   Meia   Praia da   Carvoeiro   Algar   Albufeira
E COSTA   Vila do   de Guadalupe   Lagos   Praia   Rocha   Seco   Praia da
            Bispo   Luz   Praia de   Galé
VICENTINA   Raposeira   Burgau   Porto   Dona Ana   Praia do
        Salema   de Mós   Peneco
Cabo de   Beliche   Bateria do Zavial   ATLANTIC   Praia dos
São Vicente   Praia do   OCEAN   Pescadores
        Sagres   Martinhal
    Praia da   Porto da
    Mareta   Baleeira

A   B   C

more than 1,000,000; nearly half of all visitors to Portugal head straight to this coast. The unfailing lure boils down to three essentials: a sunny year-round climate, beautiful sandy beaches, and scenic golf courses. In addition, some of Portugal's top restaurants cater to a sophisticated cosmopolitan clientele.

Faro, where the recently upgraded airport is located, constitutes the midway point between the more low-key eastern Algarve and the brasher, package-holiday heaven around Albufeira. Faro, too, is where you will get your first glimpse of the lagoons and islets of the Parque Natural da Ria Formosa. Toward the eastern end of this

NOT TO BE MISSED:

The wealth of birdlife in the lagoons of the Ria Formosa 243

Eating grilled sardines riverside in Portimão 247

Picking up a memento from Loulé market 249–250

A day at the spa in Monchique 254

Playing a round of golf at a top course 255–256

Watching the sunset from Cabo de São Vicente 262

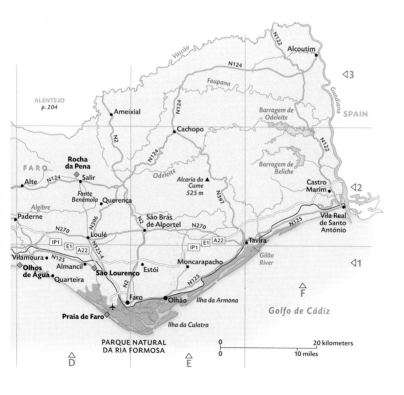

park lies the charming town of Tavira, one of the region's best kept secrets with plentiful offerings from history and gastronomy to peaceful beaches. In the far west, the Costa Vicentina is home to some of Europe's most spectacular beaches and is frequented mainly by surfers and campers.

The low, undulating *serra* (hills) to the north and east remains scenic. Between the serra and coast lies the intermediary band known as the Barrocal—the true agricultural heart of the Algarve. Local market stalls brim with cherries, strawberries, and melons in summer and grapes, figs, and almonds in fall.

You cannot really go wrong here in your choice of food, as the Moors' legacy reveals itself in local cuisine.

Try the delicious *bolinhos de amêndoa* (small marzipan cakes). Sardines and tuna have long been favorites from the deep; clams and other shellfish are steamed in the ubiquitous *cataplanas* (copper pans with domed lids) or stewed with rice. In the hills, pork and poultry enter the menu, joined in autumn by hare soup and stewed partridge. Choose a wine from one of the vineyards near Lagoa, Lagos, Tavira, or Portimão. They produce fruity, full-bodied wines, continuing a tradition first developed by the Phoenicians, and later expanded upon by the Romans.

Algarve's cornucopia of attractions for the mind, body, and spirit will certainly please even the most discerning visitor. ■

■ **The placid harbor of Faro**

FARO & COASTAL ALGARVE

Centered on the southern coast of the Algarve, Faro is the point of arrival for most visitors. To the east lie the low-key towns of Olhão and Tavira, while west as far as Lagos is a succession of idyllic beaches backed by burgeoning development.

The Faro airport lies a short distance from town, right beside the lagoons, salt pans, and sandbank islands that characterize the eastern half of the Algarve. Protected as **Parque Natural da Ria Formosa** *(natural.pt)*, they extend some 30 miles (48 km) northeast to beyond Tavira. This important habitat for birds claims the least tern and purple gallinule among its rarities, as well as more common waterbirds. Some of the Algarve's quietest beaches are found on the *ilhas* (islands) off Faro and Tavira. To the west the shoreline heaves with high-rises and holiday developments, and yet the beauty of the ocher cliffs and white sandy beaches remains undiminished. Albufeira is the hub of this stretch.

one-way road system common to many Portuguese towns, is user-friendly. Known as Ossonoba in pre-Roman days, Faro was once one of southern Portugal's most important settlements. It was much developed in the eighth century by the Moors, integrated

Idyllic beaches line the Algarve coast.

Faro

Faro has an attractive historic center that, apart from a diabolical

Coastal Algarve 🗺 240–241 B1–F2 **Visitor Information** ✉ Avenida 5 Outubro 18–20, Faro ☎ 289 800 400 **turismodoalgarve.pt • Faro** 🗺 241 D1 **Visitor Information** ✉ Rua da Misericórdia 8–11 ☎ 289 803 604

into Portugal in 1249, and later declared capital of the Algarve in the mid-1800s.

Enter the walled **Vila-Adentro** (Inner Town) from the north through the **Arco da Vila,** a monumental gateway added in 1812. This brings you past 19th-century government buildings to the impressive **Largo da Sé,** dominated by the **Sé** *(tel 289 807 590, closed Sun., $).* Only the bell tower and main entrance remain from the original 1251 church, thanks to pillaging by English troops in 1596 and the earthquake in 1755. Look at the azulejos and baroque retable, and then climb the bell tower for fabulous views. The curious shrine across the courtyard dates from before the earthquake; this area was a children's cemetery and the entire structure was constructed from skulls and bones.

The peaceful walled quarter ends to the south at defensive ramparts built by ninth-century Arab ruler Ben Bekr, with towers added three centuries later. To the northeast lies the old *mouraria* (Arab quarter) and a network of pedestrianized shopping streets centered on Rua de Santo António.

East of Faro

From Faro to Olhão, lagoons and islands edge the coastline. The most popular beaches of **Ilha da Culatra** and **Ilha da Armona** can be reached by boat from Olhão.

Olhão: This town is a bit of an anomaly—far from being a beach resort, it's the region's largest fishing port, complete with trawlers, canning factories, and a lively fish market. It has an attractive, bustling air about it, and the pedestrian streets behind the harbor are a joy to wander. Lined with picturesque, peeling facades of both humble and aristocratic buildings, these cobbled streets start at the modest 17th-century parish church on Avenida da República and end at the **Mercado Municipal** (City Market) on the waterfront, where vendors at the morning fish market hawk a fantastic array of creatures. Beside the market, the verdant grounds of the **Jardim Patrão Joaquim Lopes** host Olhão's main festival of seafood and folk music during the second week of August.

Tavira: The last stop east is Tavira, arguably Algarve's most unspoiled town. The Romans developed their fish-salting industry here, and later Tavira flourished under Moorish rule; in the 15th century, it was the chief port for supporting Portuguese overseas garrisons. This led to city status, in 1520. Decline followed in the 17th and 18th centuries, due in part to the silting of the channel, plague outbreaks, and the 1755 earthquake. Tuna fishing and canning again revived Tavira's fortunes,

Olhão 🗺 241 E1 **Visitor Information** ✉ Largo Sebastião Martins Mestre 3B ☎ 289 713 936 **turismodoalgarve.pt**

Shopping at the Olhão fish market is an immersive experience.

and recently it began dabbling in tourism. *Flor de sal* (salt flakes) is another local industry; the flakes are obtained by skimming off young crystals from the pans between May and October. The rest of the year ordinary salt is farmed.

Despite the town's attractive Mediterranean-style architecture along the Gilão River, Tavira has successfully escaped major development. It strives to achieve status as the Algarve's cultural hub through exhibitions, concerts, and innovative structures. The palm-lined river frontage—with two bridges, one of which is originally Roman, fishing boats, and low whitewashed houses—is a classic picture-postcard scene. And there are plenty of outdoor cafés from which to enjoy the view.

Towering above is the hilltop **castelo,** originally Moorish and rebuilt by Dom Dinis. The castle interior blooms with ficus, hibiscus, and bougainvillea, and the top affords panoramic views. On the way up from Rua da Liberdade, you pass the church of the **Misericórdia** *(Travessa da Fonte, Rua da Galeria, tel 281 320 500, closed Sun.)* with its beautiful Renaissance facade by André Pilarte, the master mason who also worked on Lisbon's Mosteiro dos Jerónimos (see pp. 64–67). Inside, look at the statues and gilded retable of the main altar. Just past the church, the **Museu Municipal-Núcleo Islámico** *(tel 281 320 570, museumunicipaldetavira.cm-tavira.pt, closed Sun.–Mon., $)* gives insight into Tavira's Islamic past. At the top of Rua

Tavira  241 F2 **Visitor Information** ✉ Praça da República 5 ☎ 281 322 511 **turismodoalgarve.pt**

Dusk falls over the tiled roofs of Albufeira's whitewashed cubic houses.

da Galeria, stop to see the **Palácio da Galeria** *(tel 281 320 540, closed Sun.–Mon., $)* with its exhibitions of contemporary art.

Beside the castle stands the Gothic church of **Santa Maria** *(closed Sat. p.m.–Sun.)*, dating from the 13th century but much altered since, and with huge external clocks defying all sense of proportion. Another of Tavira's numerous churches is **Igreja de Santiago,** immediately downhill from Santa Maria. It was built on a former mosque and is home to some valuable baroque statues. Just behind the church a rare camera obscura is installed inside an old water tower:

the **Torre de Tavira** *(Calçada da Galeria 12, tel 281 322 527, camera obscuratavira.com, closed Sat.–Sun., $)*. It offers a 30-minute journey through Tavira in real time, giving a fascinating overview.

West of Faro

Some 25 miles (40 km) west of Faro, **Albufeira** is Portugal's most popular package resort town; it is submerged in a sea of development as well as a bewildering network of roads. Despite souvenir shops, bar signs in English and German, and roaming packs of sunburned revelers, the old part of Albufeira to the west maintains some character, with narrow streets of whitewashed houses perched above the beach. The surrounding hills are alive with chaotic vacation apartments, while the modern eastern extension, **Montechoro,** is dedicated to eating, drinking, and entertainment.

The entire seafront is pedestrianized, so you can stroll from one beach to the next. **Praia dos Pescadores,** fronting the old town, provides a whiff of Albufeira's past in colorful, painted fishing boats. Immediately west, **Praia do Peneco** is often jampacked with sunbathers, but venture beyond to **Praia da Galé,** or east to **Praia da Oura** and **Olhos de Água,** and you come to vast stretches of sand and pretty coves that are far less crowded. Most of the Algarve's golf courses concentrate between Praia da Oura and Faro, notably at **Vilamoura.**

The most photographed beach, **Praia da Rocha,** lies farther west, due south of **Portimão,** whose only claim to fame is sardines (see sidebar below). This beach kicked off tourism in the Algarve in the 1950s and 1960s, drawing crowds to its very scenic red-ocher cliffs, craggy outcrops, and clear water. Today the central thoroughfare, Avenida Tomas Cabreira, is lined with tourist facilities, and a ruined **fort** at the mouth of the Arade River now overlooks a marina. **Carvoeiro,** 3 miles (5 km) south of Lagoa, is yet another picturesque fishing village on a cliff-backed cove that has seen a radical transformation. Immediately east is **Algar Seco,** a popular beauty spot of eroded cliffs and extraordinary rock formations. ■

Albufeira ⚠ 240 C1 **Visitor Information** ✉ Rua 5 de Outubro ☎ 289 585 279 **turismodoalgarve.pt** • **Praia da Rocha** ⚠ 240 B1 **Visitor Information** ✉ Avenida Tomas Cabreira ☎ 282 419 132 **turismodoalgarve.pt**

Sardines

Grilled sardines, one of Portugal's most typical dishes, can be found in any coastal town between May and October; however, many would argue that the best place to eat sardines is riverside in Portimão. So famous is Portimão for its grilled sardines that in 1994 it staged a Sardine Festival, now a firm fixture on its annual calendar. For a week in August, the Zona Ribeirinha (riverbank area) serves over 80,000 visitors grilled sardines with a hunk of bread, roasted green-pepper salad, and a jug of wine. Stalls sell local delicacies and crafts and the evenings feature live music and dancing. For more information, contact the Portimão Tourist Office (tel 282 430 165).

EXPERIENCE: Follow the Cork Route

As you travel around central and southern Portugal, you'll see acres upon acres of the cork oak—*Quercus suber*. The cultivation of this evergreen tree has been of vital importance to the national economy for centuries. Immerse yourself in the heritage and tradition of cork by spending a day with **Algarve Rotas** (*Eco-Cork Factory, Sítio da Mesquita Baixa, São Brás de Alportel, tel 965 561 166, algarverotas.com, $$$*), following the cork route.

North of Faro, Algarve Rotas takes visitors through the whole cork process, from the tree to the factory, explaining its heritage and traditions. You'll walk through cork groves along ancient trails, explore rural life as it has been for hundreds of years, and watch cork masters at work using traditional methods. The cork harvest is still done by hand, June through August, using age-old and totally natural methods. Harvesters use a small axe to cut sections of bark, which they then pry off in strips, using the handle of the axe. As you follow the cork route, you'll learn Portugal produces some 50 percent of the world's cork and is home to one-third of the world's cork oak forests. Today, the cork oak accounts for about 16 percent of Portugal's foreign trade income.

Cork oaks need abundant and evenly distributed rainfall as well as short dry summer periods, mild winters, clear skies, lots of sun, and deep siliceous soil. All these conditions come together especially well in central and southern Portugal, with the very best quality cork coming from the Algarve and parts of the Alentejo. The trees take 25 to 30 years to reach maturity, by which time their bark—the cork—is ready to be harvested. The tree will then take 9 to 10 years to grow new bark and be ready for harvest again. Portugal presently has some 650 companies working in the cork sector, equipped to produce all types of cork items for domestic and industrial use: cigarette tips, flooring, table mats, floats, and insulation for such diverse areas as shipping, homes, and even the space program. This in addition to the 40 million stoppers it produces daily.

Feira da Serra

Another way you can become more acquainted with the cork oak is to attend the Feira da Serra (Mountain Market), an annual event that takes place the last weekend in July in São Brás de Alportel. In addition to finding all types of regional craftwork for sale here, you will have the opportunity to see cork artisans at work, making a range of items from hats and belts to table mats and purses. For information, contact the tourist office in São Brás de Alportel (*Largo de São Sebastião 23, tel 289 843 165*).

■ Cork oaks have been a valuable Portuguese resource for centuries.

INLAND ALGARVE

Many people forget there is more to the Algarve than beaches. It also possesses captivating inland destinations and a gently rolling *serra* (hills). This is where you should head for authenticity, handicrafts, whitewashed villages, a Roman spa, and great walking territory.

It is little more than 20 miles (32 km) from the coast north to the Alentejo border, so a drive into the hills is an easy day trip. You'll also find welcome relief from the hordes. The A22 highway, which extends from the Spanish border west to Lagos, forms a frontier between the coastal infrastructure and a quieter, rural hinterland. This region, known as the Barrocal, is where fertile limestone soil nurtures the Algarve's fruit orchards.

As you head toward the hills and negotiate the web of roads encircling **Almancil,** try not to miss the church of **São Lourenço** *(tel 289 395 451, closed Sun., $),* visible beside the N125. Although remodeled during the heyday of baroque, it was originally Romanesque and is regarded as one of the Algarve's greatest cultural gems. The cupola, walls, and ceiling are faced in a masterful display of azulejos illustrating the life of St. Lawrence. This is the 1730 work of Policarpo de Oliveira Bernardes who, together with his father António, created many tiled masterpieces found throughout Portugal.

Loulé

North of Almancil, huge crowds descend upon Loulé every Saturday morning for the food and handicrafts **market** staged in a field on the west side of town.

Loulé 🗺 241 D2 **Visitor Information** ✉ Avenida 25 de Abril 9 ☎ 289 463 900 **turismodoalgarve.pt**

▪ The stunning azulejos in Almancil's São Lourenço church depict the life and martyrdom of St. Lawrence.

This tradition goes back to 1291, when the founding of a fair made Loulé a major trading crossroads. Dried figs, almonds, and honey (all favored by the Moors) are among the staples on offer, as is rock salt. Few people know that Loulé sits above miles of underground galleries where exceptionally pure salt is mined. Nonperishable items for sale at the market include copperware, leather goods, and wickerwork handmade in area villages.

Because the market is very tourist oriented, you may want to explore Loulé on another day when the sleepy atmosphere returns. The Moorish-style market hall on the corner of Praça da República has a daily **food market** (closed Sun.) as well as some handicrafts, and just behind lies the small but attractive old quarter. The **castelo** and **Museu Municipal** (Rua D. Paio Peres Correia 19, tel 289 400 885, museudeloule.pt, closed Sun.—Mon., $) houses a reconstructed traditional kitchen, in keeping with Loulé's gastronomic concerns. The museum exhibits a predictable collection of Neolithic, Roman, and Moorish artifacts, and from there steps take you up to the castle walls and turret. Far more interesting are the craft shops concentrated in the street behind the castle, Rua da Barbacã. Loulé and Almancil both have strong gastronomic reputations, so if you want a true dining experience away from the coast, indulge yourself here.

Carnaval in Portugal

Carnaval, known in some parts of the world as Mardi Gras, traditionally marks the final days of feasting and celebration before the restraint and fasting of the Christian season of Lent. Running now for more than a hundred years, the Loulé Carnaval parade claims to be the oldest in Portugal. Locals do all they can to capture the atmosphere of a Brazilian Carnaval, with samba bands, scantily clad dancers, and elaborate floats; only the tropical Rio weather evades them, as the February Carnaval falls in the middle of Portugal's winter.

North of Loulé

The typical Algarve villages of Querença and Salir nestle on either side of **Fonte Benémola.** Entered from **Querença,** Fonte Benémola is a protected, idyllic little valley crossed by walking trails. Near the Algibre River, you will pass willows, ashes, oleanders, and tamarisks, while the higher slopes foster carob trees, wild olives, oaks, and aromatic herbs. Fauna is limited to otters, bats, and a wide variety of birds. A little farther north is the very pretty whitewashed village of **Salir**—visually dominated by a rather nondescript church and water tower—that safeguards

Fonte Benémola 🗺 241 D2

the significant remains of a castle. Follow the *"ruínas"* signs to see extant ramparts now incorporated into several picturesque houses and gardens. Although modestly signposted, they are among Portugal's few surviving examples of Moorish fortifications constructed of *taipa,* a Moorish building material made of sand, pebbles, clay, and lime. The outpost was subsequently captured by the Knights of Santiago, who prepared their 1249 assault on Faro from here.

A couple of miles west of Salir, the steep walls of the limestone outcrop **Rocha da Pena**—another protected area with nature trails for visitors—rises to 1,600 feet (474 m). It offers sublime views from the summit looking north to the rugged serra and south to the sea. You may spot Bonelli's or royal eagles, as well as genets, mongooses, and foxes

---

Rocha da Pena 🗺 241 D2 • **Alte** 🗺 241 D2 **Visitor Information** ✉ Polo Museológico, Rua Condes de Alte ☎ 289 478 060 **cm-loule.pt**

EXPERIENCE: Bird-Watching in the Algarve

Bird-watching may not be what first comes to mind when you think of the sun-soaked Algarve, but the coast and interior hills actually shelter some significant birdlife. Coastal areas are home to diverse coastal and seabird species, including the rare red-billed chough; while inland, cork forests and scrubland provide the ideal habitat for bee-eaters, hoopoes, azure-winged magpies, and raptors such as kestrels and short-toed eagles.

Birding is possible at any time of year, although there are fewer species to be found between June and August. Spring marks the arrival of summer breeders and the start of the migration period, especially among waterbirds; autumn is the best time to observe large numbers of migratory seabirds and raptors. Ornithologist Simon Wates, a longtime resident of the area and owner of **Algarve Birdwatching** *(tel 912 824 053, algarvebirdman .com, $$$$$),* leads tours that are tailored to your interests and time constraints—call well in advance to arrange a trip. Or try **BeCool Travel** *(tel 308 810 671, becooltravel.com).*

If you would rather head off on your own, try to find a copy of *A Birdwatchers' Guide to Portugal and Madeira* (Prion Birdwatchers' Guide Series, 1988) by H. Costa, C. C. Moore, and G. Elias. Although old, it is still one of the best birding guides to Portugal on the market. Alternatively, check out the **Portuguese Society for the Study of Birds** *(spea .pt/en),* which offers some great information on birds and bird-watching in the area and has a visitor's center in the Azores and one in Sesimbra.

among the juniper, arbutus, and pepper trees. You can drive north of this outcrop and circle round to **Alte,** another picturesque village of whitewashed houses edged in *platibandas* (decorative plaster borders, often painted yellow or blue), clinging to a hillside. The church dates from the 13th century, when it was founded by the wife of Alte's ruler in thanks for his safe return from the Crusades; it has been altered since. The tiled walls and painted ceiling of the main chapel date from the 18th century, but the Sevillian tiles of the chapel of São Sebastião are 16th century. While the church is attractive, the most popular draws in Alte are its fountains, the **Fonte Pequena** and **Fonte Grande** (respectively small and large), signposted at the bottom of the village, which once produced water to turn the wheels of nine mills. One of them, the Moinho da Abóboda, still stands.

Silves

Another enclave of interest, the hill town of Silves, sits beside the Arade River. Once the Moorish capital of the Algarve, borne out by its towering red sandstone castle, Silves is today a prosperous, well-organized town. Your first port of call should be the massive **castelo** *(tel 282 440 837, $),* which was landscaped in the style of an Arab garden in 2005. An outsize bronze statue of Sancho I, who first conquered Silves from the Moors in

INSIDER TIP:

Café Inglês in Silves *(Rua do Castelo 11, tel 282 442 585, cafeingles.com.pt, closed Mon.)* is a charming place to stop for a bite. Enjoy the shady terrace, but don't miss the great art displays inside.

—SUSANNA REDMAN
Owner, Casacanela Food & Wine Tours

1189, greets you outside the castle's double gateway. Inside, excavations have revealed 12th- and 13th-century Almohad structures, and it is thought the Moors occupied the site for some 500 years. One of their 11th-century rulers was Al-Muthamid, a poet-king whose works are still widely read in Arab countries. Apart from archaeological excavations and the garden, the area inside houses an *aljibe* (cistern), once the town's water supply; you can climb the castle's ramparts for fabulous views.

Steps lead from the castle entrance to the **Sé** (cathedral), which dates from 1189 and preserves a simple Gothic nave with numerous tombs of Crusaders. Next door is the simple little **Igreja da Misericórdia,** a church built in the late 16th century. Down

Silves △ 240 C2 **Visitor Information** ✉ EN 124, Parque das Merendas ☎ 282 098 927 **turismodoalgarve.pt**

The lovely town of Caldas de Monchique owes its wealth to the hot springs that pour from its mountainside.

the cobbled streets at the base of the hill, the modern **Museu Municipal de Arqueologia** *(Rua da Porta de Loulé 14, tel 282 444 838, museusdoalgarve .wordpress.com, $),* illustrates the rich archaeological history of Silves from Neolithic times onward.

The **Municipal Market** in Silves, just past the Ponte Romana, is worth a visit to pick up local produce and delicacies; Saturday morning is the best, when stalls spill out onto the square.

Serra de Monchique

From Silves, the drive up into the cool Serra de Monchique, due north of Portimão, takes you into densely wooded hills of eucalyptuses, chestnuts, cork oaks, and pines, with occasional splashes of wild rhododendrons. The volcanic soil, combined with the humid climate, makes the hill range particularly fertile. Be sure to stop at the viewpoint that overlooks the

Medronho & the Arbutus Tree

Distilled from the fruit of the arbutus tree, commonly known as the strawberry tree, the *medronho* is the (exceedingly) alcoholic drink of choice in the Algarve. For generations, there were dozens of village distilleries producing medronho; with the advent of European Union health and safety legislation, most of these ancestral home breweries were forced to close. Thankfully several converted their facilities and continue to produce this excellent *aguardente*. Be sure to try a high-quality brand and do not drive afterward. To taste and buy the best, go to **Loja do Mel e do Medronho** (*Largo 5 de Outubro, Monchique, tel 967 735 783*). For the full story, head east to **Casa do Medronho** (*Rua de Aljezur 14, Marmelete, tel 282 955 121, casadomedronho.com*), a working museum where visitors can learn about the whole distilling process.

tight terracing (originally Roman) around the spa town of **Caldas de Monchique** to take in its incredibly panoramic scene.

Ancient Romans already favored this spa for treating their digestive troubles, then 19th-century Spanish bourgeois flocked to take its waters, and today resort fugitives seek out its serenity. You can indulge in a treatment at the sulfurous **Termas de Monchique** (*tel 282 910 910, monchiquetermalresort .com*), wander the quiet streets lined with pastel-hued buildings, or simply enjoy the gardens overlooking the ravine.

A few miles farther north lies the small town of **Monchique** itself, where you can explore the ruins of a 17th-century Franciscan monastery and admire the Manueline portal of the parish church. The town is a hub for hikers and horseback riders, and its good selection of basketware, leatherware, woolen garments, and honey will please any shopper. The town's monthly **market** is held on the second Friday of the month; it's a great place to pick up local crafts such as wooden and cork items and a good selection of basketware. They also sell hand-painted wooden children's chairs and the local folding scissor-style stools, thought by some to be of Roman origin. Vendors also peddle the local firewater, *medronho,* made from fermented arbutus berries (see sidebar this page).

Five miles (8 km) from Monchique is the Serra's highest point at Fóia, more than 3,000 feet (900 m) up. ∎

Monchique 🅰 240 B2 **Visitor Information** ✉ Largo de São Sebastião 📞 282 911 189 **turismodoalgarve.pt**

A GOLFING TRADITION

Portugal's love affair with golf dates from the end of the 19th century. Porto Niblicks ("niblick" is the old name for a lofted golf club, the equivalent of today's nine iron) was the first golf club, its creation linked to British involvement in the wine city of Porto. Lovers of the game, the British established courses wherever they lived—notably in the countries of their empire or, in the case of Portugal, where they had trading interests.

The Porto Golf Club (it has dropped "Niblicks") still exists 10 miles (16 km) south of Porto beside the beaches of Espinho. It's the second oldest course in continental Europe.

The number of golf clubs grew in the 1920s and '30s to accommodate wealthy Portuguese patrons and the increasing number of tourists from Britain and France flocking to fashionable Cascais and Estoril. Porto's second course, Miramar, appeared in 1932, but the main growth centered around Lisbon, notably the Estoril course, which was played on by exiled European royals such as the Duke of Windsor, the former King Edward VIII.

Golf & the Algarve

Today the Lisbon region boasts 23 courses, notably Penha Longa at Sintra, host to many European tour events; Oitavos Dunes in Cascais; Quinta do Peru, south of the Tagus; and Troia Resort, south of Setúbal. The largest expansion, however, has been in the Algarve, where there are now 37 golf courses—and with good reason: It is perfect golf country. The climate is mild in winter, and summer sea breezes cool even the most hot-tempered golfer.

The very first course on the Algarve goes back to 1921: it was a small, rudimentary course between Portimão and Praia da Rocha that was abandoned during World War II. The turning point came with the arrival of Sir Henry Cotton, a former British Open champion who began semiretirement in the Algarve in the late 1950s. He designed three courses and remained most proud of his first,

■ **The Da Balaia course commands dramatic views to the sea.**

European royals once played on the Estoril course.

ing Arnold Palmer–designed Victoria course in 2004, which hosted the 2005 World Cup championship.

Several Algarve courses are perfect for beginners, such as Pine Cliffs, just east of Albufeira. The golf club's first president was former Formula One world champion Nigel Mansell. The nine-hole course overlooking the sea might be short, but there are some hazardous holes, notably the sixth where you have to drive over a huge ravine to land on the putting green. Known as The Devil's Parlour, it is a devilish little hole that can ruin an otherwise delightful stroll over the clifftop course. With such illustrious precedents and such views, golf in the Algarve is unlikely to decline. (See p. 322 for a listing of several Algarve courses.)

Penina, which was built on a former rice field in 1964. The Portuguese Open was played there in 2004.

Today Vilamoura, with six courses, is the center of Algarve golf. The first one, the Old Course, was designed in 1969 by Frank Pennink; it was arguably the most popular course until the grand unveiling of the challeng-

---

EXPERIENCE: Improve Your Swing

With its delightful climate and wealth of courses, the Algarve is the perfect place to improve your swing if your golf game is a little over par. You can spend a few days at one of the Algarve's many golf schools or take an organized golf vacation; a wide selection of programs are available, catering to all levels. Here are three good choices.

Monte Rei Golf & Country Club *(Vila Nova de Cacela, tel 281 950 950, monte-rei.com)* includes the North Course and a second, under construction, designed by former champion Jack Nicklaus. The Academy organizes courses for all levels.

At his **Lester's Golf Academy** *(Vilamoura, tel 967 979 576, lesters-golf.com)*, PGA Tour professional Peter Lester hosts four- to seven-night golf vacations. All options include accommodation in a Vilamoura hotel, transfers to the golf course, and daily lessons.

During winter months, British golf specialist **David Short** *(tel 01 637 879 991, davidshort golf.co.uk)* brings his golf clinics to the Algarve, with guests spending the morning in class and the afternoon playing the most prestigious courses in the region. Costs run starting from $1,600 for a weeklong clinic.

LAGOS

Lagos's name reflects its role in the Portuguese age of discoveries, when the town was the operational center for Prince Henry the Navigator (1394–1460) to plan his African forays. Its status grew further in 1573, when it became the capital of the Algarve until 1756.

Today Lagos is an attractive, relaxed town, its walled harbor guarded by the modest 17th-century **Forte da Ponta da Bandeira** *(currently closed).* Here you can learn about Lagos's role during Prince Henry's time. A statue of the prince presides over the nearby **Praça do Infante,** a verdant square with an unmarked but significant arcaded building in its northwest corner—the site of Europe's first slave market, in 1444.

A short walk takes you to the fabulous **Igreja de Santo António,** entered through the **Museu Municipal** *(Rua Gen. Alberto da Silveira, tel 282 762 301, closed Sun.–Mon., $).* This displays interesting archaeological pieces as well as cork, azulejos, and vestments, but the church is the showstopper. Within its gilded baroque interior, azulejo-faced walls and a painted ceiling counterbalance the remarkable retable. To recover from this visual excess, explore the streets that run north to **Praça Gil Eanes.** Don't miss **Rua da Barroca;** its sidewalks are cobbled with marine designs.

Lovely nearby beaches include the broad sweep of **Meia Praia** to the east and a string of coves with calm waters and some impressive grottoes and sea stacks, particularly at **Praia de Dona Ana,** south of Lagos. A walking path from **Praia do Pinhão** leads around the headland as far as **Porto de Mós.**

If in need of a break from the idyllic beaches of the Algarve, head to the well-maintained **Parque Zoologico de Lagos** *(Medronhal–Quinta Figueiras, Barão de São João, tel 282 680 100, zoolagos.com, $$$)* a few minutes outside Lagos. Birds are the stars of the show here, but there are also small mammals, reptiles, and an adventure playground to keep the kids happy. Great effort has been made to keep animals in their natural habitat and enclosures are often secured by moats rather than bars. ■

The fantastically eroded coastline at Ponta da Piedade

Lagos 🅰 240 B1 **Visitor Information** ✉ Praça Gil Eanes ☎ 282 763 031

SAGRES

The reality of Sagres reinforces a distinct sensation of teetering on the edge of Europe, a final blip on the map. Little happens in this small town other than the ebb and flow of surfers, and the main attraction is a fort symbolizing its past glory.

Sagres is indelibly linked to the legacy of Prince Henry the Navigator: This is where he supposedly founded his school of navigation. Although he lived and died (in 1460) nearby and his expeditions set off from Lagos, no proof exists of this school. Yet

■ **The 16th-century Sagres fortress stands watch over a desolate but spectacular headland.**

Sagres is an extraordinarily evocative place, occupying a flat, three-pronged promontory that was for centuries one end of the known world. Surprisingly, it still has this quality about it, particularly in the off-season. Surfers and windsurfers flock here year-round, giving the town an alternative feel and spawning low-key bars and cheap restaurants. A trail of their parked campers snakes north up the Costa Vicentina.

The main site at the tip of the windswept promontory is the **For-**

INSIDER TIP:

The countryside surrounding Sagres is delightful year-round, but in spring it is filled with the color and smell of wildflowers.

—ANA CARLA CABRITA
Owner, Walkin'Sagres

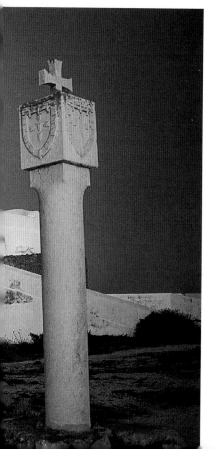

taleza de Sagres *(tel 282 620 140, $)*. Renovated in 1993, it encloses, among other things, a small 16th-century church and the famous "wind rose." This giant mariner's compass built in stone was uncovered in 1921, but little else is known about it—yet another Sagres mystery. Walk along the promontory's mile-long (1.6 km) path to enjoy fabulous views of pounding surf and soaring eagles.

A couple of miles west lies the barren **Cabo de São Vicente** (Cape of St. Vincent) with its lighthouse and, just before it, the old fort of **Beliche**, where visitors flock to watch the sun set behind the cape. Down below Sagres itself is the beach of **Mareta**, while around the headland to the east, fishing boats moor at the **Porto da Baleeira**. At the next beach along the coast, the lovely **Praia do Martinhal,** windsurfing is king. ∎

Sagres 🗺 240 A1 **Visitor Information** ✉ Rua Comandante Matoso ☎ 282 624 873
turismodoalgarve.pt

DRIVE TO CABO DE SÃO VICENTE

This leisurely drive takes you along the undeveloped western Algarve coast between Lagos and Europe's most southwesterly point—Cabo de São Vicente.

From the fort on the seafront of **Lagos** (see p. 257), drive west out of town, following signs to Sagres on the N125. Turn left at the signpost to **Luz ❶**, a small seaside town just a couple of miles off the main road. Follow signs down to the *praia* (beach). Park near the yellow-and-white church of São Vicente and take a stroll along the palm-lined promenade, overlooking rock pools and the crescent-shaped beach backed by cliffs.

Follow the one-way system out of town and signs to Burgau past a stretch of vacation apartments before regaining the countryside. At **Burgau,** cross an intersection and then follow signs to Forte de Almádena. A rough road leads you into empty hills dotted with farms. At a sign for **Praia das Cabanas Velhas ❷**, turn left down a dirt road to an idyllic little cove, and the discreetly designed modern **Cabanas Beach Restaurant** *(tel 968 871 974)*.

Back up on the road, continue west for a half mile (0.8 km) before turning left along another dirt road to **Forte de Almádena.** This ruined 16th-century fort was built for João III and commands beautiful views west from its headland position. The coastal road winds downhill before crossing the old riverbed of the Almádena, now full of

pampas grass and oleanders. This rutted road ends at a junction where you turn left onto a steep paved road to **Salema ❸**, a charming fishing port.

Leave by returning uphill and following signs to Vila do Bispo. At the main road (N125) turn right, then left

opposite a huge tourist development. Keep driving until you see a sign for **Guadalupe** to the right, where you take a parallel road past grazing donkeys. After about a mile (1.6 km) you come to a tiny 13th-century chapel venerating **Nossa Senhora de Guadalupe ❹**; this is where Prince Henry the Navigator is said to have prayed while living in Raposeira, a short distance farther west. Keep driving on this side road to rejoin the N125, and

NOT TO BE MISSED:

Praia das Cabanas Velhas • Salema • Nossa Senhora da Conceição

then follow a sign, just after Raposeira, left to the **"monumentos megalíticos."** Here, numerous ancient menhirs lie scattered in the shrub of a high

▬ Cabo de São Vicente's cliffs rise nearly vertically some 246 feet (75 m).

headland, and sweeping views take in the lighthouse at Cabo de São Vicente. The **Bateria do Zavial,** a ruined 17th-century fortification, lies at the end of this road, from where you circle back to Raposeira. At the N125, follow signs to nearby Vila do Bispo.

Vila do Bispo to the Cape

Drive into **Vila do Bispo** ⑤ and park near the beautiful yellow-and-white baroque church, **Nossa Senhora da Conceição,** on the main square. If it is open, you will see a dazzling early 1700s interior of azulejos, gilded woodwork, painted ceilings, and ornate retables. Wander the side streets before rejoining the main road to continue to Sagres (see pp. 258–259). After driving through town, turn right at a traffic circle to Cabo de São Vicente, and then cross a barren heath to the 1632 fortress of **Beliche.** Beyond is the lighthouse of **Cabo de São Vicente.**

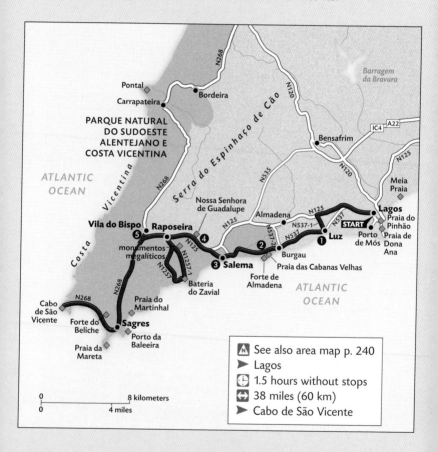

See also area map p. 240

Lagos

1.5 hours without stops

38 miles (60 km)

Cabo de São Vicente

COSTA VICENTINA

Europe's most spectacular beaches edge this wild coastline that descends the Alentejo coast and wraps around into the Algarve. This is an area for surfing and hiking; the Atlantic waves are rarely safe for swimming.

This inviting coast—protected as part of the **Parque Natural do Sudoeste Alentejano e Costa Vicentina**—is noted as much for its geologic formations as for its plants, birdlife, and estuaries.

Rough roads end at breathtaking viewpoints over deserted beaches backed by craggy cliffs and edged by breakers. Infrastructure is still occasional—only a few restaurants or beach bars, and accommodations are limited to private rooms or guesthouses. There is an easy though rough road from **Carrapateira,** on the main N268, to the beach of **Pontal,** a blissfully broad sweep of sand. **Arrifana,** 9 miles (14 km) farther north, is a long stretch of white sand with a pretty little fishing harbor and the ruins of a 17th-century fort built to protect the tuna fishermen. Farther north again, the neighboring beaches of **Amoreira** and the 5-mile-long (8 km) **Monte Clérigo** have striking rock formations and some visitor facilities.

Aljezur, the crossroads for this stunning string of beaches, makes a pleasant place for lunch. Two rivers, the Aljezur and the Cerca, meet at the center of town. The ramparts of a tenth-century Moorish fort, badly damaged in the 1755 earthquake, stand atop the hill, while downhill, the **Museu Municipal** displays local items that highlight the history of this evocative region. ■

■ **Blissfully unspoiled low hills border the Costa Vicentina.**

Parque Natural do Sudoeste Alentejano e Costa Vicentina

🗺 240 A1–A3 **Visitor Information** ✉ Rua João Mendes Dias 46 A, Aljezur ☎ 282 998 673 **natural.pt** • **Museu Municipal de Aljezur** ✉ Largo 5 de Outubro ☎ 282 991 011 🕐 Closed Sun.–Mon. 💲 $ **cm-aljezur.pt**

An island hothouse for subtropical plants, where botanical beauties clad breathtakingly steep cliff edges

MADEIRA

Strelitzia, or bird-of-paradise—one of Madeira's floral exports

MADEIRA

Madeira's benign weather has helped transform this rugged volcanic island into one vast, verdant garden—a botanical storehouse whose natural splendors and stunning vistas have been enjoyed by travelers since it was first discovered in the 15th century.

Madeira is one of Portugal's most intriguing outposts. Set in the eastern Atlantic, it lies closer to Morocco than to Portugal, and this southerly latitude gives it a warm subtropical climate, which helps make the island a popular year-round vacation destination, as the ocean here is significantly warmer than in the rest of the country. The tip of a submerged mountain chain, it is part of an

■ Looming out of the sea, the cliffs at Porto Moniz are protected by reefs and black lava rocks.

archipelago, also called Madeira, which comprises Porto Santo, the Ilhas Desertas, and the Ilhas Selvagens. Madeira is the largest island, with an area of 286 square miles (740 sq km) and a population of around 250,000.

Porto Santo was the first island discovered in the archipelago by Portuguese explorers. In 1418, João Gonçalves Zarco and Tristão Vaz Teixeira, leading an expedition to explore the West African coast, sought shelter on this tiny landmass when they were blown off course. They returned two years later and found the main island, which they christened Ilha Madeira (Wooded Island) because of its thick forest cover. The forests were set alight to clear land for settlement, and the resultant ash and underlying volcanic soil proved fertile ground for the grapevines and sugarcanes that were introduced. Slaves were imported to terrace the steep hillsides and dig an extensive network of irrigation canals—the famous *levadas.* The capital, Funchal, soon developed into a port of call for transatlantic ships. During the 17th century, Madeira abandoned sugar in favor of winemaking, establishing the basis for a trade that still flourishes today. The unique characteristics of Madeiran wine result from a long, hot maturing process. This was

■ The thrill of a *carrinho de cesto* ride
from Monte to Funchal

discovered by accident when it was found that barrels of wine sent as ballast on long sea voyages in the tropics were actually improved by the journey.

The island's mild climate attracted an increasing number of wealthy visitors in the 19th century—particularly well-to-do British citizens, who enjoyed stopping here on the way to and from their colonies. Funchal's famous Reid's Hotel opened in 1891 to cater to this growing market. British visitors also introduced the crafts of embroidery and making cane furniture.

Madeira Today

Tourism is still Madeira's economic mainstay. The island is famous for its wonderful walking alongside the levadas that crisscross the lush hills. More energetic pursuits, such as scuba diving, rappelling, and canyoneering, are also popular. If one thing is lacking, it is a sandy beach, but that is provided across the waves on Porto Santo.

An abundance of fruits and vegetables combines with fresh fish for a memorable cuisine, and a calendar of festivals ensures a lively cultural scene. Nearly two-thirds of this island, with its dramatic scenery and colorful flora, is protected as a nature reserve.

Madeira has two recent highways that literally run through the middle: the island, though small, is a succession of highlands and mountains that in the past made travel from one location to another slow; now—with a Via Rápida—you can save time, however, you must drive through long stretches of tunnels. ■

FUNCHAL

The island capital has a glorious setting, sprawling across a wide amphitheater of mountains and hillsides with the glittering, boat-studded
bay below. Often shrouded in clouds, the hills protect the city from the
northeasterly winds, making it the warmest location on the island.

Home to about one-third of
Madeira's inhabitants, Funchal was
named for the wild fennel (funcho)
early settlers found here. Today it
is sometimes dubbed "little Lisbon" for its elegant architecture,
lively cafés, and smart shops. Luxuriant vegetation perfumes its winding streets. The old town fronts
the harbor and marina, while the

modern extension—home to most
hotels—lies due west along the
seafront. After destructive fires in
2016, Funchal and its inhabitants
have returned to a general sense
of normality.

Start your visit at the main square,
Praça do Município, with its distinctive black-and-white patterned
stone pavement. Note the **Câmara**

Funchal 🗺 266 B2 **Visitor Information** ✉ Avenida Arriaga 16 ☎ 291 145
305 • ✉ Estrada Monumental 175 ☎ 291 620 028 **visitmadeira.com**

Madeira Wine

The island of Madeira has been
producing world-famous wine for
hundreds of years. In the 16th
century, sailors headed to the
New World took aboard barrels
of local wine; as the wine traveled
into tropical climates, it was heat-
ed in the hold of the ship and its
taste greatly improved. By the
18th century, following the example of the port shippers, young
wines were fortified with brandy
to stabilize them and wine producers began to cut costs and
heat the wines in their own cel-
lars; a process still used today and
known as *estufagem*. There are
four types of Madeira, named af-

ter the white grapes used in their
production. The driest is Sercial,
made from grapes grown above
2,600 feet (800 m); it is best
served chilled as an aperitif. The
white Verdelho, grown at 1,300 to
2,000 feet (400–600 m), produces a medium-dry, tawny wine best
served with meat dishes. Bual is a
rich and nutty, medium-sweet
wine made from grapes grown on
terraces below 1,300 feet (400
m); it is particularly good with
cheeses and dessert. Finally,
Malmsey, grown in sunny vineyards below 1,300 feet (400 m),
produces a sweet, full-bodied
wine, served as a digestive.

Municipal (Town Hall), a gracious 18th-century mansion originally built for the count of Carvalhal, and, on the south side of the square, the former bishop's palace with its lovely arcaded gallery. The latter now houses the **Museu de Arte Sacra** *(Rua do Bispo 21, tel 291 228 900, masf.pt, closed Sun., $$).* Look for the beautiful processional cross donated to Funchal's cathedral by Manuel I. On the second floor, Portugal's best collection of 15th- and 16th-century Flemish paintings hangs beside Portuguese artwork, including Jan Provost's serene "St. Mary Magdalene." On the north side of the square is the 17th-century **Igreja do Colégio,** built by the Jesuits. Heading south from the praça brings you to Funchal's imposing **Sé** (cathedral), completed in 1514. Except for the azulejo-faced belfry, the exterior is fairly austere, but the interior features an intricately carved, ivory-inlaid,

■ **The Jardim Botânico includes a three-room Natural History Museum.**

wooden ceiling and flamboyant choir stalls. Funchal's main street, Avenida Arriaga, runs west from the Sé toward a seafront park, the **Jardim de Santa Catarina,** passing the **Palácio de São Lourenço,** an 18th-century fortress still used by the military. Opposite the fortress is the tourist office and Blandy's Wine Lodge, once known as **Adegas de São Francisco** *(tel 291 228 978, blandyswinelodge.com, $$$–$$$$).* Originally a Franciscan monastery, it now houses the offices of this big wine company. They offer the island's most atmospheric wine tour, concluding with a tasting of Madeira's famously sweet nectar and a visit to their museum. West of this central zone, **Madeira Film Experience** *(currently closed),* offers an audiovisual tour through 600 years of Madeira history.

In the **Vila Velha** (Old Town), take time to explore the cobbled streets lined with restaurants, cafés, fado bars, and craft shops. A highlight is the vast **Mercado dos Lavradores** *(Largo dos Lavradores, tel 291 214 080, closed Sat. p.m.–Sun.),* a market where locals sell a colorful cornucopia of island produce. Close by is the terminal for the **Teleférico** (cable car) to the hill town of Monte (see p. 273). No visit would be complete without a trip to the lovely **Jardim Botânico** *(Quinta do Bom Sucesso, Caminho do Meio, tel 291 211 200, closed Dec., $).* Bountiful native vegetation grows here in terraces overlooking the valley, and exotics such as orchids, lilies, and birds-of-paradise bloom in the gardens. In the month of July, the city comes alive with an animated Jazz Festival. ■

WESTERN MADEIRA

The breathtaking western coastline of Madeira sports villages clinging to the steep shoreline, with cultivated terracing tumbling down to the sea. Inland, more panoramic vistas await.

Heading west from Funchal, the first stop on the coastal highway is **Câmara de Lobos,** a quaint fishing village famed for its brightly painted boats. The fishermen catch *espada* (scabbard fish), a Madeiran specialty. These fishes rise from the depths at night to feed, so the boats head out in the evening.

Just past Câmara de Lobos is one of the island's most impressive sights: the magnificent **Cabo Girão.** The second highest sea cliff in Europe (beaten only by one in Norway), Cabo Girão plunges a dizzying 1,900 feet (580 m) to the sea below. Incredibly, terraced vineyards are carved into the vertiginous cliff face—further evidence of Madeira's industrious farmers. The more daring can head out onto the glass-bottomed skywalk.

Another popular stopping point is the seaside resort of **Ribeira Brava,** 20 miles (32 km) west of Funchal. Lying at the entrance to a steep-sided valley, its name (Wild River) derives from the torrential flows pouring off the mountains in the winter months. The sizable town features a 15th-century parish church, a fishing harbor, and the informative **Museu Etnográfico da Madeira** *(Rua de São Francisco 24, tel 291 952 598, closed Sun.–Mon., $),* exploring the essentials of Madeiran life over the centuries: fishing, weaving, and winemaking.

The sunniest spot on the south coast is said to be **Ponta do Sol,** 2.5 miles (4 km) west of Ribeira Brava. This "headland of the sun" is an unspoiled village straddling a deep ravine, with cobbled streets leading up toward an unusual church. A sunset stroll along the harborfront is de rigueur.

Madeira's westernmost point, **Ponta do Pargo,** is famed for its sea views: There are thousands of miles of Atlantic Ocean between you and the east coast of North America. Just as Câmara de Lobos is known for its espada fishing, Ponta do Pargo is renowned for its catches of *pargo,* or dolphinfish (no relation to dolphins).

Rounding the Northernmost Point

A short distance from the island's westernmost tip is its northernmost point—**Porto Moniz.** A series of large rock pools here attract

Western Madeira 🅼 266 A2–B2 **Visitor Information** ✉ Forte de São Bento, Ribeira Brava ☎ 291 951 675 • ✉ Rua do Príncipe D. Luís 3, Ponta do Sol ☎ 291 974 034 • ✉ Rua dos Emigrantes 2, Porto Moniz ☎ 291 853 075

weary day-trippers to soak their aching limbs while contemplating the ocean spray breaking over the northern shoreline. Cafés, restaurants, and a hotel cater to more prosaic visitor needs. Porto Moniz has one of the only protected harbors on the north coast and was once an important whaling center. Today, the cetaceans are being sighted again and there are many organized whale-watching outings.

The **Antiga ER101,** which used to link Porto Moniz to São Vicente, 12 miles (19 km) to the east, ranks as one of the most spectacular and dangerous coastal roads in Europe: Built after World War II, it clings to the cliff edge with breathtaking views and took 16 years to complete. Today it is closed to traffic because of the risk of rockfall, but it has remained an attraction for tourists who can venture there on foot. **São Vicente,** which you can reach via the new ER101, is a spruced-up agricultural crossroads with plenty of facilities for travelers, the most substantial town on the north coast. The pedestrianized center, with cobbled streets, houses decorated with flowers, and cafés, is pleasant to stroll. If you feel more adventurous, head just south of town to the **Grutas de São Vicente,** an intriguing cave system with a short guided tour of volcanic tunnels, or lava tubes, featuring lava cakes and volcanic stalactites.

A vertigo-inspiring view from the towering cliff face of Cabo Girão looks east toward Funchal.

Connecting São Vicente to Ribeira Brava on the south coast, Route 104 passes over the stupendous **Boca da Encumeada,** a popular viewing point with panoramas north to São Vicente and down to the Serra de Água valley in the south. Try to arrive at the 3,304-foot (1,007 m) pass in the morning; clouds tend to obscure the view as the day progresses. For vertigo sufferers, a tunnel dives underneath the pass. The Levada do Norte, a 38-mile-long (60 km) channel that irrigates the valley below, passes under the road. ∎

Grutas de São Vicente ⧉ 266 B2 ✉ Sítio do Pé do Passo, São Vicente
☎ 291 842 404 💲 $$ **grutasecentrodovulcanismosaovicente.com**

EASTERN MADEIRA

Eastern Madeira offers rich pickings, from the eccentric toboggan ride of Monte to outstanding botanical gardens and the attractive fishing towns of Caniçal and Machico.

Monte & Around

High above the northeastern outskirts of Funchal, the village of **Monte** is a perennial favorite for excursions. During the 19th century it was fashionable to descend from Monte to Funchal by **toboggan.** This system is still used today, with tourists riding two abreast in a sled made of wicker and wood steered back to Funchal's suburbs by two men, running and riding alongside. Alternatively, the more high-tech cable car, **Teleférico da Madeira,** runs between Funchal's Vila Velha and Monte.

Thriving at the elevation of 1,970 feet (600 m), lush vegetation surrounds Monte. The striking sight of the church of **Nossa Senhora do Monte,** with its twin towers and gray-basalt detailing on a white facade, rises from a hillock in the town center. Every August 15, pilgrims climb up 74 steps to reach this church. Inside is the iron tomb of Charles I, Austria's last emperor, who lived in the Quinta do Monte hotel during his exile, in 1921, and died the following year. Within walking distance from here are two lovely gardens: the **Jardim do Monte,** with luxuriant ferns and flowering plants, and the **Jardim Tropical Monte Palace,** which covers 17 acres (7 ha) with statuary, ponds, bridges, Asian-style gardens, and typical subtropical flora.

The **Quinta do Palheiro** lies just 5 miles (8 km) east of Funchal. Tended by successive generations of the Blandy family, the estate boasts botanical riches

Camacha Wicker

Not far from Quinta do Palheiro, reached by following Route 102 northward, the village of Camacha excels at wickerwork. The canes come from pollarded willows, which grow abundantly in the island's valleys. The **Grupo Folclórico da Casa do Povo da Camacha** *(Largo Conselheiro Aires de Ornelas 18, tel 927 103 683, grupo folcloricocamacha.com)* fosters these traditions and the music of the Madeira region, especially dance performances in traditional dress.

Eastern Madeira ⚠ 266 B2–C2 **Visitor Information** ✉ Rua do Sacristão, Sítio do Serrado, Santana ☎ 291 575 162 • **Teleférico da Madeira** ✉ Largo das Babosas 8, Monte ☎ 291 780 280 💲 $$$ (one-way only) **madeiracablecar.com**

Spring wildflowers carpet rolling meadows near Camacha.

from all over the world and is considered to be the most beautiful on the island, with more than 3,000 species.

Machico & Beyond

The largest town in eastern Madeira is **Machico,** where discoverer João Gonçalves Zarco first stepped ashore in 1420; a river divides the old town from the fishermen's quarter. In the main square, an attractive 15th-century church boasts a lateral doorway presented by Manuel I. Here, too, is a statue of Zarco's fellow navigator, Tristão Vaz Teixeira, who became Machico's governor. East of the square, the **Capela dos Milagres** (Chapel of the Miracles) is the focus of a major festival every October. This event celebrates the rescue of the chapel's crucifix after the original chapel was washed out to sea by floods in 1803.

Just north of Machico, the tiny port of **Caniçal** was the center of the island's whaling industry until the trade was banned in 1981. The whalers used small open boats and handheld harpoons to hunt their prey; the **Museu da Baleia** (*Rua Garcia Moniz 1, tel 291 961 858, museudabaleia.org, closed Mon., $$*) documents their exploits. This whaling museum also outlines conservation efforts in progress, including the creation of a 77,220-square-mile (200,000 sq km) marine mammal sanctuary around the archipelago. Caniçal now has the island's biggest tuna-fishing fleet; the brightly colored boats are berthed on the beach.

Beyond Caniçal the landscapes take on a wild, desolate quality as the road dwindles to a potholed track at the easternmost tip of the island. At **Prainha** you will find Madeira's only sandy beach, signposted down steps from the road, and very crowded on hot summer days. From the parking lot at the end of the road, a footpath leads across the **Ponta de São Lourenço,** a rugged promontory with dramatic views across the Ilhas Desertas. ■

Jardim Tropical Monte Palace ✉ Caminho do Monte 174, Monte
☎ 291 780 800 💲 $$$ **montepalacemadeira.com • Quinta do Palheiro**
🅰 266 B2 ✉ Caminho da Quinta do Palheiro 32, Monte
☎ 291 793 044 💲 $$ **palheironatureestate.com**

MADEIRA'S VEGETATION

The "pearl of the Atlantic" boasts two outstanding aspects: the first, a 1,500-mile-long (2,500 km) network of *levadas* (irrigation canals), and the second, luscious subtropical vegetation. Visitors can walk for miles on paths beside the levadas to reach remote and otherwise inaccessible areas. En route, as microclimates change, a seemingly miraculous world of hothouse plants and spectacular blooms is revealed—thriving in the wild.

Every hillside and roadside of Madeira is a mass of technicolor flowers, dominated by large-scale geraniums, hydrangeas, scarlet and pink hibiscus, mauve blue agapanthus, creamy arum lilies, torchlike red hot pokers *(Kniphofia uvaria)*, and deep crimson or orange bougainvilleas. All are backed up by flowering trees such as purple jacaranda, creamy yellow magnolia, giant pink camellia, and golden yellow mimosa. Perhaps the most spectacular blooms are the brilliant orange flowers of the tulip tree— or flame of the forest *(Spathodea campanulata)*—brought to Madeira by Capt. James Cook in the 18th century. Madeira's most famous endemic plant is the dragon tree *(Dracaena draco)*, shared with the Canary Islands and Cape Verde Islands. It now rarely grows in the wild, but can be found in gardens and parks. Like Africa's baobab, it looks as if it has been planted upside down; the straight trunk ends in a tangled mass of branches and stems. Barbary figs are encroaching along the nonirrigated areas of the warmer south

■ **Even in urban Funchal, the island's exotic blooms are never far away.**

coast, while countless fleshy succulents and flowering aloes opt to grow on rocky outcrops.

Such density and variety is hard to better—except when it comes to the cultivated varieties of cut flowers grown for export: Numerous orchid varieties, anthuriums, and spiky *Strelitzias* (birds-of-paradise) are foremost. Madeira's botanical gardens abound in imported species, offering yet another dazzling visual feast.

Ecological Variety

Levada walking (see sidebar below) is popular because the channels are easy to find and follow, and the gentle sound track of trickling water is only interrupted by the birdcalls or rustles of undergrowth courtesy of the lizards, typical island reptiles. One of the most striking features of the landscape is its tendency to suddenly change, offering walkers an electrifying experience of emerging from a damp and misty pine forest into a brilliantly sunny, verdant valley, where banana palms nestle at the base. Madeira's steep elevations have endowed it with three distinct vegetation zones: Subtropical plants flourish at sea level up to about 1,000 feet (330 m); a more temperate, Mediterranean zone nurtures grapevines, cereals, citrus fruits, mangoes, and apples up to about 2,500 feet (750 m); and ancient forest blankets elevations above the 2,500-foot (750 m) mark. Dating back some 20 million years to the Tertiary era, this type of forest once covered much of southern Europe, but it was later destroyed by glaciation. Madeira is one of the last places where its species—sesame, tree laurel, mahogany, til *(Oreodaphne jetens),* and even ironwood—still grow in their original habitat. The laurel forests (supplying bay leaves) around Faial, Portela, and Queimadas are among the last pockets of woods that escaped being burned down by Madeira's first settlers; they now stand protected as nature reserves.

EXPERIENCE: Walk the *Levadas*

Immerse yourself in Madeira's stunning landscape by walking alongside the levadas that crisscross the island. These irrigation canals, which date back as far as the 16th century, stretch some 1,500 miles (2,500 km). They take their name from the Portuguese word *levar,* which means "to carry." They funnel water from the wet northern highlands to the drier south, where it is used to irrigate banana plantations, vineyards, orchards, and vegetable gardens. Some 870 miles (1,500 km) of the levadas have adjacent, well-maintained paths, allowing walkers to easily follow the gentle contours of the hills. You can easily set off on your own (the Funchal tourist office has a leaflet of recommended walks, but better yet is Paddy Dillon's book *Walking in Madeira,* which you should bring with you), but you'll gain a greater appreciation of Madeira's flora and history on a guided walk. **Madeira Happy Tours** *(Estrada Monumental 284A, Monumental Experience Shopping Center, shop 4, Funchal, tel 291 768 426, madeirahappytours.com, $$$$$)* offers full- and half-day levada walks with qualified mountain guides. Vertigo sufferers should mention their condition as some levadas, though safe, are somewhat precipitous.

PORTO SANTO & OTHER ISLANDS

In stark contrast to Madeira, Porto Santo is quite flat and mostly arid: Very little grows here, and most of the 5,000 inhabitants depend on a steady stream of summer tourists for income.

There is just one reason for visiting Porto Santo: Its glorious beach that sweeps 5 miles (8 km) along the south coast. Twenty-three miles (37 km) northeast of Madeira, it is reached by ferry *(portosantoline.pt)* or plane.

The capital, **Vila Baleira,** was once home to the Genoese explorer Christopher Columbus, who came as a buyer for Lisbon sugar merchants in the 1470s. He later married Dona Filipa Moniz, the daughter of Porto Santo's governor. Their house is now the **Casa Colombo–Museu do Porto Santo,** where books, maps, and charts document the explorer's life. Dona Filipa died in childbirth and legend has it that while grieving, staring out to sea, Columbus became convinced that the vegetation washing ashore came from another continent; he was thus inspired to make his Atlantic crossing in 1492. From the main square, palm-fringed Rua Infante D. Henrique leads to the famous beach. En route you will pass a drinking fountain, one of many on the island that flows with local mineral water, which is bottled and sold on Madeira. Reportedly even the beach sand has healing properties.

Nineteen miles (30 km) to the southeast of Madeira, the three **Ilhas Desertas** (Empty Islands) form a protected reserve, principally to nurture the nearly extinct monk seal. The most southerly outposts of Portuguese territory are the remote **Ilhas Selvagens** (Wild Islands), some 150 miles (240 km) away, also with protected status. ∎

■ **Incongruous electric lighting lines the jetty at Porto Santo—miles and miles from anywhere.**

Porto Santo ▲ 266 D3 **Visitor Information** ✉ Praça do Barqueiro ☎ 291 985 244 • **Casa Colombo-Museu do Porto Santo** ✉ Travessa da Sacristia 2/4, Vila Baleira ☎ 291 983 405 🕐 Closed Tues. **cultura.madeira.gov.pt**

TRAVELWISE

Two-wheel transport in Lisbon

TRAVELWISE

PLANNING YOUR TRIP
When to Go

Mainland Portugal enjoys an attractive climate with long hot summers lasting roughly from May to September, and pleasantly mild winters, making it a safe-bet destination for much of the year. In the north, mountainous areas do see snow, and some ski stations function in the Serra da Estrela from January to March. The region of Trás-os-Montes experiences the harshest winters, with high rainfall in December and January. In neighboring Minho, including Porto, the pattern is similar though less extreme. Summers are hot and sunny, although there are occasional showery days. At the opposite end of the country, Algarve temperatures seldom fall below 50°F (10°C); limited rain falls mainly in December, January, and March, but it otherwise offers a very mild year-round climate. Come summer, temperatures soar to well over 86°F (30°C); July and August are peak family holiday time on the beaches, so you may wish to avoid those months. Inland in the Alentejo, temperatures are hotter, often topping 104°F (40°C). Lisbon and the country's center fall between these extremes, coolest in January and February and with the highest rainfall from November to January. Temperatures rarely drop below 46°F (8°C) and in summer they hover around 86°F (30°C). As there is always a breeze from the Atlantic and the Tejo River, midsummers are usually quite comfortable. The entire Atlantic coast offers a breezy summer climate, though the beaches get crowded and the crashing (and chilly) surf is not great for swimming. The sea here does not really warm up until July, unlike the protected coves of the Algarve. Spring and fall are the optimum time to visit to avoid domestic tourists and benefit from lower hotel rates. Spring (Apr.–May) especially is a wonderful period—wildflowers are in bloom and the countryside is seductively green. Early fall (Sep.–Oct.) is also enticing, with warm sunny days and russet vineyards. Meanwhile, offshore in the Atlantic, Madeira is quite temperate and is a popular winter destination for northern Europeans.

Festivals

Portugal's calendar is peppered with festivals, large and small, religious and secular, so whenever you travel you are bound to find one of them. Carnaval explodes across the country in February. The liveliest carnival is in Loulé and Torres Vedras, where floats are heavy on political satire. Funchal, the capital of Madeira, also hosts an extravagant Brazilian-style parade. Spring sees Easter Week, with some spectacular festivities and torchlit processions. The most memorable Easter celebrations take place at Óbidos, lasting two weeks, at Braga, and at Ourem. It is best to book hotels well in advance if you plan to attend any festivities in these cities. Spring also sees Coimbra's large student population enjoying days of revelry and excess in May before their final exams. Many local festivals occur during the summer months (June–Aug.). The Minho region has the most colorful traditional costumes. Autumn (late Sep.) is the time for grape harvest festivals, held over most of the country—inquire at local tourist offices for precise dates.

What to Take

Portuguese stores stock the same goods as any other Western city. Clothing depends very much on where you are going and at what time of year, but usually follows a European style of informal chic, unless you're hiking in the hills. You only need to dress up a bit at top restaurants in Lisbon, Porto, or at luxury hotels and *pousadas*. It's always optimal to dress in layers. Portuguese clothes are reasonably priced, so if necessary you can always buy extras.

Take enough prescribed medication to cover your stay, although Portuguese pharmacies are well stocked with non-prescription drugs, the pharmacists are very helpful, and many speak English. Most common forms of contraception are available, but may be hard to find in more remote areas. If you wear glasses, take a copy of your prescription in case you lose them.

Photographers will have no problem in finding batteries, digital peripherals, and printers in camera stores, although these are almost certainly cheaper in the United States. Video accessories are available in the large towns but take your own charger and transformer. You should also bring digital cards with you, as small towns are not necessarily well stocked. Birders should bring their binoculars, as they, too, are expensive in Portugal.

Insurance

No vaccinations are necessary to enter Portugal. The climate is healthy and the seafood generally fresh and carefully prepared, so you are unlikely to have any stomach problems. However, do make sure that you have travel insurance for medical treatment, repatriation, and baggage and money loss, and make a note of the pertinent telephone numbers to call while abroad. Keep all receipts for expenses, as you will need them to make a claim. Anything stolen should be reported to a police station where a signed statement will be given to you for insurance purposes.

Entry Formalities

Citizens of the United States, Canada, and the United Kingdom do not need a visa for stays of up to 90 days, likewise for Australians and New Zealanders, but they must have a passport that is less than 10 years old and valid for at least 3 months from the end of their stay in Portugal. European Union nationals are allowed to travel with just an ID card. Portuguese police are empowered to make identity spot checks so keep your documents on you (in a safe place) all the time. Customs formalities are the same as in all European Union countries. If a non-EU citizen, you may bring 1 liter of spirits or 2 liters of liquor (not exceeding 22 percent vol) plus 2 liters of still wine, 200 cigarettes, and 50 milliliters of perfume—but all of these goods are cheaper in Portugal. Narcotics and illegal drugs are banned and customs officers are very alert.

HOW TO GET TO PORTUGAL
By Plane

Portugal's flagship airline is **TAP** (Air Portugal, *flytap.com*). It offers direct flights from the U.S. departing from Newark, New York, Miami, San Francisco, and Boston, and from Canada departing from Montreal. Flights on major American airlines have at least one stopover, typically with a layover in Philadelphia. Indirect flights such as those by **British Airways** *(britishairways.com)* offer a wider range of departure cities in the United States and can be cheaper. British Airways provides a direct flight London-Lisbon. Budget airlines **Easyjet** *(easyjet.com)* and **Ryanair** *(ryanair.com)* fly to Lisbon, Porto, and Faro from the UK and many European cities. Easyjet and Ryanair also fly to Funchal-Madeira.

Airports

Portugal's international airports *(ana .pt)* are located in Lisbon, Porto, Faro, and Funchal (Madeira). Lisbon city center is only 4.5 miles (7 km) from the airport, and several city bus lines will take you to the city in 20 or 30 min, but if your bag is too large, you will have to take the special Aerobus. The Vermelha subway line can take you to the São Sebastião stop near Parque Eduardo

VII. In Porto, the purple E line of the metro goes to the center from the airport, 6 miles (11 km) away; it's about a 30-minute ride. At Faro, an airport bus outside the terminal takes you to the city center in about 20 minutes. Local buses Nos. 14 and 16 also run the 2.5 miles (4 km) to and from the airport. Madeira's airport at Funchal is a nerve-racking affair on a rocky outcrop quite a distance from the town center: Airport buses (local transport or shuttles) take 45 minutes and run approximately every hour. Taxis are available at all airports; expect to pay extra for luggage. In Lisbon buy a prepaid voucher from the Turismo de Lisboa counter.

By Boat

There are no scheduled ferries to Portugal, but many cruise ships stop at Lisbon and many more at Madeira.

By Bus

Long-distance buses from Europe are now cushy affairs with air-conditioning, reclining seats, and onboard toilets. However, the proliferation of budget airlines has reduced their viability. In a short time, **Flixbus** (global.flixbus.com) has become the continent's lead company for ground travel and if you reserve far enough in advance, you can find tickets at great prices.

By Car

There are numerous entry points into Portugal from neighboring Spain and rented cars can generally be taken over the border without any extra cost or paperwork. Do check, however, with the rental agency you are using. As the Schengen agreement makes passports between European countries obsolete, border posts are unmanned.

By Train

The trains that go to Portugal from Spain or France were drastically reduced during the COVID-19 pandemic and haven't been reinstated since. Currently, the only train access from Spain is from the city of Vigo (Guixar station; renfe.com), from which a train leaves for Porto, with stops in Valença and Viana do Castelo. The Spanish and Portuguese railways are improving a few lines and will possibly make a direct train between Madrid and Lisbon available in 2024.

GETTING AROUND
In Lisbon

Lisbon has an excellent public transport system. The fast-expanding subway system, **Metropolitano de Lisboa** (metro lisboa.pt), has four lines, 56 stations, and connections (correspondencia) with main and suburban railways and ferries across the Tejo River. Entrances at street level are marked with large red signs with a white M, and trains run from 6:30 a.m. to 1 a.m. To take public transportation, you need a ticket (or you can enter the turnstiles with a credit card); you can also use the convenient **Viva Viagem** card (€0.50), which is valid for the subway and buses, and you can load whatever amount you need on it. A single ticket for the subway costs €1.65, and a daily pass €6.60. Alternatively, the **Lisboa Card** (lisboacard.org) is an excellent value, giving free travel on bus, metro, tram, and Lisbon's unique lifts as well as free admission to 38 sights and a number of discounts. Valid for 24, 48, or 72 hours, it makes sense if you are trying to cover a lot in a short time. It can be purchased online then collected at all Turismo de Lisboa offices. **Carris** (tel 213 500 115, carris.pt) operates all Lisbon public transport except the metro.

Lisbon's most popular form of transport for visitors is the tram, a quaint visual feature of this hilly city. The No. 28 is the classic visitors' route that trundles up from the Baixa to the Alfama, and No. 12 takes you from Praça da Figueira through the Alfama. For Belém, pick up the modern No. 15 tram from Praça do Comercio. Be careful about your pockets and bags, however, as pickpockets target tourists. Suburban trains will whisk you on day trips out of town to Sintra (from Rossio station), to Estoril and Cascais (from Cais do Sodré), or to Setúbal, and farther south from the spectacular station of Oriente. Taxis are plentiful and can be hailed in the street; they run on meters and are reasonably priced. A tip of 10 percent is appreciated. To order a taxi, call **Radio Taxis de Lisboa** (tel 218 119 000). Alternatively, Uber functions in both Lisbon and Porto (uberportugal.pt).

By Air
Throughout the country there are a number of small airports with limited facilities. It is possible to fly from international airports to many of these smaller ones with the domestic airline Sevenair (tel 214 444 545, flysevenair .com). However, given Portugal's inspiring landscapes, it is a far better option to travel by car, train, or bus.

By Bus
Private bus routes crisscross the country, can be faster than trains, and are useful for more remote areas. The most comfortable and fastest are expressos (tel 217 524 524, rede-expressos.pt), closely followed by rápidos, but you should avoid the ultraslow carreiras. Timetables change with the seasons and school holidays so it is advisable to get information online or from the bus station.

By Car
Portugal's road network has greatly expanded and improved over the last years; the same can't be said of the drivers, who some might find a bit reckless. You can get around very safely if you remain extra alert to unexpected maneuvers by other drivers and to unannounced turnoffs. One problem is the shortage of road signs, so make sure you have a good map or navigator. One-way systems through labyrinthine towns can also present frustrations; it is generally advisable to park in a town

center and walk rather than attempt to explore by car. The six-lane highways (auto-estradas) are all toll roads (portagem). IP (itinerário principal) roads are direct routes, but sometimes only have three lanes and alternating passing lanes in each direction. Minor country roads are the most scenic and quiet— the only hazards being tractors, carts, or animals. One of Portugal's greatest pleasures is getting off the beaten track into remote villages, and having a car is the only way to do this.

Drive on the right and give priority to traffic coming from the right. Seat belts are obligatory in both front and back seats and children under 12 must sit in the back. There are strict penalties for driving under the influence (the limit is 0.5 grams per liter of alcohol in your blood), with imprisonment for more than 1.2 grams per liter. On highways, dipped headlights in daylight are compulsory. Police will impose instant fines for traffic offenses such as speeding, parking, or lack of seat belts. Speed limits are 75 miles an hour (120 kph) on toll highways, 62 miles an hour (100 kph) on IP and IC (secondary principal) roads, and 53 miles an hour (90 kph) on national roads. In towns the limit is 30 miles an hour (50 kph).

Car rental through **Hertz, Avis, National, Budget,** and **Europcar** is easy to arrange in your own country by phone or Internet. Most of these companies have counters at the international airports alongside local outfits and rates are reasonable, particularly out of season. You must be older than 21 years old (though some agencies require a minimum age of 23 or even 25) and have had a license for at least a year. An international driving license is not necessary. Rental rates usually include mileage and CDW (collision damage waiver), with optional surcharges for personal or passenger insurance. The rental company will give you details of breakdown services and what to do in case of an accident. Fuel, whether unleaded (sem chumbo) or diesel (gasóleo), is easily available with little difference in prices between vendors. International credit cards are accepted at most gas stations, but be aware that in small rural places ATMs may be less frequently available.

By Ferry

Ferries cross the Tejo River in Lisbon from Belém, Cais do Sodré, and Terreiro do Paço (Praça do Comercio). You can also try a private river cruise with **Tagus Cruises** (tel 925 610 034, tagus cruises.com). Porto is the starting point for numerous boat trips and cruises along the Douro River beginning at the Cais de Ribeira. Several companies offer tours: **Douro Cruises** (tel 226 191 090, cruzeiros-douro.pt) has a wide range; **Portowellcome** (tel 223 747 320 or 916 986 257, portowellcome .com), in Vila Nova de Gaia, organizes similar boat trips.

By Train

There is a vast range of comfort in the Portuguese train network, from fast Alfa Pendular to the more spartan regionais. The quickest Alfa Pendular trains (some only first class) cover north–south routes between Lisbon and Porto or Braga (via Coimbra) and Lisbon–Faro. Next down come directos intercidades, reasonably fast local trains with first- and second-class sections. Regionais cover the rural routes, stopping at every stop along the way. Timetables and fare information are available from **Comboios de Portugal** (tel 707 210 220, cp.pt), where seat bookings on fast trains should be made. Special tourist tickets are available. Portugal also offers quaint narrow-gauge railways in the Douro Valley.

PRACTICAL ADVICE
Communications

The word correio denotes a post office or services. First-class inland mail is correio azul. To mail packages, go to the counter marked encomendas. Also available at post offices is EMS, an express service. Post offices are normally open 8:30 a.m. to 6:30 p.m., Monday through Friday. In bigger towns they may also open on Saturday morning, while they may close at lunchtime in small towns. Public telephones are increasingly rare and are being taken down almost everywhere. Phone cards (cartão telefónico) can be bought at post offices and newsdealers. European roaming works also in Portugal, which allows you to use a European phone under whatever plan you have in your European home country.

International code for Portugal: + 351
Emergency: 112

Internet

Internet cafés and wireless areas are readily available, and you will have little trouble getting online in Lisbon and Porto. Even in smaller places public access is increasingly available in cafés and local shopping malls. Tourist offices often offer free Internet as do some municipalities elsewhere. European roaming allows you to connect under whatever plan you have in your European home country, but some might have limits on the amount of data you can use, so check with your operator beforehand.

Conversions

1 kilo = 2.2 pounds
1 liter = 0.2642 U.S. gallon
1 kilometer = 0.62 mile
1 meter = 1.093 yards
1 centimeter = 0.39 inch

Women's Clothing

U.S.	8	10	12	14	16	18
Europe	36	38	40	42	44	46

Men's Clothing

U.S.	36	38	40	42	44	46
Europe	46	48	50	52	54	56

Women's Shoes

U.S.	6–6.5	7–7.5	8–8.5	9–9.5
Europe	38	39	40–41	42

Men's Shoes

U.S.	8	8.5	9.5	10.5	11.5	12
Europe	41	42	43	44	45	46

Electricity

Voltage is 220V or 225AC. Plugs have two round pins. American appliances will need an adapter and a transformer.

Etiquette & Local Customs

The Portuguese are relaxed and self-confident, particularly the younger generation. Although formality and politeness are still important, much of the Portuguese lifestyle is comparable to any Western country. Many Portuguese speak English, French, or both, but they will appreciate your effort if you learn a few greetings in Portuguese. Their age-old enmity with Spain means that the Spanish language is less welcome, although it is understood. Above all, the Portuguese are extremely helpful; you will never be at a loss for assistance.

Holidays

Regional festivals and saints' days are celebrated locally but the main public holidays are the following:

January 1 (New Year's Day)
February (Shrove Tuesday)
March/April (Good Friday)
April 25 (1974 Revolution Day)
May 1 (Labor Day)
Early June (Corpus Cristi)
June 10 (Portugal and Camões Day)
August 15 (Assumption)
October 5 (Republic Day)
November 1 (All Saints' Day)
December 1 (Restoration of Independence)
December 8 (Immaculate Conception)
December 25 (Christmas)

Media

There are four main daily newspapers, either Lisbon- or Porto-based, and two weeklies, in Portuguese. A weekly English-language newspaper, the Portugal News (*theportugalnews.com*) contains useful local information as well as a roundup of Portuguese news stories. English and American newspapers can be found in the main towns of Lisbon, Porto, Coimbra, and Funchal, as well as more widely in the Algarve. Most hotels have satellite TV bringing international channels to your bedroom. The country's channels are in Portuguese, with the exception of movies, usually broadcast in their original languages.

Money Matters

The currency in Portugal is the euro, like most other European countries. Exchange counters can be found at airports, otherwise most banks change foreign currency—although rates and charges vary considerably. ATMs are widespread and accept all major international cards. Large hotels will exchange currency but generally at lower rates. A sales tax known as IVA (VAT) in Portugal is at present 23 percent. Persons from outside the European Union, when visiting for fewer than 180 days, can reclaim this tax by requesting the form "Isenção de IVA" and presenting it to customs when leaving Portugal.

Opening Times

Banks are open from Monday to Friday, 8:30 a.m. to 3 p.m., except on public holidays. Shopping hours are 9:30/10 a.m. to 7 p.m. Monday to Friday, but in smaller towns most close for lunch 12:30/1 p.m. to 2:30 p.m. Saturday opening is 9 a.m. to 1 p.m., however, this is now changing and many reopen in the afternoon. Shopping centers are open 10 a.m. to 12 a.m. all week except possibly for the Christmas and Easter Day holidays. Many museums are closed on Mondays, and some on Sunday afternoons as well. Attractions in smaller towns may close for lunch. For all sights, check ahead if you are planning a visit on a holiday.

Places of Worship

Catholic churches are found throughout Portugal, but it is rare to find facilities for other denominations, except in the Algarve and on Madeira. When visiting churches, be sensitive to local worshippers, dress conservatively, and keep your voices low.

Time Differences

Portugal runs on GMT (Greenwich Mean Time), so it is one hour behind Spain, the same as the United Kingdom, and five hours ahead of Eastern Standard Time. Between the end of March and end of October, it operates on GMT plus one hour.

Tipping

When tipping at restaurants, the Portuguese tend to leave approximately 5 percent. A foreign tourist is generally expected to leave 10 percent, though there is no law stating what you should leave. When tipping, bear in mind that one euro does not go very far, and good service helps to make the meal.

Travelers With Disabilities

Accessibility is becoming more widespread, not only through parking spots but also with reserved seats on public transportation. The **Accessible Portugal** association has created a website and app, **TUR4all** *(tur4all.com)* that has valuable information and tours for travelers with disabilities.

In the United States, the best source of information for the blind is the **American Foundation for the Blind** *(tel 212 502 7600 in the U.S., afb.org)*.

Numerous tour operators are specialized in trips for people with various types of disabilities, including **Tapooz Travel** *(tapooztravel.com)*, which operates from the U.S., and **Disabled Holidays** *(disabledholidays.com)* in the U.K., which also offers accessible vacations, from city breaks to more active tours.

Visitor Information

The Portuguese National Tourist Office has some useful tourist literature, but it is, above all, their large network of offices throughout the country that are to be commended. Bi- or trilingual staff in even the smallest of towns will talk you through whatever you want to see and comment intelligently on recent changes.

Portuguese National Tourist Office
866 2nd Ave., 8th fl., New York
Tel 646 723 0213
info.usa@turismodeportugal.pt
visitportugal.com

EMERGENCIES

Crime & Police

Portugal is a generally safe, law-abiding country and the greatest crimes are petty thefts and pickpocketing, mainly in the touristic areas of the cities. Drivers should not leave belongings visible inside the car: Lock everything up in the trunk.

By calling 112 from anywhere in Portugal you will be connected to fire, police, and ambulance services. Every fire brigade also maintains one or more ambulances for emergencies. Security in cities and towns is handled by the Polícia de Segurança Pública (PSP), in rural areas by the Guarda Nacional Republicana (GNR), and the traffic by the GNR's Brigada de Trânsito. On motorways and several major roads there are SOS phone boxes for help in accidents or breakdowns.

Embassies & Consulates

U.S. Embassy
Avenida das Forças Armadas, Lisbon
Tel 217 273 300 or 210 942 000
(after hours/emergency dial either telephone number and press 0 to speak to embassy official)
pt.usembassy.gov

Canadian Embassy
Avenida da Liberdade 196–200 3rd fl., Lisbon
Tel 213 164 600
lsbon.consular@international.gc.ca
travel.gc.ca

Canadian Consulate
Rua Frei Lourenço de Santa Maria 1,
Faro
Tel 289 803 757

British Embassy & Consulate (Lisbon)
Rua de São Bernardo 33, Lisbon
Tel 213 924 000
(in case of emergency, also Tel 213 924 000)
gov.uk/contact-consulate-lisbon

Embassy of Ireland, Portugal
Avenida da Liberdade 200, 4th floor,
Lisbon
Tel 213 308 200
ireland.ie/en/portugal/lisbon

Health
Pharmacists can give advice on simple health problems and suggest treatment. They are also allowed to sell many medicines without a doctor's prescription. A green cross on a white background denotes a pharmacy. A red cross on a white background denotes a Red Cross station. In most towns there are Emergency Treatment Centers (SAP), providing assistance 24/7.
Ambulance, tel 112

Lost Property
In Lisbon, property lost on trams or buses is centralized at the police station in Praça Cidade Salazar *(tel 218 535 403)*. The subway lost and found office is located in Praça da Figueira, near the Baixa-Chiado station *(tel 213 500 115)*. In the case of theft, you will need to make a police report at any station for insurance purposes.

What to Do in Case of a Car Accident
In the case of a minor accident, fill out a *Constat Amiable* (European Accident Statement), which is an exchange of basic information with the other driver. One of these forms should be included in your rental documents. In the case of a serious accident, dial 112.

FURTHER READING
The number one Portuguese author is undoubtedly the poet Fernando Pessoa, whose posthumous international best-seller *Book of Disquiet* revolves around his melancholic ruminations in Lisbon, although its underlying sense of tragedy is perhaps not the most uplifting for vacations. Luís Vaz de Camões's 16th-century classic, *The Lusiads,* is Portugal's national epic in the style of Homer's *Odyssey;* it relates Vasco da Gama's sea voyage to India. In contemporary literature, António Lobo Antunes's novels should be read for a lucid perspective with a strong psychological bent. Some are harrowing indictments of society; all are deep, including *The Inquisitor's Manual* (which recreates Salazar's regime and its iniquities). José Cardoso Pires's exciting thriller *Ballad of Dog's Beach* is, on the surface, a detective story, yet it reveals the underside of the Salazar regime and its secret police. José Saramago is considered the doyen of Portuguese literature, and his books vary considerably. His personal travel guide, *A Journey to Portugal,* is an insightful read. Saramago's best seller *Baltasar and Blimunda* gives a surrealistic reflection of life in 18th-century Portugal during the building of the Mafra palace. Miguel Torga's books *The Creation Days One and Two* and *Tales from the Mountain* (banned under the Salazar regime) should be read by anyone traveling in the Trás-os-Montes area, where they are set. Marion Kaplan's book, *The Portuguese: The Land and Its People* (rev. ed., 2006), somewhat overambitiously tries to cover everything under the sun but gives great insight into the Portuguese way of life and recent history. Jean Andersen's *Food of Portugal* (1994), although older, remains a standard for information on regional food, wine, markets, restaurants, and, of course, recipes. Barbara Segall's illustrated book *The Garden Lover's Guide to Spain and Portugal* (1999) will inspire you to discover Portugal's beautiful private and public gardens.

HOTELS & RESTAURANTS

Finding comfortable and interesting places to sleep and eat can make all the difference in your visit. Portugal offers a wide range of hotel and restaurant selections in all price categories and styles—there's something for every taste.

HOTELS

Portuguese hotel classification is a minefield defying all logic, but luckily moves are afoot to simplify the system. Taxes are included in the rates unless stated otherwise. (Breakfast is generally included but should be confirmed when booking.) There are, however, huge rate variations from season to season. April through September sees the highest rates, peaking in August, while November through February has the lowest.

You can rely on the state-owned but privately managed *pousadas* (inns) for upscale comfort and atmosphere. These converted palaces, monasteries, and castles (*pousada charme, histórica, or histórica design*) or relatively modern hotels in exceptional locations (*pousada natureza*) offer individualized decors, excellent service, and reliable restaurants serving regional cuisine. If you intend to visit several, consider the Pousadas Passport discount program. For more information, contact **Pousadas de Portugal** *(tel 210 158 100, pousadas.pt)*.

Private hotels range from luxurious palaces to basic accommodations. In between, *estalagens* (country inns) and *albergarias* (city or town inns) are generally very acceptable, but some can be frayed at the edges. The smaller scale *residencial* (denoted by an R) and *pensão* (P) can be an excellent value and are generally well maintained. In recent years an almost countless number of trendy hostels have opened up, primarily in the larger cities. Some are cheap and basic, others offer quirky and often very comfortable lodging. For booking, visit *hostel world.com*. At the bottom of the scale are rooms in restaurants or private houses, which can also be perfectly acceptable.

State-monitored, privately owned guesthouses fall into further categories: *turismo de habitação* (TH), in houses of architectural interest, *turismo rural* (TR), and *agro-turismo* (AT), the latter two offering rural and farmhouse accommodations respectively. These establishments provide good opportunities to meet local people and to experience Portuguese home life and generosity. Breakfasts can be epicurean feasts with home-baked pastries, local cheeses and sausages, freshly squeezed orange juice, and strong coffee or tea. Some places will also provide dinner for a modest charge. Many of these establishments are available through **Solares de Portugal** *(Praça da República, Ponte de Lima, tel 258 931 750, solaresdeportugal.pt)*, an association offering self-catering cottages or guest rooms in some superb manor houses and country estates. For an excellent choice of private accommodation in manor houses and guesthouses, as well as well-vetted hotels, all of which can be reserved on its website, contact **Pousadas of Portugal** *(Rua Ricardo Marques 41, Viana do Castelo, tel 258 821 751, pousadasofportugal.com)*.

RESTAURANTS

Each region of Portugal has a plethora of restaurants that range from the lowly *tasca* (tavern) or *cervejaria* (beerhouse with simple food) to a *restaurante* (more upscale, offering a choice of dishes), a *marisqueira* (specializing in fish and shellfish), or a *churrasqueira* (featuring spit-roasted or grilled foods). Appearances can be deceiving: You may see smart businessmen lunching in a somewhat scruffy tasca—they are drawn by the quality of the food, the price, and the friendliness of the owners, not the decor. Cafés and some restaurants often serve a lunchtime *prato do dia* (dish of the day), which is generally homemade and a good value.

Depending on location and style, Portuguese restaurant prices are very reasonable compared with other European countries and servings can be gigantic. It may be possible to order a half portion—*meia dose*—particularly at lunch at more traditional, casual places. A law passed in 2007 prohibited smoking in public places. Bars and restaurants are now nonsmoking, though some proprietors allow smoking in covered outdoor areas.

Hours of Eating

Generally speaking, lunch is eaten between 12:30 and 2:30 p.m.; dinner between 8 and 10 p.m. (sometimes later in large towns). If you wish to dine at one of the upscale city restaurants, you should make a reservation.

How to Order

At the table in most places, you'll be served bread, butter, olives, and assorted appetizers. These are not free; you can refuse them with a smile—though unless very elaborate they do not add much to the bill. And you may regret sending them back: It may take a while for your food to be prepared—always a good sign of freshness. Vegetarians are not well catered to beyond soups and omelets. It may be necessary to special request vegetable side dishes. Fish dishes are plentiful throughout Portugal.

Drinks

Portuguese grapes produce some excellent, little-known wines—reds, whites, and rosés—and the *vinho da casa* (house wine) can generally be relied upon to be an excellent choice. In the north, enjoy the refreshing young *vinho verde* (white or red), with its low alcohol content. Portuguese beer, a strong lager, comes in three brands: Sagres, Crystal, and Super Bock. Mineral water *(agua mineral)* is always available either *com gas* (carbonated) or *sem gas* (still). After eating (although rarely done by locals), you may wish to sample one of Portugal's famous fortified wines, like port or Madeira.

Check & Tip

A conta (the check) may be slow in coming, and is sometimes known to contain the odd error, so best to give it a quick look. The Portuguese leave small tips—barely 5 percent—but if you like the service and food you should leave more.

Credit Cards

Many hotels and restaurants accept major credit cards. If the credit card icon is shown, then American Express, MasterCard, and Visa are all accepted. Those that accept some or none are noted.

ORGANIZATION

Hotels and restaurants are listed first by chapter area and town, then by price category, then in alphabetical order with hotels listed first. Hotel restaurants of note have been boldfaced in the hotel entries and indicated by a restaurant icon beneath the hotel icon (if they're unusually special, they are treated in a separate entry within the restaurant section).

▶ **LISBON**

🏨 **BAIRRO ALTO HOTEL**
$$$$$
PRAÇA LUIS DE CAMÕES 2,
BAIRRO ALTO
TEL 213 408 288
bairroaltohotel.com
Situated on the Praça de Camões, between the Chiado and Bairro Alto districts, this elegant boutique hotel is in a very good location if

---

🔵 Air-conditioning 🏊 Indoor Pool 🏊 Outdoor Pool 🏋 Health Club 📶 Wi-Fi 💳 Credit Cards

---

PRICES

HOTELS

An indication of the cost of a double room in the high season is given by **$** signs.

$$$$$	Over $250
$$$$	$200–$250
$$$	$150–$200
$$	$80–$150
$	Under $80

RESTAURANTS

An indication of the cost of a three-course meal without drinks is given by **$** signs.

$$$$$	Over $65
$$$$	$40–$65
$$$	$28–$40
$$	$15–$28
$	Under $15

---

you want to explore the city. It offers well-appointed rooms with a sophisticated decor in muted tones and classic, wood-paneled bathrooms. Its rooftop terrace enjoys outstanding views.

🏨 55 🅿 ⬍ 🚭 📺 📶 Free 🛗

🏨 POUSADA DE LISBOA
$$$$$

PRAÇA DO COMÉRCIO 31–34,
BAIXA

TEL 210 407 640

pousadas.pt

For a first-rate hotel that has a terrace unlike any other and consistently high standards, not to mention the prime location, check into one of the latest Pestana hotels to open in the capital. The well soundproofed rooms look out over the Praça do Comércio and the river Tejo beyond. Rooms are of a good size for a European capital, decorated in a minimal style with luxury bathrooms.

🏨 90 ⬍ 🏔 📺 📶 Free 🛗

🏨 MY STORY HOTEL ROSSIO
$$$–$$$$

PRAÇA D. PEDRO IV 59,
BAIXA

TEL 213 400 380

mystoryhotels.com

Opened in 2015, perfectly located in the central Rossio square and set over four floors, this is one of Lisbon's new wave of fashionable establishments catering to the design-conscious on a mid-range budget.

🏨 46 ⬍ 🚭 📶 Free 🛗

SOMETHING SPECIAL

🏨 YORK HOUSE
🍴 $$$

RUA DAS JANELAS VERDES 32

TEL 213 962 435

yorkhouselisboa.com

Arguably one of Lisbon's most attractive hotels, this establishment—partly converted from a 17th-century convent—maintains its position in the upper echelons of style. Terraced patios and ivy-clad walls introduce a dramatic interior of vaulted corridors painted in deep oxblood and Prussian blue, yet the rooms have been given a discreet contemporary makeover. Graham Greene and John le Carré stayed here. The restaurant currently opens for a minimum of 15 guests.

🏨 32 🅿 🚭 📶 Free 🛗

🏨 AS JANELAS VERDES
$$

RUA DAS JANELAS VERDES 47,
BAIRRO ALTO

TEL 213 968 143

lisbonheritagehotels.com

Plush and ornate, this 18th-century mansion is now a boutique hotel. Well situated between Lapa and the docks in an area of embassies, this longtime favorite is close to the Museu Nacional de Arte Antiga. The top-floor library and terrace make relaxing

---

escapes. Room sizes vary, and some offer views over the Tejo River.

ⓘ 29 🅿 ⮁ 🚫 🔆 📶 Free 🚭

🏨 LISBON DESTINATION HOSTEL
$$
LARGO DO DUQUE DE CADAVAL 17,
BAIRRO ALTO
TEL 213 466 457
destinationhostels.com

Inside the 19th-century Rossio train station (despite this, a quiet accommodation) is a hostel with rooms of various capacities and types, for all budgets, even designed for families. It has a beautiful winter garden and nooks for relaxing, modern and sensible "capsule" style rooms and beds with all amenities, and kind and helpful staff.

ⓘ 35 📶 Free 🚭 All major cards

🍴 ALMA
$$$$$
RUA ANCHIETA 15, CHIADO
TEL 213 470 650
almalisboa.pt

In 2015, chef Henrique Sá Pessoa reopened his restaurant Alma, in the Chiado, within the stone-arched, former warehouse of Livraria Bertrand (one of the oldest bookstores in Europe). His innovative creations are influenced by traditional Portuguese cuisine and by his personal travels, particularly to the Far East. The work of the chef and his staff has been rewarded with two Michelin stars. Reservations required.

🕐 Closed Sun.–Mon. 🚫 🔆 🚭

🍴 BELCANTO
$$$$$
RUA SERPA PINTO 10A,
BAIRRO ALTO
TEL 213 420 607
belcanto.pt

One of the few restaurants in the country to boast two Michelin stars,

Belcanto is the flagship restaurant of Portuguese chef José Avillez, who takes diners on a gastronomic and sensory journey where, as he likes to say, "each dish tells a story and stirs the emotions of those willing to try it." Reservations essential. It has an excellent wine list with over 350 selections.

🕐 Closed Sun.–Mon. 🚫 🔆 🚭

SOMETHING SPECIAL

🍴 100 MANEIRAS
$$$$–$$$$$
RUA DO TEIXEIRA 39,
BAIRRO ALTO
TEL 910 918 181
100maneiras.com

This fashionable Bairro Alto restaurant only offers a ten-course, fixed-price tasting menu from a kitchen headed up by the highly acclaimed, Sarajevo born, Ljubomir Stanisic. His highly creative dishes fuse traditional Portuguese ingredients with French sophistication; for the complete experience, splash out on the accompanying wine-tasting menu. Alternatively, you can try the 100 Maneiras Bistro *(Largo da Trindade 9)*, open until 2 a.m., with its more affordable prices.

🕐 Closed L 🚫 🔆 🚭

🍴 MINI BAR
$$$$–$$$$$
RUA NOVA DA TRINDADE 18,
BAIRRO ALTO
TEL 211 305 393
minibar.pt

One of chef José Avillez's Lisbon restaurants, this is an excellent pick if Belcanto is out of reach or fully booked. The ambience is informal, yet dramatic; the cocktails are prepared to perfection (arguably the best pisco sour this side of the Andes); and the tasting menu is 12 courses of tapa-sized sensory overload (à la carte menu also available). Reservations advised.

🕐 Closed L 🚭 🚫 📵

🍴 PALÁCIO CHIADO
$$$$
RUA DO ALECRIM 70, CHIADO
TEL 210 101 184
palaciochiado.pt
For something a little different, try Lisbon's food court in a palace. Built in 1781, this elegant building reopened in 2016—its frescoes, elaborate cornices, and stained-glass windows carefully restored—then completely renewed in 2018. Its glorious salons are now home to several fine-dining experiences. Start on the ground floor with a drink and an appetizer before heading to the more sumptuous (and more expensive) rooms on the top floor.

🚭 🚫 📵

🍴 CERVEJARIA TRINDADE
$$$–$$$$
RUA NOVA DA TRINDADE 20,
BAIRRO ALTO
TEL 213 423 506
cervejariatrindade.pt
Worth it for the location alone, this medieval monastery has experienced earthquakes and fires throughout its history and was completely renovated in the 19th century. It has spacious rooms decorated with azulejos. Trindade is the oldest brewery in the country; today you can eat at the restaurant with an à la carte menu of excellent Portuguese cuisine, or more informally at the bar or on the terrace.

📵

🍴 CHAPITÔ À MESA
$$$
RUA COSTA DO CASTELO 7, ALFAMA
TEL 218 875 077
chapito.org
Just down from the castle, this young and cheerful tapas bar is part of the Chapito circus school cooperative. The attractive terrace is a good spot for a salad or grilled lamb on warm evenings; a smarter upstairs restaurant (with an excellent view, especially at sunset) serves international cuisine. Live music most evenings.

📵

🍴 CLUBE DE FADO
$$$
RUA SÃO JOÃO DA PRAÇA 92–94
TEL 218 852 704
clubedefado.pt
Tucked in the lower part of the Alfama, this bar/restaurant is geared to nightly fado sessions. Eat and drink traditional fare until 2 a.m. while listening to some of the capital's top voices. Be sure to note the Moorish arch integrated into the bare stone walls.

🏠 120 🕐 Closed L 🚫 📵

🍴 MARTINHO DA ARCADA
$$–$$$
PRAÇA DO COMÉRCIO 3
TEL 218 879 259
martinhodaarcada.pt
In this elegant antique café, founded in 1782, you can breathe in the history of the literature and writers of this grand country. Pessoa stopped by often on his way home from work and events were held with José Saramago and the Brazilian author Jorge Amado. Get a seat at a table outside under the portico, order a cup of coffee or a snack, and savor your surroundings.

🚫 📵

🍴 BONJARDIM
$$
TRAVESSA DE SANTO ANTÃO 7–11
TEL 213 427 424 OR 213 424 389
Tourists flock to this Lisbon classic; a simple, no frills eatery with its several dining rooms and terraces. Try the typical Portuguese *piri-piri* chicken,

served with generous portions of fries and tomato salad.

🕐 Closed Mon. 🔆 🗝️

🍴 TIME OUT MARKET
$–$$$
MERCADO DA RIBEIRA, AVENIDA 24 DE JULHO
TEL 210 607 403
timeoutmarket.com
Part traditional food market, part gastro-food hall, this is a great place to pick up produce and deli items or explore at the approximately 50 food stalls next door, each representing well-established and highly regarded Lisbon restaurants and food outlets. You'll find everything from seafood, wood-fired pizza, exotic cuisine, and experimental modern Portuguese food.

🍴 A BRASILEIRA
$
RUA GARRETT 120
TEL 213 469 541
Part of a venerable old chain, this café has strong literary associations. Poet Fernando Pessoa, whose bronze statue sits outside, used to frequent this showpiece of wood paneling and ornate details. The café serves delectable pastries and coffee, although service can be offhand.

🔆 🗝️

▶ PORTO & NORTE

AMARANTE

🍴 CONFEITARIA DA PONTE
$
RUA 31 DE JANEIRO 186
TEL 255 432 034
confeitariadaponte.pt
Supplying the Amarante people with fluffy *pão de ló* (light eggy sponge cake) since 1930, this establishment, overlooking the river near the old

bridge, is an obligatory stop for your morning coffee or an afternoon tea. In addition, there is a huge selection of typical *doces conventuais* (sweet, egg-based delicacies) to sample.

🗝️

BRAGA

🏨 HOTEL BRACARA AUGUSTA
$$–$$$
AVENIDA CENTRAL 134
TEL 253 206 260
bracaraaugusta.com
Centrally located downtown, offering exceptionally friendly service and superb value. Rooms are simple but clean and comfortably furnished and the breakfast is generous.

🛏️ 18 🅿️ 🛗 🔆 🗝️ Free 🗝️

🏨 HOTEL DO PARQUE
$$–$$$
LARGO DO SANTUÁRIO DO BOM JESUS
TEL 255 603 470
hoteisbomjesus.pt
High on the hilltop above the city of Braga, next to the church of Bom Jesus do Monte, are the Hotel do Parque and its sister hotels, **Hotel do Elevador** and **Hotel do Templo.** All three offer the same standard of service and amenities, though the rooms at the Elevador can claim the most spectacular views and the Parque benefits from a quieter setting backed by the park.

🛏️ 49 🅿️ 🛗 🔆 📺 🗝️ Free 🗝️

🏨 HOTEL RESIDENTIAL DONA SOFIA
$
LARGO DE SÃO JOÃO DO SOUTO 131
TEL 253 263 160
hoteldonasofia.com
Well located on an attractive square in central Braga within minutes of

the sights. Rooms are bright and comfortable; a good, budget-friendly stopover.

🛈 34 🅿 🛗 🚭 📶 Free 🖼

🍴 COZINHA DA SÉ
$$
RUA DOM FREI CAETANO BRANDÃO 129
TEL 253 277 343
cozinhadase.pt
Arguably Braga's best restaurant, located around the corner from the cathedral, its traditional, northern granite interior reflects the northern cuisine, served in generous portions. Pork with chestnuts and apple puree or the local Barrosã beef are very good choices.

🕐 Closed Sun. D & Mon. 🚭 🖼

🍴 RESTAURANTE PANORAMICO
$$
HOTEL DO ELEVADOR, BOM JESUS DO MONTE
TEL 253 603 400
hoteisbomjesus.pt
This is the perfect spot to watch the sunset from high above Braga. Book a table by the window and indulge in the local cuisine, whether octopus or kid goat with rice, both preceded by classic cabbage or bacalhau soup. Helpful service and good wines will complete the evening.

🅿 🚭 🖼

🍴 A BRASILEIRA
$
LARGO BARÃO DE SÃO MARTINHO 17
TEL 253 262 104
Step into the past at one of Braga's oldest cafés, its interior retaining all its original architectural features. This city icon first began selling coffee in 1907; drinks and light snacks are served throughout the day.

🚭

BRAGANÇA

🏨 POUSADA BRAGANÇA
🍴 $$–$$$
ESTRADA DO TURISMO
TEL 273 331 493
pousadas.pt/en/hotel/pousada -braganca
It's one of the more modern *pousadas,* designed in the 1950s, offering efficiency and comfort. It lies just outside the city center of Bragança, across the Fervença River, and enjoys superb views over the valley to the distant mountains. All rooms have balconies and nice views.

🛈 28 🅿 🛗 🚭 🚭 🏊
📶 Free 🖼

🏨 A LAGOSTA PERDIDA
$$
RUA DO CIMO 4
ALDEIA DE MONTESINHO
TEL 273 919 031
lagostaperdida.com
A great base for those wanting to explore the countryside around Bragança by car or on foot, this family-run guesthouse provides spacious, clean rooms with rustic features and modern bathrooms. Renovated to a high standard, the property added a lovely heated pool and attractive landscaped patios. Standard prices include breakfast and a three-course dinner with wine, water, and coffee. Basketball net and toys for children.

🛈 6 🅿 🚭 🏊 📶 Free in public areas 🖼

🏨 HOTEL TULIPA
$
RUA DR. FRANCISCO FELGUEIRAS 8–10
TEL 273 331 675
hoteltulipa.com
This friendly, well-maintained, and well-managed hotel is located right in the town center and is an excellent choice for those traveling on a

budget. The clean, simply furnished rooms have all the essentials for a comfortable stay.

[1] 30 ⊟ 🖸 📶 Free 🖴

SOMETHING SPECIAL

SOLAR BRAGANÇANO
$$
PRAÇA DA SÉ 34
TEL 273 323 875
admr.sb@gmail.com
Located in an 18th-century mansion, this gem of a restaurant seems to step back in time with chandeliers, heavy linen tablecloths, and classical music. Feast on game and regional dishes such as rabbit, pheasant with chestnut, partridge with grapes, wild boar, or venison; fish is on offer, too. Wines are local, *vinho verde* or Barca Velha from the Douro. The owners ensure that everyone is happy. There is a garden for warmer days.

🞢 75 🕒 Closed Mon. 🖸 🖴

CHAVES

SOMETHING SPECIAL

FORTE DE SÃO FRANCISCO
$$
RUA TERREIRO DE CAVALARIA
TEL 276 333 700
fortesaofrancisco.com
An unusual place converted from a former convent inside the walls of a fort. Patios are filled with antiques, architectural features, and paintings. Rooms are classically tasteful, but interest lies in the spacious public areas, including a huge pool with views. The restaurant **Cozinha do Convento** serves seasonal Trás-os-Montes specialities such as chestnut soup, veal and chorizo, and Chaves smoked ham.

 [1] 58 🅿 ⊟ 🖸 🖸 🞢 📶 Free 🖴

DOURO VALLEY

VINTAGE HOUSE
$$$$
RUA ANTÓNIO MANUEL SARAIVA, PINHÃO
TEL 254 730 230 OR 220 133 137
vintagehousehotel.com
This hotel occupies a breathtaking site in Pinhão, on the banks of the Douro River. Generous public areas are decorated in traditional Portuguese fashion and chintz prevails in the bedrooms, all of which overlook the river. Excellent amenities (tennis court, activities, tours) make it popular with boat cruises from Porto.

[1] 43 🅿 ⊟ 🖸 🖸 🞢 📶 Free in public areas 🖴

CASA DOS VISCONDES DA VÁRZEA
$$$
VÁRZEA DE ABRUNHAIS, LAMEGO
TEL 254 690 020 OR 967 606 385
hrcvv@netcabo.pt
This well-appointed rural hotel sits in a lovely vineyard setting. The owner has virtually rebuilt her family manor house and added lavish and antique furnishings, making your stay feel slightly akin to staying with an aristocratic friend. Pool, horseback riding, and tennis are available.

[1] 29 🅿 🖸 🞢 📶 Free in public areas 🖴

GUIMARÃES

SOMETHING SPECIAL

HOTEL DA OLIVEIRA
$$–$$$
LARGO DA OLIVEIRA
TEL 253 514 157
hoteldaoliveira.com
Smack in the middle of the monuments, this hotel retains the ambience of its former manor house status. Creaky wooden floors and

whitewashed walls contrast delightfully with contemporary furnishings. Reserve a room on the top floor, as evening carousing in the square below can be noisy. The excellent restaurant serves regional specialities.

🚹 20 ➐ 🅢 🅢 📶 Free 🕸

🍴 SÃO GIÃO
$$$$
AVENIDA C. JOAQUIM DE ALMEIDA
FREITAS 56, MOREIRA DE CÓNEGOS
TEL 253 561 853
sgiao.com

For something sophisticated, head 20 minutes south of Guimarães to the village of Moreira de Cónegos. Considered to be one of the best restaurants in the region, São Gião's elegant dining room looks out over vineyards; its food is traditional yet refined and its wine list is extensive.

🔲 80 🕐 Closed Mon. 🅢 🕸

PENEDA-GERÊS

🍴 ESPIGUEIRO DO SOAJO
$–$$
SOAJO, ARCOS DE VALDEVEZ
TEL 258 576 136

The perfect place to stop for a well-deserved break from the national park's tortuous roads. Sit inside the rustic restaurant or in its garden to sample such local specialties as chicken and rice, *bacalhau* (salted cod), or roast kid. The owner speaks fluent English.

🅿 🕐 Closed Mon., also Nov. 🕸

PORTO

SOMETHING SPECIAL

🏨 INTERCONTINENTAL PORTO
🍴 PALACIO DAS CARDOSAS
$$$$
PRAÇA DA LIBERDADE 25
TEL 220 035 600
ihg.com

This luxurious, five-star hotel sits on Porto's main square within a converted 18th-century palace and within walking distance of the city's main attractions. Guest rooms are beautifully furnished, marble bathrooms are packed with fluffy towels, and many rooms have views over the square. Staff are friendly and knowledgeable.

🚹 121 🅿 ➐ 🅢 🅢 🍽
📶 Free 🕸

🏨 PESTANA VINTAGE
🍴 PORTO HOTEL
$$$$
PRAÇA DA RIBEIRA 1
TEL 223 402 300
pestanacollection.com/en/hotel/pestana-porto

The setting is hard to beat as this top hotel stands directly opposite the port lodges on the main quay of the Douro River. Built into a section of medieval wall and occupying houses dating from the 16th to 18th centuries, it still manages to maintain an intimate feel. Most rooms overlook the river.

🚹 90 🅿 ➐ 🅢 🅢
📶 Free 🕸

🏨 HOTEL EUROSTARS
DAS ARTES
$$
RUA DO ROSÁRIO 160–164
TEL 222 071 250
eurostarsdasartes.com

A short walk or tram ride from the city center, this hotel offers a great base for those wishing to escape the bustle of downtown. Easily recognized by its period blue-tile façade, its interior is modern with all the expected amenities and comforts of a four-star hotel. Don't miss the excellent buffet breakfast. If you have a car, book a place in the underground parking lot.

🚹 89 🅿 ➐ 🅢 📶 Free 🕸

🏨 CATS HOSTEL PORTO
🍴 $
RUA DO CATIVO 26–28
TEL 220 043 030
catshostels.com/porto
In recent years, as in Lisbon, Porto has seen a wave of design hostels open their doors to the more discerning budget traveler. In addition to dorm beds, many offer private rooms with ensuite bathroom facilities and family rooms, as well as self-catering facilities. The hostel is centrally located with a pleasant roof bar terrace.

ⓘ 16 🔁 🔲 📶 Free 🗝

🍴 PEDRO LEMOS
$$$$$
RUA DO PADRE LUÍS CABRAL 974
TEL 220 115 986
pedrolemos.net
Inside this Foz town house, Michelin-starred chef Pedro Lemos takes seasonal ingredients and traditional recipes and transforms them into works of art. Do not expect huge portions, but do expect exceptional quality and creativity. The tasting menu is a good option and there is an extensive list of Portugal's best wines, available by the glass.

🔲 44 🕐 Closed Sun. & Mon.
🔲 🗝

🍴 THE YEATMAN
$$$$$
RUA DO CHOUPELO,
VILA NOVA DE GAIA
TEL 220 133 100
the-yeatman-hotel.com
Inside the hotel of the same name, chef Ricardo Costa is at the helm of this two-Michelin-starred restaurant's kitchen. The location is elegant and charming (the view of the Douro helps) and the cuisine highly regarded. A lot of fish and a celebration of tradition are astutely revisited,

in an unforgettable journey between regions. The tasting menu is recommended. The wine list, mainly Portuguese, is unrivaled in the country, and one of the restaurant's strengths is its wine and food pairing.

🔲 50 🕐 Closed L & Sun.–Mon.
🅿 🔲 🔲 🗝

🍴 CANTINHO DO AVILLEZ
$$$
RUA MOUZINHO DA SILVEIRA 166
TEL 223 227 879
cantinhodoavillez.pt
This is one of star-chef José Avillez's restaurants and, like its Lisbon counterpart *(Rua dos Duques de Bragança 7, Chiado, tel 211 992 369)*, it produces simple, well-executed dishes rooted in Portuguese tradition. Service is friendly and well informed.

🔲 🔲 🗝

🍴 FLOW
$$–$$$
RUA DA CONCEIÇÃO 63
TEL 222 054 016
flowrestaurant.pt
A restaurant that's very elegant, very chic, and very good. Its modern style has traditional touches and great attention to detail is evident in all of its dishes. If you're looking for a romantic evening and the opportunity to enjoy Mediterranean fusion specialties, this is the place to be.

🕐 Closed L 🔲 🗝

🍴 DAMA PÉ DE CABRA
$
PASSEIO DE SÃO LÁZARO 5
TEL 223 196 776
damapedecabra@gmail.com
Deli-café offering fresh snacks at great prices throughout the day. Sit out on the terrace to watch the world go by.

🕐 Closed Sun.–Mon. & Tues.–Thurs. D 🔲 🗝 Cash only

⁍ MERCADO DO BOM SUCESSO

$

PRAÇA DO BOM SUCESSO 132
TEL 226 056 610
mercadobomsucesso.pt

To sample some of the best food the city has to offer, all under one roof, head to the Bom Sucesso market, south of the Boavista roundabout. Built in the 1940s, the building is home both to traditional market vendors selling fresh produce from across the region, and now a fashionable, urban food hall where some of the city's most renowned restaurants have set up stalls.

⁍ PEDRO DOS FRANGOS

$

RUA BONJARDIM 223
TEL 222 008 522

Portuguese fast food at its best. There are other options but most come for the excellent no-frills *frango* (chicken) and fries with optional hot *piri-piri* sauce. An icy-cold *imperial* (draft beer) goes well with it.

🔄 🚭

VIANA DO CASTELO

SOMETHING SPECIAL

⌂ CASA MELO ALVIM

$$$

AVENIDA CONDE DA CARREIRA 28
TEL 258 808 200
hotelmeloalvim.com

This palatial boutique hotel makes a stylish base for exploring the northern Minho region. Each room is furnished in a different period style, integrating modern fittings; bathrooms are in marble and polished granite. The restaurant serves new Portuguese cuisine as well as traditional fare. A courtyard garden adds to the charms.

🛏 20 🅿 🔁 🔄 🛜 Free 🚭

⌂ QUINTA DA BOUÇA D'ARQUES

$$$

RUA ABREU TEIXEIRA 333,
VILA DE PUNHE
TEL 968 044 992
boucadarques.com

A 20-minute drive south of Viana do Castelo, and 10 minutes from the Atlantic beaches, this beautiful *quinta* makes the perfect base for exploring the region. The owners have ingeniously married centuries-old architecture with chic lines of glass and steel to create this tranquil haven full of personality.

🛏 7 self-catering cottages
🅿 🔄 🚗 🛜 Free 🚭 Cash only

⁍ TASQUINHA DA LINDA

$$$

DOCA DAS MARÉS A-10
TEL 963 012 360
tasquinhadalinda.com

For the freshest of seafood head toward the fishermen's quarter near the docks and the fort. Tasquinha da Linda is frequented by locals and visitors alike thanks to its quality and good service. The latest catch is always on display and once selected, comes grilled with potatoes and vegetables. When in season, try the highly prized and rather pricey *percebes* (goose barnacles).

🕐 Closed Sun. 🔄 🔄 🚭

⁍ O CAMELO

$$

RUA DE SANTA MARTA 119,
SANTA MARTA DE PORTUZELO
TEL 258 839 090
camelorestaurantes.com

For the best in Minho fare, drive 10 minutes east of Viana, along the road EN202, to this local landmark. If visiting at lunchtime, sit outside under the vines and enjoy delicious, tapas-style starters, succulent roast meats, and mouthwatering desserts, perfectly accompanied by a glass of fresh *vinho verde*.

P 🕒 Closed Mon. 🔆 🖾

🍴 LIZ CAFFE BAR
$
RUA GAGO COUTINHO 17
TEL 963 062 529

As their slogan implies, this establishment serves primarily "tapas and toast." The tapas include platters of cheeses, quince jam, and regional sausages; the toasts are hearty slabs of local bread topped with cured hams, cheese, tomato, and more. Try to accompany this with a carafe of sangria, a cold beer, or a house cocktail.

🕒 Closed L & Sun.–Mon. 🔆 🖾

▶ CENTRO

AVEIRO

🏨 AVEIRO PALACE HOTEL
$$
RUA DE VIANA DO CASTELO 4
TEL 234 421 885
hotelaveiropalace.com

Located opposite the bridge over Aveiro's central canal in the heart of town with classically furnished rooms and a large TV lounge. Noisier front rooms have double-glazed windows. Good value and friendly.

ⓘ 48 😄 🔆 🕿 Free 🖾

🏨 HOTEL MOLICEIRO
$$
RUA BARBOSA DE MAGALHÃES 15–17
TEL 234 377 400
hotelmoliceiro.pt

Centrally located and overlooking Aveiro's main canal, this independently owned, modern hotel with abundant artworks welcomes with a glass of port wine and *ovos moles* (local pastry), served upon arrival.

ⓘ 49 😄 🔆 🕿 Free 🖾

🍴 CASA DE CHÁ ARTE NOVA
$
CASA MAJOR PESSOA, RUA DR. BARBOSA MAGALHÃES 9
TEL 916 842 029

Located on the ground floor of its outstanding art nouveau building, the Museu de Arte Nova's tearoom, with both indoor and patio seating and a range of teas, coffees, local cakes, salads and sandwiches, is the perfect place to take a break. Some evenings, there are live music events.

🕒 Closed Mon. 🔆 🖾

COIMBRA

🏨 PALACE HOTEL
🍴 BUSSACO
$$$
MATA DO BUÇACO, LUSO
TEL 231 937 970
almeidahotels.pt

This classic fairy-tale hotel sits in the wonderful Buçaco forest. Built in 1885 in neo-Manueline style, it has since 1917 been a luxury hotel with all the expected trimmings—marble, antiques, azulejos, tapestries, chandeliers—with service to match.

ⓘ 64 **P** 😄 🔆 🕿 Free in public areas 🖾

🏨 PALÁCIO DA LOUSÃ
🍴 BOUTIQUE HOTEL
$$$
RUA VISCONDESSA DO ESPINHAL
TEL 239 990 800
palaciodalousa.com

With a new and modern wing, this village manor house is full of charm, about 14 miles (23 km) southeast of Coimbra. Antiques and contemporary styles mix well, and many original baroque features remain. Views over the mountains from the bar, restaurant, and pool.

ⓘ 46 **P** 😄 🏊 🕿 Free in public areas 🖾

SOMETHING SPECIAL

▦ QUINTA DAS
▮ LÁGRIMAS
$$$
RUA ANTÓNIO AUGUSTO
GONÇALVES
TEL 239 802 380
quintadaslagrimas.pt
Fully renovated in 2016, this historic manor house on the Mondego River is an absolute gem. It features romantic botanical gardens, a designer spa, two restaurants (one fusion and the other award-winning gourmet), indoor and outdoor pools, and a golf course. The elegant salons and supposed aristocratic ghosts create a refined atmosphere.

🛈 54 🅿 ⊟ 🕄 ☎ ⛱ 👕 📶 Free in public areas ⊗

▦ ASTÓRIA HOTEL
$$
AVENIDA EMÍDIO NAVARRO 21
TEL 239 853 020
almeidahotels.pt
Centrally located by the river, this art deco hotel is one of Coimbra's landmarks, a 1919 flatiron building with a good standard of rooms and service.

🛈 62 ⊟ 🕄 📶 Free in public areas ⊗

▮ RESTAURANTE
DOM PEDRO
$$$
AVENIDA EMÍDIO NAVARRO 58
TEL 239 820 814
Steps lead down to this traditional, appreciated (although somewhat touristy) restaurant, where tiled walls, a fireplace, and copper pans give a timeless appeal. Specialties include roast kid and lamb, but there is plenty of seafood, too.

🕄 ⊗

▮ DUX PETISCOS E VINHOS
$$
RUA DOS COMBATENTES
DA GRANDE GUERRA 102
TEL 239 402 818
Describing itself as an "urban taverna," Dux takes regional specialities and gives them a modern twist, a welcome break from the delicious, yet often heavy, traditional fare. Dishes are served on wooden boards or wrapped in brown paper. Extensive and complete wine list.

⊗ ⊗

▮ NOTES BAR & KITCHEN
$$
RUA DR. MANUEL RODRIGUES 17
TEL 239 151 726
This tapas bar 10 minutes north of Coimbra's center is worth the walk. Among others, try the *ameijoas à bulhão pato* (clams with coriander and garlic broth) or the black açorda with clams. Good selection of artisan beers, and quality wines by the glass.

🕒 Closed Sun.–Mon. ⊗ ⊗

▮ CAFÉ SANTA CRUZ
$
PRAÇA 8 DE MAIO
TEL 239 833 617
cafesantacruz.com
Open since 1923, Coimbra's classiest café is found inside a wing of the Santa Cruz Monastery. The palatial vaulted hall and wooden features give it character, while outside tables have a great view of the square. Drinks, coffee, and snacks served until midnight.

⊗ Cash only

▮ ZÉ MANEL DOS OSSOS
$
BECO DO FORNO 12
TEL 239 823 790
Arrive early at this popular, rustic *tasca* tucked behind the Hotel

Astória; it doesn't take reservations. Tables are cramped but the food is honest, portions generous, and prices cheap. Soups and roast meats recommended.

🕐 Closed Sun. 🔲

GUARDA

🏨 SOLAR DE ALARCÃO
$$
RUA D. MIGUEL DE ALARCÃO 25
TEL 271 214 392
solardealarcao.pt

The rooms in this unusual 17th-century family guesthouse opposite Guarda's cathedral feature dark wood and a general surfeit of furnishings. Garden, pergola, game room, and café also on hand.

ⓘ 3 🅿 🛜 Free 🔲 Cash only

SERRA DA ESTRELA

SOMETHING SPECIAL

🏨 POUSADA DO
🍴 CONVENTO DE BELMONTE
$$$$
SERRA DA ESPERANÇA, BELMONTE
TEL 275 910 300
pousadas.pt

Perched on the far end of Belmonte's outcrop, this stylishly converted medieval monastery is a real dream. When you can see them through the clouds, the mountain views are hard to beat. Granite is omnipresent, but the rooms and public spaces have subtle modern touches. Excellent restaurant serves regional cuisine.

ⓘ 24 🅿 🔵 🔵 🏊 🛜 Free 🔲

VISEU

🏨 HOTEL GRÃO VASCO
$$
RUA GASPAR BARREIROS 1

TEL 232 423 511
hotelgraovasco.pt

Classic in style, with a sense of grandeur despite its relative youth, this hotel is perfectly located by the old quarter in leafy gardens. Facilities are excellent, for the price, with spacious rooms comfortably appointed, some with balconies.

ⓘ 109 🅿 🔄 🔵 🏊 🎾 🛜 Free 🔲

SOMETHING SPECIAL

🍴 CORTIÇO
$$
RUA AUGUSTO HILÁRIO 47
TEL 916 461 576
restaurantecortico.pt

It's worth the trip to eat here. Two restaurants on both sides of a narrow cobbled street serve mouthwatering regional fare in a rustic setting; hams hang from the ceiling, yet tablecloths are embroidered white linen. Try the three-day-old rabbit bean stew or, better still, the divine duck rice baked with *chouriço* sausage and bacon. Excellent wines accompany the hearty dishes, and the service is warm, yet professional.

🕐 Closed Mon. 🔵 🔲

▶ LISBOA E REGIÃO

BATALHA

🏨 CASA DO OUTEIRO ARTS & CRAFTS HOTEL
$$
LARGO CARVALHO DO OUTEIRO 4
TEL 244 765 806
hotelcasadoouteiro.com

This modern establishment sits opposite Batalha's monastery. Good facilities and prices for immaculate white rooms, some with balconies and monastery views. A 2017 renovation gave each room a personal

PRICES

HOTELS

An indication of the cost of a double room in the high season is given by **$** signs.

$$$$$	Over $250
$$$$	$200–$250
$$$	$150–$200
$$	$80–$150
$	Under $80

RESTAURANTS

An indication of the cost of a three-course meal without drinks is given by **$** signs.

$$$$$	Over $65
$$$$	$40–$65
$$$	$28–$40
$$	$15–$28
$	Under $15

touch with the use of handcrafted originally made pieces. Inside there is a shop selling jams and handicrafts.

🅿 🚫 🏊 📶 Free 🚭

🍴 SOPAS & C.
$
TRAVESSA ALVARO SAMPAIO 1
This small, simple restaurant is unpretentious and inexpensive. Why should you go there? With an excellent location, behind the monastery, the cuisine is light and very good. Serving Portuguese specialties, along with excellent steak, it also offers delectable vegetarian dishes.

🚫 🚭

CALDAS DA RAINHA

🍴 ADEGA DO ALBERTINO
$$
RUA JÚLIO SOUSA 7
TEL 262 835 152
adegadoalbertino.pt
Checkered tablecloths, tiled floors, and a multitude of rustic objects suspended from the rafters make this a welcoming restaurant. Specialties include *bacalhau* (salted cod), shrimp rice, and entrecôte steak served with an unusual wine, honey, and almond sauce.

🅿 🕐 Closed Sun. D & Mon.
🚫 🚭

CASCAIS

SOMETHING SPECIAL

🏨 FAROL DESIGN HOTEL
🍴 $$$$$
AVENIDA REI HUMBERTO II
DE ITALIA 7
TEL 214 823 490
farol.com.pt
Right beside the lighthouse at the western end of Cascais, this hotel is part century-old mansion, part sleek glass box jutting out over the waves. Rooms have balconies or glazed walls; all have hydromassage tubs. Hip interiors styled by different Portuguese designers impress in scarlet, black, and white. The funky bar **The Mix** and adjoining restaurant **Sushi Design** *($$$)* prepare Mediterranean fusion dishes and sushi respectively.

ℹ 33 🅿 ⬍ 🚫 🏊 📶 Free 🚭

🏨 FORTALEZA DO
🍴 GUINCHO
$$$$
ESTRADA DO GUINCHO
TEL 214 870 491
fortalezadoguincho.com
This mock medieval fortress built in 1956 occupies a prime position at the end of the lovely and otherwise wild beach, Praia da Guincho. The rooms are ornately decorated. The Michelin-starred French restaurant's panoramic windows overlook the waves, and the central patio is just the place for a relaxing drink.

🅿 🚫 🚫 🏊 📶 Free 🚭

PESTANA CIDADELA
CASCAIS
$$$$
FORTALEZA DA CIDADELA,
AVENIDA DOM CARLOS I
TEL 214 814 300
pestanacollection.com
Set within the 16th-century Cidadela fortress, this hotel offers every state-of-the-art comfort in airy rooms, some with spectacular views over the sea and bay area. Several terraces and an indoor swimming pool that opens in warmer months allow you to enjoy the sea breeze.

🛈 126 🔽 💲 🏊 📶 Free 💳

CASA DA PERGOLA
$$
AVENIDA VALBOM 13
TEL 214 840 040
thepergola.pt
A turn-of-the-20th-century mansion cascading in bougainvilleas and decorated in traditional Portuguese style. Lots of character and a friendly staff make this guesthouse shine in keeping with Cascais's aristocratic past. A large living room can be used by guests and the pretty front garden has plenty of sitting areas.

🛈 15 💲 📶 Free 💳

CAFÉ GALERIA HOUSE OF WONDERS
$$
LARGO DA MISERICÓRDIA 53
TEL 911 702 428
With a delightful roof terrace for warmer days and a cozy ground-floor dining room with a blazing log burner for chillier evenings, this café is warm, welcoming, and full of colors. The friendly staff serves homemade vegetarian dishes, mezze platters, fresh juices, and tasty cakes. It also acts as a gallery for local artists.

💲 💳

MERCADO DA VILA
$–$$
RUA PADRE MOISÉS DA SILVA
TEL 911 702 428
As is the trend, Cascais's municipal market now, in addition to the traditional stalls, has several trendy eateries and juice bars, some under cover, others in the central courtyard. Try **Marisco na Praça** *(tel 214 822 130)* for seafood and **Páteo do Petisco** *(tel 218 002 663)* for tapas.

SOMOS UM REGALO
$
AVENIDA VASCO DA GAMA 36
TEL 214 865 487
With its recognizable chimney, this popular restaurant offers some of the best grilled chicken in the area; for the real deal, order with *piri-piri.*

🕐 Closed Wed. 💲 💳 Cash only

LEIRIA

RESTAURANTE O MANEL
$$
RUA DR CORREIA MATEUS 50
TEL 244 832 132
This old-fashioned classic, popular with local business people at lunch, has an open fireplace at the back used to barbecue fresh fish—in particular sea bass—priced by the kilo. *Bacalhau* (salted cod) is another house specialty and there is a good wine list.

🕐 Closed Sun. 💲 💳

ÓBIDOS

HOTEL REAL D'ÓBIDOS
$$$$
RUA DOM JOÃO DE ORNELAS
TEL 262 955 090
hotelrealdobidos.com
Medieval themes run riot in this hotel just outside the castle walls. Men in velvet tunics, tights, and pointy shoes proffer your room key on a heavy

chain, while armor rattles in the corridor. The pool has fabulous views toward the castle and the surrounding countryside.

🏨 18 ⬘ 🔄 🌊 📶 Free 🚭

🏨 POUSADA CASTELO
🍴 ÓBIDOS
$$$$
PAÇO REAL
TEL 262 248 980
pousadas.pt
Portugal's first castle converted into a *pousada* in 1951, this unique place is a real eyrie, reached by steep steps. As well as rooms within the castle, there are also rooms set in adjoining village houses. The restaurant offers superb views.

🏨 18 🅿 🚭 🔄 📶 Free 🚭

🏨 CASA DE S. THIAGO DO CASTELO
$$
LARGO DE S. THIAGO
TEL 262 959 587
casasthiagodocastelo.com
This pretty little corner guesthouse nestles under a cascade of bougainvilleas on the main street inside the castle walls. Cozy rooms are arranged around a common sitting room and breakfast patio.

🏨 8 📶 Free 🚭

🍴 A NOVA CASA DE RAMIRO
$$$
RUA PORTA DO VALE
TEL 967 265 945
Attractively decorated in warm colors with large stone urns and archways, the Casa de Ramiro is an excellent address for a romantic dinner. It has won local gastronomic awards for specialties such as *arroz de pato* (duck rice), *cabrito assado* (roast kid), and *bife com pimenta* (pepper steak).

🕑 Closed Sun. & Mon. L 🔄 🚭

PENICHE

🏨 CASA DO CASTELO TURISMO DE HABITAÇÃO
$$
ESTRADA NACIONAL 114 NO. 16, ATOUGUIA DA BALEIA
TEL 262 750 647
vistavillas.eu/casa-do-castelo-da-atouguia-peniche-portugal
These picturesque 17th-century buildings originated in a Moorish castle. In season, oranges from the beautiful shady garden are squeezed into your breakfast juice. Rooms are decorated with good taste. It is located only about 4 miles (6.5 km) from Peniche, and Óbidos lies a short distance in the opposite direction. There is a minimum three-night stay.

🏨 8 🅿 📶 Free in public areas
🚭 Cash only

🏨 MH PENICHE
🍴 $$
AVENIDA MONSENHOR M. BASTOS
TEL 262 780 500
mh-hotels.pt
This huge five-story modern hotel, among the best at Peniche, overlooks a pool and gardens beside Praia da Consolação, a beach just south of town. All rooms have balconies.

🏨 120 🅿 ⬘ 🔄 🌊 📶 Free 🚭

🍴 ESTELAS
$$
RUA ARQUITECTO PAULINO MONTEZ 21
TEL 262 782 435
Peniche's best seafood restaurant consistently wins local gastronomic awards. Easily located on the street that runs inland from the tourist office. Anyone tiring of lobster or fish stew should try the juicy Tournedos steak accompanied by one of the excellent local wines.

🅿 🔄 🚭

🍴 MARISQUEIRA MIRANDUM
$$
RUA DOS HEROIS DO ULTRAMAR
TEL 963 270 017
Not much to look at from the outside and set back from the shore in a rather run-down part of town, Marisqueira Mirandum serves some of the best seafood in the area, including clams, crab, lobster, and fish grilled to perfection. The fish selection will be limited to what was available from the local fishermen that day. It is also popular among locals, so book ahead.
🕐 Closed Wed. *&* Thurs. L 🗺 🏚

🍴 RESTAURANTE A SARDINHA
$$
RUA VASCO DA GAMA 81
TEL 262 781 820
restauranteasardinha.com
In addition to sardines (when in season), A Sardinha is renowned for its excellent fish stew (*caldeirada de peixe*) and rice with mixed seafood or monkfish (*arroz de marisco* or *arroz de tamboril*). Meat lovers should try the highly prized *porco preto* (pork from free-range Alentejo black pigs). Portions are big—leave some room for the delicious desserts.
🗺 🏚

SANTARÉM

SOMETHING SPECIAL

🏨 CASA DA ALCÁÇOVA
$$$
LARGO DA ALCÁÇOVA 3, PORTAS DO SOL
TEL 243 304 030 OR 936 080 100
alcacova.com
Guarded by the citadel ramparts, this 18th-century manor house offers imaginatively but classically decorated rooms (each different in style and furniture) with great views of the river and plains. Original artworks adorn the walls, the bathrooms have Jacuzzis, and the furnishings are of high quality; you will more than likely sleep in a four-poster bed. A minimum stay of two nights is requested.
🛏 8 🅿 🗺 🌊 🏝 Free in public areas 🏚

🏨 CORINTHIA SANTARÉM HOTEL
$$
AVENIDA MADRE ANDALUZ
TEL 243 330 800
santaremhotel.net
A large modern hotel with predictable facilities geared to business travelers. Rooms have good views over the Tejo River and the city.
🛏 105 🅿 🔄 🗺 🌊 🏝 🍴 🏝 Free 🏚

SÃO MARTINHO DO PORTO

🏨 QUINTA DA VIDA SERENA
$$
RUA PRINCIPAL 115, CASAL DE MACALHONA, ALFEIZERÃO
TEL 262 989 287
quinta-serena.com
This guesthouse, surrounded by nature and a few minutes' drive outside São Martinho do Porto, has farm animals, organic fruit trees, vineyards, and complete quiet. The kind management offers both self-catering apartments and studios, plus an outdoor plunge pool and private beach for swimming in the Dão River.
🛏 4 🅿 🗺 🌊 🏝 Free in public areas 🏚

SESIMBRA

🍴 MARISQUEIRA O RODINHAS
$$–$$$
RUA MARQUÊS DE POMBAL 25
TEL 212 231 557
marisqueiraorodinhas.pt

Simple, with no frills, this traditional Portuguese restaurant offers quality food and prompt and efficient service. Opt for the seafood platter or the grilled prawns or, for something a little unusual, try the house specialty *chocos fritos* (fried cuttlefish). Arrive early or book in advance.

🕐 Closed Wed. 🔊

🍴 O CANHÃO
$$
RUA DA FORTALEZA 13
TEL 212 231 442 OR 969 188 786
restauranteocanhao.pt
Just behind the fortress, this welcoming seafood restaurant serves regional classics such as fish stew and *cataplana*. The interior has partly tiled walls and a traditional style plus a few tables for outside dining.

🔄 🔊

SETÚBAL

🏨 B&B HOTEL SADO
🍴 SETÚBAL
$$
RUA IRENE LISBOA 1
TEL 265 542 800
hotel-bb.com
Run by a chain that offers accommodation for those without a need for many services, this property retains the charm of its history. It is a comfortable accommodation with beautiful views of the Sado Estuary. The rooms are really bright and many of them are suitable for guests with reduced mobility.

🛈 66 🅿 🔄 🔊 📶 Free 🔊

🍴 COPA D'OURO II
$$
AVENIDA LUISA TODI 530
TEL 265 232 942
Traditional and professional, this well-established seafood restaurant is a favorite with the locals. It's on the main bayside road, with a big glass-sided dining room; the menu features the morning's catch, from red mullet to sea bass.

🕐 Closed Tues. 🔊 🔊

🍴 PEROLA DA MOURISCA
$$
RUA DA BAIA DO SADO 9
TEL 265 793 689
A few minutes' drive west of Setúbal, this restaurant is popular among locals in the know for serving some of the best seafood in the region (meat lovers are also well catered for). Staff are efficient and friendly.

🕐 Closed Tues. 🔊 🔊

SINTRA

SOMETHING SPECIAL

🏨 VALVERDE PALÁCIO
🍴 DE SETEAIS
$$$$–$$$$$
RUA BARBAROSA DU BOCAGE 8
TEL 219 233 200
valverdepalacioseteais.com
This magical 18th-century palace with extensive gardens is just a 10-minute walk from central Sintra. The interiors of the numerous salons and guest rooms are stunning, spacious, and decorated in fittingly regal style. Guests are cosseted with a choice between a pool with valley views, tennis courts, or a long drink at the terrace bar.

🛈 30 🅿 🔄 🔊 🏊 📶 Free 🔊

🏨 SINTRA BOUTIQUE HOTEL
$$$–$$$$
RUA VISCONDE DE MONSERRATE 40
TEL 219 244 177
sintraboutiquehotel.com
In the center of Sintra, with rooms looking out over the old town or nature park, it boasts beautifully designed interiors, attentive service

and excellent dining; and all rooms, from standard to junior suite, are spacious and cozy.

🏨 18 ❄ 🛜 Free 🗝

🏨 LAWRENCE'S
🍽 HOTEL
$$$

RUA CONSIGLIÉRI PEDROSO 38–40
TEL 219 105 500
lawrenceshotel.com

This privately owned boutique hotel trades on its age and brief association with Lord Byron. Rooms are cozy, and quite small, but the hotel is quaint with enjoyable patios and terraces. Centrally located with views, it also has a gourmet restaurant (*$$$$*).

🏨 17 ❄ 🛜 Free 🗝

🍽 CAFÉ SAUDADE
$

AVENIDA MIGUEL BOMBARDA 6
TEL 212 428 804
saudade.pt

A three-minute walk from the train station, this café serves homemade snacks and light meals into the early evening. Its popular fixed breakfast and brunch menus offer good value; afternoon tea offers scones and other homemade pastries.

🔵 🗝

🍽 NAU PALATINA
$

CALÇADA DE SÃO PEDRO 18
TEL 219 240 962
naupalatina.pt

This cozy little eatery serves a variety of delicious tapas, either in individual portions on a slab of bread or in dishes to share. The attentive staff are happy to talk you through the menu of cured meats, regional cheeses, wild prawns, and more—and don't miss desserts! Arrive early or book in advance.

🕐 Closed L & Sun.–Mon. 🔵 Cash only

TOMAR

🏨 HOTEL DOS
🍽 TEMPLÁRIOS
$$

LARGO CÂNDIDO DOS REIS 1
TEL 239 310 100
hoteldostemplarios.pt

Pleasantly located, this efficient large-scale hotel's grandiose lobby is something straight out of Bollywood. All the rooms are well laid out, most of them with generous balconies and both river and castle views.

🏨 176 🅿 ❄ 🔵 🏊 🏊 🏋
🛜 Free 🗝

🏨 THOMAR STORY GUEST
HOUSE
$

RUA DE JOÃO CARLOS EVERARD 53
TEL 249 327 268
thomarstory.pt

Its location within a historic 19th-century building in the heart of the old town makes this an ideal base for exploring the town on foot. Decor is modest but clean and modern, with some rooms equipped with their own kitchenette.

🏨 12 🔵 🔵 🛜 Free 🗝

SOMETHING SPECIAL

🍽 CAFÉ PARAISO
$

RUA SERPA PINTO 127
TEL 249 312 997
cafeparaiso.pt

This unexpected art deco jewel in an otherwise resolutely medieval town opened in 1911 and is still in the same family. It's a rare relic of the days when Portugal's intellectuals and artists would meet over coffee. Don't miss your turn sitting beneath whirring ceiling fans in this grandiose mirror-and-marble setting.

🗝 Cash only

▶ ALENTEJO

BEJA

🏨 POUSADA CONVENTO
🍴 DE BEJA–SÃO FRANCISCO
$$$$
LARGO D. NUNO ÁLVARES PEREIRA
TEL 284 313 580
pousadas.pt
This impressive, rambling *pousada,* a Franciscan convent back in the 13th century, stands in the heart of the old town, though the one-way streets make access tricky. The massive proportions are decorated firmly in the classical style. Guests can enjoy the tennis court, pool, and billiards room.

ℹ 35 🅿 ⬍ 🚫 🔆 🏊 📶 Free 🚭

🍴 DOM DINIS
$$
RUA DOM DINIS 11
TEL 965 337 578
Typical Alentejano fare. Fish and seafood are on the menu, but the grilled meats—lamb or pork—are the best bet; all with generous sides of vegetables.

🕐 Closed Tues. D & Wed. 🔆 🚭

ESTREMOZ

SOMETHING SPECIAL

🏨 POUSADA CASTELO
🍴 ESTREMOZ
$$$$
LARGO DE DOM DINIS
TEL 268 332 075
pousadas.pt
This castle-palace has a seven-century-long story of deaths, murder, and explosions—with Vasco da Gama, star-struck Crown Prince Pedro, and his grandmother, saintly Queen Isabel (for whom the palace was built), all thrown in at different moments. This *pousada* is one of the best, with

vast, palatial proportions, antiques, character, comfort, gardens, pool, and stupendous views. You'll feel like a Liliputian in the enormous restaurant.

ℹ 29 🅿 ⬍ 🚫 🔆 🏊 📶 Free 🚭

🍴 CAFÉ ALENTEJANO
$$
ROSSIO MARQUÊS DE POMBAL
13–15
TEL 268 322 834
There's plenty of atmosphere at this venerable café, a favorite with the local old men. A marble staircase leads to an excellent little restaurant serving Alentejano bread soup *(açorda),* lamb and chickpea stew, and pig's feet. Comfortable en suite guest rooms *($)* are also available.

🔆 🚭

ÉVORA

🏨 CONVENTO DO
ESPINHEIRO
$$$$
ESTRADA DOS CANAVIAIS,
APARTADO 594
TEL 266 788 200
conventodoespinheiro.com
This luxury hotel stands in a rural setting a few miles northeast of Évora. Once a 15th-century convent, the hotel offers slick service, extensive landscaped gardens, a gourmet restaurant, and luxury.

ℹ 93 🅿 ⬍ 🚫 🔆 🏊 🏊
📺 📶 Free 🚭

SOMETHING SPECIAL
🏨 POUSADA CONVENTO
🍴 DE ÉVORA
$$$$
LARGO DO CONDE DE VILA FLOR
TEL 266 730 070
pousadas.pt
This superb converted convent is part of Évora's main historic cluster. Tiled

---

🏨 Hotel 🍴 Restaurant ℹ No. of Guest Rooms 🅿 Parking 🕐 Closed ⬍ Elevator 🚭 Nonsmoking floors, stone steps, a cloister garden, and tasteful antiques contribute to the atmosphere. The downside is the size of the "cell" rooms; try the main suite where a sitting room has painted walls and ceiling. The restaurant *($$$$)*, overlooking the cloister, has excellent regional dishes and, unusually, caters to vegetarians.

🛈 33 🅿 🆂 🆂 🏊 🛜 Free 💳

🏨 ÉVORA OLIVE HOTEL
$$$–$$$$
RUA DE EBORIM 18
TEL 961 829 481
artsoulgroup.com
/evoraolivehotel/en
This hotel inside the city walls is modern and offers every comfort. The very cordial staff will make you feel pampered.

🛈 69 🅿 🆂 🏊 🍽 🛜 💳

🏨 ALBERGARIA DO CALVÁRIO
$$
TRAVESSA DOS LAGARES 3
TEL 266 745 930
adcevora.com
Located inside the old city gates, the warm staff at this charming inn serve a great breakfast. Enjoy a leisurely coffee in the lovely courtyard.

🛈 22 🆂 🛜 Free 💳

🍴 O FIALHO
$$$
TRAVESSA DAS MASCARENHAS 16
TEL 266 703 079
restaurantefialho.pt
In the same family for three generations, O Fialho has been serving traditional Alentejo food since 1945. Located in the historic center of the city, this restaurant is known across the region and beyond for its use of quality prime ingredients sourced locally. It also boasts an excellent wine cellar. Reservations advised.

🕐 Closed Mon. 🆂 💳

SOMETHING SPECIAL
🍴 A CHOUPANA
$$
RUA DOS MERCADORES 16–20
TEL 266 704 427
Locals queue for lunch here, as the food is delicious and amazingly good value. The cozy interior has two sections, a dining room and a long bar; turnover is fast, but there is no pressure. Specialties include Alentejano pork and roast lamb with onion, garlic, and white wine; in winter they feature game dishes. Portions are gigantic; consider ordering the half portion—*meia dose.*

🕐 Closed Sun. 🆂 💳

ÉVORAMONTE
🍴 CAFE RESTAURANTE O EMIGRANTE
$
TRAVESSA DO MONTINHO
TEL 268 950 053
This excellent little restaurant is inexpensive and comfortable. It has indoor and outdoor seating, meticulous service, and offers appetizing traditional cuisine. It is open every day from morning until evening, and here you can savor what many consider the best Alentejo pork in the area.

🆂 💳

MONSARAZ
🍴 XAREZ RESTAURANTE BAR
$$
RUA DE SANTIAGO 33
TEL 266 557 052
Near the castle, this friendly, popular small-scale restaurant in rural style has alfresco eating on a stone-paved terrace overlooking the plains. Daily specials include Alentejo tapas, such

as asparagus with egg and bread crumbs (*migas*).

🕐 Closed Thurs. 🔾 🔾

PORTALEGRE

🏨 POUSADA MOSTEIRO
🍴 DO CRATO
$$$$
MOSTEIRO DA FLOR DA ROSA,
CRATO
TEL 245 997 210
pousadas.pt
Yet another surprising *pousada*, hidden away in an imposing monastery complete with nesting storks in the hamlet of Flor da Rosa. West of Portalegre near Crato, the pousada is in the center of a rural region. Furnishings have an elegant and modern yet classic style with strong personality. Nearby is the Alter do Chão stud farm, famed for Lusitanian horses.

ⓘ 24 🅿 ➌ 🔾 🔾 🏊
🛜 Free 🔾

🏨 ROSSIO HOTEL
$$
RUA 31 DE JANEIRO 6
TEL 245 082 218
rossiohotel.com
Conveniently located on the edge of the old town, the Rossio is an environmentally friendly hotel, including solar panels, LED lighting, rainwater recycling, and more. Guest rooms are well equipped with spacious bathrooms. Head to the rooftop terrace for views of the Serra de São Mamede.

ⓘ 18 🅿 ➌ 🔾 🔾 🔾 🛜 Free 🔾

🍴 TOMBALOBOS
$$$$
RUA 19 DE JUNHO 2
TEL 245 906 111
On the eastern side of town (off the N246-2), this is Portalegre's most sophisticated dining option. Chef José Júlio Vintém varies the menu daily, depending on what he finds at the local market, creating innovative dishes with unusual combinations. Don't miss the quality Alentejo wines.

🕐 Closed Sun. D & Mon. 🔾 🔾

🍴 RESTAURANTE SOLAR DO
FORCADO
$$
RUA CÂNDIDO DOS REIS 14
TEL 245 330 866
If you are not averse to the framed bullfighting photos that grace the walls, O Forcado offers some of the best traditional cooking in town and some amazing regional wines. Housed in a former coach house, it is slightly more sophisticated than the competition. Dishes here are plated with care and service is very attentive.

🕐 Closed Sat. L & Sun. 🔾 🔾

SANTIAGO DO CACÉM

🏨 HERDADE DO FREIXIAL
$$
ESTRADA DE SÃO LUIS,
VILA NOVA DE MILFONTES
TEL 963 697 680
Check in here for a rural retreat from which to explore the Alentejo coast. With spectacular views overlooking the river Mira, choose between self-catering accommodation or guest suites. The infinity pool (with poolside bar) and Jacuzzi offer plenty of opportunity for relaxation.

ⓘ 8 🅿 🔾 🏊 🛜 Free 🔾

SERPA

🏨 CASA DA MURALHA
$$
RUA DAS PORTAS DE BEJA 43
TEL 284 543 150
casa.muralha@sapo.pt

423978110419

This very unusual private guesthouse is built into the walls of Serpa, with aqueduct arches looming overhead. Large, tasteful rooms with Alentejano painted furniture all open onto a lovely courtyard of orange trees. Access from outside the walls is from Rua dos Arcos.

🛈 4 🅲 📶 Free 🅒

🍴 RESTAURANTE O ALENTEJANO
$$
PRAÇA DA REPÚBLICA 6
TEL 284 544 335

This restaurant, popular with locals, sits above a café on Serpa's main square. Lofty vaulted ceilings lend style, and the wine list is impressive. Tasty Alentejano fare includes a delicious *ensopada de borrega* (lamb stew), pork with clams, and of course *bacalhau* (cod).

🪑 48 🕐 Closed Sun. D & Mon. 🅒 🅒

SERRA DE SÃO MAMEDE

🏨 POUSADA DE 🍴 MARVÃO SANTA MARIA
$$$
RUA 24 DE JANEIRO 7, MARVÃO
TEL 245 993 201
pousadas.pt

Friendly and small in scale, two adjoining houses have been converted into this cozy, fairly simple *pousada*. Rooms are cheerful and some have great views over the countryside, as does the restaurant.

🛈 31 🅲 🅒 🅲 📶 Free 🅒

🏨 HOTEL CASTELO 🍴 DE VIDE
$
AVENIDA DA EUROPA, CASTELO DE VIDE
TEL 245 908 210
hotelcastelodevide.com

This small modern hotel on the edge of town offers good value rooms with balconies overlooking the hills. Though a little worn, rooms are well furnished and immaculate; cuisine is satisfactory.

🛈 53 🅿 🅲 🅲 🅲 🌊 📶 Free 🅒

VILA VIÇOSA

SOMETHING SPECIAL

🏨 POUSADA CONVENTO 🍴 VILA VIÇOSA
$$$
CONVENTO DAS CHAGAS
TEL 268 980 742
pousadas.pt

Located next to the royal palace in this elegant town, this *pousada*, built within a handsome Renaissance convent, maintains the cloister, oratories, and frescoed niches balanced by contemporary elements and a garden. White marble is rampant. Guest rooms have secluded balconies and public areas are generously scaled.

🛈 39 🅿 🅲 🅲 🅲 🌊 🅒

▶ ALGARVE

ALBUFEIRA

🏨 PINE CLIFFS RESORT 🍴 $$$$$
PINHAL DO CONCELHO
TEL 289 500 300
pinecliffs.com

Commanding a prime clifftop spot and designed in spacious Moorish style, Pine Cliffs offers excellent service and facilities. A glass elevator transports you down to a fabulous beach, while up among the pines await three pools, a nine-hole golf course, a tennis academy, and a children's village.

🛈 215 🅿 🅲 🅲 🅲 🌊 🌊 🅗 📶 Free 🅒

🅲 Air-conditioning 🌊 Indoor Pool 🌊 Outdoor Pool 🅗 Health Club 📶 Wi-Fi 🅒 Credit Cards

VILA JOYA
$$$$$
PRAIA DE GALÉ
TEL 289 591 795
vilajoya.com
This delicious two-star Michelin restaurant is part of a small luxury hotel, so book your table ahead. The evening five-course meal may include such specials as lobster with citrus fruit. 45 ⊕ Closed one month Nov.–Mar. (dates vary) 🔒 🚭

COSTA VICENTINA

PONT'A PÉ
$
LARGO DA LIBERDADE 12, ALJEZUR
TEL 282 998 104
pontape.pt
This great little restaurant sits just inland from Portugal's wildest coast. A table inside the rural interior or outside by the footbridge makes a perfect spot to indulge in grilled meats, fresh shellfish, fish, and delicious homemade desserts. Occasionally live music is hosted.
⊕ Closed Sun. 🔒 🚭

FARO

POUSADA PALÁCIO
DE ESTOI
$$$$
RUA SÃO JOSÉ, ESTOI
TEL 210 407 620
pousadas.pt
Set within the restored 18th-century palace of the Count of Cadaval, 7 miles (11 km) north of Faro, this *pousada* retains all its former rococo splendor. Public rooms are a riot of ornate stucco, chandeliers, and mirrors; a modern wing houses the more minimalist bedrooms.
63 🛗 🔒 ♨ 🏊 📺 📶 Free 🚭

LOULÉ

PEQUENO MUNDO
$$$$
CAMINHO DAS PEREIRAS, APARTADO 3618
TEL 289 399 866
pequeno-mundo.com
In a beautiful, elegantly furnished building, you will find an experience that ignites all the senses: colors, scents, and flavors under the trees of a romantic interior garden. The cuisine is well crafted and makes excellent use of Algarve ingredients, expertly interpreted with a taste for French gastronomy.
⊕ Closed L & Sun. 🔒 🚭 🔒 🚭

MONCHIQUE

A CHARRETTE
$$
RUA DOUTOR SAMORA GIL 30–34
TEL 282 912 142
After exploring the Algarve interior, head to this welcoming rustic establishment for hearty, traditional, mountain cuisine such as *farinheira* (sausage made with corn-flour and paprika) or pork with chestnuts.
⊕ Closed Wed. 🚭 🚭

SAGRES

POUSADA SAGRES
$$$
PONTA DA ATALAIA
TEL 282 620 240
pousadas.pt
In splendid isolation, this cliffside *pousada* draws its theme from Henry the Navigator, with maps and globes omnipresent. Comfortable rooms are enlivened with vividly colored accessories, but their best asset is the view from the balcony: far-reaching vistas of Atlantic waves.
51 🔒 🛗 🚭 🔒 🏊 📶 Free 🚭

🏨 Hotel 🍴 Restaurant 🛏 No. of Guest Rooms 🅿 Parking ⊕ Closed 🛗 Elevator 🚭 Nonsmoking

🍴 RETIRO DO PESCADOR
$
RUA DOS MURTÓRIOS
TEL 282 624 438
retirodopescador.com
"If it comes from the sea, it can come to the table," is the philosophy behind this no-frills, great-value eatery. The *cataplana de amêijoas* (clam stew) is the house specialty, but there are plenty of options from the large coal-fired grill.
🕐 Closed Sun. D & Mon.
🚫 Cash only

SILVES

🍴 RUI MARISQUERIA
$$
RUA COMENDADOR
VILARINHO 23–27
TEL 282 442 682
marisqueirarui.pt
It's one of the Algarve region's most famous seafood restaurants. This place packs people in with its vast selection of fresh shellfish, grilled fish, seafood rice, and special *cataplana*.
🕐 Closed Tues. 🔵 🔶

🍴 CAFÉ INGLÊS
$
ESCADA DO CASTELO
TEL 282 442 585
cafeingles.com.pt
Pizzas, fresh juices, homemade soups, and desserts are served on the sunny terrace or inside the brightly painted rooms. Live music on weekends, in season.
🔩 60 🕐 Closed Mon. 🔵 🔶

TAVIRA

🏨 POUSADA DE TAVIRA
🍴 CONVENTO DA GRAÇA
$$$$$
RUA D. PAIO PERES CORREIA
TEL 210 407 680
pousadas.pt

Well located, only a short walk from the center of the town, this restored 16th-century monastery provides comfortable, spacious rooms plus an outdoor pool and pleasant gardens.
ⓘ 36 🅿 🔄 🔵 🏊 �📶 Free 🔶

🍴 ZECA DA BICA
$
RUA ALMIRANTE CANDIDO DOS REIS 22
TEL 281 323 843
Whether you find a table outside in the picturesque alleyway or inside this traditional but a bit atypical restaurant, you'll feel at home at the Zeca da Bica. The personnel may seem a bit rough but they always have a smile for you, and the dishes that come out of the kitchen are the quintessence of genuine Portuguese cuisine.
🕐 Closed Wed. 🔵 🔶 Cash only

VILA DO BISPO

🏨 HOTEL MIRA SAGRES
$$
RUA 1° DE MAIO 3
TEL 282 639 160
hotelmirasagres.com
Located at the entrance to the town, this hotel, once an old pension and now restored, will surprise you with the simplicity of its décor and its relaxing atmosphere, together with a number of comforts such as a spa, a gym, and a pool. It's great for a visit to the city or as a starting point for a trip to the beach.
ⓘ 21 🅿 🔄 🔵 🏊 🍸 📶 🔶

🍴 RIBEIRA DO POÇO
$$
RUA RIBEIRA DO POÇO 11
TEL 282 639 075
ribeiradopoco.com
This family-run restaurant in a former hay barn serves all kinds of fresh fish and seafood, including *lapas* (limpets) and the highly prized *percebes*

(goose barnacles). Finish with fig cheese and a shot of medronho, the local fruit brandy.

🕐 Closed Mon. & Jan. 🚫 ⬧

▶ MADEIRA

FUNCHAL

🏨 BELMOND REID'S PALACE
🍴 $$$$$
ESTRADA MONUMENTAL 139
TEL 291 717 171
belmond.com
For more than a century this palatial clifftop hotel has welcomed royalty, heads of state, and celebrities; some guests still don black tie for dinner. Stroll through the delightful lush gardens or luxuriate in the spa. The wicker furniture suits the dowager character.

ⓘ 163 🅿 ⬧ 🚫 ⬧ ⬧ 🛜 Free ⬧

🏨 HOTEL THE
🍴 CLIFF BAY
$$$$$
ESTRADA MONUMENTAL 147,
SÃO MARTINHO
TEL 308 804 221
portobay.com
This exquisite, high-quality hotel is located in a splendid position, just outside the city center, and offers beautiful views of both the city and the Atlantic Ocean. Completely renovated in 2021, it is home to the two-Michelin-starred **Il Gallo d'Oro**

restaurant. You will be pampered with an infinity of services and small delightful comforts that include private access to the beach, the wellness center, the pools, the whirlpool baths, and the specialties served at the hotel's restaurants and bars. You may never want to go home.

🅿 ⬧ 🚫 ⬧ ⬧ ⬧ 🍴 🛜 ⬧

🏨 QUINTA DA PENHA DE FRANÇA
$$
RUA IMPERATRIZ DONA AMÉLIA 85
TEL 291 204 650
penhafrancahotels.com
Nestled in a verdant garden just a 15-minute stroll from downtown, this family-run hotel breathes old-time Madeira. Ask for a room in the atmospheric old house rather than in the modern wing.

ⓘ 109 🅿 ⬧ 🚫 ⬧ 🛜 Free in public areas ⬧

SOMETHING SPECIAL

🍴 RESTAURANTE DO FORTE
$$$
RUA PORTÃO SÃO TIAGO
TEL 291 215 580
forte.restaurant
Service here is attentive and the food beautifully presented, with à la carte as well as a fixed three-course menu with drinks included, offering good value. At lunchtime, weather permitting, you can sit out by the battlements looking over the ocean.

🚫 ⬧

SHOPPING

Portugal's shopping offerings range from regional food and drink specialties, such as goat and sheep cheese or port wine, to an imaginative range of traditional handicrafts. Nearly every small town has a handful of specialty stores selling local products, while Lisbon is, of course, the mecca for more up-to-date designs. Outside the capital, you will see some local crafts at weekly markets, but better-quality goods are sold in the specialty shops.

Throughout Portugal, craftspeople excel at making household linen and towels: In the northern Minho area you will find fantastic quality, delicately embroidered or otherwise (Amarante and Viana do Castelo are good sources). People in the know look for cotton bedspreads and lace from Guimarães and the much prized *colchas* (silk-embroidered bedspreads) of Castelo Branco—these are real investments, as they take months to make. Close rivals are the stunning appliqué bedspreads made in Nisa, in the Alentejo.

Lace is big business from the seaside resort of Peniche as far as Madeira, as lacemaking is the traditional occupation of seamen's wives during their husbands' absences. The Serra da Estrela mountains are known for beautiful woolen blankets in subtle, natural tones and countless sheepskin products.

To the south, the Alentejo produces handwoven shawls and blankets and, at Arraiolos, wool-embroidered rugs made with techniques going back to the Middle Ages. And Portalegre is home to Portugal's tapestry industry. Another major Alentejo handicraft is woodwork, from painted furniture (Évora and Nisa) to colorful children's toys. Cork products are typical, too, in a wide variety of wares. Tourist offices have lists of workshops that can be visited, making shopping far more interesting. Farther south still, the Algarve is where to find wickerwork, copper, and brassware.

Portugal is above all a country of potters, whether making traditional forms of *barro* (basic terra-cotta), bis-cuit-ware porcelain, colorful glazed tableware, or cutting-edge designer objects. Although ceramics are not the easiest items to carry home, large outlets can arrange to ship them abroad. Head into the center to Caldas da Rainha to find Portugal's most whimsical range of ceramics, above all majolica tableware in vegetable or animal forms by Bordallo Pinheiro. Contemporary designs have been developed here, too. Coimbra is another town with a strong ceramics tradition; here you can pick up quality glazed ceramics decorated with fine floral patterns, traditionally in blue.

Outside Aveiro is the factory for a national institution: Vista Alegre porcelain. It has been produced here since 1824, but you can find the exquisite, pricey ceramic in shops all over the country. More unusual and localized is the black pottery from Bisalhães, near Vila Real, and from Viseu. In the Alentejo, Estremoz specializes in charming pottery figurines and unglazed terracotta, and Santiago do Cacém in tiles.

If you're interested in glassware, we suggest you head to Marinha Grande, just north of Caldas da Rainha (outlets in Porto and Lisbon). Designs range from the traditional to ultramodern.

For clothing, Portugal is a great place to buy good value leather accessories. The sharpest designs are found in Lisbon. Look, too, for old-fashioned haberdashery and ironmongers' shops, both of which stock unusual and seemingly outdated items. Upscale jewelry shops, found in all large towns, sell traditional gold and silver filigree designs (produced near Porto) or, alternatively, imaginative and stylish contemporary designs. Aim to catch at least one street market. The vast Thursday market at Barcelos, near Braga, is Portugal's largest market for handicrafts.

■ LISBON

A Vida Portuguesa, Rua Anchieta 11, Bairro Alto, tel 213 465 073, *avida portuguesa.com.* Top quality, traditional Portuguese products make for original gifts (other stores in the city).

Arcadia, Rua Castilho 65, tel 213 880 273, *arcadiachocolates.com.* Delicious artisan chocolates made with traditional recipes and only natural ingredients. In the same family since 1933.

Associação dos Artesãos da Região de Lisboa, Rua de Entrecampos 66, tel 217 962 497. A good selection of local handicrafts.

Caza das Vellas Loreto, Rua do Loreto 53, Bairro Alto, tel 213 425 387, *caza vellasloreto.com.pt.* Every conceivable type of candle for sale in a beautiful 18th-century store.

Colombo Shopping Center, Avenida Lusiada, *colombo.pt.* One of the largest shopping malls in Iberia; it has around 420 stores that are open until midnight daily.

Confeitaria Nacional, Praça da Figueira 18B, tel 213 424 470, *confeitarianacional .com.* All types of confectionery set in tempting rows in wooden cabinets in the original ornate 1820s store.

Conserveira de Lisboa, Rua dos Bacalhoeiros 34, tel 218 864 009, *conserveira delisboa.pt.* East of Praça do Comércio, this small shop sells traditional canned goods tied in brown paper and string.

Deposito da Marinha Grande, Rua de São Bento 234–236, tel 213 963 234, *dmg.com.pt.* It is impossible not to buy

something at this outlet for Portugal's best glassmakers.

El Corte Inglés, Avenida António Augusto de Aguiar 31, tel 213 711 700, *el corteingles.pt.* A branch of the Spanish department store stocks fashionwear, gourmet food, and household goods.

Figurado de Barcelos, Rua de São Nicolau 81, tel 215 831 977. A tribute to Minho ceramic art in the capital city. Colorful creations to admire and take home.

Isabel Lopes da Silva, Rua da Escola Politécnica 67, tel 213 425 032. Rare objects, designer furnishings, and jewelry from the 1920s through 1950s.

Leitão & Irmão, Largo do Chiado 16–17, tel 213 257 870, *leitao-irmao.com.* Producing high-quality jewelry and filigree for royalty and others since the 18th century.

Luvaria Ulisses, Rua do Carmo 87, Chiado, tel 213 420 295, *luvariaulisses.com.* Superlative kid gloves in wonderful hues and designs—unbeatable chic offerings.

Vista Alegre, Largo do Chiado 20–23, tel 213 461 401, *vistaalegre.com.* The flagship showroom for Portugal's superb manufacturer of fine porcelain.

■ PORTO E NORTE

A Oficina, Rua da Rainha 126, Guimarães, tel 253 515 250, *aoficina.pt.* Municipal outlet for fine linens and other quality crafts. The association organizes various cultural events, from dance and music to workshops.

A Pérola do Bolhão, Rua Formosa 279, Porto, tel 222 004 009. For more than 100 years, historic grocers selling a great array of cured meats and cheeses.

Arcadia, Rua do Almada 63, Porto, tel 222 001 518, *arcadiachocolates.com.* Best chocolate in town, 100 percent natural; in business since 1933.

Casa Ferreira da Cunha, Largo do Toural 38–39, Guimarães, tel 253 412 223, *ferreiradacunha.net*. Carry home an ornate iron doorknocker—it will be unique!

Chocolateria Delícia, Avenida Alberto Sampaio 10, Viseu, tel 232 431 950, *chocolateriadelicia.com*. Fine artisan chocolates made on the premises for all to see.

Depósito da Marinha Grande, Rua do Bonjardim 133, Porto, tel 222 030 752, *dmg.com.pt*. Glassware in every shape and form: carafes, vases, glasses, bowls.

Garrafeira do Carmo, Rua do Carmo 17, Porto, tel 222 003 285, *garrafeira carmo.com*. An exhaustive range of national wines, including rare port wine vintages.

Livraria Lello e Irmão, Rua das Carmelitas 144, Porto, tel 222 002 037, *livrarialello.pt*. A neo-Gothic, palatial bookstore with ornate wood paneling and sweeping stairs; a Porto landmark.

Mercado de Barcelos, Largo Campo da Republica, Barcelos. Held in the main square every Thursday, this market is a sprawling affair selling clothing, shoes, local handicrafts, ceramics, and delicious local delicacies.

Oficina do Ouro, Sobradelo da Goma, Póvoa de Lanhoso, tel 253 943 945, *oficinadoouro.com*. Tour the gold filigree workshop (*$*) then visit the store at this traditional Minho jewelry center 20 minutes east of Braga.

Ourivesaria Freitas, Rua Sacadura Cabral 16, Viana do Castelo, tel 258 801 230, *ourivesariafreitas.com*. Selling quality filigree and traditional Portuguese jewelry since 1920.

▦ CENTRO

Casa dos Linhos, Rua Visconde da Luz 103–105, Coimbra, tel 239 822 465, *casadoslinhos.com.pt*. Good selection of household linen with traditional and modern designs.

Celeiro dos Sonhos, Avenida Capitão Silva Pereira 161, Viseu, tel 965 405 206. Good choice of regional products: cheeses, mountain honey, Dão wines.

O Sotão, Rua das Olarias 48, Castelo Branco, tel 272 342 048. A small, unassuming store that hides quality handmade items, especially woven fabrics and baskets.

▦ LISBOA E REGIÃO

Chapelaria e Sapataria Liz, Rua Barão de Viamonte 14 A (Rua Direita), Leiria, tel 244 823 244. Founded in 1928 and located in the center of the old town, this old-world establishment specializes in quality head- and footwear.

Made in Alcobaça, Praça 25 de Abril 64, Alcobaça, tel 262 585 402. Small craft shop selling bags, aprons, and decorative items made from the traditional all-cotton Chita de Alcobaça fabric.

Piriquita, Rua das Padarias 1–18, Sintra, tel 219 230 626, *piriquita.pt*. Do not leave Sintra without trying the local *queijadas*. The best are to be found at Piriquita, serving since 1862.

▦ ALENTEJO

A Chapelaria, Rua da República 7–9, tel 965 770 207, Évora. Come here for every conceivable type of hat.

A Roda da Fortuna, Praça 10 de Maio 10, Évora, tel 266 752 619. Regional crafts including jewelry, ceramic, and cork items, many with a contemporary design element.

Ameixas de Elvas, Fábrica Museu da Ameixa, Rua Martim Mendes 16, Elvas, tel 268 628 364, *ameixas-elvas.com*. This workshop, founded in 1919, is still in operation. Visit it, and you will find jams and other original foods, especially ones made from the prized local plums.

Arabe, Rua Jorge Raposo 25, Beja, tel 961 276 559 or 968 718 872. A wide choice of local artisans' wares, ranging from ceramics to embroidery, wicker, and copper.

éNisa, Nisa, tel 245 410 000, *nisaglobal .cm-nisa.pt*. The city of Nisa has founded its own brand that certifies the authenticity of the area's handicraft products to protect some unique techniques, such as *olaria pedrada*, a special terracotta making process. Look for the trademark when you shop here.

Fábrica de Tapetes Hortense, Rua Alexandre Herculano 22, Arraiolos, tel 965 632 589, *hortensegalleryarraiolos.pt*. One of many shops in town selling the world-famous Arraiolos carpets.

Loja Coisas de Monsaraz, Largo do Castelo 2, Requengos de Monsaraz, tel 266 557 484, *olaria-carrilho.com*. Rustic village shop selling colorful pottery in traditional Alentejo designs.

Mizette, Rua do Celeiro, Monsaraz, tel 266 502 179. The most authentic shop in this touristy village, offering beautiful, locally made, handwoven wool blankets, scarves, and mats.

Mont'Sobro, Rua 5 de Outubro, Évora, tel 266 704 609. *montsobro .com*. In a town full of cork-item shops Mont'Sobro is in a league of its own with tasteful quality jewelry, watches, and bags.

O Cesto, Rua 5 de Outubro 77, Évora, tel 266 703 344, *ocesto.com.pt*. Wide selection of cork goods, ceramics, and painted wood items.

■ ALGARVE

Artesanato (craft) shops along the main N125 road abound with gift items, especially pottery.

About Wine, Rua Horta Machado 20, Faro, tel 965 006 735, *aboutwine.pt*. Extensive selection of fine wines and port, with bar area and organized tastings.

Casa das Portas, Rua 5 Outubro 1–3, Tavira, tel 281 328 772. Top-quality and original souvenirs at top prices.

Mar d'Estorias, Rua Silva Lopes 30, Lagos, tel 282 792 165, *mardestorias.com*. Innovative new venue incorporating a gift shop, art gallery, bar and bistro, and rooftop terrace with amazing views over the town and water.

■ MADEIRA

Blandy's Wine Lodge, Avenida Arriaga 28, Funchal, tel 291 228 978, *blandys winelodge.com*. The widest possible choice of Madeira wines, including vintage versions.

D'Oliveiras, Rua dos Ferrerios 107, Funchal, tel 291 220 784. A quaint and atmospheric wine lodge.

Grupo Folclórico da Casa do Povo da Camacha, argo Conselheiro Aires de Ornelas 18, Camacha, tel 927 103 683, *grupofolcloricocamacha.com*. Camacha is the center of the island's wickerwork trade, and at the headquarters of this association (which supports local customs and traditions with music and dance) you can find quality products.

Patricio & Gouveia, Rua do Visconde de Anadia 34, Funchal, tel 291 222 928. One of Madeira's biggest and best embroidery outlets, with high-quality clothes and table linens.

ENTERTAINMENT

The hottest nightlife and cultural life is in Lisbon: Pick up the monthly listings magazine *Follow Me Lisboa* at the tourist office, as new venues are always opening. Lisbon's nightlife is closely followed by that of Porto, while Coimbra boasts fun, young venues. Most discos and clubs close on Sunday nights and/or Mondays. Outside the big cities, Portugal's entertainment concentrates on the summer months, when seaside nightclubs open their doors to throngs of visitors, particularly in the Algarve.

◼ LISBON

Adega do Ribatejo, Rua do Diario de Noticias 23, Bairro Alto, tel 213 468 343. Attractive tiled interior with a relaxed crowd listening to fado serenades at dinner.

Casa de Linhares, Beco dos Armazéns do Linho 2, tel 218 239 6600 or 910 188 118, *casadelinhares.com*. Atmospheric fado restaurant and bar at the base of the Alfama. Open every night; plenty of choice also for vegetarians.

Cinco Lounge, Rua Ruben A. Leitão 17A, Príncipe Real, tel 213 424 033 or 914 668 242, *cincolounge.com*. Arguably the best cocktail bar in Lisbon.

Docas de Alcântara, Doca de Santo Amaro, Alcântara. Former warehouses overlooking the marina, now home to many bars and restaurants.

Park, Calcada do Combro 58, tel 215 914 011. With no signs, this bar on the roof of a Bairro Alto carpark is tricky to find, but the amazing views make it memorable.

Pensão Amor, Rua do Alecrim 19, tel 213 143 399, *pensaoamor.pt*. Former well-known city brothel, Pensão Amor retains its air of decadence with intimate lounges and attentive staff.

Portas Largas, Rua da Atalaia 105, Bairro Alto, tel 213 466 379. Bar on the top of the hill with a pleasant retro atmosphere and good music.

Red Frog Speakeasy, Rua do Salitre 5A, tel 215 831 120, *redfrog.pt*. Inspired by the American Prohibition era, with a nod to 1950s and 1960s tropical influences.

Senhor Vinho, Rua do Meio, Lapa 18, tel 213 972 681, *srvinho.com*. More restaurant than club, an elegant setting to listen to nightly fado singers. Excellent wine list.

◼ PORTO

Casa da Musica, Avenida da Boavista 604–610, Porto, tel 220 120 220, *casa damusica.com*. Wide variety of musical events.

Hot Five Jazz & Blues Club, Rua Guerra Junqueiro 495, tel 934 640 732, *hot five.pt*. Top musicians play live jazz and blues in a friendly atmosphere.

Portologia, Rua do Almada 315, tel 222 011 050, *portologia.com*. More than 200 port wines available to taste, aided by a knowledgeable staff.

The Wall, Rua Cândido dos Reis 90, tel 936 916 301. Cool and contemporary bar attracting Porto's hip crowd.

Rooftop Bar Ontop, Rua de Serralves 124, Hotel HF Ipanema Park, tel 225 322 121. Great city views from this

15th-floor rooftop bar. Good music, cocktails, and pool complete the package. *(May–Sep.)*

COIMBRA

À Capella, Rua Corpo de Deus, Largo da Vitória, tel 239 833 985, *acapella.com.pt*. This former 14th-century chapel offers a superb setting for live fado shows.

Bar Diligência, Rua Nova 30, tel 911 763 722. One of the oldest fado venues where fado is sung in its Coimbra version.

Rugby Lounge Club, Rua Castro Matoso 17, tel 913 582 907. Young atmosphere with music for dancing in a nice space with an outdoor courtyard and good drinks.

ALGARVE

Note: Out of season *(Oct.–May)*, most Algarve nightspots operate limited opening hours; some are only open in July and August.

Caniço, Aldeamento da Prainha, Praia dos Três Irmãos, Alvor, tel 282 458 503, *canicorestaurante.com*. A picture-perfect bar and restaurant nestled into the cliff edge serving cocktails until late night.

Casino Vilamoura, Praça Casino Vilamoura, Quarteira, tel 289 310 000, *gruposolverde.pt*. Gaming machines and tables as well as nightly shows.

Le Club Santa Eulália, Praia de Santa Eulália, Albufeira, tel 289 598 000, *leclubalgarve.com*. Bar areas, lounge, dance floor, and a sushi restaurant with veranda overlooking the sea *(Open Fri.–Sat. in Aug.)*.

No Solo Água, Marina de Portimão, tel 282 498 180, *nosoloagua.com*. Beach club with occasional live music.

ACTIVITIES

From hiking or rock climbing in the Serra de Peneda-Gerês to scuba diving, windsurfing, surfing, canoeing, tennis, and golf, Portugal has something for everyone in the way of physical activities.

Sport Federations

The following organizations are good sources of information on all things related to their sport in Portugal.

Federação Equestre Portuguesa (horseback riding), Avenida Manuel da Maia 26, Lisbon, tel 218 478 775, *fep.pt*

Federação Portuguesa de Actividades Subaquaticas (scuba diving), Rua do Alto Lagoal 21A, Caxias, Lisbon, tel 211 910 868, *fpas.pt*

Federação Portuguesa de Canoagem (canoeing), Rua Antonio Pinto Machado 60, Porto, tel 225 432 237, *fpcanoagem.pt*

Federação Portuguesa de Ciclismo (cycling), Rua de Campolide 237, Lisbon, tel 213 802 140, *fpciclismo.pt*

Federação Portuguesa de Golfe (golf), Rua Santa Teresa do Menino 948, Algés, tel 214 123 780, *portal.fpg.pt*

Federação Portuguesa de Surf (surfing), Avenida Marginal, Edificio Narciso, Praia de Carcavelos, tel 219 228 914, *surfingportugal.com*

Federação Portuguesa de Ténis (tennis), Rua Actor Chaby Pinheiro 7A, Linda-a-Velha, tel 214 151 356, *tenis.pt*

Federação Portuguesa de Vela (sailing), Doca de Belém, Lisbon, tel 213 658 500, *fpvela.pt*

Golf

There are some 75 golf courses in mainland Portugal, with the majority in the Algarve (see pp. 255–256).

An informative website for this area is *algarvegolf.net;* for all of Portugal try *portugalgolf.pt.* The Lisbon area is well served by the coastal resorts, from Estoril north to Quinta da Marinha (Guincho), and there are more courses south of the Tejo River. Although less concentrated, northern Portugal has its share of courses, and Madeira has three.

Here is a selected listing:

Lisbon Area

Beloura Pestana Golf Resort, Rua das Sesmarias 3, Quinta da Beloura, Sintra, tel 219 106 350, *pestanagolf.com*
18 holes, par 72
6,251 yards/5,716 m
Architect: Rocky Roquemore
One of the more appreciated courses on the Estoril coast, with views of the Sintra mountain range.

Clube de Golf do Estoril, Avenida da República, Estoril, tel 214 680 176, *www.clubegolfestoril.com*
18 holes, par 69
5,728 yards/5,238 m
Architect: Mackenzie Ross
There's also a nine-hole course.

Clube de Golf do Montado, Algeruz, Palmela, tel 265 708 150, *montado resort.com*
18 holes, par 72
6,961 yards/6,366 m
Architect: Duarte Sottomayor
Maybe not for the beginners, but very pleasant and surrounded by vineyards and cork tree groves.

Lisbon Sports Club, Casal de Carregueira, Belas, tel 214 310 077, *lisbonclub .com*

18 holes, par 69
5,772 yards/5,278 m
Architect: Hawtree & Sons
One of Portugal's oldest golf courses; the club, founded in 1861, originally focused on cricket.

Oitavos Dunes, Quinta da Marinha, Casa do Quinta 25, Cascais, tel 214 860 020, *oitavosdunes.com*
18 holes, par 71
6,526 yards/5,967 m
Architect: Arthur Hills
Links-type holes in woodland with views of the ocean. Considered to be one of the best courses in Portugal.

Penha Longa Clube de Golf, Caesar Park, Penha Longa, Estrada da Lagoa Azul, Linhó, Sintra, tel 219 249 031, *penhalonga.com*
18 holes, par 72
6,878 yards/6,290 m
Architect: Robert Trent Jones Jr
Host of the 1994–95 Portuguese Open Championships. Also has a nine-hole course on property.

Quinta do Perú Golf Course, Alameda da Serra 2, Quinta do Conde, tel 212 134 320, *quintadoperugolf.com*
18 holes, par 72
6,601 yards/6,036 m
Architect: Rocky Roquemore
The Arrábida mountain range acts as a backdrop to this course south of the Tejo River.

Troia Golf, Troia Resort, Troia Carvalhal, tel 265 494 112, *troiaresort.pt*
18 holes, par 72
6,930 yards/6,337 m
Architect: Robert Trent Jones Sr
It is thought to be one of the most difficult layouts in the country.

Algarve
Golf Santo Antonio, Vale do Poço, Budens, Vila do Bispo, tel 282 690 054, *www.saresorts.com*
18 holes, par 72
6,041 yards/5,524 m

Dramatic, rugged course, a contrast with the usual parkland layouts of the Algarve.

Monte Rei, Monte Rei Golf & Country Club, Sesmarias, Vila Nova de Cacela, tel 281 950 960, *monte-rei.com*
18 holes, par 72
7,182 yards/6,567 m
Architect: Jack Nicklaus
Set in the rolling foothills of the eastern Algarve with views of the Atlantic.

Pine Cliffs Golf and Country Club, Pine Cliffs Resort, Albufeira, tel 289 500 300, *pinecliffs.com*
9 holes, par 32
2,541 yards/2,324 m
It enjoys a memorable position overlooking the sea.

Quinta do Lago, Sociedade do Golfe da Quinta do Lago, Almancil, tel 289 390 700, *quintadolago.com*
Three 18-hole courses, all par 72
Not only the Algarve's first golf course, but also one of the country's largest golf clubs.

The Old Course Golf Club, Vilamoura, tel 289 310 341, *dompedrogolf.com*
18 holes, par 73
6,839 yards/6,254 m
Architect: Frank Pennink, remodeled by Martin Hawtree
One of the oldest golf courses in the Algarve.

Northern & Central Portugal
Amarante Golf Club, Quinta da Deveza, Fregim, Amarante, tel 255 446 060, *golfedeamarante.com*
18 holes, par 68
5,561 yards/5,085 m
Architect: Jorge Santana da Silva

Estela Golf, Lugar Rio Alto, Estela, Póvoa de Varzim, tel 252 601 567, *estela golf.pt*
18 holes, par 72
6,724 yards/6,148 m
Architect: Duarte Sottomayor

Montebelo Golfe, Farminhão, Viseu, tel 232 856 464, *montebelogolfe.pt*
18 holes, par 72
6,903 yards/6,312 m
Architects: Mark Stilwell and Malcolm Kenyon
Mountainous course with excellent views over Serra da Estrela and Serra do Caramulo.

Praia del Rey, Avenida Dom Afonso Henriques, Vale de Janelas, Óbidos, tel 262 905 005, *praia-del-rey.com*
18 holes, par 73
7,072 yards/6,467 m
Architect: Cabell B. Robinson

Quinta da Barca Golf Course, Quinta da Barca, Gemeses, Esposende, tel 253 966 723
9 holes, par 31
2,140 yards/1,957 m
Architect: Jorge Santana de Silva

Madeira
Palheiro Golf, Rua do Balancal 29, Funchal, tel 291 790 120, *palheironature estate.com*
18 holes, par 72
6,655 yards/6,086 m
Architect: Cabell B. Robinson

Guided Activities
Algarve Birdwatching, tel 912 824 053, *algarvebirdman.com*
Expert guide Simon Wates offers well-informed and well-organized bird-watching trips across the region.

Turaventur, Caminho Municipal 1182–2, Senhor dos Aflitos, Évora, tel 266 743 134 or 966 758 940, *turaventur .com*
A dynamic Alentejo adventure tourism company which organizes guided treks, mountain biking, and kayaking, as well as cultural tours.

Walkin'Sagres, Aldeamento de S. Vicente, Bl. A-1o C, 8650 Sagres, tel 925 545 515, *walkinsagres.com*

Informative family hikes with enthusiastic guide Ana Carla through the Parque Natural Sudoeste Alentejano e Costa Vicentina.

Horseback Riding
Portugal has a special feeling for horses and is the home of the Lusitano breed. This agile, hot-blooded horse has been bred in the Ribatejo region for hundreds of years and is a mixture of the Arab and English Thoroughbred. Visitors will find stables easily, in particular in the Algarve, Alentejo, and Ribatejo.

Albufeira Riding Centre, Caminho do Vale Navio, Vale Navio, Albufeira, tel 961 269 526, *albufeiraridingcentre.com*
Offers a range of activities including lessons and treks of 20 minutes to a full day.

Centro Hípico Quinta da Marinha, Rua São Rafael 715, Cascais, tel 214 860 006, *quintadamarinhahipico.com*

Coudelaria Rita Cotrim, Quinta dos Álamos, Golegã, tel 918 599 360
Horseback-riding excursions and courses for all levels (even beginners) in the heart of the Lusitanian horse country.

Ecotura, Lugar do Queimadelo, Castro Laboreiro, Melgaço (Peneda-Gerês National Park), tel 967 442 217, *eco tura.com*
An introduction to the small Portuguese Garrano horse, which lives wild in the Peneda-Gerês National Park, and horseback riding for the whole family.

Escola Portuguesa de Arte Equestre, Palácio Nacional de Queluz, tel 219 237 300, *parquesdesintra.pt*
This is the sharpest show of Portuguese dressage you can enjoy, held at the Picadeiro Henrique Calado in Belém, Monday through Friday from 10 a.m. to 1 p.m.

Morgado Lusitano, Quinta da Portela, Cabeço da Rosa, EN116, Alverca do Ribatejo, tel 219 936 520, *morgado lusitano.pt*
Classical dressage on superb stallions near Lisbon.

Tiffany's Riding Centre, Vale Grifo, 1677 E. Almádena, Luz, Lagos, tel 919 231 975, *teamtiffanys.com*
Riding center for beginners to advanced, a couple hours to a full day.

Tennis
Tennis is the third most played sport in Portugal. The center of this sport is the Clube de Ténis do Estoril (Avenida Condes Barcelona 808, *ctestoril .pt)*, where the annual clay-court Estoril Open is held. Other important centers can be found in Porto, Coimbra, Évora, and the Algarve. Some clubs offer special packages that include accommodations and coaching. Courts range from all-weather artificial grass to American clay.

Water Sports
Along the Atlantic coast, the obvious sports are windsurfing, sailing, surfing (see p. 170 for more surf schools), and scuba diving. Water temperatures range from 61° to 71°F (16°–22°C); wet suits are advisable. Portugal is recognized as the best place in Europe for surfing; Guincho Beach (near Cascais) is the most challenging thanks to its considerable undertow. Other popular places are Aveiro farther north and the Algarve's Costa Vicentina.

Algarve Watersport, Estrada da Albardeira, Lagos, tel 960 460 800, *algarvewatersport.com*
Camps, lessons, and equipment rental for surfing, kitesurfing, and windsurfing in western Algarve.

Carcavelos Surf School, Avenida Marginal, Praia de Carcavelos, tel 962 850 497 or 966 131 203, *carcavelossurf school.com*
Surf lessons and equipment for all levels; it's one the first surf schools established in the Lisbon area.

Haliotis, Casal Ponte, Atouguia da Baleia, Peniche, tel 262 781 160 or 913 054 926, *haliotis.pt*
Scuba diving around Peniche and the Berlengas.

LANGUAGE GUIDE

The Portuguese themselves admit they have a fiendish language, so they will make every attempt to speak yours. As a language based on Latin, Portuguese shares common roots with Spanish, French, and Italian, but all similarity stops there. Pronunciation is the big stumbling block, so be ready to mouth "sh" and "ow" sounds every other word. Masculine and feminine subjects and words have agreements: The most obvious you will encounter is the word for "thank you": *obrigado* (for a man) and *obrigada* (for a woman). English is spoken in tourist areas, in hotels, upscale restaurants, and in pharmacies. In more remote places, among older generations, French is often the only foreign language spoken. Spanish is understood but few people feel like using it, as their rivalry goes back for centuries.

Basic Words & Phrases

yes/no	*sim/não*
please	*faz favor*
thank you	*obrigado/a*
You're welcome	*de nada*
good morning	*bom dia*
hi	*olá*
good afternoon	*boa tarde*
goodbye/bye	*adeus/tchao*
See you	*Até logo*
Excuse me/sorry	*Desculpe*
How are you?	*Como está?*
very well, thank you	*muito bem, obrigado/a*
My name is	*Chamo me*
I'm from the USA	*Sou dos Estados Unidos*
Do you speak English?	*Fala inglês?*

Getting Around

Where is?	*Onde está?*
Where are?	*Onde estão?*
When?	*Quando?*
Turn left	*Vire à esquerda*
Turn right	*Vire à direita*
straight on	*sempre emifrente*
opposite	*em frente*
traffic lights	*semáforo*
train station	*estação ferroviária*
metro station	*estação de metro*
market	*mercado*
Do you have?	*Tem?*
a single room	*um quarto individual*
a double room	*um quarto de casal*
a twin-bed room	*um quarto duplo*
with bathroom	*com casa de banho*
Can I see the room?	*Posso ver o quarto?*

Time

What time?	*A que horas?*
leave/arrive	*parte/chega*
morning	*manhã*
afternoon	*tarde*
When do you open/close?	*Quando abrem/fecham?*
yesterday	*ontem*
today	*hoje*
tomorrow	*amanhã*
now	*agora*
later	*mais tarde*
Monday	*segunda feira*
Tuesday	*terça feira*
Wednesday	*quarta feira*
Thursday	*quinta feira*
Friday	*sexta feira*
Saturday	*sábado*
Sunday	*domingo*

Shopping

Do you sell?	*Vendem?*
How much is it?	*Quanto custa?*
Can I look at it?	*Posso ver?*
open/closed	*aberto/encerrado*
Do you take credit cards?	*Aceitam cartões de crédito?*
I'll take this	*Levo isto*

Numbers

1	*um*
2	*dois*
3	*tres*
4	*quatro*
5	*cinco*
6	*seis*
7	*sete*
8	*oito*
9	*nove*
10	*dez*
11	*onze*
12	*doze*
13	*treze*
14	*catorze*
15	*quinze*
16	*dezasseis*
17	*dezassete*
18	*dezoito*
19	*dezanove*
20	*vinte*
30	*trinta*
40	*quarenta*

100	cem
1,000	mil

Menu Reader

I'd like	Queria
breakfast	pequeno almoço
lunch	almoço
dinner	jantar
the check please	a conta se faz favor
daily special	prato do dia
half portion	meia dose
spoon	colher
fork	garfo
knife	faca

Food Basics

açucar	sugar
azeite	olive oil
azeitonas	olives
limão	lemon
manteiga	butter
pão	bread
pimenta	pepper
piri-piri	chili sauce
queijo	cheese
sal	salt
vinagre	vinegar

Cooking Methods

assado	roast
bem passado	well cooked
cozido	boiled
estufado	stewed/ steamed
frito	fried
grelhado	grilled
mal passado	rare
no carvão	barbecued
no espeto	on the spit
no forno	in the oven/ baked

Peixe e Mariscos/ Fish & Seafood

arroz de marisco	seafood rice
arroz de polvo	octopus rice
atum	tuna
bacalhau	salted cod
caldeirada de peixe	fish stew
camarões	shrimps
cataplana	shellfish and ham cooked in a sealed pan
chocos	cuttlefish
espadarte	swordfish
gambas	prawns
lagosta	lobster
lampreia	lampreys (baby eels)
linguado	sole
lulas	squid
pargo	sea bream
robalo	sea bass
rodovalho	halibut
salmão	salmon
salmonete	red mullet
sardinhas	sardines
truta	trout

Carne e Aves/ Meat & Poultry

bife	steak (not necessarily beef)
borrego	lamb
cabrito	kid goat
carne assada	roast beef
chouriço	spicy smoked sausage
churrasco	spit-roasted pork
coelho	rabbit
costeleta	cutlet/ chop
cozido	meat & vegetable stew
entrecosto	rump steak
feijoada	bean stew with rice and meats
fiambre	cooked ham
figado	liver
frango	chicken
leitão assado	roast suckling pig
lombo	pork fillet
pato	duck
porco	pork
salsicha	sausage
tripas	tripe
vaca	beef
vitela	veal

Legumes/Vegetables

alface	lettuce
alho	garlic
batatas	potatoes
cebola	onion
cenoura	carrot
cogumelos	mush-rooms
ervilhas	green peas
espargos	asparagus
espinafres	spinach
favas	broad beans
feijão	dried beans
lentilhas	lentils
pepino	cucumber
pimentos	peppers
salada/mista	salad/ mixed
tomate	tomato

Ovos/Eggs

cozido	hard boiled
escalfado	poached
estrelado	fried
mexido	scrambled
omelete	omelet
quente	boiled

Fruitas/Fruit

alperces	apricots
ameixas	plums
amendoas	almonds
ananas	pineapple
bananas	bananas
figos	figs
framboesas	raspberries
laranjas	oranges
limões	lemons
maças	apples
meloa	melon
morangos	strawber-ries
pessegos	peaches
uvas	grapes

INDEX

ILLUSTRATIONS CREDITS

All photographs by Tino Soriano unless otherwise noted below:

2–3, Zyankarlo/Shutterstock; 4, Michele Falzone/AWL Images/Getty Images; 8, InavanHateren/
Shutterstock; 10, Mirlo/Shutterstock.com; 18, hugon/Shutterstock; 22, AP Photo/Frank Augstein;
25, Goran Bogicevic/Shutterstock.com; 28, NORTH DEVON PHOTOGRAPHY/Shutterstock; 32,
Ann Ronan Picture Library/Heritage Images/Corbis; 34, Alexandre Rotenberg/Shutterstock.com; 38,
Luis Santos/Shutterstock.com; 42, Museu de Arte Antiga, Lisbon, photo by James L. Stanfield; 44,
Alex Segre/Alamy Stock Photo; 47, Sophie Bassouls/Sygma/Corbis; 48, Pinghung Chen/EyeEm/
Getty Images; 54, trabantos/Shutterstock.com; 55, Joe Dunckley/Getty Images; 57, Patricia De Melo
Moreira/AFP/Getty Images; 77, Sonia Bonet/Shutterstock.com; 85 saiko3p/Shutterstock.com; 92,
Vadim Petrakov/Shutterstock; 99, Nandi Estevez/Shutterstock.com; 100, Vector99/Shutterstock;
107, LuisCostinhaa/Shutterstock.com; 108, Alex Livesey/Getty Images; 112, Dolores Giraldez
Alonso/Shutterstock.com; 116, RS-74/Shutterstock.com; 120, rui vale sousa/Shutterstock.com; 123,
Zacarias da Mata/Shutterstock.com; 127, Josep Curto/Shutterstock.com; 134, Mirlo Shutterstock
.com; 137, Spencer Grant/Science Source/Getty Images; 140, Jan Butchofsky/Corbis; 141, VR2000/
Shutterstock.com; 144, Sergio Azenha/Alamy Stock Photo; 145, byruineves/Shutterstock.com;
148, Oleksandra Gnatush-Kostenko/iStockphoto; 153, photolocation 2/Alamy Stock Photo; 160,
Alexandre Rotenberg/Shutterstock.com; 163, Zoonar GmbH/Nikolai Sorokin/Alamy Stock Photo;
168, Sopotnicki/Shutterstock.com; 170, R.M. Nunes/Shutterstock.com; 179, James L. Stanfield/
National Geographic Creative; 182, Freesurf/Adobe Stock; 186, André Gonçalves/age fotostock/
Getty Images; 187, Sean Pavone Photo/Getty Images; 191, saiko3p/Adobe Stock; 193, Marko
Stavric/Getty Images; 200, StockPhotosArt/Shutterstock.com; 208, Celli07/Shutterstock.com; 226,
LuisPinaPhotography/Shutterstock.com; 232, amnat30/Shutterstock.com; 235, Mauro Rodrigues/
Shutterstock.com; 242, Matyas Rehak/Shutterstock.com; 243, Carlos Caetano/Shutterstock.com; 245,
David MG/Shutterstock.com; 246, Roberto Soncin Gerometta/Lonely Planet Images/Getty Images;
248, Inacio Pires/Shutterstock; 255, Yann Arthus-Bertrand/Corbis; 268, Nikiforov Alexander/
Shutterstock.com; 270, Vlada Z/Adobe Stock.